Tom Sharpe was born in 1928 and educated at Lancing College and at Pembroke College, Cambridge. He did his National Service in the Marines before going to South Africa in 1951, where he did social work for the Non-European Affairs Department before teaching in Natal. He had a photographic studio in Pietermaritzburg from 1957 until 1961, when he was deported. From 1963 to 1972 he was a lecturer in History at the Cambridge College of Arts and Technology. He is married and li

Tom Sharpe

THE THROWBACK
ANCESTRAL VICES
VINTAGE STUFF

PAN BOOKS
IN ASSOCIATION WITH SECKER & WARBURG

The Throwback first published 1978 by Martin Secker & Warburg Ltd and first published by Pan Books Ltd 1980 in association with Martin Secker & Warburg Ltd

Ancestral Vices first published 1980 by Martin Secker & Warburg Ltd and first published by Pan Books Ltd 1982 in association with Martin Secker & Warburg Ltd

Vintage Stuff first published 1982 by Martin Secker & Warburg Ltd and first published by Pan Books Ltd 1983 in association with Martin Secker & Warburg Ltd

This combined edition published 1994 by Pan Books

an imprint of Macmillan General Books
Cavaye Place London SW10 9PG
and Basingstoke
in association with Martin Secker & Warburg Ltd

Associated companies throughout the world

ISBN 0 330 34191 X

9 8 7 6 5 4 3 2 1

A CIP catalogue record for this book is available from
the British Library

Printed and bound in Great Britain by
Cox & Wyman Ltd, Reading, Berkshire

The Throwback

Chapter one

It could be said of Lockhart Flawse when he carried his bride, Jessica, *née* Sandicott, across the threshold of 12 Sandicott Crescent, East Pursley, Surrey, that he was entering into married life with as little preparedness for its hazards and happiness as he had entered the world at five past seven on Monday, 6 September 1956, promptly killing his mother in the process. Since Miss Flawse had steadfastly refused to name his father even on the stinging nettles that composed her deathbed and had spent the hour of his delivery and her departure alternately wailing and shouting 'Great Scot!', it had devolved upon his grandfather to name the infant Lockhart after the great Scott's biographer and, at some risk to his own reputation, to' allow Lockhart to assume the surname Flawse for the time being.

From that moment Lockhart had been allowed to assume nothing, not even a birth certificate. Old Mr Flawse had seen to that. If his daughter had been so obviously devoid of social discretion as to give birth to a bastard under a dry-stone wall while out cub-hunting, which dry-stone wall her horse had, more sensibly than she, refused, Mr Flawse was determined to ensure that his grandson grew up with none of his mother's faults. He had succeeded. At eighteen Lockhart knew as little about sex as his mother had known or cared about contraception. His life had been spent under the care of several housekeepers and later half a dozen tutors, the former chosen for their willingness to endure the bed and board of old Mr Flawse, and the latter for their other-worldliness.

Since Flawse Hall was situated on Flawse Fell close under Flawse Rigg some seventeen miles from the nearest town and on the bleakest expanse of moorland north of the Roman Wall, only the most desperate of housekeepers and other-worldly of tutors accepted the situation for long. There were other rigours than the natural. Mr Flawse was an extremely irritable man and the succession of tutors who had provided Lockhart with the most particular of general educations had done so under the strict proviso that Ovid was not to be included among the classics and that literature was to be dispensed with entirely.

Lockhart was to be taught the ancient virtues and mathematics. Mr Flawse was particularly hot on mathematics and believed in numbers as ferociously as his forefathers had believed in predestination and cattle-rustling. They formed in his opinion a firm foundation for a commercial career and were as entirely without obvious sexual connotations as were the features of his housekeepers. Since tutors, and other-worldly tutors at that, seldom combined a knowledge of both maths and the classics, Lockhart's education proceeded by fits and starts but was sufficiently thorough to defeat every attempt by the Local Authorities to provide him with a more orthodox schooling at public expense. The School Inspectors who ventured to Flawse Hall to obtain evidence that Lockhart's education was deficient came away confounded by his narrow erudition. They were unused to small boys who could recite their nineteen-times table in Latin and read the Old Testament in Urdu. They were also unused to conducting examinations in the presence of an old man who appeared to be toying with the trigger of an ostentatiously loaded shotgun aimed absent-mindedly in their direction. In the circumstances they felt that Lockhart Flawse, while hardly in safe hands, was educationally in excellent ones and that there was nothing to be gained, except in all probability a volley of buckshot, by attempting to take him into public care, a point of view that was shared by his tutors, who came less frequently with every passing year.

Mr Flawse made good their absence by teaching Lockhart himself. Born in 1887 at the height of the Empire, he still held those tenets to be true which had been commonplace in his youth. The British were the finest specimens of animal life that God and Nature had created. The Empire was still the greatest that had ever existed. Wogs began at Calais, and sex was necessary for procreation but was otherwise unmentionable and generally disgusting. The fact that the Empire had long since ceased to exist and that wogs, far from beginning at Calais, had reversed the process and in large measure ended at Dover, Mr Flawse ignored. He took no newspaper and, lacking any electricity at Flawse Hall, used this as an excuse for refusing to have even a transistor radio, let alone a television set, in the house. Sex, on the other hand, he couldn't ignore. Even at ninety he was consumed by guilt at his own excesses and the fact that these, like the Empire, had largely passed from reality to fantasy only made matters worse. In his mind Mr Flawse remained a profligate and maintained a regimen of cold baths and long walks to exercise his body and exorcize his soul. He also hunted and fished and shot and encouraged his bastard grandson in these healthy outdoor pursuits to the point where Lockhart could bring down a running hare at five hundred yards with a First World War 303 Lee-Enfield and a grouse at a hundred with a 22. By the time he was seventeen Lockhart had so decimated the wild life on Flawse Fell and the fish in the North Teen that even the foxes, carefully preserved from relatively painless death by gunshot to be hunted and torn to pieces by the hounds, found it difficult to make ends meet, and brought meets to an end by moving off to less exacting moors. It was largely in consequence of this migration, which coincided with the departure of his latest and most desirable housekeeper, that old Mr Flawse, resorting too heavily to the port bottle and the literary companionship of Carlyle, was urged by his personal physician, Dr Magrew, to take a holiday. The doctor was supported by Mr Bullstrode, the solicitor, at one of the monthly dinners at Flawse Hall which the old man had given for thirty years and which allowed him a forum for those vociferous disputations on things eternal, metaphysical, biological and generally slanderous. These dinners were his substitute for church attendance, and his arguments afterwards were his nearest approach to any recognizable religion.

'Damned if I will,' he said when Dr Magrew first mooted the idea of a holiday. 'And the fool who first said a change is as good as a rest didn't live in this benighted century.'

Dr Magrew helped himself to more port. 'You can't live in an unheated house without a housekeeper and expect to last another winter.'

'I've got Dodd and the bastard to look after me. And the house isn't unheated. There's coal in the drift mine up Slimeburn and Dodd brings it down. The bastard does the cooking.'

'And that's another thing,' said Dr Magrew, who rather suspected that Lockhart had cooked their dinner, 'your digestion won't stand the strain and you can't expect to keep the boy cooped up here for ever. It's time he saw something of the world.'

'Not till I find out who his father is,' said Mr Flawse malevolently. 'And when I do I'll horsewhip the swine to within an inch of his life.'

'You'll not be fit to horsewhip anyone unless you take our advice,' said Dr Magrew. 'Isn't that your opinion, Bullstrode?'

'Speaking as your friend and legal adviser,' said Mr Bullstrode glowing in the candlelight, 'I would say that I would regret the premature ending of these pleasant occasions by virtue of an obstinate disregard for the weather and our advice. You're not a young man and the question of your will . . .'

'Damn my will, sir,' said old Mr Flawse, 'I'll make a will when I know whom I'm settling my money on and not before. And what is this advice you offer so readily?'

'Take a cruise,' said Mr Bullstrode, 'somewhere hot and sunny. I'm told the food is excellent.'

Mr Flawse stared into the depths of the decanter and considered the proposition. There was something in what his friends advised and besides there had recently been complaints from several tenant farmers that Lockhart, lacking any more fleet-footed quarry, had taken to pot-shooting sheep at fifteen hundred yards, complaints that had been confirmed by Lockhart's cuisine. They had had underdone mutton too frequently of late for Mr Flawse's digestion and conscience, and besides Lockhart was eighteen and it was high time he got shot of the lad before someone got shot by him. As if to reinforce this opinion there came the sound from the kitchen of Mr Dodd's Northumbrian pipes playing a melancholy air while Lockhart sat opposite him listening, just as he listened to Mr Dodd's stories of the grand old days and the best way to poach pheasant or tickle trout.

'I'll think about it,' Mr Flawse said finally.

That night a heavy fall of snow decided him, and Dr Magrew and Mr Bullstrode came down to breakfast to find him in a more amenable mood.

'I'll leave the arrangements to you, Bullstrode,' he said as he finished his coffee and lit a blackened pipe. 'And the bastard will go with me.'

'He'll need a birth certificate to get a passport,' said the solicitor, 'and . . .'

'Born in a ditch and die in a dyke. I'll only register him when I know who his father is,' said Mr Flawse glowering.

'Quite,' said Mr Bullstrode who didn't want to go into the question of horsewhipping so early in the morning. 'I suppose we could still have him put on your passport.'

'Not as his father,' snarled Mr Flawse, the depths of whose feelings for his grandson were partly to be explained by the terrible suspicion that he himself might not altogether be devoid of responsibility for Lockhart's conception. The memory of one drunken encounter with a housekeeper who had seemed on recollection to have been younger and more resistant than her daytime appearance had led him to expect still haunted his conscience. 'Not as his father.'

'As his grandfather,' said Mr Bullstrode. 'I'll need a photograph.'

Mr Flawse went through to his study, rummaged in a bureau drawer and returned with one of Lockhart aged ten. Mr Bullstrode studied it dubiously.

'He's changed a lot since then,' he said.

'Not to my knowledge,' said Mr Flawse, 'and I should know. He was ever a gormless lout.'

'Aye, and for all practical purposes a non-existent one,' said Dr Magrew. 'You know he's not registered on the National Health system, and if he's ever taken ill I can foresee considerable difficulties in the matter of obtaining treatment.'

'He's never known a day's illness in his life,' Mr Flawse retorted. 'A healthier brute it would be difficult to find.'

'He could have an accident,' Mr Bullstrode pointed out.

But the old man shook his head. ' 'Tis too much to be hoped for. Dodd's seen to it he knows how to handle himself in an emergency. You'll have heard the saying that a poacher makes the best gamekeeper?' Mr Bullstrode and Dr Magrew had. 'Well, Dodd's the reverse. He's a gamekeeper who would make the best poacher,' continued Mr Flawse, 'which is what he has made of the bastard. There's not a bird nor beast safe within twenty miles when he's abroad.'

'Talking of abroad,' said Mr Bullstrode, not wishing as a solicitor to be privy to Lockhart's illegal activities, 'where would you like to go?'

'Somewhere South of Suez,' said Mr Flawse whose memory

for Kipling was not what it had been. 'I'll leave the rest to you.'

Three weeks later Lockhart and his grandfather left Flawse Hall in the ancient brougham Mr Flawse used for his more formal means of transport. As with everything else modern he eschewed the motor car. Mr Dodd sat up front at the reins, and behind was tied the cabin trunk Mr Flawse had last used in 1910 on a voyage to Calcutta. As the horses clattered down the metalled track from the Hall, Lockhart was in a state of high expectation. It was his first journey into the world of his grand-father's memories and his own imagination. From Hexham they took the train to Newcastle and from Newcastle to London and Southampton, Mr Flawse all the way complaining that the London North-Eastern Railway wasn't what it had been forty years before and Lockhart astonished to discover that not all women had partial beards and varicose veins. By the time they reached the ship old Mr Flawse was exhausted to the point of twice supposing, thanks to the complexion of two ticket col-lectors, that he was already back in Calcutta. It was with the greatest difficulty and the least examination of his passport that he was helped up the gangway and down to his cabin.

'I shall dine here in the stateroom,' he told the steward. 'The boy will sup aloft.'

The steward looked at the 'boy' and decided not to argue that the cabin was not strictly a stateroom, nor that dinners in cabins were things of the past.

'We've got one of the old sort in Number 19,' he told the stewardess afterwards, 'and when I say old I mean old. Wouldn't surprise me if he sailed on the *Titanic*.'

'I thought they all drowned,' said the stewardess, but the steward knew better. 'Not all. That old sod's a survivor if ever I saw one and his ruddy grandson's like something out of the Ark and I don't mean something cuddly.'

That evening as the *Ludlow Castle* sailed down the Solent, old Mr Flawse dined in his stateroom, and it was Lockhart, dressed conspicuously in tails and white tie which had once belonged to a larger uncle, who made his way up to the First Class Dining Saloon and was conducted to a table at which sat Mrs Sandicott and her daughter Jessica. For a moment, stunned by Jessica's beauty, he hesitated, then bowed and sat down.

Lockhart Flawse had not fallen in love at first sight. He had plunged.

Chapter two

And Jessica followed suit. One look at this tall, broad-shouldered young man who bowed and Jessica knew she was in love. But if with the young couple it was love at first sight, with Mrs Sandicott it was calculation at second. Lockhart's appearance in white tie and tails and his general air of incoherent embarrassment had a profound effect upon her, and when during the meal he managed to stammer that his grandfather was dining in their stateroom Mrs Sandicott's suburban soul thrilled to the sound.

'Your stateroom?' she asked. 'You did say your stateroom?'

'Yes,' mumbled Lockhart, 'you see he's ninety and the journey from the Hall fatigued him.'

'The Hall,' murmured Mrs Sandicott and looked significantly at her daughter.

'Flawse Hall,' said Lockhart. 'It's the family seat.'

Once again Mrs Sandicott's depths were stirred. The circles in which she moved did not have family seats and here, in the shape of this angular and large youth whose accent, acquired from old Mr Flawse, went back to the late nineteenth century, she perceived those social attributes to which she had long aspired.

'And your grandfather is really ninety?' Lockhart nodded. 'It's amazing that such an elderly man should be taking a cruise at his time of life,' continued Mrs Sandicott. 'Doesn't his poor wife miss him?'

'I really don't know. My grandmother died in nineteen thirty-five,' said Lockhart, and Mrs Sandicott's hopes rose even higher. By the end of the meal she had winkled the story of

11

Lockhart's life from him, and with each new piece of information Mrs Sandicott's conviction grew that at long, long last she was on the brink of an opportunity too good to be missed. She was particularly impressed by Lockhart's admission that he had been educated by private tutors. Mrs Sandicott's world most certainly did not include people who had their sons educated by tutors. At best they sent them to Public Schools. And so, as coffee was served, Mrs Sandicott was positively purring. She knew now that she had not been wrong to come on the cruise and when finally Lockhart rose and lifted her chair back for her and then for Jessica, she went down to her cabin with her daughter in a state of social ecstasy.

'What a very nice young man,' she said. 'Such charming manners and so well brought up.'

Jessica said nothing. She did not want to spoil the savour of her feelings by revealing them. She had been overwhelmed by Lockhart but in a different way to her mother. If Lockhart represented a social world to which Mrs Sandicott aspired, to Jessica he was the very soul of romance. And romance was all in all to her. She had listened to his description of Flawse Hall on Flawse Fell close under Flawse Rigg, and had garnished each word with a new significance that came from the romantic novels with which she had filled the emptiness of her adolescence. It was an emptiness that amounted to vacuity.

At eighteen Jessica Sandicott was endowed with physical charms beyond her control and an innocence of mind that was both the fault and despair of her mother. To be more precise, her innocence resulted from the late Mr Sandicott's will in which he had left all twelve houses in Sandicott Crescent 'to my darling daughter, Jessica, on her reaching the age of maturity'. To his wife he bequeathed Sandicott & Partner, Chartered Accountants and Tax Consultants, of Wheedle Street in the City of London. But the late Mr Sandicott's will had bequeathed more than these tangible assets. It had left Mrs Sandicott with a sense of grievance and the conviction that her husband's premature death at the age of forty-five was proof positive that she had married no gentleman, the proof of his ungentlemanliness lying in his failure to depart this world at least ten years earlier when she was still at a reasonably remarriageable age, or, failing that, to have left her his entire fortune. From this misfortune Mrs Sandicott had formed two resolutions. The first was that her next husband would be a very rich man with a life expectancy of as few years as possible and preferably with a terminal illness; the second to see that Jessica reached the age of maturity as slowly as a religious education could delay. So far she had failed in her first objective and only partly succeeded in her second.

Jessica had been to several convents, and the plural was indicative of her mother's partial failure. At the first she had developed a religious fervour of such pronounced proportions that she had decided to become a nun and subtract her own worldly possessions by adding them to those of the Order. Mrs Sandicott had removed her precipitately to a less persuasive convent and for a time things looked distinctly brighter. Unfortunately, so did several nuns. Jessica's angelic face and innocence of soul had so combined that four nuns fell madly in love with her and the Mother Superior, to save their souls, had requested that Jessica's disturbing influence be removed. Mrs Sandicott's self-evident argument that she wasn't to blame for her daughter's attractions and that if anyone ought to be expelled it was the lesbian nuns cut no ice with the Mother Superior.

'I do not blame the child. She was made to be loved,' she said with suspicious emotion and in direct contradiction to Mrs Sandicott's views on the subject. 'She will make some good man a wonderful wife.'

'Knowing men rather more intimately than I hope you do,' riposted Mrs Sandicott, 'she will marry the first scoundrel who asks her.'

It was a fatefully accurate prediction. To protect her daughter from temptation and to maintain her own financial income from the rents of the houses in Sandicott Crescent, Mrs Sandicott had confined Jessica to her home and a correspondence course in typing. By the time Jessica reached eighteen it was still impossible to say of her that she had reached the age of maturity. If anything she had regressed and while Mrs Sandicott supervised the running of Sandicott & Partner, the partner being a Mr Treyer, Jessica sank back into a literary slough of romantic novels populated entirely by splendid young men. In short she lived in a world of her imagination, the fecundity of which was proven one morning when she announced that she was in love with the milkman and intended to marry him. Mrs Sandicott studied the milkman next day and decided that the time had come for desperate measures. By no stretch of her own imagination could she visualize the milkman as an eligible young man. Her arguments to this effect, backed by the fact that the milkman was forty-nine, married and the father of six children, and hadn't been consulted by his bride-to-be in any case, failed to influence Jessica.

'I shall sacrifice myself to his happiness,' she said. Mrs Sandicott determined otherwise and promptly booked two tickets on the *Ludlow Castle* in the conviction that whatever else the ship might have to offer in the way of possible husbands for her daughter, they couldn't be less eligible than the milkman. Besides, she had herself to think of, and cruise liners were notoriously happy hunting-grounds for middle-aged widows with an eye to the main chance. That Mrs Sandicott's own eye was fastened on an ancient and potentially terminal old man with money only made the prospect of the voyage the more desirable. And Lockhart's appearance had heralded the mainest chance of all, an eligible and evidently half-witted young man for her idiot daughter and in his stateroom a gentleman of ninety with an enormous estate in Northumberland. That night Mrs Sandicott went to sleep a cheerful woman. In the bunk above Jessica sighed and murmured the magical words, 'Lockhart Flawse of Flawse Hall on Flawse Fell close under Flawse Rigg.' They formed a litany of Flawse to the religion of romance.

On the boat-deck Lockhart leant on the rail and stared out over the sea, his heart filled with feelings as turbulent as the white wake of the ship. He had met the most wonderful girl in the world and for the very first time he realized that women were not simply unprepossessing creatures who cooked meals, swept floors and, having made beds, made strange noises in them late at night. There was more to them than that but what that something more was Lockhart could only guess.

His knowledge of sex was limited to the discovery, made while gutting rabbits, that bucks had balls and does didn't. There appeared to be some connection between these anatomical differences that accounted for ladies having babies and men not. On the one occasion he had attempted to explore the difference further by asking the tutor in Urdu how Mizriat begat Ludin in Genesis 10:13 he had received a clout across the ear that had temporarily deafened him and had given him the permanent impression that such questions were better left unasked. On the other hand he was aware that there was such a thing as marriage and that out of marriage came families. One of his distant Flawse cousins had married a farmer from Elsdon and had subsequently raised four children. The housekeeper had told him as much and no more, except that it had been a shotgun marriage which had merely deepened the mystery, shotguns in Lockhart's experience being reserved for putting things to death rather than bringing them to life.

To make matters even more incomprehensible, the only occasions on which his grandfather had permitted him to visit his relatives, had been to their burials. Mr Flawse enjoyed funerals immensely. They reinforced his belief that he was hardier than any other Flawse and that death was the only certainty. 'In any uncertain world we can take consolation in the verity, the eternal verity, that death comes to us all in the end,' he would tell a bereaved widow to terrible effect. And afterwards, in the jaunting-cart he used for such outings, he would expatiate glowingly to Lockhart on the merits of death as preserver of moral values. 'Without it we would have nothing to stop us from behaving like cannibals. But put the fear of death up a man and it has a wondrously purgative effect.'

And so Lockhart had continued in ignorance of the facts of life while acquiring extensive knowledge of those of death. It was left to his bodily functions and his feelings to guide him in quite contrary directions in the matter of sex. Lacking a mother and loathing most of his grandfather's housekeepers, his feelings for women were decidedly negative. On the more positive side he got a great deal of pleasure from nocturnal emissions. But their significance escaped him. He didn't have wet dreams in the presence of women and he didn't have women at all.

And so leaning on the guard rail staring down at the white foam in the moonlight Lockhart expressed his new feelings in images he knew best. He longed to spend the rest of his life shooting things and laying them at Jessica Sandicott's feet. With this exalted notion of love Lockhart went down to the cabin where old Mr Flawse, clad in a red flannel nightgown, was snoring noisily, and climbed into bed.

If Mrs Sandicott's expectations had been aroused by Lockhart's appearance at dinner they were confirmed by old Mr Flawse at breakfast. Dressed in a suit that had been out of fashion as far back as 1925, he cut a swathe through subservient waiters with an arrogance far older than his suit and, taking his place with a 'Good morning to you, ma'am', surveyed the menu with disgust.

'I want porridge,' he told the headwaiter who hovered nervously, 'and none of your half-boiled mush. Oats, man, oats.'

'Yes, sir, and what to follow?'

'A double ration of eggs and bacon. And find some kidneys,' said Mr Flawse to the prognostic delight of Mrs Sandicott, who knew all there was to know about cholesterol. 'And by double I mean double. Four eggs and a dozen rashers. Then toast and marmalade and two large pots of tea. And the same goes for the boy.'

The waiter hurried away with this lethal order and Mr Flawse looked over his glasses at Mrs Sandicott and Jessica.

'Your daughter, ma'am?' he inquired.

'My only daughter,' murmured Mrs Sandicott.

'My compliments to you,' said Mr Flawse without making it clear whether he was praising Mrs Sandicott for her daughter's beauty or her singularity. Mrs Sandicott blushed her acknowledgement. Mr Flawse's old-world manners were almost as enchanting to her as his age. For the rest of the meal there was silence broken only by the old man's denunciation of the tea as weaker than well-water and his insistence on a proper pot of breakfast tea you could stand your spoon up in. But if Mr Flawse appeared to be concentrating on his bacon and eggs and tea that contained enough tannin to scour its way through a blocked sewer-pipe, his actual thoughts were elsewhere and moved along lines very similar to those of Mrs Sandicott though with a rather different emphasis. In the course of his long life he had learnt to smell a snob a mile off and Mrs Sandicott's deference suited him well. She would, he considered, make an excellent housekeeper. Better still, there was her daughter. She was clearly a gormless girl, and just as clearly an ideal match for his gormless grandson. Mr Flawse observed Lockhart out of the corner of a watery eye and recognized the symptoms of love.

'Sheeps' eyes,' he muttered aloud to himself to the confusion of the hovering waiter, who apologized for their not being on the menu.

'And who said they were?' snapped Mr Flawse and dismissed the man with a wave of a mottled hand.

Mrs Sandicott absorbed all these details of behaviour and calculated Mr Flawse to be exactly the man she had been waiting for, a nonagenarian with an enormous estate, and therefore an enormous bank account, and an appetite for just those items on the menu best suited to kill him off almost immediately. It was therefore with no affectation of gratitude that she accepted his offer of a stroll round the deck after breakfast. Mr Flawse dismissed Lockhart and Jessica to go and play deck quoits, and presently he and Mrs Sandicott were lapping the promenade deck at a pace that took her breath away. By the time they had covered the old man's statutory two miles, Mrs Sandicott's breath had been taken away for other reasons. Mr Flawse was not a man to mince his words.

'Let me make myself plain,' he said unnecessarily as they took their seats in deckchairs, 'I am not overgiven to delaying my thoughts. You have a daughter of marriageable age and I have a grandson who ought to be married. Am I right?'

Mrs Sandicott adjusted the blanket round her knees and said with some show of delicacy that she supposed so.

'I am so, ma'am,' said Mr Flawse, 'I know it and you know it. In truth we both know it. Now, I am an old man and at my age I cannot expect a sufficient future to see my grandson settled according to his station. In short, ma'am, as the great Milton expressed it "in me there's no delay". You take my meaning?'

Mrs Sandicott took it and denied it simultaneously. 'You're quite remarkably fit for your time of life, Mr Flawse,' she said encouragingly.

'That's as may be, but the Great Certainty looms,' said Mr Flawse, 'and 'tis equally certain that my grandson is a nincompoop who will in a short time, being my only heir, be a rich nincompoop.'

He allowed Mrs Sandicott to savour the prospect for a moment or two. 'And being a nincompoop he needs a wife who has her head screwed on the right way.'

He paused again and it was on the tip of Mrs Sandicott's tongue to remark that Jessica's head, if screwed on at all, had been screwed on against the thread, but she restrained her words.

'I suppose you could say that,' she said.

'I can and I do,' continued Mr Flawse. 'It has ever been a Flawse trait, ma'am, in choosing our womenfolk, to take cognizance of their mothers, and I have no hesitation in saying that you have a shrewd head for business, Mrs Sandicott, ma'am.'

'It's very kind of you to say so, Mr Flawse,' Mrs Sandicott simpered, 'and since my poor husband died I have had to be the breadwinner. Sandicott & Partner are chartered accountants and I have run the business.'

'Exactly,' said Mr Flawse. 'I have a nose for these things and it would be a comfort to know that my grandson was in good hands.' He stopped. Mrs Sandicott waited expectantly.

'And what hands did you have in mind, Mr Flawse?' she asked finally, but Mr Flawse had decided the time had come to feign sleep. With his nose above the blanket and his eyes closed he snored softly. He had baited the trap. There was no point in watching over it and presently Mrs Sandicott stole quietly away with mixed feelings. On the one hand she had not come on the cruise to find a husband for her daughter; she had come to avoid one. On the other, if Mr Flawse's words meant anything he was looking for a wife for his grandson. For one wild moment Mrs Sandicott considered Lockhart for herself and instantly rejected him. It was Jessica or no one, and the loss of Jessica would mean the loss of the rent of the twelve houses in Sandicott Crescent. If only the old fool had proposed to her she would have seen things in a different light.

'Two birds with one stone,' she murmured to herself at the thought of a double killing. It was worth calculating about. And so, as the two young lovers gambolled on the sun-deck, Mrs Sandicott ensconced herself in a corner of the First Class Lounge and calculated. Through the window she could keep an eye on the blanketed figure of Mr Flawse recumbent in the deckchair. Every now and again his knees twitched. Mr Flawse had given way to those sexual excesses of the imagination which were the bane of his non-conformist conscience, and for the first time Mrs Sandicott figured in them largely.

Chapter three

Imagination played a large part in the love that blossomed between Lockhart and Jessica. Having plunged they sported like water babies in the swimming pool or frolicked at deck tennis and as each day passed, and the ship steamed slowly south into equatorial waters, their passion grew inarticulately. Not entirely inarticulately but when they spoke during the day their words were matter-of-fact. It was only at night, when the older generation danced the quickstep to the ship's band and they were left alone to stare down at the white water swirling from the ship's side and invest one another with those qualities their different upbringings had extolled, that they spoke their feelings. Even then it was by way of other people and other places that they told one another what they felt. Lockhart talked of Mr Dodd and how at night he and the gamekeeper would sit at the settle in the stone-flagged kitchen with the black iron range glowing between them while the wind howled in the chimney outside and Mr Dodd's pipes wailed inside. And of how he and Mr Dodd would herd the sheep or stalk game in the wooded valley known as Slimeburn where Mr Dodd dug coal from a drift mine that had first been worked in 1805. Finally there were the fishing expeditions on the great reservoir fringed with pine that stood a mile from Flawse Hall. Jessica saw it all so clearly through a mist of Mazo de la Roche and Brontë and every romantic novel she had ever read. Lockhart was the young gallant come to sweep her off her feet and carry her from the boredom of her life in East Pursley and away from her mother's cynicism to the ever-ever land of Flawse Hall on Flawse Fell close under Flawse Rigg where the wind blew fierce and the snow lay thick outside but all within was warm with old wood and dogs and the swirl of Mr Dodd's Northumbrian pipes and old Mr Flawse sitting at the oval mahogany dining-table disputing by candlelight questions of great moment with his two friends, Dr Magrew and Mr Bullstrode. In the tapestry woven from Lockhart's words she created a picture of a past which she dearly longed to make her future.

Lockhart's mind worked more practically. To him Jessica was an angel of radiant beauty for whom he would lay down, if not his own life, at least that of anything which moved within range of his most powerful rifle.

But while the young people were only implicitly in love, the old were more outspoken. Mr Flawse, having baited the trap for another housekeeper, waited for Mrs Sandicott's response. It came later than he had expected. Mrs Sandicott was not a woman to be hustled and she had calculated with care. Of one thing she was certain. If Mr Flawse wanted Jessica for his daughter-in-law he must take her mother for his wife. She broached the subject with due care and by way of the mention of property.

'If Jessica were to marry,' she said one evening after dinner, 'I would be without a home.'

Mr Flawse signalled his delight at the news by ordering another brandy. 'How so, ma'am?' he inquired.

'Because my poor dear late husband left all twelve houses in Sandicott Crescent, including our own, to our daughter and I would never live with the young married couple.'

Mr Flawse sympathized. He had lived long enough with Lockhart to know the hazards of sharing a house with the brute. 'There is always Flawse Hall, ma'am. You would be very welcome there.'

'As what? A temporary guest or were you thinking of a more permanent arrangement?'

Mr Flawse hesitated. There was an inflexion in Mrs Sandicott's voice which suggested that the permanent arrangement he had in mind might not be at all to her liking. 'There need be nothing temporary about your being a guest, ma'am. You could stay as long as you liked.'

Mrs Sandicott's eyes glinted with suburban steel. 'And what precisely would the neighbours make of that, Mr Flawse?'

Mr Flawse hesitated again. The fact that his nearest neighbours were six miles off at Black Pockrington, and that he didn't give a tuppenny damn what they thought, presented a prospect that had lost him too many housekeepers already and was unlikely to appeal to Mrs Sandicott.

'I think they would understand,' he prevaricated. But Mrs Sandicott was not to be fobbed off with understandings. 'I have my reputation to think of,' she said. 'I would never consent to staying alone in a house with a man without there being some legal status to my being there.'

'Legal status, ma'am?' said Mr Flawse and took a swig of brandy to steady his nerves. The bloody woman was proposing to him.

'I think you know what I mean,' said Mrs Sandicott.

Mr Flawse said nothing. The ultimatum was too clear.

'And so if the young couple are to be married,' she continued remorselessly, 'and I repeat "if", then I think we should consider our own futures.'

Mr Flawse did and found it an uncertain one. Mrs Sandicott was not a wholly unattractive woman. Already in his dozing fantasies he had stripped her naked and found her plump body very much to his taste. On the other hand wives had disadvantages. They tended to be domineering and while a domineering housekeeper could be sacked a wife couldn't, and Mrs Sandicott for all her deference seemed to be a strong-minded woman. To spend the rest of his life with a strong-minded woman was more than he had bargained for, but if it meant getting the bastard Lockhart off his hands it might be worth the risk. Beisdes there was always the isolation of Flawse Hall to tame the strongest-minded woman and he would have an ally in Mr Dodd. Yes, definitely an ally in Mr Dodd and Mr Dodd was not without resource. And finally if he couldn't sack a wife nor could the wife leave like a housekeeper. Mr Flawse smiled into his brandy and nodded.

'Mrs Sandicott,' he said with unaccustomed familiarity, 'am I right in supposing that it would not come averse to you to change you name to Mrs Flawse?'

Mrs Sandicott beamed her assent. 'It would make me very happy, Mr Flawse,' she said, and took his mottled hand.

'Then allow me to make you happy, ma'am,' said the old man, with the private thought that once he'd got her up to

Flawse Hall she'd get her fill of happiness one way or another. As if to celebrate this forthcoming union of the two families the ship's band struck up a foxtrot. When it had finished Mr Flawse returned to more practical matters.

'I must warn you that Lockhart will need employment,' he said. 'I had always intended to keep him to manage the estate he will one day inherit but if your daughter has twelve houses . . .'

Mrs Sandicott came to his rescue. 'The houses are all let and at rents fixed by the Rent Tribunal on long leases,' she said, 'but dear Lockhart could always join my late husband's firm. I understand he is clever with figures.'

'He has had an excellent grounding in arithmetic. I have no hesitation in saying so.'

'Then he should do very well at Sandicott & Partner, Chartered Accountants and Tax Consultants,' said Mrs Sandicott.

Mr Flawse congratulated himself on his foresight. 'Then that is settled,' he said. 'There remains simply the question of the wedding.'

'Weddings,' said Mrs Sandicott, emphasizing the plural. 'I had always hoped that Jessica would have a church wedding.'

Mr Flawse shook his head. 'At my age, ma'am, there would be something incongruous about a church wedding to be so closely followed by a funeral. I would prefer a more cheerful venue. Mind you, I disapprove of registry offices.'

'Oh so do I,' Mrs Sandicott agreed, 'they are so unromantic.'

But there was nothing unromantic about the old man's reluctance to see Lockhart married in a registry office. It had dawned on him that without a birth certificate it might be impossible to marry the swine off at all. And besides there was still the fact of his illegitimacy to be concealed.

'I see no reason why the Captain shouldn't marry us,' he said finally. Mrs Sandicott thrilled at the notion. It combined speed and no time for second thoughts with an eccentricity that was almost aristocratic. She could boast about it to her friends.

'Then I'll see the Captain about it in the morning,' said Mr Flawse, and it was left to Mrs Sandicott to break the news to the young couple.

She found them on the boat-deck whispering together. For a moment she stood and listened. They so seldom spoke in her presence that she was curious to know what they did say to one another in her absence, What she heard was both reassuring and disturbing.

'Oh, Lockhart.'

'Oh, Jessica.'

'You're so wonderful.'

'So are you.'

'You really do mean that?'

'Of course I do,'

'Oh, Lockhart.'

'Oh, Jessica.'

Under the gleaming moon and the glittering eye of Mrs Sandicott they clasped one another in their arms and Lockhart tried to think what to do next. Jessica supplied the answer,

'Kiss me, darling.'

'Where?' said Lockhart.

'Here?' said Jessica and offered him her lips.

'There?' said Lockhart. 'Are you sure?'

In the shadow of the lifeboat Mrs Sandicott stiffened. What she had just heard but couldn't see was without doubt nauseating. Either her future son-in-law was mentally deficient or her daughter was sexually more sophisticated, and in Mrs Sandicott's opinion positively perverse, than she had ever dreamt. Mrs Sandicott cursed those damned nuns. Lockhart's next remark confirmed her fears,

'Isn't it a bit sticky?'

'Oh, darling, you're so romantic,' said Jessica, 'you really are.'

Mrs Sandicott wasn't. She emerged from the shadows and bore down on them. 'That's quite enough of that,' she said as they staggered apart. 'When you're married you can do whatever you like but no daughter of mine is going to indulge in obscene acts on the boat-deck of a liner. Besides, someone might see you.'

Jessica and Lockhart stared at her in amazement. It was Jessica who spoke first.

'When we're married? You really did say that, mummy?'

'I said exactly that,' said Mrs Sandicott. 'Lockhart's grandfather and I have decided that you should . . .'

She was interrupted by Lockhart who, with a gesture of

chivalry that so endeared him to Jessica, knelt at his future mother-in-law's feet and reached out towards her. Mrs Sandicott recoiled abruptly. Lockhart's posture combined with Jessica's recent suggestion was more than she could stomach.

'Don't you dare touch me,' she squawked and backed away. Lockhart hastened to his feet.

'I only meant . . .' he began but Mrs Sandicott didn't want to know.

'Never mind that now. It's time you both went to bed,' she said firmly. 'We can discuss arrangements for the wedding in the morning.'

'Oh, mummy . . .'

'And don't call me "mummy",' said Mrs Sandicott. 'After what I've just heard I'm not at all sure I *am* your mother.'

She and Jessica left Lockhart standing bemused on the boat-deck. He was going to get married to the most beautiful girl in the world. For a moment he looked round for a gun to fire to announce his happiness but there was nothing. In the end he unhooked a lifebelt from the rail and hurled it high over the side into the water and gave a shout of joyful triumph. Then he too went down to his cabin oblivious of the fact that he had just alerted the bridge to the presence of 'Man Overboard' and that in the wake of the liner the lifebelt bobbed frantically and its warning beacon glowed.

As the engines went full astern and a boat was lowered, Lockhart sat on the edge of his bunk listening to his grandfather's instructions. He was to marry Jessica Sandicott, he was to live in Sandicott Crescent, East Pursley, and start work at Sandicott & Partner.

'That's marvellous,' he said when Mr Flawse finished, 'I couldn't have wished for anything better.'

'I could,' said Mr Flawse, struggling into his nightgown. 'I've got to marry the bitch to get rid of you.'

'The bitch?' said Lockhart. 'But I thought . . .'

'The mother, you dunderhead,' said Mr Flawse and knelt on the floor. 'Oh Lord, Thou knowest that I have been afflicted for ninety years by the carnal necessities of women,' he cried. 'Make these my final years beneficent with the peace that passes all understanding and by Thy great mercy lead me in the paths

24

of righteousness to the father of this my bastard grandson, that I may yet flog the swine within an inch of his life. Amen.'

On this cheerful note he got into bed and left Lockhart to undress in the darkness, wondering what the carnal necessities of women were.

Next morning the Captain of the *Ludlow Castle*, who had spent half the night searching for the Man Overboard and the other half ordering the crew to check the occupants of all cabins to ascertain if anyone had indeed fallen over the side, was confronted by the apparition of Mr Flawse dressed in a morning suit and grey topper.

'Married? You want me to marry you?' said the Captain when Mr Flawse had made known his request.

'I want you to conduct the ceremony,' said Mr Flawse. 'I have neither the desire to marry you nor you to marry me. Truth be told, I don't want to marry the damned woman either, but needs must when the devil drives.'

The Captain eyed him uncertainly. Mr Flawse's language, like his costume, not to mention his advanced age, argued a senility that called for the services of the ship's doctor rather than his own.

'Are you sure you know your own mind on this matter?' he asked when Mr Flawse had further explained that not only was the marriage to be between himself and Mrs Sandicott but between his grandson and Mrs Sandicott's daughter. Mr Flawse bristled. 'I know my own mind, sir, rather better than it would appear you know your own duty. As Master of this vessel you are empowered by law to conduct marriages and funerals. Is that not so?'

The Captain conceded that it was, with the private reservation that in Mr Flawse's case his wedding and burial at sea were likely to follow rather too closely for comfort.

'But wouldn't it be better if you were to wait until we reach Capetown?' he asked. 'Shipboard romances tend to be very transitory affairs in my experience.'

'In your experience,' said Mr Flawse, 'I dare say they do. In mine they don't. By the time you reach four-score years and ten any romance is in the nature of things bound to be a transitory affair.'

'I see that,' said the Captain. 'And how does Mrs Sandicott feel about the matter?'

'She wants me to make an honest woman of her. An impossible task in my opinion but so be it,' said Mr Flawse. 'That's what she wants and that's what she will get.'

Further argument merely resulted in Mr Flawse losing his temper and the Captain submitting. 'If the old fool wants the wedding,' he told the Purser later, 'I'm damned if I can stop him. For all I know he'll institute an action under Maritime Law if I refuse.'

And so it was as the ship sailed towards the Cape of Good Hope that Lockhart Flawse and Jessica Sandicott became Mr and Mrs Flawse while Mrs Sandicott achieved her long ambition of marrying a very rich old man with but a short time to live. Mr Flawse for his part consoled himself with the thought that whatever disadvantages the ex-Mrs Sandicott might display as a wife, he had rid himself once and for all of a bastard grandson while acquiring a housekeeper who need never be paid and would never be able to give notice. As if to emphasize this latter point he refused to leave the ship while she lay in Capetown, and it was left to Jessica and Lockhart to spend their honeymoon chastely climbing Table Mountain and admiring one another from the top. When the ship set out on the return voyage only their names and their cabins had changed. Mrs Sandicott found herself closeted with old Mr Flawse and prey to those sexual excesses which had previously been reserved for his former housekeepers and of late for his imagination. And in her old cabin Jessica and Lockhart lay in one another's arms as ignorant of any further purpose in their marriage as their singular upbringings had left them. For another eleven days the ship sailed north and by the time the two married couples disembarked at Southampton, it could be said that, apart from old Mr Flawse, whose excesses had taken some toll of his strength and who had to be carried down the gangway in a wheelchair, they were all entering upon a new life.

Chapter four

If the world of Flawse Hall on Flawse Fell close under Flawse Rigg, Northumberland, had played a large part in persuading Jessica that Lockhart was the hero she wanted to marry, the world of Sandicott Crescent, East Pursley, Surrey, had played no part in Lockhart's choice at all. Used as he was to the open moors of the Border country where the curlews, until he shot them, cried, Sandicott Crescent, a cul-de-sac of twelve substantial houses set in substantial gardens and occupied by substantial tenants with substantial incomes, was a world apart from anything he knew. Built in the thirties as an investment by the foresighted if late Mr Sandicott, the twelve houses were bordered to the south by the Pursley Golf Course and to the north by the bird sanctuary, a stretch of gorse and birch whose proper purpose was less to preserve bird life than to maintain the property values of Mr Sandicott's investment. In short it was an enclave of large houses with mature gardens. Each house was as different in style and similar in comfort as the ingenuity of architects could make it. Pseudo-Tudor prevailed, with an admixture of Stockbroker Spanish Colonial, distinguished by green glazed tiles, and one British Bauhaus with a flat roof, small square windows and the occasional porthole to add a nautical air. And everywhere trees and bushes, lawns and rockeries, rose bushes and ramblers were carefully clipped and trimmed to indicate the cultivation of their owners and the selectness of the district. All in all, Sandicott Crescent was the height of suburbia, the apex of that architectural triangle which marked the highest point of the topographical chart of middle-class ambition. The result was that the rates were enormous and the rents fixed. Mr Sandicott for all his prudence had not foreseen the Rent Act and Capital Gains Tax. Under the former there was no way of evicting tenants or increasing the rent they paid to a financially profitable sum; under the latter the sale of a house earned more for the Exchequer than it did for the owner; together the Rent Act and the tax nullified all Mr Sandicott's provisions for his daughter's future. Finally, and most aggravatingly of all, from Mrs Sandicott's point of view, the inhabitants of the Crescent took plenty of exercise, ate sensible diets and generally refused to oblige her by dying.

It was in large part the knowledge that she was saddled with twelve unsaleable houses whose combined rents barely covered the cost of their maintenance that had persuaded Mrs Sandicott that Jessica had reached the age of maturity she had so assiduously delayed. If Mr Flawse had rid himself of the liability of Lockhart, Mrs Sandicott had done much the same with Jessica and without further inquiry into the extent of Mr Flawse's fortune. It had seemed enough that he owned five thousand acres, a Hall and had but a short life expectancy.

By the time they had disembarked she had begun to have doubts. Mr Flawse had insisted on immediately catching a train to London and thence to Newcastle and had absolutely refused to allow Mrs Flawse to collect her belongings first or to drive him north in her large Rover.

'Ma'am,' he said, 'I place no faith in the infernal combustion engine. I was born before it and I do not intend to die behind it.' Mrs Flawse's arguments had been countered by his ordering the porter to put their baggage on the train. Mr Flawse followed the baggage and Mrs Flawse followed him. Lockhart and Jessica were left to move straight into Number 12 Sandicott Crescent with the promise to have her belongings packed and sent by removal van to Flawse Hall as quickly as possible.

And so the young couple started their married but unorthodox life in a house with five bedrooms, a double garage and a workshop in which the late Mr Sandicott, who had been handy with tools, had made things. Each morning Lockhart left the house, walked to the station and caught the train to London. There in the offices of Sandicott & Partner he began his apprenticeship under Mr Treyer. From the start there were difficulties. They lay less with Lockhart's ability to cope with figures – his limited education had left him mathematically exceedingly proficient – than in the directness of his approach to the problems of tax avoidance, or as Mr Treyer preferred to call it, Income Protection.

'Income and Asset Protection,' he told Lockhart, 'has a more positive ring to it than tax avoidance. And we must be positive.'

Lockhart took his advice and combined it with the positive simplicity his grandfather had adopted towards matters of income tax. Since the old man had transacted all possible business in cash and had made a habit of hurling every letter from the Income Tax authorities into the fire without reading it while at the same time ordering Mr Bullstrode to inform the bureaucratic swine that he was losing money not making it, Lockhart's adoption of his methods at Sandicott & Partner, while initially successful, was ultimately catastrophic. Mr Treyer had been delighted at first to find his IN tray so empty, and it was only his early arrival one morning to discover Lockhart using the toilet as an incinerator for all envelopes marked, 'On Her Majesty's Service' that alerted him to the cause of the sudden cessation of final demands. Worse still, Mr Treyer had long used what he called his Non-Existent Letter device as a means of confusing Income Tax officials to the point where they had nervous breakdowns or demanded to be transferred to other correspondence. Mr Treyer was proud of his Non-Existent Letter technique. It consisted of supposed replies which began 'Your letter of the 5th refers . . .' when in fact no letter of the 5th had been received. The consequent exchange of increasingly acrimonious denials by tax officials and Mr Treyer's continued assertions had been extremely beneficial to his clients if not to the nerves of Income Tax officials. Lockhart's arson deprived him of the ability to start letters beginning 'Your letter of the 5th refers . . .' with any confidence that one didn't.

'For all I know there may well have been half a dozen bloody letters of the 5th and all of them referring to some vital piece of information I know nothing about,' he shouted at Lockhart who promptly suggested that he try the 6th instead. Mr Treyer regarded him with starting eyes.

'Which since you burnt those too is a bloody useless suggestion,' he bawled.

'Well, you told me it was our business to protect our clients' interests and to be positive,' said Lockhart, 'and that's what I was doing.'

'How the hell can we protect clients' interests when we don't know what they are?' Mr Treyer demanded.

'But we do,' said Lockhart. 'It's all there in their files. I mean take Mr Gypsum, the architect. I was looking in his file the other day and he made £80,000 the year before last and all he paid in income tax was £1,758. The rest went in expenses. Let me see. He spent £16,000 in the Bahamas in May and . . .'

'Stop,' yelled Mr Treyer, on the verge of apoplexy, 'I don't want to hear what he spent . . . Dear Christ!'

'Well, that's what he said he did,' objected Lockhart. 'It's there in his letter to you. £16,000 in four days. Whatever do you think he did with all that money in only four days?'

Mr Treyer leant forward and clutched his head with a hand. To be lumbered with a mentally deficient creature with a photographic memory who went around burning Her Majesty's Official correspondence with a disregard that bordered on the insane was shortening his life.

'Look,' he said as patiently as he could, 'from now on I don't want you to go anywhere near those files, you or anyone else, do you understand?'

'Yes,' said Lockhart. 'What I don't understand is why the richer you are the less tax you pay. There's Gypsum earning a whacking £80,000 and paying £1,758.40 pence while Mrs Ponsonby who only got £6,315.32 pence in income had to shell out £2,472. I mean . . .'

'Shut up,' screamed Mr Treyer, 'I don't want to hear any more of your questions and I don't want to catch you within ten yards of a filing cabinet. Is that clear?'

'If you say so,' said Lockhart.

'I do say so,' said Mr Treyer. 'If I so much as see you glancing towards the files . . . Oh get out.'

Lockhart got out and Mr Treyer tried to restore his shattered nerves by taking a pink pill and a paper cup of whisky. Two days later he had cause to regret his instructions. A series of terrible screams from the room which contained the Value Added Tax records sent him scurrying through to find an officer of the Customs and Excise VAT department trying to extricate his fingers from the drawer of a filing cabinet which Lockhart had slammed shut just as he was reaching for a file.

'Well, you told me not to let anyone go near those files,' Lockhart explained as the VAT man was led away to have four broken fingers attended to by a doctor. Mr Treyer stared at him frenziedly and tried to think of an adequate phrase to describe his detestation.

'I mean,' continued Lockhart, 'if he had laid a hand on Mr Fixstein's VAT records . . .'

'Laid a hand!' screamed Mr Treyer almost as loudly as the VAT man. 'The poor sod won't have a hand to lay after what you've just been and done to him. And what's worse we'll have a hundred Excise men descend on us tonight and go through our books with a fine-tooth comb.' He paused and tried to think of a way out of the ghastly mess. 'Now you just go through and apologize and tell him it was an accident and perhaps . . .'

'I won't,' said Lockhart. 'It wasn't.'

'I know it bloody wasn't,' yelled Mr Treyer. 'I suppose if he had stuck his fucking head inside you'd have done the same.'

'I doubt it,' said Lockhart.

'I don't. Still it's a relief to know . . .' Mr Treyer began but Lockhart ended what little relief he had known.

'I would have kicked the door shut,' he said.

'Christ,' said Mr Treyer, 'it's like living with a murderer.'

That night the staff at Sandicott & Partner worked late transferring records to a Rent-A-Van to be taken to a barn in the country until the VAT storm was over. And next day Lockhart was taken off all accounting and given an office of his own.

'From now on you will stay in there and if there is anything I think I can trust you not to make a hash of I'll give it to you,' said Mr Treyer. Lockhart sat at his desk and waited but it was four days before Mr Treyer could think of anything for him to do.

'I've got to go to Hatfield,' he said, 'and there's a Mr Stoppard coming in at twelve-thirty. I'll be back by two so all I want you to do is to take him out and give him an expense-account lunch until I get back. That should be easy enough. Just buy him lunch. Right?'

'Buy him lunch?' said Lockhart. 'Who pays?'

'The firm pays, you fool. I said an expense-account lunch, didn't I?' He went away dejectedly but with the feeling that Lockhart could hardly make a total cock-up of a lunch with one of the firm's oldest clients. Mr Stoppard was a reticent man at the best of times and, being a gourmet, seldom spoke during a meal. When Mr Treyer returned Mr Stoppard was voluble to a degree. Mr Treyer tried to appease him and having finally got rid of him sent for Lockhart.

'What in the name of heaven made you take that bloody man

to a fish and chip shop?' he asked trying to control his blood pressure.

'Well, you said it was an expense-account lunch and we'd got to pay and I thought there was no point in wasting money so—'

'Thought?' yelled Mr Treyer letting his blood pressure go to hell and gone. 'Thought? And wasting money? What the hell do you think an expense-account lunch is for if it isn't to waste money? The meal is tax-deductible.'

'You mean the more a lunch costs the less we pay?' said Lockhart.

'Yes,' sighed Mr Treyer, 'that is precisely what I mean. Now the next time . . .'

The next time Lockhart took a Leicester shoe manufacturer to the Savoy Grill and wined and dined him to the tune of one hundred and fifty pounds, only to refuse to pay more than five when the bill was presented. It had taken the combined efforts of the shoe manufacturer and Mr Treyer, hastily summoned from a bout of flu, to persuade Lockhart to pay the one hundred and forty-five pounds' difference and make good the damage done to three tables and four waiters in the altercation that had ensued. After that Mr Treyer wrote to Mrs Flawse threatening to resign unless Lockhart was removed from the firm, and while waiting for a reply he barred Lockhart from leaving his office except to relieve himself.

But if Lockhart, to put it as mildly as modern parlance will allow, was having a job adjustment problem in Wheedle Street, his marriage proceeded as sweetly as it had started. And as chastely. What was lacking was not love – Lockhart and Jessica were passionlessly in love – but sex. The anatomical differences between males and females he had detected while gutting rabbits proved accurate in humans. He had balls and Jessica didn't. Jessica had breasts, large ones at that, and he didn't – or only of the most rudimentary kind. To further complicate matters, when they went to bed at night and lay in one another's arms he had an erection and Jessica didn't. The fact that he also had what are crudely termed 'lovers' balls' and spent part of the night in agony he was too brave and gentlemanly to mention. They simply lay in one another's arms and kissed. What happened after that he had no idea and Jessica had no idea either. Her mother's determination to retard her age of maturity had succeeded as completely as had Mr Flawse's equal determination that his grandson should inherit none of his mother's sexual vices. To compound this ignorance Lockhart's education, grounded in the most ancient of classical virtues, complemented Jessica's taste for the sickliest of historical romances in which sex was never mentioned. Taken together this fearful combination led them to idealize one another to the extent that it was impossible for Lockhart to conceive of doing anything more positive than worship Jessica and for Jessica to conceive at all. In brief, their marriage was never consummated and when after six weeks Jessica had her period rather more publicly than before, Lockhart's first impulse was to phone for an ambulance. Jessica in some distress managed to deter him.

'It happens once a month,' she said clutching a sanitary napkin to her with one hand while holding the phone down with the other.

'It doesn't,' said Lockhart, 'I've never bled like that in my life.'

'To girls,' said Jessica, 'not to boys.'

'I still say you ought to see a doctor,' insisted Lockhart.

'But it's been going on for ever so long.'

'All the more reason for seeing the doctor. It's obviously something chronic.'

'Well, if you insist,' said Jessica. Lockhart did. And so one morning when Lockhart had gone to his lonely vigil in the office, Jessica visited the doctor.

'My husband is worried about my bleeding,' she said. 'I told him not to be silly but he would insist.'

'Your husband?' said the doctor five minutes later, having discovered that Mrs Flawse was still a virgin. 'You did say "your husband"?'

'Yes,' said Jessica proudly, 'his name is Lockhart. I think that's a wonderful name, don't you?'

Dr Mannet considered the name, Jessica's manifest attractions, and the possibility that Mr Flawse, far from having a locked heart, must have a padlocked penis not to have been driven sexually berserk by the proximity of such a beautiful wife. Having run through this sequence he assumed the air of a counsellor and leant on the desk to conceal his own physical reaction.

'Tell me, Mrs Flawse,' he said with an urgency that was impelled by the almost certain feeling that he was about to have a spontaneous emission, 'has your husband never . . .' He stopped and shuddered violently in his chair. Dr Mannet had. 'I mean,' he began again when the convulsion was over, 'well . . . let me put it this way, have you refused to let him . . . er . . . touch you?'

'Of course not,' said Jessica who had watched the doctor's throes with some concern, 'we're always kissing and cuddling.'

'Kissing and cuddling,' said Dr Mannet with a whimper, 'Just kissing and . . . er . . . cuddling? Nothing more?'

'More?' said Jessica. 'What more?'

Dr Mannet looked despairingly into her angelic face. In a long career as a General Practitioner he had never been faced by such a beautiful woman who did not know that there was more to marriage than kissing and cuddling.

'You don't do anything else in bed?'

'Well, we go to sleep of course,' said Jessica.

'Dear Lord,' murmured the doctor, 'you go to sleep! And you do absolutely nothing else?'

'Lockhart snores,' said Jessica, thinking hard, 'but I can't think of anything else in particular.'

Across the desk Dr Mannet could and did his damnedest not to.

'And has no one ever explained where babies come from?' he asked, lapsing into that nursery whimsy that seemed to emanate from Mrs Flawse.

'Storks,' said Jessica bluntly.

'Stalks?' echoed the doctor, whose own stalk was playing him up again.

'Or herons. I forget which. They bring them in their beaks.'

'Beaks?' gurgled the doctor, now definitely back in the nursery.

'In little cradles of cloth,' continued Jessica, oblivious of the effect she was having. 'They have these little cradles of cloth and they carry them in their beaks. Surely you've seen pictures of them. And their mummies are ever so pleased. Is something the matter?'

34

But Dr Mannet was holding his head in his hands and staring at a prescription pad. He had shot his bolt again.

'Mrs Flawse, dear Mrs Flawse,' he whimpered when the crisis was past, 'if you'll just leave your telephone number . . . Better still, would you mind if I had a word with your husband, Lock-prick . . .'

'Hart,' said Jessica, 'Lockhart. You want him to come and see you?'

Dr Mannet nodded feebly. He had always previously disap-proved of the permissive society but just at that moment he had to admit that there were things to be said in its favour.

'Just ask him to come and see me, will you? Excuse me for not rising. You know the way out.'

Jessica went out and made an appointment for Lockhart. In the consulting-room Dr Mannet worked feverishly on his trousers and donned a white lab coat to cover the havoc Jessica had provoked.

But if Mrs Flawse had been a disturbing if pleasurable patient, her husband was even more disturbing and definitely not pleasurable. From the start he had eyed the doctor with danger-ous suspicion brought on by Jessica's account of Dr Mannet's poking and prodding and general gynaecological curiosity. By the time Dr Mannet had spoken for five minutes the suspicion had gone and the danger doubled.

'Are you suggesting,' said Lockhart with a grimness that made one of the more awful Aztec gods look positively amiable, 'that I should intrude what you have chosen to call my penis into the person of my wife and that this intrusion should take place through the orifice between her legs?'

Dr Mannet nodded. 'More or less,' he muttered, 'though I wouldn't put it quite like that.'

'Which orifice,' continued Lockhart more ferociously than ever, 'being too small will then split and cause her pain and suffering and . . .'

'Only temporarily,' said Dr Mannet, 'and if you object I can always make a slight incision myself.'

'Object?' snarled Lockhart and grabbed the doctor by the tie. 'If you think for one moment I'm going to let you touch my wife with your foul John Willie—'

'Not my John Willie, Mr Flawse,' gurgled the strangulated doctor, 'with a scalpel.'

It was an unwise suggestion. As Lockhart's grip tightened Dr Mannet turned from puce to purple and was passing to black when Lockhart released his grip and hurled him back into his chair.

'You come near my wife with a scalpel,' he said, 'and I'll gut you like a dead rabbit and have your balls for breakfast.'

Dr Mannet tried to get his voice back while considering this awful end. 'Mr Flawse,' he whispered finally, 'if you will just bear with me a moment. The purpose of what I call your penis and what you prefer to regard as your John Willie is not solely to pass water. I hope I make myself plain.'

'You do,' said Lockhart. 'Very plain, not to say downright ugly.'

'That's as may be,' continued the doctor. 'Now in the course of your adolescence you must at one time or another have noticed that your pen ... John Willie gave you pleasurable sensations.'

'I suppose you could say that,' said Lockhart grudgingly. 'At night.'

'Precisely,' said the doctor. 'At night you had wet dreams.'

Lockhart admitted that he had had dreams and that the results had sometimes been wet.

'Good,' said the doctor, 'now we're getting somewhere. And in those dreams were you not conscious of an overwhelming desire for women?'

'No,' said Lockhart, 'I most certainly wasn't.'

Dr Mannet shook his head carefully to rid himself of the feeling that he was dealing with some violent and wholly unconscious homosexual who having turned nasty once might turn murderous a second time. He trod warily.

'Would you mind telling me what you did dream about?'

Lockhart consulted his memory for a moment. 'Sheep,' he said finally.

'Sheep?' said Dr Mannet faintly. 'You had wet dreams about sheep?'

'Well, I don't know about the wet part,' said Lockhart, 'but I certainly dreamt about sheep a lot.'

'And did you do anything to these sheep you dreamt about?'

'Shot them,' said Lockhart bluntly.

Dr Mannet's sense of unreality grew alarmingly. 'You shot sheep in your sleep,' he said with involuntary alliteration. 'Is that what you're slaying . . . saying?'

'I shot them anyway,' said Lockhart. 'Wasn't anything much else to shoot so I took to potting them at fifteen hundred yards.'

'Potting them?' said the doctor slipping paediatrically. 'You potted sheep at fifteen hundred yards? Isn't that a bit difficult?'

'Well, you've got to aim up and off a bit, but at that range they've got a running chance.'

'Yes, I suppose they do,' said the doctor, who wished he had. 'And having potted them you then had spontaneous emissions about them?'

Lockhart studied him with concern now mixed with his disgust. 'I don't know what the hell you're talking about,' he said. 'First you fiddle with my wife and then you ask me here and start talking about fucking sheep . . .'

Dr Mannet seized on the expression. 'Ah,' he said, heading for bestiality, 'so having shot sheep you fucked them?'

'Did I?' said Lockhart who had picked up the six-letter word from Mr Treyer who used it frequently in its seven-letter variety when speaking to or about Lockhart. It was usually suffixed by idiot.

'Well, you should know,' said Dr Mannet.

'I may have done,' said Lockhart, who didn't. 'Anyway afterwards we had them for dinner.'

Dr Mannet shuddered. Much more of these appalling revelations and he would be in need of therapy himself.

'Mr Flawse,' he said determined to change the subject, 'what you did or did not do with sheep is beside the point. Your wife consulted me because she said you were concerned about her menstrual discharge . . .'

'I was concerned about her bleeding,' said Lockhart.

'Quite so, her monthly period. We call it menstruation.'

'I call it bloody horrible,' said Lockhart. 'And worrying.'

So did Dr Mannet but he took pains not to say so. 'Now the facts are simply these. Every woman—'

'Lady,' said Lockhart irritably.

'Lady what?'

'Don't call my wife a woman. She is a lady, a radiant, beautiful, angelic—'

Dr Mannet forgot himself. More particularly he forgot Lockhart's propensity for violence. 'Never mind all that,' he snapped. 'Any woman who can bring herself to live with a man who openly admits a preference for fucking sheep has got to be an angel, never mind the radiant or beautiful ...'

'I mind,' said Lockhart and brought the outburst to a sudden end.

Dr Mannet remembered himself. 'All right, given that Mrs Flawse is a lady it is nevertheless true that as a lady she naturally produces an ovum every month and this ovum descends her Fallopian tubes and unless it is fertilized it passes out in the form of ...'

He ground to a halt. Lockhart had gone Aztec again.

'What do you mean fertilized?' he snarled.

Dr Mannet tried to think of some way of explaining the process of fertilizing an ovum without causing further offence. 'What you do,' he said with an unnatural calm, 'is you put your pen ... Jesus ... your John Willie into her vagina and ... Dear God.' He gave up in despair and rose from his chair.

So did Lockhart. 'There you go again,' he shouted. 'First you talk about dunging my wife and now you're on about shoving my John Willie—'

'Dung?' screamed the doctor backing into a corner. 'Who said anything about dung?'

'Dung's fertilizer,' bawled Lockhart. 'Dig it and dung it. That is what we do in our kitchen garden and if you think ...'

But Dr Mannet was past thought. All he wanted to do was obey his instincts and get the hell out of his consulting-room before this sheep-obsessed maniac laid hands on him again. 'Nurse, nurse,' he screamed as Lockhart strode towards him. 'For God's sake ...' But Lockhart's fury had abated.

'Call yourself a doctor,' he snapped and went out the door. Dr Mannet sank back into his chair and called his partner. By the time he had prescribed himself thirty milligrams of Valium washed down with vodka and was able to put his words into coherent order he was determined to strike Mr and Mrs Flawse off his books for ever.

'Don't let either of them into the waiting-room ever again,' he told the nurse. 'On pain of death.'

'But isn't there something we can do for poor Mrs Flawse?' said the nurse. 'She seemed such a sweet girl.'

'My advice to her would be to get a divorce as quickly as possible,' said Dr Mannet fervently. 'Failing that, a hysterectomy would be the only thing. The thought of that man breeding . . .'

Outside in the street Lockhart slowly unclenched his jaw and fists. Coming at the end of a day in which he had been confined to an otherwise empty office with nothing whatsoever to do, the doctor's advice had been the last straw. He loathed London, Mr Treyer, Dr Mannet, East Pursley and everything about this insane rotten world into which he had been launched by his marriage. Every single thing about it conflicted absolutely with what he had been brought up to believe. In place of thrift there were expense-account lunches and rates of inflationary interest that were downright usury; instead of courage and beauty he found arrant cowardice in men – the doctor's squeals for help had made him too contemptible to hit – and in every building he saw only ugliness and a sordid obeisance to utility; and finally to cap it all there was this omnipresent concern with something called sex which grubby little cowards like Dr Mannet wanted to substitute for love. Lockhart walked along the street thinking of his love for Jessica. It was pure and holy and wonderful. He saw himself as her protector and the notion that he must hurt her to prove himself a dutiful husband was utterly repellent to him. He passed a newsagent's shop on whose racks were magazines displaying largely nude girls, dressed in the briefest of briefs or plastic macintoshes, and his gorge rose with disgust at their supposed appeal. The world was rotten and corrupt and he longed to be back on Flawse Fell with his rifle in his hands and some identifiable target between his sights while his darling Jessica sat in the stone-flagged kitchen by the black iron range waiting for him to come home with their supper. And with that longing there came the determination to make it come true.

One of these days he would take on the whole rotten world and impose his will on it, come hell or high water, and then people would learn what it meant to cross Lockhart Flawse. In the meantime he had to get home. For a moment he thought of catching the bus but it was only six miles to Sandicott Crescent and Lockhart was used to covering thirty in a day across the grassy fells of the Border country. With rage against everyone except Jessica and his grandfather and Mr Dodd, Lockhart strode off down the street.

Chapter five

At Flawse Hall the ex-Mrs Sandicott shared none of Lockhart's feelings. She would have given anything, most specifically strychnine, to old Mr Flawse, to be back in the cosy confines of Sandicott Crescent and the company of her acquaintances. Instead she was trapped in a large cold house on an empty wasteland, where the snow lay deep and the wind howled incessantly, with a horrid old man and his even more horrid gamekeeper-cum-handyman, Mr Dodd. Her husband's horridness had manifested itself almost as soon as they had taken their seats on the train from Southampton, and with each mile north it had increased while Mrs Flawse's conviction that she had made a terrible mistake grew into a certainty.

Old Mr Flawse on land had none of that old-world charm that had so affected her at sea. From being an eccentric and outspoken old man in his dotage, he had relapsed into an eccentric and outspoken old man with more faculties at his command than his age warranted. Porters scurried with their luggage, ticket collectors cringed, and even hardened taxi-drivers notorious for their rudeness when given an inadequate tip held their tongues while Mr Flawse disputed the fare and grudgingly gave them an extra penny. Mrs Flawse had been left speechless by his authority which flaunted a disregard for every tenet of her suburban creed and treated the world as his oyster.

Since Mrs Flawse had already been treated, almost literally, as his sexual oyster to be prised open on their honeymoon, she

40

should not have been surprised. It had been bad enough to discover on their first night that Mr Flawse wore a red flannel nightgown with an odour all his own and that he failed three times to distinguish between the washbasin and the lavatory bowl. Mrs Flawse had put these failings down to his age and deficient eyesight and sense of smell. She had been similarly dismayed when he knelt by the bed and implored the good Lord to forgive him in advance the carnal excesses he was about to inflict 'upon this the person of my wedded wife'. Little suspecting what he had in mind, Mrs Flawse found this prayer rather complimentary. It confirmed her belief that she was still at fifty-six an attractive woman and that her husband was a deeply religious man. Ten minutes later she knew better. Whatever the good Lord might feel about the matter of forgiveness, Mrs Flawse's feelings were implacable. She would never forgive or forget the old man's carnal excesses and any notion that he was at all religious had gone by the board. Smelling like an old fox, Mr Flawse had behaved like a young one, and had roamed about her body with as little discrimination between points of entry, or as she more delicately put it, 'her orifices', as he did between the washbasin and the toilet and with much the same intent. Feeling like a cross between a sexual colander and a cesspit, Mrs Flawse had endured the ordeal by consoling herself that such goings-on, and the old man had indeed gone on and on and on, must end abruptly in his having either a heart attack or a hernia. Mr Flawse obliged her on neither count and when she awoke next morning it was to find him sitting up smoking a foul old pipe and regarding her with undisguised relish. For the rest of the voyage Mrs Flawse had waddled the deck by day and straddled the bed by night in the dwindling hope that the wages of his sin would leave her shortly a rich and well-endowed widow.

And so she had travelled north with him determined to see the ordeal out to the end and not to be deterred by his behaviour. By the time they reached Hexham her determination had begun to sag. The grey stone town depressed her and she was only briefly revived by the spectacle outside the station of an immaculate brougham drawn by two black horses with a gaitered and tunicked Mr Dodd holding the door open for her. Mrs Flawse climbed in and felt better. This was what she called

riding in style and smacked of a world far removed from anything she had known before, an aristocratic world with uni-
formed servants and smart equipages. But as the carriage
rattled through the streets of the little market town Mrs Flawse
began to have second thoughts. The carriage bounced and
wobbled and shook and when after crossing the Tyne they took
the road to Wark by way of Chollerford she was well into her
third and fourth thoughts about the advantages of broughams.
Outside the country varied by the mile. At times they passed
along roads lined with trees and at others climbed bleak hills
where the snow still lay in drifts against dry-stone walls. And all
the time the carriage swayed and bounced horribly while beside
her Mr Flawse was savouring her discomfort.

'A splendid prospect,' he commented as they crossed a particularly unpleasant piece of open ground without a tree in
sight. Mrs Flawse kept her thoughts to herself. Let the old man
relish her misery while there was breath left in him but once she
was firmly ensconced in Flawse Hall he would learn just how
uncomfortable she could make his remaining days. There
would be no more sex for one thing. Mrs Flawse had determined on that, and being a vigorous woman, was capable of
giving as good as she got. And so the two of them sat side by
side contemplating the other's discomfiture. It was Mrs Flawse
who got the first shock. Shortly after Wark they turned down a
half-metalled track that led along a nicely wooded valley
towards a large and handsome house set in a spacious garden.
Mrs Flawse's hopes rose prematurely.

'Is that the Hall?' she asked as they rattled towards the gates.

'It is not,' said Mr Flawse. 'That's the Cleydons.'

For a moment his spirits seemed to sink. Young Cleydon had
been an early candidate for Lockhart's paternity and only the
certainty that he had been in Australia during the months that
covered Lockhart's conception had saved him from being
flogged within an inch of his life.

'It seems a nice house,' said Mrs Flawse, noting her husband's
change of mood.

'Aye, 'tis better than the occupants, God rot their souls,' said
the old man. Mrs Flawse added the Cleydons to the imaginary
list of neighbours he disliked whose friendship she would cul-
tivate. That the list seemed likely to be imaginary dawned on

her a short time later. Past the house the road wound out of the woods and climbed the steep bank of a bare hillside; a mile beyond the rise they came to the first of many gates in drystone walls. Mr Dodd climbed down and opened the gate. Then he led the carriage through and shut it. Mrs Flawse searched the horizon for a sign of her new home but there was not a house in sight. Here and there a few dirty sheep showed up against the snow but for the rest there was emptiness. Mrs Flawse shivered.

'We've another ten miles yet,' said Mr Flawse cheerfully. For the next hour they bumped along the broken road with nothing more enchanting to view than an abandoned farmhouse standing within a garden wall and surrounded by fireweed and stinging nettles. Finally they arrived at another gate and beyond it Mrs Flawse could see a church standing on a knoll and around it several houses.

'That's Black Pockrington,' said Mr Flawse. 'You'll do your shopping there.'

'There?' said Mrs Flawse tartly. 'I most certainly won't. It doesn't look big enough to have shops.'

'It has a wee store and the cholera explains its size.'

'Cholera?' said Mrs Flawse, somewhat alarmed.

'The epidemic of 1842 or thereabouts,' said the old man, 'wiped out nine-tenths of the population. You'll find them buried in the graveyard. A terrible thing, the cholera, but without it I doubt we Flawses would be where we are today.'

He gave a nasty chuckle that found no echo in his wife. She had not the least desire to be where she was today.

'We bought the land around for a song,' continued Mr Flawse. 'Dead Man's Moor they call it now.'

In the distance there came the sound of an explosion.

'That'll be the artillery wasting good taxpayers' money on the firing-range. You'll get used to the noise. It's either that or they're blasting over Tombstone Law in the quarries.'

Mrs Flawse hugged her travelling rug to her. The very names were filled with dread.

'And when are we getting to Flawse Hall?' she asked, to drive away her fear. The old man consulted a large gold Hunter.

'About another half an hour,' he said, 'by half past four.'

Mrs Flawse stared out the window even more intently looking for the houses of neighbours but there were none to be seen only the unbroken expanse of open moor and the occasional outcrop of rock that topped the hills. As they drove on the wind rose. Finally they came to another gated wall and Mr Dodd climbed down again.

'The Hall is over yonder. You'll not get a better view,' said the old man as they drove through. Mrs Flawse wiped the mist from the window and peered out. What she could see of the home she had set such store by had nothing to recommend it now. Flawse Hall on Flawse Fell close under Flawse Rigg lived up to its name. A large grey granite building with a tower at one end, it reminded her of Dartmoor Prison in a miniature way. The high stone wall that surrounded three sides of the house had the same air of deliberate containment as that of the prison and the gated archway in the wall was large and ominous. A few stunted and wind-bent trees huddled beside the wall and far away to the west she caught sight of dark pinewoods.

'That's the reservoir over there,' said Mr Flawse. 'Ye'll see the dam below.'

Mrs Flawse saw the dam. It was built of blocks of granite that filled the valley and from its base there ran a stone-sided stream that followed the valley floor, passed under a gated bridge, wound on another quarter of a mile and disappeared into a dark hole in the hillside. All in all the prospect ahead was as grim as nature and nineteenth-century waterworks could make it. Even the iron gate on to the little bridge was spiked and locked. Again Mr Dodd had to climb down and open it before the carriage moved through. Mr Flawse looked up the hill proudly and rubbed his hands with glee. 'It's good to be home again,' he said as the horses began the slow ascent to the house.

Mrs Flawse could see nothing good about it. 'What's that tower at the end?' she asked.

'That's the old peel tower. Much restored by my grandfather but the house is structurally much as it was in the sixteenth century.'

Mrs Flawse had few doubts about that. 'A peel tower?' she murmured.

'A refuge for man and beast when the Scots raided. The walls are ten feet thick and it took more than a passel of marauding Scotsmen or moss troopers to break their way in where they weren't wanted.'

'And what are moss troopers?' Mrs Flawse inquired.

'They aren't any more, ma'am,' said the old man, 'but they were in the old days. Border raiders and cattle thieves from Redesdale and North Tynedale. The king's writ didn't run in the Middle Marches until well into the seventeenth century and, some say, later. It would have taken a brave law officer to come into these wild parts much before 1700.'

'But why moss troopers?' Mrs Flawse continued to take her mind off the looming granite house.

'Because they rode the moss and built their strongholds of great oak trunks and covered them with moss to hide them away and stop them being fired. It must have been a difficult thing to find them in among the bogs and swamps. Aye, and it needed a courageous man with no fear of death in his heart.'

'I should have thought that anyone who chose to live up here must have had a positive longing for death,' said Mrs Flawse.

But the old man was not to be diverted by the Great Certainty from the great past. 'You may well say so, ma'am, but we Flawses have been here since God alone knows when and there were Flawses with Percy at the Battle of Otterburn so celebrated in song.'

As if to emphasize the point another shell exploded to the west on the firing-range and as its boom died away there came another even more sinister sound. Dogs were baying.

'My God, what on earth is that?' said Mrs Flawse, now thoroughly alarmed.

Mr Flawse beamed. 'The Flawse Pack, ma'am,' he said and rapped on the window with his silver-headed stick. Mr Dodd peered down between his legs and for the first time Mrs Flawse saw that he had a cast in one eye. Upside-down, it gave his face a terrible leering look. 'Dodd, we'll gan in the yard. Mrs Flawse would like to see the hounds.'

Mr Dodd's topsy-turvy smile was horrible to behold. So too were the hounds when he climbed down and opened the heavy wooden gates under the archway. They swarmed out in a great seething mass and surrounded the brougham. Mrs Flawse stared down at them in horror. 'What sort of hounds are they? They're certainly not foxhounds,' she said to the old man's delight.

'Those are Flawse hounds,' he said as one great beast leapt up and slobbered at the window with lolling tongue. 'Bred them myself from the finest stock. The hounds of spring are on winter's traces as the great Swinburne has it, and ye'll not find hounds that'll spring so fierce on anything's traces as these beasts. Two-thirds Pyrenean Mountain Dog for their ferocity and size. One-third Labrador for the keenness of scent and the ability to swim and retrieve. And finally one-third Greyhound for their speed. What do ye make of that, ma'am?'

'Four-thirds,' said Mrs Flawse, 'which is an absurdity. You can't make four-thirds of anything.'

'Can ye not?' said Mr Flawse, the gleam in his eye turning from pride to irritation that he should be so disproved. 'Then we'll have one in for your inspection.'

He opened the door and one of the great hybrids vaulted in and slavered in his face before turning its oral attentions to its new mistress.

'Take the horrid thing away. Get off, you brute,' shouted Mrs Flawse, 'stop that at once. Oh my God . . .'

Mr Flawse, satisfied that he had made his point, cuffed the dog out of the coach and slammed the door. Then he turned to his wife. 'I think ye'll agree that there's more than three-thirds of savage hound in him, my dear,' he said grimly, 'or would you care for another closer look?'

Mrs Flawse gave him a very close look indeed and said she would not.

'Then ye'll not contradict me on the matter of eugenics, ma'am,' he said, and shouted to Mr Dodd to drive on. 'I have made a study of the subject and I'll not be told I am wrong.'

Mrs Flawse kept her thoughts to herself. They were not nice ones. But they would keep. The carriage drew up at the back door and stopped. Mr Dodd came round through a sea of hounds.

'Get them out the way, man,' shouted Mr Flawse above the barks. 'The wife is afraid of the creatures.'

The next moment Mr Dodd, flailing around him with the horsewhip, had cowed the hounds back across the yard. Mr Flawse got out and held his hand for Mrs Flawse. 'You'll not expect a man of my age to carry you across the door-stone,' he said gallantly, 'but Dodd will be my proxy. Dodd, carry your mistress.'

'There's absolutely no need ...' Mrs Flawse began but Mr Dodd had obeyed orders, and she found herself staring too closely for her peace of mind into his leering face as he clutched her to him and carried her into the house.

'Thank you, Dodd,' said Mr Flawse, following them in. 'Ceremony has been observed. Put her down.'

For a horrid moment Mrs Flawse was clutched even tighter and Dodd's face came closer to her own, but then he relaxed and set her on her feet in the kitchen. Mrs Flawse adjusted her dress before looking round.

'I trust it meets with your approbation, my dear.'

It didn't but Mrs Flawse said nothing. If the outside of Flawse Hall had looked bleak, bare and infinitely forbidding, the kitchen, flagged with great stones, was authentically medieval. True there was a stone sink with a tap above it, which signified running if cold water, and the iron range had been made in the later stages of the Industrial Revolution; there was little else that was even vaguely modern. A bare wooden table stood in the middle of the room with benches on either side, and there were upright wooden seats with backs beside the range.

'Settles,' said Mr Flawse when Mrs Flawse looked inquiringly at them. 'Dodd and the bastard use them of an evening.'

'The bastard?' said Mrs Flawse. 'What bastard?' But for once it was Mr Flawse's turn to keep silent.

'I'll show ye the rest of the house,' he said and led the way out down a passage.

'If it's anything like the kitchen ...' Mrs Flawse began but it wasn't. Where the kitchen had been bleak and bare, the rest of the Hall lived up to her expectations and was packed with fine furniture, tapestries, great portraits and the contributions of many generations and as many marriages. Mrs Flawse breathed a sigh of relief as she stood below the curved staircase and looked around her. In marrying old Mr Flawse she had done more than marry a man in his dotage, she had wedded herself to a fortune in antique furniture and fine silver. And from every wall a Flawse face looked down from old portraits, wigged Flawses, Flawses in uniform and Flawses in fancy waistcoats, but the Flawse face was ever the same. Only in one corner did she find a small dark portrait that was not clearly identifiable as a Flawse.

'Murkett Flawse, painted posthumously, I'm afraid,' said the old man. Mrs Flawse studied the portrait more closely.

'He must have died a peculiar death from the look of him,' she said. Mr Flawse nodded.

'Beheaded, ma'am, and I have an idea the executioner had a bad head that morning from over-indulgence the night before and took more chops than were rightly called for.'

Mrs Flawse withdrew from the horrid portrayal of Murkett Flawse's head, and together they went from room to room. In each there was something to admire and in Mrs Flawse's case to value. By the time they returned to the entrance hall she was satisfied that she had done well to marry the old fool after all.

'And this is my inner sanctum,' said Mr Flawse opening a door to the left of the entrance. Mrs Flawse went inside. A huge coal fire blazed in the hearth and, in contrast to the rest of the house which had seemed decidedly damp and musty, the study was warm and smelt of book-leather and tobacco. An old cat basked on the carpet in front of the fire and from every wall books gleamed in the firelight. In the centre of the room stood a kneehole desk with a greenshaded lamp and an inkstand of silver. Mrs Flawse went to the lamp to switch it on and found a handle.

'You'll need a match,' said Mr Flawse, 'we're not on the electricity.'

'You're not . . .' Mrs Flawse began and stopped as the full significance of the remark dawned on her. Whatever treasures in the way of old silver and fine furniture Flawse Hall might hold, without electricity it held only transitory attractions for Mrs Flawse. No electricity meant presumably no central heating, and the single tap above the stone sink had signified only cold water. Mrs Flawse, safe from the hounds and in the inner sanctum of her husband's study, decided the time had come to strike. She sat down heavily in a large high-backed leather chair beside the fire and glared at him.

'The very idea of bringing me here and expecting me to live in a house without electricity or hot water or any mod cons . . .' she began stridently as the old man bent to light a spill from the fire. Mr Flawse turned his face towards her and she saw it was suffused with rage. In his hand the spill burnt lower. Mr Flawse ignored it.

'Woman,' he said with a soft and steely emphasis, 'ye'll learn never to address me in that tone of voice again.' He straightened up but Mrs Flawse was not to be cowed.

'And you'll learn never to call me "woman" again,' she said defiantly, 'and don't think that you can bully me because you can't. I'm perfectly capable . . .'

They were interrupted by the entrance of Mr Dodd bearing a silver tray on which a teapot stood under a cosy. Mr Flawse signalled to him to put it on the low table beside her chair and it was only when Mr Dodd had left the room closing the door quietly behind him that the storm broke once again. It did so simultaneously.

'I said I'm—' Mrs Flawse began.

'Woman,' roared Mr Flawse, 'I'll not—'

But their unison silenced them both and they sat glowering at one another by the fire. It was Mrs Flawse who first broke the truce. She did so with guile.

'It's perfectly simple,' she said, 'we need not argue about it. We can install an electrical generator. You'll find it will make a tremendous improvement to your life.'

But Mr Flawse shook his head. 'I have lived without it for ninety years and I'll die without it.'

'I shouldn't be at all surprised,' said Mrs Flawse, 'but I see no reason why you should take me with you. I am used to hot water and my home comforts and—'

'Ma'am,' said Mr Flawse, 'I have washed in cold water . . .'

'Seldom,' said Mrs Flawse.

'As I was saying . . .'

'We can have Calor gas if you won't have electricity . . .'

'I'll have no modern contraption . . .'

They wrangled on until it was time for dinner and in the kitchen Mr Dodd listened with an interested ear while he stirred the stewed mutton in the pot.

'The auld divil's bitten off a sight more than he's teeth in his heid to chew,' he thought to himself, and tossed a bone to his old collie by the door. 'And if the mither's so rigid what's the lassie like?' With this on his mind he moved about the kitchen which had seen so many centuries of Flawse womenfolk come and go and where the smells of those centuries which Lockhart pined for still clung. Mr Dodd had no nose for them, that musk of unwashed humanity, of old boots and dirty socks, wet dogs and mangy cats, of soap and polish, fresh milk and warm blood, baked bread and hung pheasant, all those necessities of the harsh life the Flawses had led since the house first was built. He was part of that musk and shared its ancestry. But now there was a new ingredient come to the house and one he had no mind to like.

Nor after a glum dinner had Mr Flawse when he and Mrs Flawse retired to a cold bedroom and a featherbed redolent of damp and too recently plucked chicken. Outside the wind whistled in the chimneys and from the kitchen there came the faint wail of Mr Dodd's Northumbrian pipes as he played 'Edward, Edward'. It seemed an appropriate ballad for the evil hour. Upstairs Mr Flawse knelt by the bed.

'Oh Lord . . .' he began, only to be interrupted by his wife.

'There's no point in your asking forgiveness,' she said. 'You're not coming near me until we've first come to an understanding.'

The old man regarded her balefully from the floor. 'Understanding? What understanding, ma'am?'

'A clear understanding that you will have this house modernized as quickly as possible and that until such time I shall return to my own home and the comforts to which I have been accustomed. I didn't marry you to catch my death of pneumonia.'

Mr Flawse lumbered to his feet. 'And I didn't marry you,' he thundered, 'to have my household arrangements dictated to me by a chit of a woman.'

Mrs Flawse pulled the sheet up round her neck defiantly. 'And I won't be shouted at,' she snapped back. 'I am not a shit of a woman. I happen to be a respectable . . .'

A fresh wail of wind in the chimney and the fact that Mr Flawse had picked up a poker from the grate stopped her.

'Respectable are ye? And what sort of respectable woman is it that marries an old man for his money?'

'Money?' said Mrs Flawse, alarmed at this fresh evidence that the old fool wasn't such an old fool after all. 'Who said anything about money?'

'I did,' roared Mr Flawse. 'You proposed and I disposed and

if you imagine for one moment that I didn't know what you were after you're sadly misguided.'

Mrs Flawse resorted to the stratagem of tears. 'At least I thought you were a gentleman,' she whimpered.

'Aye, you did that. And more fool you,' said the old man as livid as his red flannel gown. 'And tears will get you nowhere. You made it a condition of the bastard's marrying your numb-skull daughter that you were to be my wife. Well, you have made your bed, now you must lie in it.'

'Not with you,' said Mrs Flawse. 'I'd rather die.'

'And well you may, ma'am, well you may. Is that your last word?'

Mrs Flawse hesitated and made a mental calculation between the threat, the poker and her last word. But there was still stub-bornness in her Sandicott soul.

'Yes,' she said defiantly.

Mr Flawse hurled the poker into the grate and went to the door. 'Ye'll live to rue the day you said that, ma'am,' he muttered malevolently and left.

Mrs Flawse lay back exhausted by her defiance and then with a final effort got out of bed and locked the door.

Chapter six

Next morning after a fitful night Mrs Flawse came downstairs to find the old man closeted in his sanctum and a note on the kitchen table telling her to make her own breakfast. A large pot of porridge belched glutinously on the stove and having sampled its contents she contented herself with a pot of tea and some bread and marmalade. There was no sign of Mr Dodd. Outside in the yard the grey products of Mr Flawse's experi-ments in canine eugenics lolled about in the wintry sunshine. Avoiding them by going out of the kitchen door, Mrs Flawse made her way round the garden. Enclosed by the high wall against the wind and weather, it was not unattractive. Some earlier Flawse had built greenhouses and a kitchen garden and Capability Flawse, whose portrait hung on the landing wall, had created a miniature Southern landscape in the half-acre not devoted to vegetables. Stunted trees and sanded paths wound in and out of rockeries and a fountain played in an oval fishpond. In one corner there was a gazebo, a little belvedere of flint and sea shells embedded in cement with a tiny Gothic window paned with coloured glass. Mrs Flawse climbed the steps to the door, found it unlocked and went inside to discover the first signs of comfort at the Hall. Lined with oak panels and faded velvet plush seats the little room had an ornately carved ceiling and a view out across the fell to the reservoir.

Mrs Flawse seated herself there and wondered again at the strangeness of the family into which she had so unwisely married. That it was of ancient lineage she had already gathered and that it had money she still suspected. Flawse Hall might not be an attractive building but it was filled with treasures filched from long-lost colonies by those intrepid younger sons who had risked malaria and scurvy and yellow fever to make their fortunes or meet untimely deaths in far-flung corners of the Empire. Mrs Flawse envied and understood their enterprise. They had gone south and east (and in many cases west) to escape the bleakness and boredom of home. Mrs Flawse yearned to follow their example. Anything would be preferable to the intolerable isolation of the Hall and she was just trying to think of some way of making her own departure when the tall gaunt figure of her husband emerged from the kitchen garden and made its way between the rockeries and miniature trees to the gazebo. Mrs Flawse steeled herself for this encounter. She need not have bothered. The old man was evidently in a genial mood. He strode up the steps and knocked on the door. 'May I come in?'

'I suppose so,' said Mrs Flawse.

Mr Flawse stood in the doorway. 'I see you have found your way to Perkin's Lookout,' he said. 'A charming folly built in 1774 by Perkin Flawse, the family poet. It was here that he wrote his famous "Ode to Coal", inspired no doubt by the drift mine you see over yonder.'

He pointed through the little window at a mound on the

opposite hillside. There was a dark hole beside the mound and some remnants of rusting machinery.

' "By Nature formed by Nature felled
'Tis not by Nature now expelled.
But man's endeavour yet sets free
The charred remains of many a tree
And so by forests long since dead
We boil our eggs and bake our bread."

A fine poet, ma'am, if little recognized,' continued the old man when he had finished the recitation, 'but then we Flawses have unsuspected gifts.'

'So I have discovered,' said Mrs Flawse with some acerbity.

The old man bowed his head. He too had spent a wakeful night wrestling with his conscience and losing hands down.

'I have come to beg your pardon,' he said finally. 'My conduct as your husband was inexcusable. I trust you will accept my humble apologies.'

Mrs Sandicott hesitated. Her former marriage had not disposed her to forfeit her right to grievance too easily. There were advantages to be gained from it, among them power. 'You called me a shit of a woman,' she pointed out.

'A chit, ma'am, a chit,' said Mr Flawse. 'It means a young woman.'

'Not where I come from,' said Mrs Flawse. 'It has an altogether different meaning and a very nasty one.'

'I assure you I meant young, ma'am. The defecatory connotation which you attributed to the word was entirely absent from my intention.'

Mrs Flawse rather doubted that. What she had experienced of his intentions on their honeymoon gave her reason to think otherwise, but she had been prepared to suffer in a good cause. 'Whatever you intended, you still accused me of marrying you for your money. Now that I won't take from anyone.'

'Quite so, ma'am. It was said in the heat of the moment and in the humble consciousness that there had to be a more sufficient reason than my poor self. I retract the remark.'

'I'm glad to hear it. I married you because you were old and lonely and needed someone to look after you. The thought of money never entered my head.'

'Quite so,' said Mr Flawse, accepting these personally insulting attributes with some difficulty, 'as you say I am old and lonely and I need someone to look after me.'

'And I can't be expected to look after anyone with the present lack of amenities in the house. I want electricity and hot baths and television and central heating if I am to stay here.'

Mr Flawse nodded sadly. That it should have come to this. 'You shall have them, ma'am,' he said, 'you shall have them.'

'I didn't come here to catch my death of pneumonia. I want them installed at once.'

'I shall put the matter in hand immediately,' said Mr Flawse, 'and now let us adjourn to my study and the warmth of my fire to discuss the matter of my will.'

'Your will?' said Mrs Flawse. 'You did say "your will"?'

'Indeed I did, ma'am,' said the old man and escorted her down the steps of the gazebo and across the stunted garden to the house. There, sitting opposite one another in the great leather armchairs, with a mangy cat basking before the coal fire they continued their discussion.

'I will be frank with you,' said Mr Flawse. 'My grandson, your son-in-law, Lockhart is a bastard.'

'Really?' said Mrs Flawse, uncertain whether or not to give that word its literal meaning. The old man answered the question.

'The product of an illicit union between my late daughter and person or persons unknown, and I have made it my life's work to determine firstly his paternal ancestry and secondly to eradicate those propensities to which by virtue of his being partly a Flawse I have access. I trust you follow my line of reasoning.'

Mrs Flawse didn't but she nodded obediently.

'I am, as you may have surmised from a perusal of my library, a firm believer in the congenital inheritance of ancestral characteristics both physical and mental. To paraphrase the great William, there is a paternity that shapes our ends roughhew them how we will. Paternity, ma'am. Not maternity. The mating of dogs, of which I have considerable experience, is a pointer to this end.'

Mrs Flawse shivered and stared wildly at him. If her ears did not deceive her, she had married a man with perversions beyond belief.

Mr Flawse ignored her stunned look and continued. 'The female bitch when on heat,' he said, adding, 'I trust this somewhat indelicate subject does not offend you?' and taking Mrs Flawse's shaking head as an assurance that she wasn't in the least put out, went on, 'the female bitch on heat attracts the attention of a pack of males, which pack pursues her up hill and down dale fighting among themselves for the privilege accorded to the fiercest and strongest dog of fecundating her *prima nocte*. She is thus impregnated by the finest specimen first but to assure conception she is then served by all the other dogs in the pack down to the smallest and weakest. The result is the survival of the species, ma'am, and of the fittest. Darwin said it, ma'am, and Darwin was right. Now I am an hereditarist. The Flawse nose and the Flawse chin are physical proof of the inheritance over the centuries of physical attributes evolved from our Flawse forefathers and it is my firm conviction that we not only inherit physical characteristics by way of paternal ancestry but also mental ones. To put it another way, the dog is father to the man, and a dog's temperament is determined by his progenitors. But I see that you doubt me.'

He paused and studied Mrs Flawse closely; there was certainly doubt on her face. But it was doubt as to the sanity of the man she had married rather than an intellectual doubt of his argument.

'You say,' continued the old man, 'as well you may, if inheritance determines temperament what has education to do with what we are? Is that not what you are thinking?'

Again Mrs Flawse nodded involuntarily. Her own education had been so pasteurized by permissive parents and progressive teachers that she found it impossible to follow his argument at all. Beyond the fact that he seemed obsessed with the sexual habits and reproductive processes of dogs and had openly admitted that in the Flawse family a dog was evidently the father to the man, she had no idea what he was talking about.

'The answer is this, ma'am, and here again the dog is our determinant, a dog is a domestic animal not by nature but by social symbiosis. Dog and man, ma'am, live together by virtue of mutual necessity. We hunt together, we eat together, we live together and we sleep together, but above all we educate one another. I have learnt more from the constant companionship of dogs than ever I have from men or books. Carlyle is the exception but I will come to that later. First let me say that a dog can be trained. Up to a point, ma'am, only up to a point. I defy the finest shepherd in the world to take a terrier and turn him into a sheepdog. It can't be done. A terrier is an earth dog. Your Latin will have acquainted you with that. Terra, earth; terrier, earth dog. And no amount of herding will eradicate his propensity for digging. Train him how you will he will remain a digger of holes at heart. He may not dig but the instinct is there. and so it is with man, ma'am. Which said, it remains only to say that I have done with Lockhart my utmost to eradicate those instincts which we Flawses to our cost possess.'

'I'm glad to hear it,' muttered Mrs Flawse, who knew to her cost those instincts the Flawses possessed. The old man raised an admonitory finger. 'But, ma'am, lacking a knowledge of his father's ancestry I have been handicapped. Aye, sorely handicapped. The vein of vice that runs in Lockhart's paternal line I know not and knowing not can but deduce. My daughter could by no stretch of the imagination be described as a discriminating girl. The manner of her death suffices to prove that. She died, ma'am, behind a dyke giving birth to her son. And she refused to name the father.'

Mr Flawse paused to savour his frustration and to expel that nagging suspicion that his daughter's obstinacy in the matter of Lockhart's paternity was a final gesture of filial generosity designed to spare him the ignominy of incest. While he stared into the depths of the fire as into hell itself, Mrs Flawse contented herself with the realization that Lockhart's illegitimacy was one more arrow to the bow of her domestic power. The old fool would suffer for the admission. Mrs Flawse had garnered a fresh grievance.

'When I think that my Jessica is married to an illegitimate man, I must say I find your behaviour inexcusable and dishonourable, I do indeed,' she said taking advantage of Mr Flawse's mood of submission. 'If I had known I would never have given consent to the marriage.'

Mr Flawse nodded humbly. 'You must forgive me,' he said, 'but needs must when the devil drives and your daughter's saintliness will dilute the evil of Lockhart's paternal line.'

'I sincerely hope so,' said Mrs Flawse. 'And talking about

inheritance I believe you mentioned remaking your will.' And so from things theoretical they moved to practicalities. 'I will send for my solicitor, Mr Bullstrode, and have him draw up the new will. You will be the beneficiary, ma'am. I assure you of that. Within the limits imposed by my obligations to my employees, of course, and with the proviso that on your demise the estate will go to Lockhart and his offspring.'

Mrs Flawse smiled contentedly. She foresaw a comfortable future. 'And in the meantime you will see to it that the Hall is modernized?' she said. And again Mr Flawse nodded.

'In that case I shall stay,' said Mrs Flawse graciously. This time there was the flicker of a smile on Mr Flawse's face but it died instantly. There was no point in giving his game away. He would buy time by affecting submission.

That afternoon Mrs Flawse sat down and wrote to Jessica. It was less a letter than an inventory of her possessions to be forwarded by road haulage to Flawse Hall. When she had finished she gave the letter to Mr Dodd to post in Black Pockrington. It was still unposted that night when she went up to bed. In the kitchen Mr Flawse boiled a kettle and steamed the envelope open and read its contents.

'You can post it,' he told Mr Dodd as he resealed the envelope. 'The auld trout has taken the bait. It just remains to play her.'

And so for the next few months he did. The amenities of Flawse Hall remained unimproved. The central heating firm was always coming next week and never did. The electricity remained in abeyance and the Post Office refused to connect the telephone except at a cost that even Mrs Flawse found prohibitive. There were hitches everywhere. The arrival of her private possessions was delayed by the inability of the furniture removal van to negotiate the bridge at the bottom of the valley and the refusal of the removal men to carry boxes and trunks half a mile uphill. In the end they unloaded the van and went away, leaving it to Mrs Flawse and Mr Dodd to bring the pieces up one by one, a slow process made slower by Mr Dodd's other multifarious occupations. It was late spring by the time every knick-knack and gewgaw from 12 Sandicott Crescent had been installed in the drawing-room where they competed in vain with the antique plunder of the Empire. Worst of all Mrs Flawse's Rover was dispatched by rail, and thanks to Mr Dodd's intervention with the stationmaster, in which transaction money passed hands, was rerouted back to East Pursley by way of Glasgow, and delivered to Lockhart and Jessica mechanically inoperable and with a label attached saying 'Addressee unknown'. Without her car Mrs Flawse was lost. She could accompany Mr Dodd in the dog-cart as far as Black Pockrington, but no one in Pockrington had a telephone and farther he refused to go.

After three months of discomfort, uncertainty, and procrastination on Mr Flawse's part in the matter of the will, she had had enough. Mrs Flawse delivered her ultimatum.

'You will either do the things you promised to do or I will leave,' she said.

'But, ma'am, I have done my best,' said Mr Flawse. 'The matter is in hand and . . .'

'It were better it were afoot,' said Mrs Flawse who had adapted her speech to that of her husband. 'I mean what I say. Mr Bullstrode, the solicitor, must draw up your will in my favour or I will up sticks and return to where I am appreciated.'

'Where there's a will there's a way,' said the old man, musing on the possible permutations implied in the maxim and thinking of Schopenhauer. 'As the great Carlyle said . . .'

'And that's another thing. I'll have no more sermonizing. I have heard enough of Mr Carlyle to last me a lifetime. He may be the great man you say he was but enough's as good as a feast and I've had my fill of Heroes and Hero Worship.'

'And is that your last word?' asked Mr Flawse hopefully.

'Yes,' said Mrs Flawse, and contradicted herself, 'I have endured your company and the inconveniences of this house long enough. Mr Bullstrode will put in an appearance within the week or I shall make myself absent.'

'Then Mr Bullstrode will be here tomorrow,' said Mr Flawse. 'I give you my word.'

'He'd better be,' said Mrs Flawse and flounced out of the room leaving the old man to regret that he had ever urged her to read Samuel Smiles on Self Help.

That night Mr Dodd was dispatched with a sealed envelope bearing the Flawse crest, a moss trooper pendant, imprinted in wax on the back. It contained precise instructions as to the contents of Mr Flawse's new will, and when Mrs Flawse came down to breakfast next morning it was to learn that for once her husband had lived up to his word.

'There you are, ma'am,' said Mr Flawse, handing her Mr Bullstrode's reply, 'he will be here this afternoon to draw up the will.'

'And just as well,' said Mrs Flawse. 'I meant what I said.'

'And I mean every word I say, ma'am. The will shall be drawn and I have summoned Lockhart to be present next week when it is to be read.'

'I can see no good reason why he should be present until after your death,' said Mrs Flawse. 'That's the usual time for reading wills.'

'Not this will, ma'am,' said Mr Flawse. 'Forewarned is forearmed as the old saying has it. And the boy needs a spur to his flank.'

He retired to his sanctum leaving Mrs Flawse to puzzle this riddle, and that afternoon Mr Bullstrode arrived at the bridge over The Cut and was admitted by Mr Dodd. For the next three hours there came the sound of muted voices from the study, but though she listened at the keyhole Mrs Flawse could gain nothing from the conversation. She was back in the drawing-room when the solicitor came to pay his respects before leaving.

'One question before you go, Mr Bullstrode,' she said. 'I would like your assurance that I am the chief beneficiary of my husband's will.'

'You may rest assured on that point, Mrs Flawse. You are indeed the chief beneficiary. Let me go further, the conditions of Mr Flawse's new will leave his entire estate to you until your death.'

Mrs Flawse sighed with relief. It had been an uphill battle but she had won the first round. All that remained was to insist on modern conveniences being installed in the house. She was sick to death of using the earth closet.

Chapter seven

Lockhart and Jessica were sick, period. The Curse, as Jessica had been brought up to call it, blighted what little physical bond there was between them. Lockhart steadfastly refused to impose his unworthy person on his bleeding angel and, even when not bleeding, his angel refused to insist on her right as his wife to be imposed upon. But if they lived in a state of sexual stalemate, their love grew in the fertile soil of their frustration. In short, they adored one another and loathed the world in which they found themselves. Lockhart no longer spent his days at Sandicott & Partner in Wheedle Street. Mr Treyer, forced to decide whether to implement his threat to resign if Lockhart didn't leave, a decision thrust upon him by Mr Dodd who hadn't delivered his letter to Mrs Flawse, finally resorted to more subtle tactics and paid Lockhart his full salary plus a bonus to stay away from the office before he brought ruin to the business by killing a Tax Inspector or alienating all their clients. Lockhart accepted this arrangement without regret. What he had seen of Mr Treyer, VAT men, the contradictions between income and income tax and the wiles and ways of both tax collectors and tax evaders, only confirmed his view that the modern world was a sordid and corrupt place. Brought up by his grandfather to believe what he was told and to tell what he believed, the transition to a world in which the opposites held true had had a traumatic effect.

Left fully paid to his own devices Lockhart had remained at home and learnt to drive.

'It will help to kill time,' he told Jessica, and had promptly done his best to kill two driving instructors and a great many other road users. More accustomed to the ways of horses and buggies than to the sudden surges and stops of motor cars, Lockhart's driving consisted of putting his foot flat down on the accelerator before letting out the clutch and then putting his foot flat down on the brake before smashing into whatever stood in his path. The effect of this repeated sequence had been to leave his instructors speechless with panic and in no position to communicate an alternative procedure to their pupil. Having wrecked the front ends of three Driving School cars and the back ends of two parked cars plus a lamp-post, Lockhart had found it difficult to get anyone to instruct him.

'I just don't understand it,' he told Jessica. 'With a horse you climb into the saddle and away she goes. You don't keep bumping into things. A horse has got more sense.'

'Perhaps if you listened to what the instructors say you'd get on better, darling. I mean they must know what you ought to do.'

'According to the last one,' said Lockhart, 'what I ought to do is have my bloody head examined and I wasn't even bleeding. He was the one with the fractured skull.'

'Yes, dear, but you had just knocked down the lamp-post. You know you had.'

'I don't know anything of the sort,' said Lockhart indignantly. 'The car knocked it down. All I did was to take my foot off the clutch. It wasn't my fault the car shot off the road like a scalded cat.'

In the end, by paying one of the instructors danger money and allowing him to sit in the back seat with a crash helmet and two safety belts, Lockhart had got the hang of driving. The fact that the instructor had insisted on Lockhart providing his own vehicle had led him to buy a Land-Rover. It had been the instructor who installed a governor on the accelerator and together they had practised on an abandoned airfield where there were few obstacles and no other cars. Even in these unobstructed circumstances Lockhart had managed to puncture two hangars in ten places by driving straight through their corrugated walls at forty miles an hour and it was testimony to the Land-Rover that it took so well.

Not so the instructor. He had taken it extremely badly and had only been persuaded to come out again by being offered even more money and half a bottle of Scotch before he got into the back seat. After six weeks Lockhart had overcome his manifest desire to drive at things rather than round them and had graduated to side roads and finally to main ones. By that time the instructor pronounced him ready to take the test. The examiner thought otherwise and demanded to be let out of the car half-way through. But on his third attempt Lockhart had got his licence, largely because the examiner couldn't face the prospect of having to sit beside him a fourth time. By then the Land-

Rover had begun to suffer from metal fatigue and to celebrate the occasion Lockhart traded what remained of it in for a Range Rover which could do a hundred miles an hour on the open road and sixty cross-country. Lockhart proved the latter to his own satisfaction and the frenzied distraction of the Club Secretary by driving the thing at high speed across all eighteen holes of the Pursley Golf Course before plunging through the hedge at the end of Sandicott Crescent and into the garage.

'It's got four-wheel drive and goes through sand holes like anything,' he told Jessica, 'and it's great on grass. When we go to Northumberland we'll be able to drive right across the fells.'

He went back to the showroom to pay for the Range-Rover and it was left to Jessica to confront a partially demented Club Secretary who wanted to know what the hell her husband meant by driving a bloody great truck across all eighteen greens to the total destruction of their immaculate and painstakingly preserved surfaces.

Jessica denied that her husband had done any such thing. 'He's very fond of gardening,' she told the man, 'and he wouldn't dream of destroying your greens. And anyway I didn't know you grew vegetables on the golf course. I certainly haven't seen any.'

Faced by such radiant and disconcerting innocence the Secretary had retired muttering that some maniac had put paid to the Ladies Open, not to mention the Mixed Doubles.

Mr Flawse's letter summoning the couple to Flawse Hall to hear the contents of his will therefore came at an opportune moment.

'Oh, darling,' said Jessica, 'I've been dying to see your home. How marvellous.'

'It rather sounds as if grandfather were dying anyway,' said Lockhart studying the letter. 'Why does he want to read his will now?'

'He probably just wants you to know how generous he's going to be,' said Jessica, who always managed to put a nice interpretation on the nastiest actions.

Lockhart didn't. 'You don't know grandpa,' he said.

But next morning they left very early in the Range-Rover and managed to avoid the morning traffic into London. They were less fortunate at the traffic lights at the entrance to the motorway which happened to be red at the time. Here Lockhart slammed into the back of a Mini before reversing and driving on.

'Hadn't you better go back and say you're sorry?' asked Jessica.

But Lockhart wouldn't hear of it. 'He shouldn't have stopped so suddenly,' he said.

'But the lights were red, darling. They changed just as we came up behind him.'

'Well, the system lacks logic then,' said Lockhart. 'There wasn't anything coming on the other road. I looked.'

'There's something coming now,' said Jessica, turning to look out of the back window, 'and it's got a blue light flashing on the top. I think it must be the police.'

Lockhart put his foot hard down on the floor and they were doing a hundred in no time at all. Behind them the police car turned on its siren and went up to a hundred and ten.

'They're gaining on us, darling,' said Jessica, 'we'll never be able to get away.'

'Oh yes we will,' said Lockhart, and looked in the rear-view mirror. The police car was four hundred yards behind them and coming up fast. Lockhart switched up an overpass on to a side road, squealed round a corner into a country lane and putting his hunting instincts to good use charged a five-barred gate and bucketed across a ploughed field. Behind them the police car stopped at the gate and men got out. But by that time Lockhart had negotiated another hedge and had disappeared. Twenty miles and forty hedges farther on he doubled back across the motorway and, proceeding by back roads to the east, drove on.

'Oh, Lockhart, you're so manly,' said Jessica, 'you think of everything. You really do. But don't you suppose they'll have taken our licence number?'

'Won't do them much good if they have,' said Lockhart. 'I didn't like the one it had on it when I bought it so I changed it.'

'You didn't like it? Why not?'

'It said PEE 453 P so I had another one made up. It's much nicer. It's FLA 123.'

'But they'll still be looking for a Range-Rover with FLA 123,' Jessica pointed out, 'and they've got radios and things.'

Lockhart pulled into a lay-by. 'You really don't mind us being PEE 453 P?' he asked. Jessica shook her head.

'Of course not,' she said, 'you are silly.'

'If you're quite sure,' said Lockhart doubtfully, but in the end he got out and changed the number plates back again. When he climbed back into the car Jessica hugged him.

'Oh darling,' she said. 'I feel so safe with you. I don't know why it is but you always make things look so simple.'

'Most things are simple,' said Lockhart, 'if you go about them the right way. The trouble is that people never do what's obvious.'

'I suppose that's what it is,' said Jessica, and relapsed into the romantic dream of Flawse Hall on Flawse Fell close under Flawse Rigg. With each mile north her feelings, unlike those of her mother before her, grew mistier and more hazy with legend and the wild beauty she longed for.

Beside her Lockhart's feelings changed too. He was moving away from London and that low country he so detested and was returning, if only briefly, to those open rolling fells of his boyhood and to the music of guns firing in the distance or close at hand. A feeling of wildness and a strange surge of violence stirred in his blood and Mr Treyer assumed a new monstrosity in his mind, a vast question-mark to which there was never any answer. Ask Mr Treyer a question and the answer he gave was no answer at all; it was a balance sheet. On one side there were debits, on the other credits. You paid your money and took your choice, and Lockhart had been left none the wiser. The world he understood had no place for equivocation or those grey areas where everything was fudged and bets were hedged. If you aimed at a grouse it was hit or miss and a miss was as good as a mile. And if you built a dry-stone wall it stood or fell and in falling proved you wrong. But in the south it was all slipshod and cover-up. He was being paid not to work and other men who did no work were making fortunes out of buying and selling options on cocoa yet to be harvested and copper still unmined. And having made their money by swapping pieces of paper they had it taken away from them by Income Tax officials or had to lie to keep it. Finally there was the Government which in his simple way he had always thought was elected to govern and to maintain the value of the currency.

Instead it spent more money than was in the Exchequer and borrowed to make good the deficit. If a man did that he would go bankrupt and rightly so. But governments could borrow, beg, steal or simply print more money and there was no one to say them Nay. To Lockhart's arithmetical mind the world he had encountered was one of lunacy where two and two made five, or even eleven, and nothing added up to a true figure. It was not a world for him, with all its lying hypocrisy. 'Better a thief than a beggar,' he thought and drove on.

It was almost dark when they turned off the main road beyond Wark on to the half-metalled track that led to Black Pockrington. Above them a few stars speckled the sky and the headlamps picked out the gates and occasionally the eyes of a night animal, but everything else was dark and bare, a shape against the skyline. Jessica went into raptures.

'Oh, Lockhart, it's like another world.'

'It is another world,' said Lockhart.

When finally they breasted the rise of Tombstone Law and looked across the valley at the Hall, it was ablaze with lights in every window.

'Oh how beautiful!' said Jessica. 'Let's stop here for a moment. I want to savour it so.'

She got out and gazed ecstatically at the house. From its peel tower to its smoking chimneys and the lights gleaming from its windows it was everything she had hoped for. As if to celebrate this fulfilment the moon came out from behind a cloud and glinted on the surface of the reservoir and in the distance there came the baying of the Flawse hounds. The reading matter of Jessica's retarded adolescence was making itself manifest.

Chapter eight

It might be said that old Mr Flawse's reading matter made itself manifest next morning in the hall of the peel tower which his grandfather had restored to more than its former elegance. A contemporary of Sir Walter Scott and a voracious reader of his novels, he had turned what had been a fortified byre for cattle into a banqueting hall with plaster chasing and ornamental crests, while from the rafters there hung the tattered and entirely concocted battle-flags of half a dozen fictitious regiments. Time and moths had lent these standards a gauzelike authenticity while rust had etched a handiwork into the suited armour and armoury that they had never possessed when he had bought them. And armour and arms were everywhere. Helmeted figures stood against the walls and above them, interspersed with the stuffed heads of stags, moose, antelope and bear, and even one tiger, were the swords and battle-axes of bygone wars.

It was in this bellicose setting, with a great fire blazing in the hearth and smoke filtering up among the flags, that Mr Flawse chose to have his will read. Seated before him at a huge oak table were his nearest and supposedly dearest: Lockhart, Mrs Flawse, Jessica in a coma of romance, Mr Bullstrode the solicitor, who was to read the will, two tenant farmers to witness its signature, and Dr Magrew to certify that Mr Flawse was, as he proclaimed, of sound mind.

'The ceremony must be conducted under the most stringent of legal and jurisprudent conditions,' Mr Flawse had instructed, and so it was. He might just as well have added that the late and great Thomas Carlyle would lend the weight of his rhetorical authority to the proceedings, and certainly there were strains of the Sage of Ecchilfeccan in the old man's opening address. His words rang in the rafters and while for legal reasons the will contained few commas, Mr Flawse made good this deficiency by larding his speech with semi-colons.

'You are gathered here today,' he announced raising his coat-tails to the fire, 'to hear the last will and testament of Edwin Tyndale Flawse; once widowed and twice married; father of the late and partially lamented Clarissa Richardson Flawse; grandfather of her illegitimate offspring, Lockhart Flawse, whose father being unknown, I have out of no greatness of heart but that innate and incontrovertible practicality of mind which congenitally the family Flawse numbers most firmly among its features, adopted as my heir in the male line. But of the consequentiality of that anon; 'tis not of such low bestial matters that I speak; more lofty themes become my song, if song it be that old men sing out of their memories of what might have been; and I am old and near to death.'

He paused for breath and Mrs Flawse stirred expectantly in her seat. Mr Flawse regarded her with a gleaming predatory eye. 'Aye, ma'am, well may you squirm; your turn for dotage won't delay; death's bony finger beckons and we must obey; that black oblivion is our certain destination. Certain beyond all other certainties; the one fixed star in the firmament of man's experience; all else being loose and circumstantial and inco-ordinate, we can but set our sextant by that star of non-existence, death, to measure what and where we are. Which I being ninety now see shining brighter and more darkly brilliant than before. And so towards the grave we move along the tramlines of our thoughts and deeds, those grooves of character which we, being born with them, are much beholden to and by, but which by virtue of their tiny flaws allow us unintentionally to exercise that little freedom which is man. Aye, is man, is. No animal knows freedom; only man; and that by fault of gene and chemical congeneracy. The rest is all determined by our birth. So like an engine is a man, all steam and fire and pressure building up, he yet must move along predestined lines towards that end which is the end of all of us. Before you stands a semi-skeleton, all bones and skull with but a little spirit to ligature with life these odds and ends. And presently the parchment of my flesh shall break; all spirit flown; and shall my soul awake? I know not nor can ever know till death decides to answer yes or no. Which said I do not dis-esteem myself. I am yet here before you in this hall and you are gathered now to hear my will. My will? A strange word for the dead to claim; their will; when matters of decision are lost to those they leave behind. Their will; the supposition only of a wish. But I forestall that chance by setting forth before you now my will; and will it be in all the many meanings of that word. For I have laid conditions down which you will shortly hear and hearing do or forfeit all that fortune I have left to you.'

The old man paused and looked into their faces before continuing. 'You wonder why I look?' he asked. 'To see one spark of some defiance in your eyes. One spark, that's all, one spark that yet might tell this partial skeleton to go to hell. Which it would at the least be ironical to conclude was indeed my destination. But I see it not; greed snuffs the candle of your courage out. You, ma'am,' he pointed a finger at Mrs Flawse, 'an undernourished vulture has more patience perched upon an upas tree than you with your squat backside on that bench.'

He paused but Mrs Flawse said nothing. Her little eyes narrowed with calculating hatred.

'Does nothing then provoke you to reply? No, but I know your thoughts; time runneth on; the metronome of heartbeats swings more slow and soon my threnody, a little premature perhaps, will cease. The grave I lie in will give you satisfaction. Let me forestall it for you, ma'am. And now the bastard Flawse. Have you defiance, sir, or did your education din it out of you?'

'Go to hell,' said Lockhart.

The old man smiled. 'Better, better, but prompted all the same. I told you what to say and you obeyed. But here's a better test.' Mr Flawse turned and took a battle-axe from the wall and held it out.

'Take it, bastard,' he said. 'Take the axe.'

Lockhart rose and took it.

'It was the custom of the Norsemen when a man grew old to cleave him headless with an axe,' continued Mr Flawse, 'it was the duty of his eldest son. Now having none but you, a ditch-born bastard grandson, take on the onus of this act and—'

'No,' said Jessica rising from her chair and grabbing the axe from Lockhart. 'I won't have it. You've got no right to put temptation in his way.'

The old man clapped his hands. 'Bravo. Now that's more like it. The bitch has better spirit than the dog. A flicker of spirit but spirit all the same. And I salute it. Mr Bullstrode, read the will.' And exhausted by his rhetoric old Mr Flawse sat down. Mr Bullstrode rose theatrically and opened the will.

'I, Edwin of Tyndale Flawse, being of sound mind and feeble yet sufficient body to sustain my mind, do hereby leave bequeath and devise all my worldly goods chattels property and land to my wife, Mrs Cynthia Flawse, for to have and to hold in trust and in use until her own death demise departure from this place which place being defined more closely is the radius of one mile from Flawse Hall and on condition that she do not sell mortgage rent borrow pledge or pawn a single or multiple of the possessions so bequeathed left and devised and in no way improves alters adds or amends the amenities of the said property possession chattels and house but subsists upon the income alone in recognition of which undertaking she signs herewith this will as being a binding contract to obey its strictures.'

Mr Bullstrode put down the will and looked at Mrs Flawse. 'Will you so sign?' he asked, but Mrs Flawse was in a flux of emotions. The old man had lived up to his word after all. He had left her his entire estate. Coming so shortly after being compared to a vulture this act of generosity had thrown her calculating compass off course. She needed time to think. It was denied her.

'Sign, ma'am,' said Mr Flawse, 'or the will becomes null and void in so far as it appertains to you.'

Mrs Flawse took the pen and signed and her signature was witnessed by the two tenant farmers.

'Continue, Mr Bullstrode,' said the old man almost gaily and Mr Bullstrode took up the will again.

'To my grandson Lockhart Flawse I leave nothing except my name until and unless he shall have produced in physical form the person of his natural father which father shall be proved to the satisfaction of my executor Mr Bullstrode or his successors to be the actual and admitted and undoubted father of the said Lockhart and shall have signed an affidavit to that effect which affidavit having been signed he shall be flogged by the said Lockhart to within an inch of his life. In the event of these aforestated conditions in regard to the proof of his paternity having been met the terms of the will in respect of my wife Cynthia Flawse as stated above her freely given signature shall and will become automatically null and void and the estate property chattels land and possessions pass *in toto* to my grandson Lockhart Flawse to do with whatsoever he chooses. To my servant Donald Robson Dodd I leave the use of my house and provender meat drink dogs and horse for as long as he shall live and they survive.'

Mr Bullstrode stopped and old Mr Flawse stepping up to the table picked up the pen. 'Am I in sound mind?' he asked Dr Magrew.

'Yes,' said the doctor, 'I attest that you are in sound mind.'

'Hear that,' said Mr Flawse to the two tenant farmers who nodded accordingly. 'You will witness that I am in sound mind when I sign this will.'

There was a sudden scream from Mrs Flawse. 'Sound mind? You're as mad as a hatter. You've cheated me. You said you would leave everything to me and now you've added a clause saying that I forfeit all right to inherit if ... if ... if that illegitimate creature finds his father.'

But Mr Flawse ignored her outburst and signed the will. 'Away with you, woman,' he said, handing the pen to one of the farmers, 'I kept my word and you'll keep mine or lose every penny I've left you.'

Mrs Flawse eyed the axe lying on the long table and then sat down defeated. She had been hoodwinked. 'There's nothing to say that I have to stay here while you are still alive. I shall leave first thing tomorrow.'

Mr Flawse laughed. 'Ma'am,' he said, 'you have signed a contract to remain here for the rest of your life or redress me for the loss of your presence to the tune of five thousand pounds a year.'

'I have done nothing of the sort,' screamed Mrs Flawse. 'I signed—'

But Mr Bullstrode handed her the will. 'You will find the clause on page one,' he said.

Mrs Flawse gaped at him incredulously and then followed his finger down the page. 'But you didn't read that out,' she said as the words swam before her eyes. 'You didn't read out "In the event of my wife Cynthia Flawse leaving ..." Oh my God!' And she sank back into her chair. The clause was there in black on white.

'And now that the thing is signed, sealed and delivered,' said Mr Flawse as Bullstrode folded the extraordinary document and slipped it into his briefcase, 'let us drink a health to Death.'

'To Death?' said Jessica, still bemused by the bizarre romance of the scene.

Mr Flawse patted her radiant cheek fondly. 'To Death, my dear, the only thing we have in common,' he said, 'and the great leveller! Mr Dodd, the decanter of Northumbrian whisky.'

Mr Dodd disappeared through the door.

'I didn't know they made whisky in Northumberland,' said Jessica warming to the old man, 'I thought it was Scotch.'

'There are many things you don't know and Northumbrian whisky's among them. It used to be distilled in these parts by the gallon but Dodd's the only man with a still left. You see these walls? Ten feet thick. There used to be a saying here-abouts, "Six for the Scots and four for the Excise men." And it would be a canny man who would find the entrance but Dodd knows.'

In proof of this remark Mr Dodd reappeared with a decanter of whisky and a tray of glasses. When the glasses were all filled Mr Flawse rose and the others followed. Only Mrs Flawse remained seated.

'I refuse to drink to Death,' she muttered stubbornly. 'It's a wicked toast.'

'Aye, ma'am, and it's a wicked world,' said Mr Flawse, 'but you'll drink all the same. It's your only hope.'

Mrs Flawse got unsteadily to her feet and regarded him with loathing.

'To the Great Certainty,' said Mr Flawse and his voice rang among the battle-flags and armour.

Later after a lunch served in the dining-room Lockhart and Jessica walked across Flawse Fell. The afternoon sunlight shone down on the coarse grass and a few sheep stirred as they climbed Flawse Rigg.

'Oh, Lockhart, I wouldn't have missed today for all the world,' said Jessica when they reached the top. 'Your grand-father is the darlingest old man.'

It was not a superlative Lockhart would have applied to his grandfather and Mrs Flawse, white-faced in her room, would have used its opposite. But neither voiced their opinion. Lock-hart because Jessica was his beloved angel and her opinion was not to be disputed and Mrs Flawse because she had no one to voice it to. Meanwhile Mr Bullstrode and Dr Magrew sat on with Mr Flawse at the mahogany table sipping port and en-gaged in that philosophical disputation to which their common background made them prone.

'I did not approve your toast to Death,' said Dr Magrew. 'It goes against my Hippocratic oath and besides it's a contradiction in terms to drink to the health of that which by its very nature cannot be called healthy.'

'Are you not confusing health with life?' said Mr Bullstrode. 'And by life I mean the vital element. Now the law of nature has it that every living thing shall die. That, sir, I think you will not deny.'

'I cannot,' said Dr Magrew, 'it is the truth. On the other hand I would question your right to call a dying man healthy. In all my experience as a practitioner of medicine I cannot recall being present at the deathbed of a healthy man.'

Mr Flawse rapped his glass to gain attention and the decanter. 'I think we are ignoring the factor of unnatural death,' he said refilling his glass. 'You doubtless know the conundrum of the fly and the locomotive. A perfectly healthy fly is travelling at twenty miles an hour in exactly the opposite direction to a locomotive travelling at sixty. The locomotive and the fly collide and the fly is instantaneously dead but in dying it stopped travelling forward at twenty miles per hour and reversed its motion at sixty. Now, sir, if the fly stopped and began reverse progress is it not also true that for it to do so the locomotive must also have stopped if for but the millionth of a second of the fly's stopping, and more germane to our argument is it not true that the fly died healthy?'

Mr Bullstrode poured himself more port and considered the problem but it was the doctor who took up the cudgels. 'If the locomotive stopped for a millionth of a second and about that, being no engineer, I cannot speak and must take your word for it, then it is also true that for that millionth of a second the fly was in an extremely unhealthy state. We have but to extend time in proportion to the life-expectancy of a fly to see that this is so. A fly's natural term of life is, I believe, limited to a single day, whereas the human term is three-score years and ten, present company excepted. In short a fly can look forward to approximately eighty-six thousand four hundred seconds of conscious existence whereas the human being can count on two billion one hundred and seven million five hundred and twenty seconds between birth and death. I leave it to you to discern the difference in lifetime of one millionth of a second for the fly and its equivalent length in a human's. At short notice I calculate the latter to be of the order of magnitude of five and a half minutes. Certainly sufficient time in which to diagnose the patient as being unhealthy.'

Having disposed of the fly argument and the rest of the contents of his glass Dr Magrew sat back in his chair triumphantly.

It was Mr Bullstrode's turn to apply the methods of the law to the problem. 'Let us take the question of capital punishment,' he said. 'It was one of the proudest boasts of the penal system that no man went to the gallows unless he was fit to be hanged. Now a fit man is a healthy man and since death by hanging is instantaneous a murderer died healthy.'

But Dr Magrew was not to be put down so easily. 'Semantics, sir, semantics. You say that a murderer going to the gallows is fit to be hanged. Now I would have it that no man who murders is fit to live. We can turn these things on their heads. It all depends on one's viewpoint.'

'Aye, there's the rub,' said Mr Flawse, 'from what viewpoint should we look at things? Now, lacking any firmer ground than that afforded by my own experience, which has been largely confined to dogs and their habits, I would say we should start a little lower on the evolutionary scale than primates. It is a common saying that dog eats dog. The man who said it first did not know dogs. Dogs do not eat dogs. They work in packs and a pack animal is not a cannibal. It depends upon its fellows to bring down its prey and being dependent has the morality of a social being, an instinctive morality but morality for all that. Man on the other hand has no natural or instinctive morality. The process of history proves the contrary and the history of religion reinforces it. If there were any natural morality in man there would be no need for religion or indeed for law. And yet without morality man would not have survived. Another conundrum, gentlemen; science destroyed the belief in God upon which morality depended for its source; science has likewise substituted the means for man's destruction; in short we are without that moral sense that has saved us from extinction in the past and in possession of the means of extinguishing ourselves in the future. A bleak future, gentlemen, and one I trust I shall not be here to experience.'

'And what advice would you offer the future generation, sir?' inquired Mr Bullstrode.

'That which Cromwell gave his Roundheads,' said Mr

Flawse. 'To put their faith in God and keep their powder dry.'

'Which is to suppose that God exists,' said Dr Magrew.

'Which is to suppose no such thing,' said Mr Flawse. 'Faith is one thing; knowledge quite another. It were too easy otherwise.'

'Then you fall back on tradition, sir,' said Mr Bullstrode approvingly. 'As a lawyer I find much to commend your attitude.'

'I fall back on my family,' said Mr Flawse. 'The inheritance of characteristics is a fact of nature. It was Socrates who said "Know thyself." I would go further and say to know thyself one must first know thy ancestry. It is the key to my instructions to the bastard. Let him find out who his father was and then his grandfather and even further back and then he'll find himself.'

'And having found himself, what then?' asked Mr Bullstrode.

'Be himself,' said Mr Flawse, and promptly fell asleep.

Chapter nine

Upstairs in the solitude of her bedroom Mrs Flawse was beside herself. For the second time in her life a husband had cheated her and the occasion called for wailing and gnashing of teeth. But being a methodical woman and knowing the expense of a new pair of dentures, Mrs Flawse first removed her teeth and put them in a glass of water before gnashing her gums. Nor did she wail. To have done so would have afforded her husband too much satisfaction and Mrs Flawse was determined he should suffer for his sins. Instead she sat toothless and considered her revenge. It lay, she realized, in Lockhart. If in his will Mr Flawse had saddled her with the perpetual occupation of the Hall without amenities, he had likewise saddled his grandson with the task of finding his father. Only then could he deprive her of her inheritance and failing in his search and following the old man's death she would make what improvements she liked to the Hall. Better still, the income from the estate would be hers to do with as she pleased. She could accumulate it year by year and add it to her savings and one fine day she would have saved enough to leave and not return. But all this only if Lockhart failed to find his father. Deny Lockhart the means to search, and here Mrs Flawse's thoughts flew to money, and she would be secure. She would see that Lockhart had no means.

Reaching for her writing-case she put pen to paper and wrote a short, concise letter to Mr Treyer instructing him to dismiss Lockhart from Sandicott & Partner without notice. Then having sealed the envelope she put it away to give to Jessica to post or, more ironically, for Lockhart to deliver by hand. Mrs Flawse smiled a toothless smile and went on to consider other ways of taking her revenge, and by the time the afternoon had waned she was in a more cheerful mood. The old man had stipulated in his will that there should be no improvements to the Hall. She intended to stick to the letter of his instructions. There would be no improvements and for the rest of his un-natural life there would be the reverse. Windows would be opened, doors unlatched, food cold and damp beds damper still until with her assistance the infirmities of age had been acceler-ated to his end. And the old man had toasted Death. It was appropriate. Death would come sooner than he dreamt. Yes, that was it, delay Lockhart at all cost and hasten her husband's dying and she would be in a position to dispute the will and maybe, better still, bribe Mr Bullstrode to amend its dis-positions. She would have to sound the man out. In the mean-time she would put a fine face on things.

If Mrs Flawse had been disturbed by the reading of the will so had Lockhart. Sitting on Flawse Rigg with Jessica he did not share her romantic view of his bastardy.

'I didn't know it meant I had no father,' he told her. 'I thought it was just another word he used for me. He's always calling people bastards.'

'But don't you see how exciting it all is,' said Jessica. 'It's like a paper chase, or Hunt the Father. And when you find him you'll inherit the whole estate and we can come and live up here.'

'It isn't going to be easy to find a father who's got to be flogged within an inch of his life the moment he admits it,' said

Lockhart practically, 'and anyway I don't know where to start.'

'Well, at least you know when you were born and all you've got to find out then is who your mother was in love with.'

'And how do I find out when I was born?'

'By looking at your birth certificate, silly,' said Jessica.

'I haven't got one,' said Lockhart, 'grandpa wouldn't let me be registered. It's awfully inconvenient and Mr Treyer wasn't able to pay my National Insurance stamps or anything. That's one of the reasons he wouldn't let me go to work. He said that for all practical purposes I don't exist and wished I didn't for impractical ones. I can't vote or serve on a jury or get a passport.'

'Oh, darling, there must be something you can do,' said Jessica, 'I mean once you do find your father he'll let you have a birth certificate. Why don't you have a word with Mr Bullstrode about it? He seems the sweetest old gentleman.'

'Seems,' said Lockhart gloomily, 'just seems.'

But when as the sun began to set over the firing-range they walked hand-in-hand back to the house they found Mr Bullstrode examining the front of the Range-Rover with a legal eye.

'It would appear that you have been in some sort of collision,' he said.

'Yes,' said Jessica, 'we hit a little car.'

'Indeed?' said Mr Bullstrode. 'A little car. I trust you reported the accident to the police.'

Lockhart shook his head. 'I didn't bother.'

'Indeed?' said Mr Bullstrode more legally still. 'You simply hit a little car and then continued on your way. And the owner of the other vehicle, did he have something to say about it?'

'I didn't wait to find out,' said Lockhart.

'And then the police chased us,' said Jessica, 'And Lockhart was ever so clever and drove though hedges and across fields where they couldn't follow us.'

'Hedges?' said Mr Bullstrode. 'Am I to understand that having been involved in an accident which you failed to stop and report you were then chased by the police and committed the further felony of driving this remarkable vehicle through hedges and across, by the look of the tyres, ploughed and doubtless planted fields thus damaging property and leaving yourselves liable to criminal prosecution on grounds of trespass?'

'Yes,' said Lockhart, 'that just about sums it up.'

'Good God,' said Mr Bullstrode and scratched his bald head. 'And did it never occur to you that the police must have taken your number and can trace you by it?'

'Ah, but it wasn't the right number,' said Lockhart and explained his reasons for changing it. By the time he had finished Mr Bullstrode's legal sensibilities were in tatters. 'I hesitate to add to the proscriptions attendant upon your grandfather's will by describing your actions as wholly criminal and without the law but I must say . . .' He broke off unable to give words to his feelings.

'What?' said Lockhart.

Mr Bullstrode consulted commonsense. 'My advice is to leave the vehicle here,' he said finally, 'and to travel home by train.'

'And what about finding my father?' said Lockhart. 'Have you any opinion to offer on that?'

'I was not alerted to your mother's death or your delivery until some months had passed,' said Mr Bullstrode. 'I can only advise you to consult Dr Magrew. Not, of course, that I impute any interest other than the professional to his concern for your dear mother's condition at the time of her demise, but he may be able to help in the matter of timing your conception.'

But Dr Magrew when they found him in the study warming his feet at the fire could add little.

'As I remember the occasion,' he said, 'you were, to put it mildly, a premature baby distinguished largely by the fact that you appeared to be born with measles. A wrong diagnosis, I have to confess, but understandable in that I have seldom if ever been confronted by a baby born in a stinging-nettle patch. But definitely premature and I would therefore put your conception no earlier than February 1956 and no later than March. I must therefore conclude that your father was in close proximity to these parts and those of your mother during these two months. I am glad to be able to say that I do not qualify as a candidate for your paternity by the good fortune of being out of the country at that time.'

'But didn't he look like anyone you knew when he was born?' asked Jessica.

'My dear,' said Dr Magrew, 'a premature infant expelled from the womb into a stinging-nettle patch as a result of his mother's fall from her horse can only be said to look like nothing on earth. I would hesitate to defame any man by saying that Lockhart at birth looked like him. An orang-outang possibly, but an unsightly one at that. No, I am afraid your search will have to proceed along other lines than family likeness.'

'But what about my mother?' said Lockhart. 'Surely she must have had friends who would be able to tell me something.'

Dr Magrew nodded. 'Your presence here today would seem conclusive evidence of the former proposition,' he said. 'Unfortunately your grandfather's will makes the second highly unlikely.'

'Can you tell us what Lockhart's mother was like?' asked Jessica.

Dr Magrew's face grew solemn. 'Let's just say she was a wild lassie with a tendency to rush her fences,' he said. 'Aye, and a beauty too in her day.'

But that was as much as they could get out of him. And next morning, accepting a lift from Mr Bullstrode, who had stayed overnight, they left the Hall carrying Mrs Flawse's letter to Mr Treyer.

'My dear,' said old Mr Flawse patting Jessica's hand rather more pruriently than their relationship called for, 'you have married a numbskull but you'll make a man of him yet. Come and see me again before I die. I like a woman of spirit.'

It was a tearful Jessica who got into the car. 'You must think me awfully sentimental,' she said.

'Of course ye are, hinnie,' said the old man, 'which is what I admire about you. Where there's mush there's grit beneath. You must have got it from your father. Your mother's grit all over and as soft as a slug at the core.'

And with these parting words they left the Hall. In the background old Mrs Flawse added slugs to the menu of her revenge.

Two days later Lockhart presented himself for the last time at Sandicott & Partner and handed Mr Treyer the envelope containing Mrs Flawse's instructions. Half an hour later he left again while behind him Mr Treyer praised whatever Gods there be, and in particular Janus, in the environs of Wheedle Street that he had at long last been instructed to fire, sack, dismiss and generally send packing the ghastly liability to the firm of Sandicott & Partner that marched under the name of Lockhart Flawse. His mother-in-law's letter had been couched in much the same terms as the old man's will and for once Mr Treyer had no need to equivocate. Lockhart left the office with his head ringing with Mr Treyer's opinions and returned home to explain this strange turn of events to Jessica.

'But why should mummy have done such a horrid thing?' she asked. Lockhart could find no answer.

'Perhaps she doesn't like me,' he said.

'Of course she does, darling. She would never have let me marry you if she hadn't liked you.'

'Well, if you had seen what she wrote in that letter about me you'd have second thoughts about that,' said Lockhart. But Jessica had already summed her mother up.

'I think she's just an old cat and she's cross about the will. That's what I think. What are you going to do now?'

'Get another job, I suppose,' said Lockhart but the supposition came easier than the result. The Labour Exchange in East Pursley was already swamped with applications from ex-stockbrokers and Mr Treyer's refusal to grant that he had ever been employed at Sandicott, combined with his lack of any means of identification, made Lockhart's position hopeless. It was the same at the Social Security office. His non-entity in any bureaucratic sense became obvious when he admitted he had never paid any National Insurance stamps.

'As far as we are concerned you don't statistically speaking exist,' the clerk told him.

'But I do,' Lockhart insisted, 'I am here. You can see me. You can even touch me if you want to.'

The clerk didn't. 'Listen,' he said with all the politeness of a public servant addressing the public, 'you've admitted you aren't on the Voters' Roll, you haven't been included in any census count, you can't produce a passport or birth certificate, you haven't had a job . . . Yes, I know what you're going to say but I've a letter here from a Mr Treyer who states categorically you didn't work at Sandicott & Partner, you haven't paid a penny in National Insurance stamps, you haven't got a health card. Now then do you want to go your non-existent way or do I have to call the police?' Lockhart indicated that he didn't want the police to be called.

'Right then,' said the clerk, 'let me get on with some other applicants who've got a better claim on the Welfare State.'

Lockhart left him coping with an unemployed graduate in Moral Sciences who had for months been demanding to be treated rather more generously than an old-age pensioner while at the same time refusing any job that was not consistent with his qualifications.

By the time Lockhart got home he was utterly despondent.

'It's no use,' he said, 'I can't get anyone to employ me at any sort of job and I can't get social benefits because they won't admit I exist.'

'Oh dear,' said Jessica. 'If only we could sell all the houses daddy left me, we could invest the money and live off the income.'

'Well, we can't. You heard what the Estate Agent said. They're occupied, unfurnished and on long leases and we can't even raise the rent, let alone sell them.'

'I think it's jolly unfair. Why can't we just tell the tenants to go?'

'Because the law says they don't have to move.'

'Who cares what the law says?' said Jessica. 'There's a law which says unemployed people get free money, but when it comes to paying you they don't do it, and it isn't even as if you didn't want to work. I don't see why we have to obey a law which hurts us when the Government won't obey a law which helps us.'

'What's good for the goose is good for the gander,' Lockhart agreed and so was born the idea which, nurtured in Lockhart Flawse's mind, was to turn the quiet backwater of Sandicott Crescent into a maelstrom of misunderstandings.

That night, while Jessica racked her brains for some way to supplement their income, Lockhart left the house and, moving with all the silence and stealth he had acquired in pursuit of game on Flawse Fell, stole through the gorse bushes in the bird sanctuary with a pair of binoculars. He was not bird-watching in its true sense but by the time he returned at midnight the occupants of most of the houses had been observed and Lockhart had gained some little insight into their habits.

He sat up for a while making notes in a pocket book. It was carefully indexed and under P he put 'Pettigrew, man and wife aged fifty. Put dachshund named Little Willie out at eleven and make milk drink. Go to bed eleven-thirty.' Under G there was the information that the Grabbles watched television and went to bed at ten-forty-five. Mr and Mrs Raceme in Number 8 did something strange which involved tying Mr Raceme to the bed at nine-fifteen and untying him again at ten. At Number 4 the Misses Musgrove had entertained the Vicar before supper and had read the *Church Times* and knitted afterwards. Finally, next door to the Flawse house, Colonel Finch-Potter in Number 10 smoked a cigar after a solitary dinner, fulminated loudly at a Labour Party political broadcast on television, and then took a brisk walk with his bull-terrier before retiring.

Lockhart made notes of all these practices and went to bed himself. Something deep and devious was stirring in his mind. What exactly it was he couldn't say, but the instinct of the hunt was slowly edging its way towards consciousness and with it a barbarity and anger that knew nothing of the law or the social conventions of civilization.

Next morning Jessica announced that she was going to get a job.

'I can type and take shorthand and there's lots of firms wanting secretaries. I'm going to a bureau. They're advertising for temporary typists.'

'I don't like it,' said Lockhart. 'A man should provide for his wife, not the other way round.'

'I won't be providing for you. It's for us, and anyway I might even find you a job. I'll tell everyone I work for how clever you are.'

And in spite of Lockhart's opposition she caught the bus. Left to himself, he spent the day brooding about the house with a sullen look on his face and poking into places he hadn't been before. One of these was the attic and there in an old tin trunk he discovered the papers of the late Mr Sandicott. Among them he found the architect's drawings for the interiors of all the houses in the Crescent together with details of plumbing, sewers, and electrical connections. Lockhart took them downstairs and studied them carefully. They were extremely informative and by the time Jessica returned with the news that she was starting next day with a cement company, one of whose typists was away with flu, Lockhart had mapped in his head the exact location of all the mod cons the houses in Sandicott Crescent boasted. He greeted Jessica's news without enthusiasm.

'If anyone tries anything funny,' he said, remembering Mr Tryer's tendencies with temporary typists, 'I want you to tell me. I'll kill him.'

'Oh, Lockhart darling, you're so chivalrous,' said Jessica proudly. 'Let's have a kiss and cuddle tonight.'

But Lockhart had other plans for the evening and Jessica went to bed alone. Outside, Lockhart crawled through the undergrowth of the bird sanctuary to the foot of the Racemes' garden, climbed the fence and installed himself in a cherry tree that overlooked the Racemes' bedroom. He had decided that Mr Raceme's peculiar habit of allowing his wife to tie him to their double bed for three-quarters of an hour might provide him with information for future use. But he was disappointed. Mr and Mrs Raceme had supper and watched television before having an early and less restrained night. At eleven their lights went out and Lockhart descended the cherry tree and was making his way back over the fence when the Pettigrews at Number 6 put Little Willie out while they made Ovaltine. Attracted by Lockhart's passage through the gorse the dachshund dashed down the garden with a series of yelps and stood barking into the darkness. Lockhart moved away but the dog kept up its hullabaloo and presently Mr Pettigrew came down the lawn to investigate.

'Now, Willie, stop that noise,' he said. 'Good dog. There's nothing there.'

But Willie knew better and, emboldened by his master's presence, made further rushes in Lockhart's direction. Finally Mr Pettigrew picked the dog up and carried him back into the house leaving Lockhart with the resolution to do something about Willie as soon as possible. Barking dogs were a hazard he could do without.

He progressed by way of the Misses Musgrove's back garden

– their lights had gone out promptly at ten – and crossed into the Grabbles' where the downstairs lights were on and the living-room curtains partly open. Lockhart stationed himself beside the greenhouse and focused his binoculars on the gap in the curtains and was surprised to see Mrs Grabble on the sofa in the arms of someone who was quite clearly not the Mr Grabble he knew. As the couple writhed in ecstasy Lockhart's binoculars discovered the flushed face of Mr Simplon who lived at Number 5. Mrs Grabble and Mr Simplon? Then where was Mr Grabble and what was Mrs Simplon doing? Lockhart left the greenhouse and slipped across the road to the golf course, past the Rickenshaws at Number 1 and the Ogilvies at Number 3 to the Simplons' mock-Georgian mansion at Number 5. A light was on upstairs and since the curtains were drawn, the Simplons kept no dog and the garden was well endowed with shrubs, Lockhart ventured down a flowerbed until he was standing beneath the window. He stood as still as he had once stood on Flawse Fell when a rabbit had spotted him, and he was still as motionless when headlights illuminated the front of the house an hour later and Mr Simplon garaged his car. Lights went on in the house and a moment later voices issued from the bedroom, the acrimonious voice of Mrs Simplon and the placatory one of Mr Simplon.

'Working late at the office my foot,' said Mrs Simplon. 'That's what you keep telling me. Well, I phoned the office twice this evening and there was no one there.'

'I was out with Jerry Blond, the architect,' said Mr Simplon. 'He wanted me to meet a client from Cyprus who is thinking of building a hotel. If you don't believe me, phone Blond and see if he doesn't confirm what I say.'

But Mrs Simplon scorned the idea. 'I'm not going to advertise the fact that I have my own ideas about what you get up to,' she said. 'I've got more pride.'

Down in the bushes Lockhart admired her pride and was inspired by her reluctance. If she wasn't going to advertise what she correctly thought Mr Simplon was getting up to, namely Mrs Grabble, it might be to his own advantage to do it for her. And where was Mr Grabble? Lockhart decided to explore that gentleman's movements more closely before acting. Evidently there were nights when Mr Grabble stayed away from home.

He would have to find out when. In the meantime there was no more to be gained from the Simplons, and leaving them to their quarrel he returned to the golf course; passing the Lowrys who lived at Number 7 and Mr O'Brain, the gynaecologist, who inhabited the Bauhaus at Number 9 and was already in bed, he found himself at the bottom of the Wilsons' garden at Number 11. Here the lights were on, though dimly, in the downstairs lounge and the french windows open. Lockhart squatted in a bunker on the seventeenth hole and lifted his binoculars. There were three people in the room sitting round a small table with their fingers touching, and as he watched the table moved. Lockhart eyed it beadily and his keen ear detected the sound of knocking. The Wilsons and their friend were engaged in some strange ritual. Every now and again Mrs Wilson would put a question and the table would rock and knock. So the Wilsons were superstitious.

Lockhart crawled away and presently was adding this and all the other gleanings of the night's prowl to his notebook. By the time he went to bed, Jessica was fast asleep.

And so for the next fortnight Lockhart spent his evenings patrolling the bird sanctuary and the golf course and amassed dossiers on the habits, fads, foibles and indiscretions of all the tenants of the Crescent. By day he pottered about the house and spent a good many hours in his late father-in-law's workshop with lengths of wire, transistors and a Do-It-Yourself *Manual of Radio Construction*.

'I don't know what you do with yourself all day, darling,' said Jessica, who had moved from the cement company to a firm of lawyers who specialized in libel actions.

'I'm making provision for our future,' said Lockhart.

'With loudspeakers? What have loudspeakers got to do with our future?'

'More than you know.'

'And this transmitter thing. Is that part of our future too?'

'Our future and the Wilsons' next door,' said Lockhart. 'Where did your mother keep the keys to the houses?'

'You mean the houses daddy left me?'

Lockhart nodded and Jessica rummaged in a kitchen drawer.

'Here they are,' she said and hesitated. 'You're not thinking of stealing things, are you?'

'Certainly not,' said Lockhart firmly, 'if anything I intend to add to their possessions.'

'Oh, well, that's all right then,' said Jessica and handed him the bundle of Yale keys. 'I wouldn't want to think you were doing anything that wasn't legal. Working at Gibling and Gibling I've learnt just how easy it is to get into terrible trouble. Did you know that if you write a book and say nasty things in it about somebody they can sue you for thousands of pounds? It's called libel.'

'I wish someone would write nasty things about us then,' said Lockhart. 'We've got to get thousands of pounds if I'm ever going to start looking for my father.'

'Yes, a libel case would help, wouldn't it?' said Jessica dreamily. 'But you do promise you aren't doing anything that can get us into trouble, don't you?'

Lockhart promised. Fervently. What he had in mind was going to get other people into trouble.

In the meantime he had to wait. It was three days before the Wilsons went out for the evening and Lockhart was able to slip over the fence into their garden and let himself into Number 11. Under his arm he carried a box. He spent an hour in the attic before returning empty-handed.

'Jessica, my sweet,' he said, 'I want you to go into the workshop and wait five minutes. Then say "Testing. Testing. Testing" into that little transmitter. You press the red button first.'

Lockhart slipped back into the Wilsons' house and climbed to the attic and waited. A short time later the three loudspeakers hidden under the glass-fibre insulation and connected to the receiver concealed in a corner resounded eerily to Jessica's voice. One loudspeaker was placed over the Wilsons' main bedroom, a second over the bathroom and a third above the spare room. Lockhart listened and then climbed down and went home.

'You go up to bed,' he told Jessica, 'I shouldn't be long.' Then he stationed himself at the front window and waited for the Wilsons to return. They had had a good evening and were in an intensely spiritual state. Lochart watched the lights come on in their bedroom and bathroom before contributing his share to their belief in the supernatural. Holding his nose between finger and thumb and speaking adenoidally into the microphone he whispered, 'I speak from beyond the grave. Hear me. There will be a death in your house and you will join me.' Then he switched the transmitter off and went out into the night the better to observe the result.

It was, to put it mildly, electrifying. Lights flashed on in every room in the house next door and Mrs Wilson, more used to the gentler messages of the ouija board, could be heard screaming hysterically at this authentic voice of doom. Lockhart, squatting in an azalea bush next to the gateway, listened to Mr Wilson trying to pacify his wife, a process made more difficult by his evident alarm and the impossibility of denying that he too had heard there was going to be a death in the house.

'There's no use saying you didn't,' wailed Mrs Wilson, 'you heard it as clearly as I did and you were in the bathroom and look at the mess you made on the floor.'

Mr Wilson had to agree that his aim had been put off and, by way of Mrs Wilson's infallible logic, that the mess was in consequence of his having learnt that death was so close at hand.

'I told you we should never have started fooling with that damned table-rapping!' he shouted. 'Now look what you've been and let loose.'

'That's right, blame me,' screamed Mrs Wilson, 'that's all you ever do. All I did was ask Mrs Saphegie round to see if she really had psychic gifts and could get answers from our dear departed.'

'Well, now you bloody know,' shouted Mr Wilson. 'And that wasn't the voice of any of my dear departed, that's for sure. No one on our side of the family suffered from such an awful nasal condition. Mind you, I don't suppose being decomposed in a coffin does anything for sinusitis.'

'There you go again,' whined Mrs Wilson, 'one of us going to die and you have to go on about coffins. And don't hog all the brandy. I want some.'

'I didn't know you drank,' said Mr Wilson.

'I do now,' said his wife and evidently poured herself a stiff one. Lockhart left them consoling themselves somewhat unsuccessfully that at least the terrible prophecy proved that there was life after death. It didn't seem to comfort Mrs Wilson very much.

But while the Wilsons speculated on this imminent question about the afterlife and its existence, Little Willie, the Pettigrews' dachshund, went still further and found out. At precisely eleven o'clock Mr Pettigrew put him out and just as precisely Lockhart, lurking in the bird sanctuary, tugged on the nylon fishing-line that stretched under the fence and down the lawn. At the end of the line a lump of liver purchased that morning from the butcher pursued its erratic course across the grass. Behind it, for once unwisely soundless, came Willie in hot pursuit. He didn't come far. As the liver slid past the snare Lockhart had set at the end of the lawn, Willie stopped and, after a brief struggle, gave up both the pursuit and his life. Lockhart buried him under a rose bush at the bottom of his own garden where he would do most good and having accomplished his first two intentions went to bed in a thoroughly cheerful mood, made all the more lively by the fact that the lights were still on in every room of the Wilsons' house when he turned over at three in the morning, and from the house there could be heard the sound of drunken sobbing.

Chapter ten

While Lockhart began to make life uncomfortable for the tenants of his wife's houses, her mother was doing her damnedest to make life unbearable for Mr Flawse. The weather was not on her side. From a bright spring they passed into a hot summer and Flawse Hall showed itself to advantage. Its thick walls had more functions than the keeping out of the Scots and the keeping in of the whisky; they soothed the summer's heat. Outside, the hybrid hounds might slobber and loll in the dung-dry dust of the yard; inside, Mr Flawse could sit contentedly upright at his desk poring over the parish registers and ancient enclosure deeds to which he had lately become so addicted. Knowing that in the fullness of time he was about due to join his ancestors he thought it as well to acquaint himself with the faults and failings of his family.

That he looked only on the worst side of things came from his natural pessimism and knowledge of himself. He was therefore surprised to find that the Flawses were not all unconscionably bad. There were Flawse saints as well as Flawse sinners and if as he expected the latter predominated there was still a streak of generosity to their actions he could not but admire. The Flawse, one Quentin Flawse, who had murdered, or by the more polite usage of the time done to death in a duel, one Thomas Tidley in consequence of the latter implying at the sheep shearing at Otterburn that the name Flawse derived from the Faas, a notorious family of gipsies known best for their thieving, had yet had the generosity to marry his widow and provide for his children. Then again Bishop Flawse, burnt at the stake in the reign of Bloody Mary for his apostasy from Rome, had refused the bag of gunpowder which his brother had brought to tie round his neck on the sensible grounds of economy and its better use to fire muskets into the body of damned Papists when the time was ripe. It was this sort of practicality that Mr Flawse most admired in his forebears and showed that to whatever end they came they wasted no time on self-pity but sustained an indomitable will to do unto others as they were having done to them. Thus Headman Flawse, private executioner to the Duke of Durham in the fourteenth century, had, when his time came to lay his own head on the block, gallantly offered to sharpen the axe for his successor, a gesture so generous that it had been granted: to the extinction of the new headman, fifteen bodyguards, twenty-five bystanders and the Duke himself, all of whom lay headless while Headman Flawse put his expertise to private use and escaped on the Duke's own charger to spend his days as an outlaw among the moss troopers of Redesdale.

Old Mr Flawse thrilled to the account just as he thrilled to the verse that sang in the blood of the Flawse balladeers. Minstrel Flawse was renowned for his songs and Mr Flawse found himself almost unconsciously saying aloud the first stanza of 'The Ballad of Prick 'Em Dry' which the Minstrel was supposed by some authorities to have composed beneath the gibbet at Elsdon on the occasion of his hanging, drawing and quartering for misguidedly climbing into bed with Sir Oswald Capheughton's wife, Lady Fleur, when that noble lord was not only in it but in her at the same time. Minstrel Flawse's introduction of himself into Sir Oswald had met with that reaction known as dog-knotting on the part of all concerned, and it had taken the combined efforts of seven manservants to prise Sir Oswald from Lady Fleur and the sole resources of the local barber and surgeon to sever the connection between Sir Oswald and his Minstrel. The Eunuch Flawse had gone to his subsequent dismemberment relatively cheerfully and with a song in his heart.

I gan noo wha ma organs gan
   When oft I lay abed
So rither hang me upside doon
   Than by ma empty head.

I should ha' knoon 'twas never Fleur
   That smelt so mooch of sweat
For she was iver sweet and pure
   And iver her purse was wet.

But old Sir Oswald allus stank
   Of horse and hound and dung
And when I chose to breech his rank
   Was barrel to my bung.

So hang me noo fra' Elsdon Tree
   And draw ma innards out
That all the warld around may see
   What I have done without.

But ere ye come to draw ma heart
   Na do it all so quick
But prise the arse of Oswald 'part
   And bring me back ma prick.

So prick 'em wet or prick 'em dry
   'Tis all the same to me
I canna wait for him to die
   Afore I have a pee.

Mr Flawse found the poem heartening, if crude. He knew exactly how the Minstrel had felt: his prostate had lately been giving him trouble. But it was the dour gaiety of the ballads that gave him the greatest pleasure. The Flawses might, and indeed, had been thieves and robbers, cut-throats and moss troopers, even saints and bishops, but whatever their calling they had laughed the devil to scorn and made a mockery of misfortune, and their religion had been less Christian than that of personal honour. To call a Flawse a liar was to die or to defend yourself to the death and a Flawse who flinched in the face of adversity was an outcast without hame or name, as the old saying had it.

But there was more to old Mr Flawse's ancestral interest than mere curiosity concerning his own relations. There was still the great question-mark that haunted his nights as to the paternity of Lockhart. And behind it lay the horrifying feeling that Lockhart was as much his son as his grandson. It was with this in mind that he added the flagellant clause to the will in part-recognition that if his suspicions were true he deserved to be flogged within an inch of his life and more properly a yard beyond. The question had to be answered, if not in his own lifetime, in that of Lockhart and as he worked his way through ancient deeds and documents Mr Flawse continued to consider possible candidates. They all had this in common: that at the time of Lockhart's conception, which Mr Flawse calculated to be eight months before his birth, they had lived within riding distance of the Hall and had been between the ages of sixteen and sixty. He refused to believe that his daughter, whatever her vices, would willingly have taken to herself an old man. Much more likely the father had been in his twenties. Beside each name Mr Flawse put the age of the candidate, the colour of his eyes and hair, his features, height and, where possible, his cephalic index. Since the latter required the suspect to submit to Mr Flawse measuring his head both back to front and from side to side with a pair of unnecessarily pointed calipers, not everyone was willing to undergo the operation and those who didn't had registered against their names the letters VS, which signified Very Suspicious. Over the years the old man had collected an immense amount of anthropologically interesting information, but none of it fitted Lockhart's features. They were Flawsian in every particular from the Roman nose to the ice-blue eyes and the flaxen hair and thus increased the old man's sense of guilt and his determination to absolve himself even at the risk of failing and going down in the family history as Incest Flawse. So absorbed was he in his studies that he failed to notice the change that had occurred in his wife.

Mrs Flawse had, as part of her plan for his early death, decided to play the role of dutiful wife. Far from repulsing his advances she positively encouraged him to strain his heart by sleeping with her. Mr Flawse's prostate redressed the balance and prevented him from rising to these frequent occasions. Mrs Flawse took to bringing him his early-morning cup of tea in bed having first laced it with powdered paracetamol tablets which she had once read affected the kidneys adversely. Mr Flawse didn't drink tea in bed, but, not to hurt her feelings, emptied his cup into the chamber pot with the result that Mrs Flawse's hopes were aroused quite fortuitously by the colour of the contents when she emptied it later in the day. The fact that the potion contained tea leaves, and that she was too fastidious to examine it closely, led her to the vain hope that there was something seriously amiss with his bladder. Finally she put him on an even higher cholesterol diet than usual. Mr Flawse had eggs for breakfast, fried eggs with lamb chops for lunch, pork for dinner and zabaglione for dessert, and an eggnog before retiring. Mr Flawse thrived on eggs.

Mrs Flawse, following Professor Yudkin's advice in reverse, added sugar to her list of dietetic poisons and having pressed Mr Flawse to another egg or some more pork crackling, served sweets, cakes and biscuits that consisted almost entirely of sugar. Mr Flawse's energy increased enormously and when not sitting in his study he strode across the fell with renewed vigour. Mrs Flawse watched his progress in despair and her own increased weight with alarm. It was all very well trying to poison the old man by over-indulgence but she had to share the same diet and it didn't agree with her. Finally, in a last desperate effort, she encouraged him to hit the port bottle. Mr Flawse followed her advice cheerfully and felt all the better for it. Mrs Flawse fortified the port decanter with brandy and Mr Flawse, whose nose for a fine wine was acute, recognized the addition and congratulated her on her ingenuity. 'Gives it more body,' he declared. 'I wonder I hadn't thought of it before. Definitely more body.'

Mrs Flawse silently cursed but had to agree. Port with more than its normal quota of brandy did have more body. On the other hand so did she, and her dresses were beginning to look as though they belonged to another woman. Mr Flawse found her greater girth a source of amusement and made uncalled-for remarks to Mr Dodd about breasts, bottoms and bitches being all the better for bed when broad. And all the while Mrs Flawse was conscious that Mr Dodd kept his uncast eye upon her. She found it unnerving and Mr Dodd's collie had a nasty habit of snarling whenever she passed too close.

'I wish you'd keep the creature out of the kitchen,' she told Mr Dodd irritably.

'Aye and me with her I dare say,' said Mr Dodd. 'You'd be hard put to it to keep yoursel' warm without my going down the drift mine for coal. If you dinna want me in the kitchen, you'll have to gan dig it yoursel'.'

Mrs Flawse had no intention of going down the drift mine to dig coal and said so.

'Then the dawg stays,' said Mr Dodd.

Mrs Flawse promised herself to see that the collie didn't, but Mr Dodd's habit of feeding the beast himself prevented her from putting ground glass in the dog's food. All in all it was a trying summer for Mrs Flawse and she found herself uncharacteristically yearning for the bleak winter ahead. She would have more opportunity for making things uncomfortable at the Hall.

Lockhart had already succeeded at Sandicott Crescent. Having dispatched Little Willie, the Pettigrews' dachshund, to that afterlife about which the Wilsons now had no doubts, he was able to move more easily about the gardens and the bird sanctuary on his solitary expeditions. Mr Grabble, whose wife he had seen in Mr Simplon's arms, was the European manager for a firm of electronics engineers and regularly went abroad. It was during his absences that Mrs Grabble and Mr Simplon kept what Lockhart called their trysts. Mr Simplon left his car two streets away and walked to the Grabble house; when he had finished trysting he went back to the car and drove home to Mrs Simplon at Number 5. Further investigation revealed that Mr Grabble had left an emergency number in Amsterdam where he could always be reached should need arise. Lockhart discovered this by the simple expedient of unlocking the front door to Number 2 with the late Mr Sandicott's key and consulting the Grabbles' bureau and telephone directory. Accordingly, on a hot afternoon in June, he went to the trouble of sending a telegram to Mr Grabble in Amsterdam recommending him to return home at once as his wife was dangerously ill, too ill in fact to be moved from the house. Having signed it in the name of a fictitious doctor Lockhart quietly shinned a telegraph pole in the bird sanctuary and neatly severed the line to the Grabbles' house. After that he went home and had tea before going out as dusk fell and making his way to the corner of the road in which Mr Simplon left his car. The car was there.

It was not there twenty-five minutes later when Mr Grabble, driving with more reckless concern for his wife than her behaviour justified and less for other road users, hurtled through East Pursley and into Sandicott Crescent. It was not there when Mr Simplon, naked and covering his previously private parts with both hands, scampered down the Grabbles' drive and shot frenziedly round the corner. It was sitting in the Simplons' garage where Lockhart had parked with a cheerful toot of the horn to alert Mrs Simplon that her husband was home, before crossing to the golf course and making his way sedately back to Jessica at Number 12. Behind him Numbers 5 and 2 were a holocaust of domestic understanding. The discovery that his wife, far from being dangerously ill, was copulating ardently with a neighbour he had never much liked anyway, and that he had been brought anxiously all the way back from Amsterdam to have this ugly fact thrust under his unsuspecting nose, was too much for Mr Grabble's temper. His shouts and Mrs Grabble's screams, as he used first his umbrella, and then, having broken it, an Anglepoise lamp that stood on the bedside table, to express his feelings, could be heard far down the street. They were particularly audible next door where the Misses Musgrove were entertaining the Vicar and his wife to dinner. They were also audible to Mrs Simplon. The fact that her husband, having just driven into the garage, figured so largely in Mr Grabble's invective provoked her to investigate how he could possibly be in two places at the same time. Mr Grabble's commentary supplied a third occupation, that of Mrs Grabble.

Mrs Simplon emerged from the front door at the very same moment as the Vicar, driven as much by the Misses Musgroves' curiosity as by any desire to interfere in a domestic disaster, came out of Number 4. His collision with a naked Mr Simplon who had taken his courage in both hands and was scampering back to his own house had at least the merit of explaining exactly what and whom her husband had been doing in the Grabble house. Not that she needed much telling. Mr Grabble was singularly lucid on the subject. The Rev. Truster was less well-informed. He had never met Mr Grabble in the flesh and naturally supposed that the naked man cowering on the ground at his feet was a sinner, and a wife-beater, come to repentance.

'My dear man,' said the Vicar, 'this is no way to conduct your domestic life.'

Mr Simplon was fully aware of the fact. He stared frantically up at the Rev. Truster and clutched his scrotum. Over the road his wife went indoors and slammed the front door.

'Your wife may have done all the things you say she's done but to beat a woman is the act of a cad.'

Mr Simplon thoroughly agreed but was spared the need to explain that he had never so much as laid a finger on Mrs Simplon by the crash of breaking french window and the emergence of a large and very heavy piece of Waterford glass. Mrs Grabble, in fear for her life, was fighting back to some effect. Mr Simplon took the opportunity to get to his feet and rush across the road to Number 5, a progress that took him past the Ogilvies, the Misses Musgrove and the Pettigrews, none of whom he knew at all intimately but who now knew him by rather more than the cut of his coat. As he stood under the mock-Georgian portico of his front door and beat on the Cupid-head knocker with one hand while pressing the bell with his elbow at the same time, Mr Simplon knew that his reputation as a consultant engineer was at an end. So was Mrs Simplon's tolerance. Her husband's constant absences and lame excuses had combined with her own sexual frustration to leave her a bitter woman. She had emerged to save what she could of her marriage but at the sight of her husband cowering naked in front of a clergyman had decided to end it. And not with a whimper.

'You can stay out there till hell freezes over,' she shouted through the letter box at her nearest, 'but if you think I'm letting you into my home ever again you've got another think coming.'

Mr Simplon had had enough thoughts coming without this additional one and he particularly disliked the use of the possessive adjective. 'What do you mean "my home"?' he yelled, momentarily forgetting his other lost possessions. 'I've as much right—'

'Not any more,' screamed Mrs Simplon adding an extra sting to the statement by squirting the contents of an aerosol can of De-Icing Fluid, which Mr Simplon kept on a shelf in the hall for quite other purposes, through the letter box on to those shrivelled organs Mrs Grabble had recently found so attractive. The screams that followed this remarkable initiative were music to her ears. They were certainly music to Lockhart, who had last heard their like at a pig-killing without use of a humane killer. He sat in the kitchen with Jessica and smiled over his Ovaltine.

'I wonder what can be going on,' said Jessica anxiously. 'It sounds as if someone is dying. Hadn't you better go and investigate? I mean perhaps you could do something.'

Lockhart shook his head. 'Strong fences make good neighbours,' he said complacently, a maxim that was in some dispute at the far end of the Crescent. There Mr Simplon's screams and Mr Grabble's denunciations and Mrs Grabble's absurd denials had been joined by the siren of a police car. The Pettigrews, already in communication with the police following the loss of Little Willie, had phoned again. This time the police took their complaint more seriously and, with that fine discrimination for anything vaguely homosexual, had taken both the Rev. Truster and Mr Simplon into custody, the former on the grounds that he was soliciting and the latter for indecent exposure, a charge Mr Simplon, who had been playing the garden sprinkler rather erratically on his inflamed penis when they arrived, was incapable of finding words to deny. It was left to the Rev. Truster to explain as best he could that far from soliciting Mr Simplon's sexual favours, such as they remained, he was simply doing his utmost to prevent him actually castrating himself with the revolving sprinkler. It didn't sound a likely explanation to the

Duty Sergeant, and Mr Simplon's inability to specify with any precision what he had got on his private parts to cause him to act in this peculiar manner didn't help matters.

'Put the sods in separate cells,' said the Duty Sergeant, and the Rev. Truster and Mr Simplon were dragged away.

With their going Sandicott Crescent resumed its interrupted routine. Mrs Simplon went unrepentantly to bed alone. Mr and Mrs Grabble went to bed separately and shouted abuse at one another. The Misses Musgrove did their best to console Mrs Truster who kept repeating hysterically that her husband wasn't queer.

'No, dear, of course he isn't,' they said in unison and without the slightest notion what Mrs Truster actually meant. 'He was taken queer when the policemen came but then who wouldn't be.'

Mrs Truster's attempt to explain by saying he wasn't gay either brought them no nearer to understanding what she was talking about.

But there were other less innocent reactions to the events of the evening. Mr and Mrs Raceme had been exhilarated by the sound of beating and for once forgetful of the curtains in the bedroom had allowed Lockhart a full view of their particular perversion. He had watched with interest first Mr Raceme tying his wife to the bed and beating her lightly with a cane and then allowing her to repeat the performance on himself. He went home and added the details to their dossier and finally to round the evening off had gone into the garage and promised the Wilsons next door an imminent death to such effect that once again their lights remained on all night. All in all, he thought, as he climbed into bed beside his radiant angel, Jessica, it had been a most rewarding and informative day, and if he could keep the impetus of his campaign up the For Sale boards would shortly be in evidence in Sandicott Crescent. He cuddled up to Jessica and presently they were engaged in that chaste lovemaking that characterized their marriage.

Chapter eleven

It was Jessica, returning from her work as a temporary typist next day, who brought a further development.

'You'll never guess who lives in Green End,' she said excitedly.

'I never will,' Lockhart agreed with that apparent and literal frankness that masked the devious depths of his mind. Green End was not his concern, and lay a mile away beyond the golf course in West Pursley, an even more substantial suburb with larger houses, larger gardens and older trees.

'Genevieve Goldring,' said Jessica.

'Never heard of her,' said Lockhart swishing the air with a riding crop he had constructed out of a length of garden hose bound with twine and thonged at the end with a number of leather strips.

'You must have,' said Jessica, 'she's just the most wonderful writer there ever was. I've got dozens of her books and they're ever so interesting.'

But Lockhart had his mind on other things, and whether or not to splice the leather strips with lead shot.

'A girl in our office had been working for her and she says she's really weird,' Jessica continued. 'She walks up and down the room and talks and Patsy just has to sit at the typewriter and write down everything she says.'

'Must be boring work,' said Lockhart, who had decided lead shot would be overdoing things a bit.

'And do you know what? Patsy's going to let me go and work over there in her place tomorrow. She wants the day off and they haven't found a job for me. Isn't that wonderful?'

'I suppose so,' said Lockhart.

'It's marvellous. I've always wanted to meet a real live author.'

'Won't this Goldring woman want to know why Patsy hasn't come?' asked Lockhart.

'She doesn't even know Patsy's name. She's so inspired she just starts talking as soon as Patsy comes and they work in a garden shed that revolves to catch the sun. I'm so excited. I can't wait.'

Nor could Mr Simplon and the Rev. Truster. Their appearance in court had been brief and they had been released on bail to await trial. Mr Simplon returned home in clothes borrowed from the body of a tramp who had died the previous week. He was almost unrecognizable and certainly not by Mrs Simplon, who not only refused him entry to her house but had locked the garage. Mr Simplon's subsequent action of breaking a back window in his own house had been met by the contents of a bottle of ammonia and a further visit to the police station on a charge of making a public nuisance of himself. The Rev. Truster's reception had been more gentle and understanding, Mrs Truster's understanding being that her husband was a homosexual and that far from being a crime homosexuality was simply a freak of nature. The Rev. Truster resented the imputation and said so. Mrs Truster pointed out that she was merely repeating his own words in a sermon on the subject. The Rev. Truster retorted that he wished to God he'd never given that damned sermon. Mrs Truster had asked why, if he felt so strongly on the matter of being a fag, he had ever ... The Rev. Truster told her to shut up. Mrs Truster didn't. In short, discord reigned almost as cruelly as it did in the Grabble household, where Mrs Grabble finally packed her bags and took a taxi to the station to go to her mother in Hendon. Next door the Misses Musgrove shook their heads sadly and spoke softly of the wickedness of the modern world while speculating separately on the size, shape and subsequent colour change of Mr Simplon's genitalia. It was the first glimpse they had ever had of a naked man and those parts which played so large a role, they understood, in marital happiness. And having glimpsed, their appetite, though too late in life to lead them to hope it would be satisfied, was whetted. They need not have been so pessimistic. It was soon to be sated.

Lockhart, intrigued by what he had seen in the Racemes' bedroom, had decided to acquaint himself more fully with the sexual peccadilloes of the human race and, while Jessica went joyfully off next day to her rendezvous with literary fame in Miss Genevieve Goldring's garden hut, Lockhart took the train to London, spent several hours in Soho leafing through magazines and returned with a catalogue from a sex shop. It was full of the most alarming devices which buzzed, vibrated, bounced and ejaculated *ad nauseam*. Lockhart began to understand more fully the nature of sex and to recognize his own ignorance. He took the magazines and the catalogue up to the attic and hid them for future reference. The Wilsons next door were a more immediate target for his campaign of eviction and it had occurred to him that something more than the sound of a voice from beyond the grave might add urgency to their departure. He decided to include smell and taking a spade he dug up the putrefying body of Little Willie, dismembered it in the garage, and distributed its portions in the Wilsons' coal cellar while they were out drowning their memories of the previous night at the local pub. The effect, on their return later and drunker that evening to a house that not only prophesied death but now stank of it more eloquently than words, was immediate. Mrs Wilson had hysterics and was sick and Mr Wilson, invoking the curse of the ouija board and table-knocking, threatened to fulfil the prophecy that there would soon be a death in the house by strangling her if she didn't shut up. But the smell was too strong even for him and rather than spend another night in the house of death they drove to a motel.

Even Jessica noticed the stench and mentioned it to Lockhart. 'It's the Wilsons' drains,' he said impromptu, and having said it promptly began to wonder if he couldn't make use of the drains and the sewage system to introduce noxious matter into the houses of other unwanted tenants. It was worth thinking about. Meanwhile he was having his job cut out comforting Jessica. Her experience of acting as amanuensis to the literary heroine of her youth, Miss Genevieve Goldring, had filled her with a terrible sense of disillusionment.

'She's just the most horrible person you ever met,' she said almost sobbing, 'she's cynical and nasty and all she thinks about is money. She didn't even say "Good Morning" or offer me a cup of tea. She just walks up and down dictating what she calls "The verbal shit my public likes to lick its chops over". And I'm part of her public and you know I'd never . . .'

'Of course you wouldn't, darling,' said Lockhart soothingly.

'I could have killed her when she said that,' said Jessica, 'I really could have. And she writes five books a year under different names.'

'How do you mean, under different names?'

'Well she is not even called Genevieve Goldring. She's Miss Magster and she drinks. After lunch she sat and drank crème de menthe and daddy always said people who drank crème de menthe were common and he was right. And then the golf ball went wrong and she blamed me.'

'Golf ball?' said Lockhart. 'What the hell was she doing with a golf ball?'

'It's a typewriter, a golf-ball typewriter,' Jessica explained. 'Instead of having separate letters on bars that hit the paper it has this golf ball with the alphabet on it that goes round and runs along the paper printing the letters. It's ever so modern and it wasn't my fault it went wrong.'

'I'm sure it wasn't,' said Lockhart intrigued by this mechanism, 'but what's the advantage of a golf ball?'

'Well, you can just take the golf ball with the alphabet on it off and put on another one when you want a different typeface.'

'You can? That's interesting. So if you took the golf ball off her typewriter and brought it home you could put it on your own typewriter and it would look exactly the same, the stuff you wrote I mean?'

'You couldn't do it with an ordinary typewriter,' said Jessica, 'but if you had the same sort as hers nobody could tell the difference. Anyway she was just beastly and I hate her.'

'Darling,' said Lockhart, 'you remember when you were working for those solicitors, Gibling and Gibling, and you told me about writing nasty things in books about people and libel and all that?'

'Yes,' said Jessica, 'I just wish that horrid woman would write something nasty about us . . .'

The gleam in Lockhart's eye stopped her and she looked questioningly at him.

'Oh Lockhart!' she said. 'You are clever.'

Next day Lockhart went to London once again and came back with a golf-ball typewriter of exactly the same make as Miss Genevieve Goldring's. It had been a costly purchase but what he had in mind would make it cheap at the price. Miss Goldring, it appeared, never bothered to correct her proofs.

Jessica had learnt that from Patsy. 'Sometimes she has three books on the go at the same time,' said the innocent Patsy. 'She just dashes them off and forgets all about them.'

An additional advantage was that Miss Goldring's daily output remained in a drawer in the desk in the shed at the bottom of her garden and since she switched from crême de menthe to gin at six she was seldom sober by seven and almost always pooped by eight.

'Darling,' said Lockhart when Jessica came home with this news, 'I don't want you to go to work as a temporary typist any more. I want you to stay at home and work at night.'

'Yes, Lockhart,' said Jessica obediently, and as darkness fell over the golf course and East and West Pursley, Lockhart made his way to Green End and the shed at the bottom of the great authoress's garden. He returned with the first three chapters of her latest novel, *Song of the Heart*, plus the golf ball from her typewriter. And late into the night Jessica sat and retyped the chapters. The heroine, previously called Sally, was now called Jessica and the hero, such as he was, was transformed from David to Lockhart. Finally, the name Flawse figured largely in the revised version which at three in the morning Lockhart placed in the drawer in the shed. There were other changes, too, and none of them to the advantage of Miss Goldring's characters. Lockhart Flawse in the new version liked being tied to the bed and whipped by Jessica, and when not being whipped stole money from banks. All told, *Song of the Heart* had ingredients added that were extraordinarily libellous and were calculated to make a hole in Miss Goldring's purse and a dirge in her heart. Since she wrote her novels at top speed Lockhart was so busy fetching her daily output and replacing it by Jessica's nightly amendments that his campaign for the eviction of the tenants in Sandicott Crescent had to be temporarily suspended. It was only when the novel was finished a fortnight later that Lockhart could relax and put Phase Two into operation. This involved a further outlay of money and was aimed simultaneously at the mental stability of the Misses Musgrove, and the physical ill-health of either, or both, depending on the degree of recrimination they indulged in, Mr and Mrs Raceme. But first he made further use of Jessica's typewriter by purchasing a fresh golf ball with a different typeface and composing a letter to the manufacturers of those artifacts of sexual stimulation that had intrigued and disgusted him in the catalogue. The letter was addressed from 4 Sandicott Crescent, enclosed postal orders to the tune of eighty-nine pounds and was signed with a squiggle over the typed name of Mrs Musgrove. In it Mrs Musgrove ordered an ejaculatory and vibrating dildo of adjustable proportions, the bottom half of a plastic man complete with organs, and finally a studded rubber pad with battery attached which called itself a clitoral stimulator. Not to spoil the ship for a ha'porth of tar, Lockhart also subscribed to *Lesbian Lusts, Women Only*, and *Pussy Kiss*, which three magazines he had been so appalled by that their effect on the Misses Musgrove month after month would be devastating. But having sent the letter he had to wait for the postal delay before observing any result.

In the case of the Racemes results were more immediate. Lockhart's methodical observations compiled in their dossier showed that Wednesday was the night the couple favoured for their horseplay and that it was usually Mr Raceme's turn first. With that gallantry that his grandfather had observed in his ancestors, Lockhart decided that it would be ungentlemanly to strike a lady. He had also noted that Mrs Raceme was friendly with a Mrs Artoux who lived in a flat in the centre of East Pursley. Mrs Artoux was not in the phone book and therefore presumably had no phone. And so on Wednesday night Lockhart waited in the bird sanctuary with a stopwatch and gave Mrs Raceme ten minutes in which to attach her husband to the bed with the leather straps they seemed to favour before going to the phone box on the corner and dialling the Raceme number. Mrs Raceme took the call.

'Can you come at once?' said Lockhart through a handkerchief, 'Mrs Artoux has had a stroke and is asking for you.'

He emerged from the phone box in time to see the Racemes' Saab shoot out of the drive, and consulted his stopwatch. Two minutes had elapsed since he had made the call and two minutes would not have given Mrs Raceme time to untie her husband. Lockhart sauntered down the street to their house, unlocked the door and went quietly inside. He turned out the light in the hall, climbed the stairs and stood in silence on the landing. Finally he peered into the bedroom. Naked, hooded, bound and gagged,

Mr Raceme was in the grip of those obscure masochistic emotions which gave him so much peculiar satisfaction. He squirmed ecstatically on the bed. A second later he was still squirming but the ecstasy had gone. Used to the exquisite pain of Mrs Raceme's light birch, the application of Lockhart's patent horsewhip at maximum velocity to his rump produced a reflex that threatened to lift both his body off the bed and the bed off the floor. Mr Raceme spat the gag out of his mouth and tried to express his feelings vocally. Lockhart suppressed his yell by pushing his head into the pillow and applied his horsewhip to full advantage. By the time he had finished Mr Raceme had passed from masochism to sadism.

'I'll murder you, you fucking bitch,' he screamed as Lockhart shut the bedroom door and went downstairs, 'so help me God, I'll kill you if it's the last thing I do.'

Lockhart let himself out of the front door and went round to the garden. From inside the house Mr Raceme's screams and threats had begun to alternate with whimpers. Lockhart installed himself in the bushes and waited for Mrs Raceme to return. If half of the threats her husband was making were carried out he might well have to intervene once again to save her life. He debated the point but decided that whatever Mr Raceme might say the state of his backside would deter him from putting anything into practice. He was on the point of leaving when the Saab's headlights shone in the drive and Mrs Raceme let herself into the house.

The ensuing sounds surpassed even those that had enlivened Sandicott Crescent on the evening of the Grabbles' domestic tiff. Mrs Raceme's statement, even before she entered the bedroom and saw Mr Raceme's condition, that there was absolutely nothing the matter with Mrs Artoux and that she certainly hadn't had a stroke was greeted by a scream of rage that shook the curtains and was followed by a second scream of almost equal proportions from Mrs Raceme. Lacking Lockhart's clear understanding of what Mr Raceme had promised to do to her the moment he got free, she made the mistake of untying his legs. A second later, disproving Lockhart's supposition that he wasn't in any fit state to put theory into practice, Mr Raceme was on his feet and clearly raring to go. Unfortunately his hands were still lashed to the double bed and

Mrs Raceme, recognizing almost instantaneously her mistake in untying his feet, refused to undo his hands.

'What do you mean I did this to you?' she shrieked as the double bed wedded to Mr Raceme's feet blundered towards her. 'I got this phone call from someone saying Mrs Artoux had had a stroke.'

The word was too much for Mr Raceme. 'Stroke?' he yelled in a muffled sort of way through the pillow and the mattress that obstructed his view of things. 'What in the name of hell do you mean by stroke?'

In the garden Lockhart knew precisely. His patent horsewhip had needed no lead weights added to the leather thongs.

'Well all I'm telling you,' shrieked Mrs Raceme, 'is that if you think I did that to you, you're out of your mind.'

Mr Raceme was. Impeded by the bed and driven insane by the pain he hurtled across the room in the general direction of her voice, smashed through the dressing-table behind which Mrs Raceme was sheltering and carrying all before him, dressing-table, bed, bedside lamp and teamaker, not to mention Mrs Raceme, shot through the curtains of the patio window, smashed the double glazing and cascaded down into the flowerbed below. There his screams were combined with those of Mrs Raceme herself, lacerated in much the same part of her anatomy by the double glazing and a rose bush.

Lockhart hesitated and crossed into the bird sanctuary, and as he moved silently towards Number 12 the sound of sirens could be heard above the shouts and yells of the Racemes. The Pettigrews had exercised their social conscience once again and phoned for the police.

'What on earth was all that noise?' Jessica inquired as he came in from the garage where he had deposited his horsewhip. 'It sounded as if someone had fallen through a greenhouse roof.'

'Most peculiar tenants we've got,' said Lockhart, 'they seem to kick up such a rumpus.'

Certainly Mr and Mrs Raceme were kicking up a rumpus and the police found their predicament most peculiar. Mr Raceme's lacerated posterior and his hood made instant identification difficult but it was the fact that he was still tied to the bed that intrigued them.

'Tell me, sir,' said the sergeant who arrived and promptly phoned for an ambulance, 'do you make a habit of wearing hoods when you go to bed?'

'Mind your own bloody business,' said Mr Raceme inadvisedly. 'I don't ask you what you do in the privacy of your home and you've got no right to ask me.'

'Well, sir, if that's the line you're going to take, we'll take the line that you've used obscene language to a police officer in the execution of his duty and have issued menaces against the person of your wife.'

'And what about my person?' yelled Mr Raceme. 'You seem to have overlooked the fact that she thrashed me.'

'We haven't overlooked it, sir,' said the sergeant, 'the lady seems to have made a good job of it.'

The arrival of a constable who had been investigating the contents of the Racemes' bedroom and was now carrying a bundle of rods, whips, canes and cats-o'-nine tails merely confirmed the police in their suspicion that Mr Raceme had got what he asked for. Their sympathy was all for his wife and when Mr Raceme tried to renew his assault on her they dispensed with the need for handcuffs and carried him bed and all into the Black Maria. Mrs Raceme went away in an ambulance. The sergeant following in a police car was frankly puzzled.

'Something bloody odd going on down there,' he said to the driver. 'We'd better keep an eye on Sandicott Crescent from now on.'

From that night on a patrol car was stationed at the bottom of the Crescent and its presence there forced Lockhart to adopt new tactics. He had already given some thought to the use of the sewage system and the police lent him the incentive. Two days later he purchased a wet-suit for underwater diving and an oxygen mask and, making use of the late Mr Sandicott's detailed plans of the Crescent's amenities, lifted the cover of the main sewer opposite his house, descended the ladder and closed it behind him. In the darkness he switched on his torch and made his way along, noting the inlets from each house as he went. It was a large main sewer and afforded him fresh insight into the habits of his neighbours. Opposite Colonel Finch-Potter's subsidiary were deposited a number of white latex objects which didn't accord with his supposedly bachelor status, while Mr O'Brain's meanness was proven by his use of a telephone directory for toilet paper. Lockhart returned from his potholing determined to concentrate his attention on these two bachelors. There was the problem of the Colonel's bull-terrier to be considered. It was an amiable beast but of as ferocious an aspect as that of its owner. Lockhart knew the Colonel's habits already, though the discovery of so many contraceptives in the vicinity of his drain came as something of a surprise. There was more to the Colonel than met the eye. He would have to observe him more closely. Mr O'Brain presented less of a problem. Being Irish, he was a relatively easy target, and when Lockhart had divested himself of his wet-suit and had washed it, he resorted to the telephone yet again.

'This is the Pursley Brigade of the Provisional IRA,' he said in a supposedly Irish voice. 'We'll be expecting your contribution in the next few days. The code-word is Killarney.'

Mr O'Brain's reply went unheard. A retired gynaecologist, he was sufficiently anglicized and wealthy to feel resentful of this call on his time and resources. He promptly phoned the police and asked for protection. Lockhart from the window of his bedroom saw the patrol car at the end of the street move forward and stop outside the O'Brain house. It would be as well not to use the telephone again, he decided, and went to bed with a different scheme in mind. It involved the use of the sewer and was likely to disprove Mr O'Brain's claim to have nothing to do with any organization that sought to achieve its ends by violence.

The following morning he was up early and on his way to the shopping centre when the mail van arrived and delivered several packets to the Misses Musgrove. Lockhart heard them express some surprise and the hope that these were fresh donations to the church jumble sale. Lockhart doubted the suitability of the contents for any church function, a view shared a moment or two later by the Misses Musgrove who, having glimpsed Mr Simplon's penis, recognized some awful similarity between it and the monstrous objects that they found inside the packets.

'There must be some mistake,' said Miss Mary, examining the address. 'We didn't order these frightful things.'

Her elder sister, Maud, looked at her sceptically.

'I didn't anyway. I can assure you of that,' she said icily.

'Well you don't supposed for one moment that I did, do you?' said Mary. Maud's silence was answer enough.

'How perfectly horrid of you to entertain such a suspicion,' continued the outraged Mary. 'For all I know you did and you're just trying to throw the blame on me.'

They threw the blame on one another for the next hour but finally curiosity prevailed.

'It says here,' said Maud, reading the instructions for the ejaculatory and vibrating dildo of adjustable proportions, 'that the testicles can be filled with the white of egg and double cream in equal proportions to attain the effect of a lifelike ejaculation. Which do you think the testicles are?'

Miss Mary correctly discovered them and presently the two spinsters were busy mixing the necessary ingredients, using the vibrating dildo to best advantage as an egg-beater. Having satisfied themselves that the texture was that recommended in the instructions, they had just filled the testicles to capacity and were arguing from their little observation of Mr Simplon's un-obtrusive organ what proportion to adjust the dildo to, when the doorbell rang.

'I'll answer it,' said Mary and went to the front door. Mrs Truster was there.

'I've just dropped in to say that Henry's solicitor, Mr Watts, is confident that the charge will be dropped,' she said sweeping in her accustomed way down the passage and into the kitchen, 'I thought you'd be glad to know that .. '

Whatever the Misses Musgroves might be glad to know, Mrs Truster was horrified at the spectacle that greeted her. Maud Musgrove was holding an enormous and anatomically exact penis in one hand and what appeared to be an icing syringe in the other. Mrs Truster stared wildly at the thing. It had been bad enough to suspect that her husband was a homosexual; to discover with absolute certainty that the Misses Musgrove of all people were lesbians who mixed slight culinary gifts with gigantic sexual ones was too much for her poor mind. The room swam for a moment and she collapsed into a convenient chair.

'Dear God, oh Lord,' she whimpered, and opened her eyes. The beastly thing was still there and from its . ;. whatever you called a dildo's opening ... there dribbled ... 'Jesus,' she said calling on the Almighty yet again before reverting to more appropriate speech, 'what in hell's name is going on?'

It was this question that alerted the Misses Musgrove to their socially catastrophic predicament.

'We were just ...' they began in unison when the dildo answered for them. Triggered by Miss Maud's sitting on the mechanism that controlled its functions the dildo expanded, vibrated, jerked up and down and fulfilled the guarantee of its manufacturer to the letter. Mrs Truster stared at the terrible thing as it gyrated and expanded and the mock veins stood out on its trunk.

'Stop it, for hell's sake, stop the fucking thing,' she yelled, forgetting her own social position in the enormity of her horror. Miss Maud did her best. She grappled with the creature and tried desperately to stop it jerking. She succeeded all too well. The dildo lived up to its promise and shot half a pint of mixed egg white and double cream across the kitchen like some formidable fire extinguisher. Having achieved this remarkable feat it proceeded to go limp. So did Mrs Truster. She slid off her chair on to the floor and mingled with the dildo's recent contents.

'Oh dear, what do we do now?' asked Miss Mary. 'You don't think she's had a heart attack, do you?'

She knelt beside Mrs Truster and felt her pulse. It was extremely weak.

'She's dying,' Miss Mary moaned, 'We've killed her.'

'Nonsense,' said Miss Maud practically, and put the deflated dildo on the draining board. But when she knelt beside Mrs Truster she had to admit that her pulse was dangerously weak.

'We'll just have to give her the kiss of life,' she said and together they lifted the Vicar's wife on to the kitchen table.

'How?' said Mary.

'Like this,' said Maud, who had attended a first aid course, and applied her knowledge and her mouth to the resuscitation of Mrs Truster. It was immediately successful. From her swoon Mrs Truster regained consciousness to find Miss Maud Musgrove kissing her passionately, an activity that was entirely in sexual keeping with what she had already observed of the two spinsters' unnatural lusts. Her eyes bulging in her head and her breath reinforced by that of Miss Maud, Mrs Truster broke away and screamed at the very top of her voice. And once again Sandicott Crescent resounded to the shrieks of an hysterical woman.

This time there was no need for the Pettigrews to phone the police. The patrol car was at the front door almost immediately and, breaking the glass panel in the window beside it, the police unlocked the door and swarmed down the passage into the kitchen. Mrs Truster was still shrieking and crouching in the far corner, and, on the draining board beside her, motivated a second time by Miss Maud's slumping into the chair on which its mechanism stood, slowly swelling and oozing, the dreadful dildo.

'Don't let them come anywhere near me with that thing,' screamed Mrs Truster as she was helped out of the house, 'they tried to ... oh God ... and she was kissing me and ...'

'If you wouldn't mind just stepping this way,' said the sergeant to the Misses Musgrove in the kitchen.

'But can't we put that ...'

'The constable will take that and any other evidence he finds into possession,' said the sergeant, 'Just put your coats on and come quietly. A policewoman will come for your night clothes, etc.'

And following in the footsteps of Mr Simplon, the Rev. Truster and Mr and Mrs Raceme, the Misses Musgrove were taken to the police car and driven off at high speed to be charged.

'What with?' Lockhart asked as he passed the constable on duty outside the house.

'You name it, sir, you've got it. They'll throw the book at them and two nicer old ladies to meet you couldn't imagine.'

'Extraordinary,' said Lockhart and went on his way with a smile. Things were working remarkably well.

When he got home Jessica had prepared lunch.

'There was a phone message for you from Pritchetts, the ironmongers,' she told him as he sat down. 'They say they'll send round the two hundred yards of plastic piping you asked for some time later this afternoon.'

'Great,' said Lockhart. 'Just what I needed.'

'But, darling, the garden's only fifty yards long. What on

earth can you want with two hundred yards of hosepipe?'

'I wouldn't be surprised if I don't have to go and water the Misses Musgrove's garden at Number 4. I think they're going to be away for some considerable time.'

'The Misses Musgrove?' said Jessica. 'But they never go away.'

'They've gone this time,' said Lockhart. 'In a police car.'

Chapter twelve

That afternoon, on Lockhart's suggestion, Jessica went round to the Wilsons to ask if there was anything she could do as their landlady to rectify the state of their drains.

'There's a very nasty smell,' she said to the wild-eyed Mrs Wilson. 'It's really most offensive.'

'Smell? Drains,' said Mrs Wilson, who hadn't considered this practical reason for the stench of death in the house.

'Surely you can smell it?' said Jessica as Little Willie wafted from the coal cellar.

'The grave,' said Mrs Wilson, sticking firmly to first principles. 'It is the smell of afterlife.'

'It smells more like that of afterdeath,' said Jessica. 'Are you sure something hasn't died? I mean things do, don't they? We had a rat die once behind the fridge and it smelt just like this.'

But though they looked behind the fridge and under the oven, and even inside the Wilsons' tumbler drier, there was no sign of a rat.

'I'll ask my husband to come over,' Jessica said, 'and see if it isn't the drains. He's very practical.'

Mrs Wilson thanked her but doubted there was anything practical Mr Flawse could do. She was wrong. Lockhart arrived ten minutes later with two hundred yards of plastic piping, and proceeded to investigate the drainage system with a thoroughness that was entirely reassuring. His conversation wasn't. Lapsing into his broadest Northumbrian as he worked he

110

spoke of ghosties and ghouls and things that went bump in the night.

'I ha' the gift of second sight,' he told a gibbering Mrs Wilson. ' 'Twas given me as ma birthright. 'Tis death I smell and not the drain, aye, not one death but e'en the twain.'

'Twain? Don't you mean two?' shuddered Mrs Wilson.

Lockhart nodded grimly. 'Aye twain it is depart this life, with blude red throats and bludier knife, so runs the rune my heart espied, 'tis murder first then suicide.'

'Murder first? Then suicide?' said Mrs Wilson in the grip of a terrible curiosity.

Lockhart glanced significantly at a carving knife hanging from a magnetic board. 'A woman screams without a tongue, and then from rafter man is hung. I see it all as I ha' said, ye both mun leave ere both be dead. The hoose it is that has the curse, I smell your death and soomat worse.'

His eyes lost their glazed look and he busied himself about the drains. Upstairs Mrs Wilson was packing frantically and when Mr Wilson returned she had already left. On the kitchen table there was a hardly legible note in her shaking hand to say that she had gone to her sister's and that if he was wise he'd leave at once too. Mr Wilson cursed his wife, the ouija board and the smell, but being of a more insensitive nature refused to be daunted.

'I'm damned if I'll be driven out of my own house,' he muttered, 'ghost or no ghost.' And went up to have a bath, only to find a rope with a noose on it hanging from the rafter in the mock-Tudor ceiling in the bedroom. Mr Wilson stared at it in horror and recalled his wife's message. The smell in the bedroom was equally alarming. Lockhart had retrieved portions of the putrefying Willie and distributed them in the wardrobe, and as Mr Wilson stood sickened by the bed the voice he had heard before spoke again, and this time closer and more convincingly. 'Hanged by your neck till ye be dead, the grave tonight shall be your bed.'

'It bloody well won't,' quavered Mr Wilson but he too packed and left the house, stopping briefly at Number 12 to hand Jessica the key and his notice. 'We're going and we're never coming back,' he said, 'that bloody house is haunted.'

'Oh surely not, Mr Wilson,' said Jessica, 'it's just got a nasty smell, but if you are leaving would you mind saying so in writing?'

'Tomorrow,' said Mr Wilson who didn't want to dally.

'Now,' said Lockhart emerging from the hall with a form.

Mr Wilson put down his suitcase and signed a formal statement to the effect that he renounced his tenant-right to Number 11 Sandicott Crescent immediately and without condition.

'But that's marvellous,' said Jessica when he had gone. 'Now we can sell the house and have some money.'

But Lockhart shook his head. 'Not yet,' he said. 'When we sell we sell them all. There's such a thing as Capital Gains Tax.'

'Oh dear, why are things always so complicated,' said Jessica, 'why can't they be simple?'

'They are, darling, they are,' said Lockhart. 'Now don't worry your sweet little head about anything.' And he crossed to the Wilsons' house and began to work again. His work involved the hosepipe, the drains and the gas system, and that night when he slipped down the manhole entrance to the sewer in his wet suit with a large lump of putty in one hand and his torch in the other there was murder in Lockhart's heart. Mr O'Brain was about to rue the day he ignored the threat of the Pursley Brigade of the IRA. Dragging the hosepipe behind him he crawled down to the outlet from Mr O'Brain's lavatories. There was one on the ground floor and one in the bathroom upstairs. Working swiftly Lockhart fed the pipe up the outlet and then cemented it in place with the putty. Then he crawled back, emerged from the manhole, replaced the cover and entered the Wilsons' empty house. There he switched on the gas main to which he had connected the pipe and waited. Outside all was quiet. The police car at the entrance to the Crescent burbled occasionally with radio messages but there was no criminal activity in East Pursley to warrant their attention, only a slight burbling, bubbling sound in the U bend of Mr O'Brain's downstairs toilet. Upstairs Mr O'Brain slept soundly, secure in the knowledge that he had police protection. Once during the night he got up for a pee and thought he smelt gas but, since he didn't use it himself but relied on electricity, imagined sleepily that he must be mistaken and went back to bed. Mr O'Brain slept more soundly still, but when he awoke in the morning and went downstairs the smell was overpowering. Mr O'Brain groped for the telephone and less wisely for a cigarette and, while dialling Emergency Services, struck a match.

The resulting explosion dwarfed all Sandicott Crescent's previous catastrophes. A ball of fire enveloped Mr O'Brain, billowed through the kitchen, blew out both front and back doors and every downstairs window, destroyed the conservatory, ripped plaster from the ceiling and turned to shrapnel the thick glazed porcelain of the downstairs lavatory pan which hurtled through the door and embedded itself in the wall of the hall outside. In an instant Number 9 was turned from British Bauhaus into Berlin bunker by a series of sequential explosions that ripped cupboards from walls, Mr O'Brain from the telephone, the telephone from its connection box, books on gynaecology from their shelves and finally sweeping upstairs lifted the flat roof off its moorings and deposited fragments of concrete in the road at the front and the garden at the back. By some extraordinary miracle Mr O'Brain survived the blast and was catapulted, still clutching the receiver, through the drawing-room window on to the gravel of his drive as naked as ever Mr Simpson had been but blackened beyond belief and with his moustache and fringe of hair scorched to a tinder. He was found there raving about the IRA and the ineffectuality of the British police force by Colonel Finch-Potter and his bull-terrier.

It was an unfortunate rendezvous. Colonel Finch-Potter held the firmest views about the Irish and had always regarded Mr O'Brain as a pussy-prying Paddy on account of the consultant's profession. Assuming, with some slight justification, that Mr O'Brain had brought this holocaust on himself by making bombs, Colonel Finch-Potter exercised his right as a citizen to make a citizen's arrest and Mr O'Brain's demented resistance only exacerbated matters. The bull-terrier, resenting his resistance and particularly the punch Colonel Finch-Potter had just received on the nose, turned from the amiable beast it had previously been into a ferocious one and sank its implacable teeth in Mr O'Brain's thigh. By the time the police car arrived, a matter of two minutes, Mr O'Brain had escaped the clutches of the Colonel and was climbing the lattice-work of his magnolia with an agility that was surprising for a man of his age and sedentary profession, but was to be explained by the bull-terrier's adherence to his backside. His screams, like those of Mr

Raceme, Mrs Truster and Mrs Grabble, could be heard beyond the bird sanctuary and below the surface of the road where Lockhart was busily removing the putty from the outlet and dragging the hosepipe back to the Wilsons' house. Ten minutes later, while more police cars sealed-off the entrance to Sandicott Crescent and only allowed the ambulance through, Lockhart emerged from the sewer and crossing the Wilsons' back garden went home for a bath. Jessica met him in her dressing-gown.

'What was that awful bang?' she asked.

'I don't know,' said Lockhart, 'I thought it might have been the Wilson's drains.' And having explained his noisome odour he shut the bathroom door and undressed. He came out twenty minutes later and went down the street with Jessica to survey his handiwork. Mr O'Brain had still to be coaxed from the lattice-work, a process that required the cooperation of the bull-terrier, but which, having at long last got its teeth into something juicy, the dog seemed disinclined to give. Colonel Finch-Potter was likewise uncooperative. His loathing for Mr O'Brain and his admiration for his bull-terrier's British tenacity plus the punch he had received on the nose all combined to add weight to his opinion that the bloody Irishman had got what was coming to him and that if swine like him chose to make bombs they deserved to be hoist with their own petards. In the end it was the lattice-work which gave way. Mr O'Brain and the bull-terrier flaked off the wall and landed on the drive where the police tried to prise them apart. They failed. The bull-terrier seemed to have developed lock-jaw and Mr O'Brain rabies. He foamed at the mouth and shouted expletives with a fluency and particularity that came presumably from his professional interest in women's anatomy. By the time he had abused all ten policemen, who between them were holding his shoulders and the dog's hind legs, they were in no mood to exercise their renowned moderation.

'Put them both in the ambulance,' ordered the sergeant, ignoring the Colonel's claim to his pet, and Mr O'Brain and the bull-terrier were bundled into the ambulance and driven off at high speed. As they went forensic experts moved cautiously through the rubble of the house and sought the cause of the explosion.

'The IRA have been threatening him,' the sergeant told them.

'It looks as if they got him too.' But when the experts finally left they were still puzzled. No sign of explosives had been found and yet the house was a shambles.

'Must have been using something entirely new,' they told the Special Branch officers at the police station. 'See if you can get something out of the man himself.'

But Mr O'Brain was in no mood to be helpful. The vet who had been called to sedate the bull-terrier into relaxing his grip had found his job made all the more difficult by Mr O'Brain's refusal to lie still and having twice tried to inject the dog, the vet had finally lost his nerve and short-sightedly given Mr O'Brain a jab sufficient to placate a rhinoceros. In the event it was the gynaecologist who relaxed first and passed into a coma. The bull-terrier, convinced that his victim was dead, let go and was led away with a self-satisfied look on its muzzle.

At Number 12 Sandicott Crescent Lockhart had much the same look on his face.

'It's quite all right,' he told Jessica, who was worried that one of her houses had been largely destroyed. 'It's in the lease that the occupier has to make good any damage done during his tenancy. I've checked that out.'

'But whatever can have caused it to blow up like that? I mean it looked as if it had been hit by a bomb.'

Lockhart supported Colonel Finch-Potter's argument that Mr O'Brain had been making bombs and left it at that.

He also left his activities at that for the time being. The Crescent was swarming with police who had even invaded the bird sanctuary in search of hidden caches of IRA arms and besides he had other things to think about. A telegram had arrived from Mr Dodd. It said quite simply and with that economy of expression that was typical of the man, 'COME DODD'. Lockhart went, leaving a tearful Jessica with the promise that he would be back soon. He caught the train to Newcastle and on to Hexham and then took a bus to Wark. From there he walked in a straight line across the fells to Flawse Hall with the long stride of a shepherd, climbing the dry-stone walls nimbly and leaping across the boggy patches from one hard turf to another. And all the while his mind was busy pondering the urgency of Mr Dodd's message while at the same time he was glad of the excuse to be back in the land of his heart. It was not an idle expression. The isolation of his boyhood had bred in Lockhart a need for space and a love of the empty moorlands of his happy hunting. The havoc he was wreaking in Sandicott Crescent was as much an expression of his hatred for its closeness, its little snobberies and its stifling social atmosphere, as it was for the recovery of Jessica's right to sell her own property. The south was all hypocrisy and smiles that hid a sneer. Lockhart and the Flawses seldom smiled and when they did it was with due cause, either at some inner joke or at the absurdity of man and nature. For the rest they had long faces and hard eyes that measured man or the range of a target with an exactitude that was un-erring. And when they spoke, as opposed to making speeches or arguing disputatiously at dinner, they used few words. Hence Mr Dodd's message was all the more urgent by its brevity and Lockhart came. He swung over the final wall, across the dam and down the path to the Hall. And, by that instinct that told him Mr Dodd had bad news, he knew better than to approach the Hall by the front door. He slipped round the back and through the gate into the garden shed where Dodd kept his tools and himself to himself. Mr Dodd was there whittling a stick and whistling softly some ancient tune.

'Well, Mr Dodd, I'm here,' said Lockhart.

Mr Dodd looked up and motioned to a three-legged milking stool. 'It's the auld bitch,' he said, not bothering with pre-liminaries, 'she's set hersel' to kill the man.'

'Kill grandfather?' said Lockhart recognizing the man for what he was. Mr Dodd always called Mr Flawse 'the man'.

'Aye, first she overfeeds him. Then she waters his drink with brandy and now she's taken to wetting his bed.'

Lockhart said nothing. Mr Dodd would explain.

'I was in the whisky wall the other night,' said Mr Dodd, 'and the auld bitch comes in with a pitcher of water and sprinkles it on his sheets afore he gan to bed.'

'Are you sure it was water?' said Lockhart who knew the cavity in the bedroom that Mr Dodd called the whisky wall. It was behind the panelling and Mr Dodd stored his privately distilled whisky there.

'It smelt like water. It touched like water and it tasted like water. It was water.'

'But why should she want to kill him?' said Lockhart.

'So she'll inherit afore ye find your father,' said Mr Dodd.

'But what good will that do her? Even after grandfather dies I've only to find my father and she loses her inheritance.'

'True,' said Mr Dodd, 'but who's to say ye'll find him, and even then she'll have possession and nine points of the law. You will have the devil's own job getting her out the place once the man dies and you've no father to your name. She'll gan to litigation and you've no money to fight her with.'

'I will have,' said Lockhart grimly. 'I'll have it by then.'

'By then's too late, man,' said Mr Dodd, 'you mun do something now.'

They sat in silence and considered possibilities. They were none of them nice.

'It was an evil day the man married hisself to a murderous wife,' said Mr Dodd, and sliced the stick in half to express his desire.

'What if we tell grandfather?' said Lockhart, but Mr Dodd shook his head.

'He's all consumed with guilt and fit to die,' he said. 'He'd laugh to leave the widow to dree her weird as the auld books have it. He does not care to live o'er long.'

'Guilt?' said Lockhart, 'What guilt?'

Mr Dodd gave him a quizzical look and said nothing.

'There's surely something we can do,' Lockhart said after a long silence. 'If she knows that we know ...'

'She'll find another way,' said Mr Dodd. 'She's a canny old bitch but I have her measure.'

'Then what?' said Lockhart.

'My mind's been running to accidents,' said Mr Dodd. 'She should never go swimming in the reservoir.'

'I didn't know she did,' said Lockhart.

'But she yet might.'

Lockhart shook his head.

'Or she could have a fall,' said Mr Dodd looking across at the top of the peel tower, 'it's been known to happen.'

But Lockhart refused. 'She's family,' he said. 'I wouldn't want to kill my wife's mother before I had to.'

Mr Dodd nodded. He approved the sentiment. Having so little family himself he treasured what he had.

'You mun do something, else he'll not see the spring.'

Lockhart's finger drew a gibbet in the dust at his feet.

'I'll tell her the story of Elsdon Tree,' he said finally. 'She will think twice about hurrying grandfather to his grave after that.' He got to his feet and moved towards the door but Mr Dodd stopped him.

'There something you've forgotten,' he said. 'The finding of your father.'

Lockhart turned back. 'I haven't got the money yet, but when I have . . .'

Dinner that night was a sombre affair. Mr Flawse was in a guilty mood and the sudden arrival of Lockhart had enhanced it. Mrs Flawse was effusively welcoming but her welcome died in the glower of Lockhart's scowl. It was only after dinner when Mr Flawse had retired to his study that Lockhart spoke to his mother-in-law.

'You'll take a walk with me,' he said as she dried her hands at the sink.

'A walk?' said Mrs Flawse, and found her arm gripped above the elbow.

'Aye, a walk,' said Lockhart and propelled her into the dusk and across the yard to the peel tower. Inside it was dark and gloomy. Lockhart shut the great door and bolted it and then lit a candle.

'What do you mean by this?' said Mrs Flawse. 'You've got no right . . .'

But she was stopped by an unearthly sound that seemed to come from above, a shrill weird sound that echoed the wind and yet had a melody. In front of her Lockhart held the candle high and his eyes were gleaming as weirdly as the music. He set the candle down and taking a long sword from the wall leapt upon the thick oak table. Mrs Flawse shrank back against the wall and the candle flickered a great shadow among the tattered flags and as she stared at Lockhart he began to sing. It was no such song as she had ever heard before but it followed the tune above.

'From Wall to Wark you canna call
   Nor voice to heaven from hell
But follow the fell to old Flawse Hall
   And list the tale I tell.

For old Flawse Hall has tales anew
    And walls can sometimes see
The deeds that wicked women do
    And what their thoughts may be.

Aye silent stones can weep their woe
    With never a word between
But those that read their tears can know
    The murder that ye mean.

An old man's taken a wicked wife
    And the murd'ress to his bed
While all the while she'd take his life
    And see him shortly dead.

The grave's a place we all must gan
    When Time has rolled away
But finish the deed ye've just begun
    And you shall rue the day.

Take heed, take heed and keep your head
    For I your daughter doat
And would not want her mother dead
    Because I slit your throat.

So warm your husband's bed aright
    And see the sheets are dry
Or else I'll seek ye out the night
    Wherever ye may hie.

But slowly, slowly shall ye die
    Lest hell forgetful be
So e'en the devil himself shall cry
    Such tortures shall he see.

So Wife of Flawse remember well
    When next in bed you lie
The Widow Flawse will pray for hell
    Afore she comes to die.

Aye Wife of Flawse of Flawse's Fell
    Look straight upon this sword
For 'tis the honest truth I tell
    As honour is my word.

And I would die to see thee die
    Should any harm befall
The Flawse who heard my birthday cry
    Beneath a dry-stone wall.'

Outside in the darkness Mr Flawse called from his study by the

sound of the pipes played on the battlements of the peel tower, stood by the door and listened intently as the ballad ended. Only the breeze rustling the leaves of the wind-bent trees and the sound of sobbing remained. He waited a moment and then shuffled back to the house, his mind swirling with a terrible series of new certainties. What he had just heard left no room in his mind for doubt. The bastard was a true Flawse and his ancestry was impeccably of the same line that had produced the Minstrel Flawse who had improvised beneath the Elsdon gibbet. And with that certainty there came a second. Lockhart was a throwback born by eugenic circumstances out of time, with gifts the old man had never suspected and could not but admire. And finally he was no bastard grandson. Mr Flawse went into his study and locked the door. Then sitting by the fire he gave way privately to his grief and pride. The grief was for himself; the pride for his son. For a moment he considered suicide, but only to reject it out of hand. He must dree his weird to the bitter end. The rest was left to providence.

Chapter thirteen

But on at least two points the old man was wrong. Lockhart was leaving nothing to providence. While Mrs Flawse cowered in the darkness of the banqueting hall and wondered at the re-markable insight he had shown into the workings of her own mind and hands, Lockhart climbed the stone turret to the first storey and then by way of wooden ladders up on to the battle-ments. There he found Mr Dodd casting his one good eye over the landscape with a fondness for its bleak and forbidding aspect that was somehow in keeping with his own character. A rugged man in a dark and rugged world, Mr Dodd was a servant with-out servility. He had no brief for fawning or the notion that the world owed him a living. He owed his living to hard work and a provoked cunning that was as far removed from Mrs Flawse's calculation as Sandicott Crescent was from Flawse Fell. And if any man had dared despise him for a servant he would have told him to his face that in his case the servant was master to the man before demonstrating with his fists the simple truth that he was a match for any man, be he master, servant or drunken braggart. In short Mr Dodd was his own man and went his own way. That his own way was that of old Mr Flawse sprang from their mutual disrespect. If Mr Dodd allowed the old man to call him Dodd, he did so in the knowledge that Mr Flawse was dependent on him and that for all his authority and theoretical intelligence he knew less about the real world and its ways than did Mr Dodd. It was thus with an air of condescension that he lay on his side in the drift mine and hewed coal from a two-foot seam and carried scuttles of it to the old man's study to keep him warm. It was with the same certainty of his own worth and superiority in all things that he and his dog herded sheep on the fells and saw to the lambing in the snow. He was there to protect them and he was there to protect Mr Flawse and if he fleeced the one of wool, he fed and housed himself upon the other and let no one come between them.

'You'll have scared the wits out of the woman,' he said when Lockhart climbed on to the roof, 'but it will not last. She'll have your inheritance if you do not act swift.'

'That's what I've come to ask you, Mr Dodd,' said Lockhart. 'Mr Bullstrode and Dr Magrew could remember none of my mother's friends. She must have had some.'

'Aye, she did,' said Mr Dodd stirring on the parapet.

'Then can you tell me who they were? I've got to start the search for my father somewhere.'

Mr Dodd said nothing for some moments.

'You might inquire of Miss Deyntry down over Farspring way,' he said at last. 'She was a good friend of your mother's. You'll find her at Divet Hall. She maybe could tell you something to your advantage. I canna think of anyone else.'

Lockhart climbed down the ladder and out of the peel tower. He went round to say goodbye to his grandfather but as he passed the study window he stopped. The old man was sitting by the fire and his cheeks were streaked with tears. Lockhart shook his head sadly. The time was not ripe for farewells. Instead he let himself out the gate and strode off along the path that led to the dam. As he crossed it he looked back at the house. The light was still burning in the study and his mother-in-law's bedroom was bright but otherwise Flawse Hall was in darkness. He went on into the pinewoods and turned off the path along the rocky shore. A light wind had risen and the water of the reservoir lapped on the stones at his feet. Lockhart picked a pebble up and hurled it out into the darkness. It fell with a plop and disappeared as completely as his own father had disappeared, and with as little chance of his ever finding it or him again. But he would try, and following the shoreline for another two miles he reached the old Roman military road that ran north. He crossed it on to more open country and the dark pinewoods round the reservoir dwindled behind him. Ahead lay Britherton Law and eighteen miles of empty countryside. He would have to sleep out but there was a long-abandoned farmhouse with hay in the byre. He would stay the night there and in the morning drop down into Farspring Valley to Divet Hall. And as he walked his mind filled with strange words that came from some hidden corner of himself that he had always known about but previously ignored. They came in snatches of song and rhyme and spoke of things he had never experienced. Lockhart let them come and did not bother to inquire the why or wherefore of their coming. It was enough to be alone at night striding across his own country again. At midnight he came to the farm called Hetchester and passing through the gap in the wall where the gate had hung made his bed in the hay in the old byre. The hay smelt musty and old but he was comfortable and in a short while fast asleep.

He was up again at dawn and on his way but it was half past seven before he crossed the Farspring Knowe and looked down into the wooded valley. Divet Hall stood a mile away and smoke was coming from a chimney. Miss Deyntry was up and about surrounded by dogs, cats, horses, parrots and a tame fox she had once waded through a pack of hounds to rescue while its vixen mother was being torn to pieces. In middle age Miss Deyntry disapproved of bloodsports as heartily as she had once pursued them in her wild youth. She also disapproved of the human species and was known for her misanthropy, a reversal of opinions that was generally explained by her having three times been jilted. Whatever the cause, she was known as a woman with a sharp tongue and people tended to avoid her. The only ones who didn't were tramps and the few wandering gipsies who still followed the ancient ways. Known as muggers in the past because they made pots and mugs during the winter and sold them in the summer, there were a few caravans left in the country and autumn would find them camped in the meadow behind Divet Hall. There was a caravan there now as Lockhart loped sideways down the steep hillside and their dog began to bark. Before long Miss Deyntry's menagerie had followed suit. Lockhart opened the gates to a cacophony of dogs but he was as mindless of them as he was of almost everything else and he walked past them and knocked on the door. After an interval Miss Deyntry appeared. Dressed in a smock she had designed without regard for appreciation but solely for convenience (it was fitted with pockets all down the front), she was more ornamental than attractive. She was also brusque.

'Who are you?' she asked as soon as she had taken stock of Lockhart and noted with imperceptible approval the straw in his hair and his unshaven chin. Miss Deyntry disapproved of too much cleanliness.

'Lockhart Flawse,' said Lockhart as bluntly as she had put the question. Miss Deyntry looked at him with more interest.

'So you're Lockhart Flawse,' she said and opened the door wider. 'Well, don't just stand there, boy. Come in. You look as if you could do with some breakfast.'

Lockhart followed her down the passage to the kitchen which was filled with the smell of home-cured bacon. Miss Deyntry sliced some thick rashers and put them in the pan.

'Slept out, I see,' she said. 'Heard you'd been and married. Walked out on her, eh?'

'Good Lord, no,' said Lockhart. 'I just felt like sleeping out last night. I've come to ask you a question.'

'Question? What question? Don't answer most people's questions. Don't know that I'll answer yours,' said Miss Deyntry staccato.

'Who was my father?' said Lockhart, who had learnt from Mr Dodd not to waste time on preliminaries. Even Miss Deyntry was taken by surprise.

'Your father? You're asking *me* who your father was?'

'Yes,' said Lockhart.

Miss Deyntry prodded a rasher. 'You don't know?' she said after a pause.

'Wouldn't be asking if I did.'

'Blunt too,' she commented, again with approval. 'And why do you think I know who your father was?'

'Mr Dodd said so.'

Miss Deyntry looked up from the pan. 'Oh, Mr Dodd did, did he now?'

'Aye, he said you were her friend. She'd be likely telling you.'

But Miss Deyntry shook her head 'She'd as soon have confessed to the priest at Chiphunt Castle, and he being a Papist and a Highlander to boot while she and your grandfather were ever godless Unitarians; it's as likely as spaniels laying eggs,' said Miss Deyntry, breaking eggs on the edge of the iron pan and dropping them into the fat.

'Unitarians?' said Lockhart. 'I never knew my grandfather was a Unitarian.'

'I doubt he does himself,' said Miss Deyntry, 'but he's forever reading Emerson and Darwin and the windbags of Chelsea and the ingredients of Unitarianism are all there, mix them in proper proportions.'

'So you don't know who my father was?' said Lockhart not wishing to be drawn into theology before he had had his fill of bacon and eggs. Miss Deyntry added mushrooms.

'I did not say that,' she said, 'I said she did not tell me. I have a mind who he was.'

'Who?' said Lockhart.

'I said I had a mind. I didna say I'd tell. There's many a slip 'twixt cup and lip as no better than I should know and I would not want to cast aspersions.'

She brought two plates across to the table and ladled eggs and bacon and mushrooms onto them. 'Eat and let me think,' she said and picked up her knife and fork. They ate in silence and drank from large cups of hot tea noisily. Miss Deyntry poured hers into a saucer and supped it that way. When they had finished and wiped their mouths, she got up and left the room, returning a few minutes later with a wooden box inlaid with mother-of-pearl.

'You'll not have known Miss Johnson,' she said laying the

124

box on the table. Lockhart shook his head. 'She was the post-mistress over Ryal Bank, and when I say postmistress I don't mean she had a wee shop. She carried the mail herself on an old bicycle and lived in a cottage before you reach the village. She gave me this before she died.'

Lockhart looked at the box curiously.

'The box is nothing,' said Miss Deyntry, 'It's what's in it that is pertinent. The old woman was a sentimental body though you'd not have thought it to hear her. She kept cats and when she had finished her round of a summer day she'd sit out beside her door in the sun with the cats and kittens around her. One day a shepherd called with his dog and the dog took a mind to kill one of these kittens. Miss Johnson never moved an eyelid. She just looked at the man and said, "Ye should feed your dawg." That was Miss Johnson. So you wouldn't credit her with o'ermuch sentiment.'

Lockhart laughed and Miss Deyntry studied him.

'You're afful like your mither. She had a bray like that but there's something more besides.' She pushed the box towards him and opened the lid. Inside, wrapped neatly in an elastic band, was a pile of envelopes.

'Take them,' she said but kept her hand on the box. 'I promised the old woman I'd never let the box fall into anyone else's hands but she said nothing of the contents.'

Lockhart picked the bundle out and looked at the envelopes. They were all addressed to Miss C. R. Flawse, c/o The Post-mistress, Ryal Bank, Northumberland, and they were still sealed.

'She wouldn't open them,' Miss Deyntry explained. 'She was an honest old soul and it would have been against her religion to meddle with the Royal Mail.'

'But why didn't my mother have them sent to Black Pock-rington and Flawse Hall?' Lockhart asked. 'Why have them care of The Postmistress, Ryal Bank?'

'And have your grandfather lay his hands on them and know what she was doing? Are ye so soft in the head? The old devil was so jealous of her he'd never have hesitated to censor them. No, your mother was too canny for him there.'

Lockhart looked at the postmark of one letter and saw that it came from America and was dated 1961.

'This was sent five years after she died. Why didn't Miss Johnson send it back?'

'It would have meant opening it to find the return address and she would never have done that,' said Miss Deyntry. 'I told you the Royal Mail was a sacred trust to her. Besides she did not care to have your mother's only friend to know that she was dead. "Better to live in hope than abide in sorrow," she used to say and she knew what she was talking about. The man she was affianced to went missing at Ypres but she would never admit that he was dead. Love and life eternal she believed in, more power to the old woman. I would that I believed in either but I have not the faith.'

'I suppose I have the right to open them,' said Lockhart. Miss Deyntry nodded.

'She did not leave you much else except your looks but I doubt you'll find your father's name in any of them.'

'I may get a clue.'

But Miss Deyntry would not have it. 'You'll not. I can tell you that now. You would be better advised to ask the old Romany woman in the caravan who claims she can tell fortunes. Your father never wrote a letter in his life.'

Lockhart looked at her suspiciously.

'You seem very sure of your facts,' he said, but Miss Deyntry was not to be drawn. 'You can at least tell me why you . . .'

'Begone with you,' she said rising from the table. ' 'Tis too much like looking at Clarissa to have you sitting there moping over letters from the long-dead past. Go ask the spaewife who your father was. She'll more likely tell you than I will.'

'Spaewife?' said Lockhart.

'The fortune-teller woman,' said Miss Deyntry, 'who would have it that she is a descendant of old Elspeth Faas of the old stories.' She led the way down the passage to the door and Lockhart followed with the bundle of letters and thanked her.

'Don't thank me,' she said gruffly. 'Thanks are words and I've had my fill of them. If you ever want help, come and ask me for it. That's the sort of thanks I can appreciate, being of some use. The rest is blathering. Now go and ask the old woman for your fortune. And don't forget to cross her palm with silver.'

Lockhart nodded and went round the back of the house into the meadow and presently he was squatting on his haunches

126

some twenty yards from the caravan saying nothing but waiting, by some ancient instinct of etiquette, to be spoken to. The gipsies' dog barked and was silent. Smoke filtered up into the still morning air from the open fire and bees hummed in the honeysuckle of Miss Deyntry's garden wall. The Romanies went about their business as if Lockhart didn't exist but after half an hour an old woman came down the steps of the caravan towards him. She had a brown wind-burnt face and her skin was as wrinkled as the bark of an old oak. She squatted down in front of Lockhart and held out her hand.

'Ye'll cross my loof with silver,' she said. Lockhart reached in his pocket and brought out a ten-pence piece but the woman would not touch it.

'Na silver there,' she said.

'I have no other silver,' said Lockhart.

'Then better still gold,' said the old woman.

Lockhart tried to think of something gold and finally remembered his fountain pen. He took it out and uncovered the nib. 'It's all the gold I have.'

The gipsy's hand with standing veins like ivy took the pen and held it. 'You have the gift,' she said and as she said it the pen seemed to take on a life of its own and twitched and swung in her fingers like a water diviner's dowsing rod or hazel twig. Lockhart stared as it writhed and the gold nib pointed straight at him. 'Ye have the gift of words, aye, and a tongue for a song. The pen a compass point will be and yet ye'll get its message wrong.' She turned the pen away but the nib swung round again to him. Then she handed it back to him.

'Is there anything else you see?' asked Lockhart. The gipsy did not take his hand but stared at the ground between them.

'A death, twa deaths and maybe more. Three open graves and one unfilled. I see a hanged man on a tree and more that have been killed. No more. Be gone.'

'Nothing about my father?' asked Lockhart.

'Your father is it? Ye search him out and search him long. And all the time you'll find his name in song. I'll not say more.'

Lockhart put the pen back in his pocket and took out a pound note. The old woman spat on the ground as she took it. 'Paper,' she muttered, 'it would be paper as paper's wood but paper and ink will do you no good till ye come to your gift

127

again.' And with that she was up and away back to the caravan while Lockhart, hardly knowing that he was doing it, crossed the air where she had been with his two fingers. Then he too turned and set off down the valley towards the old military road and Hexham. That night he was back in Sandicott Crescent. He found Jessica in a state of alarm.

'The police have been,' she said as soon as he entered the house, 'they wanted to know if we'd seen or heard anything unusual lately.'

'What did you tell them?'

'The truth,' said Jessica. 'That we'd heard people screaming and Mr O'Brain's house explode and windows breaking and everything.'

'Did they ask about me?' said Lockhart.

'No,' said Jessica, 'I just said you were away at work.'

'They didn't search the house then?'

Jessica shook her head and looked at him fearfully. 'What has been going on, Lockhart? The Crescent used to be such a nice quiet place and now everything seems to have gone haywire. Did you know that someone cut the telephone wire to the Racemes' house?'

'I did,' said Lockhart both answering her question and stating the fact.

'It's all most peculiar, and they've had to put the Misses Musgrove in a mental home.'

'Well, that's one more house you can sell,' said Lockhart, 'and I don't suppose Mr O'Brain will be coming back.'

'Mr and Mrs Raceme aren't either. I had a letter from him this morning to say that they were moving.' Lockhart rubbed his hands happily. 'That only leaves the Colonel and the Pettigrews on this side of the street. What about the Grabbles and Mrs Simplon?'

'Mr Grabble has kicked his wife out and Mrs Simplon came round to ask if I'd accept no rent until her divorce comes through.'

'I hope you told her no,' said Lockhart.

'I said I'd have to ask you.'

'The answer is no. She can clear out with the others.'

Jessica looked at him uncertainly but decided not to ask any questions. Lockhart was her husband, and besides, there was a look on his face that did not invite questions. All the same she went to bed troubled that night. Beside her Lockhart slept as soundly as a child. He had already made up his mind to deal with Colonel Finch-Potter next, but first there was the problem of the bull-terrier to be overcome. Lockhart was fond of bull-terriers. His grandfather kept several at the Hall and like the Colonel's dog they were amiable beasts unless aroused. Lockhart decided to arouse the bull-terrier again but in the meantime he had a vigil to keep on Number 10. The quantity of contraceptives deposited in the sewer below the Colonel's outlet suggested that the old bachelor had private habits that were amenable to use.

And so for the next week Lockhart sat in a darkened room that overlooked Number 10 and watched from seven till midnight. It was on the Friday that he saw the Colonel's ancient Humber drive up and a woman step out and enter the house with him. She was rather younger than Colonel Finch-Potter and more gaudily dressed than most of the women who came to Sandicott Crescent. Ten minutes later a light shone in the Colonel's bedroom and Lockhart had a better look at the woman. She came into the category his grandfather had described as Scarlet Women. Then the Colonel drew the curtains. A few minutes later the kitchen door opened and the bull-terrier was hustled out into the garden. The Colonel evidently objected to its presence in the house at the same time as his Scarlet Woman.

Lockhart went downstairs and across to the fence and whistled quietly and the bull-terrier waddled over. Lockhart reached through and patted it and the bull-terrier wagged what there was of its tail. And so while the Colonel made love to his lady friend upstairs, Lockhart made friends with the dog in the garden. He was still sitting stroking the dog at midnight when the front door opened and the couple came out and got into the Humber. Lockhart noted the time and made his plans accordingly.

Next day he travelled to London and hung around Soho. He sat in coffee bars and even strip shows which disgusted him and finally by dint of striking up acquaintance with a sickly young man he managed to buy what he had come to look for. He came home with several tiny tablets in his pocket and hid them in the garage. Then he waited until the following Wednesday before making his next move. On Wednesdays Colonel Finch-Potter played eighteen holes of golf and was absent all morning. Lockhart slipped next door into Number 10 carrying a tin of oven cleaner. The label on the tin advised the use of rubber gloves. Lockhart wore them. For two reasons; one that he had no intention of leaving fingerprints in the house with so many police in the vicinity; two because what he had come to do had nothing whatsoever to do with oven cleaning. The bull-terrier welcomed him amiably and together they went upstairs to the Colonel's bedroom and through the drawers of his dressing-table until Lockhart found what he was after. Then with a pat on the head of the dog he slipped out of the house and back over the fence.

That night, to while away the time, he blew all the lights in the Pettigrews' house. His procedure was quite simple. Using a piece of nylon cord he attached some stiff wire from a coat-hanger to the end and lobbed it over the twin electric cables that led from the post into the house. There was a flash and the Pettigrews spent the night in darkness. Lockhart spent it telling Jessica the story of the old gipsy woman and Miss Deyntry.

'But haven't you looked at the letters?' Jessica asked.

Lockhart hadn't. The gipsy's prophecy had driven all thought of them out of his mind and besides her final prophecy that paper was wood and paper and ink would do no good till he came to his gift again had startled him superstitiously. What had she meant by his gift of tongue and song and three graves open and one unfilled? And a hanged man on a tree? All auguries of some frightening future. Lockhart's mind was too engrossed in the present and the gift he foresaw was to come from the sale of all twelve houses in Sandicott Crescent, which he had already calculated would gross Jessica over six hundred thousand pounds at present-day prices.

'But we'll have to pay taxes on them, won't we?' said Jessica when he explained that she would shortly be a rich woman. 'And anyway we don't know that everyone is going to leave . . .'

She left the question open but Lockhart didn't answer it. He knew.

'Least said soonest mended,' he said cryptically and waited

for his preparations for Colonel Finch-Potter's self-eviction to take effect.

'I still think you should see what is inside those letters,' Jessica said as they went to bed that night. 'They might contain proof of your father's identity.'

'There's time enough for that,' said Lockhart. 'What's in those letters will keep.'

What was in the French letter that Colonel Finch-Potter nudged over his penis at half past eight the following night had certainly kept. He was vaguely aware that the contraceptive felt more slippery than usual when he took it out of the box but the full effect of the oven cleaner made itself felt when he had got it three-quarters on and was nursing the rubber ring right down to achieve maximum protection from syphilis. The next moment all fear of that contagious disease had fled his mind and far from trying to get the thing on he was struggling to get the fucking thing off as quickly as possible and before irremediable damage had been done. He was unsuccessful. Not only was the contraceptive slippery but the oven cleaner was living up to its maker's claim to be able to remove grease baked on to the interior of a stove like lightning. With a scream of agony Colonel Finch-Potter gave up his manual efforts to get the contraceptive off before what felt like galloping leprosy took its fearful toll and dashed towards the bathroom in search of a pair of scissors. Behind him the Scarlet Woman watched with growing apprehension and when, after demonically hurling the contents of the medicine cabinet on to the floor, the Colonel still screaming found his nail scissors she intervened.

'No, no, you mustn't,' she cried in the mistaken belief that the Colonel's guilt had got the better of him and that he was about to castrate himself, 'for my sake you mustn't.' She dragged the scissors from his hand while the Colonel had he been able to speak would have explained that for her sake he must. Instead, gyrating like some demented dervish, he dragged at the contraceptive and its contents with a mania that suggested he was trying to disembowel himself. Next door but one the Pettigrews, now quite accustomed to things that went bump in the night, ignored his pleas for help before he burst. That they were mingled with the screams of the Scarlet Woman didn't surprise them in the least. After the Racemes' disgusting display of perversion they were prepared for anything. Not so the police at the end of the road. As their car screeched to a halt outside Number 10 and they were bundled out to the scene of the latest crime they were met by the bull-terrier.

It was not the amiable beast it had been previously; it was not even the ferocious beast that had bitten Mr O'Brain and clung to him up his lattice-work; it was an entirely new species of beast, one filled to the brim with LSD by Lockhart and harbouring psychedelic vision of primeval ferocity in which policemen were panthers and even fence posts held a menace. Certainly the bull-terrier did. Gnashing its teeth, it bit the first three policemen out of the Panda car before they could get back into it, then the gatepost, broke a tooth on the Colonel's Humber, sank its fangs into the police car's front radial tyre to such effect that it was knocked off its own feet by the blow-out while simultaneously rendering their escape impossible, and went snarling off into the night in search of fresh victims.

It found them aplenty. Mr and Mrs Lowry had taken to sleeping downstairs since the explosion of Mr O'Brain's Bauhaus next door and the new explosion of the blown-out tyre brought them into the garden. Colonel Finch-Potter's illuminated bull-terrier found them there and, having bitten them both to the bone and driven them back into the house, had severed three rose bushes at the stem with total disregard for their thorns. If anything it felt provoked by creatures that bit back and was in no mood to trifle when the ambulance summoned by Jessica finally arrived. The bull-terrier had once travelled in that ambulance with Mr O'Brain and residual memories flickered in its flaming head. It regarded that ambulance as an offence against Nature and with all the impulsion of a dwarf rhinoceros put its head down and charged across the road. In the mistaken belief that it was the Pettigrews at Number 6 who needed their attention the ambulance men had stopped outside their house. They didn't stop long. The pink-eyed creature that knocked the first attendant over, bit the second and hurled itself at the throat of the third, fortunately missing and disappearing over the man's shoulder, drove them to take shelter in their vehicle, and ignoring the plight of Mr and Mrs Lowry, three policemen and the Colonel whose screams had somewhat subsided as he slashed at his penis with a breadknife in the kitchen, the ambulance men drove themselves as rapidly as possible to hospital.

They should have waited. Mr Pettigrew had just opened the front door and was explaining that for once he didn't know who was making such a fuss in the Crescent to the ambulance man who had rung the bell when something shot between his legs and up the stairs. Mr Pettigrew misguidedly shut the door, for once acting with a degree of social conscience he hadn't intended. For the next twenty minutes Colonel Finch-Potter's bull-terrier ravaged the Pettigrew house. What it saw in tasselled lampshades and velvet curtains, not to mention furbelowed dressing-tables and the mahógany legs of the Pettigrews' dining suite, it alone knew, but they had evidently taken on some new and fearful meaning for it. Acting with impeccable good taste and unbelievable savagery it tore its way through these furnishings and dug holes in a Persian rug in search of some psychedelic bone while the Pettigrews cowered in the cupboard under the stairs. Finally it leapt at its own reflection in the french windows and crashed through into the night. After that its howls could be heard horrifically from the bird sanctuary. Colonel Finch-Potter's howls had long since ceased. He lay on the kitchen floor with a cheese-grater and worked assiduously and with consummate courage on the thing that had been his penis. That the corrosive contraceptive had long since disintegrated under the striations of the breadknife he neither knew nor cared. It was sufficient to know that the rubber ring remained and that his penis had swollen to three times its normal size. It was in an insane effort to grate it down from a phallic gargoyle to something more precise that the Colonel worked. And besides, the pain of the cheese-grater was positively homeopathic compared to oven cleaner and came as something of a relief albeit a minor one. Behind him garnished in suspender belt and bra the Scarlet Woman had hysterics in a kitchen chair and it was her shrieks that finally drove the three policemen in the patrol car to their duty. Bloody and bowed they broke the front door down in a wild rush provoked as much by fear of the bull-terrier as by any desire to enter the house. Once in they were in half a dozen minds whether to stay or go. The sight of a puce-faced old gentleman sitting naked on the kitchen floor using a cheese-grater on what looked like a pumpkin with high blood pressure while a woman wearing only a suspender belt shrieked and gibbered and in between whiles helped herself to a bottle of neat brandy, was not one to reassure them as to anyone's sanity. Finally to add to the pandemonium and panic the lights failed and the house was plunged into darkness. So were all the other houses in Sandicott Crescent. Lockhart, under cover of the concentration of police and ambulance men on Number 6 and 10, had slipped on to the golf course and hooked his patent fuseblower over the main power lines. By the time he got back to the house even Jessica was in a state of shock.

'Oh, Lockhart, darling,' she wailed, 'what on earth is happening to us?'

'Nothing,' said Lockhart, 'it's happening to them.' In the pitch darkness of the kitchen Jessica shuddered in his arms.

'Them?' she said. 'Who's them?'

'Them's the warld that is not us,' he said involuntarily slipping into the brogue of his native fells, 'For arl that's them the good Lord curse. And if ma prayer he doesna heed, It's up to me to do the deed.'

'Oh, Lockhart, you are wonderful,' said Jessica, 'I didn't know you could recite poetry.'

Chapter fourteen

No more did anyone else in Sandicott Crescent. Poetry was the last thing on their minds. Colonel Finch-Potter had no mind to have anything on, and it was doubtful if his Scarlet Woman would ever be the same again. Certainly the Pettigrews' house wouldn't. Torn to shreds by the bull-terrier, the house was in a state of total chaos. The Pettigrews, emerging finally from the closet under the stairs just after the lights had failed, supposed that they alone had suffered this misfortune and it was only when Mr Pettigrew, trying to reach the phone in the living-room, tripped over the hole in the Persian carpet and landed on a savaged lampshade that the true extent of the damage began to dawn on them. By the light of a torch they surveyed the remnants of their furniture and wept.

'There's some terrible curse on the street,' wailed Mrs Pettigrew, echoing Lockhart's prayer, 'I won't stay here a moment longer.' Mr Pettigrew tried in vain to adopt a more rational approach but he wasn't helped by the demented howls of the bull-terrier in the bird sanctuary. Having lost a tooth it had fortunately lost its way as well and after gnawing several large trees in the archetypal belief that they were mammoths' legs had given up to wail at five multi-coloured moons that squirmed in the sky above its imagination. Mr and Mrs Lowry were busily trying to bandage one another in portions of anatomy least amenable to bandaging and were considering suing Colonel Finch-Potter for his dog's damage when they too were plunged into darkness. Next door, Mrs Simplon, convinced that her husband had deliberately fused the lights so that he could the more easily break in to retrieve his belongings, proceeded to warn him off by loading the shotgun he kept in the cupboard in the bedroom and firing it out of the window twice at nothing in particular. Not being the best shot in the world and lacking the light of the bull-terrier's imaginary moons, she managed with the first shot to blast the greenhouse in the garden of the Ogilvies at Number 3 and with the second, fired from the front, to add to the Pettigrews' problems by peppering those windows the bull-terrier had left unscathed. Only then did she realize her mistake and the fact that the entire street was in darkness. Not to be dissuaded but rather encouraged by the screams and yells of the Scarlet Woman, who was being dragged into the police car, and convinced now that the IRA had struck again, she reloaded and loosed off two more barrels in the general direction of Mr O'Brain's former house. This time she missed the house and fired point-blank into the Lowrys' bedroom which happened to intervene between the Simplons' and Mr O'Brain's residence. Outside Colonel Finch-Potter's the policemen hastily dropped their burden, took cover and radioed for armed assistance.

It was no time at all coming. Sirens sounded, police cars converged and under covering fire a dozen men surrounded

Mrs Simplon's mock-Georgian mansion and ordered everyone inside to come out with their hands up. But Mrs Simplon had finally discovered her mistake. The volley of revolver shots that seemed to come from all quarters and through every window, and the winking lights of the police cars, not to mention the voice on the loudhailer, persuaded her that absence was the best defence. Dressing as swiftly as she could and grabbing her jewels and what money she had, she went through the connecting door in the garage and hid in the sump pit which Mr Simplon, who liked tinkering with the underbodies of cars as well as Mrs Grabble's, had thoughtfully constructed. There, with the wood pulled over her head, she waited. Through the wood and the garage door she could hear the loudhailer declare that the house was surrounded and there was no point in further resistance. Mrs Simplon had no intention of resisting. She cursed herself for her stupidity and tried to think of an excuse. She was still trying in vain when dawn finally broke over the Crescent and fifteen policemen broke cover, the front and back door, four windows and found the house to be empty.

'There's no one there,' they told the Superintendent who had come to take charge. 'Searched the attic but there's not a soul.'

Mr Pettigrew protested that there must be. 'I saw the flash of the guns myself,' he said, 'and you've only got to look at my house to see what they did.'

The Superintendent looked and expressed some doubt that gunshot had ripped lampshades from their stands, cushions from sofas and curtains from windows, and had sunk what looked like fangs into the mahogany dining-tables.

'That was the dog,' said Mr Pettigrew, 'the dog the ambulance men brought with them.'

The Superintendent looked even more doubtful 'Are you trying to tell me that all this devastation was caused by a dog and that the aforesaid dog was introduced into your house by ambulance men?' he asked.

Mr Pettigrew hesitated. The Superintendent's scepticism was contagious.

'I know it doesn't sound likely,' he admitted, 'but it looked like a dog.'

'I certainly find it hard to believe that a dog can have created this degree of havoc on its own,' said the Superintendent, 'and if you're suggesting that the ambulance men ...' He was interrupted by a howl from the bird sanctuary. 'What in God's name is that?'

'That's the thing that wrecked my house,' said Mr Pettigrew. 'It's coming from the bird sanctuary.'

'Bird sanctuary my foot,' said the Superintendent. 'More like a banshee sanctuary by the sound of things.'

'I didn't think banshees wailed,' said Mr Pettigrew inconsequentially. A sleepless night, most of it spent in a broom cupboard, and the rest in the darkness of his devastated house, had not helped to make him clear-headed and Mrs Pettigrew was wailing too. She had discovered the remnants of her underwear shredded in the bedroom.

'I tell you it wasn't a dog,' she screamed, 'some sex maniac's been chewing my undies.'

The Superintendent looked at Mrs Pettigrew dubiously. 'Anyone who chewed your undies, madam, would have to be ...' he began before checking himself. Mrs Pettigrew had only her vanity left and there was no good to be done by removing that too. 'You've got no idea who might have a grudge against you?' he asked instead. But the Pettigrews shook their heads in unison. 'We've always lived such quiet lives,' they said. It was the same in every other occupied house the Superintendent visited. There were only four. At Number 1 Mr and Mrs Rickenshaw had nothing to add except gratitude that the police car was always parked outside their house. 'It makes us feel much safer,' they said.

The Ogilvies didn't share their opinion. The blast of the shotgun that had smashed every pane of glass in their greenhouse had given them a sense of grievance they voiced to the Superintendent. 'What's the world coming to when peaceful citizens can't rest easy in their beds, that's what I want to know,' said Mr Ogilvie indignantly. 'I shall complain to my MP, sir. The country is going to the dogs.'

'So it would appear,' said the Superintendent soothingly, 'but you're not suggesting that a dog destroyed your greenhouse?'

'Certainly not,' said Mr Ogilvie, 'some damned swine with a shotgun did.'

The Superintendent breathed a sigh of relief. He was getting sick of hearing all the blame put on dogs. Mrs Simplon wasn't.

Cowering beneath the wooden beams in the inspection pit under her car her nerves, like Mrs Pettigrew's undies, were in tatters. She fumbled in her bag for her cigarettes, found one and was in the process of striking a match to light it when the Super-intendent, thanking the Ogilvies for their cooperation and being trounced by Mr Ogilvie for the lack of police protection made his way past the garage door.

In fact the garage door made its way past him. Mrs Simplon had discovered to her cost that inspection pits filled with oil waste and petrol fumes were not the best place to light ciga-rettes. With several explosions, first of the fume-laden air in the pit, second of the petrol tank of the car above, and third of the half-empty oil tanks that had served to provide Number 5 Sand-icott Crescent with hot water and central heating, Mrs Sim-plon's hopes of calming her nerves succeeded beyond her wildest dreams. She was no longer conscious after the first ex-plosion and by the time the oil tanks exploded she had passed into the great beyond. With her went portions of the garage, the car and the oil tanks. A ball of flame containing elements of all three billowed out where the garage door had been and hurtled round the head of the Superintendent before pocking still more the Pettigrews' already-acned façade. In the middle of this holocaust the Superintendent kept his head. He kept little else. What the blast hadn't stripped from his little authority the flames did. His moustache crinkled and turned black under his nose. His eyebrows streaked, flaming, past the top of his ears, themselves sufficiently hot to suggest that several million people were thinking about him at the same time, and he was left standing in his boots and leather belt, a blackened, scorched and thoroughly disenchanted copper.

Once again the sirens sounded on the approaches to Sandicott Crescent but this time it was the fire brigade. As they worked frantically to extinguish the flames, which flames had already extinguished Mrs Simplon so thoroughly that she was in no need of a more ceremonial cremation, the bull-terrier made its last sortie. The flames that had flickered in its head had been dying down when the Simplons' garage revived them. With blood-red eyes and lolling tongue it lumbered out of the bird sanctuary, through the Misses Musgroves' herb garden, and having whetted its appetite on the calf of a fireman, proceeded to engage one of the fire brigade's hosepipes in mortal combat in the belief that it was wrestling with an anaconda in the ancestral forest of its dreams. The hosepipe fought back. Punctured in a dozen places, it shot water into the air with enormous pressure, and carried the bull-terrier several feet off the ground where it hung a moment snarling ravenously. By the time the dog hit the ground again the Superintendent no longer disbelieved the Pettigrews. He had seen it with his own two scorched eyes, a dog that wailed, snarled, slobbered and snapped like a crocodile with St Vitus' dance. Convinced that the animal had rabies the Superintendent stood still according to instructions. He would have been better advised to move. Baffled by the liquid resistance of the writhing hosepipe the bull-terrier sank its teeth into the Superintendent's leg, let go momentarily to re-engage the hose which it savaged in several more places and then hurled itself at the Superintendent's throat. This time the Superintendent moved and his juniors, twenty firemen, the Ogilvies and Mr and Mrs Rickenshaw were privileged to see a naked (and badly scorched) policeman in boots and belt cover one hundred metres in under ten seconds from a standing start. Behind him with starting eyes and scrabbling paws came, bullet-like, the bull-terrier. The Superintendent hurdled the Grabbles' gate, clobbered across their lawn and into the bird sanctuary. And presently in harmony with the dog he too could be heard howling for help.

'Well, at least he knows we were telling the truth,' said Mr Pettigrew and told his wife to shut up wailing like some woman for her demon lover, a remark hardly calculated to restore domestic peace to their sufficiently demented lives.

From their bedroom at the end of the street Lockhart and Jessica watched the chaotic scene. The Simplons' garage still blazed, largely thanks to the intervention of the dog, the hosepipe still writhed and spouted water from a score of holes high into the air like a lawn sprinkler with megalomania, firemen huddled on their engines and policemen in their cars. Only the armed men, brought in to deal with whoever had fired from the house, were still abroad. Convinced that the blazing garage was a diversion to allow the gunmen inside the house, who had eluded their search, to make good their escape under cover of the smoke, they lurked in the adjacent gardens and in the foliage of the bushes by the golf course. It was in consequence of this and of the smoke that obscured their view and that of an early foursome, one of whom had an incurable slice, that a ball hit an armed constable on the head.

'They're coming at us from the rear,' he yelled and emptied his revolver into the drifting smoke, hitting the man with the now terminal slice and the Club House. He was followed by several other policemen who fired in the general direction of the screams. As the bullets ricocheted round the East Pursley Golf Course and punctured the windows of the bar, the Secretary lay on the floor and dialled the police.

'We're under attack,' he screamed, 'bullets are coming from every direction.' So were other golfers. As they dashed through the smoke they were met by a hail of bullets from the Simplons' back garden. Four fell on the eighteenth, two on the first, while on the ninth a number of women clustered together in a bunker they had previously done their best to avoid. And with each fresh volley the police, unable to observe who was firing from where, engaged in warfare among themselves. Even the Rickenshaws at Number 1 who had only an hour before been congratulating themselves on the presence of police protection came to regret their premature gratitude. The contingent of police who arrived at the Club House armed now with rifles as well as revolvers and stationed themselves in the bar, the Secretary's office and the changing-room, answered their comrades' desultory fire with a positive barrage of their own. A hail of bullets screamed across the heads of the women cowering in the sandtrap on the ninth and through the smoke into the Rickenshaws' sitting-room. In the sandtrap the women screamed, in the sitting-room Mrs Rickenshaw shot through the thigh screamed and the fire engine driver, mindless of his extended ladder, decided the time had come to get out while the going was good. The going was not good.

'Never mind that fucking fire,' he yelled at the men huddled on the back, 'it's gunfire we've got now.' At the top of the ladder a fireman didn't share his point of view. Clutching his dribbling hose he suddenly found himself moving backwards. 'Stop,' he yelled, 'for God's sake stop!' But the roar of the flames and the rifles drowned his protest and the next moment the fire engine was off at top speed down Sandicott Crescent. Fifty feet above it the fireman clung to the ladder. He was still clinging when having cut a swathe through half a dozen telephone wires and an overhead electric cable the fire engine, travelling at seventy miles an hour, shot under the main railway line to London. The fireman on the ladder didn't. He shot over and landed in the path of an oncoming petrol tanker, missing the London to Brighton express by inches on the way. The tanker driver, already unnerved by the careering fire engine, now ladder-less, swerved to avoid the catapulting fireman, and the tanker ploughed into the railway embankment and exploded in time to shower flaming petrol over the last five coaches of the express above. In the guards van, now engulfed in flames, the guard did his duty. He applied the emergency brake and the express's wheels locked at eighty miles an hour. The subsequent screech of scored metal drowned even the sound of gunfire and the Police Superintendent's howls in the bird sanctuary. Inside every compartment passengers sitting with their fronts to the engine shot into the laps of those with their backs to it and in the dining-car, where breakfast was being served, coffee and waiters mingled with diners to shoot everywhere. Meanwhile the last five coaches blazed away.

So did the police in the golf club. The sight of the burning train emerging from what appeared to be a napalm bomb exploded in the centre of East Pursley only lent weight to their conviction that they were dealing with an outbreak of urban and golf-course terrorism unprecedented in the annals of British history. They radioed for army help and explained that they were pinned down in the East Pursley Club House by suburban guerrillas firing from the houses in Sandicott Crescent who had just exploded a bomb under the London to Brighton express. Five minutes later helicopter gunships were hovering over the golf course searching for the enemy. But the policemen in the Simplons' garden had had their fill. Three lay wounded, one was dead and the rest were out of ammunition. Dragging their wounded they wormed their way across the lawn and round the side of the house. and ran for the police cars.

'Get the hell out of here,' they yelled as they scrambled in, 'there's a fucking army out there.' A minute later, their sirens receding into the distance, the patrol cars had left the Crescent and were heading towards the police station. They didn't reach it. The tanker that had exploded on to the express had doused the road beneath and the tunnel was an inferno. Behind them Sandicott Crescent was in little better shape. The fire in the Simplons' garage had spread to the fence and from the fence to the Ogilvies' potting shed. It was well named. Riddled with bullet holes it added its flames and smoke to the general pall that hung over Jessica's inheritance and lent a grisly light to the scene. The Ogilvies clung to one another in the cellar listening to the whine of bullets ricocheting round their kitchen, and at Number 1 Mr Rickenshaw, tightening a tourniquet round his wife's leg, promised her that if they ever got out of this alive they'd get out of the house.

It was the same at the Pettigrews'. 'Promise me we'll move,' whined Mrs Pettigrew. 'Another night in this awful house and I'll go mad.'

Mr Pettigrew needed no urging. The series of events that had swept through Sandicott Crescent, and in particular their house, like the plagues that had affected Egypt inclined him to renounce his rationalism and return to religion. His social conscience had certainly deserted him and when Mr Rickenshaw, unable to phone for medical assistance thanks to the scythe-like activities of the fire engine's ladder, crawled across the street to ring the Pettigrews' doorbell to ask for help, Mr Pettigrew refused to open the door on the reasonable grounds that the last time anyone had asked for medical help, namely the ambulance men, of all people, they had introduced a mad dog into the house and that as far as he was concerned Mrs Rickenshaw could bleed to death before he opened his door again.

'You can think yourself lucky,' he shouted, 'your fucking wife's only got a hole in her leg, mine's got one in her head.' Mr Rickenshaw cursed him for his bad neighbourliness and, wholly unaware that Colonel Finch-Potter, having been relieved of his penis-grater, was now in intensive care at the Pursley Hospital, tried to knock him up. It was Jessica who finally came to his aid, and braving the slackening gun-fire from the Club House went down to Number 1 and applied her knowledge of first aid to Mrs Rickenshaw's wound. Lockhart took advantage of her absence to make a last sally into the sewer. Donning his wet-suit he crawled along to the outlet of Mr Grabble's house with a bucket and a World War II stirrup pump that Mr Sandicott had kept in his workshop for watering plants. Lockhart had another purpose in mind, and having introduced the nozzle into the discharge pipe and cemented it there with putty, filled the bucket from the sewer and began to pump vigorously. He worked steadily for an hour and then undid his apparatus and crawled home. By that time Mr Grabble's ground floor was awash with the effluent from every other house in the street and all his attempts to get his ground-floor lavatory to behave in the normal manner and discharge excreta out of the house rather than pump it in had failed disastrously. Driven to desperate measures and wading through sewage with his trousers rolled up, Mr Grabble had seized on the idea of using caustic soda. It was not a good idea. Instead of going down the pipe to unblock whatever infernal thing was blocking it, the caustic soda erupted from the pan in an extremely vindictive fashion. Fortunately Mr Grabble had had the good sense to foresee this possibility and was out of the tiny room when it happened. He was less sensible in resorting to an ordinary lavatory cleanser and when that failed, adding to it a liquid bleach. The two combined to produce chlorine and Mr Grabble was driven from his house by the poisonous gas. Standing on the back lawn he watched his living-room carpet lap up the foul liquid and the caustic soda eat into his best armchair. Mr Grabble took the unwise step of trying to dam the flood and the caustic soda dissuaded him. He sat on the edge of the fishpond bathing his feet and cursing.

In the bird sanctuary the Superintendent was still shouting for help, though less loudly, and at the far end the bull-terrier was sleeping it off on the mat outside his master's back door.

Lockhart, divesting himself of the wet-suit, ran himself a bath and lay in it contentedly. On the whole he thought he had done rather well. There could be no doubting now that Jessica would be in full possession of her inheritance and with the right to sell every house whenever she chose. He lay thinking about the tax problem. His experience at Sandicott & Partners had told him that Capital Gains Tax was levied on every extra house an individual owned. There had to be some way round it. The tax on twelve houses would be enormous. By the time he got out of the bath he had found a simple solution.

Chapter fifteen

Nobody else could find a simple solution to the problem of what had occurred in East Pursley. The discovery by an army helicopter of the Superintendent of Police hanging to the upper branches of a monkey-puzzle tree which would have defied the efforts of any but the most insane men to climb it didn't help to clarify matters. He kept screaming about mad dogs being loose in the neighbourhood and his statement was supported by Mr Pettigrew and the Lowrys who had wounds to prove it.

'It hardly explains how six golfers and five of my own men came to be shot,' said the Commissioner of Police. 'Mad dogs and Englishmen may go out in the midday sun but the former don't carry side-arms. And what the hell do we say about that fire engine and the petrol tanker, not to mention the London to Brighton express? How many passengers went west in that inferno?'

'Ten,' said the Assistant Commissioner, 'though accurately speaking they were going south. The Southern Region caters ...'

'Shut up,' snarled the Commissioner, 'I've got to explain this to the Home Secretary and it's got to sound good.'

'Well, I suppose we could divide the two incidents into separate areas,' suggested the Assistant Commissioner, but the Commissioner only looked at him the more lividly.

'Two? Two?' he yelled rattling the windows of his office. 'One, we have an utterly insane half-pay colonel whittling his prick with a cheese-grater in the company of a high-class whore. Two, we have a mad dog roaming the district biting everything in sight. Three, someone looses off firearms into several houses and then explodes a fucking garage with an unidentifiable woman in the inspection pit. Do I have to spell it *all* out for you?'

'I take your point,' said the Assistant Commissioner, 'which according to Miss Gigi Lamont is what Colonel Finch-Potter ...'

'Shut up,' said the Commissioner savagely and crossed his legs. They sat in silence and considered a convincing explanation.

'At least the TV people and the press weren't present,' said the Assistant Commissioner, and his superior nodded thankfully.

'What about blaming the IRA?'

'And give them something else to boast about? You must be out of your tiny mind.'

'Well, they did blow up Mr O'Brain's house,' said the AC.

'Nonsense. The sod blew himself up. There wasn't a trace of explosive in the house,' said the Commissioner, 'he was fiddling with the gas stove . . .'

'But he wasn't connected to the gas main . . .' the AC began.

'And I won't be connected to my job unless we come up with something before noon,' shouted the Commissioner. 'First of all we've got to stop the press going in there and asking questions. Got any ideas on the subject?'

The Assistant Commissioner considered the problem. 'I don't suppose we could say the mad dogs had rabies,' he said finally. 'I mean we could put the area in quarantine and shoot anything . . .'

'We've already shot half the police in that patch,' said the Commissioner, 'and while I'm inclined to agree that they were mad you still don't go round shooting people who've contracted rabies. You inoculate the brutes. Still, it would serve to keep the press and the media out. And how do you explain the six bleeding golfers? Just because some fool slices his drive you don't have a drive to slice him and five others with multiple gunshot wounds. We've got to come up with some logical explanation.'

'Sticking to the rabies theory,' said the Assistant Commissioner, 'if one of our men contracted rabies and went berserk . . .'

'You can't contract rabies instantaneously. It takes weeks to come out.'

'But if there were a special sort of rabies, a new variety like swine fever,' persisted the Assistant. 'The dog bites the Colonel . . .'

'That's out for a start. There's no evidence that anybody bit Colonel Finch-Fucking-Potter except himself and that in an anatomically impossible place unless the bastard was a contortionist as well as a pervert.'

'But he's not in a fit condition to deny the rabies theory,' said the Assistant Commissioner. 'He's clean off his rocker.'

'Not the only thing he's off,' muttered the Commissioner, 'but all right, go on.'

'We start with galloping rabies and the dog and everything follows quite logically. The armed squad go off their heads and start shooting . . .'

'That's going to sound great on the nine o'clock news. "Five officers of the Special Squad, organized to protect foreign diplomats, this morning went mad and shot six golfers on the East Pursley Golf Course." I know there's no such thing as bad publicity but in this case I have my doubts.'

'But it doesn't have to be announced on the news,' said the Assistant Commissioner. 'In a case of this sort we invoke the Official Secrets Act.'

The Commissioner nodded approvingly. 'We'd need the co-operation of the War Office for that,' he said.

'Well, those helicopters could have come from Porton Down and the Biological Warfare Research Station is there.'

'They just happen to have come from somewhere else, and anyway they came after the show was over.'

'But they don't know that,' said the Assistant Commissioner, 'and you know how dim the Army Command is. The main thing is that we can threaten to put the blame on them and . . .'

In the end it was agreed at a Joint Meeting of the Home Secretary, the Minister of Defence and the Commissioner of Police that the happenings at Sandicott Crescent were subject to official silence and, invoking the Defence of The Realm Act together with the Official Secrets Act, the editors of all papers were ordered not to publicize the tragedy. The BBC and ITV were similarly warned and the news that night contained only the story of the petrol tanker that had exploded and set the London to Brighton express on fire in the process. Sandicott Crescent was sealed off and army marksmen went through the bird sanctuary with rifles killing anything that moved as an exercise in stopping the spread of rabies. They found only birds and from a sanctuary the wood became a mortuary. Fortunately for the bull-terrier it didn't move. It slept on and on outside the Colonel's kitchen door. It was about the only creature apart from Lockhart and Jessica who didn't move. Mr

Grabble, driven from his house by the upsurge of the sewer, handed in his notice that afternoon wearing a pair of bedroom slippers over his chemically cauterized feet. Mr Rickenshaw finally managed to get his wife to hospital and the Pettigrews spent the afternoon packing. They too left before dark. The Lowrys had already left and were being given rabies inoculations in the company of several firemen, the Police Superintendent and a number of his men at the local isolation hospital. Even Mrs Simplon had gone, in a small sinister plastic bag which so upset Mrs Ogilvie that she had to be sedated.

'There's only us left,' she moaned, 'everyone else has gone. I want to go too. All those dead men lying out there . . . I'll never be able to look out at the golf course without seeing them on the dogleg ninth.'

This remark put Mr Ogilvie in mind of both dogs and legs. He too would never feel the same about Sandicott Crescent. A week later they too left and Lockhart and Jessica could look out their bedroom window at eleven empty houses, each standing (with the exception of Mr O'Brain's Bauhaus, which had slumped somewhat) in substantial and well-kept grounds in an apparently desirable neighbourhood within easy reach of London and adjoining an excellent golf club whose waiting list had been conveniently shortened by recent events. As the builders moved in to restore the houses to their pristine state, and in the case of Mr Grabble's to a sanitary one, Lockhart had time to turn his attention to other things.

There was, for instance, the little matter of Miss Genevieve Goldring's forthcoming novel, *Song of the Heart*, to be considered. Lockhart took to buying the *Bookseller* to check when it was due to be published. Since Miss Goldring managed to write five books a year under various pseudonyms, her publishers were forced by the impetus of her output to bring out two Goldring books in the same period. There was a Spring List Goldring novel and an Autumn one. *Song of the Heart* appeared in the Autumn List and came out in October. Lockhart and Jessica watched it climb from nine on the best-sellers list to two within three weeks and finally to Top. It was then that Lockhart struck. He travelled to London with a copy of the novel and spent part of an afternoon in the office of the younger of the two Giblings, and the rest of it in the office of the older with young Mr Gibling in attendance. By the time he left, the Giblings were in transports of legal rhapsody. Never in all their experience, and old Mr Gibling had had a great deal of experience in matters concerning libel; never had they come across a more blatant and outrageously wicked libel. Better still, Miss Genevieve Goldring's publishers were immensely rich, thanks in large part to her popularity, and now they were going to be immensely generous out of court in their settlement, thanks to Miss Goldring's wicked libel, or best of all they would be immensely stupid and fight the case in court, a prospect so eminently to be desired that Mr and Mr Gibling proceeded with a delicate hesitancy that was calculated to allure.

They wrote politely to Messrs Shortstead, Publishers, of Edgware Road, apprising them of an unfortunate fact that had been brought to their notice by a client, one Mr Lockhart Flawse, that his name appeared in that extremely successful novel, *Song of the Heart*, by Miss Genevieve Goldring and published by Messrs Shortstead, and that in consequence of this unfortunate error they were forced into the regrettable course of having to request Messrs Shortstead to make good the damage done to the private, professional and marital reputation of Mr Flawse by the aspersions cast on his character in the book by a financial payment and legal costs, at the same time withdrawing all copies unsold from circulation and destroying them.

'That should set the trap,' said Mr Gibling to Mr Gibling. 'It is to be devoutly hoped that they will employ the services of some up-and-coming young man in our profession who will advise them to contest.'

Messrs Shortstead did. The reply from the least senior member of the firm of solicitors, Coole, Poole, Stoole and Folsom and Partners, one Mr Arbutus, stated that while Messrs Shortstead and the author of *Song of the Heart*, hereafter termed the novel, were prepared to offer Mr Flawse their apologies and his legal costs and if necessary some small sum for his pain and injury, they were in no way obliged nor would consider much less agree to the withdrawal of all unsold copies, etc. The letter ended on the cordial note that Coole, Poole, Stoole and Folsom and Partners looked forward to hearing from Mr Gibling. Mr Gibling and Mr Gibling rather doubted it. They held the matter in abeyance for a fortnight and then struck.

'Four hundred thousand pounds damages? Do my ears deceive me?' said Mr Folsom when Mr Arbutus showed him their reply. 'I have never in all my career read anything so monstrous. Giblings have gone mad. Of course we will contest.'

'Contest?' said Mr Arbutus, 'They must have something . . .'

'Bluff, boy, bluff,' said Mr Folsom, 'I haven't read the book of course but such a sum is unheard-of in innocent libel. Come to that, it's unheard-of in deliberate libel. Probably a typist's error.'

But for once Mr Folsom erred. Mr Shortstead, taking his advice, instead of his own intuition which told him that *Song of the Heart* was somehow a little different in tone from Miss Goldring's other numerous novels, instructed Mr Arbutus to answer in kind and reversing the natural order of things to tell Mr Gibling and Mr Gibling to sue and be damned. And next day on the third floor of Blackstones House, Lincoln's Inn, London, when the mail was brought before him and opened by the senior clerk, that aged and austere gentleman discovered for the very first time in his life that Mr Gibling the Elder could do the hornpipe very creditably on his desktop; having done so he demanded the immediate production of two, no, three bottles of the best champagne to be sent for at no matter what cost.

'We have them by the nose,' he sang gleefully when Mr Gibling the younger arrived. 'O Lord that I should live to see this day. The nose, brother o' mine, the nose. Read it again. I must hear it.'

And Mr Gibling trembled in litigious ecstasy as the words 'Sue and be damned' quivered in the air.

'Sue and be damned,' he gibbered. 'Sue and be damned. I can hardly wait to hear that threat pronounced by counsel in court. Ah, the judge's face. The beauty, brother, the beauty of it all. The legal life is not without its precious moments. Let us savour the pleasure of this splendid day.'

Mr Partington, the senior clerk, brought in the champagne and Mr Gibling and Mr Gibling sent him to fetch a third glass. Only then did they solemnly toast Mr Lockhart Flawse of 12 Sandicott Crescent for stepping so simultaneously into their lives and out of the pages of Miss Genevieve Goldring's novel with its oh-so-appropriate title. That day there was little work done in Blackstones House, Lincoln's Inn. The drawing-up of writs is not an arduous job and the one issued by Gibling and Gibling between Lockhart Flawse, Plaintiff, and Genevieve Goldring and Messrs Shortstead, Defendants, was no different from other writs and merely stated that Elizabeth the Second, by the Grace of God, of the United Kingdom of Great Britain and Northern Ireland and of Our other Realms and Territories Queen, Head of the Commonwealth, Defender of the Faith; To Genevieve Goldring properly named Miss Magster c/o Messrs Shortstead ... 'WE COMMAND YOU that within fourteen days after the service of this Writ on you, inclusive of the day of service, you do cause an appearance to be entered for you in an action at the suit of Lockhart Flawse and take notice that in default of you doing so the Plaintiff may proceed therein, and judgement may be given in your absence.'

It was served the following day and caused little consternation in the offices of Messrs Shortstead and a great deal in those of Coole, Poole, Stoole and Folsom and Partners where Mr Arbutus, having read *Song of the Heart*, had discovered the horrid nature of the libel published on the aforesaid Lockhart Flawse; namely that he made a habit of being tied by his wife to the bed and being whipped by his wife, Jessica, and vice versa, and when not whipping or being whipped, stole money from banks in the process of which he shot dead several bank cashiers.

'We can't even plead innocent libel,' he told Mr Folsom but that worthy man had reason to think otherwise.

'No authoress in her right mind would deliberately set out to write a book in which she named a person she knew and ascribed all these perversions and crimes to him. The thing's a nonsense.' It was a view shared by Genevieve Goldring. 'Never heard of the creature,' she told Mr Shortstead and Mr Arbutus, 'and besides it's an improbable name. Frankly I can't remember having written about anyone called Lockhart Flawse with a wife named Jessica.'

'But it's down there in *Song of the Heart*,' said Mr Arbutus, 'you must have read it. After all, you wrote it.'

Genevieve Goldring snorted. 'I write five novels a year. You can't expect me to read the wretched things as well. I leave the matter in the competent hands of Mr Shortstead here.'

'But don't you check your own proofs?'

'Young man,' said Miss Goldring, 'my proofs don't need checking. Correct me if I'm wrong, Mr Shortstead.'

But Mr Shortstead, while he was beginning to hold a different point of view, held his tongue.

'Then we are to plead innocent libel?' asked Mr Arbutus.

'I see no reason to plead libel at all,' protested Miss Goldring. 'For all we know this man Flawse does tie his wife to the bed and whip her and with a name like Jessica she thoroughly deserves it. After all it's up to him to prove he doesn't.'

Mr Arbutus pointed out that truth was no defence unless in the public interest.

'I should think a bank robber and pervert was of very considerable public interest. It will probably increase the sales of my novels.'

Counsel thought otherwise. 'We haven't a leg to stand on,' said Mr Widdershins, QC. 'I advise settlement. We can't hope to win in court.'

'But won't the publicity do us good even if we pay?' asked Mr Shortstead, pushed into adopting this line by Miss Goldring who was always complaining that her novels were never sufficiently advertised. Mr Widdershins doubted it but, since he was being paid to conduct the defence, he saw no good reason to deprive himself of the financial remuneration a prolonged case was bound to bring him. 'I leave the decision to you,' he said, 'I have given my opinion and that opinion is that we will lose.'

'But they are demanding four hundred thousand pounds in settlement out of court,' said Mr Shortstead, 'and surely no court is going to award damages to that amount. It's outrageous.' It was.

The trial was held in The High Court of Justice, Queen's Bench Division, before Mr Justice Plummery. Mr Widdershins acted for the defendants and Mr Fescue had been instructed by Mr Gibling and Mr Gibling. The latter were in raptures. Mr Justice Plummery had a reputation for barbarous impartiality and a loathing for quibbling barristers. There was no recourse open to Mr Widdershins but to quibble, and to add to the difficulties of the defence there was Miss Goldring who, if she couldn't win the case, was determined to lose it as flamboyantly as possible.

Mr Shortstead sat beside her shivering in the shade of her crimson hat. One look at the plaintiff, Lockhart Flawse, had been enough to tell him that here was a clean upstanding young man of a type he had forgotten existed; who more probably owned banks than robbed them and who, if he was married, treated his wife with a tenderness that was positively chivalrous. Mr Shortstead was a good judge of character.

Mr Fescue rose to present the plaintiff's case. It was an impeccable one. Mr Lockhart Flawse of 12 Sandicott Crescent, East Pursley – and here Mr Widdershins was seen to cover his eyes with his hands and Miss Goldring's hat to quiver – was a close neighbour of the defendant, so close that he was known to her and had on one occasion been invited to tea by her. A note passed to Mr Widdershins from Miss Goldring simply said, 'Liar, bloody liar. I've never seen the little shit in my life,' at which Mr Widdershins' hopes rose a little. They were lowered by Mr Fescue's continued description of Lockhart Flawse's virtue and tribulations subsequent to the publication of *Song of the Heart.* Among these tribulations the most important had been his sacking from the firm of Sandicott & Partner, Chartered Accountants, where he had been previously employed. Evidence would be produced that his forced retirement from the lucrative profession had been the direct result of Miss Goldring's infamous attack on his private life and his wholly fictitious propensity for robbing banks and murdering cashiers. Mr Fescue, lacking the knowledge, did not mention that Mr Treyer's readiness to provide such evidence had been obtained in a private interview in which Lockhart had explained that unless Mr Treyer was evidentially co-operative he, Lockhart, would be forced by his conscience into revealing the true facts about Mr Gypsum's tax evasion and VAT avoidance to the appropriate authorities, a threat which had been made the stronger by his production of copies of all Mr Gypsum's files, both dummy and real.

Furthermore, said Mr Fescue, the plaintiff had been shunned by his neighbours to the extent that eleven houses adjacent to his address or in the same street had been left by their occupants to avoid any connection between them and a supposed murderer. And finally there was Mrs Flawse, correctly named in the novel as Jessica, who would testify that she had never once tied her husband or been tied by him to their marital bed and that there wasn't a whip in the house. Mrs Flawse's distress was of so great an order of magnitude that she had recently taken to wearing a veil to avoid being accosted (in the street) by men with a taste for bondage and flagellation, or alternately insulted by women she had formerly been able to invite to her house but who now refused her entry to their own. By the time Mr Fescue had finished he had portrayed an accurate picture of the young couple's social isolation for quite the wrong reasons, and an inaccurate one of their future financial prospects as a result of the publication of *Song of the Heart* for the right reasons, namely that the damages to be paid would be enormous.

When Mr Fescue sat down Mr Justice Plummery and the jury were clearly impressed and Mr Widdershins rose for the defence extremely handicapped. It was all very well for Miss Goldring to claim that Lockhart Flawse was a liar. It was going to be another matter to prove it. Mr Flawse did not look a liar. If anything he looked the opposite while, even behind her veil, Mrs Jessica Flawse radiated an innocence that was in marked contrast to the raddled flamboyance of his client. Booze, books and bed had all left their marks on Miss Goldring. Mr Widdershins did his best. The libel, he claimed, was entirely innocent. The defendant had no knowledge of the plaintiff's existence and had never so much as set eyes on him. The imputation that she had once invited him to tea was utterly without foundation and the fact that Miss Goldring lived in West Pursley while the plaintiff occupied a house in East was purely coincidental. However in the light of the statements made by his learned friend, Mr Fescue, the defence were prepared to apologize and make financial reparation for the damage done to the plaintiff and his wife and for the scorn, ridicule and consequential loss of his profession ... Here Miss Goldring broke away from the restraining hand of Mr Shortstead and rose to say that never, never, never would she pay one penny, one single penny to a man she had never written about in her life and that if anyone thought she would they were mistaken. Mr Justice Plummery regarded her with an immense distaste that would have withered the Sphinx at fifty yards and rendered it articulate at a hundred.

'Kindly sit down, madam,' he snarled with blood and iron in

his voice. 'What you will or will not do it is up to the Court to decide. But one thing I do assure you, a second interruption and I shall have you held for contempt. Proceed with what there is of your case, Mr Witherspin.'

Mr Widdershins' Adam's apple bobbed like a ping-pong ball on a waterspout in a fairground shooting-gallery as he tried to find words. He had no case.

'My clients plead innocent libel, m'lud,' he squeaked in direct contradiction to his instructions. Mr Justice Plummery looked at him dubiously.

'That is not what I understood,' he said.

Mr Widdershins asked for an adjournment to consult with his clients. It was granted and was spent in exultation by Mr Fescue and Mr Gibling and Lockhart, and in acrimonious arguments by Mr Widdershins and Miss Goldring. Mr Shortstead was ready in the face of the plaintiff's case to settle out of court. Miss Goldring in the face of his pusillanimity and the judge's distaste was not.

'It's all a damned lie,' she shouted, 'I never had that little shit to tea and I never used the name Lockhart fucking Flawse in any of my books.'

'But it's there in *Song of* . . .' Mr Shortstead began.

'Shut up,' said Miss Goldring. 'If it's there you must have put it there because it wasn't in the manuscript I sent you.'

'You're quite sure about that?' said Mr Widdershins, looking for some ray of hope in an otherwise hopeless case.

'I swear by Almighty God,' said Miss Goldring with a vehemence that was convincing, 'that I have never ever heard the name Flawse in my life, let alone used it in a book.'

'May we see a copy of the manuscript?' said Mr Widdershins, and Mr Shortstead sent for it. The name Flawse was there in bold pica type.

'What do you say to that?' said Mr Widdershins.

Miss Goldring said a great deal and most of it true. Mr Shortstead said little and all of it true.

'Then we shall contest the authenticity of this document,' said Mr Widdershins. 'Are we all agreed on that?'

Miss Goldring was. Mr Shortstead wasn't. 'That is the manuscript we received,' he maintained.

'That was not, is not, nor ever will be the manuscript I dictated. It's a fucking forgery.'

'You're absolutely sure about that?' said Mr Widdershins.

'I swear by Almighty God . . .'

'Very well. We will contest the case on those grounds, that this document which came into the possession of Mr Shortstead was not the original manuscript you wrote.'

'Precisely,' said Miss Goldring, 'I swear by Almighty God . . .'

She was still swearing by Almighty God and by lesser deities when she entered the witness box the following day to be cross-examined by an ebullient Mr Fescue. Mr Gibling and Mr Gibling could hardly contain themselves. In fact Mr Gibling the Elder couldn't at all and had to leave the court hurriedly while she was still in the witness box.

'Now Miss Magster,' Mr Fescue began before being stopped by the judge.

'I understood the witness's name to be Miss Genevieve Goldring,' he said, 'now you address her as Miss Magster. Which is it?'

'Miss Genevieve Goldring is an alias,' said Mr Fescue, 'her real . . .' He was interrupted by a squawk from the witness box.

'Genevieve Goldring is my pen name, my *nom de plume*,' she said.

Mr Justice Plummery studied the feather in her hat with disgust. 'No doubt,' he said, 'no doubt your profession requires an assortment of names. The court requires your real one.'

'Miss Magster,' said Miss Goldring, sullenly aware that this revelation would disillusion a large section of her public. 'But I am best known to my admirers as Miss Genevieve Goldring.'

'Again no doubt,' said the judge, 'but then from what I have gathered your admirers have peculiar tastes.'

Mr Fescue took his cue from the judge. 'I am prepared to call you Genevieve Goldring if you so prefer,' he said, 'it is not my intention to harm your professional reputation. Now is it or is it not true that in *Song of the Heart* you describe the character named Flawse as being addicted to what is known among prostitutes and their clients as bondage and flage?'

'I did not write *Song of the Heart*,' said Miss Goldring.

'But I thought you had already admitted writing it,' said the judge. 'Now I hear ...'

What he heard was a tirade from the witness box on the iniquities of publishers and editors. When she had finished, Mr Fescue turned to Mr Justice Plummery. 'Would it not be as well to examine the original manuscript and compare it with others submitted by the defendant to her publishers, m'lud?' he asked.

'The defendants have no objections,' said Mr Widdershins, and the Court adjourned once again.

Later that afternoon two experts on graphology and typography testified that the manuscript of *Song of the Heart* had been written, typed and produced by precisely the same machine as *King's Closet* and *Maid of the Moors*, both books written by Miss Goldring. Mr Fescue continued his cross-examination of the defendant.

'Having established beyond all possible doubt that you wrote *Song of the Heart*,' he said, 'is it not also true that you were and are acquainted with the plaintiff, Mr Lockhart Flawse?'

Miss Goldring began a violent denial but Mr Fescue stopped her. 'Before you commit perjury,' he said. 'I would ask you to consider the evidence given under oath by Mr Flawse that you invited him into your house and plied him with crème de menthe?'

In the witness box Miss Goldring stared at him with starting eyes. 'How did you know that?' she asked.

Mr Fescue smiled and looked to the judge and jury. 'Because Mr Flawse told me under oath yesterday,' he said gaily.

But Miss Goldring shook her head. 'About the crème de menthe,' she said weakly.

'Because the plaintiff also told me, though in private,' said Mr Fescue. 'You do, I take it, drink crème de menthe?'

Miss Goldring nodded miserably.

'Yes or no,' said Mr Fescue fiercely.

'Yes,' said Miss Goldring. Below her Mr Widdershins and Mr Shortstead both covered their eyes with their hands. Mr Fescue resumed his rout. 'Is it not also true that the carpet in your bedroom is blue flecked with gold, that your bed is heart shaped, that beside it stands a mauve pleated lampshade, that your cat's name is Pinky? Are these facts not all true?'

There was no doubting their veracity. The look on Miss

Goldring's face spoke for her. But Mr Fescue had the *coup de grâce* ready.

'And finally is it not a fact that you possess a chow named Bloggs for the sole purpose of preventing anyone you wish to keep out from entering your house without your permission and presence?' Again there was no need for an answer. Mr Fescue had his facts right: he had heard them from Lockhart who in turn had them from Jessica.

'So that,' continued Mr Fescue, 'without your permission Mr Flawse could not have been able to testify in a signed affidavit that when you invited him into the house you did so of your own free will and with the intention of seducing him and having failed of that purpose you set out deliberately and with malice aforethought to destroy his marriage, reputation and means of livelihood by portraying him in a novel as a thief, a pervert and a murderer. Is that not also true?'

'No,' shrieked Miss Goldring, 'no it isn't. I never invited him in. I never . . .' She hesitated catastrophically. She had invited a number of young men to share her bed but . . .

'I have no more questions of this witness,' said Mr Fescue and sat down.

In his summing up Mr Justice Plummery maintained that ferocious impartiality for which he was famous. Miss Goldring's evidence and behaviour in and out of the witness box had left no doubt in his mind that she was a liar, a prostitute in both the literary and sexual meanings of the word, and that she had maliciously set out to do what Mr Fescue had maintained. The jury retired for two minutes and found the libel proved. It was left to the judge to estimate the damages both personal and financial to the plaintiff as being of the order, due consideration being given to the level of inflation which presently and for the foreseeable future stood and would continue to stand at eighteen per cent, of one million pounds sterling, and that furthermore he was sending papers of the case to the Director of Public Prosecutions with the hope that the defendant would be charged with perjury. Miss Genevieve Goldring fainted and was not helped to her feet by Mr Shortstead.

That afternoon there was jubilation in the offices of Mr Gibling and Mr Gibling.

'A million with costs. A million. The highest damages ever awarded in a libel case. And with costs. Dear God, let them appeal, please let them appeal,' said Mr Gibling the Elder.

But Miss Goldring was past appealing. Mr Shortstead's insurers had communicated with him immediately following the award and had made it clear that they intended to sue both him and Miss Goldring for every penny they were being asked to pay.

And at Number 12 Sandicott Crescent Lockhart and Jessica had no qualms.

"Beastly woman,' said Jessica, 'and to think I used to love her books. And they were all lies.'

Lockhart nodded. 'And now we can start to sell the houses too,' he said. 'After so much unfortunate publicity we can't possibly stay in this neighbourhood.'

Next day the sign boards For Sale began to go up in Sandicott Crescent and Lockhart, feeling himself financially secure, decided to open the letters Miss Deyntry had given him.

Chapter sixteen

He did so with due ceremony and in the dim consciousness that he was tempting fate. 'Paper and ink will do you no good,' the old gipsy had told him and while her prediction had not been borne out by the paper and ink of Miss Goldring's novel, Lockhart harking back to her words felt that they applied more to these letters to his dead mother than to anything else. He had received them from Miss Deyntry in the hour of the gipsy's forecast and he felt that this was no coincidence. He would have been hard put to explain why but there lurked in his mind the vestigial superstitions of his ancestors and a time when a Romany's warning was taken seriously. And in other respects she had been right. Three deaths there had been and if she had rather underestimated there was still the fact that she had been precise about the unfilled grave. The remains of the late Mrs

Simplon had needed no grave. And what about the hanged man on a tree? Certainly the Police Superintendent had hung from a tree but not in the manner of the old woman's sinister prediction. Finally there was the matter of his gift. 'Till ye come to your gift again.' Possibly that referred to the million pounds' damages from the libel suit. But again Lockhart doubted it. She had meant another kind of gift than money.

Nevertheless Lockhart took courage and opened the letters one by one, starting from the first which was dated the year of his birth and came from South Africa and ended with the last dated 1964 and addressed from Arizona. His father, if father the writer was, had been a travelling man and Lockhart soon realized why. Miss Deyntry had been right. Grosvenor K. Boscombe had been a mining engineer and his work had taken him across the globe in search of precious metals, oil, gas and coal, anything in fact that the millenniums had covered and modern mining methods could discover. Possibly he was a mining engineer and a highly successful one at that. His last letter from Dry Bones, Arizona, in which he announced his marriage to a Miss Phoebe Tarrent also indicated that he had struck it rich in natural gas. But whatever his success as a mining engineer, Grosvenor K. Boscombe had little talent for writing letters. There was no glimmer of that passion or sentiment Lockhart had expected, and certainly no suggestion that Mr Boscombe had done anything to qualify as Lockhart's long-lost father. Mr Boscombe stuck to the occupational hazards of his profession and spoke of his boredom. He described sunsets over the Namibian, Saudi Arabian, Libyan and the Sahara deserts in almost identical terms in letters years apart. By the time he had ploughed his way through all the letters Lockhart had crossed correspondentially most of the major deserts of the world, a laborious process made more so by virtue of Mr Boscombe's inability to spell any word with more than four syllables correctly or even consistently. Thus Saudi Arabia went through half a dozen permutations from Sordy Rabier to Sourday Ayrabbia. The only word the man could spell was 'Bore' and it was appropriate. Grosvenor K. Boscombe was boring wherever he went and apart from regarding the world as a gigantic pin cushion into which it was his profession to push immensely long hollow pins, his only moment of even approximate passion came when he and the boys, whoever they were, punctured some underground pressure point and 'then she fare blue'. The phrase recurred less frequently than the sunsets, and dry holes predominated over gushers but she blue farely often all the same and his strike at Dry Bones, Arizona, put Mr Boscombe in his own words 'up amung the lucky ones with mor greenbacks than a man wuld nede to carpit the moon.' Lockhart interpreted that as meaning his possible father was rich and unimaginative. Lockhart knew exactly what he intended to do with his money and carpeting the moon didn't enter his list of priorities. He meant to find his father and do old Mrs Flawse out of any part of the estate and if Boscombe was his father, he was going to thrash him within an inch of his life in accordance with his grandfather's will.

Having read all the letters he allowed Jessica to read them too.

'He doesn't seem to have had a very interesting life,' she said. 'The only things he talks about are deserts and sunsets and dogs.'

'Dogs?' said Lockhart. 'I missed that bit.'

'It's at the end of each letter. "Please rember me to yure father and the dawgs it sure was a priv ledge nowing youall. Ever thyne, Gros." and there's another bit here about just luving dawgs.'

'That's reassuring,' said Lockhart, 'his loving dogs. I mean if he is my father it shows we've got something in common. I've never had much time for sunsets. Dogs are another kettle of fish.'

On the carpet in front of the fire Colonel Finch-Potter's ex-bull-terrier snoozed contentedly. Adopted by Lockhart he had, unlike his master, recovered from the effects of his night of passion and while the Colonel fought legal battles and wrote to his MP to get himself released from the mental hospital to which he had been committed, his pet settled cheerfully into his new home. Lockhart looked at him with gratitude. The bull-terrier had played a very considerable part in clearing Sandicott Crescent of unwanted tenants and Lockhart had appropriately renamed him Bouncer.

'I suppose we could always tempt this Boscombe man over here by offering him some extra-special sort of pedigree dog,' he pondered aloud.

'Why do you have to tempt him over?' said Jessica. 'We can

afford to fly to America to see him ourselves with all the money we've got.'

'All the money isn't going to buy me a birth certificate and without one I can't get a passport,' said Lockhart who had never forgotten his experience of non-entity at the National Insurance office and besides, he meant to put this disadvantage to good use in other matters. If the State was not prepared to contribute to his well-being when in need, he saw no need to contribute one penny by way of taxes to the State. There were virtues to non-existence after all.

And as the winter months rolled by the money rolled in. Messrs Shortstead's insurance company paid one million pounds into Lockhart's bank account in the City and money rolled into Jessica's account at East Pursley and the For Sale notices came down and new occupiers moved in. Lockhart had timed his campaign of eviction with financial precision. Property values were up and not one of the houses went for less than fifty thousand pounds. By Christmas Jessica's account stood at £478,000 and her standing with the bank manager even higher. He offered her financial advice and suggested she should invest the money. Lockhart told her not to do anything so foolish. He had plans for that money and they had nothing to do with stocks and shares and even less to do with Capital Gains Tax which the bank manager was at pains to point out she would inevitably have to pay. Lockhart smiled confidently and went on footling about in the workshop in the garden. It helped to pass the time while the houses were sold and besides, ever since his success as a radio mechanic in the Wilsons' attic, he had become quite an expert and had bought all the necessary ingredients for a hi-fi system which he then constructed. In fact he went in for gadgetry with all his grandfather's enthusiasm for breeding hounds and in no time at all Number 12 was wired for sound so that Lockhart, moving from room to room could, by the mere manipulation of a pocket tuner, switch one loud-speaker off and another one on and generally accompany himself musically wherever he went. On tape recorders he went hog wild and indulged his fancy from minute ones with batteries to vast ones with specially constructed drums a yard wide that held a tape that would play continuously for twenty-four hours and then reverse themselves and start all over again *ad infinitum*.

And in just the same way he could play his tapes all day he could record as long and in whatever room he happened to be. Every so often he would find himself breaking out into song, strange songs of blood and battle and feuds over cattle which were as surprising to him as they were out of place in Sandicott Crescent and seemed to spring spontaneously from some inner source beyond his comprehension. Words reverberated in his head and increasingly he found himself speaking aloud a barely intelligible dialect that bore but little resemblance even to the broadest brogue of the North Tyne. And rhyme came with the words and behind it all a wild music swirled like the wind haunting the chimney on a stormy night. There was no compassion in that music, no pity or mercy, any more than there was in the wind or other natural phenomena, only harsh and naked beauty which took him by force out of the real world in which he moved into another world in which he had his being. His being? It was a strange notion, that one had one's being in much the same way as his grand-uncle, an apostate from the ethical religion of self-help and hero-worship which his grandfather espoused, had the living of St Bede's Church at Angoe.

But Lockhart's mind dwelt less on these subtleties than on the practical problems facing him and the words and the wild music came out only occasionally when he was not feeling himself. And here it had to be admitted he was increasingly feeling himself in ways which his grandfather, a devotee of that Fouler whose great work, *Usage and Self-Abusage*, was the old man's guide in matters of masturbation, would have deplored. The strain of not imposing himself upon his angelic Jessica had begun to tell and sexual fantasies began to fester in his mind as he tinkered in his workshop with a soldering iron. They had the same ancestral and almost archetypal quality as the primeval forests that had flickered in Bouncer's mind under the influence of LSD and with them came guilt. There were even moments when he considered assuaging his desire in Jessica but Lockhart thrust the idea from him and used the sheepskin buffer on the electric drill instead. It was not a satisfactory remedy but it sufficed for the present. One day when he was master of Flawse Hall, and owner of five thousand acres, he would raise a family, but not till then. In the meantime he and Jessica would live chaste lives and resort to the electric drill and manual methods. Lockhart's reasoning was primitive but it stemmed from the feeling that he had yet to master his fate and until that moment came he was impure.

It came sooner than he expected. In late December the phone rang. It was Mr Bullstrode calling from Hexham.

'My boy,' he said in sombre tones. 'I have bad news. Your father, I mean your grandfather, is dangerously ill. Dr Magrew sees little hope of his recovering. I think you should come at once.'

Lockhart with death in his heart for old Mrs Flawse drove north in his new car, a three-litre Rover, leaving Jessica in tears.

'Is there nothing I can do to help?' she asked but Lockhart shook his head. If his grandfather was dying thanks to anything old Mrs Flawse had done, he did not want the presence of her daughter to hinder his plans for the old witch. But when he drove over the track to the gated bridge below the Hall it was to learn from Mr Dodd that the man had fallen, if not of his own volition at least unassisted by his wife who had been in the kitchen garden at the time. Mr Dodd could vouch for that.

'No banana skins?' said Lockhart.

'None,' said Mr Dodd. 'He slipped in his study and hit his head on the coal scuttle. I heard him fall and carried him upstairs.'

Lockhart went up the stairs and brushing Mrs Flawse's lamentations aside with a 'Hush, woman' went into his grandfather's bedroom. The old man was lying in bed and beside him sat Dr Magrew feeling Mr Flawse's pulse.

'His heart's strong enough. It's his head I'm worried about. He should be X-rayed for a fracture but I dare not move him over the broken road,' he said. 'We must trust to the good Lord and the strength of his constitution.'

As if to give a demonstration of that strength old Mr Flawse opened an evil eye and damned Dr Magrew for a scoundrel and a horse thief before shutting it and sinking back into a coma. Lockhart and Dr Magrew and Mr Dodd went downstairs.

'He could go at any moment,' said the doctor, 'and then again he may linger for months.'

'It is a hope much to be desired,' said Mr Dodd looking significantly at Lockhart, 'he canna die before the father's found.' Lockhart nodded. The same thought was in his mind. And that night after Dr Magrew had left with the promise to return in the morning, Lockhart and Mr Dodd sat in the kitchen without Mrs Flawse and conferred.

'The first thing to see to is that woman doesna go near him,' said Mr Dodd. 'She'd stifle the man with a pillow had she but half the chance.'

'Gan lock her door,' said Lockhart, 'we'll feed her through the keyhole.'

Mr Dodd disappeared and returned a few minutes later to say that the bitch was chained in her kennel.

'Now then,' said Lockhart, 'he mustn't die.'

' 'Tis in the lap of the Gods,' said Mr Dodd, 'you heard the doctor.'

'I heard him and I still say he mustn't die.'

A bellow of oaths from upstairs indicated that Mr Flawse was living up to their hopes.

'He does that every now and then. Shouts and abominates the likes of all around.'

'Does he indeed?' said Lockhart. 'You put me in mind of an idea.'

And the next morning before Dr Magrew arrived he was up and away over the broken road and down through Hexham to Newcastle. He spent the day in radio and hi-fi shops and returned with a carload of equipment.

'How is he?' he asked as he and Mr Dodd carried the boxes into the house.

'Ever the same. He shouts and sleeps and sleeps and shouts but the doctor doesna hold out too much hope. And the old bitch has been adding her voice to the din. I told her to still herself or she'd have no food.'

Lockhart unpacked a tape recorder and presently he was sitting by the old man's bed while his grandfather shouted abominations into the microphone.

'Ye damned skulking swine of a blackhearted Scot,' he yelled as Lockhart fixed the throat mike round his neck, 'I'll have no more of your probing and pestering. And take that satanic stethoscope from me chest, ye bluidy leech. 'Tis not my heart that's gan awry but my head.'

And all night he blathered on against the infernal world and its iniquities while Lockhart and Mr Dodd took turns to switch the tape recorder on and off.

That night the snow set in and the road across Flawse Fell became impassable. Mr Dodd heaped coals on the fire in the bedroom and Mr Flawse mistook them for the flames of hell. His language became accordingly more violent. Whatever else, he was not going gently into that dark underworld in which he had professed such unbelief.

'I see you, you devil,' he shouted, 'by Lucifer I'll have ye by the tail. Get ye gone.'

And ever and anon he rambled. ' 'Tis hunting weather, ma'am, good day to ye,' he said quite cheerfully, 'the hounds'll have the scent na doubt. Would that I were young again and could ride to the pack.'

But as each day passed he grew weaker and his thoughts turned to religion.

'I dinna believe in God,' he murmured, 'but if God there be the old fool made an afful mess in the making of this world. Old Dobson the stonemason of Belsay could have made better and he was a craftsman of small talent for all the Grecians taught him in the building of the Hall.'

Lockhart sitting by the tape recorder switched it off and asked who Dobson was but Mr Flawse's mind had gone back to the Creation. Lockhart switched the tape recorder on again.

'God, God, God,' muttered Mr Flawse, 'if the swine doesna exist he should be ashamed of the fact and that's the only creed a man must hold to. To act in such a way that God be put to shame for not existing. Aye, and there's more honour among thieves than in a rabble of godly hypocrites with hymnbooks in their hands and advantage in their hearts. I havena been to church in fifty years save for a burial or two. I willna go now. I'd as soon be bottled like that heretical utilitarian Bentham than be buried with my bloody ancestors.'

Lockhart took note of his words and none of Mrs Flawse's complaints that they had no right to lock her in her room and that it was insanitary to boot. Lockhart had Mr Dodd hand her a roll of toilet paper with instructions to empty the contents of her pot out the window. Mrs Flawse did, to the detriment of Mr Dodd who was passing underneath at the time. After that Mr Dodd gave the window a wide berth and Mrs Flawse no dinner for two days.

And still it snowed and Mr Flawse lingered on blaspheming and blaming the absent Dr Magrew for meddling with him when all the time it was Lockhart or Mr Dodd with the tape recorder. He heaped coals of fire on Mr Bullstrode's head too and called out that he never wanted to see that litigious blood-sucker again which, considering that Mr Bullstrode was unable to make his way to the Hall thanks to the snow, seemed highly probable.

Between these outbursts he slept and slowly slipped away. Lockhart and Mr Dodd sat in front of the kitchen fire and laid their plans for his imminent end. Lockhart had been particularly impressed by the old man's repeated wish not to be buried. Mr Dodd on the other hand pointed out that he didn't want to be cremated either if his attitude to the fire in the bedroom was anything to go by.

'It's either one or t'other,' he said one night. 'He'd keep while the cold lasts but I doubt he'd be pleasant company come the summer.'

It was Lockhart who found the solution one evening as he stood in the peel tower and stared at the dusty flags and the ancient weapons and heads that hung on the wall, and when in the cold hour before dawn old Mr Flawse, muttering a last imprecation on the world, passed from it, Lockhart was ready.

'Keep the tape recorders going today,' he told Mr Dodd, and let no one see him.'

'But he's nothing left to say,' said Mr Dodd. But Lockhart switched the tape from record to play and from beyond the shadow of death old Mr Flawse's voice echoed through the house. And having shown Mr Dodd how to change the cassettes to avoid too much repetition, he left the house and struck across the fells towards Tombstone Law and Miss Deyntry's house in Farspring. It took him longer than he expected. The snow was deep and the drifts against the stone walls deeper still and it was already afternoon when he finally slid down the slope to her house. Miss Deyntry greeted him with her usual gruffness.

'I thought I'd seen the last of you,' she said as Lockhart warmed himself in front of the stove in her kitchen.

'And so you have,' said Lockhart, 'I am not here now and I am not going to borrow your car for a few days.'

Miss Deyntry regarded him dubiously. 'The two statements do not fit together,' she said, 'you are here and you are not going to borrow my car.'

'Rent it then. Twenty pounds a day and it never left your garage and I was never here.'

'Done,' said Miss Deyntry, 'and is there anything else you'd be needing?'

'A stuffer,' said Lockhart.

Miss Deyntry stiffened. 'That I can't provide,' she said. 'Besides, I understood you to be married.'

'Of animals. Someone who stuffs animals and lives a fair way off.'

Miss Deyntry sighed with relief. 'Oh, a taxidermist,' she said. 'There's an excellent one in Manchester. I know him only by repute of course.'

'And you'll not know even that from now on,' said Lockhart and wrote down the address, 'your word on it.' He placed a hundred pounds on the table and Miss Deyntry nodded.

That night Mr Taglioni, Taxidermist & Specialist in Permanent Preservation, of 5 Brunston Road was interrupted in his work on a Mrs Pritchard's pet and late poodle, Oliver, and called to the front door. In the darkness outside stood a tall figure whose face was largely obscured by a scarf and a peaked hat.

'Yes,' said Mr Taglioni, 'can I help you?'

'Perhaps,' said the figure. 'Do you live alone?'

Mr Taglioni nodded a trifle nervously. It was one of the disadvantages of his occupation that few women seemed disposed to share a house with a man whose livelihood consisted of stuffing other things and those dead.

'I am told you are an excellent taxidermist,' said the figure pushing past Mr Taglioni into the passage.

'I am,' said Mr Taglioni proudly.

'You can stuff anything?' There was scepticism in the voice.

'Anything you care to mention,' said Mr Taglioni, 'fish, fox, fowl or pheasant, you name it I'll stuff it.'

167

Lockhart named it. 'Benvenuto Cellini!' said Mr Taglioni lapsing into his native tongue, 'Mamma mia, you can't be serious?'

But Lockhart was. Producing an enormous revolver from his raincoat pocket he pointed it at Mr Taglioni.

'But it's not legal. It's unheard of. It's . . .'

The revolver poked into his belly. 'I named it, you stuff it,' said the masked figure. 'I'll give you ten minutes to collect your tools and anything else you need and then we'll go.'

'What I need is brandy,' said Mr Taglioni and was forced to drink half the bottle. Ten minutes later a blindfolded, drunk and partially demented taxidermist was bundled into the back seat of Miss Deyntry's car and driven north and by three o'clock in the morning the car was hidden in an abandoned lime kiln near Black Pockrington. Across the fell there stalked a tall black figure and over his shoulder he carried the insensible Mr Taglioni. At four they entered the Hall and Lockhart unlocked the door to the wine cellar and laid the taxidermist on the floor. Upstairs Mr Dodd was awake.

'Make some strong coffee,' Lockhart told him, 'and then come with me.'

When half an hour later Mr Taglioni was coaxed back to consciousness by having scalding hot coffee poured down his throat, the body of the late Mr Flawse lying on the table was the first thing to meet his horrified gaze. Lockhart's revolver was the second, a masked Mr Dodd the third.

'And now to work,' said Lockhart. Mr Taglioni gulped.

'Liebe Gott, that I should have to do this thing . . .'

'That is not a thing,' said Lockhart grimly and Mr Taglioni shuddered.

'Never in my life have I been called upon to stuff a person,' he muttered, rummaging in his bag. 'Why not ask an embalmer?'

'Because I want the joints to move.'

'Joints to move?'

'Arms and legs and head,' said Lockhart. 'He must be able to sit up.'

'Legs and arms and neck maybe but hips is impossible. Either sitting or standing. It must be one or the other.'

'Sitting,' said Lockhart. 'Now work.'

And so while his widow lay sleeping upstairs unaware of her recent but long-awaited bereavement, the grisly task of stuffing Mr Flawse began in the cellar. When she did wake, the old man could be heard shouting from his bedroom. And in the cellar Mr Taglioni listened and felt terrible. Mr Dodd didn't feel much better. The business of carrying buckets upstairs and disposing of their ghastly contents in the cucumber frames where they wouldn't be seen because of the snow on the glass above was not one he relished.

'They may do the cucumbers a world of good,' he muttered on his fifth trip, 'but I'm damned if they do me. I won't be able to touch cucumbers again without thinking of the poor old devil.'

He went down to the cellar and complained to Lockhart. 'Why can't we use the earth closet instead?'

'Because he didn't want to be buried and I'll see his wishes carried out,' said Lockhart.

'I wish you'd carry out a few of his innards as well,' said Mr Dodd bitterly.

What Mr Taglioni said was largely unintelligible. What he had to say he muttered in his native Italian and when Lockhart inadvisedly left the cellar for a moment he returned to find that the taxidermist had, to relieve the strain of emptying Mr Flawse, filled himself with two bottles of that late gentleman's crusted port. The combination of a drunk taxidermist elbow-deep in his lamented employer was too much for Mr Dodd. He staggered up the stairs and was greeted by the unearthly voice of the late Mr Flawse bellowing imprecations from the bedroom.

'The devil take the lot of you, ye bloodsucking swine of Satan. You couldn't be trusted not to steal the last morsel of meat from a starving beggar,' the late man bawled very appositely, and when an hour later Lockhart came up and suggested that something substantial for lunch like liver and bacon might help the taxidermist sober up, Mr Dodd would have none of it.

'Ye'll cook whatever you damned well please,' he said, 'but I'll not be eating meat this side of Candlemas.'

'Then you'll go back down and see he doesn't help himself to more wine,' said Lockhart. Mr Dodd went gingerly down to the cellar to find that Mr Taglioni had helped himself to just about everything else. What remained of Mr Flawse was not a pleasant sight. A fine figure of a man in his day, in death he was not at his best. But Mr Dodd steeled himself to his vigil while Mr Taglioni babbled on unintelligibly and delving deeper into the recesses finally demanded more lights. The expression was too close to the bone for Mr Dodd.

'You've had his bloody liver,' he shouted, 'what more bleeding lights do you need? They're in the fucking cucumber frame and if you think I'm going to get them, you can think again.'

By the time Mr Taglioni had managed to explain that by lights he meant more illumination, Mr Dodd had been sick twice and the taxidermist had a bloody nose. Lockhart came down to separate them.

'I'm not staying down here with this foreign ghoul,' said Mr Dodd vehemently. 'The way he goes on you'd not think he knew his arse from his elbow.'

'All I ask for is lights,' said the Italian, 'and he goes berserk like I asked for something terrible.'

'You'll get something terrible,' said Mr Dodd, 'if I have to stay down here with you.'

Mr Taglioni shrugged. 'You bring me here to stuff this man. I didn't ask to come. I asked not to come. Now when I stuff him you say I get something terrible. Do I need telling? No. That I don't need. What I got is something terrible enough to last me a lifetime, my memories. And what about my conscience? You think my religion permits me to go round stuffing men?'

Mr Dodd was hustled upstairs by Lockhart and told to change the tapes. The late Mr Flawse's repertoire of imprecations was getting monotonous. Even Mrs Flawse complained.

'That's the twenty-fifth time he's told Dr Magrew to get out of the house,' she shouted through her bedroom door. 'Why doesn't the wretched man go? Can't he see he's not wanted?'

Mr Dodd changed the cassette to one labelled 'Heaven and Hell, Possible Existence of.' Not that there was any possibility in his own mind of doubting the existence of the latter. What was going on in the cellar was proof positive that Hell existed. It was Heaven he wanted to be convinced about, and he was just listening to the old man's deathbed argument borrowed in part from Carlyle about the unseen mysteries of the Divine Spirit when he caught the sound of steps on the stairs. He glanced out the door and saw Dr Magrew coming up. Mr Dodd slammed the door and promptly switched the cassette back to the previous one. It was marked 'Magrew and Bullstrode, Opinions of.' Unfortunately he chose Mr Bullstrode's side and a moment later Dr Magrew was privileged to hear his dear friend, the solicitor, described by his dear friend, Mr Flawse, as litigious spawn of a syphilitic whore who should never have been born but having been should have been gelded at birth before he could milk the likes of Mr Flawse of their wealth by consistently bad advice. This opinion had at least the merit of stopping the doctor in his tracks. He had always valued Mr Flawse's judgement and was interested to hear more. Meanwhile Mr Dodd had gone to the window and looked out. The snow had thawed sufficiently to let the doctor's car through to the bridge. Now he had to think of some means of denying him access to his departed patient. He was saved by Lockhart who emerged from the cellar with the tray on which stood the remnants of Mr Taglioni's lunch.

'Ah, Dr Magrew,' he called out, shutting the cellar door firmly behind him, 'how good of you to come. Grandfather is very much better this morning.'

'So I can hear,' said the doctor as Mr Dodd tried to change the cassette and Mr Taglioni, revivified by his lunch, burst into a foul imitation of Caruso. 'Quite remarkably better by the sound of it.'

From her bedroom Mrs Flawse demanded to know if that damned doctor was back again.

'If he tells Dr Magrew to get out of the house just one more time,' she wailed, 'I think I'll go off my head.'

Dr Magrew hesitated between so many injunctions. From the bedroom Mr Flawse had switched to politics and was berating the Baldwin government of 1935 for its pusillanimity while at the same time someone in the cellar was bawling about Bella bella carissima. Lockhart shook his head.

'Come down and have a drink,' he said. 'Grandfather's in an odd frame of mind.'

Certainly Dr Magrew was. In the course of separating Mr Dodd from the taxidermist Lockhart had, to put it mildly, been bloodied and the presence in a coffee cup on the tray of what from Dr Magrew's experience he could have sworn to be a human appendix dropped there absent-mindedly by Mr Taglioni, left him badly in need of a drink. He staggered down the staircase eagerly and presently was gulping down Mr Dodd's special distilled Northumbrian whisky by the tumbler.

'You know,' he said when he felt a little better, 'I had no idea your grandfather had such a low opinion of Mr Bullstrode.'

'You don't think that could just be the result of his concussion? The fall affected his mind as you said yourself.'

Down below Mr Taglioni, left to himself, had hit the crusted port again and with it Verdi. Dr Magrew stared at the floor.

'Am I imagining things,' he asked, 'but is there someone singing in your cellar?'

Lockhart shook his head. 'I can't hear anything,' he said firmly.

'Christ,' said the doctor looking wildly round, 'you really can't?'

'Only grandfather shouting upstairs.'

'I can hear that too,' said Dr Magrew. 'But ...' He stared demoniacally at the floor. 'Well, if you say so. By the way, do you always wear a scarf over your face in the house?'

Lockhart took it off with a sanguine hand. From the cellar came a fresh burst of Neapolitan.

'I think I had better be gone,' said the doctor, staggering to his feet, 'I'm delighted your grandfather is making such good progress. I'll call again when I feel a little better myself.'

Lockhart escorted him to the door and was seeing him out when the taxidermist struck again.

'The eyes,' he shouted, 'my God I forgot to bring his eyes. Now what are we going to do?'

There was no doubting what Dr Magrew was going to do. He took one last demented look at the house and trundled off at a run down the drive to his car. Houses in which he saw human appendixes in otherwise empty coffee cups and people announced that they had forgotten to bring their eyes were not for him. He was going home to consult a fellow practitioner.

Behind him Lockhart turned blandly back into the Hall and calmed the distraught Mr Taglioni.

'I'll bring some,' he said, 'don't worry. I'll fetch a pair.'

'Where am I?' wailed the taxidermist. 'What is happening to me?'

Upstairs Mrs Flawse knew exactly where she was but had no idea what was happening to her. She peered out of the window in time to see the persistent Dr Magrew running to his car and then Lockhart appeared and walked to the peel tower. When he returned he was carrying the glass eyes of the tiger his grandfather had shot in India on his trip there in 1910. He thought they would do rather well. Old Mr Flawse had always been a ferocious man-eater.

Chapter seventeen

All that day and the next and the one following Mr Taglioni continued his gruesome task while Lockhart cooked and Mr Dodd sat in his shed and stared resentfully at the cucumber frames. In her bedroom Mrs Flawse had stood all she could of her blasted husband's voice echoing from across the landing about Heaven and Hell and guilt, sin and damnation. If the old fool would either die or stop repeating himself she wouldn't have minded but he went on and on and on, and by the third night Mrs Flawse was prepared to brave snow, sleet and storm and even heights to escape. She tied her sheets together and then tore her blankets into strips and knotted them to the sheets and the sheets to the bed and finally, donning her warmest clothes, she clambered out of the window and slid rather than climbed to the ground. The night was dark and the snow melted and against the black background of mud and moor she was invisible. She slushed off down the drive towards the bridge and had just crossed it and was trying to undo the gates when behind her she heard the sound that had welcomed her to Flawse Hall, the baying of hounds. They were still in the yard but a light shone in the window that had been her bedroom and the light had been off when she left.

She turned from the gate and ran or rather stumbled alongside The Cut in a desperate attempt to reach the hillside by the tunnel, and as she ran she heard the creak of the wooden gates to the yard and the louder baying of the hounds. The Flawse pack was on the scent again. Mrs Flawse fled on into the darkness, tripped and fell, got up, tripped again and this time fell into The Cut. It wasn't deep but the cold was intense. She tried to climb the far bank but slipped back and giving up, waded on knee-deep in the icy water towards the dark shadow of the hill and the darker hole of the great tunnel. It loomed larger and more awful with each uncertain step she took. Mrs Flawse hesitated. The black hole ahead spoke to her of Hades, the baying pack behind of Pluto, no gay cartoon of Disneyland, but rather that dread god of the infernal regions at whose altar of mere wealth she had unconsciously worshipped. Mrs Flawse was not an educated woman but she knew enough to tell that she was caught between the devil and, by way of taps, toilets, and sewers provided by the Gateshead and Newcastle Waterworks, the deep blue sea. And then as she hesitated the baying hounds were halted in their tracks and against the skyline she could see in silhouette a figure on a horse thrashing about him with a whip.

'Get back, ye scum,' shouted Lockhart, 'back to your kennels, ye scavengers of hell.'

His voice drifting with the wind reached Mrs Flawse and for once she felt grateful to her son-in-law. A moment later she knew better. Addressing Mr Dodd as he had addressed the hounds, Lockhart cursed the man for his stupidity.

'Have you forgotten the will, you damned old fool?' he demanded. 'Let the old bitch but go one mile beyond the radius of the Hall and she will forfeit the estate. So let her run and be damned.'

'I hadna thought of that,' said Mr Dodd contritely and turned his horse to follow the pack back to Flawse Hall while Lockhart rode behind. Mrs Flawse no longer hesitated. She too had forgotten the clause in the will. She would not run and be damned. With a desperate effort she scrambled from The Cut and stumbled back to the Hall. Once there she had not the strength to climb the sheets to her bedroom but tried the door. It was unlocked. She went inside and stood shivering in the darkness. A door was open to the kitchen and a light shone beneath the cellar door. Mrs Flawse needed a drink, a strong drink to warm her blood. She stepped quietly to the cellar door and opened it. A moment later her screams echoed and re-echoed through the house for there before her very eyes, naked and with an enormous scar from groin to gullet, sat old Mr Flawse on a bare wood table stained with blood and his eyes were the eyes of a tiger. Behind him stood Mr Taglioni with a piece of cotton waste which he appeared to be stuffing into her husband's skull and while he worked he hummed a tune from *The Barber of Seville*. Mrs Flawse took one look and having screamed passed out. It was Lockhart who carried her gibbering dementedly back to her room and dropped her on the bed. Then he hauled up the sheets and blankets and knotted her to the bedstead.

'Ye'll go no more a-wandering by the light of the moon,' he said cheerfully and went out locking the door. It was true. When Mr Dodd took her breakfast up he found Mrs Flawse staring dementedly at the ceiling, gibbering to herself.

Down in the cellar Mr Taglioni gibbered too. Mrs Flawse's eruption and hysteria in the cellar had completed his demoralization. It had been bad enough to stuff a dead man but to have his work interrupted in the middle of the night by a wailing widow had been too much for him.

'Take me home,' he pleaded with Lockhart, 'take me home.'

'Not before you've finished,' said Lockhart implacably. 'He's got to speak and wave his hands.'

Mr Taglioni looked up at the masked face.

'Taxidermy's one thing. Marionettes another,' he said. 'You wanted him stuffed, you got him stuffed. Now you say I got to make him speak. What you want? Miracles? You better ask God for those.'

'I'm not asking anyone. I'm telling,' said Lockhart and produced the small loudspeaker. 'You put that where his larynx is . . .'

'Was,' said Mr Taglioni, 'I no leave nothing inside.'

'Was then,' continued Lockhart, 'and then I want this receiver put in his head.' He showed Mr Taglioni the miniature receiver. Mr Taglioni was adamant.

'No room. His head is stuffed with cotton wool.'

'Well take some out and put this in and leave space for the

batteries. And while you're about it I want his jaw to move. I've an electric motor here. Look, I'll show you.'

For the rest of the morning, the late Mr Flawse was wired for sound and by the time they had finished it was possible to hear his heart beat when a switch was pulled. Even his eyes, now those of the tiger, swivelled in his head at the touch of a button on the remote control. About the only thing he couldn't do was walk or lie down flat. For the rest he looked rather healthier than he had done of late and certainly sounded as articulate.

'Right,' said Lockhart when they had tested him out, 'Now you can drink your fill.'

'Who?' said Mr Taglioni, by this time thoroughly confused. 'Him or me?'

'You,' said Lockhart and left him to his own devices and the contents of the wine cellar. He went upstairs to find that Mr Dodd was also drunk. The sound of his Master's voice issuing from that fearful effigy in the cellar had been too much even for his sturdy soul and he was half-way through a bottle of his own Northumbrian brew. Lockhart took the whisky from him.

'I'll need your help to get the old man to bed,' he said, 'he's stiff in the hip joints and needs levering round corners.'

Mr Dodd demurred but eventually between them they got Mr Flawse, clad in his red flannel nightgown, into bed where he sat up bellowing and calling on the Almighty to save his soul.

'You've got to admit he's very realistic,' said Lockhart. 'It is just a pity we didn't think of taping his utterances earlier.'

'It's more a pity we ever thought of taping them at all,' said Mr Dodd drunkenly, 'and I wish his jaw wouldna go up and down like that. It puts me in mind of a goldfish with asthma.'

'But the eyes are about right,' said Lockhart. 'I got them from the tiger.'

'Ye dinna have to tell me,' said Mr Dodd and surprisingly broke into Blake. 'Tiger, tiger burning bright in the forests of the night. What demented hand and eye framed thy awful circuitry?'

'I did,' said Lockhart proudly, 'and I'm fixing him a wheelchair so that he can move about the house on his own and I'll direct it by remote control. That way no one will suspect he isn't still alive and I'll have time to see if this Mr Boscombe in Arizona is my father.'

'Boscombe? A Mr Boscombe?' said Mr Dodd. 'And for why would you be thinking he was your father?'

'He wrote a great many letters to my mother,' said Lockhart and explained how he had got them.

'Ye'll be wasting your time ganning after the man,' said Mr Dodd. 'Miss Deyntry was right. I recall the little man and he was a poor wee thing that your mither had no time for. You had best look closer home.'

'He's the only lead I've got,' said Lockhart, 'unless you can suggest a more likely candidate.'

Mr Dodd shook his head. 'I'll tell you this though. The auld bitch has got wind of what ye're up to and knows the old man is dead. If ye gan off to America she'll find a way out of the house to alert Mr Bullstrode. Ye saw what she did the other night. The woman's desperate dangerous and there's the Italian down below is a witness to the deed. Ye hadna thought of that.'

Lockhart pondered a while. 'I was going to take him back to Manchester,' he said. 'He has no idea where he has been.'

'Aye but he's a fine knowledge of the house and he's seen our faces,' said Mr Dodd, 'and with the woman hollering that the man was stuffed it will take no time for the law to put two and two together.'

Down in the cellar Mr Taglioni had put far more than two and two together and was drinking himself insensible on crusted port. He sat surrounded by empty bottles proclaiming in garbled tones that he was the finest stuffer in the world. It was not a word he liked to use but his tongue could no longer wrap itself round anything so polysyllabic as taxidermist.

'There he goes again with his blathering and boasting,' said Mr Dodd as they stood at the top of the cellar steps, 'the finest stuffer in the world indeed. The word has too many meanings for my liking.'

Mrs Flawse shared his distaste. Tied to the bed on which she herself had been stuffed by her late stuffed husband Mr Taglioni's repertoire filled her with dread. Mr Flawse did not help. Mr Dodd had inserted a tape cassette labelled 'Family History, Findings In', which thanks to Lockhart's electronic ingenuity no sooner ended than it rewound itself and repeated its findings *ad nauseam.* Since the tape was forty-five minutes long and took three to rewind Mrs Flawse was subjected from below to Mr Taglioni's drunken boasts and from the bedroom across the landing to endless re-runs of the tale of Headman Flawse, Bishop Flawse going to the stake, and a recitation of Minstrel Flawse's song beneath the gibbet. It was this last which affected her.

'I gan noo wha ma organs gan
　When oft I lay abed,
So rither hang me upside doon
　Than by ma empty head.'

The first stanza was bad enough but the rest were even worse. By the time Mrs Flawse had heard the old man apparently demand fifteen times that Sir Oswald's arse be prised apart and he be given back his prick because he couldn't wait for Oswald to die before he had a pee, his widow was in much the same condition. Not that she wanted a prick, but she certainly couldn't wait much longer to have a pee. And all day Lockhart and Mr Dodd sat out of earshot in the kitchen debating what to do.

'We canna let the Latin go,' said Mr Dodd. 'It would be better to dispose of him altogether.'

But Lockhart's mind was working along more economical lines. Mr Taglioni's repeated boast that he was the world's finest stuffer and the ambiguity of that remark gave him pause for thought. And Mr Dodd's attitude was strange. His adamant denial that Mr Boscombe in Dry Bones was Miss Flawse's lover and his own father had been convincing. When Mr Dodd said something it was invariably true. Certainly he didn't lie to Lockhart – or hadn't in the past. And now he was stating categorically that the letters were no clue. It was what Miss Deyntry and the old Romany had warned him. 'Paper and ink will do you no good.' Lockhart accepted the fact and yet without Mr Boscombe he was without the possibility of finding his father before it was known that his grandfather was dead. Mr Dodd was right on that point. Mrs Flawse knew and knowing would tell as soon as she was released. Her screams rising to a crescendo that drowned even old Mr Flawse's Family History and Mr Taglioni's garbled utterances decided Lockhart to go to her relief. By the time he unlocked the bedroom door she was screaming that if she didn't have a pee soon it was less a question of anyone else dying than of her bursting. Lockhart untied her and she wobbled to the earth closet. When she returned to the kitchen Lockhart had made up his mind.

'I have found my father,' he announced. Mrs Flawse stared at him with loathing.

'You're a liar,' she said, 'a liar and a murderer. I saw what you had done to your grandfather and don't think . . .'

Lockhart didn't. Between them he and Mr Dodd dragged Mrs Flawse up to her room and tied her again to the bed. This time they gagged her.

'I told you the auld witch knew too much,' said Mr Dodd, 'and since she's lived for money she'll not die without it, threaten her how you may.'

'Then we must forestall her,' said Lockhart and went down to the cellar. Mr Taglioni, on to his fifth bottle, regarded him hazily through bloodshot eyes.

'Finest taxi . . . stuffer in the world. Me,' he burbled, 'fox, flowl, phleasant, you name it I'll stuff it. And now I've stuffed a man. Whatcha think of that?'

'Daddy,' said Lockhart and put his arm round Mr Taglioni's shoulder affectionately, 'my own dear daddy.'

'Daddy? Whose flucking daddy?' said Mr Taglioni, too drunk to appreciate the new role he was being cast in. Lockhart helped him to his feet and up the stairs. In the kitchen Mr Dodd was busy at the stove making a pot of coffee. Lockhart propped the taxidermist up against the settle where he tried to focus his eyes on these new and circling surroundings. It took an hour and a pint of black coffee together with a great deal of stew to sober him up. And all the time Lockhart insisted on calling him daddy. If anything more was needed to unnerve the Italian it was this.

'I'm not your flucking daddy,' he said, 'I don't know what you're talking about.'

Lockhart got up and went to his grandfather's study and unlocked the safe hidden behind the collected works of Surtees. When he returned he was carrying a washleather bag. He beckoned to Mr Taglioni to come to the table and then emptied the bag's contents out in front of him. A thousand gold sovereigns littered the scrubbed pine table. Mr Taglioni goggled at them.

'What's all that money doing there?' he asked. He picked a sovereign up and fingered it. 'Gold. Pure gold.'

'All for you, daddy,' said Lockhart.

For once Mr Taglioni didn't question the word. 'For me? You're paying me in gold for stuffing a man?'

But Lockhart shook his head. 'No, daddy, for something else.'

'What?' said the taxidermist suspiciously.

'For being my father,' said Lockhart. Mr Taglioni's eyes swivelled in his head almost as incredulously as the tiger's did in the old man.

'Your father?' he gasped. 'You want me to be your father? For why should I be your father? You must have one already.'

'I am a bastard,' said Lockhart but Mr Taglioni knew that already.

'So even a bastard must have a father. Your mother was a virgin?'

'You leave my mother out of this,' said Lockhart and Mr Dodd shoved a poker into the glowing fire of the range. By the time it was red-hot Mr Taglioni had made up his mind. Lockhart's alternatives left him little choice.

'Okay, I agree. I tell this Mr Bullstrode I am your father. I don't mind. You pay me this money. Is fine with me. Anything you say.'

Lockhart said a lot more. They concerned the likely prison sentence to be pronounced on a taxidermist who had stuffed an old man, having in all likelihood first murdered him for the thousand gold sovereigns in his safe.

'I no murdered anyone,' said Mr Taglioni frantically, 'you know that. He was dead when I came here.'

'You prove it,' said Lockhart. 'Where are his vital organs to be examined by a police surgeon and forensic expert to say when he died?'

'In the cucumber frames,' said Mr Dodd involuntarily. It was a circumstance that haunted his mind.

'Never mind that,' said Lockhart, 'the point I'm making is that you'll never be able to prove you didn't kill my grandfather and this money is the motive. Besides, we don't like foreigners in these parts. The jury would be biased against you.'

Mr Taglioni acknowledged that likelihood. Certainly everything else in whatever parts he was seemed to have a bias against him.

'Okay, okay. I say what you want me to say,' he said, 'and then I go with all this money? Right?'

'Right,' said Lockhart, 'you have my word as a gentleman.'

That night Mr Dodd went to Black Pockrington and, having first collected Miss Deyntry's car from the old lime kiln, drove to Hexham to inform Mr Bullstrode that he and Dr Magrew were required next day at the Hall to certify the sworn statement of Lockhart's father that he was indeed responsible for Miss Flawse's pregnancy. He then returned the car to Divit Hall.

Lockhart and Mr Taglioni sat on in the kitchen while the Italian learnt his lines. Upstairs Mrs Flawse struggled with her own. She had made up her mind that nothing, not even the prospect of a fortune, was going to keep her lying there in wait for a similar end to that of her husband. Come hell or high water she was going to get loose from the bed and absent from the Hall, and not even the thought of being pursued by the Flawse pack would deter her from making her escape. Unable to express herself vocally because of the gag, she concentrated on the ropes that tied her to the iron bedstead. She pushed her hands down and pulled them back over and over again with a tenacity that was a measure of her fear.

And in Hexham Mr Bullstrode pertinaciously tried to persuade Dr Magrew to return with him to Flawse Hall the next morning. Dr Magrew was not easily induced. His last visit had had a quite remarkable adverse effect on him.

'Bullstrode,' he said, 'it does not come easily to me in my professional capacity to reveal the confidences of a man I have known so many years and who may and indeed probably is at this moment on his deathbed, but I have to tell you that old Edwin had harsh things to say about you when last I heard him.'

'Indeed,' said Mr Bullstrode, 'he was doubtless rambling in delirium. You cannot rely on the sayings of a senile old man.'

'True,' said Dr Magrew, 'but there was a certain precision about some of his comments that didn't suggest senility to me.'

'Such as?' said Mr Bullstrode. But Dr Magrew was not prepared to say. 'I will not repeat slander,' he said, 'but I am not of a mind to go back to the Hall until Edwin is either dead or ready to apologize to you.'

Mr Bullstrode took a more philosophical and financially advantageous view of the matter. 'As his personal physician you know best,' he said, 'but for myself I do not intend to forgo my professional fee as his solicitor, and the estate is a large one and will take a good deal of winding up. Besides, the will is sufficiently ambiguous to provide fertile ground for litigation. Now if Lockhart has found his father I doubt very much if Mrs Flawse will not contest the issue and the pickings of such a lengthy court action would be considerable. It would be foolish after so many years amicable acquaintance with Edwin to fail him in his hour of need.'

'Be it on your own head,' said Dr Magrew. 'I will come with you but I warn you there are strange occurrences going on at the Hall and I care not for them.'

Chapter eighteen

He liked them even less when the following morning Mr Bullstrode stopped his car at the gated bridge and waited for Mr Dodd to come and unlock it. Even at this distance Mr Flawse's voice could be heard cursing the Almighty and blaming him for the state of the universe. As usual Mr Bullstrode's point of view was more pragmatic.

'I cannot say I agree with his sentiments,' he said, 'but if as you assert he has said some unkind words about me it would appear that I am at least in good company.'

He wasn't ten minutes later. Mr Taglioni's appearance did not inspire confidence. The taxidermist had been through too many inexplicable horrors to be at his best and while Lockhart had spent half the night seeing to it that his 'father' was word perfect in his new role, drink, fear and sleeplessness had done nothing to improve his looks. Mr Taglioni's clothes too had suffered. Provided by Lockhart from his grandfather's wardrobe to replace the bloodstained garments the taxidermist had been wearing before, nothing fitted at all precisely. Mr Bullstrode looked at him with dismay and Dr Magrew with medical concern.

'He doesn't look a very fit man to me,' he whispered to the solicitor as they followed Lockhart into the study.

'I cannot express an opinion on his health,' said Mr Bullstrode, 'but the word fit does not apply to his apparel.'

'It doesn't apply to a man who is shortly to be flogged within an inch of his life,' said Dr Magrew. Mr Bullstrode stopped in his tracks.

'Good Lord,' he muttered, 'that stipulation had quite passed out of my mind.'

It had never entered Mr Taglioni's. All he wanted to do was to get out of this dreadful house with his life, reputation and money still intact.

'What are we waiting for?' he asked as Mr Bullstrode hesitated.

'Quite,' said Lockhart, 'let us get on with the business.'

Mr Bullstrode swallowed. 'Would it not be more proper to have present your grandfather and his wife?' he inquired. 'After all the one drew the will and last testament up and the other would appear to be about to be deprived of those benefits she would otherwise have received under it.'

'My grandfather has stated that he does not feel up to leaving his bed,' said Lockhart and waited while Mr Flawse's voice made fresh inroads into, this time, Dr Magrew's professional reputation. 'I think I can safely say the same for my step-grandmother. She is at present indisposed and naturally my father's appearance here today, with all its consequences for her financially, might be said to chafe her more than a little.'

It was no more than the truth. A night spent rubbing the ropes that bound her hands up and down against the iron bedstead had indeed chafed her but she still persisted while down in the study Mr Taglioni repeated word for word what he had been taught. Mr Bullstrode wrote down his words and was in spite of himself impressed. Mr Taglioni stated that he had been employed as a casual labourer by the Waterworks at the time and being an Italian had naturally attracted the attention of Miss Flawse.

'I couldn't help it,' he protested, 'I am Italian and English ladies, you know how English ladies like ...'

'Quite,' said Mr Bullstrode who knew what was coming and wasn't prepared to listen to it. 'And so you fell in love?' he continued to improve upon the singularly distressing tastes in the matter of foreigners displayed by the late Miss Clarissa Flawse.

'Yes. We fall in love. You could put it like that.'

Muttering to himself that he wished to hell he couldn't Mr Bullstrode wrote this down. 'And then what?'

'What do you think? I stuff her.'

Mr Bullstrode wiped his bald head with a handkerchief while Dr Magrew's eyes blazed lividly at the Italian.

'You had sexual intercourse with Miss Flawse?' said Mr Bullstrode when he could bring himself to speak.

'Sexual intercourse? I don't know. We fuck. Right? First I fuck her. Then she fuck me. Then—'

'So help me God someone else is going to fuck you if you don't shut up,' shouted Dr Magrew.

'Now what I say wrong?' asked Mr Taglioni. 'You ...'

Lockhart intervened. 'I don't think we need go into any further details,' he said pacifically. Mr Bullstrode expressed his fervent agreement. 'And you are prepared to swear on oath that to the best of your knowledge you are the father of this man?' he asked.

Mr Taglioni said he was. 'Then if you'll just sign here,' Mr Bullstrode went on and handed him the pen. Mr Taglioni signed.

His signature was witnessed by Dr Magrew.

'And may one ask what your present occupation is?' Mr Bullstrode asked inadvisedly.

'You mean what I do?' said Mr Taglioni. Mr Bullstrode nodded. Mr Taglioni hesitated and then, after so many lies, decided to tell the truth. Before Dr Magrew could get at him Lockhart had hustled the Italian out of the room. Behind him Mr Bullstrode and Dr Magrew were left speechless.

'Did you ever hear the like?' said Dr Magew when at last his palpitations had abated somewhat. 'The bloody swine has the gall to stand there and ...'

'My dear Magrew,' said Mr Bullstrode, 'I can only say that I now understand why the old man stipulated in his will that the bastard's father should be flogged to within an inch of his life. He must have had some inkling, you know.'

Dr Magrew agreed. 'Personally I would have preferred him to have stipulated something stronger,' he said, 'like half a mile beyond it.'

'Beyond what?' asked the solicitor.

'Beyond his life,' said Dr Magrew and helped himself to some of Mr Flawse's whisky which stood on a tray in the corner. Mr Bullstrode joined him.

'That raises a very interesting point,' he said when they had drunk one another's health and the ill-health of Mr Taglioni. 'Which is quite simply what constitutes "within an inch of his life". The question of measurement would seem to me to be crucial.'

'I hadn't thought of that,' said Dr Magrew, 'and now that you mention it I can see great objections. A more exact statement would, I suppose, have been within an inch of his death.'

'That still doesn't answer the question. Life is time. We speak of a man's lifetime, not his life-space. And an inch is not a function of time.'

'But we also speak of a long life,' said Dr Magrew, 'and that surely implies spatial extension. Now if we assume that by a long life we mean eighty years, and I think that a fair estimate, I suppose we can take as our standard three-score years and ten. Personally I am glad to suspect from the colour of that wretched Italian's complexion and his general physique that the swine has a far shorter life expectancy than that laid down in the Bible. Let us say to be on the safe side, sixty years. Now we have to transfer an inch to a scale of time relative to sixty years ...'

They were interrupted by the entrance of Lockhart who announced that to avoid disturbing his grandfather and distressing Mrs Flawse he had decided to conduct the second part of the ceremony in the peel tower.

'Dodd's getting him ready for the flogging,' he said. 'The two old men followed him out still deep in disputation as to what constituted to within an inch of life.

'An inch of life,' said Dr Magrew, 'leaves us in fact two inches to play with, one before death and one after. Now death itself is an indeterminate state and before acting it would be as well to decide what we mean by it. Some authorities define it as the moment the heart stops beating; others would have it that the brain being the organ of consciousness is capable of subsisting beyond the moment of time in which the heart stops functioning. Now, sir, let us define . . .'

'Dr Magrew,' said Mr Bullstrode as they crossed the dwarf garden, 'as a lawyer I am not qualified to judge the issue. The term "to within an inch of his life" does not allow of the man dying. I would not have been party to a last will and testament which stipulated the murder of Lockhart's father no matter how strongly I may feel about the matter personally. Murder is against the law . . .'

'So is flogging,' said Dr Magrew. 'To lay down in a will that a man must be flogged to within an inch of his life is to make us both parties to a crime.'

They had entered the peel tower and his voice echoed among the dusty battle-flags and ancient armour. An eyeless tiger bared its teeth above the great open hearth. Manacled to the opposite wall, Mr Taglioni gave voice to his objections.

'What do you mean flogged?' he screamed but Mr Dodd put a bullet in his mouth.

'To give him something to bite on,' he explained. 'It was an old custom in the army.'

Mr Taglioni spat the bullet out. 'You crazy?' he yelled. 'What more do you want from me? First I got to . . .'

'Keep the bullet between your teeth,' interrupted Mr Dodd and replaced it. Mr Taglioni struggled with the bullet and finally got it into a corner of his cheek where it bulged like a quid of tobacco.

'I tell you I don't awant to be flogged. I came here to stuff someone. I stuff him. Now . . .'

'Thank you, Mr Dodd,' said Mr Bullstrode as that servant silenced the Italian with his grimy handkerchief. 'If anything persuades me that the will ought to be carried out according to the spirit of the law rather than the letter it is his constant reference to stuffing. I find the term singularly objectionable, I must say.'

'And was I not mistaken in thinking that the gender was wrong too?' said Dr Magrew, 'I could have sworn he said "Him".'

Mr Taglioni would have sworn too if he could but Mr Dodd's handkerchief in combination with the bullet was doing things to his taste buds and his breathing that took what was left of his mind off external circumstances. He turned from white to damson. In a far corner of the hall Lockhart was practising with his horsewhip on a figure in armour and the room rang to the clang of the whip. The sound recalled Mr Bullstrode to his professional rectitude.

'I am still unpersuaded that we should proceed before determining the exact measurement of an inch of life,' he said. 'Perhaps we should consult Mr Flawse himself to find out what precisely he meant.'

'I doubt you'll get a rational answer out of the man,' said Mr Dodd, all the while wondering which cassette would give an even approximate answer to the question. He was saved the trouble by Dr Magrew. Mr Taglioni's complexion had progressed from damson to off-black.

'I think it would be as well to allow your father some air,' he told Lockhart, 'my Hippocratic oath will not allow me to attend death by suffocation. Of course if this were a hanging . . .'

As Mr Dodd removed the handkerchief and bullet Mr Taglioni regained a better complexion and a volubility that was wasted on his audience. He stood shouting in Italian. Finally, unable to hear themselves dispute, Dr Magrew and Mr Bullstrode went out into the garden in disgust.

'I find his cowardice contemptible,' said Mr Bullstrode, 'but the Italians fought very badly in the war.'

'Which hardly helps us solve our present problem,' said Dr Magrew, 'and as a man of some compassion even for such swine I would suggest that we act in strict accordance to the will and flog the brute to within an inch of his life.'

'But . . .' began Mr Bullstrode. Dr Magrew went back into the hall and spoke to Mr Dodd above the din. Presently Mr Dodd left the hall and returned five minutes later with a ruler and a pencil. Dr Magrew took them and approached Mr Taglioni. Placing the ruler an inch from his shoulder and marking the point with the pencil he proceeded down the Italian's right side making pencil marks on the stucco wall and joining them together so that they formed an outline one inch from the man.

'I think that is precise,' he announced proudly. 'Lockhart, my boy, you may go ahead and flog the wall up to the pencil line and you will have flogged the man to within an inch of his life. I think that satisfies to the letter the conditions of your grandfather's will.'

But as Lockhart advanced with the whip, Mr Taglioni fulfilled the old man's last testament to the spirit. He slumped down the wall and was silent. Lockhart looked at him in annoyance.

'Why's he gone that funny colour?' he asked. Dr Magrew opened his bag and took out his stethoscope. A minute later he shook his head and pronounced Mr Taglioni dead.

'That's torn it,' said Mr Bullstrode, 'now what the hell do we do?'

But the question was to remain unanswered for the time being. From within the house there came a series of terrible shrieks. Mrs Flawse had freed herself and had evidently discovered the full extent of her late husband's dismemberment. As the little group in the peel hall stood and, with the exception of Mr Taglioni, listened, the shrieks turned to insane laughter.

'Curse the woman,' said Mr Dodd and charged towards the door, 'I should have known better than to have left the bitch alone so long.' He dashed across the yard and into the house. Lockhart and his grandfather's two old friends followed. As they entered the Hall they saw Mrs Flawse standing at the top of the stairs while Mr Dodd writhed at the bottom and clutched his groin.

'Get her from behind,' he advised Lockhart, 'she's got me in the front.'

'The woman's insane,' said Dr Magrew unnecessarily as Lockhart headed for the back stairs. Mrs Flawse was bawling about the old man being dead and not lying down.

'Go see for yourselves,' she cried and scuttled into her room. Dr Magrew and Mr Bullstrode went cautiously up the stairs.

'If as you say the woman is *non compos mentis*,' said Mr Bullstrode, 'that only makes what has just occurred all the more regrettable. Having parted with her mind she has also relinquished any right to the estate under the will thus negating the necessity for that disgusting foreigner's statement.'

'Not to mention the swine's death,' said Dr Magrew. 'I suppose we had better pay our compliments to Edwin.'

They turned towards old Mr Flawse's bedroom while at the foot of the stairs Mr Dodd tried to dissuade them.

'He's not seeing anyone,' he shouted but the truth of this remark escaped them. By the time Lockhart, coming stealthily up the back stairs to avoid being kicked in the groin by his demented mother-in-law, arrived, the landing was empty and Dr Magrew had taken his stethoscope out and was applying it to Mr Flawse's chest. It was not the wisest of moves and Mr Flawse's subsequent ones were appalling to behold. Either the doctor's bedside manner or Mr Bullstrode's accidental treading on the remote control activated the mechanism for the old man's partial animation. His arms waved wildly, the tiger's eyes rolled in his head, his mouth opened and shut and his legs convulsed. Only the sound was off, the sound and the bedclothes which his legs kicked off the bed so that the full extent of his rewiring was revealed. Mr Taglioni had not chosen the kindest spot for the wires to extrude and they hung like some terrible electronic urethra. As Mr Taglioni had said at the time, it was the last place anyone examining him would think of looking. It was certainly the last place Dr Magrew and Mr Bullstrode wanted to look but by the very complexity of the wires they couldn't take their eyes off the thing.

'The junction box and earth,' Lockhart explained adding a cricketing term to their confusion, 'and the aerial. The amplifier is under the bed and I've only got to turn the volume up . . .'

'Don't, for God's sake, don't do anything of the sort,' pleaded Mr Bullstrode, unable to distinguish between spatial volume and output and convinced that he was about to be privy to an erection. Mr Flawse's reactions were awful enough without that dreadful addition.

'I've got him on ten watts per channel,' Lockhart went on but Dr Magrew interrupted. 'As a medical man I have never been in favour of euthanasia,' he gasped, 'but there's such a thing as sustaining life beyond the bounds of human reason and to wire a man's . . . Dear God!'

Ignoring Mr Bullstrode's plea Lockhart had turned the volume up and besides twitching and jerking the old man now gave voice.

'Twas ever thus with us,' he bellowed, a statement Dr Magrew felt certain must be untrue, 'Flawse blood runs in our veins and carries with it the bacteria of our ancestral sins. Aye, sins and sanctity so intertwined there's many a Flawse gone to the block a martyr to his forebears' loves and lusts. Would that it were not so, this determinism of inheritance, but I have known myself too well to doubt the urgency of my inveterate desires . . .'

There was equally no doubting the urgency of Dr Magrew's and Mr Bullstrode's desires. They wanted to get the hell out of the room and away as fast as their legs would carry them but the magnetism of the old man's voice (the cassette was labelled 'Flawse, Edwin Tyndale, Self-Opinions of') held them – that and Lockhart and Mr Dodd standing implacably between them and the door.

'And I must say, congenitally speaking, that I am as much a moss trooper at heart as I am an Englishman and a man of so-called civilization, albeit that civilization to which I was born and bred has gone and taken with it that pride in being an Englishman which so sustained us in the past. Where is the proud craftsman now, and where the self-reliance of the working man? Where too the managers of men and great machines that were the envy of the world? All gone and in their place the Englishman a beggar has become, the world's beggar, whining cap in hand for alms to help support him though he does no work nor now produces goods the world will buy. All cloth is shoddy and all standards dropped. And this because no politician dared to tell the truth but bowed and cringed and bought their votes to empty power by promises as empty as themselves. Such scum as Wilson, aye and Tories too, would make Keir Hardy and Disraeli both agree, this was not their meaning of democracy, this bread and circuses that makes of men a mass and then despises them. So has old England gone to pot since I was born and laws being broken by the men who passed them from Bills to Acts of Parliament, being broken by the Ministers themselves, what law is left a man should now obey when all are outlawed by bureaucracy. Aye, bureaucrats who pay themselves with money begged and borrowed, or stolen from the pockets of the working man. These civil-service maggots on the body politic who feed upon the rotting corpse of England that they killed . . .'

Lockhart switched the old man off and Dr Magrew and Mr Bullstrode breathed a sigh of terrible relief. It was short-lived. Lockhart had more in store for them.

'I had him stuffed,' he said proudly, 'and you, doctor, proclaimed him healthy when he was already dead. As Dodd's my witness so you did.'

Mr Dodd nodded. 'I heard the doctor so proclaim,' he said.

Lockhart turned to Mr Bullstrode. 'And you were instrumental in the killing of my father,' he said. 'The sin of patricide . . .'

'I did nothing of the sort,' said the solicitor. 'I refuse . . .'

'Did you or did you not draw up my grandfather's will?' he asked. Mr Bullstrode said nothing. 'Aye, you did and thus we three all stand convicted of complicity in murder. I would have you consider the consequences carefully.'

Already it seemed to Dr Magrew and Mr Bullstrode that in Lockhart's voice they heard the unmistakable tone of the old man sitting stuffed beside them, the same unshakable arrogance and that dread logic that neither port nor learned disputation nor, now it seemed, even death could totally dispel. They followed his instructions to the letter and considered the consequences very well indeed.

'I must confess to finding myself perplexed,' said Mr Bullstrode finally. 'As your grandfather's oldest friend I feel bound to act to his best advantage and in a way he would have liked.'

'I doubt very much he would have liked being stuffed,' said Dr Magrew. 'I know I wouldn't.'

'But on the other hand, as an officer of the law and a Commissioner of Oaths I have my duty to perform. My friendship contradicts my duty. Now if it were possible to say that Mr Taglioni died a natural death . . .'

He looked expectantly at Dr Magrew.

'I can't believe a coroner would find the circumstances propitious to such a verdict. A man chained by his wrists to a wall may die a natural death but he chose an unnatural position to do it in.'

There was a gloomy silence and finally Mr Dodd spoke. 'We

could add him to the contents of the cucumber frames,' he said.

'The contents of the cucumber frames?' said Dr Magrew and Mr Bullstrode simultaneously, but Lockhart ignored their curiosity.

'My grandfather expressed a wish not to be buried,' he said, 'and I intend to see his wishes carried out.'

The two old men looked unwillingly at their dead friend. 'I cannot see him sitting to anyone's advantage in a glass case,' said Dr Magrew, 'and it would be a mistake to suppose we can maintain the fiction of his life perpetually. I gather that his widow knows.'

Mr Dodd agreed with him.

'On the other hand,' said Lockhart, 'we can always bury Mr Taglioni in his place. Grandfather is so jointed it would take a conspicuously right-angled coffin to fit him in and I don't suppose the publicity attached to such a contraption would do us any good.'

Mr Bullstrode and Dr Magrew were of the same opinion.

'Then Mr Dodd will find him a suitable sitting place,' said Lockhart, 'and Mr Taglioni will have the honour of joining the Flawse ancestors at Black Pockrington. Dr Magrew, I trust you have no objections to making out a certificate of death, of natural death, for my grandfather?'

Dr Magrew looked doubtfully at his stuffed patient.

'Let us just say that I won't let appearances to the contrary influence my judgement,' he said. 'I suppose I could always put it that he shuffled off this mortal coil.'

'A thousand natural shocks that flesh is heir to, would certainly seem to fit the case,' said Mr Bullstrode.

And so it was agreed.

Two days later a solemn cortège left Flawse Hall led by the brougham in which lay the coffin containing Mr Taglioni. It made its melancholy way along the gated road to the church at Black Pockrington where, after a short service in which the Vicar spoke movingly and with unconscious percipience about the dead man's love of wild life and its preservation, the taxidermist was laid to rest beneath a tombstone which proclaimed him Edwin Tyndale Flawse of Flawse Hall. Born 1887 and

Gone to His Maker 1977. Below Lockhart had had inscribed a suitably enigmatic verse for them both.

'Ask not who look upon this stone
If he who lies here, lies alone.
Two fathers share this plot of land;
The one acquired, the other grand.'

Mr Bullstrode and Dr Magrew looking upon it found it appropriate if not in the best of taste.

'I dislike the emphasis on lies,' said Dr Magrew.

'I still have grave reservations about Mr Taglioni's claim to be the bastard's father,' said Mr Bullstrode. 'That "acquired" has a nasty ring to it but I don't suppose we shall ever know the whole truth.'

'I sincerely hope no one else does,' said Dr Magrew. 'Do we know if he left a widow?'

Mr Bullstrode said he thought it best not to inquire. Certainly Mr Flawse's widow did not attend the funeral. She wandered the house dementedly and occasionally wailed, but her cries were drowned by the whines of the Flawse hounds baying the passing of their creator. And occasionally as if in royal salute there came the boom of a gun firing on the artillery range to the west.

'I wish the old bitch would go the same way herself,' said Lockhart after the funeral breakfast. 'It would save a lot of trouble.'

'Aye, it would that,' Mr Dodd agreed. 'It never does to have your mither-in-law living in the same house with a young couple. And you'll be moving in with your wife shortly na doubt.'

'As soon as I have made financial arrangements, Mr Dodd,' said Lockhart. 'I have one or two matters still to attend to in the south.'

Next day he caught the train from Newcastle and by evening was back in Sandicott Crescent.

Chapter nineteen

There everything had changed. The houses had all been sold, even Mr O'Brain's, and the Crescent was once more its quiet undisturbed suburban self. In Jessica's bank account £659,000 nestled to her credit, the manager's effusiveness and the great expectations of the Chief Collector of Taxes who could hardly wait to apply the regulations governing Capital Gains. Lockhart's million pounds in damages from Miss Goldring and her erstwhile publishers were lodged in a bank in the City acquiring interest but otherwise untouchable by the tax authorities whose mandate did not allow them to lay hands on wealth obtained by such socially productive methods as gambling, filling in football pool coupons correctly, playing the horses or winning £50,000 by investing one pound in Premium Bonds. Even bingo prizes remained inviolate. So for the time being did Jessica's fortune and Lockhart intended it to remain that way.

'All you have to do,' he told her next morning, 'is to see the manager and tell him you are withdrawing the entire sum in used one-pound notes. You understand?'

Jessica said she did and went down to the bank with a large empty suitcase. It was still large and empty when she returned.

'The manager wouldn't let me,' she said tearfully, 'he said it was inadvisable and anyway I have to give a week's notice before I can withdraw money in my deposit account.'

'Oh did he?' said Lockhart. 'In that case we will go down again this afternoon and give him a week's notice.'

The meeting in the bank manager's office did not go smoothly. The knowledge that so valued a customer intended to ignore his advice and withdraw such an enormous sum in such small denominations had rubbed away a great deal of his effusiveness.

'In used one-pound notes?' he said incredulously. 'You surely can't mean that. The work involved . . .'

'Will go some way to making good the profit you have received from my wife's deposit,' said Lockhart. 'You charge higher rates for overdrafts than you pay for deposits.'

'Yes, well we have to,' said the manager. 'After all . . .'

'And you also have to return the money to customers when they require it and in the legal tender they choose,' continued Lockhart, 'and if my wife wants used one-pound notes.'

'I can't imagine what for,' said the manager, 'I would have thought it the height of folly for you to leave this building with a suitcase of untraceable notes. You might be robbed in the street.'

'We might equally well be robbed in here,' said Lockhart, 'and to my way of thinking we have been by the discrepancy between your rates of interest. The value of that money has been depreciating thanks to inflation ever since you've had it. You won't deny that.'

The manager couldn't. 'It's hardly our fault that inflation is a national problem,' he said. 'Now if you want some advice as to the best investment . . .'

'We have one in mind,' said Lockhart. 'Now, we will abide by our undertaking not to withdraw the money without giving you a week's notice provided you let us have the money in used pound notes. I hope that is clear.'

'Yes,' said the manager for whom it wasn't but who didn't like the look on Mr Flawse's face. 'If you will come in on Thursday it will be ready for you.'

Jessica and Lockhart went back to Number 12 and spent the week packing.

'I think it would be best to send the furniture up by British Rail,' said Lockhart.

'But don't they lose things? I mean look what happened to mummy's car.'

'They have the advantage, my dear, that while things frequently don't arrive at their proper destination they invariably fail to be returned to their point of departure. I rely on this inefficiency to prevent anyone knowing where we have gone to.'

'Oh, Lockhart, you are clever,' said Jessica. 'I hadn't thought of that. But why are you addressing that packing-case to Mr Jones in Edinburgh? We don't know any Mr Jones in Edinburgh.'

'My love,' said Lockhart, 'no more we do and no more does British Rail but I will be there at the station with a rented van to collect it and I very much doubt if anyone will be able to trace us.'

'You mean we're going to hide?' said Jessica.

'Not hide,' said Lockhart, 'but since I have been classified as statistically and bureaucratically non-existent and thereby ineligible to those benefits the Welfare State is said to provide, I have not the slightest intention of providing the State with any of those benefits we have been able to accrue. In short not one penny in income tax, not one penny in Capital Gains Tax, and not one penny in anything. I don't exist and being non-existent intend to reap my reward.'

'I hadn't thought of it like that,' said Jessica, 'but you're quite right. After all fair's fair.'

'Wrong,' said Lockhart. 'Nothing is fair.'

'Well, they do say "All's fair in love and war", darling,' said Jessica.

'Which is to invert the meaning of the word,' said Lockhart, 'or to reduce it to mean that there are no rules governing one's conduct. In which case all is fair in love, war and tax evasion. Isn't that true, Bouncer?'

The bull-terrier looked up and wagged his stump. He had taken to the Flawse family. They seemed to look with favour on those ferocious attributes for which he and his fellow bull-terriers had been bred, namely the biting of things and hanging on like grim death.

And so by the following Thursday the contents of the house had been packed and dispatched to Edinburgh by British Rail to be collected there by Mr Jones and it only remained to go to the bank and fill the suitcase with the used one-pound notes. Lockhart had already withdrawn his million in the same form from his bank in the City. The manager there had been more cooperative, largely thanks to Lockhart's explanation that he needed the money immediately as he was conducting a little transaction concerning oil wells with the Sheik of Araby who wanted his money in coinage, and preferably in five penny pieces. The thought of counting one million pounds out in fivepenny pieces had so daunted the manager that he had done his utmost to persuade Lockhart to accept one-pound notes. And Lockhart had reluctantly agreed provided they were used.

'Why used?' asked the manager. 'Surely new notes would be preferable?'

'The Sheik has a suspicious mind,' said Lockhart. 'He asked

for coins to ensure that they were real money and not forged. If I take him new notes he will immediately suppose he is being swindled.'

'But he could easily check with us or the Bank of England,' said the manager, who had not kept up with Britain's declining reputation in currency matters.

'Good God,' he muttered when Lockhart explained the Sheik genuinely believed the old saying that an Englishman's word was his bond and consequently thought all Englishmen liars by virtue in the fall in the value of British bonds, 'that it should have come to this.'

But he had handed over one million pounds in used notes and had been thankful to see the back of such a disillusioning customer.

The bank manager in East Pursley was less easily persuaded.

'I still think you are acting most unwisely,' he told Jessica when she entered with the suitcase. 'Your mother, I feel sure, would never have followed such a very rash procedure. She was always extremely careful where money was concerned and she had a shrewd mind financially speaking. I can recall her advice in 1972 to buy gold. I wish now that I had followed it.'

And Mrs Flawse's interest in gold continued. As he spoke she was following its trail from the Hall and every few yards along the path she stopped to pick up another gold sovereign. Ahead of her Mr Dodd walked steadily and every so often dropped another from the late Mr Taglioni's reimbursement. By the time he had covered a thousand yards he had dropped two hundred sovereigns on the path, one every five yards. After that he lengthened the space to twenty yards but still Mrs Flawse, oblivious to all else, followed, muttering greedily to herself. By the two-thousand-yard mark Mr Dodd had dropped two hundred and fifty and Mrs Flawse had picked as many up. And all the time the trail of glittering gold led west past the pine trees by the reservoir out on to the open fell. At three thousand yards Mr Dodd had still seven hundred sovereigns left in the washleather bag. He paused beneath a sign which said 'DANGER. MINISTRY OF DEFENCE FIRING-RANGE. ENTRY STRICTLY FORBIDDEN', and considered its message and the morality of his action. Then observing the mist that drifted across the artillery range and being a man of honour decided that he must proceed. 'What's good for the goose is good for the gander,' he muttered and then changed it to what was bad for the goose necessitated some risk to the gander. He dropped more coins, this time closer together to quicken the pace. At four thousand yards he was down to five hundred sovereigns and at five thousand the washleather bag still held four hundred. And as the money thickened on the ground so did the mist above it. At eight thousand yards Mr Dodd emptied the remnants on the ground, scattering them in the heather to be searched for. Then he turned and ran. Mrs Flawse was nowhere to be seen but her demented muttering came though the mist. So did the first shell. It burst on the hillside and sent shrapnel scudding past Mr Dodd's head and he redoubled his pace. Mrs Flawse didn't. Deaf to the sound of the artillery she walked on, stopping and stooping and gathering the golden hoard which like some legend come to life held her attention to the exclusion of all else. If this trail of bullion continued she would be a rich woman. The market value of each old sovereign was twenty-six pounds and gold had been rising. And already she had collected seven hundred of the glittering coins. Mrs Flawse foresaw a splendid future. She would leave the Hall. She would live in luxury with yet another husband, a young one this time to be bullied and put to work and made to serve her sexual requirements. With each stop and stoop she was more inflamed with greed and lust and made an audit of her good fortune. Finally at eight thousand yards the trail dwindled and stopped. But the gold gleamed in the heather all round and she scrabbled with her fingers for each remaining one. 'I mustn't miss any,' she muttered.

At four thousand yards to the south the men of the Royal Artillery were equally determined not to miss their target. They couldn't see it but the range was right and having bracketed it they prepared to fire a salvo. Ahead of them Mrs Flawse found the last coin and sat on the ground with the gold gathered in her skirt and began to count. 'One, two, three, four, five . . .' She got no further. The Royal Artillery had lived up to their reputation and the six-gun salvo had scored a direct hit. Where Mrs Flawse had been sitting there was a large crater around whose perimeter lay scattered, like golden confetti from some extravagant wedding, one thousand sovereigns. But then Mrs Flawse had always married money. Or, as she had been told as a child by her avaricious mother, 'Don't marry money, my dear, go where money is.' And Mrs Flawse had gone.

Mr Dodd had too but in a much more lively manner. He went with a clear conscience. He had put his own life at risk to be rid of the auld bitch and as the poet had it 'Liberty's in every blow! Let us do or die!' and Mr Dodd had done for liberty what he could and was still alive. As he strode back to Flawse Hall he was whistling 'Gin a body meet a body, Coming through the rye. Gin a body kill a body, Need a body cry?' Aye, old Robbie Burns knew what he was talking about, he thought, even with a little amendment to his meaning. And when he reached the Hall he lit a fire in the old man's study and fetching his pipes sat on the settle in the kitchen and played 'Twa Corbies' in elegiac recognition that o'er Mrs Flawse's white bones already bare the wind shall blaw for evermair. He was still playing when the sound of a horn blown from the locked gate on the bridge sent him running down the drive to welcome Lockhart and his wife.

'The Flawses are back at the Hall,' he said as he opened the gate. 'It's a grand day.'

'Aye, it's good to be back for good,' said Lockhart.

That evening Lockhart dined in his grandfather's place at the oval mahogany table with Jessica sitting opposite him. By candlelight she looked more innocent and lovely than ever and Lockhart lifted his glass to her. He had come into his gift again as the gipsy had foretold and the knowledge that he was now truly head of the Flawse family freed him from the imposed chasteness of the past. Later while Bouncer and the collie eyed one another warily in the kitchen and Mr Dodd played a gay tune of his own composing to celebrate the occasion, Lockhart and Jessica lay not only in one another's arms but something more.

Such was their happiness that it was not until after a late breakfast that any mention was made of Mrs Flawse's absence.

'I havena seen her since yesterday,' said Mr Dodd. 'She was away across the fell in rather better spirits than of late.'

Lockhart investigated her bedroom and found the bed had not been slept in.

'Aye, there's a discrepancy there,' Mr Dodd agreed, 'but I have a notion she's taking her rest all the same.'

But Jessica was too enchanted by the house to miss her mother. She went from room to room looking at the portraits and the fine old furniture and making plans for the future.

'I think we'll have the nursery in grandfather's old dressing-room,' she told Lockhart, 'don't you think that would be a good idea? Then we'll have baby near us.'

Lockhart agreed with everything she suggested. His mind was on other things than babies. He and Mr Dodd conferred in the study.

'You've put the money in the whisky wall with the man?' he asked.

'Aye, the trunk and the suitcases are well hidden,' said Mr Dodd, 'but you said that no one will come looking.'

'But I cannot be certain,' said Lockhart, 'and it's necessary to prepare for contingencies and I dinna intend to be dispossessed of my gains. If they cannot find the money they can seize the house and everything in it. I have mind to prepare for that eventuality in advance.'

'It would be a hard place to take by force,' said Mr Dodd, 'but perhaps you have other intentions.'

Lockhart said nothing. His pen doodled on the pad in front of him and drew a moss trooper pendant.

'I would rather avoid that necessity,' he said after a long silence. 'I'll have a word with Mr Bullstrode first. He always dealt with my grandfather's tax problems. You'll go to the telephone in Pockrington and send for him.'

Next day Mr Bullstrode arrived to find Lockhart sitting at the desk in the study and it seemed to the solicitor that a more than subtle change had come over the young man he had known as the bastard.

'I would have ye know, Bullstrode,' said Lockhart when they had exchanged preliminaries, 'that I have no intention of paying Death Duties on the estate.'

Mr Bullstrode cleared his throat.

'I think we can find a way to avoid any large assessment,' he said. 'The estate has always been run at a loss. Your grandfather tended to deal only in cash without receipt and besides I have a certain influence with Wyman as his solicitor.'

'Why, man?' said Lockhart brusquely.

'Well, to be frank because I handled his divorce for him and I doubt he would want some of the details of, shall we say, his sexual propensities whispered abroad,' Mr Bullstrode explained misinterpreting the question.

'I dinna care a fig what the bloodsucker does abed,' said Lockhart, 'his name is Wyman?'

'As a matter of fact you've more or less put your finger on what he does abed. Substitute for blood a certain appendage and . . .'

'The name Wyman, Bullstrode, not the proclivity attendant on the appendage.'

'Oh, the name,' said Mr Bullstrode, brought back from those fantasies Mr Wyman so frequently fostered in his imagination. 'The name is Mr William Wyman. He is Her Majesty's Collector of Taxes for the Middle Marches. You need have no fear he'll trouble you overmuch.'

'He'll not trouble me at all. 'Twill be t'other way round if he so much as sets foot on Flawse Fell. Ye'll tell him that.'

Mr Bullstrode said he would but he said it uncertainly. The change in Lockhart had extended to his language which before had been that educated accent acquired from old Mr Flawse but had now broadened into something more akin to Mr Dodd's way of speech. Lockhart's next statement was stranger still. He stood up and glared at the solicitor. There was a wild look about his face and his voice had a dreadful lilt.

'So gan ye back to Hexham and tell the taxmen there that should they want to die abed and not the open air, they'd best steer clear of old Flawse Hall and gan anither route or else they'll not a-hunting go but be themselves the shoot. I will not have an ane of them come peering through my door or speiring after money that I had made afore. I'll pay my way and gie my due to them as has the need but let a taxman show his face I'll show it how to bleed. Aye, they can sweat and they can stew and they can gan to court but I'll hie here and I'll lie there and niver I'll be caught. So warn them, Bullstrode, heed my words. I dinna wish to kill but if they come a searching me so help me God I will.'

Mr Bullstrode had every reason to believe it. Whatever – and there was now no doubt in his mind that Lockhart was no contemporary but some congenital disaster – whatever stood before him and threatened so much in rhyme meant every syllable he uttered. And a man who could have his own grandfather stu... Mr Bullstrode sought a diversionary word and found it in preserved, was made of sterner stuff than the society in which he was living.

Further proof of this supposition came later when, having been prevailed upon to follow his former custom and stay for dinner and the night, he lay in bed. From the kitchen there came the sound of Mr Dodd's Northumbrian pipes and with it a singing voice. Mr Bullstrode got out of bed and tiptoed to the head of the stairs and listened. It was Lockhart singing, but although Mr Bullstrode prided himself on his knowledge of Border Ballads, the one he heard that night was none he knew.

'A dead man sits in old Flawse Hall
  Though buried he should be,
And there he'll sit within the wall
  Till blossoms the great oak tree.

Aye, blossoms and blooms the oak with bluid
  And the moss is gay with red,
And so he'll sit and so he'll brood
  Till all the warld be dead.

So saddle my horse and summon the pack
  And we'll answer the call of the wild
For I'll break the bounds that held me back
  Since I was a dyke-born child.

The old Flawse clan and the old Faas' gang
  And the troopers are back on the moss
And the warning bells will again be rang
  Till they hang me from Elsdon Cross.'

As the song died away and the thin call of the pipes was lost in the silence of the house. Mr Bullstrode, shivering more from future fears than present cold, crept quietly back to bed. What he had just heard confirmed his premonition. Lockhart Flawse was out of the dim and dangerous past when the moss troopers roamed Tyndale and Redesdale and raided cattle from the low country on the east coast. And having raided they had hidden in their strongholds in the high hills. With that wild lawlessness there had come too poetry as harsh and unflinchingly tragic in its view of life as it was gay in the face of death. Mr Bullstrode, crouching beneath the blankets, foresaw dire days ahead. Finally, with a silent prayer that Mr Wyman would listen to reason and not invite disaster, Mr Bullstrode managed to snatch some sleep.

Chapter twenty

But there were forces already at work to nullify the hope expressed in Mr Bullstrode's prayer. Mr Wyman was quite prepared to listen to reason next morning when the solicitor returned to Hexham with his warning but Her Majesty's Collector of Taxes for the Middle Marches was no longer in control of the situation. In London a far more formidable figure in the person of Mr Mirkin, Senior Collector Supertax Division (sub-department, Evasion of) at the Inland Revenue offices had been alerted to the possibility that Mr and Mrs Flawse, previously of Number 12 Sandicott Crescent and now of no known address, had withdrawn £659,000 in used one-pound notes with the intention of not paying Capital Gains Tax. This had been brought to his notice by the bank manager of the East Pursley branch of Jessica's bank who happened to be a close friend of Mr Mirkin and who had been piqued by her refusal to accept his advice. He had been more than piqued by Lockhart's attitude. In his opinion something very fishy was going on. In the opinion of Mr Mirkin it was more than fishy; it stank.

'Tax evasion,' he said, 'is a crime against society of the very gravest sort. The man who fails to contribute to the economic good deserves the most severe punishment.' Which, since Mr Mirkin's income derived entirely from the contributions of socially productive persons, was an opinion both understandable and self-serving. The very magnitude of the sum involved merely increased his sense of outrage. 'I shall pursue this matter to the ends of the earth if need be.'

But such lengths were not needed. The late Mrs Flawse had written to the bank manager informing him of her change of address. That she had changed it yet again made no difference to Mr Mirkin. He consulted the tax register for North-umberland and confirmed that a Mr Flawse, who had in fact paid no tax for fifty years, nevertheless lived at Flawse Hall on Flawse Fell and where the mother was, her daughter was likely to be. Leaving all other duties aside Mr Mirkin travelled first class at the country's expense to Newcastle and then, to em-phasize his status in the hierarchy of Tax Collectors, by hired car to Hexham. Within two days of Mr Bullstrode's visit and warning, Mr Wyman found himself trying to explain to a very superior superior how it was that a Mr Flawse who owned an estate of five thousand acres and seven tenant farms had failed to make his contribution to the national Exchequer by paying any income tax for fifty years.

'Well, the estate had always run at a loss,' he said.

Mr Mirkin's scepticism was positively surgical. 'You seriously expect me to believe that?' he asked. Mr Wyman answered that there was no proof to the contrary.

'We shall see about that,' said Mr Mirkin. 'I intend to make the most thorough investigation of the Flawse accounts. Per-sonally.'

Mr Wyman hesitated. He was caught between the devil of his past and the deep blue sea of the Senior Collector Supertax Division (sub-department, Evasion of). On the whole he de-cided that it might be as well for his future if Mr Mirkin learnt from personal experience how difficult it was to extract taxes from the Flawse family. He therefore said nothing and Mr Mirkin drove off unwarned.

He arrived at Wark and was directed via Black Pockrington to Flawse Hall. There he met his first obstacle in the shape of the locked gate on the bridge over The Cut. Using the intercom which Lockhart had installed he spoke to Mr Dodd. Mr Dodd was polite and said he would see if his master was at home.

'There's a man from the Inland Revenue down at the bridge,' he told Lockhart who was sitting in the study. 'He says he is the Senior Collector of Taxes. You'll not be wanting to speak to him.'

But Lockhart did speak. He went to the intercom and asked Mr Mirkin by what right he was trespassing on private property.

'By my right as Senior Collector of Taxes,' said Mr Mirkin, 'and the question of private property does not arise. I am entitled to visit you to inquire into your financial affairs and . . .'

As he spoke Mr Dodd left the house by way of the kitchen garden and crossed the fell to the dam. Mr Mirkin, by this time too irate to observe the landscape, continued his argument with Lockhart.

'Will you or will you not come down and unlock this gate?' he demanded. 'If you don't I shall apply for a warrant. What is your answer?'

'I shall be down in just a moment,' said Lockhart, 'I have an idea it's going to rain and I'll need an umbrella.'

Mr Mirkin looked up into a cloudless sky.

'What the hell do you mean you'll need an umbrella?' he shouted into the intercom. 'There's not a sign of rain.'

'Oh, I don't know,' said Lockhart, 'we get very sudden changes of weather in these parts. I have known it to pour down without warning.'

At that moment Mr Dodd undid the main sluice gates at the base of the dam and a white wall of water issued from the great pipes. Ten feet high it hurtled down The Cut just as Mr Mirkin was about to protest that he had never heard such nonsense in his life.

'Downpour indeed. . .' he began and stopped. A horrid surging noise sounded round the corner of the hillside. It was part hiss and part thunder. Mr Mirkin stood and looked aghast. The next moment he was running hell for leather past his car and up the metalled track towards Black Pockrington. He was too late. The wall of water was less than ten feet deep now but of sufficient depth to sweep the car and the Senior Collector of Taxes (Supertax Division, etc.) off their tyres and feet and carry them a quarter of a mile down the valley and into the tunnel. To be precise, the water carried Mr Mirkin into the tunnel while the car lodged itself across the entrance. Only then did Mr Dodd close the sluice gates and, taking the precaution of adding three inches to the rainwater gauge on the wall beside the dam, he made his way back to the Hall.

'I doubt he'll be coming back the same way,' he told Lockhart who had observed the Collector's submergence with relish.

'I wouldn't be too sure,' said Lockhart while Jessica, out of the kindness of her heart, hoped the poor man could swim.

There was no kindness in Mr Mirkin's heart by the time he had issued from the tunnel a mile farther on and having been bounced, bashed, trundled and sucked through several large pipes and two deep tanks, finally came to rest in the comparative calm of the subsidiary reservoir beyond Tombstone Law. Half drowned and badly grazed and with murder in his heart, not to mention water everywhere, he clambered up the granite bank and staggered towards a farmhouse. The rest of the way to Hexham he travelled by ambulance and was lodged in the hospital there suffering from shock, multiple abrasions and *dementia taxitis*. When he could speak again, he sent for Mr Wyman.

'I demand that a warrant be issued,' he told him.

'But we can't apply for a warrant unless we've sufficient evidence of tax evasion to convince a magistrate,' said Mr Wyman, 'and quite frankly...'

'Who's talking about tax evasion, you fool?' squawked Mr Mirkin. 'I'm talking about assault with intent to kill, attempted murder...'

'Just because it rained rather hard,' said Mr Wyman, 'and you got caught...'

Mr Mirkin's reaction was so violent that he had to be sedated and Mr Wyman had to lie on a couch in Accident Emergencies holding his nose tightly above the bridge to stop it bleeding.

But Mr Mirkin was not the only person to suffer a sense of loss. The discovery of the late Mrs Flawse in a shell crater surrounded by gold sovereigns came as a shock to Jessica.

'Poor mummy,' she said when an officer from the Royal Artillery brought her the sad news, 'she never had much bump of direction and it's nice to know she didn't suffer. You did say death was instantaneous?'

'Absolutely,' said the officer, 'we bracketed her first and then all six guns fired a salvo and we were bang on target.'

'And you say she was surrounded by Sovereigns?' asked Jessica. 'That would have made her very proud. She always was a great admirer of the Royal Family and to know that they were with her in her hour of need is a wonderful comfort.'

She left the officer in a state of some perplexity and went about the more urgent business of nest-making. She was two weeks' pregnant. It was left to Lockhart to offer his apologies to the Major for the inconvenience caused by Mrs Flawse's failure to look where she was going.

'I feel very strongly about trespass myself,' he said as he saw the officer to the door, 'disturbs the game no end to have people hiking all over the countryside and with absolutely no right. If you ask me, and out of the hearing of my wife of course, the woman got what was coming to her. Damned fine shooting, what!' The Major handed over the jam jar containing Mrs Flawse and left hurriedly.

'Talk about sang-bloody-froid,' he muttered as he drove down the hill.

Behind him Mr Dodd was about to empty the jam jar into the cucumber frame when Lockhart stopped him.

'Grandfather loathed her,' he said, 'and besides, there'll have to be an official funeral.'

Mr Dodd said it seemed a waste of a good coffin but Mrs Flawse was laid to rest beside Mr Taglioni two days later. This time Lockhart's inscription on the headstone was only slightly equivocal and read:

'Beneath this stone lies Mrs Flawse
Who foolishly went out of doors.
She met her end by dint of shell,
Let those that missed her wish her well.'

Jessica was particularly touched by the last line.

'Mummy was such a wonderful woman,' she told Mr Bullstrode and Dr Magrew who put in a somewhat unwilling appearance at the funeral, 'she would love to know she had been immortalized in poetry.'

Dr Magrew and Mr Bullstrode didn't share her certainty.

'I'd have preferred the relative pronoun to be a bit more personal than that,' said the doctor, looking at the wreaths and the jam jar contributed by Mr Dodd. It contained a vixen's brush. Mr Bullstrode was rather more concerned with the Army's role in the affair.

' "From the officers and mess..." ' he read underneath a

large wreath, 'from what I have heard they should have left the mess out. It would have been more tactful all things considered.' As they left the churchyard they noticed Lockhart deep in conversation with the Major.

'It does not augur well,' said the solicitor. 'You heard what happened to the Tax Collector?'

Dr Magrew had in fact treated the man. 'I doubt it will be a few days before he's up and about,' he said. 'I put both his legs in plaster.'

'I had no idea he had broken them,' said Mr Bullstrode. Dr Magrew smiled.

'He hadn't,' he said, 'but I thought it best to be on the safe side.'

'My feelings exactly,' said Mr Bullstrode, 'I wouldn't want to pit myself against the bastard with him in so close communion with the Army.'

But Lockhart's interest in military matters was by and large pacific and concerned with preventing any further accident of the sort that had happened to Mrs Flawse.

'I'd be happy to have you put your notices up a bit closer to the house and on my ground,' he told the Major. 'It would keep people from interfering with my game.'

What his game was he kept to himself but the Major was touched by his generosity.

'I'll have to get permission from the Ministry,' he said, 'but isn't there anything else we can do to help?'

'Well, as a matter of fact there is,' said Lockhart.

Next day he drove to Newcastle with a trailer behind the car and when he returned both car and trailer were loaded to the brim with fresh electronic equipment. He made two subsequent trips and each time came back with more bits and pieces.

'Oh, Lockhart,' said Jessica, 'it's so nice to know you've got a hobby. There you are in your workshop and here am I making everything ready for baby. What was that huge machine that came up yesterday?'

'An electric generator,' said Lockhart, 'I've decided to electrify the house.'

But to watch him and Mr Dodd at work on Flawse Fell suggested that it was less the house than the surrounding countryside that Lockhart had decided to electrify. As each day passed they dug fresh holes and deposited loudspeakers in them and wired them together.

'It will be a minefield of the things,' said Mr Dodd as they ran a large cable back to the house.

'And that's another thing we'll need,' said Lockhart, 'dynamite.'

Two days later Mr Dodd paid a visit to the quarry at Tombstone Law while Lockhart, finally accepting the Major's offer of help, spent several hours on the artillery range with a tape recorder listening to the guns being fired.

'There's just one thing more I'd like,' he said when he had got what he wanted, 'some tapes of authentic rifle and machine-gun fire.'

Once again the Major was obliging and detailed off some men to fire rifles and machine-guns across the fell.

'I must say I think it's an ingenious idea,' said the Major as Lockhart packed his equipment into the car and prepared to leave. 'Sort of bird scarer, what?'

'You could put it like that,' said Lockhart and thanking him once again drove away. He returned to the Hall to find Mr Dodd waiting for him with the news that he had what was needed to make the scene realistic.

'We'll just have to be sure the sheep don't tread on them,' he said but Lockhart was of a different opinion.

'A dead sheep or two won't come amiss. They'll add a touch of death to the scene. A few bullocks would, too.'

All the while Mr Mirkin hobbled about Hexham on crutches and spent hours poring over the tax returns of old Mr Flawse in the determination to find proof of tax evasion and something that would justify the issue of a warrant. But it was a hopeless task. Old Mr Flawse had made a loss. On the other hand, one of his tax-loss enterprises had been a woollen mill and tweed-making factory and tweed-making was subject to Value Added Tax. Mr Mirkin's thoughts turned to VAT. It wasn't within his jurisdiction but came under that of Customs and Excise. VAT evasion and Customs and Excise? Mr Mirkin had found what he wanted. The Excise men needed no warrant to enter and search an Englishman's house, be it castle or cot, at any time of the day or night and their powers, unlike his own, were not subject to the limitations of magistrates, courts of law or any of the legal institutions which preserved an Englishman's supposed liberties. The Excise men were a law unto themselves and as such entirely to Mr Mirkin's envy and purpose. He went to the offices of the head VAT man for the Middle Marches and enlisted his curiosity and help.

'The best time would be to go at night,' he said, 'and take them by surprise.'

The head VAT man had raised objections. 'The Excise are not too well liked in these parts,' he said. 'I would prefer to proceed in a more open and orthodox way.'

Mr Mirkin indicated his plastered legs.

'That's what happened to me when I acted in an orthodox and open manner,' he said. 'If you take my advice you'll act swiftly at night. There's no one out there to contradict your statement that you went by day.'

'Only Mr Flawse and his wife and everyone else in the neighbourhood,' said the VAT man obstinately. Mr Mirkin sniggered.

'You didn't hear what I said,' he told the VAT man. 'The house stands six miles from the nearest neighbour and there's only Mr and Mrs Flawse there. Now if you take six men. . .'

The VAT man succumbed to his persuasion and was impressed by Mr Mirkin's willingness to join the expedition in a wheelchair. His advice about avoiding the valley and approaching by way of the dam seemed sound too.

'I shall first notify them of the need to inspect their books,' he said, 'and only if they refuse will I act according to the authority invested in me by the Government.'

And so several weeks passed and as many letters from Customs and Excise were sent and received no reply. Faced with this flagrant contempt for his office and the VAT regulations, the head VAT man decided to act. And during those weeks Lockhart and Mr Dodd continued with their preparations. They moved more equipment into the valley and on to the fells surrounding the Hall. They installed numbers of tape recorders and enormously powerful amplifiers in the whisky wall and waited for the next move.

It came with the arrival of Mr Bullstrode and Dr Magrew, the solicitor to inform Lockhart that he had learnt through Mr Wyman that the Excise men intended to raid the house that night, and Dr Magrew to confirm that Jessica was expecting a baby. Neither of them expected what happened that night, when after an excellent dinner they went to bed in their old rooms. Outside a full moon shone down on to the Hall, the fell, the Rigg, several hundred sheep, one hundred bullocks, the reservoir, the dam and Cut and half a dozen Excise men together with Mr Mirkin on crutches and Mr Wyman to help him.

Chapter twenty-one

It would also be true to say that the Excise men had no idea what to expect. They had been warned by Mr Mirkin's experience but as they stole across the dam all seemed quiet and peaceful under the brilliant moon. Having crossed the dam they took the path towards the back entrance of the Hall. Around them sheep and bullocks grazed and all was silence and shadow. The only light visible came from Perkin's Lookout where Mr Dodd sat watching their approach but, refracted through the stained glass of the little folly, it had an attractive and rather charming quality about it.

What happened next hadn't. They were still a hundred yards from the Hall when the barrage broke around them, and barrage it was. And bombardment. A thousand loudspeakers bombarded them acoustically with the roar of shells, rapid machine-gun fire, screams of agony, bombs, fresh screams, larger shells, and a high-pitched whistle of such appalling frequency that several sheep went immediately insane. Like eight men suddenly awoken Rip Van Winkle-like in the middle of the Somme bombardment or at Alamein, the Excise men tried desperately to take cover only to find that lying down was even more awful than standing up from the sound point of view. Worse still, it prevented them from getting out of the way of maddened sheep and demented bullocks startled out of their senses into panic by the terrible din.

Even in the house where Dr Magrew and Mr Bullstrode had been warned that it might be more advisable to sleep with their heads under pillows rather than on top, the sounds of battle were devastating. Dr Magrew who had been on the Somme woke with the conviction that he was back there while Mr Bullstrode, convinced that he was in dire peril from Excise men gone berserk and who being determined not to suffer Mr Mirkin's fate had taken it into their heads to bombard the Hall before entering its remains without a warrant, hurled himself under his bed and smashed the chamber pot. Gashed and bleeding he lay there with his fingers in his ears to try and keep the fearful crash of guns out. Only Lockhart and Jessica and Mr Dodd enjoyed what was happening. Provided with earplugs, specially designed ear mufflers and sound-deadening helmets they were in a privileged position.

The Excise men, lacking any such aids, weren't. Nor were the Flawse hounds. Like the sheep they went crazy. It was the high-frequency whistle that got them and in the yard they slobbered and foamed and fought to get out of the gate. Mr Dodd let them. It had been in his mind that they might prove useful yet and he had tied a length of string to the bolt. Now he pulled it and the raving pack swarmed out to join the stampede of demented bullocks, insane sheep and frantic Excise men who cascaded in a horrid panic-stricken rout back towards the dam. Only Mr Mirkin stood his ground and this involuntarily. Mr Wyman, to fend off a berserk sheep, had taken his crutches. They had done him little good. The sheep had broken the crutches and quite uncharacteristically for a normally docile and ruminant creature had bitten them in half and charged on chewing the bits. Mr Wyman charged with it only to be bitten by a Flawse hound. Several Excise men suffered similar fates and all the time the artillery bombardment continued, the rifle fire increased, the high-frequency whistle blew fit to bust and Mr Mirkin clutching his head in agony took an unwise step forward, fell and lay on an extremely large loudspeaker which was resonating at an extremely low frequency. Before he knew what was happening Mr Mirkin was transformed from Senior Collector of Taxes (Supertax Division; sub-department, Evasion of) of the Inland Revenue into a sort of semi-human tuning fork, one end of which felt as if it had been sucked into a jet engine at full power while the middle lying on top of the low-frequency loudspeaker began to rumble, stir, reverberate and bounce quite horribly. Mr Mirkin's plastered legs simply vibrated involuntarily and at a frequency that was not at all to the advantage of what lay between their upper ends. Around him the fell was clear. Sheep, bullocks, hounds and Excise men, all deaf to everything but the pain in their ears, had fled the field and had scampered back across the dam or in the case of two Excise men actually dived into the reservoir where they tried to keep their noses above the water while keeping their ears under.

As they finally disappeared from view Lockhart turned the amplifiers off and the bombardment ceased as suddenly as it had begun. Not that Mr Mirkin or the fleeing Excise men either knew or cared. They were in a soundless world in any case and by the time they reached their cars on the road and were able to voice their shattered feelings they were unable to get them heard. Only sight, smell, touch and fright remained and they stared back in wonderment at Flawse Hall. It was still incredibly standing and apparently unscathed by the bombardment. Nor were there any craters to be seen and the smoke that should have obscured their view was quite extraordinarily absent. But at least the pain had gone too and the Excise men were about to climb back into their cars and leave the scene of this frightful experience when a figure appeared climbing the road from the bottom of the valley. It was Lockhart; across his shoulder like a sack with wooden legs hung Mr Mirkin.

'You've left this thing behind,' he said, and dumped the ex-Senior Collector of Taxes across the bonnet of the leading car. The Excise men saw his lips move but heard nothing. Had they heard they would have agreed that Mr Mirkin was a thing. He was certainly not a human being. Gibbering soundlessly and foaming at various orifices he had passed beyond the bounds of sanity and would clearly never be the same again. They managed to get him into the boot of one of the cars (his vibrating legs prevented his occupying a seat in the car itself) and drove off into the silent night.

Behind them Lockhart walked happily back to the Hall. His

experiment in surrogate and purely sonic warfare had worked splendidly, so splendidly in fact that as he approached the house he saw that most of the windows were broken. He would have them repaired next day and in the meantime there was something to celebrate. He went into the peel tower and lit the fire in the great hearth. As it blazed up he told Mr Dodd to fetch the whisky and went himself into the house to invite Mr Bullstrode and Dr Magrew to join him and Jessica in drinking a toast. He had some difficulty making his invitation plain to them but their sleep had been so completely interrupted that they dressed and followed him to the banqueting hall. Mr Dodd was already there with the whisky and his pipes and standing in a little group beneath the battle-flags and the swords they raised their glasses.

'What are we going to drink to this time?' asked Jessica and it was Mr Dodd who supplied the answer.

'To the Devil himself,' he said.

'The Devil?' said Jessica. 'Why the Devil?'

'Why aye, hinnie,' said Mr Dodd, ' 'tis clear you dinna ken your Robbie Burns. Do ye not ken his poem "The De'il's Awa Wi' The Excise Man"?'

'In that case, to the De'il,' said Lockhart and they drank.

And they danced by the light of the fire while Mr Dodd played on his pipes and sang

'There's threesome reels, and foursome reels,
  There's hornpipes and strathspeys, man;
But the one best dance e'er cam to our lan',
  Was – the De'il's awa wi' the Excise Man.'

They danced and drank and drank and danced and then, exhausted, sat round the long table while Jessica made them ham and eggs. When they had finished Lockhart stood up and told Mr Dodd to fetch the man.

'It wouldna be kind to let him miss this great occasion,' he said. Mr Bullstrode and Dr Magrew, too drunk to disagree, nodded. 'He would have appreciated seeing those scoundrels run,' said Lockhart, 'it would have appealed to his sense of humour.' As dawn broke over Flawse Fell Mr Dodd flung open the gates of the peel tower and old Mr Flawse, seated in a wheelchair and manifestly self-propelled, rolled into the room and took his accustomed place at the end of the table. Mr Dodd shut the doors and handed Lockhart the remote control. He twiddled with the switches and once again the room rang with the voice of old Mr Flawse. Lockhart had been editing the tapes and compiling fresh speeches and it was these that the old man now uttered.

'Let us dispute, my friends, as once we did before the man with the sickle got the better of me. I take it you've both brought your reasons with you just as I've brought mine.'

Dr Magrew and Mr Bullstrode found the question difficult to answer. They were both very drunk and in any case recent events had moved so fast that they had tended to forget that old Mr Flawse, if stuffed, still seemed to have a mind of his own. They sat and stared speechlessly at this animated *memento mori*. Lockhart assuming that they were still partially deaf turned the volume up and Mr Flawse's voice filled the room.

'I care not what argument you use, Magrew,' he yelled, 'I'll not have it that ye can change a nation's or a man's character by meddling with his environment and social circumstance. We are what we are by virtue of the precedence of birth and long-established custom, that great conglomerate of our ancestral heritage congenital and practical. The two are intertwined. What judges once pronounced we now apply; 'tis common law; and what by chemistry committed shapes our cells becomes the common man. An Englishman is yet an Englishman though centuries apart. Do you not agree, Mr Bullstrode, sir?'

Mr Bullstrode nodded. He was powerless to speak.

'And yet,' continued Mr Flawse at ten watts per channel, 'and yet we have the paradox that what's called English differs century by century as well. A strange yet constant inconsistency this is that leaves the men the same and yet divides their conduct and opinions from themselves. In Cromwell's day it was religious controversy led in the field; a century and Chatham's day the conquest of an Empire and the loss of America but faith had fled the field before a clockwork model of the universe and Frenchmen dideroting on encyclopediae. Ye ken what Sully said? That Englishmen take their pleasures sadly after the fashion of their country. A century later Voltaire, that idol *persifleur* of France, would have it that we by and large have a most serious and gloomy temperament. So where's the influence of all ideas between the sixteenth and the eighteenth century on

Englishmen? Not that I mind what Frenchmen say of us; their observations have ill-accorded with mine own; or of my reading come to that. 'Tis Merrie England all the time to me and what have the French to equal Sterne or Smollett or yet a Surtees? I've still to see a Frenchman Jorrocks ride to hounds. With them it's wit and badinage that's aye the joke. With us 'tis ever action and that war between our words and what we be which they across the Channel have named hypocrisy. And what we be is all mixed up with alien blood and refugees from tyranny like a bag pudding boiled within this pot we call the British Isles. 'Twas ever thus; 'twill ever be; a ragamuffin race of scoundrels born of pirates on the run. What say you to that, Magrew, you who have some acquaintanceship with Hume?'

But Dr Magrew, like Mr Bullstrode, had nothing to say. He was silent before this effigy of the past which uttered words in parody of its own complex self. He gaped and as he gaped the old man's voice rose louder still. It was filled with fury now and Lockhart, wrestling with the remote control, found nothing would abate his voice.

'It was some damned scoundrel versifying American,' bawled Mr Flawse, 'would have it that he'd go with a whimper not a bang. 'Twere better for the creature had he been with Whymper on the Matterhorn and learnt the meaning of a fall. Well, I'll not do the same. Damn whimpering, sir, and being the world's whining beggar, cap in hand. I've not a forelock left to touch and wouldna raise a finger to it had I one, to wheedle pennies from a foreign swine be he an Arab Sheik or the Emperor of Japan. I'm true-born English to the core and so I will remain. So keep your whimpering for womenfolk and let me have my bang.'

And as if in answer to this request there was a dull explosion in his innards and smoke poured out of his ears. Mr Bullstrode and Dr Magrew looked on appalled while Lockhart, trying the switches, shouted to Mr Dodd.

'The fire extinguisher,' he yelled, 'for God's sake get the fire extinguisher!'

But it was no good. Mr Flawse was living up to his promise not to whimper. Flailing round him with his arms and shouting incomprehensible imprecations from his clapper mouth he streaked in his wheelchair across the banqueting hall, gathered a rug over his feet on the way, bounced off an armoured figure and finally, with that practicality he had always admired in his ancestors, shot into the open hearth and burst into flames. By the time Mr Dodd arrived with fire extinguisher he was beyond extinction and had flared up the chimney in a shower of sparks and flames.

'The man was born unto trouble as the sparks fly upward. Amen,' said Mr Dodd.

And so in the great hearth old Mr Flawse, the last of his line, finally fizzled out before the eyes of his two closest friends, Jessica, Mr Dodd, and the man he had always called the bastard.

'Almost a Viking's funeral,' said Dr Magrew as the charred remains flaked to ashes and the last transistor melted. It had been made in Japan, he noted, which tended to contradict the old man's final boast that he was English to the core. He was about to point this interesting anatomical and philosophical observation out to Mr Bullstrode when he was interrupted by a cry from behind him. Lockhart was standing on the oak table among the guttering candles and tears were running down his cheeks. 'The De'il has pity in him yet,' thought the doctor but Mr Dodd, recognizing the symptoms, picked up his pipes and squeezed the bag under his arm as Lockhart began his dirge.

'The last of them all is gan fra' the Hall
   And the Flawse is fled fra' the fell
But those that are left can aye recall
   The tales he used to tell.

Twa deaths he died, twa lives he led,
   Twa men he might have been;
The ane spake words he had but read
   The ither he didna mean.

And so he struggled his whole life through
   And niver in strife he ceased.
And he allus sought what was good and true
   Though hissel' to be half a beast.

'Twas all the truth he iver knew
   Since Science and God had fled,
And you couldna shake his firm held view
   That the best of men are dead.

But their words remain to ease our pain
   And he'd have ús now rejoice
That though he's gan we can hear again
   The sound of his living voice.'

While Mr Dodd squeezed on with his tune, Lockhart jumped down from the table and left the peel tower. Behind him Mr Bullstrode and Dr Magrew looked at one another in wonderment and for once even Jessica, startled into womanly concern by Lockhart's tears, lost her sentimental streak and stood dry-eyed. She was about to follow Lockhart out when Mr Dodd stopped her.

'Let him be by hissel', hinnie,' he said. 'He gan to dree his weird awhile.'

Mr Dodd was only partly right. Lockhart was not dreeing but what came next was certainly weird. As the sun rose over Tombstone Law a thousand loudspeakers planted across the fell boomed forth again. This time the sound was not that of shell and shot but the gigantic voice of Edwin Tyndale Flawse. He was singing 'The Ballad of Prick 'Em Dry'.

Chapter twenty-two

As the final echoes of that enormous voice died away and the deafened birds in the pinewoods round the reservoir fluttered back to their perches and tried to resume their morning chorus, Lockhart and Jessica stood on the roof of the peel tower and looked over the battlements at the land that was truly theirs. Lockhart's tears were gone. They had never been entirely for the conflagration of his grandfather but more for the loss of that terrible innocence which had been the old man's intellectual legacy to him. And, like some incubus, that innocence had lain heavily upon him denying him the right to guilt and the true humanity which comes from guilt and innocence. Lockhart had stated it all unconsciously in his lament but now he felt free to be his divided self, a man of lusts as well as loves, of ingenuity mingled with compassion, of fear as well as mindless bravery, in short a man like other men. All this his grandfather's obsession with heroes and hero-worship had denied him but, in the flames that had consumed Mr Flawse, Lockhart had been born anew, his own man, never mind his ancestry or who and what his father might have been and done.

And so while Mr Bullstrode and Dr Magrew drove off down the road to Hexham and Mr Dodd with brush and dust-pan swept the ashes of his late master from the grate and, separating those foreign parts which had been the components of old Mr Flawse's posthumous animation, deposited the rest in the cucumber frame, Lockhart and Jessica stood together and were content to be themselves.

The same could hardly be said for Mr Mirkin or the Excise men now back in Hexham. Mr Mirkin in particular was not himself and no longer beside himself. He had no self to be beside. The Senior Collector of Taxes (Supertax Division; sub-department, Evasion of) was back in hospital outwardly unscathed but suffering internally the simultaneous after-effects of extremely low-frequency waves. His condition baffled the doctors who could make neither head nor tail of his symptoms. At one end he fluttered; at the other end he wowed. The combination was one they had never previously encountered and it was only with the arrival of Dr Magrew, who suggested plastering his plastered legs together to stop them oscillating, that Mr Mirkin could be kept in bed. Even so he wowed, his most insistent wow being to have his Schedule D, a demand that led to some confusion with the Vitamin. In the end he was gagged and his head encased in lead-filled icebags to stop it vibrating.

'He's clean off his rocker,' said Dr Magrew gratuitously as the Senior Collector bounced on the bed. 'The best and safest place for him would be a padded cell. Besides, it would keep the rumble down.'

'His stomach doesn't seem to be capable of keeping anything down,' said a consultant, 'and its rumble is quite revolting.'

To make the diagnosis even more difficult Mr Mirkin, unable to hear, refused to answer questions, even those concerned with his name and address, and when the gag was removed he simply wowed the louder. In the maternity ward nearby his wowing led to complaints and the demand that he be transferred out of earshot. Dr Magrew agreed at once and signed a committal order to the local mental hospital on the perfectly sensible grounds that a man whose extremities were so clearly at odds with one another, and who seemed to have lost his memory, was suffering from incurably split personality. And so with that anonymity that was entirely in keeping with his profession as a Tax Collector, Mr Mirkin, now a mere digit himself, was taken at public expense and registered under Schedule D in the most padded and soundless of cells.

Meanwhile the Excise men and the head VAT man were too taken up with their own loss of hearing to consider with any enthusiasm a return visit to Flawse Hall. They spent their time writing notes to one another and to their solicitors concerning the actions for damages which they were bringing against the Ministry of Defence for failing to draw their attention to the fact that they were, on the night of the raid, entering an artillery range. The case was a prolonged one made longer still by the Army's adamant denial that they fired at night and by the need for all cross-examination of the Excise men to be done in longhand.

Meanwhile life at Flawse Hall resumed its quiet routine. There too things had changed. The cucumbers in the frames grew larger than Mr Dodd had ever known them to and Jessica expanded likewise. And all summer long the bees in the straw hives buzzed over the heather and young rabbits gambolled outside warrens. Even the foxes, sensing the changed atmosphere, returned and for the first time in many a year curlews called over Flawse Fell. Life was returning and Lockhart had given up his previous desire to shoot things. This was partly thanks to Jessica but much more to Miss Deyntry who had taken Jessica under her wing and while instilling a dislike of bloodsports had also knocked the sentimentality out of her. Morning sickness had helped and all talk of storks had ended. Jessica had broadened out into a homely woman with a sharp tongue in her head and the Sandicott strain had reasserted itself. It was a practical strain that placed some value on comfort and the Hall had been transformed. The windows had been replaced and central heating installed to cut out the damp and the draughts but Jessica still stuck to open fires in the main rooms. And Mr Dodd still mined coal from the drift mine, though rather more easily than before. As a result of Lockhart's sonic warfare strange things had happened in the mine.

'The roof has fallen in some places,' Mr Dodd reported, 'but it's the seam itself that puzzles me. The coal has crumbled and there's an afful amount of dust down there.'

Lockhart went to inspect and spent several hours examining this strange occurrence. The coal had certainly crumbled and coal dust was thick everywhere. He emerged blackened but elated.

'It could be we've hit upon a new method of mining,' he said. 'If sonic waves can break windows and shatter glass, I can see no reason why they shouldn't be used underground to more purpose.'

'You'll not expect me to be down there with some infernal whistle, I trust,' said Mr Dodd. 'I dinna want to go out of my mind in the interest of science and there's a number of sheep and bullocks that canna rightly be called undemented yet.'

But Lockhart reassured him. 'If I'm right there will be no need for any man to risk his life and health down a coal mine ever again. One would simply install a self-propelling machine that emitted the right frequency and it would be followed by a sort of enormous vacuum cleaner to suck the dust out afterwards.'

'Aye, well I dare say there's something to be said for the idea,' said Mr Dodd. 'It's all there in the Bible had we but known it. I've always wondered how Joshua could bring down the walls of Jericho with a wee bit of a horn.'

Lockhart went back to his laboratory and began work on his sonic coal extractor.

And so the summer passed peacefully and the Hall once again became the centre of social life in the Middle Marches. Mr Bullstrode and Dr Magrew still came to dinner but so did Miss Deyntry and there were other neighbours whom Jessica invited. But it was late November when the snow lay in thick drifts against the dry-stone walls that she gave birth to a son. Outside the wind whistled and the sheep huddled in their stone shelters; inside all was warmth and comfort.

'We'll name him after his grandfather,' said Lockhart as Jessica nursed the baby.

'But we don't know who he is, darling,' said Jessica. Lockhart said nothing. It was true that they still had no idea who his father was and he had been thinking of his own grandfather when he spoke. 'We'll leave the christening until the spring when the roads are clear and we can have everyone over for the ceremony.' So for the time being the new-born Flawse remained almost anonymous and as bureaucratically non-existent as his father while Lockhart spent much of his time in Perkin's Lookout. The little folly perched on the corner of the high wall served as his study where he could sit and look through its stained-glass window at the miniature garden created by Capability Flawse. There at his desk he wrote his verse. Like his life it had changed and was more mellow and there one spring morning when the sun shone down out of a cloudless sky and the cool wind blew round the outside wall and not into the garden, he set to work on a song to his son.

'Gan, hinny, play the livelong day
And let your ways be bonnie.
I wouldna have the warld to say
I left ye only money.

For I was left no father's name
And canna now renew it,
But face and name are aye the same
And by his ways I knew it.

Some legions came, they say, fra' Spain
While ithers marched from Rome
But like the Wall their ways remain
And make in us a home.

So dinna fash yoursel', sweet son,
The name ye bear be Flawse.
'Tis so the same with everyone
And no man has nie flaws.

We're Flawse or Faas but niver fause
I pledge my word by God.
For so the ballad is my source
And my true name is Dodd.'

Down below in a warm sunlit corner of the miniature garden Mr Dodd, as happy as a skylark, sat by the pram of Edwin Tyndale Flawse and played his pipes or sang his songs while his grandson lay and chuckled with sheer delight.

Ancestral Vices

one

Lord Petrefact pressed the bell on the arm of his wheelchair and smiled. It was not a nice smile, but few of those who knew the President of Petrefact Consolidated Enterprises at all well, and they were an unlucky few indeed, would have expected him to smile nicely. Even Her Majesty, persuaded against her better judgement by the least scrupulous Prime Minister to grant Ronald Osprey Petrefact a peerage, had found his smile almost threatening. Lesser dignitaries were accorded smiles that ranged from the serpentine to the frankly sadistic depending upon their standing with him, a function purely of their temporary utility, or, in the case of his more memorable smiles, of his not needing them at all.

In short, Lord Petrefact's smile was simply the needle of his mental barometer whose scale never registered anything more optimistic than favourable and was more frequently set at stormy. And since his illness, occasioned by the combined efforts of one of his financial editors (who had unwittingly slated shares in which Lord Petrefact had recently invested) and a particularly resentful oyster, his smile had assumed such a lopsided bias that it was possible to sit on one side of him and suppose that, far from smiling, he was merely baring his dentures.

But on this particular morning his smile almost approached the genial. He had, to employ his favourite metaphor, thought of a way of killing two birds with one stone, and since one of those birds consisted of the members of his own family, it was a singularly pleasing thought. Like so many great men Lord Petrefact loathed his nearest and dearest, their nearness and in the case of his son, Frederick, certainly his dearest in financial terms, being directly proportional to his loathing. But it wasn't simply his immediate family who would be put out by what he had in mind. The numerous and infernally influential Petrefacts scattered about the world would be highly indignant, and since they had always disapproved of him he found a great deal of pleasure in anticipating their reactions.

In fact it had taken all his financial guile and the collaboration of an American company which he had surreptitiously taken over to put an end to their meddling in what had until then been the family business. Even his peerage had been a source of considerable acrimony and it had only been his argument that unless he was allowed to elevate his own name he would almost certainly desecrate that of the entire Petrefact tribe by going to gaol that had persuaded them. But then they prided themselves on being one of the oldest families in the Anglo-Saxon world and counted among their ancestors several who pre-dated the Conquest. Not that they had made themselves socially conspicuous. They had, as it were, kept themselves to themselves to the point where Uncle Pirkin, who compiled the genealogical record in Boston, Mass., had several times to invent spurious wives to obscure the taint of incest.

Certainly for some rather sinister reason the Petrefacts had produced a statistically abnormal number of supposedly male offspring. For once Lord Petrefact had to agree with old Pirkin. The evidence of abnormality, both statistical and sexual, had been brought home to him by his sons. His wife, the late Mrs Petrefact, had boasted rather prematurely that she never did things by halves and had promptly contradicted her assertion by producing twins. Their father had greeted their birth with some dismay. He had married her for her money, not for her ability to turn out twins at the drop of a hat.

'I suppose it could have been worse,' he had grudgingly admitted on hearing the news. 'She could have spawned quadruplets, and daughters at that.'

But by the time the twins, Alexander and Frederick, had reached puberty even their doting mother was beginning to have doubts.

'They'll probably grow out of it,' she told her husband when he complained that he had found them role-swapping in his *en suite* toilet. 'They've simply got an identity problem.'

'What I saw didn't suggest simplicity,' snapped Petrefact, 'and when it comes to identity I'll know one from the other when one of the little sods stops wearing ear-rings.'

'I don't want to hear.'

'And I didn't want to see. So for Chrissake lock your goddam suspender belts away some place.'

'But, Ronald, I gave up wearing them years ago.'

'Well I just wish everyone else around here would too,' said Petre Petrefact, slamming the door to emphasize his disgust. But the uncertain gender of his sons continued to haunt him and it was only when Frederick had proved his manhood, at least in part, by being seduced by one of his mother's best friends that Lord Petrefact was

6

reconciled to the thought that he had one male heir. With Alexander there was no knowing. Or not until one evening several years later when Frederick, who should have been at Oxford, sauntered into a reception being held to honour the Minister for Land Development in Paraguay who was on the point of negotiating the sale of ninety per cent of his country's mineral rights to the Petrefact subsidiary, Groundhog Parities.

'I am afraid I have to announce that we have just lost a member of the family,' he told the assembled company, looking with pointed gloom at his mother.

'Not ... you can't mean ...' began Mrs Petrefact.

Frederick nodded. 'I am afraid my brother has taken the plunge. I tried to dissuade him but....'

'You mean he's drowned himself?' Petrefact asked hopefully.

'Oh my poor Alexander,' moaned his wife.

Frederick waited until her sobs were clearly audible. 'Not yet, though doubtless when she comes round ...'

'But I thought you said he was dead.'

'Not dead but gone before,' said the appalling Frederick. 'What I actually said was that we had lost a member of the family. I can think of less delicate ways of putting it but none so exact. I didn't, for instance, say –'

'Then don't,' shouted Petrefact who had finally caught the meaning of the altered pronoun. His wife had been more obtuse.

'Then why did you say he had taken the plunge?'

Frederick helped himself to a glass of champagne. 'I've always assumed there must be some degree of plunging in that sort of operation. And Alexandra, or Alexander as she then was, certainly took it ...'

'Shut up!' yelled Petrefact but Frederick was not to be silenced so easily.

'I always wanted a sister,' he murmured, 'and while I may be a little premature you can at least console yourself, mother dear, that you haven't lost a son but gained a neuter.'

Nor was that all. As the unconscious Mrs Petrefact was carried from the room Frederick had enquired of the Minister if the Catholic Church held as strong views on sex change as it did on abortion.

'But of course not. One has only to think of church choirs of castrati,' said Frederick gaily before turning to the Minister's wife to hope with assumed sympathy that she hadn't found the operation too painful in her own case.

As the reception broke up Petrefact had formed one strong and unalterable resolution: neither his son nor his presumed daughter would ever inherit their father's estate. Nor was he reconciled by the premature death of Mrs Petrefact some six months later. Frederick had been cut off, appropriately in Lord Petrefact's view, without a penny while Alexandra, already sufficiently excised, was paid a pitiful allowance on which she ran a hairdressing salon in Croydon.

Relieved of their presence and his matrimonial duties Lord Petrefact had continued his rise to fame and enormous fortune with a ruthless drive that was fuelled by his knowledge that his will, drawn up by a team of expert lawyers, was uncontestable. He had left his entire estate to Kloone University and had already installed the most advanced computer there as evidence of his good will and proof of his good sense. Petrefact Consolidated had been spared the expense of maintaining the computer themselves and the tax avoidance advantages of channelling profits through a charitable institution had proved considerable.

And now as he sat in his office overlooking the Thames Lord Petrefact's thoughts, ever a mixture of family loathing and financial calculation, turned once more to Kloone. The University might hold his computer: it also held someone less amenable to programming in the person of Walden Yapp. And Yapp had arbitrated in too many industrial disputes to be taken lightly. He was just considering how nicely he had planned things when Croxley entered.

'You rang?'

Lord Petrefact looked at his private secretary with his usual distaste. The man's refusal to address him as 'My Lord' was a daily irritation but Croxley had been with him for almost half a century and at least his loyalty wasn't in doubt. Nor, for that matter, his memory. Before the coming of the computer Croxley had been the nearest thing to a human information storage system Lord Petrefact had ever found.

'Of course I rang. I intend to go to Fawcett.'

'Fawcett? But there's no one there to look after you. The indoor staff were dispensed with eight years ago.'

'Then make provision for a firm of private caterers to deal with matters.'

'And will you be wanting the resuscitation team?'

Lord Petrefact goggled at him. Sometimes he wondered if Croxley had the brains of a louse. Presumably he must have to possess his incredible memory, but there were moments when Lord Petrefact had his doubts.

'Of course I want the resuscitation team,' he shouted. 'What the hell do you think I have this red button for?'

Croxley regarded the red button on the wheelchair as if seeing it for the first time.

'And I want a computer forecast on production increases at the Hull plant.'

'There aren't any.'

'Aren't any? There've got to be. I don't employ that damned computer to sit on its arse and not turn out forecasts. That's what the bloody thing's ...'

'Any increases. In fact to the best of my latest knowledge since the new machinery was introduced production has fallen by almost seventeen point three recurring per cent. In the months March through April plant utilization was limited –'

'All right, all right,' snapped Lord Petrefact, 'there's no need to go on.'

And having dismissed his private secretary with the similarly private thought that the confounded man was a recurring point himself and why the hell he'd ever bothered to install the computer when he had Croxley he'd never know, Lord Petrefact settled back in his wheelchair and considered the next moves in his own interminable battle with his work-force. Closure of the Hull factory would be a well-chosen symbolic gesture. But first there was Yapp to be manipulated. And Fawcett House was near to Kloone.

two

The University Library at Kloone is not a building of outstanding beauty. It stands on a grassy mound overlooking the refinery, the propane tanks and the chemical installations from which its students had been intended to draw their inspiration and, even less successfully, the University had hoped to gain a large proportion of its income. In the event neither hope had been fulfilled. The University attracted the highest number of low-grade Arts students while earning a reputation second only to Oxford for producing the most incompetent scientists in the country.

In large part the building of the library had been responsible for this strange reversal of expectation. Originally designed in the late fifties as a relatively demure structure, it had been given its new dimensions following the accidental visit of Sir Harold Wilson, then mere Harold, in the heady days at the start of his first administration. Thanks to a fog and the political bias of the Chief Constable, the Prime Minister had arrived at Kloone instead of Macclesfield and had been so overwhelmed by the changes evidently achieved at the local Working Men's Club in so short a time since his last visit while campaigning that he had made an impassioned plea for 'the creation of a library to commemorate and indeed sustain the technological advances the vast mass of people are about to see, and if this example of radical improvement is anything to go by, have already seen under Labour'. To further this great work the Prime Minister had taken out his cheque book there and then and had made the first subscription of one hundred pounds while noting on the stub that the sum was to be deducted from his income tax as a necessary expense. From this act of fortuitous generosity there had been no turning back. To protect the Prime Minister's reputation, prominent business men with left-wing insurance policies, trade unions, party officials, multi-national companies with an eye to North Sea oil, Members of Parliament and eminent prison visitors had all poured contributions into the Kloone University Library Fund while the university council had promptly scrapped the original plans and had offered a prize to the architect whose design best expressed the technological advances the Prime Minister had so eloquently prophesied. The library fulfilled these conditions to the letter.

Built of reinforced and unnecessarily prestressed concrete, a maze of metal conduits and carbon fibre columns all of which supported nothing more substantial than an acre of glass, the library managed to break every rule in the energy conservationist's handbook. In summer it sweltered in post-tropical heat to the point where the lifts could only be prevented from seizing up between floors by the installation of an intricate and enormously expensive air-conditioning system. During the winter months it switched to Arctic and the temperature dropped so abruptly that it was frequently necessary to use microwave ovens before books, which had suffered excessive humidity during the summer, could be defrosted and opened at all. To remedy these sub-zero effects it had been essential to duplicate the air-conditioning system with central heating using the same metal conduits for which some purpose had finally been found. Even then, thanks to the architect's obsession with the idea of advanced technology and his consummate ignorance of its practical application, a slight spell of bright weather followed by a small cloud could threaten students who had been sunbathing one moment with frostbite the next.

In fact during early spring and autumn it was essential to run both cooling and heating systems at the same time or to alternate between them extremely abruptly to maintain even a moderately comfortable atmosphere. It had been during one of these sudden switches that a large section of glass, less ready to make allowances for the stresses to which it was being subjected than the human occupants, had disintegrated both itself and the deputy librarian who had been on the point of masturbating in the open-plan lavatories two hundred and thirty feet below. From that dreadful day the toilets had been known as Death Row and avoided by the more nervous readers, much to the disgust of the surviving librarians and with a disregard for hygiene not normally associated with places of higher learning.

Faced with ultimatums from the library staff and in a frantic attempt to restore ordure to more sanitary disposal points than Early English and Middle Slavonic, the authorities had erected a screen of chicken wire immediately below the vast glass roof in the hope that this would engender fresh confidence in the toilets. As an incentive it was only partially successful. While it saved a number of valuable books from being used for improper purposes it had the disadvantage of making even limited ventilation impossible and the cleaning of the inside glass a matter of infinite patience and dubious value. Before long the great glass structure had assumed a mottled and perfervid green which had at least the merit of giving the library a faintly botanical air from the outside. Inside the 'faintly' could be omitted. In the unique climate strange bacteria, lichen and the lowest forms of vegetable life proliferated. A green light filtered down on the shelves and with it a fine mist of algae which, having condensed under the roof, now made homes for themselves in the carpet of the Reading Room or more irrevocably between the covers of books. Several stacks on the fourteenth floor actually exploded and in the Manuscript room a number of irreplaceable papyri on loan from the University of Port Said were so finely composted, or formed such intractable symbiosis with their hosts, that they defied decipherment or even partial restoration.

In short, the cost of maintaining the library proved catastrophic to the economy of the University. Science and Technology languished, laboratories lacked adequate equipment, and physicists, chemists and engineers migrated to more generous establishments.

Paradoxically the Humanities, and in particular the Social Sciences, flourished. Attracted by the spirit of innovation so clearly manifest in the Library, eminent scholars ignored at Oxbridge or bored by redbrick flocked to the concrete campus. They brought with them an evangelical fervour for the experimental, the radical, the anarchic and the interpersonally permissive that was, even in the middle sixties, far in advance of their students. What was demanded by revolutionary students at other universities was imposed on the undergraduates at Kloone.

Young women from respectable working-class homes found themselves marshalled into multi-sexed hostels with unisex washing facilities. Their complaints that sharing beds, bedrooms and almost inevitably parts of themselves with young men had not been mentioned in the curriculum and was hardly conducive to serious study were met by wholly unwarranted accusations of latent lesbianism, which in those days had yet to become entirely respectable.

Having imposed the ostensible aims of Women's Liberation before anyone else, the authorities had gone on to inculcate their own classless ideals into students whose presence at the University was in itself a measure of their determination to climb the social ladder by the only means made available in the Welfare State. Lecturers fashionably extolling the virtues of the proletariat to the sons and daughters of millhands, miners and steel workers found themselves faced by a blank bewilderment and an extraordinarily high rate of neurosis. And so, while other universities became battlegrounds between A-level enragés and proto-Fascist dons, attempts to engender left-wing militancy at Kloone failed hopelessly. There were no 'sit-ins' – no one in his right mind would willingly sit in the Library and there was no other building large enough to accommodate the numbers required to create mass hysteria; no demands for student control; no invasion of the records office; and a positive refusal to attend staff self-criticism seminars. Even the graffiti sprayed so ineptly by lecturers were promptly scrubbed off by student volunteers and the only demands voiced were those asking for the end of continuous assessment, the re-imposition of exams and the introduction of strict discipline with rules and regulations which would free the student body from the agonies of decision.

'If only they wouldn't listen so attentively,' the Reader in the Mechanics of Socio-Political Engineering had complained after spending an hour fulminating against the militaristic excesses of contemporary democracy. 'They give one the entirely false impression of understanding the objective conditions under which they are media-manipulated, then hand in essays that might well have been dictated by Peregrine Worsthorne.'

The Professor of Positive Criminology sympathized. His efforts to persuade his students that murder, rape and particularly violent crimes against the person were forms of social protest, and as such only less estimable than burglary, bank robbery and fraud, had failed so hopelessly that he had twice been visited by the police investigating complaints from undergraduates that he was guilty of incitement.

'I sometimes think we would get a more sympathetic hearing at a meeting of the Monday Club. At least there would be some degree of controversy. My lot simply write down everything I say and then spew it back to me with conclusions so far at variance with my own that I can only assume they think I'm being ironical.'

'If they think at all,' said the Reader. 'In my opinion they've been so grossly indoctrinated since childhood they're incapable of conceptual thought in the first place.'

In this atmosphere of staff disillusionment and student dedication the singular figure of Walden Yapp, Professor of Demotic Historiography, stood, or more frequently strode, for that rigorous common touch on which Kloone had hoped to pride itself. Ideologically his pedigree was beyond criticism. His grandfather, Keir Yapp, had dropped dead on the march from Jarrow and his mother, while still in her teens, had served as a part-time waitress

13

in the International Brigade before being captured, raped and consigned to a nunnery by Franco's troops. Her escape in the weekly nightcart, her travels as an itinerant leper through Seville to Gibraltar where she was refused entry as a health hazard, and her desperate attempt to swim to freedom only to be picked up by a Soviet troopship and transported to Leningrad, all this had lent Elizabeth Hardy Yapp a legendary respect in extreme left-wing circles. Moreover she had spent the first two years of the War denouncing the Government as capitalistic warmongers and with the entry of Russia had used the good offices of the Ministry of Information and her own histrionic gifts to exhort factory workers to defeat Hitler and to elect a Labour Government at the next General Election.

It was as a result of a particularly emotional speech in Swindon that she had met, considered marrying, and had conceived a child by someone called Ernest. Like so much else in her stormy life the attachment had been brief. Spurred into unnatural pugnacity by his mistress' fiery rhetoric, and possibly by the thought that he might have to spend the rest of his life listening to it, Ernest had done his country no great service – he had been an extremely skilled toolmaker in a reserved occupation – by enlisting and getting himself killed at the first available opportunity.

Miss Yapp had added his death to her list of social grievances and had used the aura still surrounding the name of Yapp in Jarrow to secure a safe Labour seat in Parliament. As 'Red Beth' she had represented Mid-Shields with an extremism so unmitigated by practicality that she had never sullied her reputation by being offered a post in Government. Instead she had gone from strength to strength reviling the leaders of her own party for class treachery and the rank and file of all others as downright capitalists, while ensuring that Walden received the best education invective could buy and otherwise leaving him in the care of a deaf and religiously inclined aunt.

In the circumstances it was hardly surprising that Walden Yapp grew up into a singular young man. In fact it was surprising he grew up at all. Isolated from the ordinary world of children by his aunt's fear that he might pick up nasty habits from them and fed an intellectual diet compounded of The Book of Revelation and his mother's inflammatory rhetoric, he had by the age of ten so fused the two into a single doctrine in his own mind that he had been known to sing 'Abide With Me' at Labour Party Conferences and 'The Red Flag' in the local chapel. But his singularity did not only consist of his unquestioning confusion of religion with politics: in his own way Walden Yapp was a genius. Thanks to his aunt's determination to keep his thoughts pure and holy she had denied him any reading matter other than The Bible and the *Encyclopedia Britannica*. Walden had read both from cover to cover so many times that he was capable even at nine of stating without hesitation that a zygote was a fertilized egg or ovum. In short his knowledge was quite literally encyclopedic and, if organized solely along alphabetical lines, too prodigious for the comfort of his teachers. It also helped to put him in quarantine from other children who didn't want to know where the letter A originated or even that an abacus was an early form of computing device. Walden went his own way. When he tired of remembering what anything was he turned to the only other reading matter in the house, a series of railway timetables which had once belonged to his grandfather.

It was here that his genius first showed itself. While other boys experienced the disorientation of puberty, Walden was discovering how best to get from Euston to King's Cross by way of Peterborough, Crewe, Glasgow and Aberdeen, the best way in his view being that which was the most complicated. The fact that half the stations no longer existed and that lines had been axed was of no importance. It was enough to know that in 1908 he could have travelled the length and breadth of Britain without once having to enquire the time or destination of the next train at any booking office. Better still to lie in bed at night and visualize the effect of altering the points at three strategic junctions at exactly the same moment. According to his calculations it would have been possible to bring the entire network of the LMS, the LNER and the Great Western Railway to a catastrophic halt. It was here, in these extraordinary compounds of useless knowledge with valueless mathematical and spatial computations, that Walden Yapp's brilliant future was born. Of reality he knew nothing.

On the other hand his prodigious grasp of theory so baffled his teachers and examiners that, without knowing the limitations of his intellect, they had to pass him as rapidly as possible on through school to university and from First-Class Honours degrees to his Doctorate. In fact his doctoral thesis on 'The Incidence of Cervical

Carcinoma in Female Mineworkers in 1840', the statistics for which he had gathered from the records of hospitals and workhouses in the Newcastle area, had been so startling and in detail so repulsive that it had been accepted on first reading – and in the case of one examiner with only a cursory glance at the first few pages.

It was on the strength of his reputation for unthinking radicalism, and indeed for unthinking thought, that he was offered the fellowship at Kloone. From that unwarranted moment Walden Yapp had never looked back or, to be more precise, had never ceased looking back while moving steadily forward. His second monograph, 'Syphilis: An Instrument of Class Warfare in the 19th Century', had sustained his reputation, and his lectures proved so popular – he interspersed undiluted bias with irrefutable statistics to such an extent that his students were as untrammelled by the need to think or by intellectual uncertainty as if they had been required to learn a telephone directory off by heart – that his election to the Professorship of Demotic Historiography had been merely a matter of time and unremitting publication.

And so by the age of thirty he had established himself as the most harrowing chronicler of the horrors endured by the English Working Person in the post-Industrial Revolution since G. D. H. Cole and even Thompson. More importantly, in his own eyes at any rate, he had made demographic history almost an art form by a series of TV plays on the domestic agonies of Victorian Britain aptly named 'The Proof Of The Pudding', which, if they had done little to enhance his reputation in the stuffier circles of academe and had caused more than one viewer to vomit, had helped to make the name of Walden Yapp and keep that of Kloone University before the disgusted public.

Nor was that all. In the field of industrial relations he had left his mark. Governments, anxious to appear impartial in the war to the national death waged between management and unions, could always rely upon Walden Yapp to act as arbitrator in unduly prolonged strikes. Yapp's peace formula, while unpalatable among monetarists, invariably found favour with unions.

It was based on the simple assumption that demand must predicate supply and that what applied in the field of economics *per se* must have equal validity in wage negotiations. His application of this formula through hours, days and sleepless nights of intense discussion had resulted in the need to nationalize several previously profitable companies and the suspicion held in extreme right-wing circles that Walden Yapp was an agent of the Kremlin.

Nothing could have been further from the truth. Walden Yapp's dedication to democracy was as genuine as his belief that the poor need not always be with us but that, while they were, they must of necessity be in the right. It was a simple view, though never so simply expressed, and it saved him the trouble of having to make decisions of more than a personal nature.

But it was here that his life lacked fulfilment. He had no personal life to speak of and what there was could hardly be called natural. From a lonely childhood he had progressed to a lonely adulthood, both abstract to the point where it was impossible to say he had ever been a child or had become an adult. He remained singular in every sense of that word and if students flocked to his simple lectures, his colleagues flocked out of the common-room the moment he entered rather than suffer the boredom of the wholly inconsequential monologues he mistook for conversation. In short, Walden Yapp's personal life consisted of tutorials with his students, assisting PhD graduates with their theses, discussing his TV plays with bemused producers, and last but by no means least in playing chess with the computer Lord Petrefact had bequeathed to the University. If he had been asked to name his best friend he would truthfully have had to say the computer. Strictly speaking it was his only friend. And best of all, it was available day or night. Situated in the basement of the Library, it could never get away from him. He could either go down and sit at a keyboard there or, more conveniently, switch on the terminal beside his bed, type out his password and immediately get through to what amounted to his electronic *alter ego*. Even when he left the campus he could still take his Modem with him and, by simply installing the telephone receiver in its slot, resume his discussions with the computer. Since he programmed the computer according to his own ideas it had the inestimable merit, not to be found in human friends, of seldom disagreeing with him and then only on matters of fact but never of opinion. Into it he poured all his statistics, all his findings and theories, and from it he obtained his only companionship. About the only thing he couldn't do was sleep with it, not because he objected to its physical appearance, which he found entirely acceptable, but from fear of electrocution and the thought that his physical intrusion would almost certainly put an end to their beautiful if Platonic relationship.

That it was a genuine friendship Yapp had no doubt. The computer told him things about his colleagues' work and he could scan through their correspondence and their latest findings by the simply expedient of using their codewords. That these were supposedly secret was no deterrent. The hours and nights he had spent in the computer's company had given him an uncanny insight into the creature's peculiar dialect and mode of thought. It was as though it too, or she as Yapp preferred, had spent her formative years ingesting railway timetables and reconstituting them along lines similar to his own. Yes, there was no doubt in his mind that she was his friend and with her help he would arrive at that total knowledge of all things which his singular upbringing had taught him was the purpose of living.

In the meantime there was the bothersome business of reality to attend to.

three

Reality first intimated its intrusion into his life in the shape of an envelope with a crest of a griffon on the back. At least Walden supposed it to be a griffon, although it looked alarmingly like a vulture to him. Since he found it in his pigeon-hole at the Faculty of History it was only natural that his singular gift of association should lead him to suppose for a moment that it had perched there by mistake. But no, it was addressed to Professor Yapp and inside was a letter typed on similarly crested notepaper stating that Lord Petrefact would be staying at Fawcett House over the coming weekend and would much appreciate the company of Professor Yapp to discuss the possibility of 'your writing a history of the Petrefact family and in particular the part played by the family in the industrial sphere'.

Yapp stared at the last sentence in disbelief. He knew exactly what part the Petrefact family had played in the industrial sphere.

A remarkably foul one. A whole list of sweatshops, mines, lead-works, mills, foundries, shipyards and appalling factories jostled for pre-eminent vileness in his mind. Wherever labour was cheapest, conditions of work worst and profits highest, the Petre-fact family had been there. And he was being invited to write the family history? Considering that he had mentioned their role as exploiters of the working class in at least two of his TV plays it seemed a most unlikely invitation. About as likely in his opinion as the Rockefellers inviting Angela Davis to write a piece on their role in the sphere of race relations. In fact, even more unlikely. It was absurd and, with the thought that there must be some hoaxer who could lay his hands on Petrefact crested paper, Walden Yapp strode into the lecture room and gave a more than usually grisly account of the Match Workers Strike.

But when he returned to his office the letter was still there on his desk and the griffon looked more vulturine than ever. For a moment Walden Yapp considered discussing the question with the computer before remembering that Lord Petrefact had given it to the University and that its judgement might be tainted by this association. No, he would have to decide himself. And so picking up the phone he dialled the number of Fawcett House. The reply he got from a man who claimed that he was the frozen food auditor of a firm of contract caterers and he wouldn't know Lord Petrefact from a cod fillet if he saw him did little to put his mind at rest. His second call was answered by a voice so tinged with revulsion that it suggested that its owner was holding the receiver with a pair of surgical forceps and talking through an antiseptic mask. Yes, the voice conceded, Lord Petrefact was in residence but on no account to be disturbed.

'I merely want to confirm that he has invited me,' said Yapp. The voice agreed that this was indeed the case but it implied that as far as it was concerned the presence of Professor Yapp at Fawcett House was about as welcome as a dose of Lassa Fever.

Yapp put down the phone, finally convinced that the letter was genuine. Incivility of the order of that arrogant voice wasn't typical of a practical joker. If Lord Petrefact thought he could get away with treating Walden Yapp like some forelock-tugging millhand he was in for another think. And if he imagined for one moment that the family history as written by Walden Yapp was going to be a paean of praise and a verbal puff for a family that had made a fortune out of the miseries of ordinary decent working folk, he would learn what class solidarity really meant. To make quite sure that Lord Petrefact was under no illusions he turned to the keyboard of his automatic typewriter and composed a letter accepting the invitation but making it as abundantly and arrogantly plain as the voice he had spoken to that he disliked the idea of being a guest in the house of a capitalist bloodsucker.

Having got so far and stored the letter in his personal file in the computer for the information of his colleagues and to ensure that no one could say he wasn't sticking firmly to his principles, he changed his mind and sent a brief telegram saying that he would arrive at Fawcett House on Saturday. There were in a curious way subtleties about Walden Yapp which the world had never realized. And after all if the offer was genuine and he could lay his hands on the documentary evidence, the ledgers, the accounts of the Petrefact family in their most detestably exploitive period, he would write such an exposure of their activities as would make their name stink even in capitalist circles.

Lord Petrefact received the telegram with evident pleasure.

'Splendid, splendid,' he told Croxley whose voice had already expressed its opinion of Yapp's visit, 'he's taken the bait.'

'Bait?' said Croxley. He had once spent a very uncomfortable ten minutes watching an episode of 'The Proof Of The Pudding' before trying to erase its memory by switching uncharacteristically to 'Top of The Pops'.

Lord Petrefact pressed the express button of his wheelchair and spun it delightedly in a circle. If that damned oyster hadn't played havoc with his entire metabolism he would almost certainly have danced a jig.

'Bait, my dear Croxley, bait. Now we must prepare the net for the fellow. Got to get him properly involved. What do you suppose he'd like for dinner?'

'From what I saw of that disgusting programme of his I'd say trotters from an undernourished pig followed by last month's bread and skimmed milk.'

Lord Petrefact shook his head. 'No, no, nothing like that. After all we must feed his preconceptions too you know. You have to realize, my dear Croxley, that we plutocrats do ourselves astonish-

20

ingly well. Nothing less than an eight-course dinner will satisfy Yapp's imagination.'

'I suppose we could start with oysters,' said Croxley, who disliked being included in the plutocracy.

Lord Petrefact winced. 'You can,' he said, 'I certainly don't intend to. No, I think we'll start with genuine turtle soup served from the shell of the turtle. He's almost certainly got conservationist tendencies and that should give him pause for thought.'

'I should think it would give the contract caterers pause for thought too,' said Croxley. 'Where on earth they'd get a genuine turtle –'

'The Galapagos Islands,' said Lord Petrefact. 'They can fly one in.'

'If you say so,' said Croxley, making a mental note to tell the chef to lay his hands on a turtle-shell and fill it with tinned soup. 'And after that?'

'A large helping of caviar, genuine Beluga caviar, none of your substitute muck.'

'It's not mine,' said Croxley, 'and anyway Beluga caviar comes from Russia. He'll probably approve of it.'

'Never mind that. The thing is to give him the impression we dine like this every evening.'

'It's a mercy we don't,' said Croxley. 'Any particular wine to go with it?'

Lord Petrefact thought for a moment. 'Château d'Yquem,' he said finally.

'Dear God,' said Croxley, 'that's a dessert wine. It's as sweet as hell and with caviar ...'

'Of course it's sweet. That's the whole point of it. What you don't seem to realize is that our ancestors drank sweet wines with every damned course.'

'Not mine,' said Croxley. 'They had more sense. Stuck to small beer.'

'Mine didn't. You've only got to look at the menu they served up for the Prince of Wales's visit in 1873.'

'I'd just as soon not. They must have had constitutions like oxen.'

'Never mind about their constitutions,' said Lord Petrefact who disliked reminders about his own almost as much as Croxley disliked being classed as a plutocrat. 'Now with the sucking pig we'll have –'

'Sucking pig?' said Croxley. 'We've got a firm of frozen-food specialists downstairs and if you think they can rustle up a deep-freeze sucking pig at the drop of a hat ...'

'Listen Croxley, if I say I want sucking pig I mean I want sucking pig. And anyway they don't rustle the sucking things. At least to the best of my knowledge they don't. They snatch the little buggers from their mother's teats and –'

'Yes, sir,' said Croxley hurriedly, cutting short the terrible explanation he could see coming. 'Sucking pigs it is.'

'No it isn't. It's one, one with an apple between its gums.'

Croxley shut his eyes. Lord Petrefact's morbid interest in the details of sucking pigs was almost as unpleasant as the prospect of the dinner. 'And the dessert after that, sir?' he asked hopefully.

'Dessert? Certainly not. An eight-course dinner needs eight courses. Now after the roast sucking pig I think we'll move onto higher things.'

He paused while Croxley prayed silently. 'Game pie,' said Lord Petrefact finally, 'a thoroughly high game pie. That shall be the *pièce de résistance*.'

'I shouldn't be at all surprised,' said Croxley. 'If you ask me, this Yapp will have run for his life by the time you get to the sucking pig –'

Lord Petrefact interrupted lividly. 'I'm not getting anywhere near that bloody pig,' he shouted, 'you know that as well as I do. My digestion wouldn't stand it and in any case I'm under doctor's ...'

'Quite so, sir. One game pie.'

'Two,' said Lord Petrefact. 'One for you and one for him. Both of them high. I shall enjoy the aroma.'

'Yes sir,' said Croxley after a brief colloquy with himself in which he considered raising the objection that the deep-freeze artists in the kitchen might find it as difficult to prime their game products to the heights demanded as to rustle up a sucking pig and deciding against it.

'And make sure their tails drop off,' continued Lord Petrefact.

'Their tails?'

'Their tails. You hang pheasants until their tails drop off.'

'Christ,' said Croxley, 'aren't you getting a bit confused? I shouldn't have thought pheasants had –'

'Tail feathers, you oaf. They've got to be so rotten their tail feathers come away in your hand. Any good chef knows that.'

'If you say so,' said Croxley deciding once and for all that he was going to see that the contract caterers forgot all about game pie.

'Right, now how many courses is that?'

'Six,' said Croxley.

'Four,' said Lord Petrefact adamantly. 'Now after the pie I think we'll have champagne-flavoured zabaglione followed by Welsh rarebit gorgonzola ...'

Croxley tried to still his imagination and wrote down the instructions. 'And where will Professor Yapp be trying to sleep?' he asked finally.

'In the North wing. Put him in the suite the King of the Belgians used in 1908. That should stir his historical imagination a bit.'

'I doubt if he'll have much time for his historical imagination after dinner,' said Croxley, 'I'd put him nearer the resuscitation team.'

Lord Petrefact waved his objections away. 'The trouble with you, Croxley, is that you lack vision.'

Croxley didn't but he knew better than to say so.

'Vision, Croxley, that's the hallmark of a great man. Now here we have this fellow Yapp and we want something from him so ...'

'What?' said Croxley.

'What do you mean, what?'

'What on earth could we possibly want from a raving socialist radical like Yapp?'

'Never mind what we want from him,' said Lord Petrefact, who knew his secretary's devotion to the family too well to provoke a prolonged argument, 'the fact is we want something. Now the man without vision would suppose that the best way of going about it would be to put the request to him in a roundabout fashion. We know he's an extreme left-winger and he loathes our guts.'

'After that dinner I shouldn't think he'll be particularly fond of his own, come to that.'

'That's beside the point. As I was saying, he regards us as capitalist swine and there's nothing we can do to disillusion him. So we must act the part and play on his vanity. Is that clear?'

'Yes, sir,' said Croxley for whom nothing was at all clear except that he was almost certainly in for a bout of convulsive indigestion unless he came to an agreement with the caterers as quickly as possible. 'And now if you don't mind I'll go and attend to the arrangements.'

He hurried from the room while Lord Petrefact pressed the button on his wheelchair and crossed to the window to stare with intense dislike at the garden his grandfather had laid out so meticulously. 'The runt of the litter,' the old brute had called him. Well, the runt was head of the litter now and nicely poised to shatter the public image of the family which had always despised him. In his own way Lord Petrefact loathed his family almost as fervently as Walden Yapp, though for more personal reasons.

four

Walden Yapp travelled to Fawcett by hire car. He usually went everywhere by train but Fawcett House was nowhere near a railway station and consultation with Doris, the computer, had merely confirmed that there was no bus or other form of public transport he could use to get there. And Yapp refused to own a private car, partly because he believed the State should own everything, partly because of those conservationist tendencies Lord Petrefact had so rightly diagnosed, but most of all because Doris had pointed out that the £12–75 required to run a car could provide enough food and medical aid to keep 24 children alive in Bangladesh. On the other hand she countered this argument by demonstrating that if he bought a car he would provide jobs for five British car workers, two Germans, or half a Japanese, depending on what make he chose. After a struggle with his conscience about making five British workers redundant Yapp had chosen not to own a car at all and had donated the money saved to Oxfam, with the sad reflection that it was more likely to keep two administrators behind desks than feed the starving anywhere else.

But his thoughts as he turned up the drive were not concerned with the underdeveloped world. They were centred on the gross, vulgar and thoroughly overdeveloped sense of their own importance the Petrefacts had displayed in building the enormous mansion in front of him. Fawcett House was a misnomer. It was a repulsive palace, and to think that there were still people rich enough to live in such a vast establishment disgusted him. He was even more disgusted when he stopped outside the front door and was immediately confronted by a genteel lady in a twin-set who said the charge per visit was £2.

'It isn't,' said Yapp, 'I'm here on business.'

'You'll find the servants' entrance round the back.'

'With his majesty,' said Yapp descending to sarcasm. It was wasted on the twin-set.

'Then you're fifty years too late. The last time Royalty visited was in 1929.'

She turned back into the house while Yapp took his borrowed Intourist bag out of the car, cast a disparaging eye on the bent figure of a gardener who was weeding a flower-bed, and finally strode into the house.

'In case I didn't make myself plain enough ...'

'You don't have to try,' said twin-set.

'I've come to see the old bugger himself,' said Yapp, maintaining his proletarian origins with some violence.

'There's no need to be vulgar.'

'It would be hard not to be in these surroundings,' said Yapp looking at the marble pillars and gilt-framed paintings as pointedly as possible. 'The whole place stinks of a gross abuse of wealth. Anyway I'm here at his Lordship's invitation.' He rummaged in his pocket for the letter.

'In that case you'll find him in the private wing to your right,' said twin-set, 'though I can't say I envy him the company he keeps.'

'And I don't much care for his servants,' said Yapp and made his way down a long corridor to a green baize door with a sign that said Private. Yapp shoved it open with his foot and stepped inside. Another long corridor, this time carpeted, greeted him and he was about to start down it when a small dapper man appeared from a door to his right and studied him briefly.

'Professor Yapp?' he enquired, with a deference that was in its own way as insulting as the woman at the door.

'That's me,' said Yapp not to be outdone.

'If you'll just step this way, sir. I'll get one of the servants to show you your rooms. His Lordship will be available at six-thirty and doubtless you'll wish to change.'

'Listen, mate, let's get things straight. In the world I come from, meaning the real world like, and not Poona in 1897 or the jungle round Timbuktu, the ordinary man doesn't change for dinner. And I don't need overfed underpaid butlers showing me where my room is. Just tell me where it is and I'll find my own way.'

'If you say so, sir,' said Croxley, restraining himself from the repartee that as far as he knew the ordinary bloke never had changed for dinner and there weren't any jungles in the neighbourhood of Timbuktu. 'You're on the first floor in the King Albert suite. If there's anything you need you'll find me here.'

He went back into the study and left Walden Yapp to wander along the corridor and up a curving staircase to yet another corridor.

Twenty fruitless minutes later he was down again.

'The Prince Albert suite ...' he began after opening the door without knocking. Croxley regarded him with palpable disdain.

'The *King* Albert suite, sir,' he said heading out of the door. 'King Albert of Belgium stayed here in 1908. We've kept it for visitors with progressive views ever since.'

'Progressive views? You've got to be joking. The swine was responsible for chopping off hands of Africans in the Congo and the most appalling atrocities.'

'So I've always understood, sir,' said Croxley. 'But we ordinary blokes do like to have our little jokes, sir. It's one of the perks of being a menial.'

And leaving Yapp to work that one out he went downstairs feeling rather pleased with himself.

Behind him Yapp surveyed the King Albert suite with disgust, curiosity, and a disquieting sense of having been goaded into a quite unnecessary gaucherie. After all it was the system which was at fault and the dapper little man – and even twin-set, for all her condescension – were only servants and probably had families to support. If over the years they had succumbed to the temptation of, to quote a phrase he frequently used in lectures, 'deferential ego-identity', that was hardly to be wondered at and the surprising thing was that they retained any sense of humanity at all. And the little man with his dark suit and waistcoat and highly polished shoes had shown a nice self-awareness in calling himself a menial. Walden Yapp decided to reserve his more flamboyant class origins for Lord Petrefact.

In the meantime he inspected the room which had once housed the king who had claimed the entire Belgian Congo as his private possession. It was appropriately gross and tasteless, with an enormous bed, a vast dressing-table on which with deliberate defiance Yapp placed his Intourist bag to cover the inlaid crest of monarchy, and a fireplace over which hung a portrait of the king in military array. But it was next door, through what had evidently been the dressing-room, that he came to something that really interested him. As an historian with a particular bias towards the objective, and again to quote him 'the artefactual evidence of class disparity', the bathroom held treasures of Victorian plumbing. Mahogany fittings surrounded the bath, the water-closet and the toilet pan. There was a huge stained mirror above the washbasin, a bell-pull, a large radiator-cum-towel-rack, and a cupboard containing a number of enormous towels. But it was the bath itself, or rather the array of taps, dials and levers to one side, which fascinated him most. It was a remarkably large bath, deep-sided and fashioned like a four-poster bed with a canopy above and some sort of waterproof curtains draped along the side. Yapp leant across the bath and read the gauges. One was a temperature indicator, another gave details of water pressure, while the third, which was larger than the others, had a lever and a dial with a series of settings engraved on it. Yapp sat down on the edge of the bath to read them better and for one horrid moment felt himself slipping sideways. He leapt off and regarded the bath suspiciously. The damned thing had definitely moved. And as he watched it tilted back to the horizontal again.

Odd. Yapp reached out cautiously and pushed the mahogany surround down. The bath remained stationary. Not wishing to risk disturbing the thing again he knelt on the floor and peered across at the dial with the lever and arrow. At one end of the scale he read WAVE and at the other end STEAM. In between these two rather alarming commands – and now that he came to think of it the lever and dial reminded him of the engine-room signals he had seen in films of ships' bridges – there were others. WAVE was followed by SWELL only to revert to STRONG WAVE, then NEUTRAL and finally three sorts of JET, STRONG, MEDIUM and SLIGHT. It was all very fascinating and for a moment Yapp considered having a bath and trying what was evidently a quite remarkable example of early automation applied to domestic plumbing, and one which demonstrated the Imperialist obsession with naval supremacy, the Suez canal, trade routes and India. But it was already past six and after making a note of this comment in the diary he invariably carried when out of touch with Doris, he decided against it. Instead he made a sketch of the contraption, measured its dimensions and recorded the various settings on the dial. Finally when he had finished and was about to leave, his eye caught sight of a faded yellow paper in a glass frame on the wall next to the washbasin. It was a set of instructions for use with THE SYNCHRONIZED ABLUTION BATH. Yapp glanced through them and noted that WAVE MOTION application required the Level Of Water In The Bath to be two-thirds when combined with the Displacement ... The rest of the sentence had been eroded by steam and time.

He went through the bedroom and down the corridor to the stairs. Croxley was waiting for him in the study but his form of condescension had altered. He was wearing a sports jacket with flannels, a woollen shirt and knitted tie and looked distinctly uncomfortable.

'You needn't have bothered,' said Yapp rather testily.

'We like to make our visitors feel at home,' said Croxley, who had been ordered by Lord Petrefact to put on something casual.

'I'm not likely to feel at home in this place. It's more like a palace and it ought to be a museum.'

'As a matter of fact for most of the year it is,' said Croxley and opened a door. 'After you.'

Yapp went through and was surprised to find himself back in the mid-1970s. The drawing room was as unostentatiously comfortable as the rest of the house was the opposite. A russet carpet covered the floor, a colour television flickered in a corner, there was a wood fire burning in a stainless-steel hearth and in front of it a low table and a large modern sofa.

'Help yourself to a drink,' said Croxley, indicating a cabinet in the corner. 'I'll fetch the old man.'

Left to himself, Yapp looked round in amazement. The walls were covered with modern art. Klee, Hockney, a Matisse, two Picassos, a number of abstracts Yapp couldn't put a name to and finally, most astonishingly of all, a Warhol. But before he could convert his surprise into disgust at this financial exploitation of the art world, Walden Yapp's emotions were sent reeling again. Through a side door beyond the fireplace there came the sound of

28

a querulous voice, a pair of bedroom slippers and the chromium spokes of a wheelchair.

'Ah my dear fellow, how good of you to come all this way,' said Lord Petrefact, lending even less enchantment to Yapp's view than the abstract 'Nude In Pieces' by Jaroslav Somebody he had been studying, by attempting to smile. To a man of greater experience of reality that smile would have come as a terribly augury: to Walden Yapp's deep commitment to compassion and concern it heralded a courageous attempt to ignore physical suffering. From one moment to the next Lord Petrefact was transformed from a capitalist bloodsucker to a Senior Citizen with a disability problem.

'Not at all,' he muttered, desperately trying to sort out the tangle of conflicting emotions to which Lord Petrefact's sorry appearance had subjected him; and without quite realizing what he was doing he was shaking the limp hand of one of Britain's wealthiest and, in his previous opinion, most ruthless exploiters of the working man. The next moment he was sitting on the sofa with a whisky and soda while the old man prattled on about how rewarding it must be to give one's all to young people in a world which sorely lacked men of Professor Yapp's dedication.

'I would hardly say that,' he demurred. 'One does one's best of course but our students are not of the highest calibre.'

'All the more reason why they should have the best teaching,' said Lord Petrefact, clutching a glass of milk with one hand while wiping an eye with a handkerchief in the other the better to study this gaunt young man who represented in his view the most dangerous species of hypocritical ideologue in the modern world. If Yapp had his preconceived notions of capitalists, Lord Petrefact's prejudices were as extreme about socialists, and Yapp's reputation had led him to expect something more formidable. For a moment his resolution faltered. It was hardly worthwhile setting a man who looked like a cross between an inexperienced social worker and a curate on to make life a misery for the family. The sods would eat him alive. But then again, Yapp's appearance might be deceptive. His arbitration decisions, particularly his ninety per cent pay rise for cloakroom attendants and urinal maintenance personnel, had been so evidently motivated by political prejudices, while the parity payments with hospital consultants he had claimed for road-sweepers had been so monstrous, that they left no doubt that Yapp, whatever he might appear, was a very considerable subversive force. Lord Petrefact made these assessments while continuing to sip his milk and discuss the need for greater training opportunities for young people with a muted enthusiasm tinged with a melancholy he didn't feel.

In the corner, uncomfortably conscious of his Harris tweed jacket, Croxley listened and watched. He had seen Lord Petrefact in this role of philanthropic invalid before and it had inevitably led to extremely nasty consequences. In fact, by the time he had given Walden Yapp a second whisky and had seen him swallow it as the contract butler announced that dinner was served, he was beginning to take pity on the poor fool. Against such sympathy he had to remind himself that Yapp couldn't be quite the imbecile he appeared to have risen so high in the academic world and Croxley, who had been born and raised before the introduction of free university education, begrudged Yapp his opportunites and success.

At least Croxley had been able to mitigate the more indigestive consequences of the meal. The turtle soup had come from a tin and he had made certain that the game pie was as low as possible. Only the sucking pig remained a problem. What the butcher had delivered had clearly not been dragged from its mother's teats – or if it had the swine had never been weaned. It was in fact a full-size boar and was so far beyond the dimensions of the oven and the experience of the chef that it had only been by cutting the middle section out of the beast and sewing the head and the haunches together that the thing had been cooked at all. Croxley, who had checked its progress, had been in two minds whether or not to have it brought in with an apple between its tusks. In the end he had decided as usual to do approximately what he was told, but he wasn't looking forward to Lord Petrefact's reaction.

Now as he followed Yapp into the dining-room he was tempted to have a last word with the chef, but already Lord Petrefact had taken his place at the head of the table and was eyeing the turtle shell with genuine regret.

'I'm afraid I can't join you,' he told Yapp. 'Doctor's orders, you know. And in any case I feel strongly that wildlife should not be massacred for mere human consumption.' He turned a baleful eye on Croxley. 'I'm surprised you ordered genuine turtle soup.'

Croxley looked balefully back and decided that enough was enough. 'I didn't,' he said. 'The shell came from the Aquarium at Lowestoft and the contents from Fortnum & Mason.'

30

'Really?' said Lord Petrefact, managing to smile at Yapp with one side of his face while glaring at Croxley with the other. But it was Yapp who saved Croxley from further harassment by launching into a disquisition on the origins of mock turtle. He was beginning to enjoy himself; whatever reservations he had about the source of the Petrefact wealth, and they remained as unequivocal as ever, had been salved for the moment by the thought that he was seeing how the rich really lived. It was, as Croxley had said, like visiting a museum, and if he came away with nothing else he would have gained fresh insight into the socio-domestic psychology of the capitalist class at its most refined. He was particularly struck by the quirky relationship which existed between Lord Petrefact and his confidential secretary. It was almost as though the old man demanded or provoked defiance from Croxley, and a strange camaraderie of mutual dislike seemed to bind them together.

'No, I won't have another helping, thank you,' Croxley said when he had finished his soup. But Lord Petrefact insisted. 'We can't have you wasting away, my dear chap,' he said with his disturbingly lopsided smile, and the secretary suffered the indignity of having his plate filled by one of the waiters. It was the same with the caviar. While Lord Petrefact toyed with what looked like boiled fish fingers and Yapp had thoroughly enjoyed two helpings, Croxley clearly hadn't wanted three.

'You ought to know by now that I always have a light supper,' he said, 'I can't sleep on a full stomach.'

'You're fortunate to have a stomach to sleep on. I lie awake trying to remember when I last had a thoroughly good dinner.'

'About the time you ate that oyster,' said Croxley, a remark that evidently had some esoteric significance because it produced from Lord Petrefact a smile so reptilian that even Yapp could see that it was not entirely spontaneous. For a moment it looked as though the old man was about to explode but he managed to control himself.

'And how do you like the wine?' he enquired turning to Yapp. Yapp considered the wine for the first time.

'I'm not a connoisseur but it goes very well with the caviar.'

'Does it indeed? Not too sweet?'

'If anything a little on the dry side,' said Yapp.

Lord Petrefact looked from him to the decanter dubiously and finally to Croxley.

'Chablis,' said Croxley cryptically.

Again a glance of venomous significance seemed to pass between the two but it was with the arrival of the next dish that Lord Petrefact's shrunken figure seemed to swell and grow as monstrous as his reputation.

'And what, pray, is that?' he demanded. Yapp noted the archaic use of 'pray' and also that Croxley seemed to have taken the advice. Only then did he look at the extraordinary object that the headwaiter was holding with some difficulty on a silver platter beside him. Even to Walden Yapp's eyes, inexperienced as they were in the oddities of haute cuisine, there seemed to be something fundamentally wrong with the roast animal and for a moment he had the distinct impression that he was seeing things.

Lord Petrefact certainly was. His face had ballooned out into an awful purple. 'Sucking pig?' he yelled at the waiter. 'What do you mean "sucking pig"? That thing's no more a sucking pig than I am.'

'I daresay not, sir,' said the waiter with a courage Yapp had to admire, 'I rather think the butcher must have got it wrong.'

'Wrong? He didn't just get the thing wrong. He must have got it from the same place he got that damned turtle shell or more likely some circus specializing in deformed animals.'

'By wrong I mean he got the message wrong, sir. The chef definitely asked for sucking pig on the telephone and possibly the butcher thought he said ...' The waiter stopped and looked pathetically at Croxley for help. But Lord Petrefact had already got the message.

'If anyone's telling me that whatever's on that platter fucked anything they're out of their tiny minds,' he yelled obviously almost out of his. 'Look at its back bloody legs. It's a wonder it could hobble about, let alone fuck. It must have tripped over its own bleeding snout all the time. And where's its bloody stomach?'

'In the refrigerator, sir,' mumbled the waiter. Lord Petrefact goggled at him.

'Is that supposed to be some sort of joke?' he bellowed. 'You bring me a roast dwarf of a pig and ...'

'Porg,' said Yapp feeling rather unwisely that it was time to come to the waiter's assistance. Lord Petrefact looked at him full-face.

'Pork? Of course it's pork. Any fool can see it's pork. What I want to know is what sort of pork it is.'

'I was referring to your use of the word "dwarf",' said Yapp adamantly. 'It's not a term I would expect to find used in polite company.'

'Wouldn't you? Then may we have the privilege of learning what you would like to hear used in polite company? And take that fucking apparition of a stunted pig out of my sight.'

'Person of restricted growth,' said Yapp.

Lord Petrefact stared at him dementedly. 'Person of restricted growth? I get handed a pig that looks as though it's been concertinaed and you start blathering about polite company and people of restricted growth. If anything's ever had its growth restricted that poor damned animal ...' He gave up and slumped exhausted in his wheelchair.

'The term "dwarf" has pejorative overtones,' said Yapp, 'whereas Person of Restricted Growth, or Porg for short –'

'Listen,' said Lord Petrefact, 'you may be a guest in this house and I may be impolite but if anyone mentions anything even vaguely reminiscent of pigs again ... Excuse me.' And with a whirr he turned his wheelchair and sped from the dining-room. Behind him Yapp heaved a sigh of relief.

'I shouldn't let that worry you,' said Croxley, who had warmed to Yapp for diverting Lord Petrefact's fury. 'He'll be as right as rain by the time we've finished here.'

'I wasn't worried. I was simply interested to observe the clash of contradictions manifested in the social behaviour of the so-called upper class when confronted by the objective conditions of experience,' said Yapp.

'Oh really. The foreshortened pig being an objective condition I suppose?'

They ate the rest of the meal in silence interrupted only by the occasional sound of raised voices from the kitchen where Lord Petrefact was investigating who precisely was responsible for the deformation of the pig and his own breach of good manners.

'I think I'll nip off to bed if you don't mind,' said Croxley when they finally rose from the table. 'If you need anything in the night just ring for it.'

He slipped out into the corridor and left Yapp to return to the drawing-room. Yapp went reluctantly and with every intention of telling his host exactly what he thought of him if he spoke one rude word again but Lord Petrefact, having discovered the unnatural origins of the species he had been presented with, was in no mood to quarrel with Walden Yapp.

'You must excuse my outburst, my dear fellow,' he said with apparent geniality. 'It's this confounded digestive system of mine, you know. It's bad enough at the best of times but ... do help yourself to brandy. Of course you will. I think I'll have a small one myself.' And in spite of Yapp's protest that he had already drunk more than he usually did in a month, Lord Petrefact propelled himself across to the cabinet in the corner and handed him a very large brandy.

'Now sit yourself down and have a cigar,' he said. This time Yapp refused firmly on the grounds that he was a non-smoker.

'Very sensible. Very sensible. Still; it calms the nerves, so they tell me.' And armed with a large cigar and a sizeable brandy he manoeuvred his chair so that his relatively benevolent side was uncomfortably close to Yapp.

'Now I daresay you're wondering why I've invited you down here,' he said in an almost conspiratorial whisper.

'You mentioned something about my writing a history of the family.'

'So I did. Quite so,' said Lord Petrefact with every effort to appear absent-minded, 'but doubtless you found the idea more than a little perplexing.'

'I wondered why you had chosen me, certainly,' said Yapp.

Lord Petrefact nodded. 'Exactly. And taking, let us say, the extreme poles of our political opinion, the choice must have seemed mildly eccentric.'

'I did find it unusual and I think I ought to tell you here and now that ...'

But Lord Petrefact raised his hand. 'No need, my dear fellow, no need at all. I know what you're going to say and I agree absolutely with your pre-conditions. Precisely why I chose you. We Petrefacts may have our faults and I've no doubt you'll catalogue them in detail, but one thing you won't find in us is self-deception. I suppose another way of putting it would be to say we lack vanity, but that would be going too far. You've only got to look at this infernal house to see what lengths my grandparents went to proclaim their social superiority. And a fat lot of good it did them. Well, I'm of another generation, another epoch you might say, and if there's one thing I value above all else it is the truth.'

And managing to hold both his cigar and his brandy glass in one hand he grasped Yapp's wrist rather unnervingly with the other.

'The truth, sir, is the last repository of youth. How's that for a saying?'

Much to Yapp's relief Lord Petrefact let go of his wrist and sat back in his chair looking remarkably pleased with himself.

'Now what do you say to that?' he insisted. 'And there's no use your looking in La Rochefoucauld or Voltaire for the maxim. Mine, sir, my very own and nonetheless true for that.'

'It's certainly a very interesting notion,' said Yapp, not certain that he fully understood what the extraordinary old man was saying but feeling that it must have some significance for him.

'Yes. The truth is the last repository of youth. And while a man is prepared to look truth in the face and see the mirror of his defects, let no man call him old.'

And having delivered himself of this phrase so redolent of Churchill, Beaverbrook and possibly even Baldwin at his most meaningless, Lord Petrefact blew a smoke ring from his cigar with great expertise. Yapp watched, mesmerised, as the ring of smoke, like some ectoplasmic ripple of personality, wafted its way towards the fireplace.

'If I read you right,' he said, 'what you're saying is that you are prepared to give me a free hand to research the history of the Petrefact family with all the economic and financial data made available to me and that there will be no interference with my socio-economic deductions from that data.'

'Exactly,' said Lord Petrefact, 'I couldn't have put it better myself.'

Yapp sipped his brandy and wondered at this remarkable generosity. He had prepared himself to turn the whole proposition down if there had been the slightest suggestion of his being asked to write a puff for the Petrefacts – and in fact had been rather looking forward to this demonstration of his high principles – but the last thing he had expected was to be given a free hand. It took some getting used to. Lord Petrefact eyed him closely and savoured his confusion.

'No let or hindrance, sir,' he said evidently feeling that ham was paying off. 'You can go where you like, look at whatever documents you want, talk to anyone, read the correspondence, and there's enough of that I can tell you, most revealing stuff too, and all this for the . . .' He checked 'princely sum' just in time. There was no point in alienating the young fool just when he had him hooked. Instead he felt in his pocket and produced a document. 'One hundred thousand pounds. There's the contract. Twenty thousand on signature, a further twenty on completion of the manuscript and sixty thousand on publication. Can't put it fairer than that. Read it through carefully, have whoever you like check it out, you won't find a flaw in it. Drew it up myself, so I know.'

'I'll have to think about the offer,' said Yapp, fighting down a sense of quite extraordinary euphoria and glancing at the first page of the contract. And as if to indicate that he was the last person to bring the pressure of his personality to bear on anyone Lord Petrefact whirred across the room to the door and with a final remark about helping himself to anything he wanted and not worrying about the lights because the servants would see to them, he wished Yapp goodnight and disappeared from the room. Yapp sat on, stunned by the suddenness of it all and with the heady feeling that he had been in the presence of one of the last great capitalist robber barons. Twenty thousand pounds on signature and twenty thousand . . . And no preconditions. Not a single thing to prevent him from documenting the exploitation, the misery, and the rapacity which lay behind that misery, which the Petrefacts had caused their workforce over more than a century.

There had to be a snag somewhere. Walden Yapp emptied his glass, poured himself another brandy and settled down in comfort to read through the contract.

five

In the next room Lord Petrefact sat in the darkness for some time savouring his cigar but cursing himself for his stupidity. He also cursed Croxley for the episode of the foreshortened pig and would, if he could have reached him, have given the swine a week's notice and a piece of his mind. But Croxley had chosen to sleep upstairs. Fawcett House was ill-equipped with elevators and Lord Petrefact too sensible to even consider attempting to manoeuvre his wheel-chair up the marble staircase, particularly a marble staircase that had already demonstrated its lethal propensities in the case of great-uncle Erskine. Lord Petrefact could recall the tragedy with vivid satisfaction, though it remained a mystery why his great uncle should have first urinated against the balcony before stepping to his death clad only in a partially unveiled condom. Presumably the old goat had mistaken one of the marble statues in a niche for a housemaid.

But that was beside the point. What was closest to it was that the egregious Croxley was upstairs and he was downstairs and he would have to wait until morning before venting his fury on the idiot. No, what was particularly irking him was that he had offered the imbecile Yapp such extraordinarily generous terms for research the raving lunatic would have gladly done for free. There was the added irritation of wondering if Yapp, for all his reputation, would prove the right man for the job. His politeness at dinner hadn't suggested the ruthless hatchet-man Lord Petrefact would have chosen to let loose on his family. With the thought that he would have to point the brute in the right direction, Lord Petrefact trundled off to his bedroom and the ministrations of the resuscitation team whose female members had the unenviable task of getting him into bed at night and out in the morning.

In the drawing-room Yapp finished studying the contract and, conscious that he was keeping the servants up until a quite un-necessarily late hour, made his way along the corridor and up to his room. As far as he could tell, and he had studied the fine print with particular care, there was absolutely nothing in the contract to prevent him from writing the most scurrilous history of the family imaginable. It was most extraordinary. And for this gift of socio-economic-fiscal data he was to be paid one hundred thousand pounds. It was an unnerving thought – almost as unnerving as knowing that he was about to sleep in a bed once occupied by the tyrant of the Congo.

It was hardly surprising that Walden Yapp had difficulty in going to sleep. While Lord Petrefact lay below him considering which of his relatives would least appreciate Yapp's enquiries into their private affairs, the great Demotic Historiographer found sleep almost as awkward. He kept waking and staring at the shape of the window wondering at his good fortune before dozing off again.

When he did sleep it was to dream of pigs in wheelchairs and Lord Petrefact horribly distorted with his slippered feet more or less where his shoulder blades should have been. To make matters worse, there was no reading lamp beside the bed and he couldn't lull his imagination into a comfortable torpor by dwelling on the sufferings of knife-grinders in Sheffield in 1863, a doctoral thesis of one of his students he had brought with him to serve as bedside reading. Above all, there was no Modem. If only he could have fed the contract to Doris he felt sure she would have seen the flaw in it somewhere. But that would have to wait until he got back to his apartment at Kloone.

Even Croxley, normally an excellent sleeper, found himself for once prey to insomnia. He had managed to escape the immediate fury of Lord Petrefact in respect of the makeshift sucking pig, but the morning would undoubtedly see an explosion of wrath. Croxley resigned himself to this inevitable outburst. The old man might blast him to hell and gone, but Croxley knew his own worth and his job was not in danger. No, there was something more insidious going on, and for once he had no insight into Lord Petrefact's motives. Why had he invited this subversive scholar to Fawcett? It was beyond Croxley. And if Lord Petrefact cursed himself for having offered such a large sum to Yapp for his research, Croxley blamed himself for not having used the opportunity at dinner to find out from Yapp why he was there. Anyway, whatever the reason, Croxley disapproved of it. Searching back in his mind for a motive, he could only suppose it had to do with the proposed closure of the plant at Hull. That was certainly on the cards and perhaps Yapp was a possible arbitrator in the dispute. In which case the old man might be trying to buy him off. But that didn't explain the way in which he had fawned on the wretched creature. In half a century of self-indentured loyalty to Lord Petrefact and total devotion to the family, Croxley could remember only very few occasions when the old man had attempted so ferociously to hide his true feelings. There had been the time he needed Raphael Petrefact's holdings in American Carboils to effect a take-over, and another when he had required the collaboration of Oscar Clapperstock to bankrupt a competitor, but apart from those two vital moments in his career Lord Petrefact had been conscientiously unpleasant. It was one of the qualities Croxley most admired about him, this relentless pursuit of private profit at the expense of personal popularity. But eventually even the puzzled Croxley drifted off and Fawcett House resumed the grim silence and sepulchral splendour that seemed to commemorate so eloquently the suffering millions who had made its building possible.

But it was precisely the thought of those suffering millions that finally drove Walden Yapp from his bed. How could he possibly accept one hundred thousand ill-gained pounds from a man whose proudest and most publicized boast had been to paraphrase Churchill, 'Never in the field of private enterprise has so much been owed by so many to one man.' The whole notion of being paid in coinage that was stamped with the blood, sweat, tears and sputum of silicotic miners in Bolivia and South Africa – not to mention tea workers in Sri Lanka, lumberjacks in Canada, bulldozer drivers in Queensland and in fact workers just about anywhere you cared to mention in the world – was intolerable. And if that wasn't bad enough there was the thought of what the contract could do to his own immaculate reputation. It would be said that Walden Yapp had been bought, had become the lackey, the publicity man for Petrefact Consolidated Enterprises, and had renounced his principles for a mere hundred thousand pounds. He would be blackballed by the Tribune group, turned away from the steps of Transport House and cut in the street by such middle-of-the-roaders as Wedgie Benn. Unless, of course, he donated the entire sum to some deserving charity like the ILO or the Save Pol Pot Fund. Something of that order anyway would certainly answer his critics and he could go on with his research into methods of exploitation used by the Petrefacts. Yes, that was the answer and with the happy thought that no one could possibly decry the name Yapp in the annals of Socialism he went through to the bathroom and decided that if he couldn't sleep in the same bed as the vile monarch he might as well try out the antediluvian bath. It would be a start in his research into how the very rich had lived.

In the event it surpassed his expectations. Having read the instructions again Yapp pulled the lever marked PLUG, turned the temperature gauge tap until the dial read 70° and waited while the bath had reached the two-thirds capacity required for WAVE MOTION. Only then did he turn the tap off and step into the vast bath. Rather, he *would* have stepped if the thing hadn't suddenly lurched sideways and thrown him off his feet. The next moment he was scrabbling for the lever and the bath had lurched the other way. Yapp slid down it and collided with the spout and was trying desperately to grab hold of it when, with an appalling grinding noise, the bath changed direction and simultaneously began to vibrate. As he slid precipitously down it, helped by a bar of soap that had lodged itself between his buttocks, Yapp grabbed the lever and swung it to JET. The indicator fulfilled this promise with an enthusiasm that came presumably from years of understandable neglect. Hot rusty water hurled itself from holes beneath the mahogany surround. With a yell Yapp grasped at a curtain and tried to pull himself to his feet. But the bath clearly had other ideas of its own. As the curtain tore from its corroded railing and the devotee of computers and multiple modes of function crashed once more into the water and scalding jets, the infernal contraption combined every mode of function its insane designer had contrived for it. It waved, it jetted, it vibrated and now it demonstrated its capacity to steam. From one series of holes came the jets, from another a cloud of steam that ended all Yapp's attempts to grab the lever and shove it into neutral. He couldn't even see the lever as he hurtled past it, let alone grab the thing. And all the time there came the thump and grind of whatever antiquated mechanism – Yapp could only suppose it to be some infernal beam engine – animated the Synchronized Ablution Bath.

It was this incessant thumping that finally woke Lord Petrefact in the room below. He opened his eyes, blinked, reached for his glasses, missed them and lay staring at the ornately plastered ceiling above him. Even without his glasses it was clear that something was seriously wrong, either with his liver – and the din gave the lie to that – or with the whole damned building. On first reflection he would have said that the place had been hit by an unusually severe earthquake, except that earthquakes didn't go on and on and on. Nor, as far as he knew, were they accompanied by what sounded like a runaway steam engine.

A piece of moulding fell from the ceiling and crashed into his tooth-glass, a portrait of his grandfather detached itself from the wall and impaled itself on the back of a chair, but it was the stain of rusty brown liquid spreading across the ceiling which decided Lord Petrefact. That and the chandelier, which from bouncing had now taken to gyrating in ever-increasing circles. If the damned thing came off there was no telling what might happen and he certainly wasn't going to stay in bed to find out. With a vigour that was surprising for a man supposedly immobile, Lord Petrefact hurled himself from the bed and scrabbled for his wheelchair and the essential red button.

He was too late. The chandelier had reached the end of its tether. To be precise, the entire portion of ceiling to which it was attached had, and with an unappealing groan and a crescendo of clashing crystal it peeled away and dropped. As it came Lord Petrefact was conscious of only one thing. He had to reach that red button before he was crushed, splintered or drowned. A murky brown liquid was pouring from the hole in the ceiling and now a new hazard entered the arena. A chunk of plaster disassociating itself from the chandelier dropped onto the wheelchair and in particular onto the very buttons Lord Petrefact so desperately needed. Behind him the chandelier disintegrated against the wall and lay still. In front the wheelchair, activated by the plaster, shot forward, gathered speed and collided first with a large ornamental vase and then with an embroidered silk screen which had until then been camouflaging Lord Petrefact's portable commode. Having demolished the screen and emptied the commode the chair recoiled, with apparent disgust and evident urgency, in the opposite direction. As the damned thing scuttled past him Lord Petrefact made a final attempt to stop it but the wheelchair was intent on other things, this time a glass-fronted cabinet containing some extremely valuable jade pieces. With a horror that came in part from the knowledge that they were irreplaceable, and for all he knew underinsured, Lord Petrefact watched the wheelchair slam through the glass and spin round several times, shattering the treasures of half a dozen dynasties before heading straight towards him.

But Lord Petrefact was ready. He had no intention of being decapitated by his own wheelchair or of joining the contents of the commode in that corner of the room. He shot sideways under the bed and lay crouched in a corner staring lividly at the footrest of the wheelchair which had nudged itself under the side of the bed and was still trying to get at him. That was certainly the impression Lord Petrefact had, and having seen what the bloody machine was capable of doing when it did get at something, he wasn't having it get at him. On the other hand he didn't want to be drowned either, and what appeared to be a domestic waterfall was gushing through the ceiling and spreading across the floor. He was just debating whether to risk the wheelchair or shove it in some less lethal direction when the door opened and someone shouted, 'Lord Petrefact, Lord Petrefact, where are you?'

Under the bed the great magnate tried to make his whereabouts known, but the infernal din upstairs, now joined by screams and the splash of falling water, drowned his reply. Having no dentures didn't help. Gnashing his gums he crawled towards the wheelchair while keeping an eye on the feet of the resuscitation team who had gathered in the doorway and were surveying the shambles.

'Where the hell can the old sod have got to?' one of them asked.

'Looks as though he's blown his top with a vengeance,' said someone else. 'I always knew the old bugger was as mad as a March hare but this takes the biscuit.'

Under the bed the old bugger wished he had a better view of the speaker. He'd show him what really happened when he blew his top. With a final effort to escape he reached out and shoved the foot rest of the wheelchair to one side. For a moment the thing seemed to hesitate while its wheels spun in the murky fluid, a process that involved gathering the end of Lord Petrefact's pyjama cord round its axle. And then it was off. Behind it, now convinced he was suffering from a terminal strangulated hernia, came Lord Petrefact. But it was the wheelchair that held the attention of the resuscitation team. They had seen many weird sights in their professional lives but an empty wheelchair gone berserk was not one of them. As it smashed its way through the remnants of the silk screen, as it ploughed across the commode, as it ricocheted off the wall and demolished yet another glass cabinet, this time containing a collection of Meissen figurines, the group stood transfixed in the doorway.

It was a great mistake. The wheelchair had evidently imbibed some of the malevolent characteristics of its previous occupant, now merely an appendage and an unrecognizable one at that, and by some mechanical telepathy knew its enemies. It hurtled at the door and as the group of doctors tried to escape, ploughed into them. There was a brief moment of respite for Lord Petrefact as the machine bucketed about in the doorway and then it was off down the corridor carrying all before it. The resuscitation team it discarded, leaving them lying limply on the carpet, but the green baize door proved only a slight obstacle and one that allowed Lord

Petrefact to collide with the rear of the wheelchair. After that the thing was away again bouncing from one wall of the corridor to another in its wild career.

Behind it Lord Petrefact, now convinced that he was past the terminal stage of strangulated hernia and well into its after-effects, knew only one thing. If, and the conditional seemed hopelessly optimistic, if he survived this appalling ordeal somebody was going to pay for it with their jobs, their future, and, if he could arrange it, with their lives. Not that he was in any state to catalogue those responsible, though the inventor of the wheelchair came high on the list with the distributors of the portable and supposedly un-spillable commode not far behind. And Croxley, God, just let him lay hands on Croxley ...

But these were subliminal thoughts and even they vanished as the wheelchair hurtled frenetically out of the corridor into the great marble entrance hall. For a moment Lord Petrefact glimpsed a blurred face peering over the balcony as he slithered across the marble floor and then the wheelchair skidded sideways, banged into a large oak table, slamming Lord Petrefact against the wall in the process, and with a last dash for freedom lurched at the front door. For one terrible moment Lord Petrefact had a vision of him-self being dragged down the steps and across the gravel drive towards the lake, but his fears were not fulfilled. Misjudging the door by a foot the chair smashed into a marble column. There was a crash as the footrest crumpled, a faint whirr before the motor stopped and Lord Petrefact caught up with the machine and, col-liding with the back wheels, lay still.

six

From the balcony Croxley watched the final demise of the wheel-chair, and with it presumably that of his employer, with a mixture of dismay and satisfaction. He had already risked life and limb by rescuing the egregious Yapp from what amounted to a combina-tion of superheated sauna and a rollercoaster bath, and had finally persuaded the distraught and buffetted professor that a deliberate attempt had not been made on his life. Yapp hadn't been easily persuaded.

'How the hell was I to know the bloody thing hadn't been used for sixty years?' he had squawked as Croxley dragged him from the wreckage.

'I did warn you that it was like living in a museum.'

'You didn't say anything about the Chamber of Horrors and that fucking bath being an instrument of capital punishment. There ought to be a law against installing bathroom facilities with lethal tendencies. I might have been scalded to death.'

'Yes,' said Croxley wistfully. Walden Yapp hadn't been a pleasant sight with his clothes on, but naked, pink, bruised and exuding a sense of outrage, he was the personification of his political opinions. Or so it seemed to Croxley. He left him with the deftly timed remark that he hoped Lord Petrefact wouldn't take him to the cleaners for wrecking a very valuable piece of domestic Victoriana and, by the look of things through the hole in the floor, the entire room below.

But by the time he reached the balcony the look of things had changed. It was doubtful if Lord Petrefact would live to sue another day and if anyone needed taking to the cleaners the object that slithered out in the wake of the wheelchair was clearly that person. For one horrible second Croxley had supposed it to be a pair of pyjamas that had somehow escaped from a septic tank and was doing its damnedest to catch the wheelchair. It was only after the revolting bundle had hit the wall and the wheelchair had crunched into the marble column that Croxley recognized his employer. With a sense of duty that overcame his personal feelings he bounded down the stairs and knelt beside the corpse and tried diffidently to find its pulse. It didn't seem to have one. And where the hell had the resuscitation team disappeared to? If ever their services had been needed it was now. But after he had yelled 'Help' several times and no one had appeared Croxley was forced to take that action for which he had conscientiously prepared himself and which he had prayed he would be spared. Lifting Lord Petrefact's bleeding head, and the fact that it was bleeding seemed to argue the old swine wasn't quite dead, he shut his eyes and applied mouth-to-mouth resuscitation. It was only after his third puff that he opened his eyes and found his left one staring into the demonic eye of Lord Petrefact. Croxley dropped the head at once. He had seen that eye looking murderous before but never at such close quarters.

'Are you all right?' he asked and immediately regretted it. The question galvanized the old man. It had been awful enough to be chased and then dragged by a demented wheelchair through God alone knew what filth, but to regain consciousness to find himself being kissed by his own confidential secretary of fifty years standing, and a man moreover whose perverse sense of humour had constructed a sucking pig out of the extremities of a fucking wild boar, was beyond belief awful.

'All right?' he yelled. 'All right? You stand there and have the gall to ask me if I'm all right. And what the hell were you kissing me for?'

'Mouth-to-mouth resuscitation,' muttered Croxley feeling that it would only exacerbate matters if he pointed out that he was actually kneeling and not standing. But Lord Petrefact was wrestling with his pyjama cord. Whatever Croxley had been doing could wait until he had done the infernal knot that was threatening his bowels with gas gangrene or worse. The thing was more a tourniquet than a pyjama cord.

'Here, let me help you,' said Croxley, suddenly realizing what was the matter, but Lord Petrefact had had enough of his secretary's oral attentions.

'Oh no you don't,' he screamed and gave a terrible spasmodic lurch. The wheelchair rolled backwards and ended his attempt to free himself from its ghastly attachment. With a sob Lord Petrefact lay still and was about to order Croxley to fetch a knife when the resuscitation team arrived on the scene.

'He's caught up in the –' Croxley began before being swept aside by the medical experts who thought they knew best. While one of them undid the oxygen mask, another unclipped the electrodes of the heart stimulator. Within seconds Lord Petrefact was silenced by the mask and was learning what it felt like to have electric shocks applied to a relatively healthy heart.

'And get rid of that damned wheelchair,' ordered the head of the team. 'We can't possibly work with that thing in the way and the patient needs room to breathe.'

Inside the oxygen mask Lord Petrefact disagreed, but he was in no position to voice his opinions. As the electric shocks pulsed through his chest and oxygen was pumped into his lungs and, finally, as another member of the team tried to drag the wheelchair away, Lord Petrefact knew that he was dying. For once he didn't care. Hell itself would be blissful by comparison with what these swine were doing to him.

'You fucking murderers,' he yelled into the mask, only to be jolted by another shock and the prick of a hypodermic in his arm. As he lapsed into unconsciousness he was vaguely aware that Croxley was bending over him with something that looked ominously like a carving knife. For a moment Lord Petrefact remembered the expurgated pig and felt for it. The next he was happily unconscious and Croxley was trying to get at the pyjama cord. It was a move calculated to mislead the doctors. The insane events of the morning had been caused by someone, and, being scientists, they were disinclined to blame the wheelchair. Nor did they know that what had caused the destruction of the bedroom had been something as mechanical as the Synchronized Ablution Bath. They had lived long enough in close proximity to Lord Petrefact to understand the strain he imposed on his secretary. It seemed abundantly clear to them that the man had been goaded beyond the limits of sanity and was bent on disembowelling his master. As Croxley grabbed the pyjama cord they threw themselves on him and pinned him to the ground before wresting the carving knife from his hand.

It was this scene that greeted Yapp as he emerged from the King Albert suite with his Intourist bag, determined to get the hell out of Fawcett House as quickly as possible. It was also the scene that met the horrified eyes of Mrs Billington-Wall when she arrived to open the house to visitors. Now wearing a tweed suit in place of her twin-set she was more formidable than ever. One glance at the mêlée of doctors and Croxley on the floor, another at Yapp hesitating on the staircase, and a final disgusted look at Lord Petrefact, and she took command of the situation.

'What the devil do you think you're doing down there?' she demanded.

'He was trying to kill Lord Petrefact,' muttered one of the medical team.

'I wasn't,' squeaked Croxley, trying to recover his breath, 'I was merely going to cut the cord that ...' He ran out of breath.

46

'Yes, well we've all heard that one before,' said one of the doctors. 'A classic case of paranoid schizophrenia. Cutting umbilical cords ...'

But Mrs Billington-Wall had already sized at least a portion of the situation up. 'He's got a point,' she said, looking with a professional eye on Lord Petrefact's purpling toes. 'Something is definitely obstructing his circulation.' And with a deft practicality she undid the pyjama cord and watched the toes begin to resume their normal pallor. The doctors got to their feet rather awkwardly.

'Well, someone certainly tried to kill him. His bedroom's been wrecked. He must have put up a terrific struggle.'

'If you're looking for a culprit I'd turn your attention to him,' said Mrs Billington-Wall, indicating Walden Yapp, who was hesitating with every symptom of guilt written all over him halfway down the stairs. 'And if you don't take that mask off the old fellow's face you'll be to blame yourselves.'

Walden Yapp waited no longer. The conviction that he had been lured to the house less by a hoaxer than by someone determined to have him pulped and scalded to death in that fearful bath had been made less tenable by the sight of Lord Petrefact lying bleeding and clearly *in extremis* on the floor. He was trying to deduce why the doctors were wrestling with Croxley when that snob of a woman intervened to point the finger of guilt at him. He could see himself being made the scapegoat for whatever crime had been committed. As the doctors moved towards the stairs and Mrs Billington-Wall uncoupled Lord Petrefact from the life-support system that was slowly killing him, Walden Yapp panicked. He turned and ran back along the landing and down the corridor. Behind him the doctors' footsteps urged him on but before he could decide where to go, and anywhere was preferable to the King Albert suite, they had turned the corner. Yapp tried a door and found it unlocked. He shot inside, slammed it behind him and looked for the key. There was no key. Or if there was it was on the other side. For a second he considered barricading the door with whatever furniture he could find but the curtains were drawn and the room in semi-darkness. It was also bare and apart from what looked like a rocking-horse he could see nothing useful. Instead he stood silently against the wall and hoped to hell they hadn't seen him enter.

But the footsteps had stopped and some muttering was going on in the corridor. Those ghastly creatures in white coats were evidently conferring. Then he heard Croxley speak.

'It's the old nursery. He won't be able to get out of there.' A key turned in the lock, the footsteps retreated, and Walden Yapp was left alone with the rocking-horse and his own tormented thoughts. By the time he had examined the room more thoroughly and discovered the barred windows he could see what Croxley meant about not being able to get out, though what ferocious children had required such thick bars to contain them he couldn't imagine. But then Fawcett House was filled with so many extraordinary features that it wouldn't have surprised him to learn that the nursery had once been used to house a baby gorilla. It seemed unlikely, but that fucking bath had seemed unlikely too and he wasn't going near the rocking-horse for fear it turned into a synchronized one. Instead he sat down in a corner and tried to take his mind off his own misery by studying those of the knife-grinders in Sheffield in 1863.

By the time Croxley and the resuscitation team returned to the hall Mrs Billington-Wall had taken control.

'You'll take him upstairs and give him a bed-bath and a fresh pair of pyjamas and put him to bed,' she told the doctors. 'And don't argue with me. There's nothing the matter with him that a good rest and some disinfectant won't put right. Scalp wounds always bleed profusely. I wasn't a FANY for nothing you know.' Croxley looked at her doubtfully and wondered. Mrs Billington-Wall was not a prepossessing woman but in wartime men were desperate ... On the other hand he wasn't looking forward to Lord Petrefact's reaction when he recovered consciousness and voiced his opinions about guests who wrecked bathrooms and put his life in danger, wheelchairs, medical teams and almost certainly that damned pig, and it might be an advantage to have him immobilized upstairs on Mrs Billington-Wall's instructions. Croxley made himself scarce while the resuscitation team, urged on by her insistence that she didn't want to have visitors seeing a peer of the realm in such a disgusting condition, carried Lord Petrefact up the staircase and into a bedroom.

And so until Lord Petrefact awoke to find himself clean, clothed and bedded down in a room that looked down over the lawns to the lake, Croxley busied himself with breakfast, the Sunday papers and what the hell to do about Yapp. He had no qualms about keeping him locked in the nursery and in any case the swine had his uses. If Mrs Billington-Wall could take the can back for ordering Lord Petrefact to be put to bed on the first floor with no recourse to the communications system implanted in the arm of the wheelchair, then Yapp would be a suitable scapegoat for the rest of the catastrophe. And catastrophe it certainly was. Croxley's brief inventory of the damage done by the Synchronized Ablution Bath and the wheelchair added up to something in the region of a quarter of a million pounds and possibly more. The jade pieces, and the term applied more accurately now than it had done before the wheelchair had shattered them, had been beyond price. Now they were beyond restoration. So were several extremely valuable Oriental rugs. The bath was responsible for their destruction – the bath and the steam which had filtered down through the hole left by the chandelier. In fact Petrefact's makeshift bedroom looked as though a rather hot flashflood had been through it. Yes, Yapp could be held responsible and Croxley thanked God that he hadn't been the one to suggest lodging the brute in the King Albert suite.

He was just congratulating himself on this piece of luck when one of the doctors came downstairs with a message that Lord Petrefact had regained consciousness and wanted to see him. From the look on the man's face Croxley gained the impression that Lord Petrefact's health had improved dramatically and with it had come a marked deterioration in his temper.

'I should watch your step,' said the doctor. 'He's not what you might call himself yet.'

Croxley went upstairs wondering what this cryptic comment might mean. Much to his astonishment he found Lord Petrefact in a comparatively mild state of fury. Mrs Billington-Wall was laying down the law.

'You're to stay here until you're better,' she told the nastier side of Lord Petrefact's face with a courage that suggested she had indeed been a FANY in the war and might well have seen action on a great many fronts. 'I won't allow you to be moved until I'm satisfied you've fully recovered from this dreadful assault.'

Lord Petrefact glared at her but said nothing. He evidently knew when he had met his match.

'And I don't want you to excite him,' she told Croxley. 'Ten minutes at the most and then down you go.'

Croxley nodded gratefully. Ten minutes in Lord Petrefact's company was ample. Under present conditions it was too long but it was better than forty.

'Who the hell was that?' asked Lord Petrefact weakly when she had left.

'Mrs Billington-Wall,' said Croxley, deciding that obtusely literal answers were the best defence. 'The widow of the late Brigadier-General Billington-Wall, D.S.O., M. –'

'I don't want the bitch's family tree. I want to know what she's doing here.'

'Taking care of you, as far as I can tell. She's usually showing visitors round the house but she's taken time off today –'

'Shut up,' yelled Lord Petrefact, momentarily forgetting his head. He sank back wincingly on the pillow. Croxley shut up and sat gazing with deferential dislike at the old man.

'Well, say something,' moaned Lord Petrefact.

'If you insist. First you tell me to shut up and then when I do you complain that I'm not saying anything.'

Lord Petrefact eyed his secretary with undivided loathing. 'Croxley,' he said finally, 'there have been moments in our long association when I have seriously considered firing you but I can tell you this, never before have I considered it quite so seriously as I am at this moment. Now then, why am I on the first floor?'

'Mrs Billington-Wall,' said Croxley. 'I tried to dissuade her but you've seen for yourself what she is like.'

Lord Petrefact had. He nodded. 'And what happened before that?'

Croxley decided to avoid a replay of the mouth-to-mouth misunderstanding and to get down to basics. 'Shall I start at the beginning?'

'Yes.'

'Well it all began when that fellow Yapp decided to take a bath ...'

'A bath?' goggled Lord Petrefact. 'A bath?'

'A bath,' repeated Croxley. 'Apparently he turned on the hot tap and waited until the bath was nearly full before getting in and ...'

But Lord Petrefact was no longer listening. It was clear that he had misjudged Yapp. The man wasn't the milksop he had supposed. If the brute could begin a train of events that had ended with the total destruction of a downstairs room and its contents, not to mention bringing down an extremely heavy and valuable chandelier, simply by taking a bath, he was a force to be reckoned with. More, he was a human cataclysm, a walking disaster area, a man of such maniacal gifts as beggared the imagination. To let him loose on his Petrefact relatives would be to bring down on their heads something of such malevolent energy that they wouldn't know what had hit them.

'Where is he now?' he demanded, interrupting the flow of Croxley's account.

'We've locked him in the old nursery.'

Lord Petrefact jerked under the sheets. 'In the old nursery? What the hell for?'

'We thought it safest. After all, the insurance company are going to want to know how this ...'

But Lord Petrefact had no intention of wasting Yapp's terrible gifts on insurance companies. 'Let him out at once. I want to see that young man. Fetch him here this instant.'

'But you heard what Mrs Billington-Wall ... oh all right.' He went out and down the corridor to the Nursery and was about to unlock the door when he was interrupted by Mrs Billington-Wall.

'And what do you think you're doing?' she demanded.

Croxley looked at her with malign pathos. It was perfectly obvious what he was doing. Even the meanest intelligence could comprehend that he was unlocking a door and he was about to put these thoughts into simple words when the look in her eye deterred him. It was even meaner than her intelligence. 'Lord Petrefact has requested the presence of Professor Walden Yapp,' he said, hoping to hell that formality would quell her. It did nothing of the sort.

'Then he's far sicker than I would have supposed. Probably suffering from concussion. In any case there will be no communication with that creature in there until the police have interviewed him.'

'Police?' squawked Croxley. 'You don't mean to say ... What police?'

Mrs Billington-Wall's eyes took on the qualities of an irritated laser. 'The local police, of course. I've phoned them to come at once.' And she shepherded the astonished Croxley back down the corridor.

Only outside Lord Petrefact's room did Croxley make a stand.

'Listen,' he said, 'there's been some mistake. You may not like Professor Yapp, and I certainly don't, but for some unknown reason Lord Petrefact does and when he hears you've called in the cops he isn't going to take kindly to it. It's in your own best interest to go downstairs and phone them again ...'

'I think I know my own best interests rather better than you do,' said Mrs Billington-Wall, 'and I'm not going to be party to an affray.'

'Affray? Affray? Dear God, you didn't tell them there'd been an affray here?'

'And how would you describe the disgraceful occurrences of this morning?'

Croxley sought for a suitable word and, apart from happenstance, which was rather too frivolous to appeal to this foul woman, could think of nothing. 'I suppose you could say —'

'An affray,' interrupted Mrs Billington-Wall. 'And what you seem to forget is that I am held personally responsible for this house during Lord Petrefact's absence and as caretaker ...'

'But he isn't absent. The man's in there,' said Croxley.

Mrs Billington-Wall gave the door of Lord Petrefact's bedroom a disparaging look. 'One must suppose so,' she conceded. 'All the same my judgement is that he's not in a fit state to make a lucid assessment of the situation. Legally speaking he is absent. I am not, and in my opinion ...'

'Yes, but what about the scandal?' said Croxley now fighting with a desperation made positively ferocious by the knowledge of what Lord Petrefact would do when he learnt that the police had been invited to take a look at his private affairs. Short of actually asking Her Majesty's Income Tax Inspectors to send half a dozen of their brightest young men to browse through his third set of ledgers Croxley could think of nothing more likely to give the old man terminal apoplexy than the intrusion of the police.

'What scandal?' asked Mrs Billington-Wall. 'If there's been any scandalous behaviour here I would say that the destruction of ...'

But Croxley had taken her arm and was leading her down the corridor away from the door.

'Pigs,' he whispered conspiratorially.

'Pigs?'

'Exactly.'

'What do you mean "exactly"?'

52

'What I said,' continued Croxley, frantically trying to lure the woman into a maze of misunderstanding from which she would emerge determined to stop the police on the doorstep.

'But you said "Pigs". Now you say "Exactly". I've not the slightest idea what you're talking about.'

'A nod's as good as a wink,' said Croxley with what he hoped was a suggestive leer.

Mrs Billington-Wall ignored it. 'Not to me it isn't. Are you trying to tell me ...'

'Quite,' said Croxley. 'Say no more.'

'That that old man in there has a perverse penchant for pigs?' Croxley raised his eyes to heaven and prayed. If it ever got to the old man's ears ... Still, anything was better than the police. He ploughed on.

'Sucking pigs,' he said trying to imbue the participle with a positively revolting emphasis. He succeeded. Mrs Billington-Wall stiffened.

'I don't believe it,' she snapped.

'I'm not asking you to,' said Croxley truthfully. 'All I'm saying is that if the police come tramping round the house in their dirty great boots the name of Billington-Wall's going to hit the front page of the *News of The World* next Sunday with banner head-lines like "Brigadier General's widow in Pork Orgy". And if you don't believe me go and ask the contract chef in the kitchen. Lord Petrefact had one disembowelled last night so that it would fit.'

'Fit?' said Mrs Billington-Wall with an expression of quite extra-ordinary disgust.

'Fit,' said Croxley. 'It wasn't the right size.'

'Size?'

'Look, you surely don't want me to spell out the physiological facts for you, do you? I should have thought a woman with your experience of ...'

'Never mind my experience,' said Mrs Billington-Wall, 'and I can assure you that it doesn't extend to bestiality.'

'I suppose not. Still ...'

'And if you think I'm going to be party to a conspiracy to cover up the disembowelling of a pig for the purposes you have sug-gested ...'

'Now, wait a moment –' began Croxley but Mrs Billington-Wall was not a woman to be stopped.

'Let me assure you I'm not. As Secretary of the Fawcett branch of the RSPCA I feel deeply on these matters.'

'I'm sure you do,' said Croxley, now so enmeshed in *suggestio porcine* that he was prepared to be rude, 'and you'll feel a damned sight deeper by the time the fuzz have had their crack at you. You try and explain the presence of a good third of intersected pig in the deep freeze and see how far it gets you. And don't believe me. Go and ask the bleeding chef and see for yourself.'

Leaving the bewildered woman he stalked back to Lord Petrefact's room.

Mrs Billington-Wall tramped downstairs and presently was engaged in a frantic attempt to elicit from the contract chef exactly what had happened the previous night. The process wasn't helped by the chef's Italian origin, the confusion of consonants, the insult to his profession implicit in Croxley's insistence that he turn a full-grown pig into a baby one by truncating the bloody thing, and now Mrs Billington-Wall's peculiar line of questioning.

'How should I know what for he wanted it that way? Is not my business. If he say cut pig I cut pig. So he likes little pigs. Is all right with me.'

It wasn't all right with Mrs Billington-Wall. 'How utterly revolting. I've never heard anything so disgusting in my life.'

The chef shrugged philosophically. 'Not disgusting. Is peculiar I admit but English milords is known for being ... how you say ...?'

'Disgusting,' said Mrs Billington-Wall adamantly.

'Eccentric,' said the chef finally finding the word he was after.

'Well you may think it eccentric but as far as I'm concerned the whole thing is beyond description repulsive.'

She turned to leave the kitchen when a fresh thought struck her. 'And what did you do with the ... er ... the thing afterwards?' she enquired, now quite convinced that Croxley's advice had been sensible.

'Afterwards?' said the chef. 'So his lordship didn't like it we weren't going to waste it. We ate it, of course.'

For one terrible moment Mrs Billington-Wall stared at the chef with a look of such incredulous revulsion that he felt called upon to amplify his statement.

'Was very good. The crackling ...'

But Mrs Billington-Wall had gone. There were limits to her sense of what was right and proper and even sane and what she had just heard ... As she dashed from the kitchen fighting to keep her gorge down she knew one thing absolutely. The police must on no account be allowed to investigate the horrible sequence of events that had taken place at Fawcett House.

seven

For once her views and those of Lord Petrefact could be said to coincide. His reaction to Croxley's announcement that the police were on their way had been so violent that he was out of bed and almost on his feet before he realized the lack of a wheelchair.

'I'll have the law on the bitch,' he yelled, 'so help me God I'll ...'

Croxley helped him off the floor and back into bed before pointing out that the trouble with the police was that, colloquially speaking, they were the law and in any case tended to represent it. Lord Petrefact wasn't in the mood for fine distinctions.

'I know that, you moron. I don't mean that sort of law. I mean my sort.'

'Yours being the sort with teeth to it,' said Croxley. 'I've always been interested in the dichotomy between civil law and ...'

'Dichotomy?' yelled Lord Petrefact. 'If you so much as mention that word again after serving up that fucking dichotomized pig last night I'll ...' He ran out of threats and lay breathing heavily. 'And get me another bleeding wheelchair.'

Croxley considered the matter. It was certainly more to his liking than discussions about pigs. 'We've got a problem there,' he said finally.

Lord Petrefact took his own pulse and tried to keep calm. 'Of course we've got a problem,' he spluttered at last, 'that's why I need another fucking wheelchair.'

'It's Sunday.'

Lord Petrefact stared at him dementedly. 'Sunday? What the hell has Sunday got to do with it?'

'For one thing the shops aren't open and for another even if they were I doubt if the local Post Office runs to motorized invalid chairs. I mean this isn't London ...'

'London?' yelled Lord Petrefact, disregarding the intimations of his pulse. 'Of course it isn't London. Any fool knows that. It's the back of bleeding beyond. That doesn't mean you can't phone Harrods or some place and tell them to send one in by helicopter.'

'Some place being possibly the Galapagos Islands?' said Croxley deciding to chance his arm.

Lord Petrefact stared at him wildly but said nothing. Croxley was evidently trying to kill him. 'Never mind where. Just get me one.'

'I'll do my best but I don't suppose it will arrive before the police and there's Yapp to consider. I mean if they find him locked in the nursery I don't know what they're going to think or he to say.'

Lord Petrefact did, and could hardly find words. 'You don't mean to say he's ...' Croxley nodded.

'But I told you to let him out. I told you I wanted to see the swine.'

'It was a little difficult to persuade Mrs Billington-Wall that letting him out was an advisable course of action. She seemed to think ...'

'Seemed? That loathsome creature has no right to think. She shouldn't even have the fucking vote in my opinion. And when I say I want him out ... Go and get the bastard, Croxley, go and get him. And if that woman gets in your way you have my permission to use the utmost physical force. Kick the cow where it hurts.'

'Definitely,' said Croxley, and left the room.

But downstairs Mrs Billington-Wall was too engaged in defending her own reputation against the consequences of a police enquiry to be bothered about Yapp. The sergeant and two constables who had driven over had already entered the hall before she could stop them.

'And what brings you here, Sergeant?' she asked with an unfortunate attempt to look surprised.

'You did, Mrs Billington-Wall.'

'I did?'

'Yes,' said the Sergeant. 'If you remember, you phoned the station and said there'd been an affray ...'

Mrs Billington-Wall put a supposedly startled hand to her cultured pearls. 'You must be mistaken. I assure you I . . .' She drained off. The Sergeant was studying the crumpled wheelchair and the bloodstains on the marble floor.

'What's more, by the look of things you weren't far off,' continued the Sergeant and took out his notebook. 'One badly damaged invalid chair, one large blood patch, one deal table . . .'

'Oak,' said Mrs Billington-Wall involuntarily.

'All right, one oak table with leg missing . . . And what's that horrible pong?'

'Pong?'

'Smell, then.'

'I really can't think,' said Mrs Billington-Wall truthfully.

'I can,' said the Sergeant, and ordering a constable to stand guard by the wheelchair, the bloodstain and the oak table, followed his nose.

'His Lordship will take great exception to your intrusion,' said Mrs Billington-Wall, trying to pull rank, but the Sergeant was not to be deterred.

'Not the only thing he'll take exception to,' he said, 'I can't say I like the look of things and as for that niff . . .' He took out a handkerchief and covered his nose. 'I think we'll have a look down this corridor,' he mumbled.

Mrs Billington-Wall barred his way. 'You have absolutely no right to enter private premises without permission,' she said staunchly.

'Which, since you invited us here in the first place, I can only presume has been given,' said the Sergeant.

'But I keep telling you I didn't. I don't know what you're talking about.'

'Nor do I,' said the Sergeant, 'but I'm going to find out.' And pushing past her he headed down the foetid corridor. As he opened the shattered baize door there was no doubt in his mind that Mrs Billington-Wall had not been exaggerating when she had stated there had been an affray in Fawcett House. If anything she had been understating the case.

'One smashed door,' he noted as he stepped over the wreckage, 'one soiled mat . . .'

'One Shirvan rug,' said Mrs Billington-Wall. 'It's an extremely fine specimen of Persian rug.'

'Was,' said the Sergeant. 'I wouldn't like to be the bloke who has to clean that lot up.'

'And I wouldn't like to be in your shoes when Lord Petrefact gets to hear about your invasion of his privacy.'

'More like his privy, if you ask me.'

By the time they had reached the wrecked bedroom the Sergeant had noted several more exhibits in his book and Mrs Billington-Wall had given her reputation up for lost.

'Jesus, looks like the place has been hit by a hurricane,' said the Sergeant surveying the destruction. 'Talk about bleeding bulls in china shops. And what's that thing?'

Mrs Billington-Wall looked at the commode with disgust. 'I hesitate to say.'

'I shouldn't hesitate too long. I'm going to want a statement from you as to exactly what's gone on in here. And there's no use your looking like that. You phoned us and said there'd been an affray and we were to come immediately. Now we're here and there's blood on the floor and the place looks like a thousand football hooligans have been through it and you clam up. Now I want to know why. Has someone been putting the frighteners on you?'

Mrs Billington-Wall thought about pigs and said nothing. She was saved by the dishevelled appearance of one of the doctors who passed the door carrying a bedpan.

'Jesus wept,' said the Sergeant, 'what the hell was that?' But before Mrs Billington-Wall could answer he was out into the corridor. 'OK, hold it,' he shouted. The doctor hesitated but a glance towards the hall sufficed to tell him he was trapped. Another policeman was standing there.

'What do you want?' he asked belligerently.

'I want to know who you are and what you're doing with that thing,' said the Sergeant, eyeing the bedpan with very considerable suspicion.

'I happen to be Lord Petrefact's medical attendant,' said the doctor, 'and this is a bedpan.'

'Is it?' said the Sergeant, who disliked irony. 'And I suppose you're going to tell me next that Lord Petrefact needs it?'

'I am.'

'I should have thought it was a bit late in the day for bedpans. There's a portable loo in there and ...' He stopped. The doctor was staring over his shoulder and Mrs Billington-Wall was mouthing something at him. The Sergeant wasn't having witnesses to a serious crime interfered with.

'All right, take him in there,' he told the constable, 'I'll question him later. I'm going to drag the truth out of her first. And call the Regional Crime Squad. This is no ordinary case.'

While the doctor, still protesting that he was being prevented from carrying out his professional duties, was hustled into Croxley's study, the Sergeant turned his full attention on Mrs Billington-Wall.

'But I don't know what happened,' she said, though with rather less force than before. 'I arrived this morning to find the house ... well, you've seen what it's like but ...'

'So why did you tell that medic with the bedpan not to mention pigs?'

Mrs Billington-Wall swallowed and said she hadn't.

The Sergeant shook his head. 'Listen, when someone starts whispering about pigs over my shoulder to another witness I rate that as obstructing justice. Now what's with the pigs?'

'I think you ought to have a word with the chef,' said Mrs Billington-Wall, 'and please make a note in that beastly little book that I wasn't anywhere near this house at any time last night. I swear I wasn't.'

The Sergeant looked from her to the wrecked room. 'You're not seriously suggesting that pigs had anything to do with this?' he asked before forming an even worse impression of her. 'Or were you by any chance referring to the police as pigs?'

'No, I wasn't. I've always had the highest regard –'

'Right, so now you can demonstrate some of that high regard by telling me exactly what the hell's been going on here.'

'Officer,' said Mrs Billington-Wall, 'I can honestly say I've no idea.'

'But you say the chef does?' said the Sergeant.

Mrs Billington-Wall nodded miserably and wished to hell he didn't. They went down the corridor to the kitchen. But by the time they emerged twenty fraught minutes later the Sergeant was none the wiser. The contract chef's claim that he had no idea what on earth had caused the chaos in the bedroom or the bloodstains in the hall had been interjected with hysterical denials that he had been hired to provide perverse entertainment for Lord Petrefact by way of fucking pigs. Mrs Billington-Wall had promptly demanded the right to leave the room.

'I'm not standing here while this disgusting little man goes on about this disgraceful business,' she said, 'I've had all I can take this morning.'

'You think I like being asked these questions?' shouted the outraged chef. 'I'm not an ordinary chef ...'

'You can say that again,' said Mrs Billington-Wall and walked out.

'Never mind her,' said the Sergeant. 'Now, you say that Mr Croxley ... who the devil is Mr Croxley anyway? Lord Petrefact's secretary. Right, so this Croxley told you to cut the pig in half because Lord Petrefact wanted to fuck it? Is that what you are saying?'

'I don't know what he wanted. First he says for me to order a pig. So I get a pig. Then he says too big for sucking.'

'Sucking? You did say sucking?' said the Sergeant beginning to share Mrs Billington-Wall's misgivings.

'I didn't say anything. All I say is I work all my life as chef and I never seen such a big fucking pig. No way could I get that pig in the oven. Not even two ovens. Maybe three. I don't know. And then there was the turtle.'

'Turtle?'

'Yes, first he wants a turtle. Mr Croxley telephones the aquarium and –'

'The aquarium?'

'That's what he say. Don't ask me. If Mr Croxley tell me ...'

'This Croxley bloke's got some answering to do,' said the Sergeant and made some notes, while the chef fetched the turtle-shell and showed it to him. The Sergeant shook his head in disbelief. The notion that anyone could find anything remotely resembling carnal pleasure with an enormous turtle was even less appealing to think about than that fucking pig.

'And you say all this took place between two o'clock yesterday afternoon and nine last night?' he said, attempting to return to mundane facts.

'Two o'clock?' shouted the chef. 'How long do you think it took me to cut that pig in three pieces and sew them together again?'

The Sergeant preferred not to think. He went back down the corridor to question the doctor.

eight

If the Sergeant's quest for some sort of understanding as to what kind of crime he was supposed to be investigating led him deeper into a morass of confusion, Lord Petrefact had troubles of his own.

Walden Yapp had emerged from the Nursery with only one thought in mind. He was going to get out of this frightful building, and once out he had half a mind to sue Lord Bloody Petrefact for unlawful imprisonment, grievous bodily harm, assault and attempted murder. The other half of his mind was busily trying to discover a motive for the conspiracy and failing hopelessly. He was naturally reluctant to follow Croxley anywhere, and particularly disliked the notion of seeing Lord Petrefact again.

'But he simply wants to apologize,' said Croxley. 'There's nothing more to it than that.'

'If his apologies are anything like his bathroom facilities I can do without them.'

'I can assure you that was purely accidental.'

'Well, locking me in that room wasn't,' said Yapp, 'I heard you do it. I intend going to the police to lodge a complaint.'

Croxley gave a wan smile. 'In that case I should definitely stick around. The police are already downstairs questioning people and they'll certainly want to grill you.'

'Me?' said Yapp now distinctly alarmed. 'Why me?'

'You'd better ask Lord Petrefact that. He's in a better position to tell you than I am. All I know is that there's obviously been an exceedingly serious crime.'

He ushered the now subdued Yapp into the bedroom. Lord Petrefact raised a bandaged head and gave his awful smile. 'Ah, Yapp my dear chap,' he said, 'do take a seat. I think we ought to have a little chat.'

Yapp hesitantly took a seat by the door.

'All right, Croxley, you can leave,' said Lord Petrefact. 'Just go downstairs and see that we're not disturbed.'

'That's easier said than done,' said Croxley. 'The cops are crawling all over the place and ...'

There was no need for him to go on. Lord Petrefact was taking the news as badly as everyone else. 'Get out,' he yelled. 'And if one copper puts his nose inside that door I'll have your scalp.'

Croxley went and Lord Petrefact turned his terrible charm on Yapp. 'A most unfortunate occurrence, and I shall do everything I can to spare you from being involved,' he murmured. Yapp looked at him doubtfully.

'I must say I take exception ...' he began but Lord Petrefact raised a withered hand.

'Of course you do, of course you do. I'd feel exactly the same in your situation. The last thing you want is to have your name dragged through the mud by the media. Court actions, insurance company investigations and all that sort of thing ... No, no, we can't possibly allow that to happen.'

Yapp said he was glad to hear it. He wasn't too sure what it was he was hearing but at least Lord Petrefact seemed to bear him considerably less ill-will than he did Croxley. 'On the other hand I was locked in a room,' he began but the old man stopped him.

'That idiot Croxley's fault. I have reprimanded him very severely and you've only to say the word and I'll have the fellow sacked.'

He watched with amusement as Yapp rose to the bait.

'Certainly not,' he said. 'The last thing I'd want is for any man to lose his employment on my account.'

'Dock his pay for a couple of months then?'

Yapp looked appalled and was still searching for socially significant words to express his disgust at this act of capitalist exploitation when the old man went on.

'Now then, about the family history. You've read the contract and I hope the terms are agreeable.'

'Agreeable?' said Yapp, who, in the extraordinary circumstances of the morning, had largely forgotten the purpose of his visit and had seen it more as a trap.

'You don't consider the fee too slight? Of course I'm prepared to shoulder all expenses into the bargain.'

'I really don't know,' said Yapp. 'You seriously want me to research the entire socio-economic background of your family?' Lord Petrefact nodded. There was nothing he wanted more than to set this destructive maniac to work on his family. By the time the swine was through with them half the relatives would have died of shock.

'With no pre-conditions?'

'Absolutely none.'

'And publication guaranteed?'

'Without question.'

'Well in that case ...'

'Done,' said Lord Petrefact, 'I'll sign the contract here and now. There's no point in letting the grass grow under one's feet.'

'I suppose not,' said Yapp, who didn't find the metaphor a particularly happy one.

And presently, with Croxley to witness the signatures, the contracts were exchanged.

'Well, you'll be wanting to get on,' said Lord Petrefact sinking back on the pillow, 'but before you go ... all right Croxley, there's no need for you to hang around.'

'There is,' said Croxley. 'The Regional Crime Squad have just arrived.'

'Tell the swine to go away. There hasn't been a crime and I'm not having policemen –'

'That's not what Mrs Billington-Wall told them. She's told them you've been into pigs and the Sergeant's got the notion from the chef that that turtle was a receptacle for more than Fortnum and Mason's best ...'

'Dear God,' shouted Lord Petrefact. 'What do you mean I'm "into pigs"?'

'That's just the beginning,' said Croxley, preferring to keep off the topic. 'She's also told them that Professor Yapp tried to murder you and the doctor's evidence that there were several detonations hasn't exactly helped.'

Lord Petrefact nudged himself up the bed. 'Croxley,' he said in tones of such implicit menace that Yapp shuddered, 'either you will go downstairs and explain to those interfering lunatics of the Crime Squad that this is my property and that as far as I am concerned there has been no crime committed on it and that Professor Yapp was merely taking a bath or ...' There was no need for him to continue. Croxley had already left.

Lord Petrefact turned back to his guest. 'You will start at Buscott. It's the original family mill, you know, built in 1784 and still working to the best of my knowledge. Ghastly place. I did my apprenticeship there. Anyway it will give you a fairly good idea of the conditions under which the family made its early fortune. My youngest sister, Emmelia, runs the place now. Makes ethnic costumes, whatever they are, or something of the sort. You'll find her at the New House, Buscott. Can't miss it. And the earliest records are in the local museum. You shouldn't have any trouble and if you do refer them to me.'

'A letter of introduction might help,' said Yapp.

Lord Petrefact rather doubted it but he was prepared to compromise. 'I'll have Croxley make out a cheque for you just as soon as he's got rid of these confounded policemen. And now if you don't mind. The events of this morning have rather taken their toll of me.' And with a last reminder that Yapp was to start his research at Buscott, Lord Petrefact dismissed him and lay back wearily in bed with the comforting thought that this foul man was going to make mincemeat of Emmelia and all the other Petrefacts who littered the landscape round Buscott.

But to Walden Yapp as he threaded his way down the corridor and onto the landing there was no hint of these hidden motives. He was still too dazed by the sudden switch from misfortune to the extraordinary good fortune of being offered the opportunity to expose the social evils which had led the Petrefacts to fortune and the building of this vile house to concentrate on remote problems. Or even immediate ones. His consistently theoretical mind was so preoccupied with the statistical evidence of working-class suffering he would be able to extract from the Petrefact archives that he had reached the bottom of the great staircase before he was fully conscious that there were an inordinate number of policemen milling about. He stopped and stared suspiciously. Yapp disliked policemen. It was one of the tenets of his social philosophy that they were the bodyguards of property owners and in his more high-flown lectures he had referred to them as the Praetorian Guard of Private Enterprise.

In the present circumstances their role seemed quite the reverse. Croxley was arguing with an inspector whose attention was held by the bloodstain on the floor.

'I keep telling you the whole thing was an accident,' he said, 'there is absolutely no purpose in your being here.'

'That's not what Mrs Billington-Wall says. She says –'

'I know what she says, and if you want my opinion the woman is mad. Lord Petrefact has instructed me ...'

'I'd like to see this Lord Petrefact myself before I form any opinion,' said the Inspector dourly.

'Quite so,' said Croxley. 'On the other hand he doesn't want to see you, and his medical advisers have given orders that he isn't to be disturbed. He's not in a fit condition.'

'In that case he ought to be in hospital,' said the Inspector. 'You can't have it both ways. If he's too ill to see me he's too sick to stay here. I'll send for an ambulance and –'

'You do that and you'll live to regret it,' shouted Croxley, now thoroughly alarmed. 'You don't think Lord Petrefact goes to ordinary hospitals. It's the London Clinic or nothing.'

'In that case I'm going up to have a word with him.' The Inspector headed for the stairs and was just climbing them when Yapp decided this was a good opportunity to make himself scarce. He strode across the hall towards the doorway and might have made it if Mrs Billington-Wall hadn't chosen that moment to reappear.

'There he is,' she screamed, 'there's the man you want.' Yapp stopped in his tracks and glared at her but already several constables had converged on him and he was hustled into what had once been the main drawing-room, closely followed by the Inspector.

'I protest against this outrage,' he began, following the routine he had learnt from so many political demonstrations. But the Inspector wasn't to be fobbed off by protests.

'Name?' he said taking a seat at a table.

Yapp considered the question and decided not to answer it. 'I demand to see my legal representative,' he said.

The Inspector made a note of this lack of co-operation. 'Address?'

Yapp remained silent.

'I know my rights,' he said presently when the Inspector had finished writing down that the suspect refused to state his name and address and had adopted an aggressive manner from the start.

'I'm sure you do. Been through the drill before, eh? And got a record.'

'A record?'

'Done a stretch or two.'

'If you're suggesting I've been to prison ...'

'Listen,' said the Inspector. 'I'm not suggesting anything except that you won't answer questions and have acted in a suspicious manner. Now then ...'

While the interrogation began Croxley went upstairs with a new sense of satisfaction. Mrs Billington-Wall might be, and indeed was, a force for confusion, but the sight of Walden Yapp being dragged by three constables into the drawing-room had cheered him enormously. Croxley was still smarting under the affront to his confidentiality occasioned by not knowing what document he had seen signed. For all he knew it might be Lord Petrefact's will, though a will would hardly require Yapp's signature as well. No, it was some form of contract and as confidential private secretary he had a right to know. It was therefore with something like mild delight that he entered the bedroom.

'The fat's in the fire now,' he announced choosing his metaphor for maximum effect. Lord Petrefact's diet made him averse to any mention of fat while he had an understandable phobia about fires.

'Fire? Fat? Where?' squawked the alarmed peer.

'In the drawing-room,' said Croxley. 'The Billington woman has fingered Yapp.'

'Fingered him?' said Lord Petrefact, subsiding slightly.

'Colloquially speaking. It's police jargon for accusing someone. Anyway they've dragged him off and are presumably grilling the fellow.'

'But I told you to get rid of the bastards,' shouted Lord Petrefact, 'I specifically ordered you to ...'

'It's no use your carrying on like that. I told them to leave but they won't listen to me. I got the impression from the Inspector that he doesn't believe you exist. He insists on seeing you.'

'Then, by God, he will,' yelled the old man and hoisted himself onto the edge of the bed. 'Get me the medical team and bring me that fucking wheelchair ..' He stopped and considered the fate of great-uncle Erskine on the staircase and the demonstrably lethal qualities of the wheelchair. 'On second thoughts, don't. There's a sedan chair in the Visitors' wing. I'll use that.'

'If you insist,' said Croxley doubtfully, but it was clear that Lord Petrefact did. His imprecations followed Croxley down the corridor.

Twenty minutes later the sedan chair, borne on the shoulders of Croxley, two waiters, the chef and the male members of the resuscitation team, lurched down the staircase while inside Lord Petrefact prayed and occasionally cursed.

'If anyone drops this fucking thing they'll never hear the end of it,' he shouted rather illogically when they were halfway down. But they reached the bottom safely and lumbered into the drawing-room, to the astonishment of the Inspector who had finally got Yapp to admit that he was Professor of Demotic Historiography at the University of Kloone. That had been difficult enough to believe, but the apparition of the sedan chair and its contents unnerved the Inspector.

'What in Heaven's name is that?' he demanded.

Lord Petrefact ignored the question. When it came to dealing with public servants he had no scruples. 'What do you think you are doing on private property? There is no need to answer that question. I intend to lodge a complaint with the Home Secretary and doubtless you will be required to answer then. In the meantime I give you five minutes to get out of here lock, stock and barrel. If you are still here you will be charged with illegal entry, trespass and damage to property. Croxley, put a telephone call through to the Solicitor General. I'll take it in the study. Professor Yapp will accompany me.'

And without further ado he ordered the sedan chair to be carried out and across the hall to the study. Yapp followed in a daze of speculation. He had heard of the Influence of The Establishment and had in fact lectured on it, but never before had he seen it so flagrantly in action.

'Well, I'll be fucked,' said the Inspector as the procession departed. 'Who the hell landed us in this bloody mess?'

'Mrs Billington-Wall,' said Croxley who had stayed behind to avoid having to bear the weight of the sedan chair and to witness the dismay of the Crime Squad. 'If you want to get yourself out of trouble I would advise you to take her in for questioning.'

And having left this suggestion to cause that wretched woman the maximum inconvenience he followed Yapp to the study. Ten minutes later the police had driven off. Mrs Billington-Wall accompanied them, much against her will.

'This is a cover-up,' she shouted as she was bundled into a police car, 'I tell you that creature with the Intourist bag is behind it.'

The Inspector privately agreed. He hadn't liked Yapp from the word go, but then again he hadn't liked what the Solicitor General had said on the telephone and couldn't imagine he'd enjoy the inevitable interview with the Chief Constable. Since the weight of authority had come down against Mrs Billington-Wall he meant to concoct some form of excuse from her statement.

Behind them Fawcett House resumed its evil tenor. The notice announcing that visitors would be welcome at £2 a head was taken down. Yapp accepted a glass of brandy. Croxley accepted the immediate notice of the contract chef and dismissed the caterers. The medical team made up another bed in the private study on the ground floor and Lord Petrefact, having entered it, ordered the converted hearse to be ready to take him to London as soon as he had rested.

Finally Walden Yapp drove off down the long drive in his rented car with a cheque for twenty thousand pounds in his pocket and a new sense of social grievance to spur his research. He couldn't wait to get back to his Modem and tell Doris all about his recent experiences.

nine

The little town of Buscott (population 7048) nestles in the Vale of Bushampton in the heart of England. Or so the few guide books that bother to mention it would have the tourist believe. In fact it crouches beside the sluggish river from which it derives the first part of its name and the original Petrefacts had drawn much of their wealth. The old mill still stands beside the Bus and the remains of its wheel rust in a sump of plastic bottles and beer cans. It was here that they had for centuries past ground corn and, if Yapp's assumptions were right, the faces of the poor. But it is further down the river that the New Mill, built, as Lord Petrefact said, in 1784, looms so monumentally and provides the little town with its sole industry and presumably underpaid employment. Inside its gaunt grey walls generations of Petrefacts had done a brief apprenticeship before moving on, suitably chastened by the experience, to greater and financially more rewarding occupations.

They were about the only people who did move. For the rest Buscott, unaffectionately known to the locals as Bus Stop for the illogical reason that buses had long stopped even passing through, has changed little over the years. It remains what it was, a small mill town, isolated from the rest of Britain by its remoteness, the silting of the old canal and the axing of its railway line and, most strangely of all, by the very industriousness of its inhabitants. Whatever may be said about contemporary England, workers in Buscott work; the last strike occurred briefly in 1840 and is never mentioned. As if these oddities were not enough, climate and geography combine to cut Buscott off even more completely. TV reception is appalling and the weather so variable that in winter the roads are frequently blocked by snow and in summer are avoided by all but the hardiest hill-walkers.

It was in the guise of such a one that Walden Yapp moved towards the town. Wearing a pair of shorts which reached below his knees and which had been bequeathed him by a Fabian uncle, he strode across the moors carrying a slumped rucksack. Every now and again he stopped and surveyed the landscape with appreciation. Heather, bog, outcrop and the occasional coppice all fitted into his imagination most precisely. This was the approach to Buscott he had foreseen. Even the few tumbledown cottages he passed afforded him satisfaction and spoke nostalgically of rural depopulation in the eighteenth century. That they had never been more than shepherds' huts and sheepfolds escaped him. His sense of demotic history prevailed. This was Petrefact land and honest yeomen had been driven from these moors to provide fodder for the mill and space for grouse.

By the time he reached the Vale of Bushampton Yapp was a happy man. The memory of his stay at Fawcett had faded, his cheque had been deposited and he had received several hand-written letters from Lord Petrefact setting out the names of his various relatives who might prove mines of information. But Yapp was less interested in the personal reminiscences of plutocrats than in the objective socio-economic conditions of the working class, and with each stride forward he felt more certain that Buscott would provide in microcosm the definitive data he sought to validate the research he had already done in the University library.

Over the weeks he had fed Doris with his findings; that the census records showed that the population had remained constant, more or less, since 1801; that the New Mill had until recent times produced cotton products of such excellent quality and low price that they had been able to stand competition from foreign mills far longer than factories elsewhere in Britain; that over half the working population were employees of the Petrefacts; and that ninety percent of the households, far from holding their houses with anything approaching permanency, rented them from the damnably ubiquitous family. Even the shops in the town were Petrefact possessions and as far as Yapp could make out it seemed probable that he was going to find some form of truck system still in existence. Nothing would have surprised him, he confided to the computer in a preliminary draft of his findings; as usual Doris had obliged by agreeing.

But as in so many things Yapp's theories proved at some variance to the facts. As he breasted the last rise and looked down into the Vale he was disappointed not to see the obvious signs of squalor and opulence which marked the division between the town and its owners. From a distance Buscott looked disturbingly bright and cheerful. True, the mill cottages of his imagination were there, as was the New House on the hill. But the cottages were brightly painted, their gardens filled with flowers, while the New House had a gentle elegance about it that suggested a greater degree of good taste in the Petrefact who had built it than Yapp would have expected. It was a refined Regency house with delicately wrought iron balconies and a sloping canopy along its front. A gravelled drive ran up one side of a curved lawn and down the other and behind it there was an herbaceous border and a flowering shrubbery. Finally a large conservatory gleamed along one side of the house. Even Yapp couldn't claim that the New House dominated Buscott in the gloomy way he had expected. He turned his attention to the Mill and again was disappointed. The factory might loom over the river, but from where he sat it had a prosperous and positively cheerful air about it. As he watched, a brightly coloured van drove through the gates and stopped in the cobbled yard. The driver got out and opened the back doors and presently the van was being loaded with a speed and efficiency Yapp had never seen in any of the many factories he had studied. Worse still, the workers appeared to be laughing, and laughing workers were definitely outside his range of experience.

All in all his first impressions of Buscott were so different from his hopes that he unhitched his knapsack, seated himself on the bank and fumbled for his sandwiches. As he munched them he sifted through the statistics he had gathered about Buscott, the low wages, the high unemployment, the absence of proper medical facilities, the total lack of trade-union representation, the number of houses without bathrooms, the infant mortality rate, the refusal of the local and undoubtedly Petrefact-dominated council to provide a comprehensive school on the suspicious grounds that since Buscott didn't have a grammar school to begin with, the Secondary Modern was sufficiently comprehensive already. None of these grim facts squared with his first impressions of the place, and certainly they didn't explain the laughter that had reached him from the Mill.

And so with the thought that he had been sensible to come alone to make a preliminary study of the town before sending for the team of sociologists and economic historians he had assembled at the University, he got to his feet and set off down through the woods towards the river.

In his office at the Mill Frederick Petrefact finished finding faults with the proof of the latest catalogue, made a few comments about the false register of the colour photographs, and decided it was time for lunch. Lunch on Thursday meant Aunt Emmelia, inconsequential conversation, cats and cold mutton. Of the four Frederick could never make up his mind which he disliked most. The cold mutton had at least the merit of being dead, and from the inertia of several cats he had sat on in the past he judged that not all Aunt Emmelia's menagerie were living. No, on the whole it was the combination of Aunt Emmelia and her conversation that made Thursday a black day for him. It was made worse by the knowledge that without her favour he wouldn't be where he was, a circumstance that made it impossible for him to be downright rude to her. Not that he liked being in Buscott or running the Mill, but it did give him the chance to make another fortune to take the place of the one his father had denied him. And Aunt Emmelia shared one thing with him, she loathed his father.

'Ronald is a bounder and a cad,' she had said when he first came down to explain his problem. 'He should never have sullied the family name by taking a peerage from that vile little man and I have the gravest doubts about what he had done to deserve it. It wouldn't surprise me to hear that he had fled to Brazil. One can hardly see him following the proper example of that other creature who had the decency to shoot himself.'

It was an odd attitude to find in such an apparently homely woman, but Frederick was soon to learn that Aunt Emmelia had at least one absolute principle to which she clung. She had elevated social obscurity to a point of honour and was always quoting the seventeenth-century Petrefact who was supposed to have said that if God had been prepared to answer Moses by conceding only 'I am that I am' it behoved the family to be as modest. Petrefacts were Petrefacts and the name was title enough. In Aunt Emmelia's eyes her brother had defiled the family by adding 'Lord' to the name. It was this rather than his treatment of his son which had won Frederick a place in her peculiar affections and the sole management of the Mill.

'You can do what you like down there,' she had told him. 'It is the business of a business to make money and if you are a true Petrefact you will succeed. I make only one condition. You will not communicate with your father. I will have nothing more to do with him.'

Frederick had agreed without hesitation. His last interview with his father had been so unpleasant he had no wish to repeat it. On the other hand Aunt Emmelia's character was too subtle for his liking. He never knew what she was thinking except on the subject of his father and beneath a façade of absent-minded kindness he suspected she was no nicer than the other members of the family.

Certainly her charities were so conspicuously arrogant or downright contradictory – she had once handed a pound note to a very wealthy farmer who had celebrated the purchase of some more acres by getting so drunk that he had fallen into the gutter, and had compounded this insult by expressing the hope that he would find gainful employment as a road sweeper for the Council – that Frederick never knew where he stood with her. And as far as he could tell the rest of Buscott felt as uncertain. She refused to go to church and had rebuffed the arguments of several vicars by pointing to the loving achievements of Christians in Ireland, Mexico and Reformation Britain.

'I mind my own business and I expect others to do likewise,' she said, 'and why God should find merit in groups of people who gather in a building and sing ridiculous hymns rather badly is quite beyond my comprehension. He doesn't sound right in the head to me.'

On the other hand it was suspected that she sometimes slipped out at night and put money through the letter-boxes of pensioners, and the New House was a safe depository for unwanted kittens. Finally there was some doubt as to why she had never married. At sixty she was still a handsome woman and it was generally considered that her objection to marriage lay in having to change her name. All in all, Aunt Emmelia was a human conundrum to everyone.

But duty called and Frederick drove up to the New House as usual. For once Aunt Emmelia was not on her knees tending the herbaceous border, and the conservatory was empty.

'She's in a frightful huff ever since the letter came,' Annie told him. 'She's been in the library I don't know how long.' Frederick went across the hall to the library rather uncertainly. There were various personal reasons he could think of that might make him the cause of his aunt's foul mood, but he pushed them to the back of his mind.

He found Aunt Emmelia sitting at her writing-table staring lividly out of the window.

'I've just had the most preposterous letter from your Uncle Pirkin,' she said and thrust the thing at him. 'Of course your father's entirely to blame but that Pirkin shouldn't find it outrageous suggests to me that he is going senile.'

Frederick read the letter through. 'Delusions of grandeur again,' he said lightly, 'though why Father should hire a man like Yapp to write the family history is beyond me.'

'He's doing it because he knows it will infuriate me.'

'But Uncle Pirkin seems to think ...'

'Pirkin is incapable of thought,' said Emmelia. 'He is a collector and a hobbyist. First it was birds' eggs and then when he grew too arthritic to climb proper trees he started on the family one.'

'I was going to say that Pirkin seems to be considering some form of collaboration with this Professor Yapp.'

'Which is precisely what irritates me. Pirkin can hardly string two words together comprehensibly, let alone write a book.'

'Well at least he could prevent the Yapp man getting very far. A month trying to collaborate with Uncle Pirkin would undermine the most determined historian. And where have I heard the name Walden Yapp?'

'Possibly in a book about ponds?' suggested Aunt Emmelia.

'No, rather more recently. I have an idea he's some sort of personal Quango.'

'How very helpful. A Quango indeed. I suppose it would be too much to hope that you are suggesting a comparison with an extinct species of Australian duck?' said Aunt Emmelia with a vagueness that concealed a very considerable knowledge of current affairs.

'A Quasi Autonomous Non-Governmental Organization, as you very well know.'

'I would prefer not to. So we must assume your father has some political motive as well.'

'Almost certainly,' said Frederick. 'If I'm right Professor Yapp has been employed in the past to give strikers what they've demanded without seeming to.'

'It all sounds very unpleasant to me,' said Aunt Emmelia, 'and if the creature imagines he will receive any help from me he will soon be disillusioned. I shall do everything in my power to see that this project comes to a speedy end.'

And on this note she led the way towards the cold mutton and the latest family gossip. An hour later Frederick drove back to the Mill with relief. On the way he passed a tall angular man wearing unfashionably long shorts, but Frederick hardly noticed him. Hikers occasionally found Buscott, and he had no idea that the deadly virus of his father's invention had already arrived in the town.

Nor was Yapp aware of his role. His first impressions of Buscott had been confirmed by his second and third. Far from being the bleak, grim early industrial town of his preconceived imagining, the place looked remarkably prosperous. The town hall, which proclaimed itself to have been built in 1653, was in the process of being restored; the Scientific and Philosophical Society's building maintained at least a portion of its original purpose by combining Adult Evening Classes with Bingo in the old reading-room. But there was far worse to come. Several supermarkets competed in the main street, a shopping precinct had been converted all too tastefully from Barrack Square, the cattle market teemed with farmers gossiping over the fatstock sale, a second-hand bookshop accommodated almost as many rather fine antiques as it did books, and a glimpse through the wrought-iron gates of The Petrefact Cotton Spinning Manufactory suggested that if cotton was no longer profitable, something else was. All in all Buscott might be isolated but could hardly be described as run down.

But if Yapp's impressions were disappointing he had more

practical problems to deal with. Accommodation came first. Yapp avoided the two hotels on principle. Only the rich or reps stayed in hotels and Yapp wanted neither.

'I'm looking for a boarding-house. Bed and Breakfast will do,' he told the several ladies who manned The Buscott Bakery & Creamery where he had found a little tearoom and had ordered a coffee. A muttered discussion took place behind the counter. Yapp caught as much of the argument as he could.

'There's Mrs Mooker used to but she's given up I hear.'

'And Kathie ...'

Nobody thought Kathie suitable. 'Home cooking I don't think. Half the reason Joe walked out on her had to do with what she fed him, never minding the other half.'

The women glanced at Yapp and shook their heads.

'The only place I can think of,' said the ringleader finally, 'is Mr and Mrs Coppett up on Rabbitry Road. They do take in visitors sometimes to help out with Social Security. Willy Coppett being what he is. But I wouldn't recommend it not with her being the way she is.'

'I'm not really concerned about my meals,' said Yapp.

'It isn't so much her meals as her ...' said another but Yapp was not to hear Mrs Coppett's faults. A customer had come into the Bakery and the conversation turned to her husband's accident. Yapp paid for his coffee and went out in search of Rabbitry Road. He found it eventually thanks to an Ordnance Survey map he bought in a stationers and no thanks at all to two people he asked in the street who directed him in several and opposite directions on the off-chance that since it wasn't in any part of Buscott they knew it must be somewhere else. By then Yapp had walked twelve miles since leaving the train at Briskerton and was beginning to wish he hadn't. Buscott might be a small town but it was also a statistically low-density one and Rabbitry Road seemed about as far from the centre as it could possibly be without actually being part of the countryside.

Yapp asked for the bus centre, learned that there were no buses, and ended up in what looked like a wrecked-car dump but which claimed it was a Car Hire Service.

'I shall only want a car for a few days,' he told a fat bald man who emerged from beneath an ancient van and announced himself as Mr Parmiter 'at your service'

'Only rent by the month,' he said. 'You'd be better off buying this fine van. Going cheap at £120.'

'I don't want a van,' said Yapp.

'Let you have it for eighty without M.O.T. Can't say fairer than that.'

'I still want to hire a car.'

Mr Parmiter sighed and led the way over to a large Vauxhall. 'Five quid a day. Thirty days minimum,' he said.

'But that's £150.'

Mr Parmiter nodded. 'Couldn't put it better myself. The van's a bargain at a hundred and twenty with M.O.T. Let you have it on Monday. At eighty you can take it off now.'

Yapp stood unhappily and felt his feet. They were exceedingly sore. 'I'll hire the car,' he said and consoled himself with the thought that Lord Petrefact was paying his expenses. He took out his cheque book.

Mr Parmiter looked at it doubtfully. 'You wouldn't by any chance have cash?' he asked. 'I mean I can wait till the banks open tomorrow. And there's discount with cash, you know.'

'No,' said Yapp, whose feet reinforced his principles. 'And I don't approve of tax-dodging.'

Mr Parmiter was offended. 'Discount isn't tax-dodging. It's just that I don't trust cheques. They've been known to bounce.'

'I can assure you that mine don't.'

All the same Mr Parmiter made him write his name and address on the back and then demanded to see his driving licence.

'I've never been treated like this anywhere else,' Yapp complained.

'Then you should have bought the van. Stands to reason. A bloke walks in here and turns his nose up at a van for a hundred quid and hires a car ...'

But eventually Yapp drove away in the Vauxhall and made his way up to Rabbitry Road.

Here at last he found the sort of poverty his statistics had led him to expect. A row of squalid houses backed onto what appeared to be an abandoned quarry and the road had presumably got its name from the remarkable number of holes in its surface. The Vauxhall bounced to a halt and Yapp got out. Yes, this was exactly the sort of social environment he had hoped to find. With the cheerful thought that he'd get the lowdown on Buscott and the

Petrefacts from the genuinely deprived, he went down an untended garden and knocked on the door.

'I'm looking for Mrs Coppett,' he told the old woman who opened it.

'She's late with the rent again?'

'No,' said Yapp, 'I understand she takes in paying guests.'

'I wouldn't know what she does. Not my business is it?'

'All I want to find out is where she lives.'

'If you're from the Welfare there's ...'

'I am not from Welfare.'

'Then she's at Number 9,' said the old woman and shut the door. Yapp limped back to the road and looked for Number 9. He found it at the far end of the row and was relieved by the evidence of tidiness in the front garden. Where the other houses had tended to merge with the grim landscape, Number 9 had an individuality all its own. The little lawn was crammed with garden ornaments, most of them gnomes but with the occasional stone frog or rabbit, and while Yapp had aesthetic reservations about such things – and even political objections on the grounds that they were a form of escapism from the concrete and objective social conditions which a proletarian consciousness demanded – in Rabbitry Road they seemed somehow comforting. And the little house was nicely painted and looked cheerful. Yapp went in the gate and was about to knock on the door when a woman's voice called from the back, 'Now you come here, Willy, and get Blondie before Hector has him for his dinner.'

Yapp went round the side of the house and found a large woman hidden behind a sheet which she was hanging on the clothes line. In the background a dog of decidedly contragenic ancestry was chasing a rabbit through the patch of vegetables, most of them cabbages.

Yapp coughed discreetly. 'Mrs Coppett?' he enquired. A pink oval face peered round the sheet.

'In a manner of speaking,' she said and transferred her gaze to his shorts.

'I understand you take in paying guests.'

Mrs Coppett dragged her attention back to his face with some difficulty. 'I thought you was Willy,' she said. 'That Hector will have Blondie if I don't do something.'

And leaving Yapp standing she joined the mêlée in the cabbage patch, finally emerging with Hector's tail in her hands. Hector followed scrabbling at the earth but Mrs Coppett clung on and took him into the kitchen. She came out a few minutes later with the dog on a length of string which she tied to a water tap. 'You were wanting?' she asked.

Yapp adjusted his most concerned smile. It had dawned on him that Mrs Coppett was definitely wanting. If he had been asked to quantify he would have said an additional forty points of I.Q.

'You do do Bed and Breakfast?' he said.

Mrs Coppett gazed at him and put her head on one side. 'In a manner of speaking,' she said in a tone which Yapp had long since termed 'The Means Test Syndrome' in his lectures.

'I would like to stay with you,' he said, trying to make his point as simple as possible, 'that is, if you have room.' Mrs Coppett nodded her head several times vigorously and led the way into the house. Yapp followed with mixed feelings. There were social measures to alleviate poverty and make all men equal in material things, but mental inequalities defied his politics.

The kitchen on the other hand defied even the gnomes in the garden when it came to aesthetics. Yapp found himself gazing with involuntary dismay at walls which were covered with photographs of All-In Wrestlers, Weightlifters and Body-Builders, all of whom bulged distorted muscles and wore suggestively inadequate clothing.

'Ever so nice, aren't they?' said Mrs Coppett evidently mistaking Yapp's astonishment for admiration. 'I do like a strong man.'

'Quite,' said Yapp, and found some relief in noticing how clean and tidy the rest of the kitchen was.

'And we've got telly,' she went on, leading the way into the hall and opening a door rather proudly. Yapp looked in and had another shock. The room was as tidy and neat as the kitchen but the walls were once again papered with images. This time they were coloured pictures, presumably cut from Greeting Cards, and depicted small furry animals with unnaturally large and expressive eyes which looked back at him with a quite nauseating sentimentality.

'They're Willy's. He's ever so fond of pussies.'

Yapp found the remark gratuitous. Kittens dominated the room. At a rough estimate they were in an absolute majority over puppies, squirrels, bunnies and things that looked like remorseful skunks but which presumably weren't.

'Well, it helps take his mind off his work,' continued Mrs Coppett as they made their way upstairs.

'And what sort of work does Mr Coppett do?' asked Yapp, hoping to hell he wasn't going to find his room wallpapered with cigarette cards.

'Well, days he does the triping and nights he dries up,' said Mrs Coppett leaving Yapp with only a vague notion of Mr Coppett's daily work and the impression that he helped out in the kitchen after supper.

But at least the bedroom was relatively free from pictures. Some Confession magazines lay on a dressing table but apart from their lurid covers and a flight of plaster ducks on the wall the room was entirely to his taste.

'Like a good read,' Mrs Coppett explained, arranging the magazines more neatly in a pile.

'It all looks very nice,' said Yapp. 'How much do you charge?'

A glimmer of suggestive intelligence came into her eyes. 'Depends,' she said.

'Would five pounds a night be reasonable?'

Mrs Coppett giggled. 'I'd have to ask Willy. Five pounds would mean extras, wouldn't it?'

'Extras?'

'Supper and sandwiches and all. Of course if you was to stay in evenings early I wouldn't have to ask Willy, would I?'

'I suppose not,' said Yapp, unable to fathom the logic of her remark. 'But sandwiches would be a great help. I shall be out all day.'

He took out his wallet and extracted seven five pound notes.

'Ooh,' said Mrs Coppett, ogling the notes, 'you do want extras. I can tell that.'

'I always like to pay in advance,' said Yapp and handed her the money. 'Now that's for the week.'

And with another giggle Mrs Coppett went downstairs.

Left to himself Yapp untied his boots before remembering that his knapsack was still in the car, did them up again, trudged down and ran the gauntlet of Mrs Coppett's musclebound idols and the garden gnomes, got the bag and asked if it would be all right if he had a bath. Mrs Coppett hesitated and immediately Yapp went into convulsions of social embarrassment. The Coppetts were probably too deprived to have a bathroom. As usual he was wrong.

'It's just that I do like Willy to have a shower before he has his tea,' she explained. Yapp said he quite understood.

'If you don't use all the hot water ...' said Mrs Coppett. Yapp went back to his room and, having examined his feet and found them in better condition than they felt, crossed the landing and was about to go into the bathroom when he noticed that the door of the Coppetts' bedroom was open.

For a moment he stopped and eyed the apparent evidence of yet another domestic tragedy. Beside the double bed stood an empty cot. Since Mrs Coppett showed no signs of being pregnant and, considering her own inheritance, Yapp hoped that she never would be, the cot seemed to point to an unrealized dream or – worse still – a miscarriage. Even some fantasy of motherhood, because a diminutive pair of pyjamas were folded on the pillow. Yapp sighed and went into the bathroom. There too he was puzzled. The bath was there but no sign of a shower apart from an extension from the taps that was attached to the wall four feet above. With the thought that the human condition was in some ways irremediably sad, Yapp sat on the edge of the bath and bathed his feet.

He had just finished and was drying them cautiously when he heard voices from below. Mr Coppett had evidently come home from work, whatever that work was. Yapp opened the door and was crossing the landing when the full realization of just how irremediably sad the human condition could be, what Mrs Coppett had meant by triping, the significance of the cot, the tiny pyjamas and above all her insistence that Willy take a shower before sitting down to his tea – all these peculiarities were revealed to him. Mr William Coppett was a dwarf (in his horror Yapp forgot the polite usage of Porg) and a bloody dwarf at that. In fact if he hadn't been coming up the stairs Yapp might well have mistaken him for one of the more brilliantly painted gnomes in the garden. From his little cap to his once-white gumboots, size 3, Mr Coppett was stained with recently spilt blood and in his hands he held a particularly nasty-looking knife.

'Evening,' he said as Yapp stood transfixed. 'Work down at abattoir. Horrible work.'

Before Yapp could begin to express his agreement Mr Coppett had disappeared into the bathroom.

ten

An hour later Walden Yapp was still in a state of vicarious misery. During all his years of dedicated research into poverty traps, post-adult isolation, racial and sexual discrimination and the miseries inflicted by the affluent society he had never come across a case of alienation to equal Mr Willy Coppett's. That a deeply sensitive, animal-loving Person of Restricted Growth, married to a barren and frustrated Person of Extremely Limited Intelligence, should be forced to earn his living as a tripe-carver was a monstrous example of the failure of society to cater for the needs of the under-privileged. He was just considering how best to classify Mr Coppett's case in socio-terminology and had decided that 'an individual genetic catastrophe' was not too strong when he was stopped in his tracks by a smell. Yapp sat on the edge of his bed and sniffed.

Drifting up from the kitchen came the unmistakable odour of tripe and onions. Yapp clenched his teeth and shuddered. Mrs Coppett might be a half-wit, and more probably an eighth one, but surely there were limits to her insensitivity. Yapp had to doubt it. The garden gnomes and the All-In Wrestlers daubing the kitchen walls indicated a positively unerring, if unconscious, sense of sadism in the woman. In the dim recesses of her mind she clearly blamed her husband for his inadequacies. Domestic cruelty compounded social misery. Yapp got up and went downstairs and out to his car. By staying with the Coppetts he was helping them financially but he had no intention of sitting down and witnessing the poor Porg's humiliation over supper. Yapp drove down into town to look for a café.

But, as was so often the case, his diagnosis was wrong. In the kitchen of Number 9 all was perfectly well. Yapp might speak of Persons of Restricted Growth but Willy was more than content to be called a dwarf. It gave him status in Buscott, people were invariably polite to him and he was never short of part-time jobs. True, there were the few more genteel elements who felt it a shame that Willy should be asked to go down blocked drains with a trowel to clear them out or, on one occasion, lowered on the end of a rope into the well behind the Town Hall to retrieve the Mayor's hat which had blown down there during a particularly windy inaugural speech, but Willy was ignorant of their concern. He enjoyed himself and regularly rode with the Bushampton Hunt seated on the cantle of Mr Symonds' saddle facing the horse's tail, where he had a very fine view of the countryside and was spared the sight of the kill.

Indeed, on one hunt he had been persuaded to insert himself into the badger's sett, in which the fox had taken temporary refuge, by the argument that the terrier must have got stuck or hurt. The fact that the fox had already departed from another hole and that the terrier was engaged in a life-or-death struggle with several enraged badgers who resented first the fox's intrusion, then the terrier's and finally Willy's, escaped the notice of the Hunt. Willy was less fortunate; having been bitten on the nose by the terrier who mistook his rescue attempt for an attack from the rear, he was lucky not to lose an entire hand to an extremely disgruntled badger. In the end both Willy and the terrier had had to be dug out and carried, bleeding badly, to the local vet who disapproved violently of foxhunting. In his fury the vet was on the point of putting the unrecognizably human Willy down before attending to the terrier when Willy raised a bloodied and muddied handkerchief to his nose. The shock to the vet had been so extreme that all three had to be taken to the Buscott Cottage Hospital for treatment. Here the vet's hysterical statement that he objected to blood sports and murdering dwarves wasn't part of his job elicited little sympathy, while Mr Symonds could only account for Willy's injuries by saying he had offered to lend a hand.

'Lend a hand?' shouted the doctor. 'He'll be lucky if he keeps the thing. And what the fuck did that to his nose?'

'His handkerchief,' moaned the vet, 'if he hadn't taken out his little handkerchief ...'

The doctor turned savagely on the man. 'If you're seriously suggesting that a mere handkerchief savaged his nose in that terrible fashion you're out of your mind. And don't keep bleating you could have killed him. From the look of his injuries you've damned near succeeded.'

But Willy's stoicism and fondness for animals saved the day. He refused to blame even the badgers. 'Went down hole. Couldn't see,' he maintained in tones of acute catarrh.

For which courageous refusal to blame anyone he was given the freedom of the beer at all Buscott's pubs and earned himself fresh popularity. Only the Health Authorities took exception.

'He ought to be in a home,' they told Mrs Coppett when she visited him at the hospital.

'He would be if he weren't here,' said Mrs Coppett with impeccable logic, 'and a very nice home too.'

And, since Willy agreed, there was nothing they could do apart from send the occasional Health Inspector who invariably reported that Mrs Coppett was an excellent surrogate mother and met all Willy's needs to perfection. As to whether or not he met hers, the Health Inspector couldn't say and there was some understandable, if prurient, speculation.

'I should think the poor fellow would be hard put to it,' said the Medical Officer. 'Of course one never knows. Hidden talents and all that. I remember a giant of a fellow in the army who had the . . .'

'Let's face it,' interrupted the Chairman hurriedly, 'we're not here to go poking our noses into other people's sex lives. What the Coppetts choose to do in the privacy of their own home has nothing to do with us.'

'Blissfully,' murmured the Medical Officer. 'And talking of noses . . .'

'I think the Marriage Advice Bureau should have a word with them,' said the Senior Social Worker. 'Mrs Coppett has a mental age of eight.'

'Four on a good day.'

'She is also a not unattractive woman . . .'

'Listen,' said the Medical Officer, 'my experience with the Marriage Advice Bureau is that they do more harm than good. I've already had one moronic woman at the clinic demanding a postnatal abortion and I don't want another.'

But in spite of his objections a Marriage Counsellor was sent to call at 9 Rabbitry Road. In true bureaucratic tradition she had not been adequately briefed and had no idea that Mr Coppett was a dwarf. And when after half an hour she discovered that Mrs Coppett was still apparently a virgin she did her best to instil in her a proper sense of sexual deprivation.

'We're not living in the Middle Ages, you know. The modern wife can demand her right to a regular orgasm and if your husband refuses to give you one, you're entitled to an immediate divorce on grounds of non-consummation.'

'But I love my little Willy,' said Mrs Coppett, who hadn't a clue what the woman was on about, 'I tuck him up in his cot every night and he snores ever so sweetly. I don't know what I'd do without him.'

'But I understood you to say that you had never had sexual intercourse. Now you say you have a child called Willy,' said the woman, ploughing forward into a mass of misapprehension.

'Willy is my husband.'

'And you put him to bed in a cot?'

Mrs Coppett nodded.

'And he doesn't sleep with you?'

Mrs Coppett shook her head. 'He's ever so happy in his cot,' she said.

The woman hitched her chair forward with all the fervour of an outraged feminist. 'That's as maybe. But if you want my opinion your husband is clearly a sexually inadequate pervert.'

'Is he really?' said Mrs Coppett. 'Well I never.'

'No, and you're not likely to so long as this unhealthy relationship continues. Your husband needs the help of a psychiatrist.'

'A what?'

'A doctor who deals with mental problems.'

'He's been to ever so many doctors but they can't do no good. They wouldn't, would they? Him being the way he is.'

'No, it sounds as though he's definitely incurable. And you won't leave him?'

Mrs Coppett was adamant on the point. 'Never. Vicar said we was to stay together and Vicar's always right isn't he?'

'Possibly he wasn't aware of your husband's condition,' said the Marriage Counsellor, suppressing her own atheism in the interests of rapport.

'I think he must have been,' said Mrs Coppett. 'It was him as got Willy to sing in the boys' choir.'

The woman's eyes narrowed. 'And your husband agreed?'

'Oh yes. He likes dressing up and all that.'

'So I've gathered,' said the Marriage Counsellor, making a mental note to stop at the police station on her way back to County Hall. 'Well, my dear, if you won't leave him the best I can suggest is that you find a proper, healthy sex life in an extra-marital affair. No one could possibly blame you.'

And with this dubious counsel she got up to leave. By the time Willy came home that evening Mrs Coppett had forgotten the 'marital'. All she knew was that the lady had said she ought to have 'extra'.

'Extra what?' said Willy, tucking into his ham and eggs.

Mrs Coppett giggled. 'You know, Willy. What we do in bed on Fridays.'

'Oh that,' said Willy, whose secret fear was that one of those Fridays he'd be crushed to death or suffocated.

'You don't mind?'

'If the Marriage people say it I don't see how I can do anything about it if I did mind,' said Willy philosophically, 'though I don't want the neighbours to know.'

'I wouldn't dream of telling them,' said Mrs Coppett. And from that moment she had pursued extras as assiduously and as unsuccessfully as the police had kept a watch on the Vicar and the choirboys. Not that she really wanted extras but if the lady insisted she supposed it was her duty.

And now a gentleman had come and said he wanted extras too and he was a real gentleman. Mrs Coppett could tell a gentleman. They wore funny shorts and spoke like the clever people on 'Any Questions' which she couldn't understand. Mr Yapp was just like them and used long words. So while Willy walked down to the Horse and Barge where he helped pay for his free beer by working behind, or more accurately beneath the bar, drying glasses, Mrs Coppett prepared herself for extras. She got out her best nightie and did her face up with particularly green attention to her eyelids and studied several adverts in a three-year-old *Cosmopolitan* she'd picked up on a market stall for 2p to see what shape to make her lipstick. Having got so far she wondered about suspender belts. The girls in her Confessions magazines always wore them, though what for she couldn't imagine. On the other hand they were evidently part of extras and Mr Yapp might feel hard done by if she didn't wear them. The only trouble was that she didn't have any. Mrs Coppett searched her tiny mind for a substitute and finally remembered her Mum's corsets which she'd just bought and never worn when she was took bad. If she cut them in half ... She went downstairs and fetched a pair of scissors and set to work. By the time she had finished and had tied them at the back so that what remained stayed approximately up, she looked at herself in the mirror and was satisfied. Now just a bit of perfume and she would be ready.

*

Yapp had spent a tortured evening. He had looked for a café in Buscott and had found several. They were all shut. He had gone into a pub and ordered his usual half of bitter before enquiring if they served food and learning that they didn't. On the other hand he might get some at the Roisterers' Arms. He finished his beer and set off hopefully only to be disappointed. The pub hardly lived up to its name and the landlord had been downright surly. Yapp had ordered another half, partly to appease the man and partly in the knowledge that it was from such embittered sources that some of his most revealing information might well be gleaned. But in spite of his efforts to get the man to talk, all he learnt was that the fellow came from Wapping and was sorry he hadn't stayed there. 'A dead-and-alive hole,' had been his comment on Buscott and while not agreeing with the logic of the phrase Yapp could see what he meant. Two more pubs and he was of the same opinion. Buscott's night-life was decidedly limited and while people drank in large quantities, they seemed to do so after eating at home. They also stopped talking whenever he entered a bar and were disconcertingly reticent about the Mill, the Petrefacts and any other subject he happened to bring up in an attempt to take an interest in their exploited lives. Yapp made a mental note that they were typically cowed and in fear of losing their jobs. He would have to gain their confidence by making it clear that he was not on the side of the bosses and made a start by announcing that his father had been a toolmaker, his mother had fought in the Spanish Civil War and that he was down in Buscott to investigate the making of a TV film on low pay, long hours and lack of union representation down at Mill. The news was greeted with a lack of enthusiasm he found quite remarkable and in some cases with what he could only judge to be looks of genuine alarm.

'What did you say your name was?' asked a more articulate if pugnacious man in the last pub he visited.

'Yapp. Walden Yapp. I'm staying up Rabbitry Road with Coppetts,' Yapp answered, dropping both the preposition and the definite article in the interests of working-class solidarity. The fellow ignored these overtures.

'Well, you'd best be minding your own business,' he said and finished his pint rather threateningly. Yapp took the hint and finished his own half and was about to order another, and a pint for his friend, when the man nodded to the landlord and left. Yapp smiled wanly and presently went out himself. Perhaps after all he would have to bring the research team down to Buscott and tackle the problem statistically. In the meantime he was extremely hungry and there was bound to be some café open in Briskerton where he had left his suitcase at the railway station. Yapp returned to the Vauxhall and drove out on the Briskerton road.

But for all the sense of anti-climax that Buscott was not as he had visualized it in his mind's eye and the computer's chips, and that barriers of almost rustic suspicion had to be broken down before he could get to the essence of the Petrefact influence, the question that most disturbed him was the personal one of Mr and Mrs Coppett's inherited misfortunes. It was almost as if in some terrifying way they denied the very possibility of that happier world to which all his efforts were directed. A wave of pathos swept over Yapp and was assisted by the beer. He would have to see what he could do about finding Mr Willy Coppett a more fulfilling job than working in a slaughterhouse. It might even be possible to get through to Mrs Coppett that her husband was a sensitive man and to serve him tripe and onions for his supper must necessarily upset him.

With these well-intentioned and kindly thoughts Yapp drove into Briskerton and collected his suitcase at the station. All that remained now was to find a café. But in this respect Briskerton proved no more enlightened than Buscott and Yapp ended up drinking rather more beer than he'd intended while waiting for a plate of sandwiches in another pub.

eleven

Up at the New House Emmelia sat in the dusk writing letters. Through the open French windows she could see the blooms of Frau Karl Druschki which a long-dead aunt had planted to commemorate, somewhat ambiguously, the passing of her husband. Since the Frau was known to rosarians as 'The Scentless Cold White Wonder' and her uncle had been passionately fond of perfumed women, her aunt's choice had often led Emmelia to wonder if Uncle Rundle had been inclined to warm black mistresses as well. The knowledge would have lent a subtle piquancy to the choice of the rose and a discretion worthy of Emmelia herself. But for the moment she had no time for speculation. She was too busy warning her nephews and nieces, cousins and her three sisters, every relative scattered around the world, of Ronald's disgraceful plan for a family history.

'Our honour and, I feel sure, our strength, lie in obscurity,' she wrote repeatedly. 'That has always been our greatest asset and I would not have it desecrated now.'

With true Petrefactian arrogance she ignored the mixed metaphor. Assets could be desecrated and while wealth assured the family reputation, the reputation was a means to wealth. Put a Petrefact, however penniless, anywhere on earth and he would by dint of hard work, commercial cunning and self-esteem become a wealthy man. It was irrelevant that such a Petrefact could always borrow from the family bank or, if need be, use the credit of his name elsewhere to raise capital. Without the name he would have no credit and it was her business to see that the name remained exclusively obscure. Other great families had had similar opportunities and had disappeared into both poverty and total obscurity by profligate ostentation. The Petrefacts would not follow their example. Professor Yapp, and the name itself was an indication of her brother's depravity, would find doors barred to him wherever he went in search of information.

And having finished her last letter, one to Fiona, a niece, who lived on Corfu with an epicene contemporary sculptor in what they chose to call a single-sex family, she sat back and considered how best to influence older and more distant relatives over whom she exercised less authority. There was old Aunt Persephone, now in her nineties and confined to a private nursing-home near Bedford – partly because she was so old but more deliberately because she had emerged after forty years of widowhood to announce that she intended to marry an already wedded ex-Jamaican bus conductor who had rashly helped the old woman onto his bus on her weekly visit to the Zoo. A word to the Matron that Professor Yapp was not to be admitted to see her might be advisable. Judge Petrefact was no problem. He'd see the biographer off with a flea in his ear. So would Brigadier-General Petrefact who spent his retirement

attempting to breed Seal-Pointed gerbils by crossing them with
Siamese cats, a process that had doomed a great many female gerbils from the start and was now carried on more remotely but just as
unsuccessfully by artificial insemination of the cats by the gerbils.
Emmelia found the hobby harmless, if decidedly unpleasant, but at
least the old soldier had the merit of monomania and she couldn't
see him divulging any information to Yapp. There were still the
Irish Petrefacts but they were so subsidiary a branch of the family,
and not even financially connected, that she dismissed them at
once.

No, the danger lay in that direct line of descent from Great-great
grandfather Samuel Petrefact who had built the Mill, thus launching the family from land-owning wealth into industrial fortune
which had culminated in Petrefact Consolidated Enterprises. Not
only the danger but that flaw in character so clearly manifest in her
brother's actions. It was as though the change of occupation had
been the cause of a mutation in the family constitution or, to put it
in terms she understood more readily from her love of roses, that
somewhere along the line the family tree had grown a 'sport' like
Kathleen Harrop from Zéphirine Drouhin, only sports were improvements – which was more than could be said for Ronald. It
was all very puzzling and disturbing. If her brother was tainted she
could hardly have escaped the change herself. Which was true.

With a smile of rather more self-knowledge than her acquaintances would have given her credit for, she closed the French windows, turned out the light and went up to bed.

Under the bar of the Horse and Barge Willy Coppett was having a
good evening. He could work there washing and drying glasses
without being seen, could help himself to bottled beer when he felt
like it, and best of all could hear the discussions going on above his
head without having to join in. He had already heard Mr Parmiter
boasting about renting his old Vauxhall to a Professor and making
a tidy profit from the deal.

'Said he only wanted it for a week but he paid for a month
without arguing. Some of these scholar fellows know about as
much about business as I do about Latin.'

'Queer,' said Mr Groce, the landlord. Under the counter Willy
thought it queer too. He'd seen Mr Parmiter's old Vauxhall parked
outside the house when he'd come home from the slaughterhouse,

but he had no idea that the lodger was a professor. He certainly hadn't looked like a professor in his shorts and walking boots, and it was all the more surprising that a professor had chosen his house of all places to stay in. Queer, definitely queer. But any doubts about it were dispelled when Mr Parmiter mentioned that Professor Yapp was wearing shorts.

'Those old-fashioned things they issued us in the desert. Caught you behind the knees, they did, and the sand came up them when you slid down to keep Jerry from shooting your head off.'

Under the bar Willy considered the horrid possibility that the Professor was staying at 9 Rabbitry Road in order to make some sort of medical study of him. It was the only explanation he could think of and he didn't like the idea. He'd been studied by enough doctors to last him a lifetime and his secret fear was that one of these days they'd find a way of transplanting the bottom half of some very tall corpse onto him to bring him up to normal height. Which was all very well for dwarves that liked it, but he wasn't one of them. Under the bar Willy shivered and helped himself to another bottled beer.

But his fears were as nothing to the consternation that reigned at The Buscott Working Men's Liberal and Unionist Club. It was typical of the little town that it had managed to combine all colours of the political spectrum within a single institution. On the one hand it had the advantage of being economical, and on the other it maintained corporate unity and avoided the political wrangling that went on in other small towns. In fact Buscott had no politics and no M.P. and since the county invariably voted Tory there seemed no need to do more than pay lip-service to party allegiance by having a club that embraced them all. On a more practical level it served to keep Buscott's few alcoholics off the streets by allowing them to drink in company from morning to midnight.

It was here that Frederick Petrefact, following the family tradition to be all things to all men until one could afford to be thoroughly unpleasant to everyone, held court, played snooker and kept an eye open for the arrival of those husbands whose wives he was employing on a piecework basis on the couch of his office at the Mill. And it was here that Mr Mackett, who had warned Walden Yapp that he'd better be minding his own business, arrived with the alarming news that the Professor had come to make a film on low pay, long hours and lack of Union representation at the factory.

'The bugger's staying up at Rabbitry Road with Willy and his missus,' he told Frederick. 'Says his name is Yapp.'

'Christ,' said Frederick who hadn't taken his aunt's concern very seriously. 'What sort of film?'

'TV documentary. Something like that.'

'Someone's been opening his big mouth,' said another man. 'Must have. Stands to reason. We've got the system sewn up as watertight as a duck's arse. So whose lip's been slipping?'

In Frederick's mind there was no question. Somehow his damned father had found out where he was and what he was doing and the talk about Yapp writing the family history was merely an excuse for souring his relations with Aunt Emmelia and wrecking his chances of making a fortune. Souring was too mild a word for his Aunt's reaction. She'd flip her lid. And if his father knew then Yapp did too, in which case Aunt Emmelia would certainly find out sooner or later.

Frederick's mind followed devious lines while the other men argued.

'The first thing to do is see he doesn't set foot inside the Mill gates,' said Mr Ponder. 'He can think what he fucking likes but he can't make a film without our cooperation and he's not going to get it.'

'He's got someone's or he wouldn't be down here,' said Mr Mackett.

'Willy Coppett?'

'Not in a month of Sundays.'

'Then why's he staying with them?'

'Search me. What he said was he was making an economic-something-or-other study of small town growth.'

'He's started at the right end with Willy,' said Mr Ponder. 'You can't get much smaller than that.'

'I think I'll go over and have a word with Mr Coppett,' said Frederick. 'He may know something. In the meantime I suggest we concentrate on ways of making Professor Yapp's life as uncomfortable as possible.'

'I'd have thought he was doing that himself, staying with the Coppetts,' said Mr Mackett. 'According to Mrs Bryant who lives two houses away his missus won't let him use the toilet in case he flushes himself down the thing when he pulls the chain. I know Rosie Coppett's as thick as two planks but that takes the cake.'

Frederick left them discussing means of ensuring that Walden Yapp's attention was distracted from the Mill and went up the street to the Horse and Barge and ordered a brandy.

'Is Willy about?' he enquired.

Willy's head appeared between the pump handles and nodded.

'I hear you've got a new lodger.'

Willy nodded again. He was in some awe of Mr Frederick. Mr Frederick was a Petrefact and everyone knew what they were. Gentry.

It was Mr Parmiter who came to his rescue. 'News travels fast, don't it now? I was only just saying to our Willy here that I didn't like the look of this man Yapp and blow me if you come in and want to know about him.'

'I just wanted to confirm what I'd heard.'

'Shorts,' said Willy finally entering the discussion rather cryptically.

'Give him a brandy,' said Frederick in consequence.

Mr Groce poured Willy a brandy and handed it to him. Willy shook his head but took it all the same. 'Wearing short trousers.'

Mr Parmiter interpreted. 'The Professor, as he calls himself, was dressed like a hiker. Khaki shorts and boots. Came into my garage wanting to hire a car.'

Frederick sipped his brandy and listened to the story.

'Do you think he's genuine?' Mr Parmiter asked finally.

Frederick did. 'I'm afraid so. He's quite a well-known figure, is Professor Yapp. He's sat on Government commissions into pay awards and things of that sort.'

'No wonder he was so short-tempered about income tax and discounts when I offered him one for cash.'

'Paying five pounds a night,' said Willy. 'Given it to Rosie already.'

Frederick bought another round. 'And has he said what he's doing down here?'

Willy shook his head.

'Well, I tell you what I want you to do for me. I want you to listen very carefully to everything he says and then come and tell me. Do you think you can do that?' Frederick took a ten-pound note out of his wallet and put it on the bar. 'And there will be more like that if you let me know where he goes and what he does.'

Willy nodded very vigorously. Whatever Professor Yapp might be he was certainly a very useful source of extra income.

'Just come to my office when you learn anything,' Frederick told him as he got up to go. Willy nodded and disappeared beneath the bar.

'Odd,' said Mr Parmiter when Frederick had gone, 'must be something extra special to have Master Petrefact so interested. Mind you, it's a bit of a tall order asking Willy to tail the blighter.'

'Wouldn't surprise me to hear he's Customs and Excise,' said the landlord, 'come down to have a look at the Bondage Warehouse I daresay.'

'You could be right at that. In which case Mr Yapp is in for a very unpleasant surprise.'

And Yapp was. As he drove down Rabbitry Road and parked the old car outside Number 9 he was filled with that same sense of personal benevolence and social indignation which so inspired his students and emptied the Senior Common-Room at Kloone. But now his benevolence was directed towards the Coppetts while his indignation was centred on the squalor of the neighbourhood and the failure of the Social Services to provide Willy with a disability pension. In Walden Yapp's view Restricted Growth was a serious disability and it never occurred to him that not only would Willy Coppett's self-respect be terribly hurt were he to be offered a pension, which he would in any case have refused, but that he actually enjoyed being the only dwarf in Buscott. No, to Yapp's paradoxical way of thinking the right to work went with the right to a pension so that one didn't have to. He had long ago overcome the argument that the working class would cease from fitting the category if they didn't have to work by pointing out that the idle rich, with few exceptions, worked extremely hard, an answer that had been confirmed by the findings of Doris, the computer.

But as he got out of the car and walked sadly through the grotesque garden gnomery which in the darkness lost all semblance of individuality and startled him into thinking for one second that all Willy's relatives were waiting for him, he was wondering if there was some way he could use his influence to remove the Coppetts from these horrid surroundings and find them work at the University. He would have to talk to them about it. He went round the side of the house and in the kitchen door. The smell of tripe and onions still hung heavily in the air but it had been joined by another smell. For a moment Yapp stood still, holding his suitcase, and sniffed; as he did so an apparition appeared in the little hallway. Yapp stopped sniffing and stared. That it was an apparition he had no doubt, and logically it had to be because it appeared, but beyond that he could not go. Mrs Coppett's make-up was so lurid, particularly the green eyelids, and so clumsily applied that in the half-light she looked like something Chagall had painted in a particularly inspired mood. But the blast of smells couldn't be attributed to anyone. There was absolutely no need to sniff. Yapp's nose was incapable of sorting out the number of stimuli it was receiving except that tripe and onions now figured far down the list. In the hours she had waited for him Rosie Coppett had changed her mind about what perfume to wear a great many times. She had started with Paris Nights and gone on through various bottles her mum had bequeathed her and others Willy had bought her in miniature and had become so bemused by the combinations that she had finally tried to drown them all with Paris Nights. Nor was that all. In her boredom she had found time to clean the bathroom and spray it with a pine-scented aerosol before spotting several flies in the kitchen and ending their brief span after a necessarily prolonged saturation with the only other aerosol she could find, which had originally been intended to maintain the matte look on Hush Puppies but which she had bought to keep Hector from barking.

To Yapp all this was irrelevant. He was transfixed by what he now dimly though vividly saw to be Mrs Coppett in a state of undress, make-up, demeanour and smell that suggested she had not only been trying out every scent under the sun but had been drinking the stuff as well.

'I'm ready,' she said striking a contorted pose against the banisters that gave ghastly prominence to and positively rivetted Yapp's disgusted attention on her putative suspender belt.

'Ready?' he asked, his voice harsh with tension as well as suede restorer.

Mrs Coppett smiled. In other words her lipstick, smeared into what she had fondly, and falsely, imagined to be a Cupid's-bow style, seemed to smudge itself sideways into what was undoubtedly

becomes an overriding psychological motivation. You are forced to assert your objective value in the context of sex.'

'I am?' said Mrs Coppett, for whom his words, derived from the seminar on The Objectivization Of Interpersonal Relationships in A Consumer-Manipulated Society, were as meaningless as they were to the vast majority of his students. Yapp nodded, and to hide the embarrassment of suddenly realizing that the poor woman was incapable of comprehending such basic concepts he took her hand in his and patted it kindly. 'I respect you, Mrs Coppett. I want you to know that I respect you deeply as a person.'

But Mrs Coppett had nothing to say. What words had failed to convey to her his simple gesture did. He was a real gentleman and he respected her. And with his respect there came the feeling of shame.

'What must you think of me?' she said withdrawing her hand. And clutching the nightdress tautly over her extensive bosom she got up and rushed from the room.

Yapp sighed and looked round the pathetic gallery of All-In Wrestlers. It was from such fantastic monstrosities that so many lonely uneducated women drew their comfort. With a clear conscience and a new disgust for the commercial manipulators Yapp went upstairs to his room.

Outside in the darkness Willy stood invisible and immobile among the garden gnomes. What he had just witnessed and signally misinterpreted only reinforced his determination to find out everything he could about Professor Yapp – and not simply for Mr Frederick.

He had a personal grudge now.

twelve

Walden Yapp spent a disturbed night. This was in part due to the sounds coming from the next room. They suggested that the Coppetts were not on the best of terms and that Willy was in a vile temper. In fact if Yapp hadn't been privy to Mrs Coppett's dis-

97

proportionately powerful physique he would have said that her diminutive husband was beating the hell out of her. And if that was a disturbing thought, there were others. They concerned sex.

Here it has to be said that Walden Yapp's reputation for singularity was fully justified. He had never succumbed to the lure of students. Other Fellows and even some married Professors had, ostensibly in the name of Progressive Thinking, Radical Politics and Liberationist Sex, relieved the monotony of tutorials and family life by sleeping with their students. Not so Yapp. In fact, thanks to his Mother's high-minded neglect and his aunt's devotion to low-Church ethics, he regarded such affairs with Puritan contempt. Which was all very well but he still had to cope with his own sexuality and in all honesty he had to admit that it wasn't exactly pure either.

At one level it expressed itself in delicate feelings for, and distant devotion to, women who were already married and who took not the slightest notice of him, while on another, more sinister plane it erupted in fantasies and irrepressible daydreams in which he did and had done to him acts of such remarkable sensuality that he suffered pangs of guilt and the suspicion that he was probably a pervert. In short, Walden Yapp at thirty was still in matters sexual at the age of puberty.

As an antidote to these uncontrollable fantasies he worked harder than ever and, when the strain grew too great, indulged in what he had been brought up to call self-abuse. Fortunately he had, as part of a seminar on Sexual Discrimination in the Cotton Industry 1780 to 1850, inadvertently read R. D. Laing and had been reassured to learn that the eminent psychologist considered that masturbation could for some individuals be the most honest act in their lives. Not that Yapp was wholly convinced. Individualism conflicted with his own collectivist views and in spite of some semantic juggling with Doris, who suggested that the two views might be combined in masturbation, Yapp felt strongly that interpersonal relationships, preferably on a communal basis, were essential for human fulfilment. His instincts thought otherwise, and continued their solitary and disconcerting irrational eruptions into consciousness.

And so, lying in bed free from the actuality of Mrs Coppett's abundant presence, which had so frightened him, his imagination transformed her into the passionate creature of his fantasies. In fact she corresponded all too closely to his imagined lover, particularly in her lack of intelligence. It was one of the things that most baffled him. He might worship at a distance women of pure morality and high intellect, but his lusts were aroused by mature women with no morality or intellect at all. Mrs Coppett fitted the bill exactly. In his imagination he was in bed with her, he was kissing her extensive breasts, her mouth was on his and her tongue ...

Yapp sat up in bed and switched the light on. This wouldn't do. He must put a stop to such irrational dreams. He reached for the folder containing the family correspondence Lord Petrefact had sent him and tried to exorcise the images, but like some welcome succubus Mrs Rosie Coppett was not to be denied. In the end he gave up, turned out the light and tried to act as honestly as he could. But here again he hit a snag. The bed squeaked too rhythmically for unembarrassed concentration and he gave up the attempt. Finally he fell into a troubled sleep and awoke next morning with the feeling that something peculiar was happening to him.

He went through to the bathroom in a pensive mood and tried to concentrate on his plans for the day. He would visit the Museum and ask the Curator for the Petrefact Papers and see what he could glean about conditions of work at the Mill and rates of pay there when it was first started by Samuel Petrefact. From that solid base of statistics he would work towards the present family. Lord Petrefact might intend the history to be a more personal and almost biographical account of generations of Petrefacts, but Yapp had his principles. He would proceed in his own way from the general to the particular. He had already decided that the title of the book should be *The Petrefact Inheritance: a Study of Emergent Multi-Nationalist Capitalism*, and if the old man didn't like it, he could lump it. The contract had given Yapp a free hand and he wasn't an expert on Demotic Historiography for nothing.

In a slightly less distracted state of mind he went down to breakfast. But here his rationalism took a fresh knock. Willy had already gone to work and Mrs Coppett, having shed her dubious finery of the night before, was fresh-faced and homely and dangerously concerned and coy.

'I don't know what you must think of me,' she said placing a large bowl of porridge in front of him, 'and you a Professor and all.'

'That's nothing,' said Yapp modestly.

'Oh but it is. Willy told me last night. He was ever so cross.'

'I'm sorry to hear that. Did he say what about?'

Mrs Coppett broke two eggs into a frying-pan. 'About you being a professor. They were talking about it down at the pub.'

Yapp cursed silently through a mouthful of porridge. Once it got round Buscott, the Petrefacts would wonder why he hadn't been in touch with them. On the other hand they were bound to know fairly soon and it had been naive of him to imagine that he could conduct his researches without their learning about it.

All the time he ate and thought his attention was drawn back to Mrs Coppett, who chattered away over the gas stove, her conversation circling monotonously about his being a professor, a title she probably didn't understand but one which endowed him with a tremendous importance. Yapp's egalitarianism asserted itself.

'You mustn't think of me as someone special,' he said in direct contradiction to his feelings. Decently dressed, she was an attractive working-class woman whose physical endowments were poignantly heightened by her lack of mental ones. 'I'm just a guest in your house. I would like you to call me Walden.'

'Ooh,' said Mrs Coppett and exchanged the porridge bowl for a plate of bacon and eggs. 'I couldn't.'

Yapp concentrated on the eggs and said nothing. A waft of that perfume still lingered and this time he was aroused by its message. Besides, Mrs Coppett had very nice legs. He hurried through the rest of the meal and was on the point of leaving the house when she handed him a tin box.

'Sandwiches. You mustn't go hungry, must you?'

Yapp muttered his thanks and was once again engulfed in the terrible empathy which her simple-minded kindness evoked in him. Taken in conjunction with the appeal of the rest of her, and in particular of her legs, its effect was devastating. Muttering his thanks with an embarrassment that masked his desire to take her in his arms and kiss her, Yapp turned away and hurried through the cenotaphs of gnomes and was presently striding down the road into Buscott, his mind sorely divided between what he was going to do to the Petrefacts and what he would like to do to and for the Coppetts.

At the abattoir Willy did not reciprocate this goodwill. He best expressed his feelings by stropping his knife on the end of his belt while explaining to the manager that he wanted the day off for apparently no good reason.

'You must have some excuse,' said the manager to the upper half of the face that stared at him over the edge of his desk. 'Don't you feel well? I mean if you're sick ...'

'Not,' said Willy.

'Then perhaps your wife ...'

'Not sick either.'

'Any relatives down with the ...'

'No,' said Willy, 'don't have any.' Under the desk he stropped his knife harder which, since he couldn't tell exactly what Willy was doing, led the manager to suppose he was doing something else.

'Listen, Willy,' he said leaning forward, 'I am perfectly prepared to let you have the day off. All you've got to do is give me some good reason. You can't just come in and do whatever you are doing down there, and while we're on the subject I wish you wouldn't, and expect me to say Yes just like that.'

Willy considered this reasonable request and came to no very good conclusion. In the hierarchy of his regard Mr Frederick stood infinitely higher than the manager of the slaughterhouse, and while Mr Petrefact hadn't actually told him not to say anything to anyone about following Yapp he didn't feel like disclosing his instructions.

'Can't,' he said finally, and unintentionally tried the edge of his knife on the ball of his thumb. The manager found the gesture reason enough.

'All right. I'll just put you down as having domestic reasons for wanting time off.'

'Have,' said Willy, and left the manager even more bewildered than before. He trotted up the street towards Rabbitry Road and was just in time to spot Yapp striding down it towards him. Willy merged with a woman pushing a pram and emerged when Yapp had passed. From then on he was never far behind though it took him all his stamina to keep up and by the time Yapp marched into the Museum Willy was glad of a breather. Peering through the glass door he saw Yapp accost the Curator and then slipped inside to listen.

'The Petrefact Papers?' the Curator said. 'Yes, they're certainly here but I'm afraid I can't let you see them.'

'But I've already explained my credentials,' said Yapp, 'and I have here a letter from Lord Petrefact ...'

Willy made a note of the fact and also its failure to impress the Curator.

'I still have to say No. I have explicit instructions from Miss Emmelia not to allow anyone to see the family documents unless she has authorized their viewing. You'll have to get her permission.'

'I see. In that case I will obtain it,' said Yapp, and after glancing briefly round the Museum and complimenting the Curator on the display of early farm implements, went out into the street. Willy followed. This time their route took them down to the Mill where, much to his surprise and Yapp's premature approval, they found a line of pickets carrying placards demanding higher pay for shorter hours and threatening scabs and blacklegs. To the best of Willy Coppett's knowledge pay was high and hours short at the Mill and he couldn't for the life of him understand it. Yapp on the contrary thought he could, but disliked the suggestion that he was a scab and blackleg.

'My name is Yapp, Professor Yapp. You may have heard of me,' he told the leader of the pickets, a large man whose placard while smaller than the others had a rather heavier handle which he waved menacingly. 'I wouldn't dream of strike-breaking.'

'Then you don't cross the picket line.'

'I'm not trying to cross it,' said Yapp, 'I have come here to make a study of your working conditions.'

'Who for?'

Here Yapp hesistated. The truth, that he was working for Lord Petrefact, was hardly likely to find favour and it went against his nature to tell a downright lie, especially to a shop steward.

'I'm from Kloone University,' he equivocated, 'I'm Professor of Demotic Historiography there and I am particularly interested –'

'Tell it to the bosses, mate. We aren't.'

'Aren't what?'

'Particularly bleeding interested. Now shove off.'

To emphasize the point he raised his placard. Yapp shoved off and Willy took up his station behind him with the satisfying knowledge that whatever extras he might have been offered the night before, Professor Yapp was getting nowhere fast today. And fast was all too true. By the time they had walked, and in Willy's case dashed, for a mile along the river bank, had gone aimlessly up one street of mill houses and down another where there were no front gardens in which he could possibly conceal himself so that he had to wait until Yapp had turned the corner before he sprinted after him, and had had to run a gauntlet of abusive small boys in the process, Willy was beginning to think he was earning his ten quid the hard way. To make things even harder Yapp stopped several times to speak to people and Willy had to repeat the interview to find out what he had said.

'He wanted to know what I knew about the bloody Petrefacts,' shouted one old man when Willy had managed to convince him that he wasn't addressing a nosey child but a genuinely inquisitive dwarf. 'I told him I didn't know the buggers.'

'Anything else?'

'What it was like in the Mill, how much they paid me and such like.'

'Did you say?'

'How the bloody hell could I, lad? Never set foot in place. Worked all my life on railway up at Barnsley. Here on visit to my daughter.'

Willy dashed off, shot round the corner and was only partly relieved to find that he hadn't lost his quarry. Yapp was seated on a bench overlooking the river talking – or, more accurately, shouting questions into the hearing aid of another old-age pensioner. Willy moved behind a letterbox and listened.

'You've lived here all your life?' yelled Yapp. The old man lit his pipe with a shaking hand and nodded.

'And worked at the Mill?'

The man continued to nod.

'Can you tell me what it was like, conditions of work, long hours and low pay, things of that sort?'

The nodding went on. But evidently Yapp's hopes were rising. He opened his tin and took out a sandwich.

'You see, I'm making a study of working-class exploitation by mill owners during the Depression and I'm told that the Petrefacts are notoriously bad employers. I would appreciate any information you could give me.'

From behind the letterbox Willy listened with interest. At last he had something to report and since he had recognized the old man as being Mr Teedle who, besides being stone deaf, had contracted the habit of nodding instead of opening his mouth thanks to a long married life with a woman of strong character and a loud voice, he felt the Professor was in safe and uninformative company. Willy left his hiding-place and crossed the road to the River Inn where he could have a pork pie and several pints while keeping an eye on his quarry at the same time. But first he'd make a phone call to Mr Frederick. With the freedom that came from being the town's popular dwarf he carried a beer crate to the phone and dialled the Mill and asked for Mr Frederick.

'All he's doing is asking people what's going on here?' Frederick asked when Willy had finished. Willy nodded and Frederick had to repeat the question before he could overcome the dwarf's speech-less deference.

'Yes,' he mumbled finally.

'He isn't asking questions about anything else?'

'No.'

'Just what we're making here?'

'Yes,' said Willy who preferred to maintain his new standing with Mr Frederick by not mentioning low pay and bad working conditions. This time it was Frederick who was silent. He was debating what to do. There were a number of choices, none of them pleasant.

'Oh well, grasp the bloody nettle, I suppose,' he muttered finally.

'Which one?' asked Willy.

'Which what?'

'Nettle.'

'Nettle? What the hell are you talking about?'

Willy relapsed into mute awe and before the question could be satisfactorily answered his money ran out and the phone went dead. With a sigh of relief Willy climbed off the crate and returned to the bar. Yapp was still engaged in his interrogation of Mr Teedle and Willy settled down to his beer and pie.

In his office Frederick poured himself a stiff whisky and cursed his father for the umpteenth time. The old devil must know what he was doing, must know in fact that he was endangering not only the rest of the family but his own position in society by sending Yapp to Buscott. It didn't make sense. At least the idea of the strike had been a good one and the pickets had seen the brute off. And with the consoling thought that it was a good thing Aunt Emmelia was such a recluse and stuck to the obscurity of her im-maculate garden, he went out for lunch.

thirteen

For once he had miscalculated. Emmelia Petrefact might take the family tradition of keeping herself to herself to extremes but the same thing could not be said for her cats. They led gregarious and promiscuous night lives, usually in other people's gardens, and it was as a result of her favourite Siamese, Blueboy's, indiscreet courtship under Major Forlong's bedroom window and the Major's remarkably accurate aim with a flower vase that she was taking the partially neutered animal to the vet when she saw the pickets outside the Mill gates. For a moment she hesitated but only for a moment. Blueboy's name might have to be changed, but that of the Petrefacts must not be sullied by strikes. Ordering her chauffeur to stop and then convey the stricken cat to the vet she stepped out of her 1937 Daimler and marched across the road.

'What's the meaning of this?' she demanded and before the pickets could begin to explain she had crossed the line and was making her way into the factory.

'Where is Mr Petrefact?' she asked the woman at Enquiries so imperiously that the secretary was left speechless. Aunt Emmelia marched on. Frederick's office was empty. Emmelia passed through into the first workshop and was astonished to find the place filled with women busily at work with sewing machines. But it was less the lack of any evidence of a strike that astonished her than the nature of the garments they were producing.

'Is there anything I can do for you?' asked a forewoman. Emmelia gaped at a pair of crotchless wet-look camiknickers which one of the seamstresses was lining with chamois leather and could find no words for her horror.

'These are one of our most popular garments,' said the forewoman. 'They go down extraordinarily well in Germany.'

The words reached Emmelia only subliminally. Her revulsion had been drawn by a woman who was stitching hairs to what had all the awful appearance of being a bald pubenda.

'And where does that go down?' she asked involuntarily.

'Here,' said the forewoman indicating the groin of an all too obviously male costume model. 'The straps go round the back.'

'What for?'

'To hold the merkin in place, of course.'

'Of course,' said Emmelia in such a trance of prurient curiosity that what she had intended to be a disgusted exclamation lost its emphasis. 'And do many people buy merkins?'

'You'd have to ask sales but I suppose they must. We've increased production by thirty per cent this year.'

Emmelia dragged herself away from the repulsive object and wandered off down the line of women making merkins, plastic leotards and inflatable bras. What she was seeing was utterly revolting but it was counterpointed by the chatter which seemed to take merkins and scrotum restrainers for granted while concentrating on banal domestic dramas.

'So I said to him, "If you think you can go down the pub every night and drink the holiday money, one of these days you'll have to cook your own supper. Two can play that game."'

'What did he say to that?' asked a woman who was stitching HIS onto what until that moment Emmelia had assumed to be the sole necessity of HERS, namely a sanitary napkin.

'Wasn't much he could say, was there? Not that ...'

There was nothing Emmelia could say. She tottered on past women discussing baby foods, last night's episode of Coronation Street, where they were going for their holidays and other people's matrimonial troubles. By the time she came to a group of evident artists who were painting veins onto what she would otherwise have assumed to be rather large and unfinished salt dispensers, she was feeling decidedly mad. She sank into a chair and stared dementedly into space.

At the far end of the workshop the forewoman was holding a heated discussion with the woman from the Enquiry desk.

'Well, how was I to know? You let her through and naturally I thought she was a buyer ...'

'She's Miss Petrefact, I tell you. I saw her at the Flower Show last year. She was judging the begonias.'

'You should have stopped her.'

'I couldn't. She asked for Mr Petrefact and marched into his office. He's going to have a fit when he finds out.'

'Not the only one,' said the forewoman and hurried down to intercept Miss Emmelia who had risen from her chair and was heading for what had formerly been the Loom Repair shop.

'You can't go in there,' said the forewoman rather too imperatively, and promptly revived Miss Emmelia's tattered sense of self-importance.

'I most certainly can,' she said with new authority. 'And what is more I intend to.'

'But ...' the forewoman faltered. Emmelia went past her and opened the door and was instantly deprived of the slight hope she had held that some part of The Petrefact Cotton Spinning Manufactory maintained its original purpose. A blast of warm air hit her and with it a particularly unattractive smell. For a moment she hesitated and then her attention centred on a conveyor belt of those revolting salt pots which had so distracted her in the other room. As they moved slowly past her the sense of unreality returned with, in the vernacular she had never used before, knobs on. Or whiskers or wands, certainly protrusions of some sort whose purpose she could only vaguely define and preferred not to. In short the erstwhile Loom Repair Shop became something she was only dreaming, a nightmare assembly line of extruded plastic penises, perpetually erect. Emmelia shut the door and tried to regain her composure.

'Are you all right?' the forewoman asked anxiously. Emmelia's pride reacted.

'Of course I am,' she snapped and then, partly out of unwilled curiosity but more from the stern sense of duty so ingrained in her character, pushed the door open again and stepped inside. The forewoman followed unhappily. Emmelia regarded the penises severely.

'And what do you call those?' she enquired, and added dildos to her vocabulary.

'Do many men require them?' But the faint hope that the Mill was less what first impressions – and particularly those revolting crotchless camiknickers – suggested than an artificial limb factory for the sexually mutilated was doused by the reply.

'They're for women,' said the woman faintly.

'Ultimately I suppose they would be but initially men must ...'

'Lesbian women,' said the woman even more faintly.

Emmelia pursed her lips and then raising herself to her full height walked slowly down the line. At the end a machine was wrapping rather flimsy articles in foil.

'French ticklers,' explained the woman when Emmelia asked

with almost royally affected interest what they were.

'Remarkable.'

And so the progress continued and by the time they reached a young man who was hammering out male chastity belts Emmelia was sufficiently majestic to stop and ask him if he enjoyed his work and found it rewarding. The youth gaped at her. Emmelia smiled and moved on. From Dildo Moulding and Handcrafted Chastity Belts they advanced to Hoods, Chains and Flagellation Accessories in the Bondage Department where Emmelia took a serene interest in Inflatable Gags.

'To be used in conjunction with French ticklers no doubt,' she said and without waiting for a more accurate explanation examined several types of Whip. Even the Clitoral Stimulators failed to shake her composure.

'It must be most satisfying to know you are helping to bring so much pleasure to so many people,' she told the girl who was checking each one. Behind her the forewoman wilted still further but Emmelia merely walked on, smiling kindly and with all the outward appearance of imperturbable assurance. Inwardly she was seething and badly in need of a cup of tea.

'I'll wait in the office,' she told the woman when the tour was over. 'Be so good as to bring me a pot of tea.'

And leaving the forewoman standing in awe Emmelia went into Frederick's office and seated herself behind the desk.

At the Buscott Working Men's Liberal and Unionist Club Frederick rounded off his leisurely lunch break with a game of snooker and was about to go back to the Mill when he was called to the phone. Ten seconds later he was ashen and all desire to go anywhere near the bloody Mill had left him.

'She's what?' he shouted.

'Sitting in your office,' said his secretary. 'She's been right round the factory and now she says she'll wait until you return.'

'Oh, my God. Can't you get rid ... No, I don't suppose you can.' He put the phone down and went back to the bar.

'I want something strong and odourless,' he told the bartender, 'preferably with aunt-repellant in it.'

'Vodka's not too smelly but I've never tried it on aunts.'

'Any idea what they gave the condemned?'

The barman recommended brandy. Frederick drank a triple,

tried frantically to think of a suitable explanation for Aunt Emmelia and gave up.

'Here goes,' he muttered, and walked down the lane back to the Mill. The pickets were still outside the gates and Frederick told them to pack up. Whatever their usefulness in keeping Yapp out he could see now that they had brought his Aunt in, though why the hell she had chosen this of all days to come to town he couldn't imagine. It was a secondary problem. The fact was that she had come. With a curse that embraced Yapp, his father, Aunt Emmelia and the hypocrisy from which he had been making a fortune and which now seemed certain to take it away from him, he entered the Mill and with affected surprise found Aunt Emmelia behind his desk.

'How nice to see you,' he said summoning what he hoped was charm to his aid.

Aunt Emmelia ignored it. 'Shut the door and sit down,' she said, 'and wipe that inane grin off your face. I have seen enough repulsive objects in the last hour to last me a lifetime. I can do without smarm.'

'Quite,' said Frederick. 'On the other hand, before you start sounding off about pornography, perverts and lack of moral fibre let me say –'

'Oh, do keep quiet,' said Aunt Emmelia, 'I have far more urgent things to think about than your inverted conscience. Besides, if there is a market for such singularly tasteless contraptions as the Thermal Agitators With Enema Variations advertised in the latest catalogue I suppose it is not wholly unreasonable to supply it.'

'You do?'

Emmelia poured herself another cup of tea. 'Of course. I have never been very clear what market forces are but your grandfather held them in very high esteem and I see no reason to doubt his good judgement. No, what concerns me most is the presence of men with banners parading for all the world to see outside the gates. I want to know why they are there.'

'To keep Professor Yapp out.'

'Professor Yapp?'

'He's in Buscott and he wants to know what we're making in the Mill.'

'Does he indeed?' said Emmelia, but a new and anxious note was in her voice.

'What's more he is staying with Willy Coppett and his wife up in Rabbitry Road and he's been going round town asking everyone what we are making and so on.'

Aunt Emmelia put down her cup and saucer with a shaking hand. 'In that case we are faced with a crisis. Rabbitry Road indeed! And the Coppetts. What on earth would persuade him to stay there instead of at The Buscott Arms or some other decent hotel?'

'Lord alone knows. Presumably the wish to remain anonymous while he snoops about.'

Emmelia considered this and evidently found it more plausible than any other explanation. 'So much for the notion that he is working on the family history. Even your father, for whom I have the lowest possible regard, would not stoop to sully the name of Petrefact by revealing the fact that we are running a fetish factory. The man must be what in my youth was properly known as a muck-raker and is now called an investigative journalist. He must be got rid of.'

'Rid of?'

'That's what I said and that's what I meant.'

Frederick stared at her and wondered what the hell she did mean. There were, after all, degrees of getting rid of people and from the tone of his aunt's voice it sounded as though she had in mind the most extreme method.

'Yes but ...'

'But me no buts,' said Emmelia more sternly than ever. 'If the man's motives were honourable he would have called at the New House and announced his intentions. Instead you tell me he's staying with a mentally deficient woman and her stunted husband in so insalubrious a neighbourhood as Rabbitry Road. I find that most sinister.'

So did Frederick, though hardly so sinister as Aunt Emmelia's suggestion that he be got rid of. But before he could raise objections she went on. 'And since you have chosen to put us all in jeopardy, I am thinking of Nicholas who is standing in the by-election for North Chatterswall, not to mention your uncle the judge and everyone else, by diversifying what was a perfectly respectable pyjama factory into instruments of genuine self-abuse, I consider it your duty to get us out of it. Let me know when he has gone.'

110

And before Frederick could argue that it was impossible to diversify a factory out of pyjamas or could raise the more immediate question of how he was to get rid of Yapp, Aunt Emmelia rose and swept austerely from the room. From the entrance hall she could be heard telling his secretary that she need not call for a taxi.

'I shall walk. The fresh air will do me a power of good,' she said. Frederick watched her cross the yard and stride out of the Mill gates and wondered briefly what it was about the English character that made murder morally more respectable than masturbation. And what raving lunatic had first called women the fair sex?

It was not a question that bothered Yapp. His promenade round, across and through Buscott had been marred by a most peculiar feeling that he was somehow already a well-known figure. In the ordinary way he would have found such immediate recognition flattering and not altogether undeserved, but in Buscott there was something almost sinister about it. He had only to enter a shop or stop someone to ask the way to sense reticence. In the library, where he went to look for books on local history, the librarian froze almost immediately and was most unhelpful. Even the ladies in the teashop who had suggested Rabbitry Road for his lodgings stopped talking as soon as he entered and ordered a cup of coffee. More pointedly still, they started chatting again the moment he stepped outside the door. It was all most mysterious and not a little disturbing. For a while he wondered if he was wearing some item of clothing that was in bad taste or was regarded superstitiously as an omen of bad luck. But there was nothing about his dress that was markedly different from other people's. Had he bothered to look behind him he would have seen the cause of his isolation, an agitated Willy whose facial contortions and pointed finger were sufficient to alert even the least intelligent Yapp was not a man to associate with.

But Walden Yapp was too immersed in theoretical conjecture to notice his restricted shadow. It was one of the tenets of his ideological faith that every town could be divided into spatial categories of socio-economic class differentiation and he had once spent months programming Macclesfield into Doris, the computer, together with answers from random samples of opinion collected by his more devoted students, and had come up with the not very surprising findings that the richer areas tended to be inhabited by

Tory voters while Labour predominated in the poorer quarters.

But in Buscott these simple preconceptions were strangely at odds with the facts. Having found that no one was prepared to discuss the Mill or the Petrefacts – and Yapp had put this reluctance down to fear of losing their jobs or houses – he had tried questioning people on their political opinions only to be told to mind his own bloody business or to have doors shut in his face without any reply at all. It was all very disheartening and made the more so by his failure to discover any real cases of hardship or even grievance. One old man had got so far as to complain that he had had to give up gardening because of his arthritis before Yapp realized he was talking about his own garden and not someone else's.

'You don't think I'd work some other bugger's garden, do you? I'm not daft.'

In short Buscott was not merely a prosperous little town, it was a cheerful one and, as such, outside the range of Yapp's experience.

As the day and his disappointment wore on, his thoughts vacillated between the horrid suspicion that Lord Petrefact had sent him down with the deliberate aim of showing him what amounted to a model of beneficent capitalism, and a yearning for the warmth and peculiar sexual attractions of Mrs Coppett. He found it difficult to decide which was the more alarming, being deceived by that damnable old swine or attracted by the body of a dim-witted woman, who was already married – and to a PORG at that. Worse still, there was no longer any doubting his feelings for her. In some quite frightening way she represented everything his singular upbringing had taught him to despise and pity. And that was the trouble. He could hardly despise Rosie Coppett for her lack of the rational and intellectual when she was manifestly so educationally subnormal, but her kindly simplicity doubled and even trebled his pity and combined with her attractive legs, her abundant breasts, and (when not covered by mutilated corsets) her presumably fulsome buttocks, to transform her into a woman of his wildest fantasies and noblest dreams. To distract himself from the particularly noble dream of transporting the Coppetts from Rabbitry Road to Kloone University and a comfortable job for Willy, he walked back towards the Mill again. After all there was a strike and strikes necessitated genuine grievances. Yes, he would concentrate his enquiries there.

But when he arrived the pickets had disappeared and workers

were streaming out through the Mill gates. Yapp stopped a middle-aged woman.

'Strike? What strike? No blooming strike here, and not likely to be one either. Pay's too good,' she said and hurried on, leaving Yapp more disillusioned and puzzled than ever. He turned and made his way up the hill towards Rabbitry Road. Rosie would be getting supper ready and he was both physically and emotionally hungry.

Willy's needs were rather different. He was exhausted. In his little life he couldn't remember having walked so far in one day. In the abattoir he had hardly had to walk at all. The carcasses had come to him. Anyway he had no intention of trudging up the hill for supper and trudging down again to the Horse and Barge for beer. He'd have his supper there and then go home early to see what the long-legged Professor was up to. He went round the back of the pub and was presently busy getting as much stew inside him as he could manage before opening time.

fourteen

As dusk fell over Buscott it would have been impossible for the most acute observer to detect anything in the little town to suggest the seething emotions that lay beneath the surface. At the New House Emmelia deadheaded her roses with a rather more ruthless hand than usual. In the kitchen of Number 9, Rabbitry Road Walden Yapp consumed more hot scones than was his wont and eyed Mrs Coppett with an expression of such bewildered infatuation that it was hard to tell whether he was simply addicted to hot buttered scones or had fallen madly in love with a thoroughly unsuitable woman. For her part Rosie's simple thoughts revolved around the question of asking him to take her for a drive in the old Vauxhall. She had only been in a car three times, once when Willy had been bitten by the badger and she had been rushed to the hospital and twice when she had been given lifts by visiting social workers. And since she had spent part of the day reading a Confessions magazine and there had been several lurid stories in which cars played a remarkably important part, the notion of going for a drive was much on her mind.

But the clearest indication of seething emotions was to be found above and below the bar at the Horse and Barge where Frederick was questioning Willy about Professor Yapp's habits, a process he tried to facilitate by filling the dwarf's glass as soon as it was empty and which Willy, who only knew that Yapp walked too bloody fast for the likes of him, had to amplify by partial invention and definite exaggeration. With each bottle the invention grew wilder.

'Kissing her he was in my own fucking kitchen,' he said after his fifth bottled beer. 'Kissing my Rosie.'

Frederick looked at him incredulously.

'Go on with you,' said Mr Parmiter, evidently sharing Frederick's scepticism, 'who'd want to kiss your Rosie? I ask you.'

'I would,' said Willy, 'I'm her lawful husband.'

'Why don't you then?'

Willy stared at him lividly over the bar. 'Because she's too bloody big and I'm not.'

'Why don't you get her to sit down or stand on a chair?'

'Wouldn't make no difference,' said Willy lugubriously. 'There's no way of doing her and kissing her at the same time. It's got to be one or the other.'

'You're not suggesting that Professor Yapp was making love to your wife?' asked Frederick hopefully.

Willy picked up the intonation and answered accordingly. His glass was empty. 'He was and all. Caught them at it I did. She had on the nylon nightie I gave her Christmas before last and she was all made up with green eyeshades.'

'Eyeshades?' said Mr Parmiter. 'What the hell was she doing wearing eyeshades?'

'Betraying me,' said Willy, 'that's what. Ten years we been married and ...'

'Another bottle, Mr Groce,' said Frederick, wishing to get back to Yapp. Mr Groce filled Willy's glass. 'Now then, Willy, where did you see this happen?'

'In the kitchen.'

'In the kitchen?'

'In the fucking kitchen.'

'Surely you mean from the kitchen,' said Frederick. 'You saw them from the kitchen.'

'I never. I was in the garden. They was in the kitchen. They never saw me. But I gave her a good hiding when I got upstairs.'

Frederick and Mr Parmiter looked at him in astonishment.

'Did too. If you don't believe me, you ask Rosie if I didn't. She'll tell you.'

'Well I never,' said Mr Parmiter. Frederick said nothing. In his devious mind schemes were stirring. They involved jealous and enraged dwarves. 'And what did you do to Roger The Lodger The Sod, give him the old heave-ho too?'

'Couldn't do that. Paid a week's rent in advance he had and Mr Frederick had told me to keep an eye on him.'

'You've done that all right,' continued Mr Parmiter. 'Still, I doubt if I could have stood by watching my wife and some bugger having it off in the kitchen. I'd have fixed the bastard proper.'

'Maybe you would,' said Willy, made melancholy by his own invention and a sixth bottle of beer. 'You're big enough.'

'If you can knock the stuffing out of that missus of yours I'd have thought you'd have been more than a match for knock-kneed professors.'

'Different with women. Rosie's seen my little waggler and she don't want ten inches of that up her innards, do she?'

Mr Parmiter took a long swig of beer thoughtfully. He was clearly considering Mrs Coppett's sexual appetites and the proportions of dwarves.

'Ten inches?' he asked finally. 'Well I suppose you'd be the first to know but all the same . . .'

'Measured it myself,' said Willy proudly. 'With a ruler. And it used to be longer but it's a bit worn down now. I'll show you if you like. Ate supper with it. It's in the kitchen.'

Before Mr Parmiter could recover sufficiently from the evident ubiquity of Willy's little waggler to say he didn't want to see the damned thing, Willy shot into the kitchen. He returned with a large and extremely nasty-looking knife. Mr Parmiter gazed at it with relief, Frederick with intense interest.

'Yes, well, I see what you mean,' said Mr Parmiter. 'You could do someone a lot of mischief with that.'

Frederick nodded his agreement. 'As a matter of fact with law the way it is now a man killing his wife's lover usually gets a suspended sentence,' he said.

'Always did,' said Mr Parmiter gleefully, 'suspended with a rope round his neck. Now they wouldn't even fine you.'

Frederick bought another round of drinks and for the next hour, with Mr Parmiter's unconscious assistance, primed Willy with tales of crimes of passion. By closing time Willy was stropping his waggler on the end of his belt and had worked himself up into a lather of jealousy. For his part Frederick was positively cheerful. With any luck Aunt Emmelia's order to get rid of the egregious Yapp would be fulfilled to the letter. Urging Willy on to keep an eye on his victim, and sliding another tenner across the bar, he went out into the fading light with a clear conscience. A car passed and completed his happiness. Beside him Mr Parmiter gaped after it.

'Blimey, did you see what I saw? And I thought Willy was exaggerating.'

'It's a sad world,' sighed Frederick. 'Still, there's no accounting for tastes.'

At the wheel of the old Vauxhall Walden Yapp would have agreed with him. His taste for the company of Rosie Coppett was certainly unaccountable and the world was a sadder place for it. The childlike pleasure she took in riding in the car played havoc with his extended concern while her closeness and the car's erratic suspension made other extensions inevitable. Torn between the desire to accept those extras she had offered so vividly the night before and a conscience that would never permit him to seduce the wife of a Porg, Yapp drove ten miles along country lanes and twice through Buscott without a thought for what other people might think. Beside him Rosie swayed and giggled and once when he rounded a bend too fast grasped his arm so excitedly that he almost drove the car through the hedge into a field. When finally he stopped outside the house in Rabbitry Road and was promptly given a kiss of gratitude, he almost lost control.

'You mustn't,' he muttered hoarsely.

'Mustn't what?' asked Rosie.

'Kiss me like that.'

'Go on with you. Kissing's nice.'

'I know that but what would people think?'

'I don't care,' said Rosie and gave him another kiss so vigorously that Yapp didn't care either.

'Come inside and I'll give you a proper kiss,' said Rosie and getting out of the car announced loudly to several observant neighbours that she'd been for a ride with a real gentleman and he deserved a kiss and cuddle, didn't he? She bounced through the garden gnomes leaving Walden Yapp to struggle with his conscience and a most uncomfortable pair of underpants. He couldn't possibly go into the house in this condition. The poor woman would draw the obvious conclusion and then there was Willy to consider. He might be home by now and his conclusions would be even more fraught with danger than Rosie's. Yapp started the car again and was about to drive off when she appeared round the side of the house.

'Wait for me,' she shouted.

'Can't,' Yapp called back. 'This is something I must do myself.'

The car moved forward leaving Rosie Coppett and several interested neighbours in some uncertainty. Not that Yapp was particularly sure himself. Never before in a life dedicated to the redistribution of wealth, rational relationships and the attainment of total knowledge had he had an involuntary emission in the twilight. It was most disturbing and he could only rationally account for it by blaming the state of the road and the car's aged shock absorbers. Not even that combination, now that he came to think about it. The car had been stationary at the time. No, it had been a physiological reaction to Rosie's kiss and for the first time Yapp had to concede that there was something to be said for the theory of animal magnetism. There was also something to be said for stopping as soon as he could and discarding his underpants.

Yapp braked and pulled into the side of the road and got out. He was just about to undo his belt when headlights appeared round the corner. Yapp crouched behind the Vauxhall until the car had passed and had to repeat the process of hiding a few minutes later when a car approached from the other direction.

'Bother,' said Yapp and decided that if he was going to be floodlit every few seconds he'd better go somewhere else. But where? A gate in the hedge suggested that things might be easier on the other side. Yapp climbed over, discovered in the process that the gate was topped by barbed wire, scratched his hands and having fallen over still found that he was floodlit when a car came round the corner at the top of the hill. He stood up and blinked round Across the field there seemed to be some sort of coppice. He'd be invisible to passing traffic there. Yapp strode stickily off across the

117

field, climbed a stone wall and presently was removing his pants and doing his best to wipe the ravages of passion from his trousers. In the darkness it was not easy and to make matters more unpleasant it began to rain. Yapp crouched under the cover of a small fir tree and cursed.

Willy left the Horse and Barge drunkenly. He lurched up Tythe Lane and had an altercation with a Corgi at the back gate of Mrs Gogan's garden before stabbing several plastic dustbins with his little waggler as a way of letting off steam about dogs that yapped and about Yapp himself. From the lane he crossed the main road after debating whether there were really two cars seemingly come towards him abreast or merely one. The headlights suggested two and even when the car had passed Willy couldn't be sure. The only fixed star in his mental firmament was that if he caught Rosie doling out extras to Professor Yapp when he got home he'd show the swine what his own tripes looked like. In short it was a very nasty dwarf who weaved his way up the hill as it began to rain. Willy ignored the rain. He was used to getting soaked but his feet had begun to hurt again. That was another score he had to settle with Yapp. He wasn't going to spend the next day trotting round town after the long-legged sod. To rest his feet he climbed onto an ancient mile-post and promptly fell off it, in the process losing his beloved little waggler.

'Bugger,' said Willy and proceeded to grope about on the ground for it. But the knife had disappeared. Willy got down on all fours and crawled out into the road and had just grasped the blade of the knife and was wishing he hadn't when he became vaguely aware of a noise. Something was coming down the road towards him, something dark and large. With a desperate effort he staggered to his feet and tried to scramble up the bank. But it was too late. A moment later Willy Coppett was a badly mangled dwarf and Mr Jipson had stopped the tractor.

He climbed out of the cab and went round to disentangle whatever bloody animal had got in his way. He had in mind a sheep or even more awkwardly a cow, but a brief examination was enough to tell him it was neither. Cows didn't wear size three shoes and no sheep he had ever known had buttons down its front. Mr Jipson struck a match and before it was blown out by the wind and rain he was a terrified man. He had just killed Buscott's sole and most popular dwarf. There was no doubt about identification and in Mr Jipson's mind no doubt that Willy was dead. You didn't drive large tractors into small people at high speed without killing them. Just to make sure he felt Willy's unbloodied wrist for the pulse beat.

'Fuck,' said Mr Jipson and considered the legal consequences of the accident, not to mention his local standing. Buscott might not object to blood sports, but killing dwarves came into an altogether different category. Besides he had been driving without lights, had no number plates on the tractor and far too much alcohol in his body. By adding these factors to Willy Coppett's popularity it took him less than thirty seconds to decide that this was one accident he had no intention of reporting. He'd dump the body in the ditch and go home. But the body would be found, there would be police enquiries ... Ditches weren't enough. Besides, he had passed a car a hundred yards back up the road and while he hadn't noticed anyone in it they were bound to be about somewhere. They'd be wondering why he'd stopped. Then again ... Mr Jipson's thoughts turned to cunning. He walked up the road and peered into the car. No one there. No one over the gate. He thought for a moment and tried the door. It opened. Supposing he took the handbrake off and rolled the car forward ... No, that wouldn't do. He'd have to move the tractor first and whoever was wherever they were might come back at any moment. On the other hand there was a chance here of getting Willy's body as far away from the scene of the accident as possible. Mr Jipson opened the boot and left it open.

Then he ran down to the tractor, took a plastic sack from the cab, put on a pair of protective gloves and with all the criminal expertise of a man who had watched hundreds of episodes of 'Z Cars', 'Hawaii Five-O', 'The Rockford Files' and 'Kojak', carefully lifted the body and carried it back up the road. Three minutes later Willy Coppett was inside the boot, the plastic sack was hanging outside the tractor cab where the rain would wash the blood off, and Mr Jipson was proceeding on his way with the temporary feeling that he'd got himself nicely out of a nasty incident.

Behind him Willy Coppett's little life trickled away without pain. Even his waggler was still with him, though he no longer grasped it. Instead, impelled by the front of the tractor, it was embedded in his stomach.

*

It was almost half an hour later that Walden Yapp decided that the rain had stopped sufficiently to allow him to get back to the car without getting drenched. Clutching his Y-fronts he climbed the stone wall, trudged across the field, caught his hand yet again on the barbed wire and finally climbed into the driver's seat with a new resolution. He would leave Number 9, Rabbitry Road in the morning. To stay in so stimulating a presence as Rosie's was to court disaster and while Yapp's philosophy rejected such things as honour and conscience in any but the social sense, his innate decency told him that he could never come between a dwarf and his wife.

Not for the first time Rosie Coppett had spoken the truth. Walden Yapp was a real gentleman.

fifteen

The rainstorm that had seen Willy Coppett's demise and Walden Yapp's discomfort drove Emmelia into her lean-to greenhouse in the kitchen garden. Ever since her childhood visits to Aunt Maria she had taken refuge in the lean-to in times of stress. It was old, had a grapevine against the brick wall where it produced more foliage in summer than was necessary for its few bunches of grapes, and in winter she tended to use the place as a potting-shed. Here, hidden by the leaves of the vine and to a lesser extent by the algae that grew where the panes of glass overlapped, surrounded by old clay pots and geranium cuttings and with one or two cats who had come in out of the wet, she sat in the darkness listening to the raindrops tapping on the glass and felt almost secure. This was her inner sanctum, fragile and old but hidden away in the walled kitchen garden, itself a sanctuary within the walls surrounding the New House. Nowhere else could she savour her obscurity so religiously or rid herself of the dross of news that reached her via *The Times* and the radio. Emmelia eschewed television and left it to Annie to watch while she cleaned the silver in the old boot-room. No, she had no time for what went on in the outside world and so far as she could tell the changes that were blazoned by the jet trails across afternoon skies, or featured prominently in public debate about the need for progress, were mere ephemera which nature would one day shrug off with as little compunction as it had buried the forests or turned the Sahara into a desert. Even the threat of nuclear obliteration seemed no more menacing, in fact even less, than the Black Death must have appeared to people living in the fourteenth century. Nature was life and death and Emmelia was content to place herself at nature's disposal with a cheerful fatalism that recognized no alternative. In her order of things the Petrefacts were an ancient species of articulate plant forever in danger of extinction unless they had their roots in the rich loam of past values.

In spite of the aplomb she had shown at the Mill that afternoon Emmelia had returned to the house deeply disturbed. While she was the first to admit that past values of the family had included a disregard for the amenities provided for blacks on their slave ships, or for workers in the Mill, and a general preparedness to do whatever an age demanded, however distasteful, by contemporary standards, those methods might seem, the discovery that Frederick had sunk to the level of an artefactual pimp dismayed her. It was also quite extraordinary that she had had to find this out for herself and hadn't been told. In spite of her isolation from the social life of Buscott and largely thanks to Annie, Emmelia had prided herself on knowing a great many things about events in the neighbourhood. But when she had questioned Annie on her return the housekeeper had denied any knowledge of what they were making at the Mill. Emmelia had to believe her. Annie had been with her for thirty-two years and she had never hidden anything from her before. That being the case she had to credit Frederick with a greater degree of authority and discretion than his repulsive products suggested. She would have to question him about his methods.

Much more to the point was whether or not her wretched brother knew what his son was up to. If he did, and had sent Professor Yapp down to disclose the knowledge to the world, she could only conclude that Ronald had gone mad. It was perfectly possible. A strain of insanity ran in the family emerging occasionally and varying in intensity from the mild eccentricity of the Brigadier-General's obsession for achieving the Seal-Pointed Gerbil to the outright lunacy of a second cousin who, having been exposed at too tender an age to the unexpurgated whimsy of *Winnie The Pooh*, had grown up with the conviction that he was Roo and every sizeable woman Kanga and had so embarrassed the family at several dinners by leaping into the laps of large female guests that he had to be packed happily off to Australia. There, true to his origins, he had earned a fortune out of sheep and a notorious reputation for being into wallabies.

Sitting in the darkness of the greenhouse among the pots and plants of her own gentle mania, Emmelia made up her mind. It didn't matter whether Ronald was mad or not: by sending Professor Yapp to Buscott he was putting the family reputation in grave danger and must be stopped immediately. Nor was it enough to have told Frederick to get rid of Yapp. In fact she rather regretted her injunction now. Frederick was as impetuous and unreliable as his father. He might do something wilful, and in any case driving Yapp out of Buscott could have the effect of confirming Ronald's suspicions, if that was all they were, that there was something to hide. And, knowing Ronald, next time he wouldn't send a so-called family biographer but half a dozen ghastly reporters or, even worse, a TV team.

As the rain lessened Emmelia left the lean-to and returned to the house. There she sat at her bureau and composed one letter rather carefully and a second more abruptly, placed them in envelopes and went through to the boot-room.

'I've put two letters on the salver in the hall,' she told Annie, 'I want you to see that the postman takes them away and delivers them when he comes in the morning.'

'Yes, mum,' said Annie and almost provoked Emmelia into telling her for the thirty-second year not to call her Mum. It was one of the many little irritations that made up the routine of the household and one she could neither get used to nor wholly regret. As far as she could tell it stemmed from Annie's too literal interpretation of 'Mum's the word', and since her words were Annie's law the housekeeper was merely acknowledging the fact and, rather obliquely, her own discretion.

Emmelia climbed the stairs to her bedroom thinking about another discreet dependent. There was always Croxley and in the last resort she could always call on him. Yes, Croxley, dear Croxley. Emmelia went to sleep thinking about him.

*

Walden Yapp hardly slept at all. Where his previous night had been disturbed by Willy apparently maltreating his wife, this time he was kept awake by the dwarf's unexplained absence and Rosie's growing agitation.

'It's not like him not to come home for his supper,' she said when Yapp returned scratched and with his hands torn. 'Oh, and what have you been doing to yourself?'

'Nothing, nothing,' said Yapp who wanted to get upstairs and dispose of his soiled Y-fronts in a suitcase before they congealed in his pocket.

'That's not nothing. You've been and gone and cut yourself something fearful. All bloody you are.'

'Just a graze, I slipped on the road.'

'But it's all down your shirt front too,' said Rosie. Yapp looked down at his shirt front and for the first time realized that he must have been bleeding more profusely than he had thought. His jacket had blood on it as well. In his examination of whatever he had knocked down Mr Jipson had bloodied himself rather more than he had known in the darkness and had transferred the gore to Yapp by way of the car door.

'I'll never get it off if you don't give it to me now,' said Rosie. 'Milk's the best thing.'

But Yapp had refused to take his shirt off.

'It's not important,' he muttered, 'I can always give it to Oxfam. It's a very old one.'

In spite of his protests Rosie had insisted and when Mr Clebb, who lived four doors up Rabbitry Road, took his dog for its urinal walk he was able to witness an already suspect Yapp sitting in his string vest in the kitchen while Mrs Coppett bathed his hands in a basin of Dettol. Since the basin was on Yapp's knees Mr Clebb couldn't actually see what exactly she was bathing, but he drew his own conclusions.

Rosie's efforts with the shirt – she poured half a pint of milk on the stain and then washed it and hung it up to dry – were less successful. While Yapp went to bed with bandaged hands and the knowledge that if he had got tetanus it wasn't Rosie's fault, he was still perplexed about the intransigent bloodstain. He could have sworn he hadn't wiped his hands on his shirt front but before he had time to consider the matter more fully he was distracted by sobs from the next room. Very briefly he supposed Willy had come home and was laying into Rosie again but, when the sobs went on, his good nature got the better of him. He climbed out of bed, sneezed three times, shivered, put his trousers on over his pyjamas and went out onto the landing.

'Are you all right?' he asked, conscious that it was not a very relevant question in the circumstances. Rosie Coppett stopped sobbing and opened the bedroom door.

'It's Willy,' she wailed, 'he's never been out this late before. He said he'd do it and he's done it.'

'Done what?'

'Run off with another woman.'

'Another woman?' From the little that Yapp had seen of Willy Coppett it didn't seem a very likely explanation.

'It's all my fault,' continued the distraught widow, 'I didn't look after him properly.'

'I'm sure you did,' said Yapp, but Rosie wasn't to be comforted so easily and with that sudden change of mood that Yapp found so disconcerting she clung to him. Yapp tried to disengage her. Rosie wasn't easily removed, and this time the sight of Yapp with Mrs Coppett in his arms was viewed with disapproval by Mrs Mane who lived next door and who had come out into the back garden to see if she could make out what was happening at the Coppetts. By the time Yapp had managed to lead Rosie back to her bed Mrs Mane had no doubts.

'Disgusting,' she told her husband, climbing back into bed. 'To think of her and him taking advantage of a blooming dwarf like that. She ought to be ashamed of herself and as for him, calls himself a gentleman ...'

At Number 9 Yapp behaved like a gentleman. He did his best to reassure Rosie, thought of the storm as an excuse for Willy's failure to return – 'He's probably staying the night down at the pub' – discounted her next theory that Willy had been put down a badger's sett again or was in hospital by pointing out that if that were the case the hospital authorities would have sent word, and that, in any case, putting Persons of Restricted Growth down badgers' holes was strictly against the law.

'Not in Buscott, it isn't. They've done it before,' she said and then, having horrified Yapp by her description of the hunt and its consequences, decided against the theory. 'No, that's not right. It's not the time.'

'It's utterly barbaric, never mind the time,' said Yapp, who put hunting in the same category as private medicine and would have abolished both these prerogatives of wealth and privilege.

'Time of the year, silly,' said Rosie. 'They don't hunt in summer. But they could still be ratting.'

'Ratting?'

'Put him in a ring with a hundred rats and see how many he could kill in a minute. Then they do the same with a terrier.'

'You mean ... dear God!'

'They take bets too. Last time Willy got a hundred pounds.'

'How appalling,' said Yapp with a shudder.

'Not that he won. Old Mr Hord's dog Bitsy did. But they gave Willy the money for trying and getting bitten so often.'

By the time he managed to escape Rosie's list of horrific possibilities Yapp was incapable of sleep. He lay in the darkness, prey to the deepest depression and sudden jolts of terror in which he imagined himself in a ring with a hundred frantic rats. Buscott was, in spite of the Petrefact influence and his own computer-stored statistics, from his observations well into the twentieth century and relatively prosperous but beneath the surface there still lingered barbarous sports banned by law and wholly at odds with his faith in progressive thought. Yapp tried to think of a rational explanation for the anachronism of cruelty but as in the case of Idi Amin, Cambodia, Chile, South Africa and Ulster, could only conclude that some people liked killing for its own sake and had no regard for the historical process.

If his mind was overactive his body matched it. His hands hurt, his head ached and he had pains in his legs and back. He also had a streaming cold which had progressed rapidly from violent sneezing to snuffling and coughing. Yapp tossed and turned restlessly and then fell asleep towards dawn. He was woken at ten by Rosie.

'That's a nasty cold you've got,' she said. 'You shouldn't never have got wet last night. Whatever was you up to?' She felt his jacket on the back of a chair. 'It's all damp. No wonder you have been took ill. Now you just stay there and I'll bring you some hot tea.'

Yapp murmured his thanks and went back to sleep and when at eleven the postman delivered Emmelia Petrefact's letter he was still too feverish to be interested.

'It's from Miss Petrefact,' said Rosie with a sense of importance which would have irritated Yapp in the normal way but which he now ignored.

'I'll read it later. I just want to sleep.'

All day Yapp slept while Rosie worried, first about Willy and what he was up to and then about the Professor and what Miss Petrefact had written about in her letter. She thought about going down to the pub to see if Willy had been there, considered the abattoir and would have gone down if Yapp hadn't been ill. And what about the doctor? It wasn't even as though she could ask the neighbours. She'd never got on with Mrs Mane and she wasn't going to ask her help now. Instead to ease her mind she tidied the house, made shepherd's pie and apple dumpling for Willy's tea, and read the horoscope in the newspaper he'd brought the tripe home in three days before. She had to rootle in the dustbin for it and when she found it and had worked out she was a Pisces it didn't say anything about disappearing husbands but was very accurate on financial benefits, romantic attachments and the need to be careful about health. After that she had another good cry and gave a great deal of unrequited affection to Blondie, the rabbit. Every now and then she poked her head round the door of Yapp's room in the hope that he was awake and could give her the advice she so badly needed, but Walden Yapp slept on unaware of the reality that was looming over him.

With everyone else involved in the drama things stood very differently and in the case of Willy didn't stand at all. Lying in the boot of the Vauxhall he had stiffened rather gruesomely into a parody of a fully-clothed foetus and was beyond recalling the nature of the reality which had hit him. Mr Jipson, to make sure that his tractor couldn't be implicated, had already washed it down several times with a hose and was now busily getting it mucky again. It was up at the New House that some sort of reality was most at work. Frederick, summoned by his aunt's letter, was amazed to find she had changed her mind.

'But you told me to get rid of the chap,' he countered when she said she had written to Yapp. 'Now you're inviting him to the house!'

'Exactly. I intend to divert him and in any case I shall find out how much he knows.'

'He must know something but I'm dashed if I understand how.

We don't call ourselves Fantasy Products Anonymous for nothing.' Emmelia eyed him sceptically. 'I mean that's been the secret of our success. The main obstacle in individual marketing has always been the fact that we cater for the sexually insecure.'

'Indeed? From what I saw I should have thought quite the contrary. Anyone strapping himself into that belt with the enema attachment would appear to require nerves of steel.'

'By sexually insecure I mean they're introverted. They're often far too shy to go into shops selling sex aids or even to have the things sent through the post.'

Emmelia sympathized but said nothing.

'What they want is to be able to purchase our goods without revealing their identity and that's exactly what we do, we guarantee their total anonymity.'

'But not apparently your own.'

'As far as I know we do,' said Frederick. 'We advertise through the usual channels and have a mail-order service based on an office in London. All communication between that office and the sales despatch department at the Mill is coded via computer so that even the girls in London have no idea they're dealing with Buscott.'

Emmelia sat back and closed her eyes and listened with apparent disinterest. At least Frederick was living up to the old reputation of the Petrefacts for keeping themselves obscure, which was more than could be said for his wretched father. She awoke from the bizarre picture of Lord Petrefact in a thermal chastity belt with enema variations to hear Frederick talking about means of delivery.

'... and where there's a large railway station with a left-luggage office we deposit the order there and mail the ticket to the client from the nearest post box so again there's no possible way of tracing us. It's perfectly simple.'

'Is it?' said Emmelia, opening her eyes. 'It sounds highly complicated to me but then I'm hardly qualified to understand. If you know the client, as you call him, and his address ...'

'But I've explained that. We don't know the client's name. He phones the London office stating his requirements and is given a code number. Then he supplies a false name and we provide a box number where he can pick up his mail. Of course, not everyone requires this personalized service. It costs considerably more than the standard despatch method, but whichever method is used we never mail orders from Buscott. Every posting is done in London.'

'Foreign sales too?' asked Emmelia.

'They're handled by subsidiaries,' said Frederick complacently, 'and again with a computer coded link-up.'

'Perhaps someone in the Mill has been talking.'

Frederick shook his head. 'Every employee is thoroughly vetted and we get them to sign the Official Secrets Act document.'

'But you can't do that. It's illegal.'

'Not, you know,' said Frederick with a smile. 'The Defector Encouragement Branch of MI 9 has a standing order for dildos and whatnot.' He paused and stared into space. 'That might explain it.'

'It explains nothing to me,' said Emmelia. 'I can think of nothing less likely to encourage me to defect than one of those monstrous things. I would rather spend the rest of my days in a salt mine than ...'

'I don't mean that. I mean Yapp. The man's a homegrown Bolshevik and as bent as Blunt. The whole thing could be KGB-inspired. The Russians will go to any lengths to cause trouble.'

'Then they must be anatomically most curious,' said Emmelia. 'In any case I have invited the wretched fellow to tea and to tea he shall come. If your father has put him up to this I intend to see that he lives to regret it.'

sixteen

Lord Petrefact was already regretting it. What the oyster had begun in the way of making him relatively immobile and intensely irritable, Yapp's catastrophic use of the Synchronized Ablution Bath and the subsequent career of the wheelchair had completed. He was now doubly dependent on Croxley, not only for his infallible grasp of the myriad details of Petrefact Consolidated Enterprises, but also to push his wheelchair. Having seen what a self-animated one could do he had no intention of trusting his precious body to another.

All of which would have been bad enough, but there was the additional annoyance of knowing that he need never have paid Yapp so much. At the time it had seemed a necessary precaution. There had been the very real risk that the Trade Unions might call on Yapp to arbitrate in the small matter of putting 8000 men out of work at the plant in Hull without paying them for their redundancy, but that risk had been removed by a fire which had burnt the factory to the ground. Anyone else would have been grateful to the charred buffoon who had started it by having an extremely loud smoke in the fuel store. Not so Lord Petrefact, who felt cheated. In his old age he could afford to indulge a perverse delight in strikes, lock-outs, the use of black-leg labour, the abuse of shop stewards and union leaders and the bewilderment expressed in the editorials of even right-wing papers at his obduracy. They all helped to revitalize his sense of power and, since Petrefact Consolidated's profits stemmed in the main from the efficient use of extremely cheap labour in Africa and Asia, he considered the millions of pounds lost by strikes of his own fomenting were well spent. They infuriated his relatives and in his opinion served to restore the morale of other industrialists.

But if he was prepared to be profligate in the matter of strikes he was extremely irked by the thought that he wasn't getting value for money from Yapp. Having seen what the lunatic could do at Fawcett in the matter of a short weekend he would have expected Buscott to have been flooded, devastated – the news that parts of North England had been hit by a minor earthquake temporarily raised his hopes – and in general to have followed the example of Troy after the introduction of the wooden horse. But as the days passed and no violent protests arrived from Emmelia he was beginning to think that Yapp had reneged on his obligations as a human disaster area. It irritated him still further because he couldn't take Croxley into his confidence. The damned man's devotion to the family made him untrustworthy. There were even moments when only the conviction, born of self-knowledge, that all true Petrefacts had hidden depths of deceit and privately loathed their kith and kin persuaded him that Croxley wasn't a member of the blasted family himself. Anyway he had no intention of asking the bastard's advice on this matter. And with every day Lord Petrefact's smile became more lopsided as he tried to think of some fresh goad to spur Yapp into action. He'd already sent him the family correspondence dealing with Great-Uncle Ruskin's bigamous relationship with several goats when he was already married to Maude and bestiality was definitely not in fashion, and if that wasn't enough to give Emmelia galloping hysteria there was also the matter of Percival Petrefact's unbiased supply of arms and ammunition to both the German Army and the Allies in the First World War. All in all, Yapp had enough material to blast the Petrefacts from their obscurity several times over. And if the swine didn't start producing repercussions soon he'd have to look to his lawyers to save even the twenty thousand pounds he had already received, let alone the rest. Lord Petrefact had his reputation as the hardest-headed financier in the City to consider. To help pass the time he snarled more frequently at Croxley, conducted several managerial purges for no obvious reason, and in general made life as hellish as possible for everyone he came in touch with. Unfortunately Yapp didn't, and when, having sent Croxley on a needless errand, he phoned the Faculty of History at Kloone the only information he could obtain was that the Professor was away and had left no forwarding address.

'Well when do you expect him back?' he demanded. The secretary couldn't say. Professor Yapp's movements were always a little erratic.

'They'll be a fucking sight more erratic if the shit doesn't contact me in the course of the next day or two,' shouted Lord Petrefact, slamming down the phone and leaving the secretary in some doubt as to his identity. Being a well-brought-up girl from a working-class home she could hardly bring herself to believe that peers swore like that.

In his office Croxley monitored the call. It was one of the few advantages of Lord Petrefact's new-found loathing for motorized wheelchairs that while the old devil could hurl insults more violently than ever he couldn't hurl himself from room to room without help and Croxley could go about his business without being interrupted by more than the intercom buzzer which he could ignore. And Croxley's business had begun to alter its emphasis. Lord Petrefact's annoyance at his secretary's devotion to the family was only partly justified.

The new regime of unadulterated abuse was taking its toll on the secretary's tolerance and Croxley had reached the age when he found being called a cunt-loving son of a syphilitic whore neither appropriate nor, by inversion, vaguely flattering. To add to his resentment, the recent purges of perfectly competent executives had made him question his own future and reach the conclusion that his prospects of comfortable retirement were under threat. To counter this threat he had broken the resolution of a lifetime not to dabble on the stockmarket and by using his savings, remortgaging his house in Pimlico and monitoring Lord Petrefact's more private telephone calls, Croxley had done rather well. So well in fact that, given a little more time and private enterprise, he hoped shortly to be in a position to tell the old swine what he really thought of him. But if his own interests were beginning to burgeon, he remained loyal to that faction of the Petrefact family which detested the peer. He was particularly devoted to Miss Emmelia and it was one of his many regrets that his station in life had prevented him from devoting himself more intimately to her.

In short, Croxley's thoughts frequently wandered towards Buscott and he was alarmed to learn from this latest call that Lord Petrefact had evidently sent Walden Yapp there. It added one more puzzling factor to the whole enigma of Yapp's visit to Fawcett. The old devil was up to something unusually devious concerning the family but what it was Croxley had no idea. Yapp in Buscott? Odd, distinctly odd. And the Mill was making excellent profits from ethnic clothing, too. That was curious too. He had never thought of Miss Emmelia as a businesswoman but with the Petrefacts there were always surprises. He was just considering the idea of retiring to Buscott – the old swine would never bother him there and he'd be close to Miss Emmelia – when the buzzer went and Lord Petrefact demanded his lunch.

'And see there's a double helping of cognac in the Complan,' he yelled. 'Yesterday I couldn't even smell the fucking stuff.'

'One brandy Complan coming up,' said Croxley and switched the intercom off before Lord Petrefact could bawl him out for being familiar. He went down to the kitchen with strychnine on his mind.

At Number 9 Rabbitry Road, Yapp sat in bed and rather reluctantly finished reading the letters Lord Petrefact had sent him. He had recovered from his bout of summer flu, but had been shaken rigid by the contents of the letters. While his own demotic leanings were less towards illicit interpersonal relationships between goats and Great-Uncle Ruskin, he had to admit that the

131

revelations threw an entirely new light on the family. But it was the impartial arms dealings of Percival Petrefact in World War One that gripped his attention. Here was material that would expose the multi-national capitalism of the Petrefacts to the entire world, though he couldn't for the life of him understand why he had been given this extraordinary correspondence. But at least he was clear on one matter, he must lay his hands on the Petrefact Papers in the Museum. If they contained a fraction of the damaging admissions of these letters the family history was as good as written. He would have to see Miss Emmelia Petrefact and get her permission to view them. That was essential.

He got out of bed and staggered through to the bathroom with new resolution, but by the time he had shaved it had been diluted by sounds coming through the floor from the kitchen. Rosie Coppett was having another good cry over the absence of her Willy. Yapp sighed. If Willy had really run off with another woman, as Rosie claimed more insistently every day, it was clear that his morals were as restricted as his growth. Moreover, he had placed Yapp in a very invidious position. He could hardly leave a deserted and mentally sub-normal woman in her hour of need; at the same time, to stay on in the house would be to invite scandal and gossip. Regarding himself in the shaving mirror, a process which involved going down on his knees because Willy had fixed the mirror firmly to the wall at two feet for his own needs, Yapp decided that he had no right to put Mrs Coppett's reputation in jeopardy. Besides, his own peculiar feelings for her made staying on impossible. He would leave her a cheque for two hundred pounds and steal quietly away. That was definitely the solution. It would avoid all the heart-rending tears of a more public departure.

Having shaved and cut himself in consequence of the height of the mirror he returned to his room, dressed, packed his bag and wrote out a cheque for three hundred pounds, at the same time adding a note saying he would get in touch with her as soon as it was proper to do so. Finally, with a surge of daring that was to be his undoing, he signed himself 'Yours most affectionately, Walden Yapp.'

Twenty minutes later he saw her go down the garden path with a shopping-bag; as she disappeared towards Buscott, he left the house with his rucksack and suitcase, threw them onto the back seat of the Vauxhall and drove off in the opposite direction. The sun shone down out of a cloudless sky but Yapp had no heart for the beauties of nature. He was thinking how sad a place the world was and how strange his own nature that it should find so strong an appeal in the large body and little mind of a woman like Rosie Coppett.

There was also a rather strange smell in the car, a distinctly nasty smell suggestive of blocked drains, but Yapp dismissed it as one of the less savoury features of agriculture, possibly some farmer mucking his fields with pig dung, and concentrated on the best approach to Miss Petrefact. From what he had gathered during his walkabouts in Buscott and from Rosie he had gained the impression that she was somewhat eccentric, definitely reclusive but not unpopular. In any case she could hardly be as thoroughly disagreeable as her brother and, while he would have preferred to continue his researches at grass-roots level, it was obvious that without her consent there would be no grass-roots to research. He had just reached this conclusion and the bottom of the hill leading to the New House when he remembered that Rosie had said something about a letter from Miss Emmelia. He'd forgotten the damned thing during his illness. It was too late to go back for it now. He would just have to press ahead.

He drove on up the hill and turned in at the gates and stopped on the gravel outside the front door. For a moment he sat there grudgingly admitting to himself that Samuel Petrefact, the founder of the Mill and the family's immense fortune, had had modest and distinctly refined tastes in domestic architecture. Yapp felt aggrieved. It was a tenet of his philosophy that entrepreneur capitalists who made life a misery for the mill-hands should proclaim that awfulness in the houses they built. Samuel Petrefact hadn't. Yapp got out and was about to ring the front-door bell when he became aware that something was moving in the depths of the shrubbery across the lawn and as he watched a figure emerged above the bushes clutching a fork. It was wearing a cloth cap which came down over its ears and its hands and old apron were very largely caked with mud. Yapp moved across the lawn and the figure promptly disappeared into the undergrowth.

'I wonder if you can tell me if Miss Petrefact is in,' he said addressing himself to a large expanse of corduroy under a *Viburbum fragrans*.

The corduroy moved further into the shrubbery. 'Strictly speaking she isn't,' it said gruffly. 'And who might you be?'

Yapp hesitated. He disliked being addressed so arrogantly even by jobbing gardeners, but then the servants of the rich frequently took on the airs and lack of graces of their employers. 'My name is Yapp. Professor Yapp. I'd like to speak to Miss Petrefact.'

A series of grunts from the depths of an Australian Bottlebrush seemed to suggest that he'd just have to wait until she was in. Yapp stood on the lawn uncertainly and surveyed the garden. It was, he supposed, a very fine one though his own tastes gravitated more towards allotments, cabbage patches and the pot leeks of the provident poor than to the artifice of herbaceous borders, shrubberies and rockeries.

'Must be hard work,' he said, 'being a gardener and having all this to look after.'

'It is.' This time the voice came from a Tree Peony and sounded even brusquer than before. Yapp noted the tone and put it down to the natural resentment of the menially employed.

'Have you worked here long?'

'Just about all my working life.'

Yapp contemplated a working life spent grubbing on hands and knees in dense shrubberies and found it disagreeable. 'Is the pay good?' he asked with an inflexion that implied the opposite. Muffled tones from an Osmarea said it didn't amount to a living wage.

Yapp warmed to the topic. 'And I don't suppose the old girl gives you an allowance for travelling time, clothing or tea breaks?'

'Never heard of them.'

'Disgraceful,' said Yapp, happy to have found someone in Buscott with a genuinely proletarian sense of grievance. 'What you need is a Horticultural Workers Union to fight for your rights. I mean how many hours a week do you have to work to maintain this garden in the state the old woman demands?'

A further series of belligerent snorts ended with 'Ninety.'

Yapp was appalled. 'Ninety? That's outrageous.'

'Sometimes a hundred,' said the voice, moving on to a Sorbaria.

'But ... but that's sweated labour,' said Yapp struggling to find words for his fury. 'The old bitch has absolutely no right to treat you like that. Nobody in industry would dream of working a hundred hours a week. And of course you don't get paid overtime, do you?'

A derisive chuckle in the depths of the Sorbaria answered his question. Yapp followed the voice down the shrubbery fulminating against the evils of exploitation. 'And I daresay it's the same down in that foul Mill of theirs. The whole system is rotten to the core. Well I'm going to see that this town and what the Petrefacts are doing here hits the headlines. It's a perfect example of the vices and lengths the capitalist class will go to to screw the proletariat. Well, you can tell the filthy old bitch that I can do without her help, thank you very much, and she's going to learn what some well-organized publicity can do to change things.'

And having worked himself up into a state of righteous indignation at the plight of the workers of Buscott on the strength of this single and rather one-sided interview, Yapp strode back to the car, got in and drove away. He knew now what he was going to do; return to Kloone and set in motion the research team he had organized. There were to be no more preliminary studies on an individual basis. People were too intimidated to talk openly unless, like the old gardener, they were assured of anonymity or knew that the outside world was there to protect them. Well, the outside world would be there in force with tape-recorders and cameras.

Behind him the filthy old bitch emerged from a Mock Orange and stared after him with mixed feelings. The man was a blithering idiot but also a dangerous one and she was glad she had had the chance to see him in his true colours instead of more politely over afternoon tea. And she was certainly extremely pleased that she had remained as obscure as her forebears. Wiping her hands on her apron, Emmelia went into the house with new determination. Professor Walden Yapp had to be stopped from continuing his researches any further. He had already gone too far.

seventeen

In fact Yapp had gone some thirty-eight miles at a far higher speed than was his norm when his sense of mortal outrage at the plight of the workers of Buscott was joined and largely overwhelmed by his sense of smell. By the time he had to stop at a cross-roads because of the traffic he was in two minds whether to go on or take the car back to Mr Parmiter and complain that there was something fundamentally wrong with the thing. But having come so far, and remembering the garage proprietor's unpleasantness, he went on. Perhaps the awful stench would disappear. It certainly lessened when he drove fast with all the windows open and the de-mister on, but every time he slowed down it seemed to catch up with him again. And it was a particularly nauseous smell. Yapp couldn't put a name to it, but the notion that it had anything to do with pig-manure was definitely out of the question. Nothing he had ever experienced smelt like this, and coming so shortly after his bout of flu, it was playing havoc with his stomach. In desperation he pulled into the side of the road, got out of the car and took several deep breaths of fresh air.

Feeling slightly better, he poked his head through the car window and sniffed. The ghastly odour was still there, and now that he could compare it with unpolluted air it smelt worse than ever. Whatever was making it had something to do with the car and for the first time Yapp began to think it might have something to do with death. Perhaps he had run over a rabbit which had got caught up in the fan belt? He opened the bonnet and looked inside, but there was no sign of dead rabbits and the air in the engine compartment smelt decidedly better than that in the interior. Yapp went round to the back door and sniffed again. The fetor was positively foul there, but though he looked on the floor and felt under the seats he could find nothing to explain it. There remained the boot. Yapp climbed out again and, after taking several more deep breaths, undid the latch and opened it. A moment later he was staggering back, had caught his foot in the handle of an abandoned pram, and was lying on his back staring insanely at the sky. It was no longer a cloudless sky, the weather had changed for the worse, but at least it was infinitely better to look at than what lay in the boot. Anything was. The sky had a sanity about it, a sense of the natural and the real that was entirely lacking in a putrefying dwarf.

For several minutes Yapp lay there trying to imagine the sight away. But his imagination failed him and in the end, with the terrible feeling that he had gone mad and was hallucinating, he got to his feet, detached his torn trouser-leg from the rusty pram, and took another look. This time there could be no doubting the reality of the contents of the boot nor its identity. Distinctly dented and in a *post-mortem* foetal position, the late Willy Coppett could hardly be mistaken for anyone else, not even by Yapp who would have cheerfully exchanged him for the first symptom of lunacy. Insanity could, with the help of modern medicine, be cured but dead dwarves were beyond any form of aid. Yapp shut the boot hurriedly and stared wildly into the coppice beside the lay-by in a frantic attempt to think. It wasn't easy. The presence of a corpse, and a mangled one at that, in the boot of the car he had been driving didn't make for coherent thought. How had Willy Coppett got there? From his two brief glimpses Yapp had no doubt that he hadn't got in of his own accord. Someone had put him there and, what was even worse, someone had evidently murdered him too. Dwarves, no matter how alienated by the awful nature of their employment, didn't bash themselves over the head with blunt instruments and then crawl into the boots of other people's cars and die. Yapp felt sure about that, just as he felt sure that Willy's death had been brought about by the forceful use of a blunt instrument. In the past he had speculated about the use of the word 'blunt' and had found it imprecise but two glances at Willy's corpse had been enough to persuade him that the term was exact. In any case he had no time for such speculations now. He had to do something.

It was here that he hit another snag. Like 'blunt' the word 'do' meant, in these appalling circumstances, something quite different from what he had previously supposed. It didn't mean uttering opinions, giving lectures or even writing learned monographs. It meant getting back into that noisome vehicle, driving it to the nearest police station and explaining to a constable or sergeant that he was in possession, albeit unintentionally, of one dead, decaying and distinctly murdered dwarf. Yapp visualized the consequences of this admission and found them all exceedingly unpleasant. In the first place there would be very considerable doubts as to his story, secondly about his sanity and finally, if his experience of the police was anything to go by, no doubts whatsoever about his guilt. Now that he came to think of it, it was inconceivable that anyone with a remotely acute sense of smell could have driven that stinking car nearly forty miles without being aware that there was something long-dead in it. There would be no explaining to an ignorant rural constable that he had been so outraged by social conditions in Buscott that he had had no nose for more immediate corruption, nor that for the most part he had driven so fast as to leave smells behind. And stories about dead rabbits wouldn't do either. Whatever dead rabbits smelt like, and Yapp had no idea, he was certain they couldn't come within a mile of smelling as noxiously as dead Persons of Restricted Growth. And to add to his problems in dealing with the police, he had on numerous occasions addressed rallies of militant strikers and flying pickets, not to mention protest meetings on behalf of falsely charged criminals or persecuted minority groups, at which he had megaphonically denounced the police as a semi-para-military force dedicated to the protection of property at the expense of people and as, in one widely reported speech, 'the fuzz on the face of fascism'. In the light of his present predicament, Yapp regretted these pronouncements. They were hardly likely to gain him a sympathetic hearing in any police station. Stories of brutality in the cells circulated in his memory and to add to his panic it occurred to him that whoever had murdered Willy had chosen his temporary resting place with a degree of acumen that suggested the choice was not purely fortuitous. In short, he had been framed. Paranoia joined panic. He had definitely been framed and the reason wasn't too hard to find. He had been framed to prevent his exposure of the deplorable conditions that without a shadow of doubt existed in the Petrefact Mill. It was a typical act of political terrorism on the part of the capitalist establishment.

From that realization Yapp drew a simple conclusion. He must get rid of the body as speedily as possible and in such a way that he couldn't be connected with it. What was more, he would send it back where it properly belonged. But how? He certainly wasn't going to drive back with it to Buscott, but didn't the River Bus flow somewhere nearby? Yapp hurriedly consulted his map and found the river several miles to the east. If he drove on he would come to a side road that crossed it, and where roads crossed rivers they did so on bridges.

Yapp got back into the Vauxhall, thanked God there had been no passing traffic to see him parked in the lay-by, prayed fervently that the recent rains had turned the Bus into a deep torrent, and drove off. Twenty minutes later he had reached the bridge and as

138

he passed across it was grateful to note that the river had not dwindled to a stream but was broad and apparently deep. Best of all, the side road lived up to its name. He had met no other cars and he could see no houses in the vicinity. On either side of the Bus woods sloped up to the empty moors whose depopulation he had so incorrectly diagnosed when he had crossed them on the day of his arrival. Now he was thankful for their emptiness but to make quite sure he wouldn't be observed he drove on up the hill on the far side of the bridge and surveyed the bleak landscape. There was not a farm in sight. He turned the car round and went back to the bridge and parked in a little clearing under the trees where empty cigarette packets, squashed cans of beer and cartons indicated people came for picnics.

Yapp got out and listened but apart from the slop of the river and the occasional birdsong there was silence. No one about. Good. The next five minutes were not. The late Willy Coppett not only stank to high heaven but he also showed a marked disinclination to leave the boot. His little shoes caught under one side while he adhered to the floor in several places so that Yapp had to grapple with him rather more closely than his stomach enjoyed. Twice he had to give up the struggle to retch into the bracken and when he finally managed to drag the body from the boot he was horrified to discover that Willy had died not solely from injuries caused by a blunt instrument but also by the insertion of an extremely sharp one. This was brought home to him when the point of the knife protruding from Willy's back jabbed Yapp in the stomach so painfully that instead of carrying the corpse onto the bridge before dropping it into the river he let go of it on land and watched with horror as it rolled slowly down the bank into the water.

Even then Yapp's panic was not abated. His lack of experience in disposing of dead bodies in rivers had led him to suppose that they sank. The late Willy Coppett didn't. He drifted slowly away downstream, snagged his jacket for several seconds in an over-hanging bush, was twirled round by the current, collided with a log and finally disappeared round a bend.

Yapp didn't wait. Thankful that he was no longer the driver of an obviously illegal hearse, he got back into the driving seat of the old Vauxhall and drove back the way he had come with the slightly comforting thought that in two hours he would be in his rooms at Kloone and could have a bath. But as ever with his theories, reality proved this one wrong. An hour later two miles out of Wastely the Vauxhall came to a halt and the engine stopped. Yapp tried the starter twice without success and then noticed that the petrol gauge read empty.

'Shit,' said Yapp with uncharacteristic violence and got out.

At Number 9 Rabbitry Road Rosie Coppett had returned from her shopping expedition in that same state of mental uncertainty in which she lived her life unless there was someone around to make up what there was of her mind for her. Since Willy's mysterious departure she had relied on Yapp, and had gone on with her daily routine telling herself that the Professor would know what to do about finding Willy as soon as he got better. But the letter on the hall table, the cheque for three hundred pounds and, worst of all, his empty room finally convinced her that he too had deserted her. Rosie took the cheque and the letter into the kitchen and looked at them both with pathetic bewilderment. The enormous sum of money he seemed to be giving her didn't make sense to her. After all, he had refused her offer of extras and she hadn't done anything more for him than she would have done for any other lodger and here was three hundred pounds. What for? And why did he write that he would get in touch with her as soon as it was proper to do so and sign his letter 'Yours most affectionately, Walden'? Slowly but with dim determination she grappled with the pieces of this puzzle. The Professor had come to stay and had paid more than she asked; he had refused her extras but had said he liked her and had comforted her by holding her hand and she had known that he meant it; Willy had disappeared without a word of warning two days later; and now the Professor, who had been so ill, had gone too, leaving her all this money. He had also left the letter from Miss Petrefact unopened and finally the shirt she had so thoroughly washed in a vain attempt to get the bloodstain off it was still hanging on the clothes line where she had hoped the sunshine would bleach the stain away. She was alone with Blondie and Hector and they couldn't tell her what to do.

She got up from the kitchen table and made a pot of strong tea like her mum had told her to when anything nasty had happened. After that she ate several slices of bread and dripping, all the while wondering where to turn to for advice. The neighbours wouldn't do. Willy would be ever so cross if she went to them and told them he'd gone away, and the Marriage lady wasn't any good either. She'd told her to leave Willy and now Willy had left her she'd say it served her right and it didn't. She'd always been a good wife to him and nobody could say she hadn't and it wasn't right to tell wives to leave their hubbies. Which brought her to the Vicar, but he was all hoity-toity and didn't stop to chat to her when she left church like he did with other richer ladies, and besides, he'd made them say they would never leave one another and, now that Willy had, he'd be angry and wouldn't let Willy sing in the choir like he used to. There was really no one she knew she could go to.

In the end she remembered Miss Petrefact's letter which the Professor had never opened. She wouldn't like Miss Petrefact to think she hadn't given it to him. She'd better return it. And so, drawn all unknowingly by the custom of deference to the Petrefacts, she put all the bits of paper and the envelope in her bag, left the house, passed sadly through Willy's collection of garden gnomes whose rigor he now shared, and trudged off in the direction of the New House.

Half an hour later she was seated in the kitchen there telling an interested Annie, who had nothing better to do than string runner beans, all her troubles.

'He left you a cheque for three hundred pounds? What would he want to do that for?' said Annie, who had been most interested in the story of the blood-stained shirt on the very night Willy Coppett hadn't come home. Rosie rummaged in her bag and brought the cheque out.

'I don't know. I don't even know how to put it in the Post Office savings. Willy always does that.'

Annie studied the cheque and the letter that had been in the envelope with it. '"Yours most affectionately, Walden,"' she read out and looked at Rosie Coppett suspiciously. 'That doesn't sound like a lodger. That sounds like something else. He didn't try to get up to anything with you, did he?'

Rosie blushed and then giggled. 'Not really. Not like you mean. He was ever so nice though. He said he was very fond of me and respected me as a woman.'

Annie looked at her even more doubtfully. She couldn't remember any man, let alone a professor, telling her that he was very

141

fond of her and as for respecting Rosie Coppett as a woman when the girl was clearly a half-wit, the man who said that must definitely have been up to something not at all nice.

'I think Miss Emmelia ought to see this,' she said, and before Rosie could protest that she didn't want to get Willy or anybody into trouble Annie had gathered the cheque and the note and taken them through to the front of the house. Rosie sat on absent-mindedly stringing the rest of the runner beans. She felt very nervous but at the same time she was glad she had come because she didn't have to think what to do any more. Miss Petrefact would know.

Twenty miles away Willy's body slid over an old weir, swirled in the foam for a few minutes, bumped its way through some rocks and swept on. It was coming back to Buscott, but it never arrived by water. Some small boys playing in the shallows by the Beavery Bridge spotted it and ran along the bank in awful excitement; when Willy was thrust by the current against the trunk of a fallen tree they were there to drag him by his little feet into the side of the river. For a few minutes they stood in frightened silence before scrambling up the bank to the road and stopping the first car. Half an hour later several policemen had arrived and were staring down at the body and the C.I.D. in Briskerton had been informed that the body of a presumably murdered dwarf, unofficially identified as William Coppett, had been discovered in the Bus.

eighteen

'You mean to tell me that Professor Yapp left the house this morning without telling you, and that you found this letter and the cheque waiting for you when you came home from shopping?'

Rosie stood in the drawing-room of the New House and mumbled, 'Yes, mum.'

'And don't call me mum, girl,' said Emmelia, 'I've had enough of that from Annie over the years, I am not your mum.'

142

'No, mum.'

Emmelia gave up. She had had a trying day and had been busily and uncharacteristically using the telephone to the leading members of the family to inform them that a family council was called for, and she had heard too many objections of one sort or another to be in a good mood.

'Did he say where he was going?'

Rosie shook her head.

'Did he say anything about The Mill?'

'Oh yes, mum, he was always going on about it.'

'What sort of things did he say?'

'What the pay was like and what they made there and such-like.'

Emmelia considered this unpleasant confirmation of what she already knew and was more than ever convinced that a family consultation was needed.

'And did you tell him?'

'No, mum.'

'Why not?'

'I don't know, mum. Nobody ever told me.'

Emmelia thanked God and ignored the reiterated implication that she was Rosie Coppett's mother. The girl was quite evidently stupid and to that extent it was exceedingly fortunate that Yapp had chosen so uninformed a landlady. If that was all he had chosen; the cheque and the note signed 'Yours most affectionately, Walden' suggested a less abstemious and, to Emmelia's way of thinking, a positively perverse relationship. And what on earth did he mean when he said he would get in touch with this mentally deficient creature 'as soon as it was proper to do so'? She put the question to Rosie, but all she could say was that the Professor was a proper gentleman. Having seen Yapp for herself Emmelia had reservations on that score, but she kept them to herself.

'Well I must say it all sounds most peculiar to me,' she said finally. 'However since he's given you this money I see no reason why you shouldn't keep it.'

'Yes, mum,' said Rosie, 'but what about Willy?'

'What about him?'

'His going off like that.'

'Has he never done it before?'

'Oh no, mum, never, not in all the years we've been married.

143

Comes home for his supper ever so regular and if it's not ready he gets so cross and I ...'

'Quite so,' said Emmelia, who had more important things to think about than the domestic habits of a dwarf and his overweight wife. 'In that case you had better go to the police and report him as missing. I can't imagine why you haven't done so already.'

Rosie twisted her fingers together. 'I didn't like to, mum. Willy gets ever so fierce if I do things on my own without telling him.'

'I can hardly see how he can possibly object if he's not there for you to tell,' said Emmelia. 'Now then, be off with you and go straight to the police station.'

'Yes, mum,' said Rosie and followed Annie back to the kitchen obediently.

Seated at her bureau, Emmelia tried to put this distressing interview to the back of her mind. She had the arrangements for the family council to make and she had yet to decide where to hold it. The Judge, the Brigadier-General and her Dutch cousins, the van der Fleet Petrefacts, had all stated their preference for London while Osbert, who owned most of the Petrefact holdings in Buscott and much of the countryside around, combined her own love of obscurity with a fear amounting to a phobia about being denounced as an absentee landlord if he so much as set foot outside the district. But there was a more telling reason in Emmelia's mind for holding the meeting in Buscott. It would save her the embarrassment of having to explain in detail the exact nature of the objects being made at the Mill. They would be able to see for themselves how imperative it was that the renegade Ronald must be forced to stop Yapp's researches before the name Petrefact became indissolubly connected in the public mind with dildos, merkins, hand-made Male Chastity Belts and French Ticklers. One glimpse inside the Mill would prepare the Judge to commit murder without a second thought, while the Brigadier-General's obsession with Seal-Pointed Gerbils would dwindle in an instant. No, the meeting must be held here in the family house in Buscott. She would put her foot down. And what was more she would insist that the meeting be held the coming weekend. That way no one could object. Even the Judge didn't try people on Saturdays and Sundays.

*

In the reassuringly aseptic surroundings of his rooms at Kloone University Walden Yapp undressed and took a bath with Dettol in it. He had had a horrid journey back from Buscott, had tramped two miles to get a can of petrol from a garage and had had to endure several disconcerting remarks about smells, first of his clothes and then of the old Vauxhall, by the man who had driven him back to the car. Yapp had tried to explain them away by saying he had recently visited an activated sludge dump but the garage man had said it reminded him of something in the war and after several minutes' silence had gone on rather too appositely about the whiff of dead bodies in Monte Cassino where he'd fought. But at least he had provided enough petrol to get Yapp back to the garage to fill up and then drive back to Kloone without interruption.

Now in his antiseptic bath he considered his next actions. He would certainly have to do something about his clothes before the cleaning lady came in the morning, and just as certainly he had to clean out the boot of the old Vauxhall. But there were more abstract considerations to deal with and when he had dried himself, put on clean clothes, put the Willy-polluted ones in a plastic dustbin bag and sealed the top, his mind turned to food and Doris. He made himself a bowl of muesli as being both vegetarian and nourishing, sat down at the computer terminal and dialled in.

On the screen in front of him the comforting figures appeared in that private language he had so carefully devised for his communications with Doris. He was back in his singular world and could at last confide in a brain whose thinking matched his own. There were things he had to tell it – in fact now that he was no longer under the pressure of desperate action it occurred to him that perhaps Doris could help. Munching his muesli he contemplated the screen and made a decision. A full confession of his activities in Buscott, the times and dates on which he had done things, or on which things had happened to him, would definitely clarify his mind while at the same time providing Doris with that data from which she could, as a wholly unbiased observer, draw equally unprejudiced conclusions.

As night fell outside his white-walled rooms Yapp committed to the computer his most intimate thoughts and feelings about the late Willy Coppett and Rosie, their actions and his own, such minutiae as what the ladies in the tea-shop had said to him when he was looking for lodgings and the remarks Mr Parmiter had made about tax-dodging and the advantages of buying the Bedford. The hours passed, midnight came and went, and still Yapp sat on in mental communion with his micro-processed *alter ego* and with each finger-tap on the keyboard and its instantaneous transmission of a digit of recalled experience to the electronic labyrinth, the dangers and chaos of reality receded, were broken down into the simplest units of positive or negative electrical impulse and reassembled in a numerative complexity that took as little cognizance of the true nature of the world as Yapp had programmed it to. Only on one question were they at variance. When, at five in the morning, an exhausted Yapp turned from feeding data to its interpretation and, out of weary impulse, asked 'Who murdered Willy?' Doris answered without hesitation, 'Someone.' Yapp gaped at the answer groggily.

'I know that,' he typed, 'but who had a motive?'

'Rosie' read Doris. Yapp shook his head and typed furiously. 'Who had the means?'

Again the name 'Rosie' appeared on the screen. Yapp's fingers danced lividly on the keyboard.

'Why would she do that?' he demanded.

'In love with you.' The words seemed to waver in front of him.

'You're just jealous,' he said but the words remained unaltered on the screen. Yapp switched them off, stood up and walked unsteadily to the bed and slumped on it in his clothes.

In a room in the police station at Buscott Rosie Coppett sat on a chair and wept. She had done as Miss Petrefact had told her and had reported to the constable at the duty desk that Willy was missing, only to learn that he had been found. For a moment she had been happy, but only for a moment.

'Dead,' said the constable with the brutal stupidity of a young man who thought that because everyone knew Rosie Coppett was simple-minded she was without any feelings as well. Precisely the opposite was true. Rosie had an abundance of feelings and no way of expressing them except by crying, but it had taken some seconds for the smile that had gathered on her face to disintegrate and by that time the constable had fetched the sergeant.

'There, there,' said the Sergeant putting a hand on her shoulder, 'I'm sorry.'

It was the last kindly word anyone spoke to Rosie that day and she didn't hear it. From that moment on she had been asked to think. The detective inspector from Briskerton had arrived and had swept the sergeant aside. Rosie had been taken into a room as bare of ornaments as her little rooms in Rabbitry Road were full of them, and she had been asked questions she had no way of answering except to cry and say she didn't know. Did Willy have any enemies? Rosie said he didn't. But someone has killed him, Mrs Coppett, so that can't be true, can it? Rosie didn't know Willy had been killed. Murdered, Mrs Coppett, murdered. The word hardly made any impression on Rosie. Willy was dead. She would never have to cook his tea for him again or have him be cross with her for letting Blondie get among the cabbages. They would never go for walks again on Sunday afternoons. She would never be able to buy him cards of bunnies from the newspaper shop on the corner. Never, never, never.

This certainty came and went and came again with more force each time and the questions she was being asked had nothing to do with that terrible realization. She answered them almost unconsciously. She could not remember when she had last seen him. Was it Monday or Tuesday or Wednesday, Mrs Coppett? But time was as irrelevant as the manner of Willy's dying and her simple mind was grappling with the prospect of an endless time without Willy.

Across the table Inspector Garnet watched her closely and tried to decide if he was dealing with a stupid but innocent woman, a stupid and guilty one, or a woman whose stupidity was ravelled with cunning and who, behind the façade of mindless grief, knew almost by instinct how to hide her guilt. A long career as a detective and a short course in criminology had influenced him to think that all criminals, and particularly domestic murderers, were stupid, emotionally unstable and at least partially clever. They had to be stupid to think that they could break the law and get away with it; they had to be emotionally unstable to commit acts of appalling violence; and they had to be in part clever because the rate of unsolved crime continued to rise in spite of brilliant detection by the police.

Having examined Willy's terrible injuries the Inspector was in

147

no doubt that he was dealing with a crime of passion. Buscott had nothing to interest gangsters or organized crime while the forensic expert's preliminary report had ruled out the possibility that Willy had been interfered with sexually. No, all the evidence pointed to an ordinary, if nasty, domestic murder. And Mrs Coppett was a very strong woman while her late husband had been a very small man. Nor did the Inspector have to look far for motive. The dead man's dwarfishness constituted one motive, his acknowledged bad temper another. Finally there was the fact that Mrs Coppett had only bothered to report that her husband was missing when he had already been found. That suggested some sort of cunning on her part, and her refusal to answer his questions straightforwardly confirmed it. He was particularly bothered by her inability to say when the dead man had last left home, if he ever had before his death.

So while the Inspector continued his fruitless questioning into the night, other detectives visited Number 9 Rabbitry Road where they took note of Rosie's predilection for All-In Wrestlers and men with all the physical characteristics her late husband so evidently lacked, removed Yapp's shirt from the clothesline and studied the stain, made more notes about Willy's cot and Yapp's unmade bed in the spare room, and were volubly assisted by the neighbours in arriving at totally false conclusions.

Armed with this new evidence they returned to the police station and conferred with the Inspector.

'Some professor bloke's been staying there?' he asked. 'What the hell for?'

'That's the puzzle. None of the neighbours knew but a couple of them stated definitely that they had seen Mrs Coppett and the fellow hugging and kissing on the landing on Tuesday night. And the old girl next door and her husband say the Coppetts were always rowing. They had a particularly nasty set-to last week just after the Professor arrived.'

'Did they? Where's this Professor now? And what's his name?'

'Left this morning. Mrs Mane, she's the old biddy next door, claims she saw him leave shortly after Mrs Coppett went shopping. Driving a Vauxhall, registration number CFE 9306 D. His name's Yapp.'

'Useful,' said the Inspector and went back to Rosie while the stained shirt was sent to the forensic experts for tests.

'Now then I want to hear about this man who calls himself Professor Yapp,' he told Rosie. 'What sort of relationship have you been having with him?'

But Rosie's thoughts were still fixed on the nothing that would be her life now that Willy had gone from it and she didn't know what a relationship was. The Inspector spelt it out for her in words of one syllable. Rosie said he'd been kind to her, ever so kind. The Inspector could well believe it, but his sarcasm was wasted on her and she relapsed into a dull silence numbed by her sense of loss. Even when, in a desperate attempt to shock her out of her inability to answer his questions in accordance with accepted police procedure, the Inspector had her taken to identify Willy's body, she was not to be broken from her grief.

'That's not my Willy,' she said through her tears. 'That's not anybody.'

'She's in a state of shock, poor thing,' said the Sergeant. 'She may be as thick as two planks but she's got feelings like the rest of us.'

'She'll be a poorer thing by the time I'm through with her,' said the Inspector, but he wanted to sleep too so Rosie was given some blankets and put in a cell with a mug of cocoa.

Outside in the interrogation room a detective went through her bag and found the cheque and the letter from Yapp.

'That just about wraps it up,' Inspector Garnet told the Sergeant. 'We'll get his address from the bank in the morning and pull him in for questioning – or do you object to putting the pressure on him too?'

'You can do what you like with the sod. All I'm telling you is that Rosie Coppett couldn't murder anyone, let alone Willy. She's too soft-hearted and simple. And anyway they were a devoted couple. Everyone knows that.'

'Not the neighbours. They know something else again.'

'What neighbours don't?' said the Sergeant and went back to his desk wishing to hell the C.I.D. from Briskerton hadn't been called in. There were other things he wouldn't have minded them investigating in Buscott, but Rosie Coppett as a murderess wasn't one of them.

In his farm at the bottom of a muddy lane a mile from Rabbitry Road Mr Jipson slept almost as peacefully as Willy. It had been a week since he had put the body in the boot of the old Vauxhall and during that week Mr Jipson had coped with his conscience. He'd examined the front of his tractor for any sign of lost paint, and hadn't found any; he had hosed it down and for good measure driven it into the duck-pond beside the farmhouse and then used it to clean out the calf byre so that it was well and truly covered in dung. Best of all, his wife was in hospital having her innards out (as he described a hysterectomy) and wasn't around to watch him or ask him awkward questions. She might have noticed some change in him. But Mr Jipson was his old self again. The killing of Willy was an accident and could have happened to anyone. It wasn't his fault that the bloody dwarf had chosen his tractor to walk into and Mr Jipson couldn't see why he should be penalized by an accident. He worked hard and made a decent living and there was no point in giving it up by telling the world. It had just ... happened. And anyway the people in that old Vauxhall must have had something to hide or they wouldn't have hidden Willy Coppett so thoroughly. This last had been the most convincing argument as far as Mr Jipson's slight conscience was concerned. Nobody who wasn't guilty of something else would have driven a car around in hot weather with a dead dwarf in the boot and not reported it – and what had they been doing on the night of the accident? They hadn't been in the car and they couldn't have been anywhere nearby or they'd have seen him put the body in and raised Cain. Mr Jipson had considered the land where the car had been parked and had thought about the coppice. That was part of Mr Osbert Petrefact's estate and he'd been having trouble with poachers, hadn't he? And poaching was a crime, which was more than could be said for road accidents, and therefore the poachers deserved what they had got more than he did.

Mr Jipson slept easily.

nineteen

In spite of his ordeal the previous day and his disturbing session with Doris, Yapp woke early and, largely because of them, stayed awake. In the bright morning light of his scholastic cell he realized the stupidity of his action in disposing of Willy's body. He ought to have gone straight to the police. That was easy to see now that he was back in the sane world of the University instead of on a lonely road surrounded by the irrational and predatory influences of Nature. It was too late now to act sensibly or, if sense came into it at all, he had to continue as he had so precipitously begun.

At eight he left his rooms carrying the plastic dustbin sack containing his clothes. Having opened it and caught its dreadful aroma he had decided against taking the jacket and trousers to the drycleaners. He also decided he never wanted to wear the things again. At half-past eight he had driven to the town refuse dump and, having waited until there were no trucks about, went in and dropped the bag down the cascade of municipal muck where with any luck it would soon be buried.

Next he had to clean the boot of the old Vauxhall. Willy had leaked conspicuously all over the floor and the boot still stank. Yapp drove back into town, for the first of many times regretting that he held such strong views on private ownership and didn't have a car of his own. He also lacked a garage where he could scrub the boot out in privacy. There was nothing for it, he would simply have to use a self-service car-wash. Stopping at a chemist he bought a bottle of Dettol, and then, to make doubly sure, a small can of Jeyes Fluid. Then he drove out to a garage, opened the boot and the two antiseptic containers, poured their contents all over the floor, and with an inexpertise that came from never having had to take a car through an automatic washing machine, drove into it with the boot still open to ensure that it got a proper sluicing. For the next few minutes drivers on their way into town were interested to watch the effect of a modern, efficient and self-motivated car-washing machine at work on an old Vauxhall whose boot-lid had been left deliberately wide open. Yapp, trapped inside the vehicle by the whirling brushes and the jets of water, could only surmise from the noise what was happening. The brushes had slammed the boot down before allowing it to open again while they attended to the back bumper, but on their return journey up and over the car found the boot in their way. A less conscientious machine might have stopped but this one didn't. While the interior of the boot filled with a mixture of Jeyes Fluid and

Dettol which seeped out in a grey pool behind the car, the flailing brushes scoured the underside of the lid with admirable efficiency and then, determined to get on with the roof, tore the thing from its rusted hinges, carried it before them along the top and finally hurled it down the windscreen and across the bonnet onto the ground. Yapp sat staring through the shattered windscreen as the brushes moved back towards him. He could see now that he had made a bad mistake. He could also feel it. Water, liberally saturated with some sort of detergent, had soaked him, and the passage of the boot across the roof had deafened him. From his viewpoint there was only one thing left that this infernal contrivance could do now and that was scour his face with pieces of broken glass from the hole in the windscreen. Faced with this awful prospect Yapp ignored the instructions clearly printed beside the coin-slot, opened the door to get out and would have done so if one side of the device hadn't promptly banged it to. Yapp took one more look at the approaching brushes and hurled himself face downwards on the seat. For two dreadful minutes he lay there, soaked, spattered with broken glass and parts of the wiper while the car-wash continued its work of destruction. By the time its cycle had ended the Vauxhall no longer smelt even vaguely of Willy. The Dettol and the Jeyes Fluid had seen to that. On the other hand it was conspicuous in other respects. It not only lacked a boot lid and a windscreen, it was without the door Yapp had so incautiously opened and the interior was as drenched as Yapp himself.

Sitting up carefully to avoid any further injury from the glass, Yapp stared at the havoc with dismay. If anything was needed to prove his monotonously repeated opinion that machines should never be allowed to deprive honest craftsmen of their jobs, the automatic car-wash had done it. No clumsy-handed human car-cleaner could have achieved so much damage in so short a time even if he'd taken a sledgehammer to the car. Anyway he hadn't the time for such considerations now. He had to get the damned machine back to the University and then when it was dry arrange for it to be repaired.

Yapp got out, collected the lid and slid it into the boot and was busy trying to disentangle the door from the mechanism of the car-wash where it was firmly lodged when he was interrupted by a shout. It didn't sound like a shout to him because his eardrums seemed still to be reverberating from the clash of metal against metal, but the expression on the face of the man who uttered it suggested it was.

'You fucking idiot, can't you read instructions?' yelled the man. 'Look what you've done to my car-wash.'

Yapp looked, and had to admit that the machine hadn't come out of the confrontation unscathed. The hole in the windscreen had taken its toll of the nylon brushes while the bars which held them were definitely bent.

'I'm very sorry,' he muttered.

The man stared at him dementedly. 'You'll be a fucking sight more sorry by the time I've finished with you,' he bawled, 'I've half a mind ... no, bugger that, I've a whole fucking mind to have the police on you and the insurance assessor and ...'

But the word 'police' had had a galvanic effect on Yapp. The one group of men he'd come to the bloody garage to avoid would ask questions he had no way of answering without getting into deeper water. 'I'll pay for the damage,' he said desperately. 'There's no need to call the police. This whole unfortunate affair can be settled discreetly.'

'Like fuck it can,' shouted the man, eyeing Yapp and then the old car with utter loathing and deciding that a maniac who drove a sixteen-year-old car and went round wrecking brand-new car-washes was the last person to settle things with anything approaching discretion, 'you'll fucking well stay here till the cops arrive.'

And to make sure that Yapp didn't make his escape, however improbably, in the wrecked car, he seized the keys from the ignition and bolted into the garage office. Yapp followed lugubriously, unconscious that he was leaving a trail of detergent and broken glass.

'Look,' he said reaching in his pocket and taking out a sopping chequebook, 'I assure you that ...'

'And so do I,' snapped the man and grabbed the chequebook as added surety, 'I'm calling the cops and that's final.' He dialled and presently was talking to someone in the police station. Yapp listened half-heartedly. Perhaps the police would not be interested; even if they were it seemed likely that the car-wash which had so effectively removed the top of the boot and the door must have done even more thoroughly by the less obvious and tenacious remains of Willy Coppett. This hopeful train of thought was interrupted by a query from the proprietor.

'What's the number of your car?' he demanded.

Yapp hesitated. 'Actually it's not my own car. It's a hire car. I don't know its number.'

'Says it's a hire car,' said the man into the telephone. 'Yes, an old Vauxhall ... hang on, I'll go and have a look.'

He put the phone down and scurried out of the office. When he returned his eyes had an even more dangerous glint in them.

'That's right,' he told the police station, 'CFE 9306 D. What is he wanted for? ... What's his name?' He eyed Yapp cautiously.

'What's your name?'

'Professor Walden Yapp, I'm at the ...'

'Says his name's Yapp,' the man told the police. 'That's right ...' He dried up suddenly and edged round the counter keeping a now wary eye on the wanted man. He put the phone down and picked up a tyre lever.

'Nice day,' he remarked with nervous affability but Yapp was in no state of mind to notice. As far as he was concerned it was a positively diabolical day and his lack of eight hours sleep was catching up with him. In any case he was beginning to wonder what the effects of sharing the facilities offered by the car-wash with the old Vauxhall were likely to be on a constitution already weakened by several days in bed with flu and the discovery that he was in the noxious company of a putrefying dwarf. Thoughts of pneumonia and enteric fever concerned him.

'Look here,' he said, 'I can't wait around in these sopping clothes. I'll go back to my rooms and change and come back and discuss this matter with you later on.'

'You bloody well ...' the garage proprietor began before remembering that the police had explicitly warned him that he was dealing with a desperate and almost certainly violent man and that on no account was he to tackle him. 'If you say so, but the police will be here in a minute ...'

'Tell them I'll be back in a hour's time,' said Yapp, and promptly walked out of the office and strode off along the road towards the University. Behind him the garage proprietor was on the phone to the police station again.

'The bugger's escaped. Made a dash for it. I tried to stop him but it was no use. Hit me over the head with a blunt instrument.'

154

To lend credence to this story and to ensure that he got his photograph and some free publicity in the *Kloone Evening Guardian*, he then tore his shirt, smashed a chair and tapped his head rather harder than he had intended with the tyre lever. He was moaning quite genuinely when the first police car shot into the forecourt.

'Did me over proper and got away,' he murmured to the policemen who found him. 'Can't have got far. Tall fellow with wet clothes. Sopping wet.'

More police cars arrived, radios crackled and in the distance sirens wailed. The hunt for Walden Yapp was on. Five minutes later it was over and Yapp, who had been apprehended at a bus stop where he was arguing with a conductor that public-transport officials had no right to refuse to carry paying public persons and even less right to describe him as undried laundry, was seized, had his arms twisted behind his back, was handcuffed, told to come along quietly and shoved into the back seat of a police car which then drove off at unnecessarily high speed.

The nightmare had begun.

It continued with remorseless efficiency and in blatant ignorance of the truth. By midday the Vauxhall had been further dismantled by forensic experts whose attention had been drawn to the boot by the remarkable amount of antiseptic on the floor. This, they now announced, had not prevented them from proving conclusively that the boot had recently contained a corpse. Yapp's rooms at the University provided more evidence. A pair of muddy shoes and some socks were taken away for soil analysis and having found his inseminated Y-fronts in his case the experts impounded all other articles of clothing in the rooms and took them off for microscopic examination.

All this time Yapp sat in the Kloone police station demanding his rights, and in particular his right to telephone his solicitor.

'All in good time,' the detective-inspector told him and made a note that Yapp hadn't asked why he had been arrested. As a result, when he was allowed to phone, the call was taped while the Inspector, two sergeants and a constable listened to the conversation in another room to corroborate the evidence of the tape which might not be admissible in court. It was typical of Yapp that his solicitor was a Mr Rubicond, whom he had several times consulted in matters concerning police harassment of student protest marches. Since on each occasion the students had resolutely refused to march and the police had no one to harass, Mr Rubicond had developed a distinctly sceptical attitude to Yapp's calls for his services.

'You've been what?' he asked.

'Arrested,' said Yapp.

'What's the charge, if any?'

'Murder,' said Yapp keeping his voice low and lending it a sinister tone in the next room.

'Murder? Did you say "murder"?' Mr Rubicond sounded understandably incredulous. 'Whom are you supposed to have murdered?'

'A Person of Restricted Growth called Mr William Coppett late of Number 9 Rabbitry Road, Buscott ...'

'A person of what growth?' demanded Mr Rubicond.

'Restricted growth. In uncivil rights language, a dwarf.'

'A dwarf?'

'That's what I said,' squawked Yapp beginning to find his legal adviser's obtuseness extremely trying.

'I thought that's what you said. I just wanted to make sure. I take it that you didn't.'

'I did,' said Yapp.

'In that case I can't begin to act for you,' said Mr Rubicond, 'unless, of course, you're prepared to plead guilty. We can always put in a plea of diminished ...'

'I'm not talking of murdering him. I said I did say he was a dwarf.'

'All right. Now say nothing else until I arrive. I take it you're in the Central Police Station?'

'Yes,' said Yapp, and put the receiver down. By the time Mr Rubicond arrived he was no longer there but was back in the police car being driven down to Buscott. The transcript of his conversation together with the findings of the forensic experts had already reached Inspector Garnet, whose opinion about Rosie's cunning had been jolted by the discovery that the blood stained into the shirt undoubtedly matched that of her murdered husband.

'Five's more likely,' he told the Sergeant who still maintained that she was as thick as two planks. 'Any murderess who leaves that sort of evidence hanging on the clothesline's got to be unless, of course, she's out to pin the crime on this bastard Yapp. In which case she may be a bit more cooperative this morning.'

With his preconceptions finely adjusted the Inspector went back to question her – or, to be more precise, to programme her.

'Now then,' he said, 'we've got your precious Professor Yapp and we know for certain he had the body of your husband in the boot of his car. In fact Willy wasn't dead when he put him in. He bled in that boot and dead bodies don't bleed so much. Now can you tell me why you washed his shirt for him?'

'There was blood on it,' said Rosie.

'Willy's, Mrs Coppett, Willy's blood. We've proved that.'

Rosie stared at him. Her thoughts couldn't cope but her feelings could and she had passed from the stage of sorrow to that of anger. 'I didn't know that. I wouldn't have washed it otherwise.'

'What would you have done, Mrs Coppett?'

'Killed him,' said Rosie, 'with the carving knife.'

Inwardly the Inspector smiled but there was no change of expression on his face. This was what he wanted to hear. 'But you didn't, did you? You didn't know because he didn't tell you. What happened that night when he came home with blood on his shirt?'

Rosie struggled to remember. It was very difficult. She tried to visualize the scene again but the kitchen had been her home for so long, the centre of her life where she cooked and read her magazines and fed Willy his supper every day and Hector had his basket in the corner and she pinned up her pictures of Wrestlers because her Mum had said her father had been a Wrestler though she hadn't remembered his name and maybe one of them had been her Dad. And now it had been spoilt for her by a man who'd pretended to be fond of her and she'd looked after when he was sick and all the time he had murdered Willy and he'd had cut hands. She remembered that detail in the confusion.

'He'd cut his hands, had he? One the same night he had blood on his shirt.'

Rosie responded to his interest. It was a help to have someone to sort things out for her. 'Yes, and his coat was all damp. I said he'd get a cold and he did. He was in bed for four days. I took his dinner up to him.'

Inspector Garnet repressed the impulse to ask what else she took Yapp in bed. Just so long as she kept talking he would find the truth. And when she had spilled her beans he'd hit her again with the evidence of the neighbours who'd seen her in Yapp's arms and Mr Clebb's conviction that he'd witnessed her massaging the filthy swine's penis when he had taken his dog for a walk. And Rosie talked and with each word she uttered and each nudge from the Inspector in the direction he wanted her to go, Rosie's imagination, already primed by so many stories in Confessions magazines, gave a new gloss to the facts. The Inspector was particularly interested in her account of Yapp's arrival and his insistence that he wanted extras. By the time he had gently wheedled from her what extras were and had gone on to fix it firmly in her mind that Yapp had actually stated that he wanted to make love to her he was satisfied he had the clearest motive for the murder and was of the opinion that she'd make an excellent prosecution witness with a pathos that would influence any jury.

'Now if you'll just sign this,' he said, handing her the text of her statement, 'you should be able to go home quite soon.'

Rosie signed it and went back to her cell. She knew now why Willy had been murdered. The Professor was in love with her. She wondered why she hadn't thought of that before. Anyway, she could think about it now and it helped to take her mind off poor Willy.

twenty

'Right,' said Inspector Garnet briskly as he took his seat opposite Yapp, 'now there are two ways of going about this. The short and comfortable or the long and nasty. Make up your mind which it's to be.'

Yapp looked at him with loathing. His opinion of the police as the praetorian guards of property, privilege and the established rich hadn't been in the least mollified by his treatment since his arrest. He had been driven away from Kloone without being allowed to consult his solicitor, had spent a most uncomfortable three hours sitting in wet clothes in the back of the police car, and was now confronted by an inspector with a small moustache. Yapp particularly disliked the look of that moustache. It suggested that the Inspector was not a caring or concerned human being.

'Well, which is it to be?' snapped the Inspector. Yapp tried to adjust his thoughts to his predicament. In between bouts of shivering on the drive down he had decided that his only hope lay in being demonstrably cooperative and in telling the truth. If the police were at all perceptive they would realize that he had absolutely no motive for murdering Willy, that he had influential friends, if not at court, at least in Parliament and the Labour Party, and that it was manifestly absurd to suppose he had homicidal tendencies. The truth, the whole truth and nothing but the truth would demonstrate his innocence.

'If you mean by that question, am I prepared to answer questions and make a full statement, yes I am.'

The moustache twitched almost amiably. 'Splendid,' said the mouth below it, 'saves everyone a lot of time and trouble. I take it you've been properly cautioned and know that you need say nothing. Sergeant, read the prisoner the cautionary rigmarole.'

The Sergeant read it out while the Inspector regarded Yapp with interest. The man was mad, of course, but it made a change to have an insane professor with a public reputation to cross-examine and, having watched several of Yapp's televised productions of the horrors of nineteenth-century life, the Inspector was looking forward to his interrogation. It would be a sort of Criminal Mastermind competition and a conviction would enhance his promotion prospects.

'Right, now then, let's get the grisly bit over first,' he said. 'At what moment in time did you decide to murder the deceased?'

Yapp sat up in his chair. 'Never,' he said. 'In the first place I didn't murder him and in the second your assumption that I did shows a degree of bias that is —'

'Prisoner denies murdering deceased,' the Inspector told the stenographer. 'Accuses police of bias.' He leant across the table and put his moustache uncomfortably close to Yapp's face. 'When did you put the murdered man's body in the boot of your car?'

'Never,' said Yapp. 'I found it there.'

'Found it there, did you?'

'Yes. In an advanced state of putrefaction.'

'Extraordinary. Quite extraordinary. You found the putrefying corpse f a murdered dwarf in the boot of your car and you did not bot 1er to bring it to the police. Is that what you're saying?'

'Yes,' said Yapp, 'I know it sounds extraordinary but that's what happened.'

'What happened?'

'I panicked.'

'Naturally. First thing a highly intelligent, sensitive bloke like you would do, panic. Perfectly understandable reaction. So what did you do after panicking?'

Yapp looked at the moustache doubtfully. He couldn't decide if it was understanding or twitching with sarcasm. 'I drove to the river and dropped it in.'

'And why did you do that?'

'Obviously because I didn't want to be connected with it. I mean, Willy Coppett had been murdered and someone had tried to put the blame on me by leaving him in the boot of the car and I didn't want to be accused.'

'Something you've got in common with the murderer at any rate,' said the Inspector. 'Meaning of course the bloke who put the body in the boot in the first place.'

'Yes,' admitted Yapp.

The Inspector reached into a drawer in the desk and produced the bloodstained shirt. 'I'd like you to have a look at this and tell us what you know about it. Take your time, there's no hurry.'

Yapp looked at the shirt. 'It's mine.'

'Good. Now then did you or did you not wear that shirt on the evening of July twenty-first this year?'

Yapp took his eyes off the moustache and back to the shirt while he consulted his memory. 21 July was the night it had rained and he'd been in the coppice with his Y-fronts and had caught his cold. It was also the night he'd cut his hands on the barbed wire and gone back to Rabbitry Road with blood on his shirt-front and Rosie had insisted on washing it at once.

'Yes,' he said.

This time the Inspector actually smiled momentarily. This was a piece of cake. If all villains were so fucking stupid he'd have an easy life. 'And did you return to Rabbitry Road with blood all over that shirt?'

Yapp hesitated again. 'It wasn't all over it. Just down the front.

I'd cut my hands on some barbed wire and I thought I must have wiped them accidentally on the shirt.'

'Quite so,' said the Inspector, 'and I daresay you'd be surprised to learn that the blood on that shirt – fresh blood, mind you – has been proved to have come from the murdered man.'

Yapp focused on that vile little moustache and found no comfort in it now. 'Yes, I'd be very surprised. I don't know how it got there.'

'Could it be that when the murderer put the body of Mr Coppett into the boot of your car he didn't realize the poor little bugger was still alive and bleeding and the blood got on his shirt that way?'

Yapp said nothing. The trap was closing on him and he couldn't begin to understand why.

'Could it, Professor Yapp? Could it?'

'If you're saying that I put Willy in that boot . . .'

The Inspector raised a hand. 'Now we mustn't put words into one another's mouths, must we? I didn't say anything about you putting the murdered man in the boot. I merely asked if, when the murderer put him in, he could have got blood on his shirt front. Now, could he have or couldn't he?'

'I suppose he could have but –'

'Thank you, that's all I wanted to know. Now then, let's return to your panic on finding the body in the boot and dropping it in the river. When did this happen?'

'Yesterday,' said Yapp, amazed that it had only been the day before that his life had taken such a ghastly turn.

'And what drew your attention to the fact that you were carrying a dead dwarf round the place in your car?'

'The smell,' said Yapp. 'It was exceedingly unpleasant. I stopped beside the road to investigate its source.'

'Very sensible of you. Would you mind telling me where you stopped to make this investigation?'

Again Yapp saw the trap closing but again there was no way of avoiding it. If he said he'd noticed the smell in Buscott and had then driven nearly forty miles before ditching the body in the river . . . No, he had to tell the truth. 'It was on the road to Wastely. If you'll get me a map I'll show you.'

A map was fetched and he indicated the spot.

'And from there you took it where?'

'To the river here,' said Yapp, pointing to the side road and the bridge.

'So you drove all that way before you began to wonder what the smell was?'

'I'd wondered what it was before but my mind was preoccupied at the time and I put it down to a farmer manuring his fields.'

'With dead dwarves?' enquired the Inspector.

'Certainly not. I thought it was pig dung.'

'So for forty miles you thought that farmers were continuously mucking their fields with pig dung? Isn't that stretching it a bit far?'

'I said I was preoccupied at the time,' said Yapp.

The Inspector nodded. 'I'm not in the least surprised. I mean you'd got something to be preoccupied about, hadn't you?'

'As a matter of fact I had. I'd just had an interview with Miss Petrefact's gardener and was outraged to learn that he worked a ninety-hour week, sometimes a hundred, and is paid a pittance. That's downright sweated labour.'

'Shocking. So you shove the body into the river and head for home. Is that right?'

'Yes,' said Yapp.

'What did you do then?'

'Had a bath.'

'And then?'

'Had something to eat and went to bed,' said Yapp rapidly deciding that, since he hadn't been asked specifically about his dialogue with Doris, there was no need for him to mention it. He was still annoyed with the computer for pointing to Rosie as the person with the most logical motive for the murder of Willy, and he most certainly had no intention of providing the police with Doris' conclusions. Poor Rosie must be grief-stricken in any case and to have the police accusing her of murder was unthinkable.

'And this morning you took the car to a car-wash and did your level best to remove all traces of evidence that the boot had been used as a hiding-place for the corpse?' continued the Inspector.

'I had to. It's a hire car and I'd only rented it for a month. If I had really murdered Mr Coppett do you think I'd have used a hire car to hide the body for so long? Of course not. It's not logical.'

The Inspector nodded. 'But perhaps you hadn't intended to leave the body there so long,' he said. 'Now let's get back to the night of the murder. Would you mind giving a full account of your movements that evening?'

Yapp looked at him miserably. He minded very much but he had decided to tell the truth and there could be no going back on it now.

'You're assuming that the murder took place on the night of 21 July?' he said to delay matters.

'I am,' said the Inspector. 'That was the last time the murdered man was seen. He left the pub where he worked at eleven o'clock and never arrived home. You, on the other hand, arrived there soaking wet and with his blood on your shirt shortly after midnight. Now if you can explain in detail what you did that evening it might help to solve this case.'

'Well, earlier in the evening Mrs Coppett asked me to take her for a drive.'

'She asked you or you invited her?'

'She asked me,' said Yapp. 'As you probably know the Coppetts don't own a car because Mr Coppett's restricted growth made it impossible for him to drive an ordinary model and Mrs Coppett's educational sub-normality prevented her from taking the test. Anyway I doubt if they could have afforded one.'

'So you took her for a drive. Where?'

'Here,' said Yapp, tracing their route on the map.

'What time did this drive take place?'

'Between seven and nine, I think.'

'And what happened after that?' asked the Inspector, who had already studied the evidence of the neighbours that they had seen Yapp and Mrs Coppett kissing.

'I went for another drive,' said Yapp miserably.

'You went for another drive,' repeated the Inspector with an ominous monotony.

'Yes.'

The Inspector smoothed his little moustache. 'And would it be true to say that while outside the Coppetts' house you kissed Mrs Coppett?'

'Sort of,' said Yapp with misplaced gallantry. The thought of poor Rosie being put through this sort of interrogation was quite unbearable.

'Sort of? You wouldn't mind being more explicit? Either you kissed her or you didn't.'

'We kissed. That is true.'

'And you then drove off again. Why?'

'Um ... er ...' said Yapp.

'Yes, well that doesn't take us any further, does it? So I'll repeat my question. Why did you drive off again?'

Yapp looked dolefully around the room but the blank walls seemed to hold out no hope that if he lied now the rest of his story would be believed.

'As a matter of fact I had done something you may think a little peculiar.'

The Inspector didn't doubt it. As far as he was concerned the whole bloody business was peculiar, not least an educational system that allowed blithering young maniacs like Yapp to become professors.

'You see,' continued Yapp, whose Adam's Apple was bobbing with embarrassment, 'as a result of Mrs Coppett's close physical contiguity I had had an involuntary emission.'

'You'd had what?'

'An involuntary emission,' said Yapp squirming on his chair.

'In other words you'd come, is that what you're saying?'

'Yes.'

'As a result of her jerking you off?'

'Certainly not,' said Yapp stiffly, 'Mrs Coppett isn't that sort of a woman. What I said was that as a result of her ...'

'I heard you,' said the Inspector. 'Close physical consomething or other.'

'Contiguity. It means contact, proximity and touching.'

'Does it indeed? And I suppose you're going to tell me now that jerking off, or if you prefer, masturbation, doesn't require contact, proximity and touching?'

'I'm not saying anything of the sort. I'm merely saying that her close physical presence next to me in the car had this unfortunate effect on me.'

The Inspector regarded him beadily. He'd got the sod on the trot now and he wasn't going to let him stop. 'Are you seriously trying to tell me that having Mrs Coppett sitting beside you was enough to make you blow your fucking fuse?'

'I object to that expression. It's coarse, vulgar and quite uncalled for and I ...'

'Listen, mate,' interrupted the Inspector, leaning across the desk and shoving his face close to Yapp's, 'you're not in any position to object to anything short of physical violence and you'd have a hard time proving that, so don't come any of your student-protest crap at me. This isn't some drug-ridden intellectual arse-hole of a university and you aren't lecturing anyone, savvy? You're our Number One suspect in a particularly nasty little murder and I've enough evidence already to have you remanded in custody and tried and sentenced and have your appeal rejected. So don't start telling me what sort of fucking language to use. Just get on and tell us your story.'

Yapp sat shaken in his chair. Reality at its most horrible was intruding now and there was no mistaking the menace of that little moustache. Yapp went on with his story and told the truth and nothing but the truth, and with its telling all doubts that he might after all have been mistaken about Yapp's guilt vanished from Inspector Garnet's mind.

'Sat in a coppice with his Y-fronts in his hand for a couple of hours in the pouring rain and he expects me to believe it,' he said when Yapp had been formally charged with the murder of the late Mr William Coppett and taken to a cell, 'and he can't precisely recall where the coppice was or the gate or even the bleeding road. I like that "precisely", I do indeed. Well at least he's let the woman off the hook. Might as well let her out.'

While Yapp sat in a cell and wondered at the infamy of the Petrefacts, who were so obviously prepared to sacrifice the life of a Porg to protect their precious reputation, Rosie was led out of the police station and told she was free.

The word meant nothing to her. Without the necessity of having Willy to look after she would never know freedom again.

twenty-one

Emmelia was unaware of these developments. Already isolated from the gossip of Buscott by her seclusion, she was now preoccupied with the arrangements for the family council. She and Annie bustled in and out of bedrooms, turned mattresses and aired sheets, and all the time she had to remember the quirks of each of the Petrefacts. The Judge had peculiarly large dentures and would require an appropriately large glass beside his bed; the Brigadier-General always insisted on a decanter of malt whisky beside his and a cover for his chamberpot because a prize and surprisingly pregnant gerbil had once drowned itself in one; the Van der Fleet Petrefacts had had their house burnt down round their heads and refused to sleep in an upstairs bedroom so they'd have to go in the morning-room and, finally and least to her liking, Fiona had cabled unexpectedly from Corfu that she and her unisex spouse were flying over because Leslie simply couldn't wait to meet all her relatives at once. Emmelia had grave doubts about having them in the house at all. The Judge held such violent views on homosexuality that he had once sentenced an unfortunate burglar whose name was Gay to an exceptionally long term of imprisonment and had had his judgement set aside on appeal. No, it would be best if Fiona and Leslie were as little in evidence as possible. They could stay with Osbert at the Old Hall.

But while she supervised these arrangements and recruited several respectable women from the Mill to help, Emmelia's thoughts turned again and again to the despicable Ronald. In a last desperate and restrained letter to him she had invited him to the family gathering and had even gone so far as to state that its purpose was to consider the future of the Mill, which was true, and the possibility of the family agreeing to sell their shares in it, which was not. Lord Petrefact had not replied, but she had hardly expected him to. If he came at all he would come unannounced to enjoy the spectacle of his relatives' dismay and outrage at the prospect of having the name Petrefact dragged still further from its obscurity and thrust into the limelight as the family which owned a fetish factory. It was just the sort of situation he would most enjoy.

Emmelia was right. Lord Petrefact had decided to attend. Her letter had whetted his appetite for family rows. There was nothing he enjoyed more, and her intimation that his relatives might be prepared to sell their shares in the Mill suggested nothing of the sort to Lord Petrefact. It suggested that they wanted him down there to bring the full weight of their pressure on him to call a

halt to Yapp's evidently highly disturbing activities in Buscott.
Lord Petrefact looked forward to that pressure. He would have
to do nothing more than sit still while they raged at him and his
silence would be more devastating than words. And if by some
extraordinary chance they were prepared to sell the Mill in exchange for an end to Yapp's research he would make the sanctimonious bunch sweat while he went through the motions of
considering their offer, but in the end he would still refuse. Feeling
quite tipsy with power he rang for Croxley.

'We're going down to Buscott immediately. Make arrangements
for the journey and accommodation in the neighbourhood.'

'There's the New House,' said Croxley. 'Surely Miss Emmelia
will have room?'

Lord Petrefact fixed him with the less favoured side of his face.
'I said accommodation, not a rat's nest of relatives,' he said with a
malevolence that was persuasive. Croxley left the room puzzled.
First Yapp in Buscott and now the old devil himself. And what did
he mean by a rat's nest of relatives? To engender some more information from Lord Petrefact Croxley phoned every hotel in the
district and demanded two groundfloor suites and a guarantee of
absolute silence between 10 p.m. and 9 a.m., provision for room
service all night and an undertaking that the chef be on twenty-
four-hour duty. Armed with seven indignant refusals he returned
to Lord Petrefact's office.

'No room at the inn,' he said with mock despondency, 'unless
you're prepared to stay in a boarding-house.'

Lord Petrefact made several incomprehensible noises.

'No, well I didn't think you would but there's nothing else.'

'But the place is a dead-and-alive dump. Where did you try?'

Croxley laid the list of hotels on the desk. Lord Petrefact glanced
at it. 'Don't we own any of them?' he asked.

'The family does but ...'

'I didn't mean them. I meant me.'

Croxley shook his head. 'Now if you'd said Bournemouth ...'

'I didn't say fucking Bournemouth. I said Buscott. They're miles
apart. Well, where the hell can we stay?'

'The rat's nest?' suggested Croxley and brought on another bout
of high blood pressure. 'Of course as a last resort there's Mr
Osbert at the Old Hall.'

Lord Petrefact felt his pulse. 'And die of pneumonia,' he yelled when it was down to 130. 'That oaf's so bloody medieval he hasn't heard of central heating and his idea of a warm bed is one with a fucking whippet in it. If you think I want to share a bed with a fucking whippet you're insane.'

Croxley agreed. 'In that case I can only suggest the New House. It may have its disadvantages but Miss Emmelia would make you comfortable.'

Lord Petrefact kept his doubts on the matter to himself. 'I suppose so. In any case we may be able to get the business over in a day.'

'May we enquire the nature of the business?'

Another paroxysm ended the discussion and Croxley hurried out to order the hearse. There were times when he wished the old swine would put it to its proper use.

And so that Saturday the illustriously obscure Petrefacts gathered at the New House in Buscott to deal with a family crisis that was already over. They were not to know. Yapp had the weekend to consider the weight of circumstantial evidence against him and Inspector Garnet was in no hurry.

'Take all the time you need,' he told Mr Rubicond, who had finally discovered where his client was being held. 'If he tells you the same story he told me you'll have a hard time with your conscience if he insists on pleading not guilty. His only out is "guilty but insane".'

Two hours later Mr Rubicond shared his opinion. Yapp was still adamant in his claim that he had been framed – and by the Petrefacts, of all unlikely people.

'You can't be serious,' said Mr Rubicond. 'No sane judge is going to believe that you were hired by Lord Petrefact to write a family history and were then framed with the murder of a dwarf simply to prevent you from writing it. If they had, and I can't for one moment believe it, if they had been prepared to take such extreme measures, why on earth murder Mr Coppett when they could as easily have murdered you?'

'They wanted to discredit me,' said Yapp. 'The capitalist class is extremely devious.'

'Yes, well it must be, though while we're on the subject of anyone discrediting you I can only say that you've done an exceedingly good job yourself. I told you not to say anything.'

'I have said nothing that is not true. The facts are as I've described them.'

'Perhaps, but did you have to describe them? I mean take this business of ejaculating in the car because Mrs Coppett kissed you. Of all the incredible indiscretions I've ever come across ... Words fail me. You've handed the prosecution your motive on a plate.'

'But I had to explain why I went into that wood. I mean I had to have some good reason.'

'Changing out of a pair of soiled Y-fronts doesn't strike me as a good reason at all. It's a bloody bad one. Why didn't you change in the car?'

'I told you. Because there was a lot of traffic on the road at the time – and besides I have rather long legs and I couldn't have got them off in the confined space.'

'So you climbed a gate with barbed wire on it, cut your hands, crossed a field, and spent the next two hours sitting under a fir tree clutching your underpants and waiting for the rain to stop?'

'Yes,' said Yapp.

'And since, when you arrived back at the Coppetts' house, you were wearing a shirt stained, according to the Inspector, with Mr Coppett's blood, we must assume that during the time you say you were in that wood his body was deposited in the boot?'

'I suppose so.'

'And you don't remember where this wood is.'

'I daresay I could recognize it if I were allowed out to drive round.'

Mr Rubicond looked at his client doubtfully and wondered about his sanity. On one thing he was resolved: when it came to the trial he would advise counsel not to allow his client to go into the witness box. The blasted man seemed determined to condemn himself with every word he said.

'I somehow don't think the police would grant you that degree of freedom in the circumstances,' he said. 'However, if you want me to I'll ask the Inspector.'

Much to his surprise the Inspector agreed.

'If he's half as daft as he's been so far he'll probably lead us to the exact spot and hand us the murder weapon,' he told the Sergeant.

For two hours Yapp sat in the police car between the Inspector and Mr Rubicond while they drove round the lanes above Buscott, every so often stopping at a gate in a hedge.

'It was on a hill,' said Yapp, 'the headlights shone in my eyes.'

'They'd do that on the flat,' said the Inspector. 'Were you going up hill or down?'

'Down. The gate was on the left.'

'But you can't say how far you had gone before you stopped?'

'I was far too distraught at the time and my mind was on other things,' said Yapp, staring hopelessly out of the window at a landscape that seemed wholly unfamiliar, a consequence in part of their driving up the hill he had come down. In any case his illness and days in bed, not to mention the horrors of the past thirty-six hours, made the fateful night seem long ago and had changed his view of the district. Experience had robbed the countryside of its romantically tragic and historic associations. It was now murderous and predatory.

'Well, a fat lot of good that was,' said the Inspector when they were back at the station and Yapp had been locked in his cell. 'Still, you can't accuse us of refusing cooperation.'

Mr Rubicond couldn't. It was part of his stock-in-trade to accuse the police of brutality and of denying his clients their rights, but on this occasion they were behaving with a disconcerting rectitude which tended to confirm his own impression that Professor Yapp was indeed a murderer. They were even prepared to let him attend the post-mortem, a privilege he would happily have forgone.

'Hit over the head with the proverbial blunt instrument and then stabbed in the stomach for good measure,' said the Police Surgeon.

'Anything to suggest what sort of instrument?'

The Police Surgeon shook his head. Willy's passage down the river had removed what evidence there might have been that he had been hit by a tractor. Even his little boots had been washed clean.

'Well, there you have it, Mr Rubicond. Now if your client is prepared to make a full confession I daresay he might get off with a lighter sentence.'

But Mr Rubicond was not to be drawn. He had his own interests to consider. Professors who murdered dwarves were not an everyday phenomenon; the trial would draw an immense amount of publicity; and Walden Yapp was an eminent man and highly regarded in those progressive circles which hadn't actually met him;

he must also be a man of considerable means, and a long trial followed by an appeal would be a very profitable affair.

'I am convinced of his innocence,' he said more cheerfully and left the station. Inspector Garnet shared his enthusiasm.

'Now I don't want this fouled up by any mistakes,' he told his team, 'Professor Yapp is to be treated with the utmost consideration. He's not your ordinary villain and I don't want anyone complaining to the Press that the swine's been ill-treated. It's kid gloves all the way.'

In the bar of the Horse and Barge feelings were rather different.

'They should never have done away with hanging,' said Mr Groce, who felt particularly aggrieved at the loss of Willy. He had no one to help him wash and dry the glasses. Mr Parmiter shared his views but took a broader perspective.

'I never did agree with the way Mr Frederick went on about Willy's right to use that fucking awful knife on the bloke just because he was shafting Rosie Coppett. I reckon Willy tackled him and the fellow did for Willy.'

'I suppose they'll be calling you as a witness because of the car and hiring it from you.'

'They'll be calling you too. You must have been the last person to see Willy alive, excepting the murderer of course.'

Mr Groce considered the prospect while Mr Parmiter concentrated on the possibility that the police might require his dubious accounts as evidence.

'Buggered if I'm going to mention Willy's threats,' said Mr Groce finally. 'Might give the bastard a chance to plead self-defence.'

'True enough. On the other hand, Willy did say he'd seen Rosie having it off with the bloke. You can't get away from that.'

'Least said soonest mended. I'm still not saying anything to let that Yapp off the hook. If ever a man deserved to swing, he does.'

'And I wouldn't want to involve Mr Frederick either,' said Mr Parmiter. In the end they agreed to say nothing and to let justice take its own uncomplicated course.

twenty-two

Lord Petrefact was driven down to Buscott in a thoroughly good mood. Before leaving London he had completed an arrangement between one of his many subsidiaries, Petreclog Footwear of Leicester, and Brazilian State Beef whereby he hoped to bring home to the workers in Leicester the disadvantages of demanding a thirty per cent pay rise while at the same time increasing his profits enormously by transferring the plant to Brazil where he would have government backing for paying the local workers a quarter of what their British counterparts had previously earned.

'A splendid move, simply splendid,' he told Croxley as the converted hearse with its attendant ambulance, in which the resuscitation team were playing Monopoly, hurtled along the motorway.

'If you say so,' said Croxley, who always found riding so prematurely in a hearse an unnerving experience, 'though why you want to go to Buscott beats me. You've always said you loathed the place.'

'Buscott? What the hell are you talking about? I was talking about the Brazil deal.'

'Yes, well I daresay it will raise your popularity rating in Leicester.'

'Teach the swine not to meddle with basic economics,' said Lord Petrefact with relish. 'In any case I'm helping an underdeveloped country to stand on its own two feet.'

'In Petreclog Footwear no doubt.'

But Lord Petrefact was in too ebullient a mood to argue. 'And as far as Buscott is concerned, one owes a duty to one's family. Blood is thicker than water, you know.'

Croxley considered the cliché and had his doubts. Lord Petrefact's familial record suggested that in his case water had a decidedly more glutinous quality than blood, while his evident pleasure seemed to lend weight to the theory that he was looking forward to a first-rate row.

But when they arrived at the New House it was to find the drive cluttered with cars and no one in.

'Miss Emmelia's taken them on a tour of the Mill,' Annie explained to Croxley who had rung the front doorbell.

'A tour of the Mill?' said Lord Petrefact when the message was relayed to him. 'What the hell for?'

'Possibly to show them her ethnic clothing,' said Croxley.

Lord Petrefact snorted. He had come down to discuss the question of Yapp's researches into the family background not to be taken on a guided tour of an ethnic clothing factory. 'I'm damned if I'm budging until they get back,' he said adamantly, 'I've seen all of that fucking Mill I want to.'

For once his opinion was shared by the group of Petrefacts gathered in the fetish factory. Emmelia had proved her point that publicity was to be avoided at all costs. The Judge had been particularly hard-hit by the merkins. Coming on top of his long-held opinion that all homosexuals were congenital criminals who ought to be castrated at birth and sentenced to penal servitude as soon as legally possible, he had been so incensed that he had had to be helped to Frederick's office and several stiff brandies, and had still refused to continue the tour.

Emmelia had led the others on to dildos. Here the Brigadier-General, who had escaped the full implications of merkins thanks to an inadequate acquaintance with the sexual attributes of anything larger than female gerbils and Siamese cats, was forced to recognize what he was looking at.

'Monstrous, utterly monstrous!' he snarled, his pique evidently provoked by personal comparison. 'Even a Bengal tiger doesn't have a ... well, a thingamegig ... a watchermacallit of such fearful proportions. You could do someone a terrible mischief with a ... Anyway who on God's earth would want a thing like that hanging about the house?'

'You'd be surprised,' said Fiona, only to be herself surprised and infuriated by the Chastity Belts. 'They're outrageous. To expect anyone to hobble round in a medieval instrument of clitoral torture is an insult to modern womanhood.'

'As I understand it, dear,' said Emmelia, 'they're actually for men.'

'That's entirely different, of course,' said Fiona, provoking Osbert into a paroxysm of alarm, 'men ought to be restrained.'

'Restrained?' shouted Osbert. 'You must be insane. Put some poor blighter in a thing like that and have him go hunting and he'd be a damned gelding at the first fence.'

In the background the Van der Fleet-Petrefacts were being disabused of their hope that the Thermal Agitators with Enema

Variations were a form of personal fire extinguisher by closer examination of the garments. By the time Emmelia had led the way to the Bondage Department, nearly everyone was appalled.

Only Fiona maintained an odd combination of Women's Power and sexual permissiveness. 'After all, everyone is entitled to find her sexual satisfaction in her own personal way,' she insisted, adding with unconscious irony in the face of the gags, handcuffs, shackles and plastic straitjackets, that society had no right to impose restraints on the freedom of the individual.

'Don't keep using that word,' squealed Osbert, still maniacally obsessed with the terrible consequences certain to result from hunting in a Male Chastity Belt.

'And never mind the freedom of the individual who dons one of those thingamegigs,' roared the Brigadier-General, picking up a cat-o'nine-tails with dangerous relish, 'I'm going to find that bloody manager, Cuddlybey, and flay the hide off the swine. He must have gone off his rocker to switch from flannel pyjamas to these ...'

'You'll do no such thing, Randle,' interrupted Emmelia. 'Besides you'd have considerable difficulty. Mr Cuddlybey retired fourteen years ago and died last August.'

'Damned lucky for him. If I —'

'If you had taken a little more interest in family affairs and a little less in those of Seal-Pointers and gerbils you'd have known that.'

'Then who is the manager now?' demanded Osbert. For a moment Emmelia hesitated but only for a moment.

'I am,' she declared.

The group gazed at her in horror.

'You don't mean to say ...' began the Brigadier-General.

'I'm saying nothing more until Ronald arrives.'

'Ronald?'

'Oh really, Osbert, don't keep repeating things. I said Ronald and I meant Ronald. And now let's see if Purbeck has recovered sufficiently to be at all coherent.'

They made their way back to the office where the Judge, having taken several small pills in addition to the brandy, was engrossed in the catalogue. Coherency wasn't his problem.

'The Do-It-Yourself Sodomy Kit,' he bellowed at the cowering Frederick. 'Do you realize that you've been putting on the market an accessory before, during and after a crime punishable by death?'

'Death?' quavered Frederick. 'But surely it's legal between consenting adults?'

'Consenting? What the hell do you mean consenting? Not even the most depraved, perverted, sado-masochistic, insane, perverted, perverted ...'

'You've said that three times, Uncle,' ventured Frederick with remarkable courage.

'Said what?'

'Perverted.'

'And I meant it three times, you damned scoundrel. In fact I meant it continuously. Not even the most perverted *ad infinitum* perverted swine of an arse-bandit would consent to have that diabolical contraption rammed past his sphincter ...'

'Hear, hear,' said Osbert with feeling. The Judge turned on him lividly.

'And I don't require your comments, Osbert. I've always suspected there was something wrong with you ever since you put that pink-eyed weasel in my bed with a tin can tied to its tail and now ...'

'Never did anything of the sort. In any case it was a ferret.'

'Whatever it was it –'

'I think we should concentrate on the present,' intervened Emmelia. 'The question is what are we to do about Ronald?'

The Judge shifted his own pink eyes to her. 'Ronald? What's Ronald got to do with these inventions of the devil?'

'We all know he sent Professor Yapp down here ostensibly to do research on the family history.'

The Judge took another small pill. 'Is it your contention that Ronald knows about this ... this ...?' he croaked.

'I can't be sure. The point is that if this dreadful creature Yapp continues his researches he may well find out.'

A fearful silence fell over the little party, broken only by the sound of clanging tongs and pokers as Mrs Van der Fleet-Petrefact swooned into the empty fireplace. Her husband ignored her.

'In that case he must not be allowed to find out,' said the Judge finally.

'Absolutely. Couldn't agree more,' said the Brigadier-General and might have continued to agree even more if he hadn't been quelled by the look in his brother's eye.

'That's easier said than done,' Emmelia went on. 'He's already tried to get in here and he's asked to see the family papers. Naturally I refused permission.'

This time it was Emmelia who got the full bloodshot blast from the Judge. 'You refused him permission to see the Petrefact papers when they would have taken his mind off this?' he demanded tapping the catalogue. 'I find that a most curious decision. I do indeed.'

'But think of the scandal,' said Emmelia. 'A family history would reveal ...'

'Nothing compared to this,' yelled the Judge. 'If it ever gets known that we are the owners of a ...'

'A Merkin Manufactory?' suggested Osbert.

'Whatever you choose to call it, why, we'll be the laughing stock, and more than laughing in my opinion, the very dregs of society. Have to resign, leave the bench, consequences would be incalculable.'

Silence fell once more in the office.

'I still think ...' began Emmelia but a storm of words broke over her.

'You allowed this disgusting youth to produce these ... these ... things,' roared the Judge. 'I hold you responsible for our appalling predicament.'

The Brigadier-General and Mr Van der Fleet-Petrefact, even Osbert and Fiona, turned on Emmelia. She sat in a chair, hardly listening. The family she had protected for so long had deserted her.

'All right,' she said finally when the abuse abated, 'I accept responsibility. Now will you tell me what we should do.'

'Perfectly obvious. Let this Professor Yapp have the Petrefact papers. Let the fellow write the family history.'

'And Ronald? He must have arrived by now.'

'Where?'

'At the New House. I invited him down too, you know.'

The Judge delivered his verdict. 'I can only conclude that you must be demented, woman.'

'Perhaps,' said Emmelia sadly, 'but what are we to tell him?'

'Nothing whatsoever about this.'

'But everything about the family?'

'Precisely. We must distract him as much as possible. And I would advise you all to treat him with the greatest respect. Ronald has it in his power to destroy our entire future.' And so saying the Judge rose unsteadily and moved towards the door. The others followed. Only Emmelia remained seated, mourning that obscure past which her relatives were bent on destroying in the interests of their own present. From the courtyard she could hear Osbert telling the Brigadier-General to remind him about the story of Great-Aunt Georgette and the Japanese naval attaché.

'I'm sure that's how Uncle Oswald got the contract for the floating dock ...'

His voice trailed away. And they were going to remind the wretch Ronald of every family scandal in order to stop him from finding out about the fetish factory. For a moment Emmelia felt tempted to defy them all and present Ronald with a copy of his son's catalogue and challenge him to go ahead with the family history in the light of its contents. But there was no point in alienating the rest of the family. She got up and followed them out.

'I shall walk up,' she said. 'I feel the need for a breath of fresh air. And I don't think Frederick should put in an appearance either.'

But Frederick had already arrived at the same conclusion and was in the bar of the Club ordering a large whisky.

While the others climbed into the old Daimler Emmelia trudged wanly through the gates and into the street. It was a long time since she had seen the little town on a Saturday afternoon. The garden had been her domain, Buscott merely an extension of the garden and, at the same time, the beginning of that wide world she had so long avoided. Her occasional visits to the vet had been by car, while her nightly walks had taken her towards the countryside. It had been enough to know the gossip for her to imagine she knew the town, but this afternoon, in the knowledge that she had been abandoned by her relatives, she viewed Buscott differently. The buildings were still the same, pleasant in their suggestion of cosy interiors, and the shops much as she remembered them, though the windows were crowded with a surprising range of goods. All the same there was something she found strange and almost unrecognizable about the streets. As she paused before Cleete's, Cornmerchant and Horticultural Supplies, and studied their offering of bulbs for autumn planting, she caught sight of herself in the reflection from the window and was startled by its message. It was as though she had seen Ronald staring back at her, though not the Ronald, Lord Petrefact, who was now confined to a wheelchair. Rather, she mirrored him as he had been twenty years before. Emmelia studied the reflection without vanity and drew a message from it. If Ronald was not a nice person – and of that there could be no doubt – was it not possible that she had deluded herself that *she* was?

For a moment she remained glued to the window while her thoughts turned inward towards the very kernel of self-knowledge. She was not a nice person. The blood of those despicable Petrefacts she had so romantically endowed with virtues they had never possessed flowed as ruthlessly through her veins as it did, more transparently, through those of her brother. For sixty years she had subjugated her true nature in order to sustain her reputation and the approval of the world she fundamentally despised. It was as if she had remained a child anxious to please Nanny and her parents.

Now, at sixty, she recognized the woman she most decidedly was. As if to emphasize the void of intervening years she watched the reflection of a young mother with a pram cross the window, merge with her own tweedy substance and re-emerge on the other side. Emmelia turned away with a rage she had never experienced before. She had been cheated of her own life by hypocrisy. From now on she would exercise those gifts of malice which were her birthright.

With a firmer step she crossed the road towards New House Lane and was about to climb up it when her eye caught the placard outside the newspaper shop on the corner. It read: PROFESSOR CHARGED WITH MURDER. FULL STORY.

For the third time in the afternoon Emmelia had the conviction that something extraordinary was happening to her. She went in and bought the *Bushampton Gazette* and read the article standing on the pavement. By the time she had finished, the conviction of amazement had been validated. She strode up the hill exulting in the freedom of malice.

twenty-three

She was not alone in her feelings of strangeness. Things had manifestly changed for Lord Petrefact. He had spent a happy hour, waiting for his relatives to return, regaling Croxley with obnoxious memories of his spoilt childhood and his holidays at the New House, how here he had shot an under-gardener with an air rifle while the fellow was bending over the onions, and there in the fishpond drowned his first (and his Aunt's favourite) Pekinese, when the family arrived. Lord Petrefact regarded them with his most repulsive expression and was amazed when his loathing was not reciprocated.

'My dear Ronald, how splendid to see you looking so well,' said the Judge with a bonhomie he had never in a lifetime displayed, and before Lord Petrefact could recover from this shock he was being overwhelmed with a most alarming geniality. Osbert, who had on more than one occasion argued that if he had his way he'd put Ronald down without the use of a humane killer, was positively beaming at him.

'Marvellous idea, this of yours, for a family history,' he boomed, 'I wonder no one has thought of it before.'

Even Randle radiated a goodwill that was singularly absent from his relations with anyone other than a gerbil or Siamese cat.

'Picture of health, Ronald, absolute picture of health,' he muttered while Fiona, stifling her repugnance for men, kissed him on the cheek. For a terrible moment Lord Petrefact could only conclude that he was in much worse health than he had supposed and that their remarkable cordiality was an augury of his deathbed. As they circled round him and Croxley wheeled the chair through the french windows into the drawing-room, Lord Petrefact rallied his hatred.

'I am *not* well,' he snarled. 'In fact I am in exceedingly poor health, but I can assure you I have no intention of dying at your convenience. I am more concerned in the history of the family.'

'And so are we,' said the Judge, 'no question about that.'

A sympathetic murmur of agreement came from the group. Lord Petrefact ran a dry tongue round his mouth. Their assent was the last thing he had expected or wanted.

'And you've no objection to Professor Yapp working on it?'

For a moment Lord Petrefact's eye seemed to catch a slight

hesitation but the Judge dashed his hopes. 'I understand he's some sort of radical,' he said, 'but I daresay his bark's worse than his bite.'

Lord Petrefact tended to agree. If Yapp's presence in Buscott had done no more than generate this bizarre friendliness among the family, he hadn't bitten at all. 'And you're all agreed that he be given full access to the family correspondence?'

'Don't see how he could write the book properly without it,' said Randle, 'and I daresay it will sell well too. Osbert here was just reminding me of Uncle Oswald's stratagem for getting the Japanese contract for the floating dock. Apparently he persuaded Aunt Georgette to slip into the Nip's room one night on her way back from the loo and ...'

Lord Petrefact listened to the story with growing apprehension. If Randle was prepared to have that sort of stuff published he was prepared for anything. Again the dark suspicion that he was being conned flickered in Lord Petrefact's mind. 'What about Simeon Petrefact's penchant for goats?' he asked dredging from the mire of family gossip the foulest predilection he could find.

'As I was told it, he preferred them dead,' said Osbert. 'Warm, you know, but definitely slaughtered.'

Lord Petrefact gaped at him and the knuckles clutching the arms of the wheelchair whitened. Something had gone terribly wrong. Either that or they were humouring him in the hope that he would never live to see Yapp's scurrilous history published. He'd soon scotch that hope. 'Then since you are all agreed perhaps it would be as well for us to draw up a new contract with Professor Yapp, a family one, which you would all sign, conceding him full access to any document or information he requires.'

Again he watched for dissension but the Judge was still beaming jovially and the others seemed to be as unperturbed as before.

'Well, Purbeck, what's your answer?' he demanded brusquely in the face of that irritating smile. But it was a new voice that answered him.

'I hardly imagine Professor Yapp will have much opportunity to continue his researches into the family, Ronald dear.'

Lord Petrefact swivelled his head lividly and saw Emmelia in the doorway. Like the others she was smiling at him, but there was nothing genial about her smile; it was one of triumph and malign glee.

'What the devil do you mean?' he asked with as much menace as he could muster in so contorted a position. Emmelia said nothing. She stood, smiling and emanating a composure that was even more alarming in its way than the family's welcome.

'Answer my question, confound you,' shouted Lord Petrefact and then, unable to keep his head screwed over his left shoulder a moment longer, turned back to the Judge. Purbeck's expression was hardly enlightening. He was staring at Emmelia with as much amazement as Lord Petrefact felt himself. So were the others.

It was the Brigadier-General who repeated his question for him. 'Er ... well I mean ... what do you mean?'

But Emmelia was not to be drawn. She crossed to a bell and pressed it. 'Now why don't we all sit down and I'll tell Annie to bring us tea,' she said, seating herself with the air of one wholly in command of a slight social occasion. 'How good of you to put in an appearance, Ronald. We'd have been quite lost without you. Ah, Annie, you may serve tea in here. Unless ...' she paused and looked at Lord Petrefact, 'unless you'd prefer something a trifle stronger.'

'What the hell for? You know damned well I'm not allowed ...'

'Then just the tea, Annie,' interrupted Emmelia and leant back in her armchair. 'Of course one tends to forget your ailments, Ronald dear. You look so wonderfully youthful for an octogenarian.'

'I'm not a fucking oct ...' he began, rising to the bait. 'Never mind my age, what I want to know is why you've got it into your blasted head Professor Yapp won't write the family history.'

'Because, my dear,' said Emmelia, having savoured the suspense, 'he would appear to have ... how shall I put it? ... Let's just say that he has more time on his hands than would seem –'

'Time on his hands? What the hell are you blathering on about? Of course he's got time on his hands. I wouldn't have hired the fellow if he hadn't.'

'Not *quite* the time you'd expect. I believe the word is a stretch.'

Lord Petrefact goggled at her. 'Stretch?'

'A stretch of time. I think that's the vernacular for a long prison sentence. Purbeck, you'll know.'

The Judge nodded vacuously.

'You mean this Yapp blighter's ...' began Randle but Emmelia raised a hand.

'Professor Yapp has been arrested,' she said and smoothed her skirt in the serene knowledge that she was pushing Lord Petrefact's blood pressure up into the danger zone.

'Arrested?' he gargled. 'Arrested? My God, you've nobbled the brute.'

Emmelia stopped smiling and turned on him. 'For murder,' she snapped, 'and I'll have you know that I do not frequent race courses and nobbling –'

'Never mind what you fucking frequent,' yelled Lord Petrefact, 'who the hell's he supposed to have murdered?'

'A dwarf. A poor little dwarf who did nobody any harm,' said Emmelia, taking a handkerchief and rendering the news even more distressing by dabbing her eyes with it.

But Lord Petrefact was too dumbfounded to notice. His mind had switched back to that terrible evening at Fawcett when Yapp had manifested an unholy interest in stunted things, and particularly in dwarves. What had the sod called them? Pork? Something like that. And now the maniac had gone and murdered one. In his own mind Lord Petrefact had no doubts. After all it was precisely because the swine was capable of causing havoc wherever he went that he'd sent him down to Buscott. But dwarficidal havoc was something else again. It would mean a trial with Yapp in the witness box saying ... Lord Petrefact shuddered at the thought. It was one thing to threaten the family with publicity but quite another to be personally held responsible for sending a dwarf-killer ... He shut off the thought and looked at Emmelia, but there was no comfort to be found in her gaze. Suddenly everything fitted together in his mind. No wonder the fucking family had been so pleased to see him and so ready to cooperate on the history. Lord Petrefact came out of his frightful meditation and turned from Emmelia to the others.

'I might have guessed,' he shouted hoarsely. 'Of all the double-dyed swine you take the cake! Well, don't think I've finished. I haven't –'

'Then I wish you would,' said Emmelia sharply. 'It's too tiresome to hear you ranting on, and besides you've only yourself to blame. You sent this extraordinary man, Yapp, down here. You didn't consult me. You didn't ask Purbeck or Randle –'

It was Lord Petrefact's turn to interrupt. 'Croxley, back to the car. I'm not staying here another minute.'

'But what about your tea, Ronald dear?' asked Emmelia switching to sweetness. 'It's so seldom we have a family reunion and ...'

But Lord Petrefact had gone. The wheels of his chair crunched on the gravel and the family sat in silence until the hearse started.

'Is this true, Emmelia?' asked the Judge.

'Of course it is.' And she produced the *Bushampton Gazette* from her bag. By the time they had all read it Annie had brought the tea in.

'Well, that's a merciful release, I must say,' said the Brigadier-General with a sigh. 'It's put a stopper on Ronald. I'd stake my reputation on the fact that he doesn't know what's been going on at the Mill. Never seen him in such a tizzwhizz since he heard Aunt Mildred had left him out of her will.'

'I tend to agree with you,' said the Judge, 'but it's not only Ronald we have to consider. The point is, does this murderer Yapp know about the Mill? If he should raise the matter in court ...'

'I daresay you'll use your influence to see that he doesn't,' said Emmelia.

'Yes ... well ...' murmured the Judge, 'naturally one will do what one can.' He took a cup of tea and sipped it thoughtfully. 'Nevertheless, it would be useful to know if he made any mention of the Mill in his statement. Perhaps it would be possible to find out?'

That night, the first of many for Yapp who lay in his cell trying to order out of horror and chaos some doctrine to explain why he was there, and finding only an incredible conspiracy, the Petrefacts, gathered round the dining-table in the New House, began that process which was to justify his theory.

'I should have thought it would be easy enough for you to find out if the man Yapp made any mention of what's been going on at the Mill in his statement,' said the Judge, addressing himself to Emmelia.

But for once Emmelia displayed no interest in the family's concern. 'You can always ask Frederick. He's bound to be in the Working Men's Club at this hour of the night. For myself, I'm going to bed.'

'Shock's probably hit her badly,' said the Brigadier-General when she had left the room. In his way he was right. The shock of discovering that the family she had protected for so long could desert her, and were in fact a collection of craven cowards, had changed Emmelia's outlook entirely. She lay in bed listening to the murmur of voices from the room below and for the first time found some sympathy for Ronald. It was exceedingly little and consisted more of a shared contempt for the rest of the family, but in the scales of her mind it tipped the balance. They could deal with the problem themselves. She had played her part and from now on they must play their own.

And so for the moment they did. Towards eleven Frederick arrived with the comforting information that Yapp's statement, as relayed to him by Sergeant Richey, whose wife was in charge of plastic underwear, contained no reference to the Mill other than that it was undoubtedly a sweat-shop.

'You don't think he's making an oblique reference to those chamois-lined camiknickers?' asked Mrs Van der Fleet-Petrefact, who had taken a secret liking to the garments. 'One would un-doubtedly perspire rather profusely ...'

'Or the Thermal Agitator perhaps?' suggested her husband.

The Judge looked at Frederick with undisguised disgust. He was wondering if the brute was wearing a merkin. 'Well?' he asked.

'I don't think so,' said Frederick, 'I mean his solicitor's been to see him and he'd have mentioned something about it if Yapp did know.'

'True,' said the Judge. 'And what is the name of his solicitor?'

'Rubicond, I think, though I don't see what that has to do with the case.'

'Never mind what you don't see. The legal profession is a brother-hood and a word dropped ...' The Judge sipped his port thoughtfully. 'Well, we must just hope for the best and let Justice take its natural course.'

And Justice, of a sort, did. On Monday Yapp was brought before Osbert Petrefact in his guise as chief magistrate and two minutes later had been remanded in custody without bail. On Tuesday Judge Petrefact, in passing sentence on a school caretaker for indecently assaulting two teenagers he hadn't, gave it as his considered opinion that acts of violence against minors and small persons such as dwarves must be stamped out before the Rule of Law collapsed entirely. The caretaker went down for ten years.

But it was in Lord Petrefact's newspapers that Yapp was most fiercely, if anonymously, condemned. Each carried an editorial pointing out that dwarves were an endangered species, a minority group whose interests were not adequately catered for or, in the case of his most respectable paper, *The Warden*, that Persons of Restricted Growth deserved better of a supposedly caring and concerned society than to be treated as ordinary men and women and ought accordingly to have shorter working hours and Disability Pensions. By Thursday even the Prime Minister had been questioned on the Human Rights of dwarves and Common Market regulations in regard to the grading of individuals according to size, while a Liberal backbencher had threatened to introduce a Private Member's Bill guaranteeing proportional accommodation on public transport and in all places of entertainment.

In short the presumption that Willy Coppett had been murdered by Professor Yapp had been firmly implanted in the public mind to such an extent that a protest march of dwarves demanding protection against assaults by Persons of Excessive Growth was seen on television proving the contrary of their case by routing a police contingent sent to prevent them from clashing with a large body of women campaigning for Abortion For Dwarves. In the ensuing mêlée several women had miscarriages and one teenage dwarf, having been disentangled from beneath the skirt of an extremely pregnant woman, was rushed to hospital as a premature baby.

Nor was that all. Behind these televised scenes more sinister moves were being made to discredit Walden Yapp and to ensure that his trial was as short as possible, his conviction certain, his sentence long, and that his evidence contained no mention of the Petrefact family. By that evidently telepathic influence which so informs the English legal system, Purbeck Petrefact remotely controlled Sir Creighton Hore, Q.C., who had been briefed by Mr Rubicond. The eminent counsel honourably refused the offer of a judgeship, but took the hint. In any case he had already decided it would be an act of legal folly to allow Yapp to be cross-examined in the witness box.

'The man's clearly as mad as a hatter and the case of *Regina versus Thorpe and others* establishes sufficient precedent.'

'But can't we simply plead insanity?' asked Mr Rubicond.

'We could, but unfortunately Broadmoor's taking the case and he's not given to accepting any proof less than the McNaghten Rules.'

'But they went out years ago.'

'My dear fellow, you don't have to tell me. Unfortunately Lord Broadmoor, for whatever reasons – and one must suppose they're largely personal – has yet to accept a plea of guilty but insane. We'll be lucky to get your client off with life imprisonment.'

'It's extraordinary that Broadmoor's been given the case,' said Mr Rubicond naively. Sir Creighton Hore kept his own counsel.

The ripples of influence spread wider still. Even at Kloone University, where Yapp had once been so popular, his predicament aroused little sympathy, and that little was promptly quenched by a surprisingly large endowment from the Petrefact Foundation which created two new professors and the building of the William Coppett Hostel for Micropersons. Only two former colleagues made feeble attempts to visit him but he was too dejected to see anyone from the world that had discarded him.

Besides, he was already succumbing to the lure of a new doctrine: that of martyrdom. The word itself had honourable antecedents, but better still it protected him from the terrifying notion that he was no more than the victim of a mistake. Anything was better than that, and if he were to allow himself to be seduced by the random and chaotic nature of existence he would lose the assurance, fostered so carefully over the years, that history was imbued with purpose and that the happiness of mankind was ultimately guaranteed. Once he admitted the opposite he would be in real danger of taking Mr Rubicond's advice quite literally and going insane. Instead he repeated his belief that he had been framed and adjusted his outlook accordingly.

'But I want to be cross-examined,' he protested when the solicitor explained that he was not to go into the witness box, 'it will allow me to tell the truth.'

'And does the truth differ in any way from the signed statement you made to the police?' asked Mr Rubicond.

'No,' said Yapp.

'In that case it will be placed before the judge and jury without your having to make it any worse for yourself. Of course, if you're determined to get forty years instead of a purely nominal life sentence I can't stop you. Lord Broadmoor's been waiting for a chance to hand out the longest term of imprisonment ever awarded in this country and if you give evidence it's my opinion he'll jump at the opportunity. Are you quite sure you wouldn't rather plead guilty and get it over with quickly?'

But Yapp had stuck to his innocence and the certainty that he was the victim of a conspiracy by the capitalist Petrefacts.

'Anyway you'll get a chance to say a few words when the jury return with their verdict,' said Mr Rubicond gloomily. 'Though if you take my advice you'll keep quiet. Lord Broadmoor's hot on contempt and he might add a few more years to your sentence.'

'History will vindicate me,' said Yapp.

'Which is more than can be said for the jury. Mrs Coppett is going to make the most ghastly impression on them and from what I've been able to glean she's already confessed to adultery.'

'Adultery? With me? But she can't have. It's absolutely untrue and in any case I very much doubt if she knows the meaning of the word.'

'But the jury will,' said Mr Rubicond. 'And those mutilated corsets aren't going to do our case any good. Broadmoor's bound to draw the attention of the jury to them. Not that they need much emphasis. The disgusting things speak for themselves.'

Yapp lapsed into a mournful silence in which, with his usual goodheartedness, he compared his lot with that of poor Rosie and came to the conclusion that he was only marginally worse off.

'Without Willy to look after she must be at her wit's end,' he said finally.

'Depends where her wits begin,' said Mr Rubicond, who still found it incomprehensible that a man of Yapp's education and standing could, as he had admitted to the police, find anything remotely attractive in the mentally deficient wife of a dwarf. It was the strongest factor in leading him to suppose that his client was both guilty and insane. 'Anyway I gather she's found a post with Miss Petrefact and is being well cared for, if that's any consolation to you.'

It wasn't. Yapp returned to his cell now doubly convinced he had been framed. Two days later he dismissed Mr Rubicond and Sir Creighton Hore, and announced that he intended to conduct his own defence.

twenty-four

But if everything seemed to be moving Yapp towards his doom, one person was increasingly convinced of his innocence. Ever since Rosie Coppett had moved from Rabbitry Road and had pinned her All-In Wrestlers and a great many bunnies to the sloping walls of her attic bedroom in the New House, Emmelia had questioned her almost daily on the events before and after Willy's death. And with each new telling – she had once laced Rosie's cocoa with whisky – Emmelia had been confirmed in her belief that, whoever had killed Willy, it wasn't Yapp.

She had arrived at this conclusion on two grounds; partly because, having shaken off the mantle of her own innocence, she was better able to discern it in others; and partly because everything in Rosie's story which had so convinced the police that Yapp was guilty seemed to point her in the opposite direction. That Yapp should have harangued her in her own shrubbery on her iniquities as an employer of sweated labour while Willy's body festered in the boot of the old Vauxhall argued an insane bravado or total innocence. Similarly, only a blithering idiot would have returned to the widow of a dwarf he had just murdered with the blood of his victim all over his hands and shirt and, while from brief acquaintance Emmelia was ready to concede that Yapp was both blithering and idiotic, he hadn't struck her as a complete moron.

In any case Rosie, in spite of the detailed instructions she had received from the police, steadfastly maintained that Yapp had never been to bed with her.

'No, mum, he refused extras when I gave them to him,' she said. It had taken Emmelia some time to find out what extras were and, when she had discovered where Rosie had picked up the term, had led to an acrimonious exchange on the telephone with the Marriage Advice Bureau on the evils of encouraging extra-marital sex, as they put it, or, in Emmelia's more forthright vocabulary, adultery. It was the same with every aspect of Rosie's account. Yapp, for all his lowly origins and socialist opinions, had behaved like a gentleman – except apparently that he had gone off one night and battered Rosie's husband to death. While Emmelia had known quite a number of so-called gentlemen who wouldn't have hesitated to batter dwarfs to death, Yapp didn't come into their category.

The man was an opinionated creature but he wasn't a murderer. That was Emmelia's conclusion and she stuck to it.

Rosie stuck to the opposite view. It lent her life – and since the death of Willy she had felt doubly deprived – a glamour she had found previously only in the pages of her Confessions magazines, and it also pleased the policemen and lawyers who went over her evidence with her. By the day of the trial she had been so adequately programmed that she was almost prepared to swear she had killed Willy herself to keep them pleased, and when Inspector Garnet arrived to take her to the Court in Briskerton he was horrified to find her wearing her best.

'Jesus wept,' he said shading his eyes against a cerise dress, pink shoes and a boa she had been given by her mother who had got it in her turn from her grandmother. 'She can't go into court looking like that. It will throw Lord Broadmoor clean off course and he'll send her down for soliciting.'

'We can always find her something more suitable,' said the policewoman who accompanied him.

'I'd like to know where.'

'There's a Women's Lib. undertaker in Crag Street who has some hefty pall-bearers.'

And so Rosie was driven to the mortician's and fitted out in mourning dress. By the time she left she had all the hallmarks of a distraught widow while the proximity of so many coffins had affected her most movingly.

'Willy's was ever so tiny,' she sobbed as she was helped into the room where the witnesses waited.

Meanwhile in the Court Emmelia was watching the course of the trial. Not that it could be accurately called a trial; Lord Broadmoor saw to that. Yapp's declaration that he intended to conduct his own defence was in part responsible for the Judge's attitude.

'You intend to do what?' he asked when Yapp first announced the fact.

'Conduct my own defence,' said Yapp. Lord Broadmoor peered at him narrowly.

'Are you by any chance suggesting that the legal profession is incapable of providing you with the very best services a man in your position could possibly require?'

'No, my decision has been taken on other grounds.'

'Has it, by God? And my decision that you shall be handcuffed to a warder for the duration of this trial is taken on the grounds that I do not intend a murderer to escape from this courtroom. Warder, shackle this man.'

While Yapp was bitterly contesting the presupposition that he was a murderer, he was handcuffed to the prison officer beside him.

'You've got no right to call me a murderer,' he shouted.

'I didn't,' said Lord Broadmoor, 'I stated that I did not intend to allow a murderer to escape from this courtroom. If you choose to call yourself a murderer I can't stop you but in your circumstances I doubt if I would. The prosecution may now present its case.'

In the third row of the public seats Emmelia hardly listened. She was studying the white-faced figure in the dock with the eyes of a woman who had, until recently, spent her entire life cossetted by an unshaken conscience and the certain belief that she was a good woman. Now that she was more nearly herself she could recognize her old symptoms in Yapp's face. They were attenuated, of course, by lack of her enormous wealth and her knowledge that she would never be poor or unprotected, but his defiance and refusal to accept an unwarranted fate sprang from conviction. Yapp's arrogance in the dock clinched his innocence for her.

It did the opposite for Lord Broadmoor. As the trial progressed his unbiased disgust for the prisoner became more apparent and when Yapp tried to step from the dock to cross-examine Dr Dramble, the forensic expert, who had given evidence of the injuries inflicted on Willy Coppett, the Judge intervened: 'And where do you think you're going?'

'I have a right to cross-examine this witness,' said Yapp.

'So you have,' said the Judge, 'indeed you have. No one doubts you have. I certainly don't. But that was not the question I put to you. I asked "Where do you think you are going?" I repeat it.'

'I am going to question this witness,' said Yapp.

Lord Broadmoor removed his spectacles and polished them. 'I would cast some doubt upon your use of the word "going",' he said finally. 'For the moment you are going nowhere. If you insist on putting questions to this expert witness you will do so from the dock. I am not prepared to have innocent prison officers dragged round the courtroom by the wrist for your amusement. You have caused enough trouble already.'

And so the trial continued with Yapp shouting his questions

from the dock and Lord Broadmoor ordering the prisoner not to make a noise or attempt to intimidate the witness, and all the time Emmelia sat watching in the knowledge that she was in some way responsible for what was happening. Perhaps not personally but at least as one of the Petrefacts whose enormous influence was so heavily weighted against Yapp. In the past she had been protected from such knowledge by her seclusion and the folly of obscure grandeur. Her mirror-image in Cleete's shop window and the family's desertion had destroyed all that, and in its place she found herself identifying with the very man her brother had sent down to destroy the Petrefact reputation. It was all most peculiar and sickening, but when at the end of the first day she left the court-room she was delighted to see Lord Petrefact being bounced very uncomfortably down the steps outside.

'My dear Ronald,' she said with that affectionate duplicity she found so easy now, 'I didn't see you among the spectators.'

'Hardly fucking surprising since I wasn't,' snapped the old man resorting to the language he expected to offend her. But Emmelia merely beamed at him.

'How stupid of me. You've been called as a witness,' she said as Croxley wheeled the chair towards the waiting hearse. 'You know, I think Professor Yapp's handling his case remarkably well.'

Lord Petrefact made noises which seemed to signify that Professor Fucking Yapp could stuff his case where the fucking monkey stuffed the fucking nuts.

'That's four "fuckings",' said Emmelia sympathetically. 'It leads one to suppose you've been having trouble with your prostate again.'

'Never mind my fucking prostate,' shouted Lord Petrefact.

'Five,' said Emmelia. 'You know, if you start using that sort of language in the witness box it will make a very bad impression on the jury.'

'Fuck the jury,' said Lord Petrefact and was hoisted into the hearse.

'And where are you staying?'

'At Reginald Pouling's.'

'One of your tame MPs. Oh well, it must be a great comfort ...' But Lord Petrefact had given orders to the driver and the hearse left Emmelia standing on the pavement. She wandered thoughtfully along the street. At least Yapp had subpoenaed one of his enemies.

Emmelia's thoughts turned to other possible witnesses but without much hope. Why, for instance, hadn't Yapp called her? He had come to see her with the body in the boot of the car ... But then again he hadn't seen her. He had supposed she was her own overworked, underpaid gardener. Well, she could soon rectify that mistake. She turned and marched back into the Courthouse and demanded of an official the right to see the accused. Since the man was a Gas Board meter reader it was some time before she discovered that Yapp was being held in Briskerton police station.

Emmelia made her way there and presently was explaining to the Superintendent that she was indeed Miss Petrefact and that she had fresh evidence which could influence the outcome of the case. Even then it was not easy to see Yapp.

'He's not what you might call a cooperative prisoner,' said the Superintendent, an opinion that was almost immediately confirmed by Yapp himself who sent a message back that he'd seen enough blood-sucking Petrefacts to last him a lifetime and in any case, since he wasn't so much being tried as pilloried, any new evidence she had to offer was hardly likely to do him much good and he'd be grateful if she gave it to the prosecuting counsel.

'The man's a fool,' said Emmelia, but she left the police station convinced more than ever that he was also an innocent.

The events of the following day tended to confirm her belief.

The prosecution played their trump card in Rosie. It could hardly be said that Rosie Coppett, dressed in the widow's weeds from the undertaker, made a wholly sympathetic impression either on Lord Broadmoor, who found it difficult to believe that so substantial a woman could have been married to a dwarf, or on the jury who found it impossible to believe that a passion for such a dowdy and dimwitted woman could provide anyone, let alone a professor, with a motive for murder. But on Yapp the sight and sound of Rosie revived those feelings of pathos and pity which had, with her physical attractions for him, combined to render him so vulnerable. The process repeated itself now though with Lord Broadmoor's help and when Yapp rose to question her on the adultery she had been programmed to admit the Judge intervened.

'Mrs Coppett has suffered sufficiently at your hands already without being subjected to an inquisition on the exact physical actions involved in adultery,' he said. 'I find this lurid and bullying type of questioning most offensive and you will kindly refrain from it.'

'But I have my doubts about her knowing what she's said,' Yapp replied.

The Judge turned to Rosie. 'Do you know what you've said?' he enquired. Rosie nodded. 'And you did commit adultery with the accused?'

Again Rosie nodded. The nice policeman had said that she had and the police didn't tell lies. Her mum had always told her to go to a policeman if she was lost. She was lost now and the tears ran down her cheeks.

'In that case,' said the Judge, addressing the jury, 'you may take it that the act of adultery was committed between the accused and this witness.'

'It wasn't,' said Yapp. 'You are wrongly accusing Mrs Coppett of an act which while not illegal nevertheless –'

'I am not accusing Mrs Coppett of anything,' snarled the Judge. 'She has openly admitted, and I might add with a frankness that does her considerably more credit than it does you, that she committed adultery with you. Now it is evidently your intention to reduce the witness's morale and thereafter discredit her evidence by delving into the loathsome and prurient sexual details implicit in the very act of adultery which it is no part of the court's business to consider.'

'I'm entitled to challenge the prosecution's allegation that adultery took place,' said Yapp.

But Lord Broadmoor would have none of it. 'You are here on a charge of murder. This isn't a divorce court and the question of adultery is immaterial to the charge.'

'But it's being used to provide a motive. I am alleged to have murdered the witness's husband precisely because I was having an affair with her. The question of adultery is therefore germane to my defence.'

'Germane indeed!' roared Lord Broadmoor, for whom the word was indissolubly and prejudicially linked with the feminist movement. 'Your defence lies in convincing the jury that the evidence against you is groundless, without any foundation in fact and is insufficient to warrant their passing a verdict of guilty. Kindly continue your cross-examination without further reference to adultery.'

'But I don't think she understands what the word means,' said Yapp.

Counsel for the prosecution rose. 'My lord, Exhibit H is, I suggest, relevant to this particular argument.'

'Exhibit H?'

Counsel held up the mutilated corsets and joggled them at the jury.

'Dear God, put the damned things down,' said Lord Broadmoor hoarsely before turning a rancid eye on Yapp. 'Do you deny that the witness wore those ... er ... that garment in your presence as she has freely admitted?'

'No,' said Yapp, 'but ...'

'But me no buts, sir. We can take it that the act of adultery is established. You may continue your cross-examination of this witness, but let me warn you that there will be no more questions relating to the physical acts that took place between you.'

Yapp looked wildly round the court but there was no comfort to be found in the faces that looked back at him. In the witness box Rosie had broken down completely and was sobbing. Yapp shook his head hopelessly. 'No more questions,' he said, and sat down.

In the public gallery Emmelia stirred. That change which had begun outside Cleete's shop was continuing and, if then she had seen herself for what she was, a rich, protected and, ultimately, a smug woman, what she was now witnessing was so far removed from justice and the truth as she knew it that she was forced to do something. Impelled by her Petrefactian arrogance she rose to her feet.

'My lord,' she shouted, 'I have something to inform the court. The woman in the witness box is in my employ and she has never committed ...'

She got no further.

'Silence in court!' roared Lord Broadmoor, evidently venting feelings that had been particularly pent up by the corsets. 'Remove that virago.'

For a moment Emmelia was too shocked to reply. Never in half a century had anyone spoken to her like that. By the time she had found her voice she was already being hustled from the court-room.

'Virago indeed,' she shouted back, 'I'll have you know I am Miss

Petrefact and what is more this trial is a travesty of justice. I demand to be heard.'

The court doors closed on her protest.

'Call the next witness,' said the Judge and presently Mr Groce from the Horse and Barge was giving evidence that Willy Coppett had, in his hearing, definitely stated that the accused was having an affair with his wife, Mrs Rosie Coppett. But Yapp wasn't listening. He was too preoccupied with the strange and vaguely familiar figure of the woman who had shouted from the public gallery. She had claimed to be Miss Petrefact and Yapp had no reason to doubt her word, and yet her voice ... He had heard that voice before somewhere. But that hardly mattered. The fact remained that she had called the trial a travesty of justice. And so it was, but for a Petrefact to announce this in open court put his whole theory of a conspiracy against him in doubt. He was still wrestling with this insoluble problem when the prosecuting counsel finished his examination of Mr Groce.

'Has the defence any questions to put to this witness?' asked Lord Broadmoor. Yapp shook his head and Mr Groce stepped down.

'Call Mr Parmiter.' The car dealer stepped into the witness box and corroborated what Mr Groce had said. Again Yapp had no questions for him.

That night in his cell Yapp succumbed to doubts he had spent a lifetime evading. Emmelia's intervention threatened more than his ability to defend his innocence against the charge of murder: it put in jeopardy the social doctrine on which his innocence relied. Without a conspiracy to sustain him there was no rhyme or reason for his predicament, no certain social progress or historical force in whose service he was now suffering. Instead he was the victim of a random and chaotic set of circumstances beyond his powers of explanation. For the first time in his life Yapp felt himself to be alone in a menacing universe.

It was a haggard scholar who stood in the dock next morning and answered Lord Broadmoor's reiterated statement that the defence could now present its case with a hopeless shake of his head. Two hours later the jury returned a verdict of guilty and once again the Judge turned to Yapp.

'Have you anything to say before sentence is passed?'

Yapp swayed in the dock and tried to remember the denunciation of the social system and capitalist exploitation he had prepared so carefully but nothing came.

'I have never killed anyone in my life and I don't know why I am here,' he muttered in its place. Among those listening only Emmelia, decently incognito beneath a hat and veil, believed him. Lord Broadmoor certainly didn't and having delivered a series of vitriolic and unrelated attacks on the dangers inherent in further education for the working class, professors as a species, and student protests, he sentenced Walden Yapp to life imprisonment and went off to a cheerful lunch.

twenty-five

While Yapp was driven off to begin his sentence, life in Buscott resumed its even tempo. To be accurate, it had hardly lost it. Mr Jipson had certainly developed a positively compulsive zeal for cleaning his tractor and immediately dirtying it, and Willy was occasionally missed beneath the bar at the Horse and Barge, but for the rest the little town remained as peculiarly prosperous as it had been since Frederick first began to cater so anonymously for the lurid fantasies of the Mill's customers.

But for Emmelia things had changed dramatically. She had emerged from the court to be confronted with further proof that the world, far from being a nice place as she had formerly supposed, was an exceedingly nasty one. Lord Petrefact was being wheeled down the steps in high spirits.

'What a splendid outcome,' he told Croxley, 'Can't remember when I've enjoyed myself so much. Two damned birds with one stone. Yapp gets a life sentence and Emmelia a bum's rush. Though what the hell she wanted to make a scene for I can't imagine.'

'Possibly because she knew Yapp was incapable of murdering anyone,' said Croxley.

'Absolute nonsense. The swine practically killed me with that confounded bath at Fawcett. I always knew the brute had homicidal tendencies.'

'We all make mistakes,' said Croxley, and from the expression on his face Emmelia judged him to think that Yapp's failure with the bath was one of them.

'Only mistake he made was not to have had a go at Emmelia,' said Lord Petrefact bitterly. 'Now, if he'd had at her with a blunt instrument and a sharp knife he'd have had my sympathy.'

'Quite,' said Croxley, and expressed his own feelings on the matter by allowing the wheelchair to bounce down the last two steps unattended.

'Damn you, Croxley,' shouted the old man, 'one of these days you'll learn to be more careful.'

'Quite,' said Croxley wheeling him away towards the waiting hearse. Behind them Emmelia made a mental note that Croxley was a man with hidden talents who might come in useful. But for the moment she was more concerned with Yapp, and that evening she phoned Purbeck at his flat in London.

'I am making this call reluctantly,' she said. 'I want you to see that Professor Yapp's case goes to appeal.'

'You want me to do what?' said the Judge.

Emmelia repeated her request.

'Appeal? Appeal? I'm not some petty solicitor, you know, and in any case the fellow had a fair trial and was found guilty by the unanimous verdict of the jury.'

'All the same, he's innocent.'

'Stuff and nonsense. Guilty as sin.'

'I say that he is innocent.'

'You can say what you please. The fact remains that as far as the law is concerned he's guilty.'

'And we all know what the law is,' said Emmelia. 'I happen to know he has been sentenced to life imprisonment for a murder he did not commit.'

'My dear Emmelia,' said the Judge, 'you may think he's been wrongly convicted but you can't know. Always supposing he has been, and I don't for a moment believe it, only Yapp and the real murderer, if there is one, can possibly know it. That is the simple truth, and as for an appeal, unless the defence can produce new evidence ...'

But Emmelia was no longer listening. She replaced the receiver and sat on in the dusk obsessed with the realization that, somewhere out there beyond the garden wall, another human being knew how, when and why Willy Coppett had met his death. It had never occurred to her to think about him or to feel his existence so tangibly. And she would never know who that person was. If the police with all their men had failed to find him it was absurd to suppose she could.

From there her thoughts whirled off along new and unexpected lines into a maelstrom of uncertainty which was adolescent in its intensity but which, in her protected youth, she had never experienced. For the first time she glimpsed a world beyond the pale of wealth and privilege where people were poor and innocent for no good reason and others rich and evil for even worse. In short the jigsaw-puzzle picture of society, a long and well-arranged herbaceous border in which the great families of England were perennial species, crumbled into its separate pieces and made no sort of sense.

She wandered out into the dusk with a new and mad determination. If the world of her upbringing had collapsed and her family had revealed themselves for the craven cowards they were, she must somehow create a new world for herself. She would restore honour to the name Petrefact even if, apparently, she had to dishonour it. Of one thing she was determined, Professor Walden Yapp would not serve his prison term. She would reverse the course of so-called justice until he was exonerated and set free.

All the time she remained aware of the anonymous figure of the real murderer. If he came forward ... He wouldn't. People who murdered dwarves didn't give themselves up to the police because another man had been found guilty of their crimes. Her own family, with far less reason, had been happy to watch an innocent Yapp go to prison to save themselves from the unfavourable publicity attached to their ownership of a fetish factory. But without the real murderer ... Emmelia's thoughts were stopped in their tracks by the sudden apparition of a dozen dwarves gathered round the goldfish pond. For a moment in the twilight she had the horrid impression that they were alive. Then she remembered she had given Rosie permission to bring her garden ornaments from Rabbitry Road and set them haphazardly round the pond, where their tasteless vigour mocked the hermaphroditic fountain nymph.

Emmelia sat down on a rustic bench and stared at the grotesque memorials to the late Willy Coppett, and as she stared an idea burgeoned in her mind – burgeoned, blossomed and bore fruit.

Half an hour later Frederick, summoned from the Working Men's Liberal and Unionist Club by telephone, was standing before his aunt in the drawing room.

'Dwarves?' he said. 'What on earth do you want with dwarves?'

'Their names and addresses,' said Emmelia.

'And you want me to find them for you?'

'Exactly.'

Frederick regarded her with some suspicion. 'And you're not prepared to tell me why you want them?'

Emmelia shook her head. 'All I am prepared to say is that it will be in your best interest to find them. Naturally you will go about the business anonymously.'

Frederick considered his best interest and found it difficult to square with an anonymous search for dwarves. 'I suppose I could phone the local labour exchange but they're going to think it a bit odd if I refuse to give my name and address. And anyway, what on earth am I going to tell them I want dwarves for?'

'You'll just have to think of something, and you're certainly not to give them any idea who you are. That is the first point. The second is that you will forget all about this conversation. As far as you are concerned it has not taken place. Is that clear?'

'Only very vaguely,' said Frederick.

'In that case let me make my point in terms you will understand. I have decided to alter my will in your favour. In the past I had always intended to leave my share in the family business to all my nephews and nieces in equal portions. Now you will inherit the lot.'

'Very kind of you, I must say. Most generous,' said Frederick, beginning to understand that his best interests were definitely in doing what Aunt Emmelia said.

Emmelia regarded him with distaste. 'It's nothing of the sort,' she said finally. 'It is simply the only way I know of guaranteeing that, whatever happens, you will keep your mouth shut. In the event that you don't I shall revoke the will and leave you nothing.'

'Have no fear,' said Frederick with a smirk, 'I shan't breathe a word. If it's dwarves you want, it's dwarves you shall have.'

'Only their names and addresses, mind you,' said Emmelia, and on this distinctly odd note she dismissed him. Left to herself she sat on, steeling herself for the next move. At twelve she left the house with a large shopping bag and a torch and walked down to the Mill. There she let herself in through a side door and presently was carefully selecting those articles she needed. By the time she returned to the New House the shopping bag contained several dildos, two handcuffs from the Bondage Department, a whip, a teatless bra and a pair of open-crotch chamois-lined plastic cami-knickers. Emmelia went up to her room, locked them away in her chest of drawers, and went to bed with a strange smile. For the first time in many a long year she was feeling excited and guilty. It was as though she had raided the pantry at Fawcett House when she was a child. How she had hated Fawcett! And how extra-ordinarily exhilarating it was to be acting outside the pale of respectability! Here she was, the guardian of the family's repu-tation, intent now on redressing the balance of their sanctimonious and sinful hypocrisy. It was with the feeling that she was at long last living up to her true Petrefactian nature that she dozed off with some refrain about 'ancestral vices prophesying war' running through her tired mind.

For the next week Frederick applied himself to the tricky busi-ness of finding local dwarves without revealing his identity. He phoned round all the Employment Exchanges in the district only to discover that, curiously enough, there was no shortage of job opportunities for dwarves. Even his claim to be a representative of Disney Films interested in remaking *Snow White* along natural-istic lines with seven midget miners elicited no great interest, while his later tactics as BBC producer working on a documentary deal-ing with the dangers to dwarves as a species, particularly after the murder of Willy Coppett, met with no response. In the end he had to report his lack of success to Emmelia.

'They're short on the ground,' he said. 'I've tried hospitals and circuses and just about every place I can think of. I suppose I could try the local Education Authority. They must have a list of teenage dwarves.'

But Emmelia wouldn't hear of it. 'Young adults, yes, but I have no intention of infl ... of having anything to do with dwarves below the age of consent.'

200

'Age of consent?' said Frederick, for whom the phrase had distinctly perverse sexual connotations when combined with dwarves. 'You're surely not thinking of ... well ... er ...'

'What I am proposing remains my private business. Yours is simply to find me suitable candidates.'

'If you say so,' said Frederick. But the sexual motif solved his problem. That afternoon he used the Personal Column of the *Bushampton Gazette* to place an advert stating that he was a lonely middle-aged Gentleman of Restricted Growth with independent means seeking the companionship of a similarly constituted Lady and gave his interests, Lego, model railways and bonsai gardening. This time he was lucky, and two days later had eight replies which he took up to the New House. Emmelia studied them doubtfully.

'I should have told you to specify male dwarves,' she said, reinforcing Frederick's suspicions that whatever his aunt had in mind was some form of dwarf fetish.

'I've had enough trouble rustling this little lot up,' he protested, 'and if you think I'm going to advertise myself as a gay dwarf in this neck of the woods, I can assure you I'm not. Quite frankly I find the whole business of masquerading as a heterosexual one unpleasant enough without being a deviant dwarf into the bargain.'

Emmelia brushed his objections aside. 'I trust you didn't go to the *Gazette*'s offices in person,' she said.

'Certainly not,' said Frederick, 'I'd have had to go in on my knees or have them wondering what a five-foot-ten man was doing inserting pieces in the agony column claiming to be three-foot-nothing. I phoned them and used a box number.'

'Good. Well, these will just have to do. And remember that if you breathe a word of this to anyone, you will lose all chance of taking your father's place as head of the family firm, quite apart from becoming an accessory before the fact.'

'Before what fact?' began Frederick and promptly decided that he didn't want to know. Whatever Aunt Emmelia was up, or in this case down to, he wanted no part of it. Having said as much, he left the house and to avoid any further implication in her affairs drove to London and made hurried arrangements for a holiday in Spain.

For the next week Emmelia continued her preparations. She bought a secondhand car in Briskerton, drove round the various villages and towns looking at the houses in which the eight correspondents claimed to live, and in general behaved in so unusual a manner that even Annie commented on it.

'I can't think what's come over her,' she told Rosie, whom she had delegated to do the washing-up. 'Hardly ever out of the garden for years and years and now she's gadding about like I don't know what.'

It was an apt expression and one that corresponded at times to Emmelia's own feelings. She didn't know what either; what had become of her former self; what had happened to her family scruples; or what she now was. Only the how concerned her, that and the knowledge that she was no longer bored or driven by the dullness of life to write long letters to her relatives pretending to be what she had evidently never been, a dear, kind and gentle elderly lady.

Instead, something harsh and almost brutal had emerged in her character in response, paradoxically, to the affront done to her naively nice view of the world and its ways by the sentencing of a foolish but innocent man. And Lord Broadmoor had called her a virago. Emmelia looked the word up in her dictionary and found its original meaning: 'a woman of masculine strength and spirit. (*Latin* = a female warrior)'. All in all it was a fair description of her present state, and it was reassuring to know that the Romans had so described some women. It placed her in a tradition older even than the Petrefact genealogy. But residues of her former self remained and at night she would wake with a start of horror at the thought of the actions she had premeditated.

To quell these moments of panic she hardened her resolve by reading *The Times* most thoroughly and by joining Annie and Rosie in the boot-room of an evening to watch television. From these encounters with focused madness and violence she would come away reconciled to the relative mildness of her own intentions. A man had burnt twenty-two people to death in a Texas club 'just for kicks'; in Manchester a father of five had raped an old-age pensioner; in Teheran more people had been executed by firing squad for 'corruption against God'; another British soldier had been killed in Ulster while presumably trying to prevent Catholics and Protestants from slaughtering one another; a fourteen-year-old baby-sitter had dropped her charge from an upstairs window in a successful attempt to stop it crying. As if these acts of senseless violence were not enough to convince her that the world was mad, there were the TV series in which detectives were shot at or shot suspected villains with a gusto that was clearly shared by Annie and Rosie and presumably by millions of other viewers.

Emmelia came away from these sessions with a quiet conscience. If the rest of the world behaved so irrationally and with so little motive she had nothing to be concerned about. By the end of a month she had been transformed inwardly beyond all recognition. Outwardly she remained Miss Emmelia Petrefact, the dear old lady who loved gardening, cats and her family.

For Yapp very little remained. Since his arrival at Drampoole Prison he had lost his clothes, most of his hair, all his personal possessions, and the illusions that criminals were simply victims of the social system. Only the knowledge that they were mostly members of the working class persisted, and with it the experience of discovering what the proletariat thought of child-murderers. Yapp's frantic attempts to explain that he hadn't murdered anyone and that, even if he had, dwarves were not children hadn't saved him from being assaulted by the two genuine murderers with whom he was forced to share a cell.

'We know what to do with sods like you,' they told him and had gone to work in several revolting and exceedingly painful ways which they had evidently learnt in the grim school of life Yapp had previously revered. By the following morning his reverence had gone and with it his ability to voice a demand to see the prison doctor. He was still whispering at the end of a week and it was only then that the warders, who clearly shared his cellmates' hatred for dwarf-molesters, decided in their own interest that he needed medical attention before they had a corpse in custody.

'One fucking squeak out of you and you'll have testicles for tonsils,' said the larger murderer gratuitously as Yapp hobbled out of the cell. 'Tell the pill-popper you fell off your bunk.'

Yapp followed these instructions in a hoarse whisper.

'Off your bunk?' said the doctor shining a torch suspiciously on Yapp's serrated sphincter. 'You did say "bunk"?'

'Yes,' whispered Yapp.

'And what precisely did you land on?'

Yapp said he wasn't quite sure.

'I am,' said the doctor, who knew an arse-bandit when he saw one and was as prejudiced against the species as he was against child-murderers. 'All right you can stand up now.'

Yapp tried and squeaked pitifully.

'And what's the matter with your voice? You're not by any chance a knob-hound too?'

Yapp said he didn't know what a knob-hound was. The doctor enlarged his vocabulary.

'Then I'm certainly not,' whispered Yapp as indignantly as his vocal chords would allow, 'I resent the imputation.'

'In that case would you mind telling me how your uvula got into its present disgusting condition?' asked the doctor, prodding the thing irritably with a spatula.

Yapp made gurgling noises.

'Call the doctor "sir",' said the warder, reinforcing the order by jabbing him in the ribs.

'Sir,' gurgled Yapp. The doctor turned back to his desk and wrote out his report.

'One soluble pessary to be taken at both extremities three times a day,' he said, 'and can't you move him in with someone who's less susceptible to the ghastly creature's sexual charms?'

'There's only Watford,' said the warder dubiously.

'Thank God,' said the doctor. 'Well, we'll just have to keep the stomach-pump handy.'

'Yes sir.'

Yapp was prodded back to his cell to collect his blankets. The two murderers eyed him expectantly.

'He's going in with Watford,' said the warder. 'You two buggers have had your fun.'

'Serve the swine right,' said the small murderer.

Yapp hobbled out onto the landing again with a terrible sense of premonition. 'What's the matter with Watford?' he croaked.

'You mean to say you've never heard of the Bournemouth poisoner? And you a fucking professor. Oh well, live and learn,' said the warder, unlocking a cell door at the far end of the landing. 'Got a friend for you, Watford.'

A small chubby man sitting on the bed eyed Yapp with an interest that was in no way reciprocated.

'What are you in for?' he asked as the door shut. Yapp slumped onto the other bed and decided for the first time in his life that the truth was definitely not to be told.

'Must have been something really nasty.' continued the cheerful Mr Watford, radiating a bedside manner. 'They never give me anyone nice.'

Yapp croaked wordlessly and pointed to his mouth.

'Oh a dummy,' continued Mr Watford, 'that's handy. Silence is golden, as I alway say. Makes things so much easier. Want me to give you a medical examination?'

Yapp shook his head vigorously.

'Oh well, just as you like. Mind you, I'm better than the prison doctor, not that that's saying much. Of course that's why I'm here. I mean nature intended me to be a great physician but my background was against me. My dad being a trolley-bus driver when he was sober and a sadist when he wasn't and mum having to make ends meet by scrubbing, I wasn't allowed to stay on at school past fourteen. First job I got was with a scrap-iron merchant sorting out lead piping from other metal. Interesting stuff, lead. Gave me my first insight into the physiological effects of metallic poisons. Arsenic's a metal too you know. Well anyway from there I went to work for a photographer ...'

The tale of Mr Watford's terrible life went on while Yapp tried to stay awake. In the ordinary way he would have been interested and even sympathetic, but the knowledge that he was in all likelihood destined to become the Bournemouth poisoner's next victim counterbalanced the call of his social conscience while his previous cellmates had given him a traumatic inkling into the mentality of the common-or-garden murderer. If he was to survive in Mr Watford's lethal company he must establish an immoral superiority over the man. Above all he must be different and subtle and in some horrible category of crime that was all his own. For the very first time in his life Yapp addressed his mind to a problem that was personal, immediate and real and had nothing to do with politics, history or the inequality of class.

By the time supper arrived he had reached a decision. With genuine revulsion and a ghastly smile he handed his tray to Watford, shook his head and pointed to his mouth.

'What, don't you want this grub?' asked the poisoner.

Yapp smiled again and this time leaned forward so that his face was disturbingly close to Mr Watford's.

'Not enough blood,' he croaked.

'Blood?' said Watford, looking up from Yapp's awful smile to the sausages and back again. 'Well, now you come to mention it, you don't get much meat in prison sausages.'

'Real blood,' whispered Yapp.

Mr Watford shifted further back on his bed. 'Real blood?'

'Fresh,' said Yapp leaning forward in pursuit. 'Fresh from the jugular.'

'Jugular?' said Mr Watford, losing a good deal of his facial colour and all his bedside manner. 'What do you mean "Fresh from the jugular"?'

But Yapp merely smiled more horribly.

'Lumme, they've put a nutter in with me.'

Yapp stopped smiling.

'No offence meant,' continued Mr Watford hastily, 'all I meant was ...' He broke off and looked doubtfully at the sausages. 'Are you sure you won't have your supper? You might feel less ... well, better or something.'

But Yapp shook his head and lay down again. Mr Watford eyed him cautiously and began to eat rather slowly. For several minutes there was silence in the cell and Mr Watford's colour had begun to return to his cheeks when Yapp struck again.

'Dwarves,' he groaned. A portion of sausage that was on its way to Mr Watford's mouth quavered on the end of his fork.

'What do you mean "dwarves"?' he demanded rather belligerently this time. 'Here I am eating my supper and you have to –'

'Little dwarves.'

'Fuck me,' said Mr Watford, and immediately regretted it. Yapp was smiling again. 'Well, if you say so, though I'd have thought all dwarves were little.'

But Yapp was not to be mollified. 'Little baby dwarves' blood.'

Mr Watford put the portion of sausage back on the plate and stared at Yapp. 'Look, mate, I'm trying to eat my supper and the topic of fucking little dwarves and their blood isn't conducive to ... oh my God.'

Yapp was on his feet and looming over him. Mr Watford recoiled against the wall.

'All right, all right,' he said shakily. 'If you like little baby dwarves' blood it's fine with me. All I ask is ...'

'Straight from their little jugulars,' Yapp went on, rubbing his bony hands together and staring pointedly at Mr Watford's neck.

'Help,' yelled the prisoner and shot off the bed and beat on the door, 'get me out of here! This bloke shouldn't be in prison. He should be in a loony-bin.'

But by the time two warders bothered to investigate his complaint Yapp was sitting quietly on his bed eating sausages and mash.

'All right, all right, now what's been going on in here?' they demanded, shoving the gibbering prisoner aside.

'He's mad. He's clean off his chump. You've stuck a fucking psychopath in with me. He won't eat his grub and keeps going on about drinking dwarves' blood ...' Watford stopped and stared at Yapp. 'He wasn't eating before.'

'Well, he's eating now, and with you around I can't say I blame him not eating before,' said the warder.

'But he kept on about dwarves' blood.'

'What do you expect him to do, talk about arsenic all the time? Anyway what are you worried about? You're not a fucking dwarf.'

'The way he looks at me I might just as well be. And I'm entitled to talk about poisons. That's my speciality. Why do you think I'm here?'

'Right, so he's entitled to talk about bloody dwarves,' said the warder. 'What do you think he's here for?'

Mr Watford looked at Yapp with fresh horror.

'Oh Gawd, don't tell me –'

'That's right, Wattie. His speciality is murdering little bleeding dwarves. The Governor thought you'd get on well together. The other villains don't want him.'

And before Mr Watford could say he didn't either, the door was shut and he was warned he'd be doing punishment if he made any more noise. Mr Watford crouched in the corner and only climbed onto his bed when the light went out.

Yapp in the meantime had been considering his next move at self-preservation. It came with Mr Watford's attempt to masturbate himself to sleep. This time he decided a religious tone would help and began to sing in a sinister whisper, 'All dwarves pink and horrible, all midgets fat and small, all dwarves white and villainous, the good Lord kills them all.'

Mr Watford stopped masturbating. 'I am not a dwarf,' he said, 'I wish you'd get that into your head.'

'Dwarves masturbate,' said Yapp.

'I daresay they do,' said Mr Watford, unable to fault the logic but finding its implications as far as he was concerned exceedingly disturbing, 'the fact remains that I am not a masturbating dwarf.'

'Spilling the seed stunts your growth,' said Yapp, recalling a rather oblique remark his religious aunt had once made on the topic. 'The Lord God of Righteousness has spoken.'

In his bed Mr Watford decided not to argue the toss. If the raving lunatic he had been lumbered with chose to combine the belief that he was the Lord God with disapproval of self-abuse and a predilection for dwarf blood, that was his business. He turned on his side and failed to go to sleep.

But the horrors of the night were not yet over. Having discovered the remarkable effects of implied madness on a genuine poisoner, who must, to Yapp's way of thinking, be mad, he was determined to continue the treatment. Presently he was groping in his trouser pocket for one of the soluble pessaries the prison doctor had prescribed and Yapp had not used. For a moment he hesitated. Soluble pessaries were not to be eaten lightly but they were infinitely preferable to some deadly potion Watford was likely to add to his diet. With a resolution that stemmed in part from his ascetic background, Yapp put the pessary in his mouth and began to munch loudly. In the other bed Watford stirred.

'Here,' he muttered, 'what are you doing?'

'Eating,' said Yapp through a mouthful of gelatine and colonic lubricant.

'What the hell have you got to eat at this time of night?' asked Watford for whom the subject of ingestion was of perennial interest.

'You can have one,' said Yapp. 'Where is your hand?'

But Mr Watford knew better. 'You can put it on the stool.'

Watford took it cautiously.

'What on earth is it?' he asked after fingering the thing and failing to identify it.

'If you don't want it I'll have it back,' said Yapp. Watford hesitated. He was fond of eating things, but the experience of his victims suggested caution and the shape and texture of the pessary weren't exactly inviting.

'I think I'll keep it for the morning, thank you very much.'

'Oh no you don't,' foamed Yapp, 'either you eat it now or I'll have it back. I'm not wasting them. I've only two left.'

Watford put the pessary hurriedly back on the stool. 'I'd still like to know what they are,' he said. Yapp grabbed the thing and made bubbling noises.

'Dwarf's balls,' he mouthed. For a few seconds there was no sound from Watford as he fought to keep his supper down and then with a sickening yell he was out of bed and battering on the cell door with the wooden stool. As the other prisoners on the landing joined in the din, Yapp spat the remains of his munched pessary into the toilet, rinsed his mouth out and pulled the chain. He was lying peacefully in bed when the door opened and Watford hurled himself at the warders. This time he gave no explanation but, to ensure he was transferred to the safety of the punishment block, hit one warder over the head with the stool and bit the other.

Yapp's conversion to the *Realpolitik* of prison life had begun. It continued next morning. Summoned before the Governor to explain his part in turning the Bournemouth poisoner from a detested prisoner into a demented one, he gave it as his considered opinion that Watford's illness, manifesting itself as it had done prior to his sojourn in Drampoole Prison in the covert and libidinously oriented attempt to surrogate to himself the paternal role vis-à-vis his mother by chemically eliminating the pseudo-persons of his father, had been environmentally aggravated to terminal paranoid-schizophrenia by prolonged incarceration and the absence of normal socio-sexual relationships.

'Really?' muttered the Governor, desperately struggling to preserve his authority in the face of this socio-jargonic onslaught. Yapp delivered several more extended opinions on the subject of indefinite imprisonment and the cabbage *Gestalt* before the Governor put his foot down and had him taken back to his cell.

'Good God Almighty,' he muttered to the Deputy Governor, 'if I hadn't heard that with my own ears I wouldn't have believed it.'

'And having heard it with mine, I don't,' said the Deputy who had served in Northern Ireland and knew bullshit when it came his way. 'Look at the brute's background. He's a political fanatic and a typical H-block troublemaker and before you can say Stormont he'll have every other murderer in High Security smearing faeces all over the walls and demanding terrorist status.'

'But this used to be such a nice quiet little prison,' sighed the Governor looking sadly at a signed portrait of Pierrepoint he kept on his desk to remind him of happier days. 'Anyway, we know what broke that ghastly little poisoner. Just imagine being locked in a cell with a man with a vocabulary like that.'

Two days later the Governor made an urgent recommendation to the Home Office asking for Professor Yapp's transfer to a Grade One Prison for First Term Offenders from the Professional and Educated Classes.

twenty-six

But it was elsewhere that Yapp's future was being most profoundly decided. Emmelia's first attack was made in the village of Mapperly where a diminutive Miss Ottram worked in the Post Office. The place was twenty miles from Buscott and Emmelia had reconnoitred it several times to discover her victim's routine. Miss Ottram left home at one end of the village at a quarter past eight every morning, walked to the Post Office at the other end, spent the day behind the counter and walked home again at five, presumably, as her letter to Frederick suggested, to tend her bottle garden. On the night of the attack Miss Ottram's bottle garden went untended. As she was walking in a dark area between two street lamps a car door opened and a husky voice asked her the way to a house called Little Burn.

'I don't know anywhere called that,' said Miss Ottram, 'not round here.'

There was a rustle of paper in the car. 'It's on the Pyvil road,' said the voice. 'Perhaps you could find Pyvil on my map.'

Miss Ottram said she could and moved closer. A moment later a blanket had been thrown over her head and she was bundled into the car.

'Stop making that noise or I'll use the knife on you,' said the voice as Miss Ottram's muffled screams came from under the blanket. The screams stopped and her hands were manacled behind her back. The car then drove off, only to stop a mile further on. In the darkness Miss Ottram felt hands clasp her and then the voice spoke again.

'Damn,' it said, 'too much traffic.' And Miss Ottram was thrust out into the road still covered in the blanket while the car drove away at high speed. Half an hour later Miss Ottram was discovered by a passing motorist and taken to Briskerton police station where she told her terrible story with more graphic and inaccurate detail than it actually deserved.

'He said he was going to rape you?' asked Inspector Garnet.

Miss Ottram nodded. 'He said if I didn't do what he told me he'd use the knife on me and then he handcuffed my hands behind my back.'

The Inspector looked at the shackles the Fire Brigade had taken some considerable time to cut off. They were extremely strong and since they required the use of a key to lock them it was impossible that Miss Ottram had put them on herself.

'I didn't like the sound of that knife threat,' said the Sergeant when she had finally been allowed to go home in a police car. 'Puts me in mind of that murder we had ...'

'I'm aware of that,' said the Inspector irritably, 'but that Professor bastard's inside. I'm more interested in this blanket.'

They looked at the blanket carefully. 'Cats' hairs. An expensive blanket with cats' hairs. That tells us something. We'll have to see if Forensic can come up with any other detail indicators.'

The Inspector went home and spent a troubled night.

At the New House Emmelia had difficulty getting to sleep too. It had been one thing to plan to molest dwarves but another thing altogether to put it into practice and she was worried about Miss Ottram. With the blanket over her head she might have been run over. Then again she had certainly been terrified. Emmelia weighed her terror against the life sentence passed on Yapp and tried to console herself that Miss Ottram's horrible experience was partially justified.

'After all, life in Mapperly must be very dull,' she told herself, 'and silly women who answer Lonely Hearts advertisements are asking for trouble. Anyway she'll have something to talk about for the rest of her life.'

Nevertheless when she struck again three nights later it was at a more mature and divorced dwarf called Mrs May Fossen who lived in a council house on the outskirts of Briskerton. Mrs Fossen was just putting her chihuahua out for its nocturnal pee when she was confronted by a masked figure wearing an overcoat from which protruded the biggest you-know-what she'd ever seen in her life.

'It was gigantic,' she told Inspector Garnet, 'I wouldn't have believed it possible to have such a big one. I don't know what would have happened to me if I hadn't had the presence of mind to slam the door in his face.'

'And you say he was wearing a mask?' said the Inspector, preferring not to speculate on the probable consequences of an enormous you-know-what being inserted into the person of even a divorced dwarf.

'Yes, a horrible black shiny thing but it was the you-know ...'

'Quite so. You were very sensible to slam the door and bolt it. Very sensible indeed. Now have you any recollection of seeing this knife?'

He produced a large carving knife which had been found in the garden. Mrs Fossen shook her head.

'Then we won't keep you any longer. Two constables will drive you home and we'll keep a guard on your house until this maniac is apprehended.'

That night Emmelia had no trouble getting to sleep. She had achieved her object without having to resort to physical force and the carving knife must be giving the police something to think about.

In this she was right. Next morning Inspector Garnet held a briefing session.

'We've established three important facts about the man we're looking for. Forensic have identified the cats that have slept on the blanket used in Miss Ottram's case. Siamese, Burmese, a lot of tabbies and at least one Persian. Next the knife. It's old and well-worn and has traces of dandelion root on it. Finally there are these handcuffs. Obviously they're handmade and purpose-built by a craftsman in metalwork. Now if any of you can come up with information that will lead us to a cat-fancier and health-food addict who dabbles in ironwork in his spare time, we should be able to wrap this case up.'

'I suppose it's too much to ask if there were any fingerprints?' said the Sergeant.

'Only smudges. Anyway he'd have to be an idiot to go out on a job without gloves in these enlightened days.'

'Only a raving lunatic would go around trying to rape dwarves,' said the Sergeant, 'especially with a penis the size of a small tree-trunk the way that Mrs Fossen described it.'

Inspector Garnet looked at him pityingly. 'I shouldn't take too much notice of what she says. I mean anyone her stature is going to find a normal penis enormous. It's all a question of relativity and perspective. If you were knee-high to a Dachshund you'd think a pencil was a whopper.'

For several days the police visited local catteries, took the names of customers of two health-food shops and interviewed them, and grilled the employees of several wrought-iron works. Their investigations led them nowhere and forced Emmelia to act with the ferocious desperation she had hoped to avoid.

Her victim this time was a Miss Consuelo Smith, whose reply to Frederick's advert suggested she was a dwarf of easy virtue. It had not mentioned that she was also a Black Belt dwarf. It was left to Emmelia to discover this disconcerting fact when, having phoned Miss Smith and pretended to be the Gentleman of Restricted Growth of the agony column, they met at a rendezvous outside the Memorial Hall in Lower Busby. As the second-hand Ford drew alongside and Emmelia opened the door Miss Smith hopped nimbly into the seat before realizing she had evidently entered the wrong car.

'Here, where do you think you're going?' she shouted as Emmelia accelerated. 'You're not a fucking dwarf. You're a ruddy norm.'

'Yes, dear,' said Emmelia hoarsely, finding some difficulty in accepting the term, 'but I'm very fond of little people.'

'Well, I'm buggered if I'm going to have a colossus fondling me, so stop the car,' screamed Miss Consuelo. Emmelia groped for her knife.

'You'll do what I say or I'll stick you like I did the other one,' she said and was promptly proved wrong. With one hand Miss Consuelo chopped the knife onto the car floor and with the other delivered a rabbit punch to Emmelia's Adam's Apple which left her speechless and gasping for breath. As she struggled to control the car Miss Consuelo employed more drastic tactics and tried to get her hands on her abductor's scrotum. Instead she hit the dildo. Unlike Mrs Fossen, Consuelo was not awed by its size. On the contrary she considered it a distinct advantage and with all the experience of a truly demi-mondaine hurled herself at it and sank her teeth into the thing. To her consternation Emmelia did not scream in agony but pulled the car into the side of the road.

'All right, you can get out now,' she said finally finding her voice but Consuelo hung on with a tenacity that sprang from a new fear. A man who could speak with even comparative calm while having his glans penis bitten to the quick was either a masochist to end all masochists or a creature of such phenomenal self-control that she was taking no chances. For a fraction of a second she opened her mouth and then bit again even harder. But Emmelia had had enough. Leaning over, she opened the side door and hurled Consuelo out into the ditch, slammed the door shut and drove off.

Consuelo sat in the ditch and stared after the retreating tail lights before realizing that she still had something in her mouth. With a natural revulsion she spat it out and gave vent to her feelings.

Ten minutes later, in a state of hysterical horror at what she had done, she stumbled across the threshold of the policeman's house at Lower Busby and presently was washing her mouth out with neat disinfectant while trying at intervals to explain what had happened.

'You mean to say you bit the top of the bastard's prick off and he didn't even squeak?' said the Constable and promptly developed what amounted to lockjaw of the thighs.

'What do you think I keep telling you?' mumbled Consuelo.

'But what was it doing there in the first place. You say this man picked you up and tried to assault you –'

'I didn't give the sod a chance,' spluttered Consuelo, 'I chopped him one across the gizzard and then because he had this erection I bit the beastly thing and the top bit was still there when I fought my way out of the car.'

'Still where?'

'Between my teeth, stupid.' Consuelo washed her mouth out again. 'I spat it out and ran here.'

The policeman blanched and crossed his legs still tighter. 'Well, all I can say is that there's some poor bugger out there who must be wishing to hell he hadn't met up with you. Must be bleeding to death by now. It doesn't bear thinking about.'

Consuelo Smith bridled. 'I like that,' she said bitterly. 'Talk about a man's fucking world and a norm's at that. I bet if I'd been raped and murdered you wouldn't feel so sorry for me. But just because I bit –'

'All right, all right. I agree. It's just that ...'

'It happened to be a male norm,' continued Consuelo only to be confounded later when Inspector Garnet arrived with a search party and discovered the tip of the dildo.

'Fuck me,' he said angrily staring down at the thing. 'Just when it seemed certain the swine couldn't strike again and all we'd got to do was to go round the hospitals and pick up the first bloke without the end of his prick, what do we find? An artificial one. And what does that tell us?'

'That the bastard knew his onions when dealing with that human rat-trap,' said the Constable, who was still having difficulty walking properly.

'Balls,' said the Inspector adding to the Constable's trauma. 'It doesn't need a shrink to tell us that our man is impotent and so sexually inadequate he can't cope with a proper woman.'

'I wouldn't put it that way in front of Consuelo. She doesn't take kindly to –'

It was the Inspector's turn to squirm. 'Kindly?' he shouted. 'Having seen what she can do to a cross between a radial tyre and a penis I wouldn't dream of putting my private parts anywhere near the bitch.'

'I didn't mean that. I mean about her not being a proper woman. She's a Dwarf Libber. She talks about male norms.'

'She can talk about them till she's blue in the face but what she's done to this thing's not normal, not by a long chalk.'

They went back to the station and confronted Consuelo with the new evidence.

'You needn't worry, Miss Smith,' said the Inspector, 'you can't possibly have contracted syphilis ...'

But Consuelo wasn't listening. Her attention was fixed on the plastic glans penis. 'I knew there was something strange,' she said. 'No wonder it didn't scream blue murder.'

'"It" being the operative word,' said the Inspector. 'We're evidently dealing with a sexual psychopath who can't get it up and –'

'Rubbish,' interrupted Consuelo, 'you're dealing with a woman.'

Inspector Garnet smiled sympathetically 'Of course we are, Miss Smith. And a woman of considerable spirit too, if I may say so.'

'Not me, dummy. The person who attacked me was a woman. I should have known that. When she first spoke it was with a deep voice but at the end it was pitched several octaves higher.'

'That's understandable after what you'd ...'

'Bright-eyes,' said Consuelo contemptuously, 'this is a false one, remember? Which is why she didn't scream.'

The Inspector sank despondently into a chair. 'You're quite certain it was a woman.'

'Absolutely. And what's more she had a la-di-da voice like she was talking down to you.'

'Yes, well all things considered I daresay she ...' began the Inspector before being quelled by the look in her eyes. 'Right, so now all we've got to find is an upper-class Lesbian who keeps cats, has lost a carving knife and the top half of a surrogate penis, and is a dab hand at making handcuffs. There can't be many such women around.'

'She also drives a Cortina, is five foot five, weighs about 140 pounds and has a sore left wrist.'

'Thank you very much, Miss Smith. You've been extremely helpful and now a police car will take you home. If we require any further information from you –'

'Blimey,' interrupted Consuelo. 'if this is the way the fuzz works it's no bleeding wonder there's so much crime around. Don't you even want to know how it was I got into that car? You don't think I go around getting into strange cars in the middle of the night without a bloody good reason, or do you? I may not be half your size but I reckon my head's got more brains in it than you pack under your helmet.'

'I don't wear a helmet,' said the Inspector huffily, and glanced with something approaching sympathy at the gnawed dildo. 'Well, why did you?'

'Because I answered an ad in the *Gazette* for a lady and this afternoon I had a phone call.'

'For a lady? What sort of lady?'

'My sort, of course,' said Consuelo, rummaging in her handbag and extracting the cutting.

216

The Inspector read it. 'A lonely middle-aged Gentleman of Restricted Growth seeks . . . Do you usually answer advertisements of this kind?'

'Oh, practically every day,' said Consuelo. 'I mean you see them all the time, don't you? You can hardly pick up a paper these days without coming across appeals from lonely dwarves appealing for company. Use your loaf.'

'There's no need to be rude,' said the Inspector, 'we're here to help you.'

'Yes, well when I need your help I'll call the Fire Brigade,' said Consuelo gathering her things together and rising slightly, 'I may be a Person of Restricted Growth, though I prefer to be called a straightforward dwarf, but at least I don't have the disability of a restricted mentality. I leave that to you lot.'

There was a sigh of relief when she had gone. 'Anyway, she gave us some useful information,' said the Inspector. 'I want a check made on the previous victims to see if they answered that advert in the agony column too.'

'Agony column just about sums it up,' said the Sergeant, nudging the dildo tip into a plastic bag.

'And if we can find a few more desperate female dwarves we can stake out their homes and hopefully catch whatever's doing this redhanded.'

But the hope was short-lived. Consuelo Smith was already on the phone selling the exclusive rights to her story so successfully to several Fleet Street newspapers that the headlines 'BUSHAMPTON DWARFIST STRIKES AGAIN' appeared on the front pages of four national dailies next morning.

By noon Briskerton was awash with reporters imbued with a sense of righteous investigation, and Inspector Garnet had been provoked into denying that Professor Yapp had been wrongly arrested and tried for the murder of Willy Coppett.

'In that case would you mind telling us what measures the police are taking to protect other dwarves in your patch?' asked one reporter who had bribed the police telephonist into revealing that Consuelo Smith was the third dwarf to be attacked in recent days.

'No comment,' said the Inspector.

'Then you don't agree that there's any connection between these three latest attacks by the dwarfist and the previous murder of Mr Coppett?'

'Certainly not,' said the Inspector and went on to an exceedingly unpleasant interview with the Chief Constable who shared the reporter's opinion.

'But these new attacks have been made by a woman,' the Inspector said inconsequentially. 'The forensic experts have come up with corroborating evidence in the work on that blanket. They've found traces of face-powder and lipstick on it. And some dyed hair.'

'And I don't suppose it's crossed your so-called mind that the case against Professor Yapp was largely based on the evidence of Mrs Coppett. If you know what's good for your career you'll take her in for questioning before we have another confounded murder on our hands.'

Inspector Garnet left in a murderous mood himself. 'It's all your fucking fault,' he shouted at the Sergeant at the Buscott police station, 'all that guff about the bitch being half-witted and kind-hearted and devoted to her precious Willy.'

'She was. I'd swear to that.'

'Well, for your information she's so bloody fond of dwarves she butchered the sod and landed us in the crap by setting Yapp up for us. That's how half-witted she is.'

'But what about the body in the boot and the blood all over his shirt?'

'Which she conveniently left on the clothesline for us to find. And as for putting bodies in the boot of that car, has it occurred to you that if Yapp had murdered her husband he wouldn't have used his own car as a coffin for a week. He'd never have put the corpse there in the first place. But she would – to set the poor bugger up. So where is she now?'

'Up at the Petrefact New House,' said the Sergeant. 'But how come you've changed your mind?'

'I'll do the questioning, Sergeant. Number One is ... No, I'll give you the answer. Cats. Siamese, Burmese, one Persian and a lot of moggies. All snoozing their heads off on expensive blankets. Am I right?'

The Sergeant gaped at him and nodded. 'I wouldn't know the exact number but Miss Petrefact practically runs a cats' hostel.'

'Thank you. Second, dildos and custom-built handcuffs. There's a sex shop in Buscott that sells these things.'

'They make them at the Mill,' admitted the Sergeant.

The Inspector rubbed his hands. 'There you are. I knew it. She'd have no difficulty laying her hands on them.'

'Yes, but what's her motive?'

'Frustration,' said the Inspector, reverting to his original theory. 'Sexual frustration. Marries a bloody midget and she's a damned big woman with a sex drive to match. He can't give her more than an inch or two at most. Any more and she'd be giving birth backwards. So what does she do?'

'I'd prefer not to think.'

'Gets a complex about All-In Wrestlers and bulging musclemen. You saw the pictures she had in the kitchen. What more do you want? Goes off her rocker, knocks her husband off and stuffs him in the Professor's car and when he's been done for the murder she starts taking her frustrations out on dwarfesses. You see if I'm not right.'

'Sounds barmy to me,' said the Sergeant.

'Which is exactly what she is. So now you go up to Miss Petrefact's house and pull her in nice and quietly so that nobody notices and we'll take her over to Briskerton just as nice and quietly and Mrs Rosie Fucking Coppett is going to make a confession even if we have to work on her round the clock for a week.'

'I don't know about the nice and quietly,' said the Sergeant, 'Miss Petrefact is bound to find out and if I know her she'll raise the roof. The Petrefacts just about own this town and her cousin's a judge. You'll have solicitors breathing down your neck with writs for *habeas corpus* before you can say ...'

'Nice and quietly,' said the Inspector, 'and nice and quietly is what I meant.'

In the event there was no need to go to the New House. Rosie Coppett was spotted outside Mandrake's Pet Shop and was delighted to be asked to go for a ride in the police car. By six o'clock that evening she was supposedly helping the police with their enquiries.

twenty-seven

In any case Emmelia was in no condition to raise the roof. Consuelo Smith's karate chop to her Adam's Apple had left her speechless. When Annie brought her her tea next morning Emmelia had written, 'I have acute laryngitis and am on no account to be disturbed.' As usual Annie had obeyed her instructions to the letter and for five days Emmelia was not disturbed. She lay in bed, had clear soup for lunch, vegetable soup plus semolina pudding for dinner, and wondered if she would ever get her voice back. But at least the papers seemed to indicate that the police had reopened the case of Willy Coppett. The Chief Constable had made a statement that there had been new developments and that charges would soon be brought. Which was all very gratifying, but when on the sixth day Emmelia got up and learnt that Rosie had disappeared she was distinctly alarmed.

'You should have told me at once,' she said in a hoarse whisper to Annie.

'But you was too ill and did say you weren't to be disturbed,' said Annie. 'Anyway she was flighty, that's what she was. Always wanting romance and all that.'

'And she'd gone down to collect the bread and never came back? On the day after ... on the day I was taken ill?'

'Yes, mum. I sent her down with the list and she never came back. I had to go down myself. Flighty's what I say.'

But Emmelia put another construction on Rosie's disappearance. Perhaps the stupid girl had seen her come back from her encounter with that confoundedly powerful dwarf and for once in her silly life had put two and two together and had come up with more than three. In which case ...

'Then you had better go down and tell the police that she is missing,' she said.

'I've done that, mum. I saw the Sergeant and told him but he just mumbled something.'

'Then go down again and inform them officially,' said Emmelia and spent the hour while Annie was away wiping thoroughly with a duster everything in the car Consuelo might have touched and then using the vacuum cleaner. She had finished and had consigned the mutilated dildo to the fire in the drawing-room when she was

220

further alarmed to see Annie return in a police car with Inspector Garnet. With a racing pulse Emmelia went into the downstairs lavatory for several minutes to compose herself. When she emerged she had adopted her most arrogant manner.

'And about time too,' she told the Inspector, 'Rosie has been gone for almost a week and my housekeeper informed you while I was ill in bed. Now, what do you want to know?'

Inspector Garnet cringed under the crack of her voice. His standing with the Chief Constable was hardly high and he had no intention of lowering it still further by rubbing this influential old lady up the wrong way.

'We're interested in knowing if she ever borrowed your car, ma'am.'

'Borrowed my car? Most certainly not. I do not make a habit of lending my car to my servants and in any case I very much doubt if Rosie Coppett can drive.'

'All the same, might it not have been possible for her to have used it without your knowing?'

Emmelia pondered the question and found it puzzling. 'I suppose so,' she said finally, 'though I consider your line of enquiry most peculiar. If she was going to use it to go away I can't for the life of me imagine why she should have brought it back again. To the best of my knowledge it is still in the stables.'

'There's no knowing the way some people's minds work,' said the Inspector. 'Irrational, you know. Would you object if we checked the vehicle out for fingerprints?'

Emmelia hesitated. She objected very much but on the other hand she had just cleaned it and to refuse would be to arouse suspicion.

'You know your duty, officer. If you require anything else please say so.'

'We would like to examine her room too.'

Emmelia nodded and went into the conservatory where she over-watered the geraniums and half a dozen cacti in her agitation.

In the garage the fingerprint men were drawing conclusions from the state of the Ford.

'Not a bloody dab anywhere,' said the detective sergeant. 'And if that doesn't prove anything and in my experience it's suggestive, take a look at this.'

The Inspector examined the front bumper. It was bent and some dried mud had stuck to it. 'A hundred to one we'll find it matches the clay in the lane where the glans dildo was discovered. So much for her claim she doesn't drive.'

The Inspector sighed wearily. It was just another of those points on which his theory foundered but the Chief Constable was urging him on and the press had already raised the issue of his competence.

'I'm going up to her room,' he said and went through to the kitchen where Annie was peeling potatoes. Half an hour later he was back in the stables.

'That just about wraps it up,' he said cheerfully, tapping his notebook. 'The housekeeper's given us all we need. There's no point in aggravating the old bird until we've put our Rosie through a few more hoops.'

But as the police car drove down the drive Emmelia was already profoundly aggravated.

'You did what?' she demanded of a white-faced but defiant Annie.

'Told them she went out in the car last Wednesday night and the Friday before.'

Emmelia stared at her lividly. 'But she didn't. I did You must have known that.'

'Couldn't say, mum,' said Annie.

'You most certainly could have,' said Emmelia knocking over a hippeastrum in her agitation, 'she was sitting with you watching television. You've got her into terrible trouble.'

'She's in that already,' said Annie. 'The police think she murdered Willy. Leastways the Inspector says she did and he ought to know and now they'll think she's the dwarfist.'

'Oh no, Annie! Do you realize what you've done?'

'Yes, mum, I do,' said Annie firmly. 'It's been bad enough having her round the house all these months she's that stupid and clumsy. I wasn't going to have them know you'd been driving out of a night doing what you have to all them dwarves. I'm a respectable woman, I am, and I've got my reputation to think of. It's all very well for the likes of you to behave queer but I won't have it said I worked for the dwarfist. I'd never get another job at my age. You didn't think of that, did you?'

'No, I'm afraid I didn't,' said Emmelia contritely, 'but you surely

222

don't really believe that Rosie Coppett murdered her husband?'

'No business of mine if she did. Anyway she could have dropped him like she did the mixing bowl last Michaelmas. Ever such a mess she made. If you ask me she'll be far better off in prison from what I've heard tell. She'll have her own little cell and it won't matter if she does break things. Besides they'll probably put her in a home, her being the way she is.'

Emmelia shook her head sorrowfully. First Yapp and now Rosie, both foolish innocents, were being sacrificed for the sake of respectability and to prevent a scandal. 'Well, I think it's outrageous,' she said, 'and I refuse to have Rosie wrongfully accused. I'd rather go to the police myself.'

But Annie was still defiant. 'Wouldn't do you any good if you did. I'll swear you didn't go out and they'll think you're dotty. And you being a Petrefact they wouldn't believe you.'

It was true. No one would believe her.

'Oh well, perhaps they won't find Rosie,' Emmelia said rather hopelessly. Rosie Coppett was hardly equipped to escape a police search.

'Found her on Thursday,' said Annie. 'Sergeant Moster sent a message up asking where she was so I told him she was going down for the bread and would likely be passing Mandrake's and was bound to stop and look at the rabbits. That's where they got her.'

Emmelia looked at the housekeeper with revulsion. 'Then you're a very wicked woman,' she said.

'If you say so, mum,' said Annie. 'Will there be anything else?'

Emmelia shook her head. There would never be anything else. The world was set in its ways. As Annie left the room Emmelia sat on, wondering how she could have known so little of a woman who had shared the same house with her for thirty-two years. It was the old Petrefact fault of taking people for granted. And if she had misjudged Annie wasn't it possible she was wrong about Rosie and Yapp? Perhaps they *had* murdered Willy Coppett after all.

Deep in this slough of uncertainty she found herself staring across the lawn at the garden gnomes. They stood now not as monuments to Willy, or even to Rosie's childish innocence, but rather as a grotesque tableau grinning at her naivety. She was the fountain nymph they mocked, a relict of that ordered, self-deceiving world in which the poor were never with you and murder was a distant drama done by unimaginably wicked people who

223

ended inevitably upon the scaffold. But life wasn't like that and never had been. It was something else again.

Inspector Garnet would undoubtedly have agreed. For six days Rosie had stuck to her Mum's instructions to always ask a policeman when she was lost or in trouble and then do what he said. Since the policeman – in this case a number of policemen – kept telling her to confess, Rosie disconcertingly obliged. But never with the same story twice. It was here that her addiction to Confessions magazines came to her aid. She had described in lurid detail how she might have murdered Willy in so many contradictory ways without once admitting that she had that several detectives had asked to be taken off the case and the Inspector's confidence in his own judgement had taken a hammering. But now he had hard evidence. The mud on Miss Petrefact's car certainly matched that in the bank where the glans dildo had been found. It only remained to discover if Rosie could drive.

'Depends,' she said when the question was put to her.

'Depends on what?' demanded the Inspector.

'Well, I like going in cars,' said Rosie, 'the Welfare lady took me once and –'

'But have you ever been in Miss Petrefact's car?'

'Depends,' said Rosie.

Inspector Garnet gritted his teeth. Rosie's infernal use of the word to find out what he wanted to hear from her was becoming unbearable. 'Then you have been in it?'

'Yes.'

'Where?'

'In the garage.'

'In what garage?'

'Miss Petrefact's.'

'And where did you go after that?'

'After what?' asked Rosie whose span of attention, minimal at the best of times, had been considerably shortened by lack of sleep and too many cups of black coffee. Inspector Garnet no longer gritted his teeth, he ground them.

'After you'd been in the car in the garage?'

'Depends,' said Rosie, falling back on equivocation.

It was too much for the Inspector. Something snapped inside his head. 'Fucking hell,' he spluttered stumbling from the room and spitting out the remains of his upper dentures, 'now look what the'th done with that fucking "dependth" of herth.'

'You could always try Super Glue,' said the Sergeant incautiously, 'they claim it mends anything.'

The Inspector goggled at him lividly. 'That'th all I need,' he shouted, 'to thpend the retht of my life with falthe teeth thtuck to the top of my fucking mouth. And the nextht time anyone round here utheth a word which endth in E-N-D I'll have his gutth for garterth.'

The phone rang and without thinking he picked it up. It was the Chief Constable.

'Making any progress?' he enquired. 'I've just had a call from the Home Office and ...'

The Inspector held the phone away from his ear and looked at it. In his present condition he was in no fit state to hear what the Home Office wanted. By the time he put it back the Chief Constable was asking if he was still there.

'Only jutht,' said the Inspector.

'Only what? You sound as though you've got a cleft palate.'

'Ath a matter of fact I have broken my dentureth.'

'Extraordinary,' said the Chief Constable unsympathetically. 'Anyway, to get back to the case, has the Coppett woman confessed yet?'

'No,' said the Inspector, deciding to avoid a complicated explanation which would also involve the use of a great many sibilants.

'In that case you'll have to move quickly. I've already had an extremely irate Miss Petrefact on the line. She's instructing her solicitor to apply for an immediate writ of *habeas corpus* and if you can't break the wretched woman there's going to be the most appalling uproar in the media.'

'Thit!' said the Inspector. 'I'll do what I can.'

For the next quarter of an hour he was extremely active. On the one hand he purloined some Blu Tack from the police typing pool and managed to get his teeth back into his mouth in a makeshift and uncomfortable fashion while on the other he wrestled with the question of whether or not Rosie could drive.

'There's only one way to tell,' he mumbled to himself finally with an intelligence born of desperation. He picked up the phone and called the Chief Constable again.

'I'd like you to be present when we do a test,' he explained. 'It would be helpful and possibly conclusive. We'll be over in twenty minutes.' And before the Chief Constable could ask any awkward questions he rang off.

Twenty minutes later the Chief Constable could see exactly what the Inspector had meant about the test being conclusive.

'If you seriously imagine I'm going to get into that car and allow myself to be driven by a demented murderess down Cliffhanger Hill you must be demented yourself.'

'Yes, sir,' said the Inspector. 'On the other hand it's the only way I can think of which will tell us whether she can drive or not. If she is the dwarfist she must be able to drive and if she can't drive she can't possible be the dwarfist and we've got hard evidence that Miss Petrefact's car was used in the attacks. Now I may be a dumb copper but I'm not a bent one –'

'If she can't drive and you let her loose down Cliffhanger Hill you soon will be,' said the Chief Constable. The Inspector ignored the remark.

'I am not going to arrest a witless woman and charge her with a crime she can't have committed.'

'But isn't there some other way of finding out? You've checked she hasn't got a driving licence?'

The Inspector nodded.

'Then you've no right to let her drive on a public road,' said the Chief Constable.

The Inspector adjusted his teeth more firmly against the Blu Tack. 'If you won't allow me to conduct this test, I'll have to take Miss Petrefact in for questioning,' he said. 'That's the alternative.'

'Miss Petrefact? Good God, man, do you know what you're saying? You can't possibly suspect . . .'

'I can and I do,' interrupted the Inspector. 'As I've said we know for certain that the dwarfist's car belongs to her. The cats' fur on the blanket used on Miss Ottram has been identified as corresponding to her menagerie, and the gnawed dildo was made at the Petrefact Mill in Buscott. Finally, Miss Consuelo Smith said that her attacker had a la-di-da voice. Add that little lot up and it doesn't come out anywhere near to Rosie Coppett.'

'What about the housekeeper?'

Inspector Garnet smiled nastily. 'She's the one who may have given the game away. She told us that Rosie went out on the nights the attacks took place.'

'Well, what's wrong with that?'

'Nothing at all, sir ... if Rosie can drive. If she can't ...'

'But the housekeeper might have been the dwarfist herself.'

'Too small. She doesn't stand five foot two in her shoes and as for weighing 140 pounds ...'

'Christ,' said the Chief Constable and moved unhappily towards the car. They drove out to the top of Cliffhanger Hill.

'Now then, Rosie,' said the Inspector getting out of the driving seat, 'you see that nice hill in front of you. I want you to show us how well you can drive. Now if you'll just move over and take the wheel I'll sit here beside you and ...'

'But I can't drive,' said Rosie tearfully, 'I never said I could.'

'In that case you've got to the bottom of the hill to learn.'

'Shit,' said the Chief Constable uncharacteristically as Rosie was pushed across the seat behind the steering wheel. The Inspector climbed in beside her and fastened his safety belt.

'Now you go right ahead,' he said, ignoring the bewildered look on Rosie's face. 'The gears are the normal H and the handbrake is beside you.'

'But how do I start it?' asked Rosie.

'You turn that key.'

'Dear God,' said the Chief Constable and tried to open the back door but Rosie had turned the key. To her surprise the engine did start.

'Now the handbrake,' said the Inspector, determined to bring home to the Chief Constable the sheer lunacy of supposing that Rosie Coppett was the dwarfist and encouraged by the scrabbling noises in the back. But before he could enjoy the situation to the full the car had begun to move and was gathering momentum down the hill.

'Put the fucking thing in gear,' he yelled but Rosie was deaf to instruction. Gripping the wheel catatonically and bracing her feet against the clutch and the accelerator simultaneously, she was staring fixedly ahead. For the first time in her life she was unable to do what a policeman said, even if she could have heard him above the scream of the engine at full throttle. Behind her the Chief Constable had stopped scrabbling. As they hurtled past a sign which predicted a gradient of 1 in 6 and recommended all vehicles to engage low gear, he needed no further persuasion that Rosie couldn't possibly drive. At what he estimated to be ninety miles an hour, the car was on a fixed course for the front of a petrol tanker lumbering up the hill.

'Rock of Ages cleft for me,' he began in place of a prayer and shut his eyes. When he opened them again it was to see the Inspector, hampered by what in other circumstances might have been properly called a safety belt, trying frantically to drag the wheel from Rosie's grasp while at the same time doing his damnedest to get his right foot across onto the brake pedal, a process impeded by the gear lever in neutral. As they swerved round the wrong side of a second lorry and headed for a corner, the Inspector took his courage in both hands. More precisely, he took the gear lever, dementedly rammed it into reverse and promptly kicked Rosie's foot off the clutch. For a fraction of a second the car seemed to hesitate – but only for a fraction. The next moment the gearbox, torn between its illogical instruction, the engine speed of eight thousand revs and the wheels doing ninety miles an hour, exploded. As particles of exquisitely engineered machinery sheared through the floor like shrapnel the Chief Constable had the briefest of illusions that they had hit a land-mine. Certainly the effect seemed to be the same. There was the explosion first, the shrapnel second and, now that the drive shaft had dug itself into the tarmac, the sensation of being blown skyhigh. For a long second the car floated towards the corner before slamming down on the road with a force that wrenched off the front wheels and splayed the rear ones inwards. As silence fell or, at least, the reverberations of battered metal slowly ceased, Rosie could be heard weeping.

'I told you I couldn't drive,' she wailed. The Chief Constable took his bloodhot eyes off the shock-absorber which had nudged its way through the seat beside him and watched with awed fascination one of the front wheels tour over an oncoming Volkswagen and vault the stone wall on the corner. He nodded. What Rosie Coppett had just said was undoubtedly true. She couldn't drive. No sane driving instructor would have been found dead in the same car with her. Or wouldn't have. In his present state the Chief Constable preferred the double negative. In which case she couldn't be the dwarfist.

228

He was distracted from this dread line of thought by the Inspector who had gone a naturally horrid colour and was making strange noises. For one splendid moment the Chief Constable considered the possibility that he was dying of a coronary.

'Are you all right, Inspector?' he enquired eagerly. The remark saved Inspector Garnet's life.

'No, I'm fucking not!' he exploded, spitting a piece of Blue Tack which had been making its presence known in his windpipe through the shattered windscreen. 'Now do you believe me about her not being able to drive?'

'Yes.'

'Then I have your permithion to take Mith Petrefact in for quethioning?'

'I suppose so, if you think you must, but I would advise you to get some fresh dentures first.'

twenty-eight

For the next two days, while Inspector Garnet's new dentures were being rushed through, the Petrefacts took council among themselves at Fawcett. Emmelia was driven over by Osbert and even Lord Petrefact was forced, by the threat to his own reputation, to attend. Besides, the notion that his sister was the dwarfist redeemed Yapp in his eyes.

'I told you the sod could do it,' he said to Croxley as they drove down. 'He evidently sent the bitch clean round the bend.'

'Congratulations,' said Croxley, 'this must be a proud moment for you. And they do say there's no such thing as bad publicity.'

'Shut up,' said the peer, for whom the maxim had become an anathema.

It was almost exactly the same advice Purbeck was giving Emmelia.

'If, and I very much doubt that the police will be allowed to take you into custody, but *if* they do you will say nothing. There is no obligation on your part to provide the police with verbal evidence that can be used in court against you. The Inspector, if and when he calls, will read that warning out to you. If he fails to do so he will be in breach of the law himself.'

'In short you are telling me to thorpe,' said Emmelia.

The Judge was scandalized. 'I would remind you that Mr Thorpe was an innocent man,' he said sternly.

'Whereas I am not an innocent woman. I am a foolish and ...'

'That is not for you to say,' interrupted the Judge hurriedly. 'It is for the prosecution to prove to the satisfaction of the jury.'

'Unless I plead guilty,' said Emmelia.

The family focused their horror on her. Even Lord Petrefact was seen to change colour.

'But you can't do that,' spluttered the Brigadier-General finally, 'I mean to say, think of the family ...'

'Think of Rampton. Think of hospitals for the criminally insane,' said the Judge more sinisterly.

'Think of the publicity,' whimpered Lord Petrefact.

Emmelia rounded on him. 'You should have thought of that before you hired Professor Yapp to write the family history,' she snapped. 'If you hadn't sent the poor man to Buscott he wouldn't be where he is today.'

'I find that a wholly illogical statement,' said the Judge. 'He might well have murdered someone else.'

Emmelia raised her eyes to a portrait of her mother for support and found only the impeccable boredom of a woman who had done her duty through countless interminable dinners and weekend house parties. There was no support in her dull gaze. Only the reminder that family loyalty came before personal preference. Nothing had changed; nothing would ever change. All over England people were behaving as insanely as she had done, but she had influence and could escape the consequences because of it. Innocence had no place in so divided a world.

'I am prepared to do as you say on one condition,' she said finally, 'and that is that you will use your influence ...'

'Unless you do what I have advised we will have no influence,' interrupted the Judge. 'Without our reputation for probity we have nothing. That is the very crux of the matter.'

For a moment Emmelia verged on the edge of submission – but only for a moment. As she looked up she saw the smile of triumph on Lord Petrefact's face. It was a grotesque reminder of their days of rivalry in the nursery, a childish skull that grinned. A goad.

'I wish to discuss the matter with Ronald,' she said quietly. 'Alone.'

'As you wish,' said the Judge, rising, but Lord Petrefact was of a very different opinion.

'Don't leave me alone with her,' he yelled. 'She's mad. She's insane. For God's sake ... Croxley!'

But his two cousins had already left the room and were conferring in the corridor.

'You don't think ...' began the Brigadier-General. The Judge shook his head.

'It is something I have often felt inclined to do myself, and besides, a murder in the family is not without its merits. Far better that she should be found unfit to plead and committed to Broadmoor than that we should be embarrassed by her trial as the dwarfist.'

But Emmelia was to be cheated yet again. As she rose from her seat Lord Petrefact slumped forward from the wheelchair and lay still upon the floor. For a full five minutes she stood looking down at him before sending for Croxley and the resuscitation team. By then Lord Petrefact had joined his ancestors.

It was a hesitant Inspector Garnet who arrived at the New House the following day to question Emmelia and a distinctly disturbed one who was ushered into the drawing-room. The coffin in the hall and the empty hearse outside hardly augured well for his enquiries. Nor did the presence of Judge Petrefact in the drawing-room.

'My cousin is in mourning, Inspector,' he said austerely. 'You will be good enough to state your business to me.'

The Inspector put his notebook away. 'I merely wanted to enquire if Miss Petrefact was aware that her car had been used in the commission of a series of crimes.'

The Judge looked at him malevolently. 'The answer to that question must be obvious even to you, Inspector. Had my cousin had any inkling of that supposition she would have been the first to inform you. Since she didn't, the question is irrelevant.'

As the Inspector left he was feeling distinctly irrelevant himself.

'You've got to be poor or black to get any justice in this fucking country,' he said sourly to the Sergeant.

It was a fine spring morning when Yapp was summoned from the library at Ragnell Regis prison to the Governor's office. He had been busy working on a lecture he was due to give to the Open University prisoners. It was entitled 'Causative Environmental Factors in Criminal Psychology' and had the paradoxical merit, in Yapp's opinion, of being wholly at odds with the facts. All his fellow inmates came from excellent social environments and their crimes had been motivated almost without exception by financial greed. But Yapp had long since abandoned his adoration of the facts and with them their correlate, the truth. His obstinate adherence to the latter had landed him in prison, while his survival there had depended on ludicrous invention.

In short he had resigned himself to himself as being the only certain thing in an otherwise capricious world. Not that he could be entirely sure even of himself. His lingering passion for Rosie Coppett was a salutary reminder of his own irrational impulses, but at least they were his own to cope with as best he could. To that extent prison life suited him down to the ground. He wasn't expected to be good. On the contrary, as the only murderer in Ragnell, and a psychopathic one at that, he was expected to be extremely nasty. Certainly the warders found his presence useful and it was only necessary to hint to some bloody-minded embezzler that if he didn't behave himself he'd be sharing a cell with Yapp for the fellow to obey prison rules and regulations to the letter.

As a result of this horrible reputation Yapp's lectures were well attended, prisoners handed in their essays on time, and in the recreation room he was listened to without the overt boredom he had produced in the Common-Room at Kloone. There were other benefits to prison life. It was practically non-hierarchical except in the most abstract sense (Yapp's dwarf-killing put him at the top of the criminal league) and entirely without discrimination in matters of food and accommodation. Even the wealthiest stockbrokers and extradited politicians had the same breakfasts as impecunious burglars and deviant vicars, and wore identical clothes. They all got up at the same time, followed the same routine and went to bed at the same hour. In fact Yapp's sympathies were reserved for the warders and ancillary staff, who had to go home to nagging wives, dubious suppers, financial worries and all the uncertainties of the outside world.

He had even reached the stage where he rejected the 'cabbage effect' of indefinite sentences and had come to view prison life as being the modern equivalent of the monastic vocation during the Dark Ages. It was certainly so in his own case. Secure in the knowledge that he was entirely innocent, his spiritual assurance was complete.

It was therefore with some irritation that he followed the warder to the Governor's office and stood grimly in front of his desk.

'Ah, Yapp, I've some excellent news for you,' said the Governor. 'I have here a communication from the Home Secretary in which he states that the Parole Board have decided that the time has come for your release under licence.'

'Under what?' said Yapp.

'Under licence. You will naturally have to report . . .'

'But I don't want to leave,' said Yapp. 'I've settled in here very comfortably and I do my best to help the other prisoners, and . . .'

'Which is doubtless why the Parole Board have come to their decision,' said the Governor. 'I have repeatedly emphasized in my reports that your conduct has been exemplary and for my own part I may say I shall be sorry to see you go.'

And in spite of his protests Yapp was taken back to his cell and an hour later was ushered through the prison gates clutching a small suitcase. He was accompanied by a substantial Prison Visitor in tweeds.

'Couldn't be better,' she said briskly as they walked towards the car. 'There's nothing like starting a new life on a fine day.'

'New life, my foot,' said Yapp – and for one mad moment considered returning to his old one by hitting the damned woman. But his natural ineffectuality got the better of him, and besides, his feelings for Doris were reasserting themselves. She alone had remained constant in her loyalty. At least, he supposed so, and with all the new material of her personal experience with which to programme her it might yet be possible to discern some rational pattern in the apparent chaos of events.

'I shall return to my research at Kloone,' he said and climbed into the car.

The computer was on Croxley's mind too. He had always known

233

it would supersede him and, with the accession of Frederick, it had. That the late Lord Petrefact had done his legal damnedest to prevent his son's succession had been of little moment. The family had congealed around Frederick like some immensely influential swarm about a queen and Croxley had revenged himself on his late master by disclosing the full extent of his mental instabilities. And now he was rewarded by being offered the managership of the Mill at Buscott. For a moment he had been tempted, but discretion prevailed. Whatever had happened at Buscott it had not been to Yapp's advantage, and Frederick resembled his father too closely to be trusted. Instead Croxley had used his last few days at Petrefact Consolidated to put several 'patches' into the computer. It would take some time to find them and by then he would be a rich man. It was, he felt, a fitting tribute to the deviousness of the late Lord Petrefact, and one the old devil would have appreciated.

At the New House Rosie Coppett was busy in the kitchen making pastry for a rhubarb pie. Through the window she could see Miss Emmelia among the cloches. By the back door Annie was gossiping with the milkman. Something about old Mr Jipson selling his tractor. Rosie wasn't interested. She would never be any good with mechanical things. Besides, it was a nice day, and Miss Emmelia had said she could have a rabbit in a hutch if she promised not to let it loose among the lettuces.

Vintage Stuff

Chapter 1

The arrival of Peregrine Roderick Clyde-Browne on earth was authenticated by his birth certificate. His father was named as Oscar Motley Clyde-Browne, occupation Solicitor, and his mother as Marguerite Diana, maiden name Churley. Their address was The Cones, Pinetree Lane, Virginia Water. It was also announced in *The Times* with the additional note, 'Most grateful thanks to the staff of St Barnabas' Nursing Home.'

The thanks were premature but at the time sincere. Mr and Mrs Clyde-Browne had waited a long time for a child and were about to resort to medical help when Peregrine was conceived. Mrs Clyde-Browne was then thirty-six and her husband already forty. They were therefore understandably delighted when, after a surprisingly easy labour, Peregrine weighed in at 8 lb 5 oz at 6 a.m. on 25 March 196–.

'He's a beautiful baby,' said the Sister with greater regard for Mrs Clyde-Browne's feelings than for the facts. Peregrine's beauty was of the sort usually seen after a particularly nasty car accident. 'And such a good one.'

Here she was nearer the truth. From the moment of his birth Peregrine was good. He seldom cried, ate regularly and had just the right amount of wind to reassure his parents that he was thoroughly normal. In short, for the first five years he was a model child and it was only when he continued to be a model child through his sixth, seventh, eighth and ninth years that the Clyde-Brownes had cause to wonder if Peregrine was more model than was entirely proper for a small boy.

'Behaviour: Impeccable?' said Mr Clyde-Browne, reading his school report. Peregrine went to a very expensive preparatory school as a day-boy. 'I find that a little disturbing.'

'I can't imagine why. Peregrine has always been a very good boy and I think it does us credit as his parents.'

'I suppose so, though when I was his age nobody said my behaviour was impeccable. On the contrary . . .'

'You were an extremely naughty little boy. Your mother admitted as much.'

'My mother would,' said Mr Clyde-Browne, whose feelings for his late mother were mixed. 'And I don't much like this "Tries hard" against all the subjects. I'd rather his work was impeccable and his behaviour left something to be desired.'

'Well, you can't have everything. If he misbehaved you'd call him a hooligan or vandal or something. Be grateful he tries hard at work and doesn't get into trouble.'

So for the time being Mr Clyde-Browne left it at that and Peregrine continued to be a model child. It was only after another year of impeccable behaviour and hard trying that Mr Clyde-Browne approached the headmaster for a fuller report on his son.

'I'm afraid there's no chance of his entering for a scholarship to Winchester,' said the headmaster when Mr Clyde-Browne expressed this hope. 'In fact it's extremely doubtful if he'd get into Harrow.'

'Harrow? I don't want him to go to Harrow,' said Mr Clyde-Browne, who had a conventional opinion of Old Harrovians, 'I want him to have the best possible education money can buy.'

The headmaster sighed and crossed to the window. His was a most expensive prep. school. 'The fact of the matter is, and you must appreciate that I have had some thirty years in the teaching profession, that Peregrine is an unusual boy. A most unusual boy.'

'I know that,' said Mr Clyde-Browne, 'And I also know that every report I've had says his behaviour is impeccable and that he tries hard. Now I can face facts as well as the next man. Are you suggesting he's stupid?'

The headmaster turned his back to the desk with a deprecatory gesture. 'I wouldn't go as far as to say that,' he murmured.

'Then how far would you go?'

'Perhaps "late developer" would be more accurate. The fact of the matter is that Peregrine has difficulty conceptualizing.'

'So do I, come to that,' said Mr Clyde-Browne. 'What on earth does it mean?'

'Well, as a matter of fact . . .'

'That's the third time you've prefaced a matter of no fact whatsoever by using that phrase,' said Mr Clyde-Browne in his nastiest courtroom manner. 'Now I want the truth.'

'In short, he takes everything he's told as Gospel.'

'As Gospel?'

'Literally. Absolutely literally.'

'He takes the Gospel literally?' said Mr Clyde-Browne, hoping for a chance to vent his feelings about Religious Education in a rational world.

'Not just the Gospel. Everything,' said the headmaster, who was finding the interview almost as harassing as trying to teach Peregrine. 'He seems incapable of distinguishing between a general instruction and the particular. Take the time, for instance.'

'What time?' asked Mr Clyde-Browne, with a glazed look in his eyes.

'Just time. Now if one of the teachers sets the class some work to do and adds, "Take your own time," Peregrine invariably says "Eleven o'clock." '

'Invariably says "Eleven o'clock"?'

'Or whatever the time happens to be. It could be half past nine or quarter to ten.'

'In that case he can't invariably say "Eleven o'clock",' said Mr Clyde-Growne, resorting to cross-examination to fight his way out of the confusion.

'Well, not invariably eleven o'clock,' conceded the headmaster, 'but invariably some time or other. Whatever his watch happens to tell him. That's what I mean about him taking everything literally. It makes teaching him a distinctly unnerving experience. Only the other day I told his class they'd got to pull their socks up, and Peregrine promptly did. It was exactly the same in Bible Studies. The Reverend Wilkinson said that everyone ought to turn over a new leaf. During the break Peregrine went to work on the camellias. My wife was deeply upset.'

Mr Clyde-Browne followed his glance out of the window and surveyed the stripped bushes. 'Isn't there some way of explaining

7

the difference between metaphorical or colloquial expressions and factual ones?' he asked plaintively.

'Only at the expense of a great deal of time and effort. Besides we have the other children to consider. The English language is not easily adapted to pure logic. We must just hope that Peregrine will develop quite suddenly and learn not to do exactly what he's told.'

It was a sadder but no wiser Mr Clyde-Browne who returned to The Cones. That evening, after a heated argument with his wife, whom he blamed entirely for bringing Peregrine up too dutifully, he tried to explain to his son the hazards involved in doing exactly what he was told.

'You could get into terrible trouble, you know. People are always saying things they don't really mean and if you do what they tell you, everything they tell you, you'll end up in Queer Street.'

Peregrine looked puzzled. 'Where's Queer Street, daddy?' he asked.

Mr Clyde-Browne studied the boy with a mixture of cautious curiosity and ill-concealed irritation. Now that it had been drawn to his attention, Peregrine's adherence to the literal had about it something of the same cunning Mrs Clyde-Browne displayed when confronted by facts she preferred not to discuss. He had in mind extravagant use of the housekeeping money. Perhaps Peregrine's stupidity was as deliberate as his mother's. If so, there was still hope.

'Queer Street is nowhere. It is simply an expression meaning a bad end.'

Peregrine considered this for a moment. 'How can I go there if it's nowhere?' he asked finally.

Mr Clyde-Browne closed his eyes in silent prayer. He could appreciate the plight of the teachers who had to cope with this ghastly logic every day. 'Never mind where it is,' he said, controlling his fury with some difficulty. 'What I'm saying is, that if you don't pull yourself together . . . no, forget that.' Peregrine might go into convulsions. 'If you don't learn to make a distinction between statements of fact and mere exhortations, you'll find yourself in deep wat . . . in terrible trouble. Do I make myself plain?'

'Yes, daddy,' said Peregrine, looking at Mr Clyde-Browne's face with a critical eye that belied his father's hopes. But Mr Clyde-Browne had exhausted his repertoire of clichés. 'Then get out and don't do every damned thing you're told to,' he shouted incautiously.

Over the next few days he came to learn the full horror of Peregrine's perverse obedience. From being a model child, Peregrine became a model delinquent. He refused to pass the marmalade at breakfast when he was told to; he came home from school with a black eye precisely because the headmaster had warned the boys against fighting; he shot Mrs Worksop's cat with his airgun, thanks to his mother's injunction to be sure he didn't; and to make matters worse, told Mrs Worksop by way of inverted apology that he was glad he'd shot her pussy.

'I can't think what's got into him,' Mrs Clyde-Browne complained when she discovered that far from tidying his room as she'd asked him, Peregrine had emptied the drawers onto the floor and had practically wrecked the place. 'He's never done anything like that before. It's all most peculiar. You don't think we've got a poltergeist in the house, do you?'

Mr Clyde-Browne replied with inaudible caution. He knew only too well what they had in the house, a son with the moral discernment of a micro-processor and with an uncanny flair for misapplying logic.

'Forget what I said the other day,' he snarled, dragging Peregrine from his previously overfed pet rabbit which was now starving. 'From now on you're to do what your mother and I say. I don't care what havoc you wreak at school but I'm not having this house turned into a hellhole and the neighbours' cats shot because you're told not to. Do you understand that?'

'Yes, daddy,' said Peregrine and returned to his less disturbing model behaviour.

Chapter 2

From this discovery that their son was not as other boys were, the Clyde-Brownes drew differing conclusions. Mrs Clyde-Browne stuck to her belief that Peregrine was a genius with all a genius's eccentricities, while her husband, more practically and with far less enthusiasm for the inconveniences caused by having a pubescent prodigy about the house, consulted the family doctor, then a child psychiatrist, a consultant on educational abnormalities and finally an expert in aptitude testing. Their findings were conflicting. The doctor expressed his personal sympathy; the psychiatrist cast some unpleasant aspersions on the Clyde-Brownes' sexual life, such as it was: and the educational consultant, a follower of Ivan Illich, found fault with Peregrine's schooling for placing any emphasis at all on learning. Only the expert in aptitude testing had the practical advice Mr Clyde-Browne was seeking, and gave it as his opinion that Peregrine's best future lay in the Army, where strict obedience to orders, however insane, was highly commended. With this in mind, Mr Clyde-Browne went on to arrange for Peregrine to go to any Public School that would have him.

Here again he had trouble. Mrs Clyde-Browne insisted that her little sweetie pie needed the very best tuition. Mr Clyde-Browne countered by pointing out that if the little moron was a genius, he didn't need any tuition at all. But the chief problem lay with the Public School headmasters, who evidently found Mr Clyde-Browne's desperation almost as alarming a deterrent as Peregrine's academic record. In the end, it was only thanks to a client guilty of embezzling a golf club's funds that Mr Clyde-Browne learnt about Groxbourne, and that by way of a plea in mitigation. Since Peregrine was already fifteen, Mr Clyde-Browne acted precipitately and drove up to the school during term time.

Situated in the rolling wooded hillside of South Salop, Grox-bourne was virtually unknown in academic circles. Certainly Oxford and Cambridge claimed never to have heard of it, and what little reputation it had seemed to be limited to a few agricultural training colleges.

'But you do have a good Army entry?' Mr Clyde-Browne enquired eagerly of the retiring Headmaster who was prepared to accept Peregrine for his successor to cope with.

'The War Memorial in the Chapel must speak for our record,' said the Headmaster with mournful diffidence, and led the way there. Mr Clyde-Browne surveyed the terrible list and was impressed.

'Six hundred and thirty-three in the First War and three hundred and five in the Second,' said the Headmaster, 'I think there can be few schools in the country which have contributed their all so generously. I put our record down to our excellent sports facilities. The playing fields of Waterloo and all that.'

Mr Clyde-Browne nodded. His hopes for Peregrine's future had been vitiated by experience.

'And then again, we do have a special course for the Over-active Underachiever,' continued the Headmaster. 'Major Fetherington, M.C., runs it and we've found it a great help for the more practically endowed boy whose needs are not sufficiently met on the purely scholastic side. Naturally, it's an extra, but you might find your son benefited.'

Mr Clyde-Browne agreed privately. Whatever Peregrine's needs were, he was never going to benefit from a purely scholastic education.

They passed along the Chapel cloisters to the back of the squash court and were greeted by a volley of shots. A dozen boys with rifles were lying on the ground firing at targets in a small-bore rifle range.

'Ah, Major,' said the Headmaster to a dapper man who was slapping a swagger stick against highly polished riding boots, 'I'd like to introduce Mr Clyde-Browne whose son will be joining us next term.'

'Splendid, splendid,' said the Major, switching his swagger stick to his left arm and shaking Mr Clyde-Browne's hand while managing almost at the same time to order the boys to down rifles,

11

unload, remove bolts and apply pull-throughs. 'Your boy a keen shot?'

'Very,' said Mr Clyde-Browne, remembering the incident with Mrs Worksop's cat. 'In fact, I think he's quite good.'

'Splendid. Having pulled-through, apply an oily rag.' The boys followed his instructions and oiled barrels.

'I'll leave the Major to show you round,' said the Headmaster and disappeared. Presently, when rifles had been inspected and the little column moved off to the Armoury, Mr Clyde-Browne found himself being taken on a conducted tour of the Assault Course. A high brick wall with ropes hanging down it was succeeded by a muddy ditch, more ropes suspended from trees across a gulley, a barbed-wire entanglement, a narrow tunnel half-filled with water, and finally, built on the edge of a quarry, a wooden tower from which a tight wire hawser slanted down to a stake some thirty yards away.

'Death Slide,' explained the Major, 'Put a toggle rope in water so it won't burn, loop it over the wire, grasp firmly with both hands and away you go.'

Mr Clyde-Browne peered nervously over the edge at the rocks some fifty feet below. He could see exactly why it was called a Death Slide. 'Don't you have a great many accidents?' he asked, 'I mean what happens when they hit that iron stake at the bottom?'

'Don't,' said the Major. 'Feet touch down first and they let go. Put them through parachute landing technique first. Keep knees supple and roll over on the left shoulder.'

'I see,' said Mr Clyde-Browne dubiously, and refused the Major's offer to try it himself.

'Then there's rock-climbing. We're very good there. Lead boy goes up first and fixes the guide rope and after they've had some training we can get a squad up in two minutes.'

'Amazing,' said Mr Clyde-Browne, 'And you've never had an accident?'

'Couple of broken legs once in a while but they'd get that anyway on the rugger field. In fact, I think it's fair to say that the boys taking this course are less likely to do themselves an injury than inflict some pretty nasty ones on other people.'

They went into the gym and watched a demonstration of unarmed combat. By the time it was over, Mr Clyde-Browne had made up his mind. Whatever else Groxbourne might fail to provide, it would guarantee Peregrine's entry into the Army. He returned to the Headmaster's study well content.

'Right, well I think we'll put him in Mr Glodstone's house,' said the Headmaster, as Mr Clyde-Browne took out his cheque-book, 'Marvellous with boys, Glodstone. And as for fees . . .'

'I'll pay in advance for three years.'

The Headmaster looked at him quizzically. 'You wouldn't rather wait and see if he finds our atmosphere suits him?'

But Mr Clyde-Browne was adamant. Having got Peregrine into what approximated to a Public School, he had no intention of having him expelled. 'I've added a thousand pounds for the Chapel Restoration Fund,' he said, 'I noticed you're making an appeal.'

And having written out a cheque for ten thousand pounds, he left in an ebullient mood. He had been particularly heartened to learn that the Overactive Underachiever's Course extended into the summer holidays when Major Fetherington took the group to North Wales for 'a spot of mountaineering and cross-country compass marching'.

'It will give us a chance to get away on our own,' Mr Clyde-Browne thought happily as he drove South. But this was not the argument he used to persuade his wife, who had learned from a friend that Groxbourne was the last school she'd send her son to.

'Elspeth says it's a brutal place and the boys are nearly all farmers' sons and the teaching is appalling.'

'It's either Groxbourne or the local Comprehensive.'

'But there must be other schools . . .'

'There are. A great many, but they won't take Peregrine. Now if you want your son to mix with a lot of teenage tarts at the Comprehensive, you've merely to say the word.'

Mrs Clyde-Browne didn't. It was one of her most ingrained beliefs that only the working class sent their children to Comprehensives and Peregrine must never be allowed to pick up their deplorable habits.

'It seems such a shame we can't afford a private tutor,' she whined, but Mr Clyde-Browne was not to be deflected.

'The boy has got to learn to stand on his own feet and face up to the realities of life. He won't do that by staying at home and being mollycoddled by you and some down-at-heel unemployable posing as a private tutor.' A remark which said as much for his own view of the world's awful reality as it did for his apparent conviction that Peregrine had spent the first fifteen years of his life standing on other people's two feet or perched on one of his own.

'Well, I like that,' said Mrs Clyde-Browne with some spirit.

'And I don't,' continued her husband, working himself up into a defensive fury. 'If it hadn't been for your insistence on bringing him up like a china doll, he wouldn't be the idiot he is now. But no, it had to be "Peregrine do this and Peregrine do that" and "Don't get your clothes dirty, Peregrine." Come to think of it, it's a wonder the boy has half a mind to call his own.'

In this he was being unfair. Peregrine's peculiarities owed as much of their bias to his father as to his mother. Mr Clyde-Browne's career as a solicitor with court experience disposed him to divide the world up into the entirely innocent and the wholly guilty, with no states of uncertainty in between. Peregrine had imbibed his rigid ideas of good and bad from his father and had had them reinforced by his mother. Mrs Clyde-Browne's social pretensions and her refusal to think the worst of anyone in their circle of acquaintances, all of whom must be nice because the Clyde-Brownes knew them, had limited the range of the entirely good to Virginia Water and the entirely bad to everywhere else. Television had done nothing to broaden his outlook. His parents had so severely censored his viewing to programmes that showed cowboys and policeman in the best light, while Redskins and suspects were shown in the worst, that Peregrine had been spared any uncertainties or moral doubts. To be brave, truthful, honest and ready to kill anyone who wasn't was to be good: to be anything less was to be bad.

It was with these impeccable prejudices that he was driven up to Groxbourne and handed over to Mr Glodstone by his parents who showed truly British stoicism in parting with their son. In Mr Clyde-Browne's case there was no need for self-control, but his wife's feelings expressed themselves as soon as they had left the school grounds. She had been particularly perturbed by the housemaster.

14

'Mr Glodstone looked such a peculiar man,' she whimpered through her tears.

'Yes,' said Mr Clyde-Browne brusquely and refrained from pointing out that any man prepared to spend his life trying to combine the duties of a zoo-keeper, a prison warder and a teacher to half-wits could hardly be expected to look normal.

'I mean, why was he wearing a monocle in front of a glass eye?'

'Probably to save himself from seeing too clearly with the other one,' said Mr Clyde-Browne enigmatically and left her to puzzle over the remark until they got home.

'I just hope Peregrine is going to be happy,' she said as they turned into Pinetree Lane. 'If he isn't, I want you to promise me . . .'

'He'll go to the Comprehensive school,' said Mr Clyde-Browne, and put an end to the discussion.

Chapter 3

But Mrs Clyde-Browne's fears were groundless. Peregrine was perfectly happy. Unlike more sensitive boys, who found the school an intimation of hell, he was in his element. This was in large measure due to his size. At fifteen, Peregrine was almost six feet tall, weighed eleven stone and, thanks to the misguided advice of a physics teacher at his prep school who had observed that even if he did a hundred press-ups every morning, he still wouldn't understand the theory of gravity, he was also immensely strong. At Groxbourne, size and strength mattered.

Founded in the latter half of the nineteenth century by a hopelessly optimistic clergyman to bring Anglo-Catholic fervour to the local farmers' sons, the school had remained so obscure and behind the times that its traditions were those of an earlier age. There was fagging and beating and a good deal of bullying. There were also prefects, the ritual of morning and evening chapel, cold showers, draughty dormitories and wholesome, if inedible, food. In short, Groxbourne maintained the routine of its founder without achieving his ambitions. For Peregrine, these abstract considerations had no meaning. It was enough that he was too hefty to bully at all safely, that the school bell chimed at regular intervals throughout the day to tell him that a lesson had ended or lunch was about to begin, and that he never had to think what he was supposed to be doing.

Best of all, his tendency to take things literally was appreciated. In any case, no master ever encouraged him to take his time. It was always, 'Now shut up and get on with it.' And Peregrine got on with it to such an extent that for the first time in his life he found himself nearer the top of the class than the bottom.

But it was on the games field that his ability to take things literally paid off. In rugby, he hurled himself into scrums with a lack of fear that won him a place in the Junior XV and the admiration of the coach, himself a Welshman and well qualified to judge murderous tactics.

'I've never seen a youngster like him,' Mr Evans told Glodstone after a match in which Peregrine had followed instructions to the letter by putting the boot in, heeling the ball out with a fury that suggested he intended taking the opposing pack's with it, and tackling a fly-half so ferociously that the fellow was carried off the field with concussion while Peregrine claimed his shorts as a trophy.

It was the same with boxing. Peregrine brought a violence to the sport that terrified his opponents and alarmed the instructor. 'When I said, "Now let's see who can shove the other bloke's teeth through his tonsils," I didn't mean belt the blighter when he's unconscious,' he protested, after Peregrine, having knocked another boy stone-cold, proceeded to hold him against the ropes with one hand while punching him repeatedly in the mouth with the other.

Even Major Fetherington was impressed. Mr Clyde-Browne's boast that his son was a keen shot proved true. Peregrine had an unerring eye. On the small-bore range his bullets so seldom missed the bull that the Major, suspecting he was missing the target with all but one, put up a large paper screen behind it and was amazed to find he was wrong. All Peregrine's bullets hit the bull. And the Assault Course held no terrors for him. He scaled the brick wall with remarkable agility, dropped cheerfully into the muddy ditch, swung across the gully, and squirmed through the waterlogged tunnel without a qualm. Only the Death Slide caused him some problems. It wasn't that he found difficulty sliding down it, clinging to a toggle rope, but that he misunderstood the Major's instruction to return to the starting point and proceeded to climb back up the wire hawser hand over hand. By the time he was halfway up and hanging forty feet above the rocks at the bottom of the quarry, the Major was no longer looking and had closed his eyes in prayer.

'Are you all right, sir?' Peregrine asked when he reached the top. The Major opened his eyes and looked at him with a mixture of relief and fury. 'Boy,' he said, 'This is supposed to be an Assault Course, not a training ground for trapeze artists and circus acrobats. Do you understand that?'

'Yes, sir,' said Peregrine.

'Then in future you will do exactly what you are told.'

'Yes, sir. But you said to return to . . .'

'I know what I said and I don't need reminding,' shouted the Major and cancelled the rest of the afternoon's training to get his pulse back to normal. Two days later, he was to regret his outburst. He returned from a five mile cross-country run in the rain to discover that Peregrine was missing.

'Did any of you boys see where he got to?' he asked the little group of exhausted overactive Underachievers when they assembled in the changing room.

'No, sir. He was with us when we reached the bottom of Leignton Gorge. You remember he asked you something.'

The Major looked out on the darkening sky — it had begun to snow — and seemed to recall Peregrine asking him if he could swim the river instead of using the bridge. Since the question had been put when the Major had just stumbled over a stone into a patch of stinging nettles, he couldn't remember his answer. He had an idea it had been abrupt.

'Oh, well, if he isn't back in half an hour, we'll have to send out a search party and notify the police,' he muttered and went up to his room to console himself over a brandy with the thought that Clyde-Browne had probably drowned in the river. Twelve hours later his hopes and fears were proved to be unfounded. The police, using Alsatians, had discovered Peregrine sheltering quite cheerfully in a barn ten miles away.

'But you definitely told me to get lost, sir,' he explained when he was brought back to the school at five in the morning.

Major Fetherington fought for words. 'But I didn't mean you . . .' he began.

'And the other day you said I was to do exactly what you told me to,' continued Peregrine.

'God help us,' said the Major.

'Yes sir,' said Peregrine, and went off with the School Sister to the Sanatorium.

But if his consistency was a pain in the neck to the Major, his popularity with the boys remained high. Not only was Peregrine never bullied, but he guaranteed the safety of other new boys who could always look to him to fight for them. And thanks to his size and his looks – his battered appearance as a baby had been aggravated by boxing — not even the most frustrated sixth former found him sexually inviting. In short, Peregrine was as prodigiously a model public schoolboy as he had previously been a model child. It was this extraordinary quality that first drew the attention of Mr Glodstone to him and shaped his destiny.

Mrs Clyde-Browne had been right in her assessment of the housemaster. Mr Glodstone was peculiar. The son of a retired Rear-Admiral of such extreme right-wing views that he had celebrated the blitz on London by holding a firework display on Guy Fawkes Night, 1940, Gerald Glodstone had lost not only the presence of his father, but that of his own left eye, thanks to the patriotic if inept efforts of a gamekeeper who had aimed a rocket at his employer and missed. With the eye went Glodstone's hopes of pursuing a naval career. Rear-Admiral Glodstone went with the police to be interned on the Isle of Man where he died two year later. The subsequent punitive death duties had left his son practically penniless. Mr Glodstone had been forced to take up teaching.

'A case of arrested development,' had been the Headmaster's verdict at the time and it had proved true. Mr Glodstone's only qualifications as a teacher, apart from the fact that his late father had been Chairman of the Board of Governors at Groxbourne, had been his ability to read, write and speak English with an upper-class accent. With the wartime shortage of schoolmasters, these had been enough. Besides, Glodstone was an enthusiastic cricketer and gave the school some social cachet by teaching fencing. He was also an excellent disciplinarian and had only to switch his monocle from his glass eye to his proper one to put the fear of God up the most unruly class. By the end of the war, he had become part of the school and too remarkable a personage to lose. Above all, he got on well with the boys in a wholesome way and shared their interests. A model railway addict, he had brought his own elaborate track and installed it in the basement of the gym where surrounded by his 'chaps' he lived out in miniature his earliest ambition without the ghastly fatalities that would evidently have resulted from its fulfilment on a larger scale.

19

It was the same with his intellectual interests. Mr Glodstone's mental age was, as far as literature was concerned, about fourteen. He never tired of reading and re-reading the classic adventure stories of his youth and in his mind's eye, forever searching for a more orthodox hero than his father on whom to model himself, found one in each old favorite. He was by turns D'Artagnan, Richard Hannay, Sherlock Holmes, The Scarlet Pimpernel (who accounted for his monocle), and Bulldog Drummond, anyone in fiction who was a courageous and romantic defender of the old, the good and the true, against the new, the wicked and the false, as he and their authors judged these things.

In psychological terms, it could be said that Mr Glodstone suffered from a chronic identity problem, which he solved by literary proxy. Here again, he shared his enthusiasms with the boys, and if his teaching of English literature was hardly calculated to get them through O-level, let alone A, it had at least the merit of being exciting and easily understood by even the dullest fifteen-year-old. Year after year, Groxbourne turned out school leavers imbued with the unshakeable belief that the world's problems, and particularly the demise of the British Empire, stemmed from a conspiracy of unwashed Bolsheviks, Jews in high finance and degenerate Black men and Germans with hooded eyelids who tapped their fingers on their knees when at all agitated. In their view, and that of Mr Glodstone, what was needed was a dedicated band of wealthy young men who were prepared to reinforce the law by 'going outside it' to the extent of bayonetting left-wing politicians in their own cellars or, in more extreme cases, tossing them into baths filled with nitric acid. That they didn't put Bulldog Drummond's remedies into practice was largely due to lack of opportunity and the need to get up at dawn to do the milking and go to bed before the criminal world was fully awake. But above all, they were saved by their own lack of imagination and later by the good sense of their wives.

Mr Glodstone was less encumbered. His imagination, growing wilder with age, could imbue the most commonplace events with arcane significance, and successive school matrons with charms they most certainly did not possess. He was only prevented from proposing to them by an exaggerated sense of his own social standing. Instead, he was sexually self-sufficient, felt guilty about his partially enacted fantasies and did his damnedest to exorcise them by taking a cold bath every morning, summer and winter. During the holidays, he visited one or other of his numerous and, in some cases, still wealthy relatives or followed, as far as changed circumstances allowed, in the footsteps of his fictional heroes.

Thus, like Richard Hannay in *Thirty-Nine Steps*, though without the incentive of a murdered man in his rooms, he took the morning train from London to Scotland and spent several exceedingly uncomfortable nights trying to sleep in the heather, before deciding he was more likely to catch pneumonia than find adventure in such a bleak and rain-sodden part of the world. The following summer he had followed Richard Chandos' route to Austria, this time on a motorcycle, in the hope of locating The Great Well at Wagensburg, only to discover Carinthia was packed with coach-loads of tourists and German holiday makers. Mr Glodstone retreated to side roads and walked forest paths in a vain attempt to invest the area with its old magic. And so, each summer, he made another pilgrimage to the setting of an adventure story and came home disappointed but with a more fanatical gleam in his eye. One day he would impose the reality of his literary world on that of the existing one. In fact, by the time Peregrine came under his care, it was extremely doubtful if the housemaster had any idea what decade he was living in. The rolling stock and carriages of his model railway suggested the nineteen-twenties with their Wagons Lits and Pullman cars which were all pulled by steam engines.

But his proudest and most dangerous possession, acquired from a dead uncle, was a 1927 Bentley, in which, until he was asked by the Headmaster to spare the school a multiple tragedy, he terrified a few favoured boys and every other road-user by hurtling at tremendous speed along narrow country lanes and through neighbouring villages.

'But it was built for speed and eats the miles,' Glodstone protested, 'You won't find a car to equal it on the road today.'

'Mercifully,' said the Headmaster, 'and it can eat as many miles as it wants out of term time, but I'm not having the School Sanatorium turned into a mass morgue as a result of your insane driving.'

'Just as you say, Headmaster,' said Glodstone and he had kept the

21

Bentley in immaculate condition, locked away in his garage, awaiting the day when it would, as he put it, come into its own.

With the arrival of Peregrine Clyde-Browne at Groxbourne, that day seemed to have come closer. Mr Glodstone had found the perfect disciple, a boy endowed with the physique, courage and mental attributes of a genuine hero. From the moment he had caught Peregrine in the school bogs beating Soskins Major to a pulp for forcing a fag to wipe his arse for him, Mr Glodstone had known that his involuntary calling had not been wasted.

But, with a discretion that came from having seen what had happened to several masters in the past who had shown too early an interest in particular boys, he demonstrated his own impartiality by speaking to the House prefects. 'I want you chaps to keep an eye on Clyde-Browne,' he told them, 'we can't have him getting too big for his boots. I've known too many fellows spoilt because they're good at games and so on. Popularity goes to their heads and they begin to think they're the cat's whiskers, what!'

For the rest of the term, Peregrine's presumed ambition to be any part of the cat's anatomy was eradicated. When he wasn't doing a thousand lines for not polishing a prefect's shoes properly he was presenting his backside to the Head of House wielding a chalked cane for talking in dormitory after Lights Out, when he hadn't been, or for taking too long in the showers. In short, Peregrine was subjected to a baptism of punishment that would have caused a normally sensitive boy to run away or have a nervous breakdown. Peregrine did neither. He endured. It simply never crossed his mind that he was being singled out for special treatment. It was only when he was accused of a singularly beastly sin against Nature by the Matron, who had found blood on his pyjama trousers, that he was forced to explain.

'It's just that I got twelve strokes yesterday and eight the day before,' he said. 'A chap can't help bleeding.'

'You mean you've had twenty strokes since Tuesday?' said the Matron, utterly appalled.

'You can count them if you like,' said Peregrine matter-of-factly. 'Though actually I had sixteen last week and they're still showing so it'll be difficult to sort them out.'

Half an hour later, after his backside had been inspected by the

Matron and the doctor, Peregrine was lying face down in bed in the San. and the Headmaster had sent for Mr Glodstone. Since he was rather more progressive than his predecessor and held strong views on corporal punishment, and had been waiting to have a row with Glodstone, the meeting was acrimonious.

'Do you realize we could be sued for damages for what's been done to that poor boy?' he demanded.

'I don't see how,' said Glodstone, lighting his pipe nonchalantly. 'Clyde-Browne hasn't complained, has he?'

'Complained? No, he hasn't. Which only goes to show how brutally you run your house. The poor boy's clearly too terrified to say anything for fear he'll get another thrashing if he does.'

Mr Glodstone blew a smoke ring. 'Is that what he says?'

'No, it isn't. It's what I say and what I mean —'

'If he doesn't say it, I don't see how you can argue that he means it,' said Mr Glodstone. 'Why don't you ask him?'

'By God, I will,' said the Headmaster, rising to the bait, 'though I'm not having him intimidated by your presence. I'll speak to him alone and you'll kindly wait here while I do.'

And leaving Mr Glodstone to browse through his personal correspondence with a curiosity the Housemaster would have found disgusting in one of his 'chaps', he marched off to the San. By the time he returned, Glodstone had put some more wood on the fire, together with two unopened envelopes for the hell of it, and the Headmaster was forced to temporize. Peregrine had refused to complain about his treatment and, in spite of the Headmaster's pleading, had said he was jolly happy in Gloddie's house and anyway, chaps ought to be beaten.

'What did I tell you?' said Glodstone, and sucked noisily on his pipe. 'Boys appreciate a firm hand. And Clyde-Browne's made of the right stuff.'

'Perhaps,' said the Headmaster morosely. 'But whatever stuff he's made of, I don't want any more of it beaten this term. It may interest you to know that his father is a leading solicitor and has paid his son's fees in advance. A man in his position could bring a court action that would bankrupt the school.'

'Just as you say, Headmaster,' said Glodstone and took his leave, while the Headmaster went back distraughtly to his depleted

23

correspondence and considered desperate measures for getting rid of the ghastly Glodstone.

Outside the study, the Housemaster knocked his pipe out into a bowl of hyacinths and returned to his rooms. There he selected one of his favourite books, *Mr Standfast* by John Buchan, and took it up to the San.

'Thought you might like something to read, old chap,' he said to the back of Peregrine's head.

'Thank you very much, sir,' said Peregrine.

'And jolly good show on your part not letting the side down,' continued Mr Glodstone. 'So when you've finished that, tell Matron and I'll bring you another.'

The literary infection of Peregrine had begun.

Chapter 4

It continued. By the time he was allowed out of the Sanatorium, Peregrine had finished all the Adventures of Richard Hannay and was well into Bulldog Drummond's. He went home for the holidays with several volumes from Glodstone's library, a letter from the Headmaster explaining that he intended to abolish corporal punishment and apologizing for Peregrine having to be beaten at all, an excellent report on his term's work and a positively glowing testimony from Mr Glodstone. Mr Clyde-Browne read the Headmaster's letter with mixed feelings and didn't show it to his wife. In his opinion there was a great deal to be said for beating Peregrine, and in any case, it seemed to suggest that the brute had at last taken it into his head not to do what he was told. Mr Clyde Browne took that as a good sign. His views of the excellent report and Glodstone's testimony were different.

'He seems to be doing extremely well at his work,' said Mrs Clyde-Browne, 'He's got an Alpha for every subject.'

'One hesitates to think what the Betas must be like,' said Mr Clyde-Browne, who was surprised to learn that any of the masters at Groxbourne knew enough Greek to use Alpha.

'And Mr Glodstone writes that he has shown remarkable character and is a credit to the House.'

'Yes,' said Mr Clyde-Browne, 'He also says Peregrine is a born leader and that's a downright lie if ever I heard one.'

'You just don't have any faith in your own son.'

Mr Clyde-Browne shook his head. 'I have every faith in him except when it comes to leading. Now if that damn fool housemaster thinks . . . oh, never mind.'

'But I do mind. I mind very much, and I'm thankful that Peregrine has at last found someone who appreciates his true gifts.'

'If that's all he does appreciate,' said Mr Clyde-Browne with rather nasty emphasis.

'And what exactly does that mean?'

'Nothing. Nothing at all.'

'It does, or you wouldn't have said it.'

'I just find the letter peculiar. And I seem to remember that you found Mr Glodstone peculiar yourself.'

Mrs Clyde-Browne bridled. ''If you're thinking what I think you're thinking, you've got a filthier mind than even I would have supposed.'

'Well, it's been known to happen,' said Mr Clyde-Browne, among whose guiltier clients there had been several seedy schoolmasters.

'Not to Peregrine,' said Mrs Clyde-Browne adamantly, and for once her husband had to agree. When next day, on the pretence of having to mow the lawn in December, he questioned Peregrine on the subject, it was clear that he took a robust attitude towards sex.

'Onanism? What's that?' he shouted above the roar of the lawn-mower.

Mr Clyde-Browne adjusted the throttle. 'Masturbation,' he whispered hoarsely, having decided that auto-eroticism would meet with the same blank look.

'Master who?' said Peregrine.

Mr Clyde-Browne dredged his mind for a word his son would understand and decided not to try 'self-abuse'. 'Wanking,' he said finally with a convulsive spasm. 'How much wanking goes on at school?'

'Oh, wanking,' Peregrine shouted as the lawn mower destroyed Mr Clyde-Browne's cover by stopping, 'well, Harrison's are a lot of wankers and Slymne's go in for brown-hatting, but in Gloddie's we –'

'Shut up,' yelled Mr Clyde-Browne, conscious that half the neighbours in Pinetree Lane were about to be privy to what went on in Gloddie's, 'I don't want to know.'

'I can't see why you asked then,' bawled Peregrine, still evidently under the impression that the lawnmower was purely incidental to the discussion. 'You asked if there was a lot of wanking and I was telling you.'

Mr Clyde-Browne dragged lividly at the mower's starting cord.

'Anyway, Gloddie's don't if that's what you're worried about,' continued Peregrine, oblivious of his father's suffering. 'And when Matron thought I'd been shafted, I told her –'

Mr Clyde-Browne wrenched the lawnmower into life again and drowned the rest of the explanation. It was only later in the garage, and after he'd warned his son that if he raised his voice above a whisper, he'd live to regret it, that Peregrine finally established his innocence. He did so in language that appalled his father.

'Where the hell did you learn the term "brown-hatter"?' he demanded.

'I don't know. Everyone uses it about Slymne's.'

'I don't use it,' said Mr Clyde-Browne. 'And what's slime got to do with it. No, don't tell me, I can guess.'

'Slymne's a shit,' said Peregrine. Mr Clyde-Browne turned the statement over in his mind and found it grammatically puzzling and distinctly crude.

'I should have thought it was bound to be,' he said finally, 'though why you have to reverse the order of things and use the indefinite article into the bargain, beats me.'

Peregrine looked bewildered. 'Well, all the other chaps think Slimey's wet and he's sucking up to the Head. He wears a bow tie.'

'Who does?'

'Mr Slymne.'

'Mr Slymne? Who the hell is Mr Slymne?'

'He's the geography master and there's always been a feud between his house and Gloddie's ever since anyone can remember.'

'I see,' said Mr Clyde-Browne vaguely. 'Anyway, I don't want you to use foul language in front of your mother. I'm not paying good money to send you to a school like Groxbourne for the privilege of having you come home swearing like a trooper.'

But at least Mr Clyde-Browne was satisfied that Mr Glodstone's extraordinary enthusiasm for his son was not obviously based on sex, though what cause it had he couldn't imagine. Peregrine appeared to be as obtuse as ever and as unlikely to fulfil the Clyde-Brownes' hopes. But he seemed to be happy and rudely healthy. Even his mother was impressed by his eagerness to go

27

back to school at the end of the holidays, and began to revise her earlier opinion of Groxbourne.

'Things must have changed with the new headmaster,' she said, and by the same process which saw no bad in her acquaintances because she knew them, she now conferred some distinction on Groxbourne because Peregrine went there. Even Mr Clyde-Browne was relatively satisfied. As he had predicted, Peregrine stayed on in the summer holidays and allowed his parents to have an unencumbered holiday by going on Major Fetherington's Fieldcraft and Survival Course in Wales. And at the end of each term, Peregrine's report suggested that he was doing very well. Only in Geography was he found to be wanting, and Peregrine blamed that on Mr Slymne. 'He's got it in for everyone in Gloddie's,' he told his father, 'you can ask anyone.'

'I don't need to. If you will insist on calling the wretched man Slimey, you deserve what you get. Anyway, I can't see how you can be doing so well in class and fail O-levels at the same time.'

'Gloddie says O-levels don't matter. It's what you do afterwards.'

'Then Mr Glodstone's notion of reality must be sadly wanting,' said Mr Clyde-Browne. 'Without qualifications you won't do anything afterwards.'

'Oh, I don't know,' said Peregrine, 'I'm in the First Eleven and the First Fifteen and Gloddie says if you're good at sports –'

'To hell with what Mr Glodstone says,' said Mr Clyde-Browne, and dropped the subject.

His feelings for Glodstone were but a faint echo of those held by Mr Slymne. He loathed Glodstone. Ever since he had first come to Groxbourne some fifteen years before, Slymne had loathed him. It was a natural loathing. Mr Slymne had, in his youth, been a sensitive man and to be christened 'Slimey' in his first week at the school by a one-eyed buffoon with a monocle who professed openly that a beaten boy was a better boy had, to put it mildly, rankled. Mr Slymne's view on punishment had been humane and sensible. Glodstone and Groxbourne had changed all that. In a desperate attempt to gain some respect and to deter his classes from calling him Slimey to his face, he had devised punishments that didn't include beating. They ranged from running ten times to the school gates and back, a total distance of some five miles, to learning Wordsworth's *Prelude* off by heart and, in extreme cases, missing games. It was this last method that brought things to a head. Groxbourne might not be noted for its academic standards but rugby and cricket were another matter, and when boys who were fast bowlers or full-backs complained that they couldn't play in school matches because Mr Slymne had put them on punishment, the other masters turned on him.

'But I can't have my authority undermined by being called nicknames to my face,' Slymne complained at a staff meeting convened after he had put six boys in the First Eleven on punishment two days before the Bloxham match.

'And I'm damned if I'm going to field a side consisting of more than half the Second Eleven,' protested the infuriated cricket coach, Mr Doran. 'As it is, Bloxham is going to wipe the floor with us. I've lost more practice time in the nets this term than any summer since we had the mumps epidemic in 1952, and then we were in quarantine and couldn't play other schools, so it didn't matter. Why can't you beat boys like any decent master?'

'I resent that,' said Mr Slymne. 'What has decency to do with beating –'

The Headmaster intervened. 'What you don't seem to understand, Mr Slymne, is that it is one of the occupational facts of teaching life to be given a nickname. I happen to know that mine is Bruin, because my name is Bear.'

'I daresay,' said Mr Slymne, 'But Bruin's a pleasant name and doesn't undermine your authority. Slimey does.'

'And do you think I like being called the Orangoutang?' demanded Mr Doran, 'Any more than Glodstone here enjoys Cyclops or Matron's flattered by being known as Miss World 1914?'

'No,' said Mr Slymne, 'I don't suppose you do, but you don't get called Orangoutang to your face.'

'Precisely,' said Mr Glodstone. 'Any boy foolish enough to call me Cyclops knows he's going to get thrashed so he doesn't.'

'I think beating is barbaric,' maintained Mr Slymne, 'It not only brutalizes the boys –'

'Boys are brutal. It's in the nature of the beast,' said Glodstone.

29

'But it also brutalizes masters who do it. Glodstone's a case in point.'

'I really think there's no need to indulge in personal attacks,' said the Headmaster, but Mr Glodstone waved his defence aside with a nasty smile.

'Wrong again, Slymne. I don't beat. I know my limitations and I leave it to the prefects in my house to do it for me. An eighteen-year-old has an extremely strong right arm.'

'And I suppose Matron gets boys to do her dirty work for her when she's called Miss World 1914,' said Slymne, fighting back.

Major Fetherington spoke up. 'She doesn't need to. I remember an incident two or three years ago involving Hoskiss Minor. I think she used a soap enema – or was it washing-up liquid? Something like that. He was off games for a week anyway, poor devil.'

'Which brings us back to the main point of contention,' said the Headmaster. 'The Bloxham match is the high point in our sporting calendar. It is of social importance for the school too. A great many parents attend and we'd be doing ourselves no good in their eyes if we allow ourselves to lose it. I am therefore overriding your ban, Mr Slymne. You will find some less time-consuming means of imposing your will on the boys. I don't care how you do it, but please bear in mind that Groxbourne is a games-playing school first and foremost.'

'But surely, Headmaster, the purpose of education is to –'

'Build character and moral fibre. You'll find our purpose set out in the Founder's Address.'

From that moment of defeat, Mr Slymne had suffered further humiliations. He had tried to get a job at other, more progressive, schools, only to learn that he was regarded as totally unsuitable precisely because he had taught at Groxbourne. Forced to stay on, he had been despised by the boys and was made an object of ridicule in the common-room by Mr Glodstone who always referred to him as 'our precious little conscientious objector.' Mr Slymne fought back more subtly by raising the level of geography teaching above that of any other subject and, at the same time, exercising his sarcasm so exclusively on boys from Glodstone's house that they failed their O-levels while other boys passed.

But the main thrust of his revenge was confined to Glodstone himself and over the years had developed into almost as demented an obsession as Glodstone's lust for adventure. Mr Slymne's was more methodical. He observed his enemy's habits closely, made notes about his movements, watched him through binoculars from his room in the Tower, and kept a dossier of boys to whom Glodstone spoke most frequently. Originally, he had hoped to catch him out fondling a boy – Slymne had bought a camera with a telescopic lens to record the event incontrovertibly – but Glodstone's secret sex life remained obstinately concealed. He even failed to rise to the bait of several gay magazines which Mr Slymne had ordered in his name. Glodstone had taken them straight to the Headmaster and had even threatened to call the police in if he received any more. As a result, Mr Slymne and the entire school had had to sit through an unusually long sermon on the evils of pornography, the detrimental effects on sportsmen of masturbation, referred to in the sermon as 'beastliness', and finally the cowardly practice of writing anonymous letters. The sermon ended on the most sinister note of all. 'If any of this continues, I shall be forced, however unwillingly, to refer these matters to the police and the long arm of the law!'

For the first time in his agnostic life, Mr Slymne prayed to God that the sex-shop owner in Soho to whom he had sent his order wouldn't solicit Mr Glodstone's custom again, and that the Headmaster's threat wasn't as all-inclusive as it had sounded. It was a view evidently shared by the boys, whose sex life over the next few days became so restricted that the school laundry was forced to work overtime.

But it was thanks to this episode that Mr Slymne first glimpsed Mr Glodstone's true weakness. 'The damned scoundrel who sent that stuff ought to have known I only read decent manly books. Rider Haggard and Henty. Good old-fashioned adventure yarns with none of your filthy modern muck like *Forever Amber*,' Glodstone had boasted in the common-room that evening, 'What I say is that damned poofters ought to have their balls cut off, what!'

'Some of them appear to share your opinion, Glodstone,' said the Chaplain, 'I was reading only the other day of an extraordinary case where a man actually went through some such operation and turned himself into a woman. One wonders . . .'

But Slymne was no longer listening. He put his coffee-cup down and went out with a strange feeling that he had found the scret of Glodstone's success and his popularity with the boys. The wretched man was a boy himself, a boy and a bully. For a few extraordinary seconds things reversed themselves in Mr Slymne's mind; the boys were all adults and the staff were boys, boys grown larger and louder in their opinions and the authority they wielded but still small, horrid boys themselves in their innermost being. It was as though they had been stunted in perpetual adolescence, which explained why they were still at school and hadn't dared the risks and dangers of the outside world. As he crossed the quad with this remarkable insight, as curious in its transposition of his previous beliefs as one of the negatives held up to the light in his darkroom, Mr Slymne felt a sudden relief. He was freed from the responsibilities of his career. He was no longer a schoolmaster, no longer an elderly thirty-eight, he was eighteen, no, fifteen, and entitled to a fifteen-year-old's ebullient spirits and unfeeling harshness, but with the marvellous difference that he had years of adult experience and knowledge on which to rely in his war with Glodstone. He would destroy the bully before he had finished.

With something approaching gaiety, Mr Slymne climbed the steps in the Tower to his room two at a time and added the findings that Glodstone only read adventure yarns to his dossier on the man. Downstairs, there came the sound of fighting in the dormitory. Mr Slymne rose from his desk, descended the stairs and ten minutes later had changed the whole pattern of his life by beating three boys without a qualm.

Chapter 5

'Heard about Slimey's conversion?' Major Fetherington said at breakfast the next morning. Glodstone peered over the *Daily Express*.

'Don't tell me he's joining the Church. God help his parishioners.'

'No such luck. The fellow's finally come round to a proper way of dealing with boys. Beat three little blighters last night for pillow-fighting in dorm.'

Mr Glodstone put down his paper and glared at the Major with his gimlet eye. 'You're joking, of course.'

'Damned if I am. Cleaves, Milshott and Bedgerson. Saw their backsides this morning when they were changing for early PT. A nicer set of welts too you couldn't wish for.'

'Extraordinary. Didn't think the runt had it in him,' said Glodstone, and turned back to his paper only slightly puzzled.

But when Mr Slymne came in five minutes later, Glodstone was genuinely startled. 'Good God,' he said loudly, 'Never thought I'd live to see the day when you'd join us for breakfast, Slymne.'

Slyme helped himself to bacon and eggs and smiled almost cordially. 'Thought it would make a change,' he said, 'One tends to get stuck in a rut. I'm thinking of taking up jogging too.'

'Just don't do yourself an injury,' said Glodstone unpleasantly. 'We wouldn't know how to get along without your conscientious objections. But then I hear you don't have any now. Beat some boys last night, eh?'

'They asked for it and they got it,' said Mr Slymne, managing to ignore the sarcasm.

'Nothing like consistency,' said Glodstone, and stalked out of the dining-room. That morning his classes suffered from his short temper and were set essays to write while Glodstone brooded.

33

Slymne's change of behaviour was disconcerting. If the damned fellow could suddenly alter his habits and start beating and take up jogging, Glodstone felt hard done by. Slymne had always been a comforting standard of wetness against which Glodstone could measure his own forthright and manly behaviour. Damn it, the next thing the wretched Slymne would do was get married. Glodstone, staring out of the window, felt a new wave of resentment boiling up inside him at the thought. Adventure had eluded him. So had romance. And he was growing older.

'Might not be a bad thing to marry some woman after all,' he muttered to himself, but apart from a distant cousin with no money, who had once proposed to him on Valentine's Day, there were no women of his social background he could think of who would do. There were some divorced mothers, of course, whose presence at the beginning of term or on Open Day had excited him, but their visits were too brief for him to get to know them. Anyway, they were hardly his sort. Glodstone dismissed them from his thoughts until he remembered La Comtesse de Montcon. He had never met her, but Anthony Wanderby, her son by a previous marriage, was in his House and while Glodstone disliked the little blighter – he was a typical American spoilt brat in the Housemaster's eyes and always malingering – he appreciated the crested envelopes and notepaper on which La Comtesse wrote to him from her château in France. Glodstone had endowed La Comtesse – in his too-frequent mentions of her in the staff-room he stuck to the French – with all those qualities of beauty and nobility he had never encountered outside his books, but which had to exist somewhere. Certainly the château existed. Glodstone had looked it up in his Michelin map for Périgord and found it apparently standing above the river, La Boose, a tributary of the Dordogne. A narrow road ran down beside the river and the hillsides opposite were coloured green which meant they were forested. It had often occurred to him to take the Bentley and find some excuse for dropping in but . . . Anyway, there was no point in pining over her. There was doubtless some damned Frog, Monsieur Le Comte, in attendance.

But that evening, after a restless day, he went up to his room early and sat sucking a pipe, studying the map again and turning over La Comtesse's brief letters to him. Then he folded them carefully away and replaced them in the cigar-box he kept in his desk before knocking out his pipe on the window sill and turning in.

'Damn Slymne,' he muttered as he lay in the darkness.

He would have damned him far more had he seem Mr Slymne move from the roof of the chapel opposite and descend the circular steps holding his camera carefully with his left hand while feeling the wall with his right. He paused at the bottom, made sure the quad was empty, and crossed to the Tower with the camera and 300mm lens concealed under his jacket. Ten minutes later, after locking himself in his bathroom and pulling the dark blind over the window, he had loaded the developing tank.

For Peregrine, the strange contortions of character in Glodstone and Slymne were too complex to be noticeable. He took them as usual quite literally at face value and since Glodstone's face with its neat moustache, monocle and glass eye gave the impression of strength and authority, while Slymne's didn't, he despised the latter. Besides, he enjoyed a man-to-man friendliness with Glodstone as a result of his enthusiastic reading of every book in his library, to the present where he was allowed to help to polish the Bentley on wet Sunday afternoons. There in the garage with rain pattering on the glass cupola above them (the place had once been a coachhouse with a few old bridles still hanging on the walls) he imbibed the code of the English gentleman which was Glodstone's special mania. He had already merged Richard Hannay, Bulldog Drummond and every other upstanding hero, including James Bond, into a single figure in his mind and had conferred their virtues on Mr Glodstone. In fact, his reading had gone further than Gloddie's which stopped around 1930. James Bond was one such character. Glodstone wasn't too sure about Bond.

'The thing is,' he told Peregrine one afternoon when they had unstrapped the bonnet of the Bentley and were polishing the great engine, 'The thing is with Bond that he's not your everyday decent chap who gets caught up in an adventure quite by chance. He's a sort of paid government employee and anyway his attitude to women's pretty rotten and sordid. And he's always flying about and gambling and generally living it up. Not a gentleman, what?'

'No sir,' said Peregrine and struck Bond off his list.

Glodstone sat down on the running-board and took out his pipe. 'I mean to say, it's his job to deal with crime. The damned fellow is a professional. He's told what to do and he has official backing. Now the real thing isn't like that. It happens accidentally. A chap is driving along and he stops for a breather and he sees murder done and naturally he has to do something about it, and by Jove he does. Takes the swine on outside the law and if he gets caught that's the luck of the draw. And another thing is, he's as fit as a fiddle and he sticks to the countryside which he knows like the back of his hand and your genuine crooks don't. That's the way it really is.'

In the presence of the Bentley, Peregrine's feelings were almost religious. Mr Glodstone's clichés opened up an idyllic world where simple chaps made simple decisions and crooks were simply crooks and got what was coming to them. It corresponded exactly with his own view of life; one day he'd be lucky enough to see murder done and would do something about it.

But apart from these occasional visions of the future, he was occupied with games, with the Major's OU course of shooting, doing the assault course, swimming in cold rivers and rock-climbing in Wales during the summer holidays and generally fitting himself for the Army career his father had decided on for him. In schoolwork, he remained a failure. Each year he took his O-levels and failed. It was the only cloud on his simple horizon. There were others gathering.

On the evening after his spell on the chapel roof, Mr Slymne locked himself in his bathroom, set up his enlarger and printed the negatives. They showed Glodstone holding an envelope and placing it in a cigar box. But the 8 × 10 prints were not big enough to tell him more. Mr Slymne turned the enlarger round, put several books on the baseboard and focused on the bathroom floor. This time the negative was so enlarged that the print only included Glodstone's hand, the lower part of his face and the envelope. As it appeared in the developing dish Slymne bent over it eagerly. There was something on the back of the envelope, he could see that now, but it was only when he had transferred the print to the fixer and turned the light on that he recognized in spite of the grain the blob as a crest. A crest? Slymne's thoughts turned to Glodstone's background. The man was always boasting about his family but there'd never been any mention of a family crest, and Glodstone was just the sort of fellow to have made a big thing about it.

If it wasn't his own, what was he doing with crested envelopes? And why keep them in a cigar box?

Anyway, he had learnt something new to add to the dossier. Mr Slymne took the print and was about to wash it when his cautious mind considered the dangers if it were found. It would be extremely awkward having to think of an excuse for photographing Glodstone from the chapel roof. Far better to destroy them now. He tore the photographs into strips of soggy paper and flushed them down the lavatory. The negatives went too. As he washed the dishes and cleared away, Mr Slymne pondered his next move. It might be possible to provoke Glodstone into some discussion on heraldry. He would have to do it tactfully.

In the event, he had to do nothing more than listen. Two days later, he was passing his house room when he heard two boys.

'Tambon says it's a bloody great castle like the sort of thing you see on telly with towers and everything,' said a boy Slymne recognized to be Paitter.

'I bet he sucked up to Wanderby to get himself invited,' said Mowbray. 'He's always doing that and Wanderby's a grotty snob. Just because his mother's a countess and he gets letters with crests, he thinks he's going to marry a royal.'

'Anyway, the countess is a real old cow according to Tambon. He was scared stiff of her. You ask him what it was like.'

A group of boys clattering down the staircase forced Slymne to move. He hurried along to the staff-room deep in thought. Was it pure coincidence that Glodstone kept crested envelopes in a cigar box and that he had a boy in his house whose mother was a countess and used crested notepaper? And if it wasn't, what did it portend? Probably nothing, but it would be worth looking into. For a moment he considered bringing the subject of Wanderby up in Glodstone's presence and watching his reaction. But Slymne's mind, honed by the misery of so many years of insult and dislike, had a new edge of cunning to it. He must do nothing to arouse the slightest glimmer of suspicion in Glodstone. Besides, there was a simple way of finding out if there was any connection between

Glodstone and Wanderby's mother. Slymne bided his time.

His opportunity came at half-term.

'I'm taking a group of chaps over to the railway museum at York,' Glodstone announced one evening. 'Never like to see boys left here when their parents don't pitch up to take them out.'

'Giving the Bentley an airing, eh,' said the Major. 'The Head won't like it, old boy.'

'Not going to give him a chance to dislike it. Hired a charabanc for the trip.'

'A charabanc. Now there's a word that's gone out of fashion,' said the Chaplain.

'I stick to the old ways, Padre,' said Glodstone, rubbing his pipe against the side of his nose to give it a greasy shine. 'They are still the best.'

Mr Slymne noted the archaism. It was another of the irritating facets of Glodstone's character that he seemed to ignore that the world had changed. But it was good to know that Glodstone would be away when the school was almost empty. Very good.

And so, when the parents had been and the coach with Glodstone's steam-engine enthusiasts had left, Mr Slymne slipped quietly along the corridor that connected his house with Gloddie's, carefully checking that each study was empty and that no one was about, and arrived at the door of Glodstone's rooms. For a moment he hesitated and listened but there were none of the usual sounds of the school. He was safe but his heart was beating palpably fast. Two deep breaths to quieten it and he was inside the room and the door was shut behind him. He crossed to the desk. The cigar box had been in a drawer on the left-hand side. Slymne tried the top one and found only exercise books and a broken pipe. The box was in the second. Keeping below the level of the window, he knelt and opened it. The envelopes were inside with the letters. With sudden decisiveness Slymne reached for the bottom one, took it out, examined the crest on the back and noted the French stamp, and put it carefully into the inside pocket of his jacket. Then he shut the drawer and hurried back to his room.

There he took out the letter and read it through with a growing sense of anti-climax. It was simply a short note written in a large flowing hand informing Mr Glodstone that Anthony would be a

38

week late in returning to school because his father was in Paris and would be flying back to the States on September 10th. The letter was signed 'Yours sincerely, Deirdre de Montcon.' Mr Slymne sat staring at it trying to think why Glodstone would want to keep a business letter so carefully in a cigar box and bring it out with the almost reverential look he had seen on his face through the telescopic lens. Perhaps he ought to look at the other letters in the box. They might reveal a more intimate relationship. He would do that when he took this letter back but in the meantime he would photograph it. First he measured the envelope and made a note of its exact dimensions. Then fitting the 55mm Micro lens to his Nikon, he photographed both the letter and the envelope and finally, moving in to within a few inches, photographed the address on the notepaper and the crest on the back of the envelope. That done, he put the letter and envelope in his pocket and slipped back to Glodstone's room, all the time listening for any sound that might indicate there was anyone about. But the school was still silent and the musty smell Slymne always associated with its emptiness during the holidays seemed to pervade the place.

Inside Glodstone's room he checked the letters in the cigar box, replaced the one at the very bottom and was no wiser. Why on earth did Glodstone bring these letters out and handle them as if they were precious? Slymne looked round the room for a clue. The photograph of Rear-Admiral Glodstone on the quarter deck of H.M.S. *Ramillies* told him nothing. Nor did a water-colour of a large square Victorian house which Slymne supposed to be Glodstone's family home. A pipe-rack, another photograph of Glodstone at the wheel of his Bentley, the usual bric-á-brac of a bachelor schoolmaster, and shelves filled with books. An amazing number of books. Slymne had had no idea Glodstone was such an omnivorous reader. He was about to cross to a bookshelf when a sound outside halted him. Someone was coming up the stairs.

Slymne moved. With understandable swiftness, he was through the door of Glodstone's bedroom and wedged up against the washbasin behind it when someone entered the study. Slymne held his breath and was conscious of a horrible weakness. Who the hell could be about when the school was supposed to be empty? And how in God's name was he to explain his presence hiding in the bedroom? For a moment he supposed it might be the woman who cleaned Glodstone's room and made his bed. But the bed was made and whoever was in the study was putting a book back on a shelf. Several minutes passed, another book was withdrawn, there was silence and the sound of the door opening and shutting again. Slymne slumped against the wall with relief but stayed there for five more minutes before venturing out.

On the desk he found a sheet of paper and a message written in neat but boyish script. 'Dear sir, I've returned *Rogue Male*. It was just as good as you said. I've borrowed *The Prisoner of Zenda*. I hope you don't mind. Clyde-Browne.'

Slymne stared at the message and then let his eyes roam round the room. The books were all adventure stories.. He ran along a shelf containing Henty and Westerman, Anthony Hope, A. E. W. Mason, all of Buchan. Everywhere he looked there were adventure stories. No wonder the beastly man had boasted that he only read decent manly stuff. Taking a book from a side table, he opened it: 'The castle hung in the woods on the spur of a mountainside, and all its walls could be seen, except that which rose to the North.'

It was enough. Slymne had found the connecting link between Glodstone's treasure of mundane letters from the Comtesse de Montcon, his Bentley and his belligerent datedness.

As evening came, and with it the sounds of cars and boys' voices, Slymne sat on in the darkness of his room letting his mind loose on a scheme that would use all Glodstone's adolescent lust for violent adventure and romance, lure him into a morass of misunderstanding and indiscretion. It was a delightful prospect.

Chapter 6

For the rest of the term, Slymne soaked himself in adventure stories. It was a thoroughly distasteful task but one that had to be done if his plan was to work. He did his reading secretly and, to maintain the illusion that his interests lay in an entirely different direction, he joined the Headmaster's Madrigal Singers, bought records of Tippett and Benjamin Britten and, ostensibly to hear Ashkenazy playing at the Festival Hall, drove down to London.

'Slimey's trying to worm his way into the Head's good graces by way of so-called music,' was Glodstone's comment, but Slymne's activities in London had nothing to do with music. Carefully avoiding more fashionable stationery shops, he found a printer in Paddington who was prepared to duplicate La Comtesse de Montcon's notepaper and crested envelopes.

'I'll have to see the original if you want it done exactly,' he told Slymne, who had produced photographs of the crest and printed address. 'And it'll cost.'

'Quite,' said Slymne, uncomfortably supposing that the man took him for a forger or blackmailer or both. The following week, he found an excuse to be in the Secretary's office when the mail came, and was able to filch Wanderby's letter from his mother. That Saturday, on the grounds that he had to visit a London dentist about his gum trouble, Slymne was back at the printer's with the envelope he had carefully steamed open. He returned to Groxbourne with a lump of cotton wool stuck uncomfortably in his mouth to suggest some dental treatment. 'I'm afraid you'll have to do without me. Dentist's orders,' he explained thickly to the Headmaster. 'Not allowed to sing for the time being.'

'Dear me, well we'll just have to do our best in your absence,' said the Headmaster, with the later comment to his wife that at least they couldn't do worse.

41

Next day, Wanderby's lost letter was found, rather muddied, in the flowerbed outside the Secretary's office and the postman was blamed.

By the end of term, Slymne had completed his preliminary preparations. He had collected the envelopes and notepaper and had deposited most of them in a locked tin box at his mother's house in Ramsgate for the time being. He had renewed his passport and taken out travellers' cheques. While the rest of the staff dispersed for the Easter holidays, Mr Slymne took the cross-Channel ferry to Boulogne and hired a car. From there he drove to the Belgian frontier before turning south at a small border crossing near Armentières. The place was carefully chosen. Even Slymne had memories of old men croaking *'Mademoiselle d'Armentières, parlez-vous?'* in remembrance of their happy days of slaughter in the First World War, and the name would arouse just the right outdated emotions he required in Glodstone. So must the route. Slymne stopped frequently to consult his maps and the guidebooks to find some picturesque way through this industrial grimness, but finally gave up. Anyway, it would heighten the romance of the wooded roads and valleys further south and the slag-heaps and coal-mines had the advantage of lending the route a very convincing reality. If one wanted to enter France unobserved, this was the way to come. And so Slymne kept to side roads, well away from autoroutes and big towns during his daytime driving, only moving into a hotel in a city at night. All the time he made notes and made sure he was maintaining the spirit of Glodstone's reading without bringing him too closely in touch with the real world.

For that reason he avoided Rouen and crossed the Seine by a bridge further south, but indulged himself on Route 836 down the Eure before back-tracking to Ivry-la-Bataille and noting an hotel there and its telephone number. After that, another diversion by way of Houdan and Faverolles to Nogent-Le-Roi and Chartres. He was hesitant about Chartres, but one look at the Cathedral reassured him. Yes, Chartres would inspire Glodstone. And what about Château Renault just off the road to Tours? It had been four miles outside Château Renault that Mansel and Chandos had gassed Brevet in his own car. Slymne decided against it and chose the minor road to Meung-sur-Loire as being more discreetly surreptitious. He would have to impress on Glodstone the danger of crossing rivers in big towns. Slymne made a note 'Bridge bound to be watched,' in his notebook and drove on.

It took him ten days to plan the route and, to be on the safe side, he stayed clear of the countryside round the Château Carmagnac with one exception. On the tenth night he drove to the little town of Boosat and posted two letters in separate boxes. To be precise, he posted envelopes, each with a crest on the back and with his own address typed onto a self-adhesive label on the front. Then he turned north and retraced his route to Boulogne, checking each mark he had made on his maps against the comments in his notebook and adding more information.

By the time he sailed for Folkestone, Mr Slymne was proud of his work. There were some advantages to be had from a degree in geography after all. And the two envelopes were waiting for him at his mother's house. With the utmost care, he prised off the self-adhesive labels and steamed open the lightly gummed flaps. Then he set to work with an ink-pad to obliterate the date on the postmark while leaving Boosat clearly visible. For the next three days, he pored over the photograph of the Comtesse's letter to Glodstone and traced again and again her large flowing handwriting. When he returned to Groxbourne, even the Comtesse herself would have found difficulty in saying which of the letters she had written without reading their contents. Mr Slymne's skills had come into their own.

It was more than could be said for Peregrine Clyde-Browne. The discrepancy between his school report and his failure to pass any subject at O-level apart from the maths which, because it allowed of no alternatives to right and wrong, he had managed to scrape through with a grade C, had finally convinced Mr Clyde-Browne that sending his son to Groxbourne might have had the advantage of keeping the brute out of the house for most of the year, but that it certainly hadn't advanced the chances of getting him into the Army. On the other hand, he had paid the fees for three years, not to mention his contribution to the Chapel Restoration Fund, and it infuriated him to think that he had wasted the money.

'We're almost certain to be lumbered with the cretin at the end of the summer term,' he grumbled, 'and at this rate, he'll never get a job.'

'I think you're being very hard on him. Dr Andrews says he's probably a late developer.'

'And how late is late? He'll be fifty before he knows that Oui is French for Yes and not an instruction to go to the toilet And I'll be ninety.'

'And in your second childhood,' retorted Mrs Clyde-Browne.

'Quite,' said her husband. 'In which case you'll have double problems Peregrine won't be out of his first. Well, if you want to share your old age with a middle-aged adolescent, I don't.'

'Since I'm spending my own middle-age with a bad-tempered and callous –'

'I am not callous. I may be bad-tempered but I am not callous. I am merely trying to do the best for your   all right, our son while there's still time.'

'But his reports say –'

But Mr Clyde-Browne's patience had run out. 'Reports? Reports? I'd as soon believe a single word of a Government White Paper as give any credence to those damned reports They're designed to con parents of morons to go on shelling out good money. What I want are decent exam results.'

'In that case you should have taken my advice in the first place and had Peregrine privately tutored,' said Mrs Clyde-Browne, knitting with some ferocity.

Mr Clyde-Browne wilted into a chair 'You may be right at that,' he conceded, 'though I can't imagine any educated man staying the course. Peregrine would have him in a mental home within a month. Still, it's worth trying. There must be some case-hardened crammer who could programme him with enough information to get his O-levels. I'll look into it.'

As a result of this desperate determination, Peregrine had spent the Easter holidays with Dr Klaus Hardboldt, late of the Army Education Corps. The doctor's credentials were of the highest. He had drilled the Duke of Durham's son into Cambridge against hereditary odds and had had the remarkable record of teaching eighteen Guards officers to speak pidgin Russian without a lisp.

'I think I can guarantee your son will pass his O-levels,' he told Mr Clyde-Browne. 'Give me anyone for three weeks of uninterrupted training and they will learn.'

Mr Clyde-Browne had said he hoped so and had paid handsomely. And Dr Hardboldt had lived up to his promise. Peregrine had spent three weeks at the Doctor's school in Aldershot with astonishing results. The Doctor's methods were based on his intimate observations of dogs and a close connection with several chief examiners.

'Don't imagine I expect you to think, because I don't,' he explained the first morning. 'You are here to obey. I require the use of only one faculty, that of memory. You will learn off by heart the answers to the questions which will be set you in the exam. Those of you who fail to remember the answers will be put on bread and water; those who are word perfect will get fillet steak. Is that clear?'

The class nodded.

'Pick up the piece of paper in front of you and turn it over.'

The class did as they were told.

'That is the answer to the first question in the Maths paper you will be set. You have twenty minutes in which to learn it off by heart.'

At the end of twenty minutes, Peregrine could remember the answer. Throughout the day, the process continued. Even after dinner it resumed and it was midnight before Peregrine got to bed. He was wakened at six next morning and required to repeat the answers he had learnt the day before to a tape recorder.

'That is known as reinforcement,' said the Doctor. 'Today we will learn the answers to the French questions. Reinforcement will be done tomorrow before breakfast.'

Next day, Peregrine went hungrily into the classroom for geography and was rewarded with steak at dinner. By the end of the week, only one boy in the class was still incapable of remembering the answers to all the questions in History, Geography, Maths, Chemistry, Biology and English Literature.

Dr Hardboldt was undismayed. 'Sit, sir,' he ordered when the boy fell off his chair for the third time, owing to semi-starvation. The lad managed to get into a sitting position. 'Good dog,' said the

45

Doctor, producing a packet of Chocdrops. 'Now beg.'

As the boy put up his hands, the Doctor dropped a Chocdrop into his mouth. 'Good. Now then Parkinson, if you can obey that simple instruction, there's not the slightest doubt you can pass the exam.'

'But I can't read,' whimpered Parkinson, and evidently tried to wag his tail.

Doctor Hardboldt looked at him grimly 'Can't read? Stuff and nonsense, sir. Any boy whose parents can afford to pay my fees must be able to read.'

'But I'm dyslexic, sir.'

The Doctor stiffened. 'So,' he said. 'In that case we'll have to apply for you to take your O-levels orally. Take this note to my secretary.'

As Parkinson wobbled from the room, the Doctor turned back to the class. 'Is there any other do. . boy here who can't read? I don't want any shilly-shallying. If you can't read, say so, and we'll have you attended to by the hypnotist.'

But no one in the class needed the attentions of the hypnotist.

The second week was spent writing down verbatim the answers to the questions and in further reinforcement. Peregrine was woken every so often during the night and interrogated. 'What is the answer to question four in the History paper?' said the doctor.

Peregrine peered bleary-eyed into the ferocious moustache. 'Gladstone's policy of Home Rule for Ireland was prevented from becoming law because Chamberlain, formerly the radical Mayor of Birmingham, split the Liberal party and . . .'

'Good dog,' said the doctor when he had finished and rewarded him with a Chocdrop.

But it was in the third week that reinforcement became most rigorous. 'A tired mind is a receptive mind,' the doctor announced on Sunday evening. 'From now on, you will be limited to four hours sleep in every twenty-four, one hour in every six being allocated for rest Before you go to sleep, you will write down the answers to one exam paper and, on being woken, will write them down again before going on to the next subject. In this way, you will be unable to fail your O-levels even if you want to.'

After seven more days of conditioning, Peregrine returned to his parents exhausted and with his brain so stuffed with exam answers that his parents had their own sleep interrupted by an occasional bark and the sound of Peregrine automatically reciting the doctor's orders. They were further disturbed by Dr Hardboldt's insistence that Peregrine be prevented from returning to Groxbourne until after he had sat his exams. 'It is absolutely essential that he isn't exposed to the confusion of other methods of teaching,' he said. 'Nothing is more damaging to an animal's learning ability than contradictory stimuli.'

'But Peregrine isn't an animal,' protested Mrs Clyde-Browne. 'He's a delicate, sensitive –'

'Animal,' said her husband, whose views on his son coincided entirely with the Doctor's.

'Exactly,' said Dr Hardboldt. 'Now where most teachers go wrong is in failing to apply the methods used in animal training to their pupils. If a seal can be taught to balance a ball on its nose, a boy can be taught to pass exams.'

'But the questions are surely different every year,' said Mr Clyde-Browne.

Dr Hardboldt shook his head. 'They can't be. If they were, no one could possibly teach the answers. Those are the rules of the game.'

'I hope you're right,' said Mrs Clyde-Browne.

'Madam, I am,' said the Doctor. 'Time will prove it.'

And time, as far as Peregrine was concerned, did. He returned to Groxbourne a month late and, with the air of a sleepwalker, took his O-level exams with every sign that this time he would succeed. Even the Headmaster, glancing through the papers before sending them off to the external examiners, was impressed. 'If I hadn't seen it with my own eyes I wouldn't have believed it possible,' he muttered, and immediately wrote to the Clyde-Brownes to assure them that they could go ahead with their plans to enter Peregrine for the Army.

Mr Clyde-Browne read the letter with delight. 'He's done it. By golly, he's done it,' he whooped.

'Of course he has,' said Mrs Clyde-Browne, 'I always knew he was gifted.'

Mr Clyde-Browne stopped whooping. 'Not him . . .' he began and decided to say no more.

Chapter 7

But Peregrine's future was being decided by more subtle influences than those of the military Doctor. Mr Glodstone had spent the holidays in search, as he put it, 'of some damned woman' to marry. 'The thing is one doesn't want to marry beneath one,' he confided to Major Fetherington over several nightcaps of whisky in his rooms.

'Absolutely,' said the Major, whose wife had died of boredom ten years before. 'Still, if there's lead in your pencil, you've got to make your mark somewhere.'

Glodstone glanced at him dubiously. The Major's metaphor was too coarse for his romantic imagination. 'Perhaps, but love's got to be there too. I mean, only a cad would marry a girl he didn't love, don't you think?'

'Suppose so,' said the Major, enjoying the whisky too much to argue from his own experience. 'Still, a fellow's got to think of the future. Knew a chap once, must have been eighty if he was a day, keen tennis-player in his time, married a woman he happened to be sitting next to in the Centre Court at Wimbledon. Splendid match. Died in her arms a fortnight later desperately in love. Never can tell till you try.'

Glodstone considered the moral of this example and found it hardly illuminating. 'That sort of thing doesn't happen to me,' he said and put the cap back on the whisky bottle.

'The trouble with you,' said the Major, 'is that you've got champagne tastes and a beer income. My advice is to lower your sights. Still, you never know. Chance has a funny way of arranging things.'

For once Mr Slymne would have shared Glodstone's unspoken disagreement. He was leaving as little as possible to chance. Having discovered Glodstone's wildly romantic streak, he was determined to exploit it, but there were still problems to cope with. The first concerned Sports Day. La Comtesse de Montcon might put in an appearance, and if the wretched woman turned out to be as formidable as the conversation he had overheard in the house-room suggested, all his preparations would be wasted. Glodstone would hardly go to the aid of a woman who was manifestly capable of looking after herself. No, it was vital that the image in Glodstone's imagination should be that of a poor, defenceless, or to be exact, a rich defenceless sylph-like creature with an innocence beyond belief. Slymne had a shrewd idea that La Comtesse was more robust. Any mother who could send her son to Groxbourne had to be. Slymne checked his dossier and found that Tambon had said 'The countess is a real old cow,' and was reassured. He also surreptitiously took a look at the Visiting Parents' Book in the Bursar's office and found no evidence that La Comtesse had ever visited the school.

But to be on the safe side, he used a geography lesson to ask all those boys whose mothers were coming to Sports Day to put up their hands. Wanderby didn't. Having dealt with that problem, Slymne concentrated on the next one; how to phrase his letter to Glodstone. In the end he decided on the direct approach. It would appeal to Glodstone's gallantry more effectively than anything too subtle. On the other hand, there had to be more definite instructions as well. Slymne penned the letter, tracing La Comtesse's handwriting again and again for practice, and then on a weekend visit to London, spent the night in a hotel room making a number of direct-dialled calls to France. By the time he returned to Groxbourne, he was ready to provide the instructions. Only one uncertainty remained. Glodstone might have made arrangements for his summer holidays already. In which case, the timing of the letter would be vital. And Wanderby's own movements in the holidays might prove awkward too. Again Slymne made use of a geography lesson to find out where the boy was spending the summer.

'I'm going to Washington to stay with my father and his girl friend,' Wanderby announced brashly. Mr Slymne was delighted and used the statement in the Common Room that evening to good advantage.

'I must say we have some pretty peculiar parents,' he said loudly,

'I was discussing time zones with 2B this morning and that American boy, Wanderbury, suddenly said his father's got a mistress in Washington.'

Glodstone stopped sucking his pipe. 'Can't you even remember the names of the boys you teach?' he asked angrily. 'It's Wanderby. And what's all this about his father having a mistress?'

Slymne appeared to notice Glodstone for the first time. 'In your house, isn't he? Typical product of a broken home. Anyway, I'm merely repeating what he said.'

'Do you make a habit of poking your nose into the boy's family affairs in your lessons?'

'Certainly not. As I said, I was discussing time zones and jet-lag and Wandleby –'

'Wanderby, for God's sake,' snapped Glodstone.

'– volunteered the information that he was going to Washington at the end of term and that his father –'

'All right, we heard you the first time,' said Glodstone and finished his coffee hurriedly and left the room. Later that evening as he crossed the quad, Slymne was pleased to notice Glodstone sitting at his desk by the window with a cigar box beside him. The crack about the broken home and Wanderby's father having a mistress would enhance Glodstone's romantic image of La Comtesse. That night, Slymne completed the task of writing out her instructions and locked the letter away in his filing cabinet.

It was to remain there for another five weeks. The summer term dragged on. Sports Day came and went, cricket matches were won or lost and Glodstone's melancholy grew darker with the fine weather and the liveliness of youth around him. He took to polishing the Bentley more frequently and it was there in the old coach-house one evening that he asked Peregrine what he was going to do when he left.

'Father's got me down for the Army. But now I've got O-levels, he's talking about my going into a bank in the City.'

'Not your sort of life I would have thought. Dashed dull.'

'Well, it's on account of my maths,' said Peregrine. 'That and Mother. She's all against my going into the Army. Anyway, I've got a month free first because I'm going on the Major's course in Wales

It's jolly good fun doing those night marches and sleeping out in the open.'

Glodstone sighed at the remembrance of his youth and came to a sudden decision. 'Damn the Head,' he muttered, 'let's take the old girl out for a spin. After all, it is your last term and you've done more than your fair whack in keeping her shipshape and Bristol fashion. You go off down to the school gates and I'll pick you up there in ten minutes.'

And so for an hour they bowled along country lanes with the wind in their faces and the great exhaust murmuring gently behind them.

'You drive jolly well,' said Peregrine, as they swung round a corner and headed through an overhang of oaks, 'and she goes like a dream.'

Beside him, Glodstone smiled. 'This is the life, eh. Can't beat a vintage Bentley. She's a warhorse just raring to go.'

They came to a village and on the same impulse that had carried him so far, Glodstone stopped outside a pub. 'Two pints of your best bitter, landlord,' said Glodstone loudly, provoking the man into enquiring if Peregrine was eighteen.

'No . . .' said Peregrine but his answer was drowned by the boom of Glodstone's voice.

'Of course he is. Damnation, man, you don't imagine I'd bring an under-age drinker into your place?'

'I've known it happen,' said the barman, 'so I'll make it one bitter and a lemonade shandy and you can take your glasses outside to a table.'

'We can do better than that and take our custom elsewhere,' said Glodstone and stalked out of the pub. 'That's the trouble with the damned world today, people don't know their place any more. In my father's day, that fellow would have lost his licence and no mistake. Anyway, with a manner like that, the beer was probably flat.'

They drove on to the next village and stopped again. This time Glodstone lowered his voice and they were served. As they sat on a bench outside admiring their reflections in the shining waxed coachwork of the great car and basking in the comments it caused, Glodstone cheered up.

51

'You can say what you like but there's nothing to touch a pint of the best British bitter,' he said.

'Yes,' said Peregrine, who had hardly touched his beer and didn't much like it anyway.

'That's something you won't find in any other country. The Hun swills lager by the gallon and the Dutch have their own brew which isn't bad but it's got no body to it. Same with the Belgians, but it's all bottled beer. Mind you, it's better than the Frog muck. Charge the earth for the stuff too but that's the French all over. Dashed odd, when you come to think of it, that the wine-drinking countries have never been a match for the beer ones when it comes to a good scrap. Probably something in the saying they've got no guts and no stomach for a fight.'

Peregrine drank some more beer to mark his allegiance while Glodstone spouted his prejudices and the world shrank until there was only one decent place to be, and that was sitting in the summer twilight in an English village drinking English beer and gazing at one's reflection in the coachwork of an English car that had been made in 1927. But as they drove back to the school, Glodstone's melancholy returned. 'I'm going to miss you,' he said. 'You're my sort of chap. Dependable. So if there's anything I can ever do for you, you've only to ask.'

'That's jolly good of you, sir,' said Peregrine.

'And another thing. We can forget the "sir" bit from now on. I mean, it's the end of term and all that. All the same, I think you'd better hop out when we get to the school gates. No need to give the Head any reason to complain, eh?'

So Peregrine walked back up the avenue of beeches to the school while Glodstone parked the Bentley and morosely considered his future. 'You and I are out of place here, old girl,' he murmured, patting the Bentley's headlight affectionately, 'we were born in a different world.'

He went up to his room and poured himself a whisky and sat in the darkening twilight wondering what the devil he was going to do with himself during the holidays. If only he'd been younger, he'd be inclined to join Major Fetherington's walkabout in Wales. But no, he'd look damned silly now and anyway the Major didn't like anyone poaching on his own private ground. It was a fairly desperate Glodstone who finally took himself off to bed and spent half an hour reading *The Thirty-Nine Steps* again. 'Why the hell can't something challenging come my way for once?' he thought as he switched out the light.

A week later it did. As the last coach left for the station and the cars departed, Slymne struck. The School Secretary's office was conveniently empty when he tucked the envelope addressed to G. P. Glodstone, Esq., into the pigeonhole already jammed with Glodstone's uncollected mail. Slymne's timing was nicely calculated. Glodstone was notorious for not bothering with letters until the pigeonhole was full. 'A load of bumpf,' he had once declared. 'Anyone would think I was a penpusher and not a schoolmaster.' But with the end of term, he would be forced to deal with his correspondence. Even so, he would leave it until the last moment. It was in fact three days before Glodstone took the bundle of letters up to his room and shuffled through them and came to the envelope with the familiar crest, an eagle evidently tearing the entrails from a sheep. For a moment Glodstone gazed almost rapturously at the crest before splitting the envelope open with a paper-knife. Again he hesitated. Letters from parents were too often lists of complaints about the treatment of their sons. Glodstone held his breath as he took it out and laid it flat on the desk. But his fears were unfounded.

'Dear Mr Glodstone,' he read, 'I trust you will forgive me writing to you but I have no one else to turn to. And, although we have never met, Anthony has expressed such admiration for you – indeed maintains you are the only gentleman among the masters at Groxbourne – that I feel you alone can be trusted.' Glodstone re-read the sentence – he had never suspected the wretched Wanderby of such perception – and then continued in a ferment of excitement.

'I dare express nothing in a letter for fear that it will be intercepted, except that I am in the greatest danger and urgently need help in a situation which is as hazardous as it is honourable. Beyond that I cannot go in writing. Should you feel able to give me that assistance I so desperately require, go to the left-luggage office at Victoria Station and exchange the enclosed ticket. I can say no more but know you will understand the necessity for this precaution.'

The letter was signed, 'Yours in desperation, Deirdre de Montcon. P.S. Burn both the letter and the envelope at once.'

53

Glodstone sat transfixed. The call he had been awaiting for over thirty years had finally come. He read the letter several times and then, taking the left-luggage ticket, which he put into his wallet, he ceremoniously burnt the letter in its envelope and as an extra precaution flushed the ashes down the lavatory. Seconds later, he was packing and within the half hour the Bentley rolled from the coach-house with a rejuvenated Glodstone behind the wheel.

From the window of his rooms in the Tower, Slymne watched him leave with a different excitement. The loathsome Glodstone had taken the bait. Then Slymne too carried his bags down to his car and left Groxbourne, though less hurriedly. He would always be one step ahead of his enemy.

Chapter 8

It was late afternoon by the time Glodstone parked the Bentley in a street near Victoria Station. He had driven down in a state of euphoria interspersed with occasional flashes of insight which told him the whole affair was too good to be true. There must be some mistake. Certainly his judgement of Wanderby had been wholly wrong. What had the letter said? 'Maintains that you are the only gentleman among the masters.' Which was true enough, but he'd hardly expected Wanderby to have recognized it. Still, the boy's mother was La Comtesse, and he evidently knew a gentleman when he saw one.

But for the most part, Glodstone had spent the drive concentrating on ways of reaching the Château Carmagnac as speedily as possible. It would depend on what message he found at the left-luggage office, but if he took the Weymouth to Cherbourg ferry, he could drive through the night and be there in twenty-four hours. He had his passport with him and had stopped at his bank in Bridgnorth to withdraw two thousand pounds from his deposit account and change them into travellers' cheques. It was the sum total of his savings but he still had his small inheritance to fall back on. Not that money counted in his calculations. He was about to embark on the expedition of his dreams. He was also going alone. It was at this point that a feeling of slight disappointment crept over him. In his fantasies, he had always seen himself accompanied by one or two devoted friends, a small band of companions whose motto would be that of The Three Musketeers, 'All for one and one for all.' Of course when he was young it had been different, but at fifty Glodstone felt the need for company. If only he could have taken young Clyde-Browne with him – but there was no time for that now. He must act with speed.

55

But the message he found waiting for him at the left-luggage office changed his opinion. He had been rather surprised to find that it was in fact a piece of luggage, a small brown suitcase. 'Are you sure this is the article?' he asked the attendant rather incautiously.

'Listen, mate, it's yours isn't it? You gave me the ticket for it and that's the luggage,' said the man and turned away to deal with another customer. Glodstone glanced at a label tied to the handle and was satisfied. Neatly typed on it was his own name. He walked back to the car with a new sense of caution and twice stopped at a corner to make sure he was not being followed. Then with the case on the seat beside him he drove to the flat of an aged aunt in Highgate which he was forced to use when he was in London. In keeping with his background, Glodstone would have much preferred his club, The Ancient Automobile, but it didn't run to rooms.

'Well I never, if it isn't Gerald,' said the old lady, rather gratuitously in Glodstone's opinion, 'and you didn't even write to say you were coming.'

'I didn't have time. Urgent business,' said Glodstone.

'It's a good thing your room is still ready just as you left it, though I'll have to put a hot-water bottle in to air the sheets. Now you just sit down and I'll make a nice pot of tea.'

But Glodstone was in no mood for these domestic details. They clashed too prosaically with his excitement. All the same, his aunt disappeared into the kitchen while he went up to his room and opened the suitcase. Inside it was stuffed with French newspapers and it was only when he had taken them all out that he found the second envelope. He ripped it open and took out several sheets of notepaper. They were all crested and the handwriting was unmistakably that of La Comtesse.

'Dear Mr Glodstone, Thank you for coming thus far,' he read. 'It was to be expected of you but, though I would have you come to my aid, I fear extremely you do not appreciate the dangers you will face and I would not put you at your peril without fair warning. Desperate as my situation is, I cannot allow you to come unprepared. Those about me are wise in the ways of crime whereas you are not. This is perhaps to your advantage but for your own sake

56

and for mine, be on your guard and come, if you can, armed, for this is a matter of life and death and murder has already been done.'

'Your tea is ready, dear,' the old lady called from her cluttered sitting-room.

'All right, I'll be there in a minute,' said Glodstone irritably. Here he was about to engage in a matter of life and death and with murder already done, and aged aunts who called him dear and served tea were distinctly out of place. He read on. 'I enclose the route you must follow. The ports are watched and on no account must you appear to be other than an English gentleman touring through France. It is vital therefore that you take your time and trust no one. The men against whom you are set have agents among the gendarmerie and are themselves above suspicion. I cannot state their influence too highly. Nor dare I catalogue their crimes in writing.' This time the letter was signed 'Yours in gratitude, Deirdre de Montcon,' and as before the postscript ordered him to burn both letter and envelope.

Glodstone turned to the other page. It was typewritten and stated that he was to cross from Dover to Ostend on the early morning ferry on the 28th of July and drive to Iper before passing the frontier into France the following day. Thereafter his route was listed with hotels at which 'rooms have been booked for you.' Glodstone read down the list in amazement. Considering the terrible dangers La Comtesse was evidently facing, her instructions were quite extraordinarily explicit. Only when he turned the page was there an explanation. In her own handwriting she had written, 'Should I have need to communicate with you, my messages will be waiting for you in your rooms each night. And now that I have written this by hand, please copy and then burn.'

Glodstone reached in his pocket for a pen, only to be interrupted by his aunt.

'Your tea's getting cold, dear.'

'Damn,' said Glodstone, but went through to the sitting-room and spent an extremely impatient half an hour listening to the latest family gossip. By the time Aunt Lucy got on to the various diseases her grandnieces and nephews had been suffering from, Glodstone was practically rabid. 'Excuse me, but I have some really pressing

57

business to attend to,' he said, as she launched into a particularly clinical account of the symptoms his cousin Michael had contracted, or more precisely expanded, as a result of mumps.

'Balls,' continued Aunt Lucy implacably.

'I beg your pardon,' said Glodstone, whose attention had been fixed on La Comtesse's instructions.

'I was saying that his –'

'I simply must go,' said Glodstone and rather rudely left the room.

'What a very peculiar boy Gerald is,' muttered the old lady as she cleared away the tea things. Her opinion was confirmed some forty minutes later when she discovered the hallway was filling with smoke.

'What in heaven's name are you doing in there?' she demanded of the door to the lavatory which seemed to be the source of the fire.

'Nothing,' choked Glodstone, wishing to God he hadn't been so conscientious in following La Comtesse's instructions to burn all evidence. The letter and his itinerary had gone easily enough, but his attempt to screw the envelope into a ball and catch the flood had failed dismally. The envelope remained obstinately buoyant with the crest plainly visible. And the cistern had been no great help either. Built for a more leisurely age, it filled slowly and emptied no faster. Finally Glodstone had resorted to the French newspapers. They were incriminating too and by crumpling them up around the sodden envelope he might get that to burn as well. In the event, he was proved right, but at considerable cost. The newspapers were as fiery as their editorials. As flames shot out of the pan, Glodstone slammed the lid down and was presently tugging at the chain to extinguish what amounted to an indoor bonfire. It was at this point that his aunt intervened.

'Yes, you are,' she shouted through the door, 'You've been smoking in there and something's caught fire.'

'Yes,' gasped Glodstone, finding this a relatively plausible explanation. Nobody could say that he hadn't been smoking. The damned stuff was issuing round the edges of the lid quite alarmingly. He seized the towel from behind the door and tried to choke the smoke off before he suffocated.

'If you don't come out this minute I shall be forced to call the fire brigade,' his aunt threatened but Glodstone had had enough. Unlocking the door, he shot, gasping for air, into the hall.

His aunt surveyed the smoke still fuming from beneath the seat. 'What on earth have you been up to?' she said, and promptly extinguished the smouldering remnants of *Le Monde* with a basin of water from the kitchen before examining the fragments with a critical eye.

'You've been a bachelor too long,' she declared finally. 'Your Uncle Martin was found dead in the lavatory with a copy of *La Vie Parisienne* and you've evidently taken after him. What you need is a sensible wife to take care of your baser needs.'

Glodstone said nothing. If his aunt chose to draw such crude conclusions it was far better that she do so than suspect the true nature of his enterprise. All the same, the incident had taken a measure of the immediate glamour out of the situation. 'I shall be dining out,' he said with some hauteur and spent the evening at his club planning his next move. It was complicated by the date of his cross-channel booking, which was set for the 28th. He had five days to wait. Then there was the question of obtaining arms. The letter had definitely said 'Come armed,' but that was easier said than done. True, he had a shotgun at a cousin's farm in Devon but shotguns didn't come into the category of proper arms. He needed a revolver, something easy to conceal in the Bentley, and he could hardly go into a gunsmith in London and ask for a .38 Smith & Wesson with a hundred cartridges. The thing to do would be to approach some member of the underworld. There must be plenty of people selling guns in London. Glodstone didn't know any and had not the foggiest notion where to look for them. It was all very disconcerting and he was about to give up the notion of going armed when he remembered that Major Fetherington kept revolvers and ammunition in the School Armoury. In fact there were several old ones there. And he knew where the Major kept the keys. It would be a simple matter to take one and he could have it back before the beginning of next term. With a more cheerful air, Glodstone ordered a brandy before returning to his aunt's flat. Next morning he was on the road again and by lunchtime back at Groxbourne.

'Fancy you coming back so soon,' said the School Secretary. 'The galloping Major's back too, only he isn't galloping quite so much. Been and gone and sprained his ankle.'

'Damnation,' said Glodstone horrified at this blow to his plan, 'I mean, poor fellow. Where is he?'

'Up in his rooms.'

Glodstone climbed the staircase to the Major's rooms and knocked.

'Come in, whoever you are,' shouted the Major. He was sitting in an armchair with one leg propped up on a stool. 'Ah, Gloddie, old boy. Good to see you. Thought you'd shoved off.'

'I had to come back for something. What on earth happened? Did you slip on some scree in Wales?'

'Never got to bloody Wales. Glissaded on a dog-turd in Shrewsbury and came a right purler, I can tell you. All I could do to drive that damned minibus back here. Had to cancel the OU course and now I've got old Perry on my hands.'

'Peregrine Clyde-Brown?' asked Glodstone with rising hope.

'Parents off in Italy somewhere. Won't be back for three weeks and he's been trying to phone some uncle but the chap's never in. Blowed if I know what to do with the lad.'

'How long is that ankle of yours going to take to mend?' asked Goldstone, suddenly considering the possibility that he might have found just the two people he would most like to have with him in a tight spot.

'Quack's fixed me up for an X-ray tomorrow. Seems to think I may have fractured my coccyx.'

'Your coccyx? I thought you said you'd sprained your ankle.'

'Listen, old man,' said the Major conspiratorially. 'That's for public consumption. Can't have people going round saying I bought it where the monkey hid the nuts. Wouldn't inspire confidence, would it? I mean, would you trust a son of yours to go on a survival course with a man who couldn't spot a dog-pat when it was staring him in the face?'

'Well, as a matter of fact I don't . . .' began Glodstone, only to be interrupted by the Major who was shifting his posterior on what appeared to be a semi-inflated plastic lifebelt. 'Another thing. The

60

Head don't know, so for Lord's sake don't mention a word. The blighter's only too anxious to find an excuse for closing the OU course down Can't afford to lose my job.

'You can rely on me,' said Glodstone. 'Is there anything I can get you?'

The Major nodded. 'A couple of bottles of whisky Can't ask Matron to get it for me. Bad enough having her help me to the loo, and then she hangs about outside asking if I need any help. I tell you, old boy, everything they say about passing razor blades is spot-on.'

'I'll see to the whisky,' said Glodstone, not wishing to pursue this line of conversation any further It was obvious that the Major was a broken reed as far as the great adventure was concerned. He went downstairs in search of Peregrine. He had no difficulty. The sound of shots coming from the small-arms range indicated where Peregrine was Glodstone found him using a .22 to puncture the centre of a target. For a moment he watched with delight and then stepped forward.

'Gosh, sir, it's good to see you,' said Peregrine enthusiastically and scrambled to his feet, 'I thought you'd left.'

Glodstone switched his monocle to his good eye. 'Something's turned up. The big show,' he said.

Peregrine looked puzzled. 'The big show, sir?'

Glodstone looked cautiously round the range before replying. 'The call to action,' he said solemnly. 'I can't give any details except to say that it's a matter of life and death.'

'Gosh, sir, you mean –'

'Let's just say I've been asked to help. Now, as I understand it, your folks are in Italy and you've nothing on.'

For a moment Peregrine's literal mind struggled with the statement before he caught its meaning. 'No, sir, I've been trying to phone my uncle but I can't get through.'

'In which case you won't be missed That's number one Number two is we've three weeks in which to do the job. I take it you've got a passport.'

Peregrine shook his head. Glodstone polished his monocle thoughtfully 'In that case we'll have to think of something.'

'You mean we're going abroad?'

'To France,' said Glodstone, 'that is, if you're game. Before you answer, you must know that we'll be acting outside the law with no holds barred. I mean, it won't be any picnic.'

But Peregrine was already enthralled. 'Of course I'm game, sir. You can count me in.'

'Good man,' said Glodstone and clapped him on the shoulder. 'Now as to a passport, I have an idea. Didn't Mr Massey take the fifth-form French to Boulogne last year?'

'Yes sir.'

'And Barnes had flu and couldn't go. If I'm not wrong, the Bursar said he'd kept his temporary visitor's passport back. It could be he still has it in his office.'

'But I don't look a bit like Barnes.'

Glodstone smiled. 'You will by the time you cross,' he said, 'We'll see to that. And now for weapons. You don't by any chance have the key to armoury, do you?'

'Well, yes sir. The Major said I could keep my eye in so long as I didn't blow my head off.'

'In that case, we'll pay the gunroom a visit. We need to go armed and two revolvers won't be missed.'

'They will, sir,' said Peregrine. 'The Major always checks the guns.'

'I can't see him doing it in his present condition,' said Glodstone. 'Still, I don't like going unprepared.'

For once Peregrine had the answer. 'There's a smashing shop for replica guns in Birmingham, sir. I mean if we —'

'Splendid,' said Glodstone. 'The Major wants some whisky. We can kill two birds with one stone.'

That evening the substitutions were made and two .38 Webleys with several hundred rounds of ammunition were stored in cardboard boxes beneath the seats of the Bentley. And the problem of the passport had been solved too. Glodstone had found Barnes's in the Bursar's office.

'Now it remains to convince the Major that you're going to your uncle's. Tell him you're catching the ten o'clock train and I'll pick you up at the bus-stop in the village. We don't want to be seen leaving the school together So hop along to his room and then turn in We've got a long day ahead of us tomorrow.'

Glodstone went up to his rooms and sat on in the evening sunlight studying his route on the map and sipping pink gins. It was nine before he remembered the Major's Scotch and took him the two bottles.

'Bless you, old lad,' said the Major, 'You'll find a couple of glasses in the cupboard. Saved my life. And Perry's off to his uncle's tomorrow.'

'Really?' said Glodstone. 'Anyway, your very good health.'

'Going to need it by the feel of things. Bloody nuisance being cooped up here with no one much to chat to. Are you staying around for long?'

Glodstone hesitated. He was fond of the Major and the whisky coming on top of his pink gins had added to the intoxication he felt at the prospect of his adventure. 'Strictly between these four walls,' he said, 'and I do mean strictly, the most extraordinary thing's happened and . . .' He hesitated. The Countess had asked for the utmost secrecy but there was no harm in telling the Major and if anything went wrong, it would help to have someone know 'I've had a summons from La Comtesse de Montcon, Wanderby's mater. Apparently she's in terrible trouble and needs me . .'

'Must be,' said the Major unsympathetically, but Glodstone was too drunk to get the message. By the time he'd finished, Major Fetherington had downed several stiff whiskies in quick succession and was looking at him peculiarly. 'Listen, Gloddie, you can't be serious. You must have dreamt this up.'

'I most certainly haven't,' said Glodstone. 'It's what I've been waiting for all my life. And now it's come. I always knew it would. It's destiny.'

'Oh, well, it's your pigeon. What do you want me to do?'

'Nothing. I know how you're placed and all that But do remember, you're sworn to secrecy. No one, but no one, must know. I want your hand on that.'

'If you say so,' said the Major. 'Shake a paw. No names, no pack-drill and all that. You can rely on me. All the same . . . Pass the bottle. So you're crossing to Ostend?'

'Yes,' said Glodstone and got up unsteadily. 'Better get some shut-eye.' He wove to the door and went downstairs. On the way, he met the Matron and ignored her. She held no attractions for him now. La Comtesse de Montcon wanted him and the great romance of his life had begun. He crossed the quad. A light was burning in Peregrine's dormitory but Glodstone didn't see it.

'Fuck me,' said the Major, unfortunately just as the Matron entered.

Peregrine shut the book and turned out the light. He had just finished *The Day of the Jackal*.

Chapter 9

In Ramsgate, Slymne hardly slept. Away from Groxbourne and in the saner atmosphere of his mother's house, Slymne could see considerable weaknesses in his plan. To begin with, he had forged two letters from the Countess and if Glodstone hadn't followed instructions to burn the confounded things and actually produced them to her, things could become exceedingly awkward. The woman might well call the police in and they would probably find his fingerprints on the letters. At least Slymne supposed they could, with modern methods of forensic science, and even if they didn't there was still the matter of the hotel bookings. As far as he could see, this was his most fatal mistake. He should never have made the bookings by telephone from England. If the calls were traced the police would begin looking for motive and from there to his own progress across France during the Easter holidays . . . Slymne preferred not to think of the consequences. He'd lose his job at the school and Glodstone would gloat over his exposure. In fact he could see now that the whole thing had been a ghastly mistake, a mental aberration that was likely to wreck his career. So, while Glodstone and Peregrine drove to London next day and booked into separate rooms, one with a bathroom, Slymne concentrated on means of stopping the scheme he had so successfully started. Possibly the best way would be to send a telegram to the school purporting to come from the Countess and countermanding the instructions. Slymne decided against it. For one thing they always phoned telegrams before sending the printed message and the School Secretary would take the call, and for another Glodstone had probably left no forwarding address. To make absolutely certain, Slymne took the opportunity, while his mother was out shopping, to put a large wad of cotton wool very uncomfortably in his mouth to disguise his voice and phone the school. As he anticipated the Secretary answered.

'No, Mr Slymne,' she said, to his horror, 'you've just missed him. I mean he was here till yesterday but he's gone now and you know what he's like about letters anyway. I mean they pile up in his pigeonhole even in term-time and he never does leave a forwarding address. Is there anything I can tell him if he comes back again?'

'No,' said Slymne, 'and my name isn't Slymne. It's . . . it's . . . er . . . Fortescue. Just say Mr Fortescue phoned.'

'If you say so, Mr Fortescue, though you sound just like one of the masters here. He had ever such bad toothache the term before last and —'

Slymne had put the phone down and removed the wad of cotton wool. There had to be some way of stopping Glodstone. Perhaps if he were to make an anonymous phone call to the French Customs authorities that Glodstone was a drug smuggler, they would turn him back at the frontier? No, phone calls were out, and in any case there was no reason to suppose the French Customs officials would believe him. Worse still, the attempt might provoke Glodstone into some more desperate action such as crossing the frontier on foot and hiring a car once he was safely in France and driving straight to the Château. Having opened the Pandora's box of Glodstone's adolescent imagination it was going to prove exceedingly difficult to close the damned thing. And everything depended on Glodstone having burnt those incriminating letters. Why hadn't he considered the possibility that the man might keep them as proof of his *bona fides*? The answer was because Glodstone was such a fool. But was he? Slymne's doubts increased. Putting himself in Glodstone's shoes, he decided he would have kept the letters just in case the whole thing was a hoax. And again, now that he came to think of it, the instruction to burn every piece of correspondence was distinctly fishy and could well have made Glodstone suspicious. As his doubts and anxieties increased, Slymne decided to act.

He packed a bag, found his passport, took the file containing the photographs of the Countess's letter, together with several sheets of crested notepaper and envelopes, and was ready to leave when his mother returned from her shopping.

'But I thought you said you were going to stay at home this

66

summer,' she said. 'After all, you had a continental holiday at Easter and it's not as though you can afford to go gallivanting about . . .'

'I shall be back in a few days,' said Slymne. 'And I'm not gallivanting anywhere. This is strictly business.'

He left the house in a huff and drove to the bank for more travellers' cheques. That afternoon, he was in Dover and had joined the queue of cars waiting for the ferry when he was horrified to see Glodstone's conspicuous green Bentley parked to one side before the barrier to the booking office. There was no doubt about it. The number plate was GUY 444. The bastard was disregarding the Countess's instructions and was leaving earlier than he was meant to. Crossing to Calais and sending a telegram from the Countess addressed to Glodstone care of the Dover–Ostend ferry was out of the question. And Slymne was already committed to taking the Calais ferry himself. As the queue of cars slowly moved through Customs and Immigration and down the ramp into the ship, Slymne's agony increased. Why the hell couldn't the man have done what he was told? And further awful implications were obvious. Glodstone's suspicions had been aroused and while he was still committed to the 'adventure', he was following an itinerary of his own. More alarming still, he was travelling on the same ship and might well recognize Slymne's Cortina on the car deck. With these fears plaguing him, Slymne disappeared into the ship's toilet where he was prematurely sick several times before the ship got under way. Very furtively, he went up on deck and stared at the retreating quay in the hope that the Bentley would still be there. It wasn't. Slymne drew the obvious conclusion and spent the rest of the voyage in a corner seat pretending to read the *Guardian* and hiding his face from passers-by. He was therefore in no position to observe a young man with unnaturally black hair who leaned over the ship's rail and was travelling under a temporary passport made out in the name of William Barnes.

In the end, unable to stand the suspense, Slymne slipped down to the car deck as soon as the French coast was sighted and made a hurried inventory of the cars. Glodstone's Bentley was not among them. And when he drove off the ship at Calais and followed the *Toutes Directions* signs, he was even more confused. Presumably

Glodstone was crossing on the next ferry. Or was he going to Boulogne or even sticking to his original instructions to travel by Ostend? Slymne turned into a side road and parked beneath a block of flats, and, having considered all the permutations of times of ferry crossings and destinations, decided there was only one way to find out With a sense of doom, Slymne walked back to the office and was presently asking the overworked clerk in broken French if he could trace a Monsieur Glodstone. The clerk looked at him incredulously and replied in perfect English.

'A Mr Glodstone? You're seriously asking me if I can tell you if a Mr Glodstone has crossed, is crossing or intends to cross from Dover to Calais, Dover to Boulogne, or Dover to Ostend?'

'Oui,' said Slymne, sticking to his supposedly foreign identity, 'je suis.'

'Well you can suis off,' said the clerk, 'I've got about eight hundred ruddy cars crossing on the hour by the hour and thousands of passengers and if you think —'

'Sa femme est morte,' said Slymne, 'C'est très important .   '.

'His wife's dead? Well, that's a different matter, of course. I'll put out a general message to all ferries   .'

'No, don't do that,' Slymne began but the man had already disappeared into a back office and was evidently relaying the dreadful news to some senior official. Slymne turned and fled. God alone knew how Glodstone would respond to the news that he was now a widower when he'd never had a wife.

With a fresh sense of despair Slymne scurried back to his car and drove wildly out of Calais with one over-riding intention. Whether Glodstone arrived at Calais or Boulogne or Ostend he would still have to come south to reach the Château Carmagnac, and with any luck would stick to the route he'd been given. At least Slymne hoped to hell he would, and since it was the only hope he had he clung to it He might be able to head the swine off and the best place to start would be at Ivry-La-Bataille The place had the sort of romantic picturesqueness that would most appeal to Glodstone and the hotel he had booked him into there was Highly Recommended in the Guide Gastronomique. As he drove through the night, Slymne prayed that Glodstone's stomach would prove his ally He need not have been so concerned Glodstone was still in Britain and had worries of his own. They mostly concerned Peregrine and the discrepancy between his appearance, as altered by dyeing his hair dark brown, and that of William Barnes as depicted on his passport. The transformation had taken place in the London hotel. Glodstone had sent Peregrine out with instructions to get some dye from a chemist and had told him to get on with it. It had been a bad mistake. Peregrine had been booked into the hotel an unremarkable blond and had left it sixteen hours and ten towels later, looking, in Glodstone's opinion, like something no bigoted Immigration Officer would let out of the country, never mind allow in.

'I didn't tell you to take a bath in the blasted stuff,' said Glodstone surveying the filthy brew in the tub and the stained towels. 'I told you to dye your hair.'

'I know, sir, but there weren't any instructions about hair.'

'What the hell do you mean?' said Glodstone who wished now that he had supervised the business instead of protecting his reputation as a non-consenting adult by having tea in the lounge. 'What did it say on the bottle?'

'It was a powder, sir, and I followed what they said to do for wool.'

'Wool?'

Peregrine groped for a sodden and practically illegible piece of paper. 'I tried to find hair but all they had down was polyester/ cotton mixtures, heavy-duty nylon, acetate, rayon and wool, so I chose wool. I mean it seemed safer. All the other ones said to simmer for ten minutes.'

'Dear Lord,' said Glodstone and grabbed the paper. It was headed 'DYPERM, The Non-Fade All-Purpose Dye.' By the time he had deciphered the instructions, he looked despairingly round the room again. 'Non-Fade All-Purpose' was about right. Even the bathmat was indelibly dyed with footprints. 'I told you to get hair-dye, not something suitable for ties, batik and macramé. It's a miracle you're still alive. This muck's made for blasted washing-machines.'

'But they only had stuff called Hair Rinse at the chemist and that didn't seem much use so I –'

'I know, I know what you did,' said Glodstone. 'The thing is, how the devil do we explain these towels . . . Good God! It's even stained the shower curtains, and they're plastic. I wouldn't have believed it possible. And how on earth did it get up the wall like that? You must have been spraying the filth all over the room.'

'That was when I had a shower afterwards, sir. It said rinse thoroughly and I did in the shower and some got in my mouth so I spat it out. It tasted blooming horrible.'

'It smells singularly foul too,' said Glodstone gloomily 'If you'll take my advice, you'll empty that bath and try and get the stain off the enamel with some Vim, and then have another bath in clean water.'

And retreating to the bar for several pink gins, he left Peregrine to do what he could to make himself look less like something the Race Relations Board would find hard to qualify. In the event DYPERM didn't live up to its promise and Peregrine came down to dinner unrecognizable but at least moderately unstained except for his hair and eyebrows.

'Well, that's a relief,' said Glodstone. 'All the same, I think it best to get you on the most crowded ferry tomorrow and hope to hell you'll pass in a crowd. I'll tell the manager here you had an accident with a bottle of ink.'

'Yes, sir, and what do I do when I get to France?' asked Peregrine.

'See a doctor if you fell at all peculiar,' said Glodstone.

'No, I mean where do I go?'

'We'll buy you a rail ticket through to Armentières and you'll book into the hotel nearest the station and be sure not to leave it except to go to the station every two hours. I'll try to make it across Belgium as fast as I can. And remember this, if you are stopped at Calais, my name must not be mentioned. Invent some story about always wanting a trip to France and pinching the passport yourself.'

'You mean lie, sir?'

Glodstone's fork. halfway to his mouth, hovered a moment and returned to his plate Peregrine's peculiar talent for taking everything he was told literally was beginning to unsettle him. 'If you must put it like that, yes,' he said with an awful patience. 'And stop calling me "sir". We're not at school now and one slip of the tongue could give the game away From now on I'll call you Bill and you can address me as . . . er . . . Patton.' 'Yes, si . . . Patton,' said Peregrine.

Even so, it was a worried Glodstone who went to bed that night and who, after an acrimonious discussion with the hotel manager on the matter of towels, took the Dover road next morning with Peregrine beside him. With understandable haste, he booked him as William Barnes on the ferry and by train to Armentières and then hurried away before the ship sailed. For the rest of the day, he lay on the cliff above the terminal scanning returning passengers through his binoculars in the hope that Peregrine wouldn't be among them. In between whiles, he checked his stores of tinned food, the camping gas stove and saucepan, the picnic hamper and the two sleeping-bags and tent. Finally, he taped the revolvers to the springs below the seats and, unscrewing the ends of the tent-poles, hid the ammunition inside them. And as the weather was good, and there was no sign of Peregrine being dragged ashore by Immigration Officers, his spirits rose.

'After all, nothing ventured, nothing gained,' he replied tritely to a gull that shrieked above him. In the clear summer air he could see faint on the horizon the coastline of France. Tomorrow he'd be there. That evening, while Peregrine struggled to explain to the desk clerk that he wanted a room at the hotel in Armentières and Slymne drove desperately towards Ivry-La-Bataille, Glodstone dined at a country pub and then went down to the ferry terminal to confirm his booking to Ostend next morning.

'Did you say your name was Glodstone, sir?' enquired the clerk.

'I did,' said Glodstone, and was alarmed when the man excused himself and went to another office with an odd look on his face. A more senior official with an even odder look came out.

'If you'll just come this way, Mr Glodstone,' he said mournfully and opened the door of a small room.

'What for?' said Glodstone, now throughly worried.

'I'm afraid I have some rather shocking news for you, sir. Perhaps if you took a seat . . '

'What shocking news?' said Glodstone, who had a shrewd idea what he was in for.

'It concerns your wife, sir.'

'My wife?'

71

'Yes, Mr Glodstone. I'm sorry to have to tell you —'

'But I haven't got a wife,' said Glodstone, fixing the man with his monocle.

'Ah, then you know already,' said the man. 'You have my most profound sympathy. I lost my own three years ago. I know just how you must feel.'

'I very much doubt if you do,' said Glodstone, whose feelings were veering all over the place. 'In fact, I'd go as far as to say you can't.'

But the man was not to be denied his compassion. The years behind the booking counter had given him the gift of consoling people. 'Perhaps not,' he murmured, 'As the Bard says, marriages are made in heaven and we must all cross that bourne from which no traveller returns.'

He cast a watery eye at the Channel but Glodstone was in no mood for multiple misquotations. 'Listen,' he said, 'I don't know where you got this idea that I'm married because I'm not, and since I'm not, I'd be glad to hear how I can have lost my wife.'

'But you are Mr G. P. Glodstone booked for the Ostend boat tomorrow morning?'

'Yes. And what's more, there isn't any Mrs Glodstone and never has been.'

'That's odd,' said the man. 'We had a message from Calais just now for a Mr Glodstone saying his wife had died and you're the only Mr Glodstone on any of the booking lists. I'm exceedingly sorry to have distressed you.'

'Yes, well since you have,' said Glodstone, who was begining to find the message even more sinister than the actual death of any near relative, 'I'd like to hear who sent it.'

The man went back into the office and phoned through to Calais. 'Apparently a man came in speaking French with a strong English accent and wanted to find out on which ferry you were crossing,' he said. 'He wouldn't speak English and the clerk there wouldn't tell him where you were landing, so the man said to tell you your wife had died.'

'Did the clerk describe the man?'

'I didn't ask him and frankly, since . . .'

But Glodstone's monocle had its effect and he went back to the phone. He returned with the information that the man had disappeared as soon as he'd delivered the message.

Glodstone had made up his mind. 'I think I'll change my booking,' he said. 'Is there any space on tonight's ferries?'

'There's some on the midnight one, but –'

'Good. Then I'll take it,' said Glodstone, maintaining his authority, 'and on no account is that fellow to be given any information about my movements.'

'We don't make a habit of handing out information of that sort,' said the man. 'I take great exception to the very idea.'

'And I take exception to being told that a wife I don't have has just died,' said Glodstone.

At midnight, he took the ferry and was in Belgium before dawn. As he drove out of the docks, Glodstone kept his eyes skinned for any suspicious watchers but the place was dark and empty. Of one thing, Glodstone was now certain. La Comtesse had not been exaggerating the brilliant criminal intelligence he was up against. That they knew he was coming was proof enough of that. There was also the terrible possibility that the message had been a warning.

'If they touch one hair of her head,' Glodstone muttered ferociously and adjusted his goggles as the Bentley ate the miles towards Iper and the obscure frontier crossing beyond it.

Chapter 10

'Gosh, it's good to see you, sir . . . I mean Patton, sir,' said Peregrine when the Bentley drew up outside the railway station that morning. Glodstone peered at him from behind his one-eyed goggles, and had to admit that he was fairly pleased to see Peregrine. He was terribly tired, had had no sleep for twenty-four hours and the border crossing Slymne had chosen for him had been so obscure that he'd spent several hours trying to find it.

'I'll get some breakfast while you fetch your kit from the hotel,' he said, 'I don't want to be delayed here too long. So step lively. You see, they know I'm coming but that you're with me they do not know.'

And with this strangely accurate remark. Glodstone climbed down and entered a café where, to his disgust. he was forced to make do with café au lait and croissants. Half an hour later the Bentley, which had attracted a disconcerting number of vintage car buffs around it, was once more on the road.

'We've stolen a march on them so far,' said Glodstone, 'but there's no doubt they know La Comtesse has been in communication with me. Which goes to show she has been badly served. And so, from now on, we must be on our guard and keep our eyes open for anything suspicious.' And he recounted the story of the man who had visited the booking office at Calais and had left the warning message. 'Which means they may be holding her against our coming.'

'Your wife?' asked Peregrine. 'I didn't know you had one. For a moment Glodstone took his eye off the road to glare at him and looked back just in time to avoid crushing a herd of cows that was blocking the way.

'La Comtesse. you oaf.' he shouted as the car screeched to a halt.

'Oh, her,' said Peregrine. 'In that case, why did they say your wife was dead?'

To vent his fury and avoid actual violence, Glodstone sounded the horn. Ahead of them, the cows mooched on their way unperturbed. 'Because,' said Glodstone, with barely controlled patience, 'not even the most brazen swine would walk up to a booking clerk and say "Tell Mr Glodstone that if he comes any further La Comtesse will die." The last thing they want to do is bring the police in.'

'No, I suppose they don't. Still –'

'And another thing,' continued Glodstone before Peregrine could send his blood pressure up any further by his obtuseness, 'the fellow enquired which ferry I was taking, which tells me this: they don't know I was crossing via Ostend. At least they didn't last night and it will take them time to find out and by then we must have reached the Château. It's surprise that counts, so we'll press on.'

'When those cows get out of the way,' said Peregrine. 'You don't suppose they're blocking the road on purpose?'

For a few seconds Glodstone eyed him incredulously. 'No,' he said, 'I don't.'

Presently they were able to drive on. As they drove, Glodstone's mind wrestled with the problem of hotels. La Comtesse had arranged the bookings to enable her to communicate with him en route and if he avoided them and pushed on there was the danger that he might miss a vital message. Against that there was the need for speed. In the end, Glodstone compromised and when they reached Gisors, where he had been scheduled to spend the first night, he sent Peregrine in to cancel the room.

'Explain that I've been taken ill and won't be coming,' he said, 'and if there are any messages for me, collect them.' He parked the Bentley out of sight round the corner and Peregrine went into the hotel. He was back in five minutes. 'The manager spoke English,' he said.

'So the blighter should. After all we've saved them from the Hun in two World Wars and a fat lot of thanks we've had for it. Bloody butter mountains and wine lakes and the confounded Common Market,' said Glodstone, who had been looking forward to a short nap. 'And no message or letter for me?'

Peregrine shook his head and Glodstone started the Bentley again. All day, the great car ate the miles and a vast quantity of petrol, but Glodstone pushed along the side roads of Slymne's tortuous route. It was afternoon by the time they came to Ivry-La-Bataille and Glodstone was able to totter into the hotel and remove his goggles. 'I believe you have a room reserved for me. The name is Glodstone,' he said in French that was a shade less excruciating than Slymne's and infinitely more comprehensible than Peregrine's.

'But yes, monsieur. Number Four.'

Glodstone took the key and then paused. 'Has any message come for me?'

The clerk looked through a stash of envelopes until he came to the familiar crest. 'This was delivered this afternoon, monsieur.'

Glodstone took the letter and tore it open. Five minutes later the key to his room was back on the board and Glodstone had left. 'You can stop bringing the baggage in,' he told Peregrine, 'La Comtesse has sent a message.'

'A message?' said Peregrine eagerly.

'Shut up and get in,' said Glodstone casting a suspicious eye round the street, 'I'll explain while we go.'

'Well?' said Peregrine when they were clear of the little town.

'Take a good look at that,' said Glodstone and handed him the letter.

'It's from the Countess asking you on pain of her death not to come,' he said when he had read it through.

'In that case why was it delivered by a man with an English accent who refused to speak English? In short, our friend who left the warning at Calais. And another thing, you've only to compare her handwriting with that of the earlier letters to see that the devils have tortured her into writing it.'

'Good Lord, you mean –' began Peregrine. But Glodstone's mind has already fabricated a number of new conclusions. 'Just this, that they know the route we're following and where we're going to stay the night, which may be to their liking but doesn't suit my book.'

'Which book?' asked Peregrine, browsing through a mental library from *The Thirty-Nine Steps* to The Day of the Jackal with more insight into the workings of Glodstone's mind than he knew.

Glodstone ignored the remark. He was too busy planning a new strategy. 'The thing is to put yourself in the other fellow's shoes,' he said, 'I'm sure we're being watched or waited for. And they know we've had that message yet we're going on. And that will give them pause for thought. You see, we've been warned off twice now. I think it's time we played their game. We'll turn back at Anet and head for Mantes and there we'll spend the night. Tomorrow we'll rest up and tour the sights and then tomorrow night we'll take the road again as soon as it is dark and drive for Carmagnac.'

'I say, that will confuse them,' said Peregrine as the Bentley turned left across the Eure and headed north again.

But Slymne was already confused. Having driven all night to reach Ivry-La-Bataille, he hadn't dared stay there but had gone on to Dreux. There in a hotel he had penned the letter from La Comtesse and had slept briefly before returning with the ominous message for Glodstone to pick up. After that, he had watched the road from a track and had seen the Bentley go by. With a muttered curse he started his Ford Cortina and followed at a discreet distance in time to see the Bentley cross the bridge and turn a little later onto the Mantes road. For a few minutes Slymne was delighted before it dawned on him that, if Glodstone had intended to give up the expedition, there would have been no need for him to have left the hotel or to have taken the road south in the first place. The natural thing to do would have been to spend the night in Ivry-La-Bataille and head back towards Calais next morning. But Glodstone hadn't done the natural thing and moreover, to complicate matters, he wasn't alone. There had been another passenger in the Bentley. Slymne hadn't been able to glimpse his face but evidently Glodstone had persuaded some other damned romantic to join him on his adventure. Another bloody complication. With a fresh sense of exasperation, he followed the Bentley and wondered what to do next. At least the great car wasn't difficult to spot and was in fact extremely conspicuous while his own Cortina was relatively anonymous and could easily match the Bentley for speed.

As they reached the outskirts of Mantes, Slymne made another plan. If Glodstone left the town travelling north, well and good, but if he turned south, Slymne would drive for the Château and be ready to take action before Glodstone could get to see the Countess.

What action he would take he had no idea, but he would have to think of something. In the event, he was forced to think of other things. Instead of leaving Mantes, the Bentley pulled up outside a hotel. Slymne turned into a side street. Five minutes later, the Bentley had been unloaded and then driven into the hotel garage.

Slymne shuddered. Obviously Glodstone was spending the night but there was no telling when he would leave next morning and the idea of staying awake in case the blasted man decided to make a dawn start was not in the least appealing. Slymne wasn't remaining where he was in a sidestreet. Glodstone might, and, by all the laws of nature, must be exhausted but he was still capable of taking a stroll round the neighbourhood before going to bed and would, if he saw it, immediately recognize the Cortina. Slymne started the car and drove back the way he had come before stopping and wondering what the hell to do the next. He couldn't send yet another message from the Countess. Unless the old cow possessed second sight she couldn't know where Glodstone had got to, and anyway letters didn't travel several hundred miles in a couple of hours.

Slymne consulted the map and found no comfort in it. All roads might lead to Rome, but Mantes was a contender when it came to roads leading from it. There was even a motorway running into Paris which they had driven under on the way into town. Slymne dismissed it. Glodstone loathed motorways and if he did turn south again his inclination would be to stick to minor roads. By watching the intersection on the outskirts of the town he would be in a position to follow if Glodstone took one. But the 'if' was too uncertain for Slymne's liking and in any case following was insufficient. He had to stop the idiot from reaching the Château with those damning letters.

Slymne drove on until he found a café and spent the next hour gloomily having supper and cursing the day he had ever gone to Groxbourne and even more vehemently the day he had set up this absurd plan. 'Must have been mad,' he muttered to himself over a second brandy and then, having paid the bill, went back to his car and consulted the map again. This time his attention was centred on the district round the Château. If Glodstone continued on his infernal mission he would have to pass through Limoges and Brive

78

or find some tortuous byroads round them. Again Slymne considered Glodstone's peculiar psychology and decided that the latter course would be more likely. So that put paid to any attempt to stay ahead of the brute. He would have to devise some means of following him.

But for the moment he needed sleep. He found it eventually in a dingy room above the café where he was kept awake by the sound of a jukebox and by obsessive thoughts that Glodstone might already have left his hotel and be driving frantically through the night towards Carmagnac. But when he got up groggily at six and, after drinking several black coffees, walked back into town he was reassured by the sight of the Bentley being washed down by a young man with black hair who looked strangely familiar.

Slymne, passing on the other side of the street, did not linger but went into the first clothing shop he could find and emerged wearing a beret and the blue jacket he supposed would make him look like a typical French peasant. For the rest of the day Slymne lurked round corners, in cafés that commanded a view of the hotel, in shop doorways even further down the street, but Glodstone put in no appearance.

He was in fact faced with almost the same dilemma as Slymne. Having driven for twenty-four hours without sleep, he was exhausted and his digestion had taken a pounding from rather too many champignons with his steak the night before. In short, he was in no condition to do any sightseeing and was having second thoughts about La Comtesse's letter. 'Clearly the swine forced her to write it,' he told Peregrine,' and yet how did they know we would be staying at Ivry-La-Bataille?'

'Probably tortured her until she told them,' said Peregrine. 'I mean, they're capable of anything.'

'But she is not,' said Glodstone, refusing to believe that even a helpless heroine, and a Comtesse at that, would give in to the most fiendish torture. 'There's a message for us here if we could read it.'

Peregrine looked at the letter again. 'But we've already read it. It says   . '

'I know what it seems to say,' snapped Glodstone, 'What I want to know is what it's trying to tell us.'

'To go back to England and if we don't she'll be –'

'Bill, old chap,' interrupted Glodstone through clenched teeth, 'what you don't seem to be able to get into that thick head of yours is that things are seldom what they appear to be. For instance, look at her handwriting.'

'Doesn't look bad to me,' said Peregrine, 'it's a bit shaky but if you've just been tortured it would be, wouldn't it? I mean if they used thumbscrews or red-hot pokers —'

'Dear God,' said Glodstone, 'what I'm trying to tell you is that La Comtesse may have written in a trembling hand with the intention of telling us she is still in trouble.'

'Yes,' said Peregrine, 'and she is, isn't she? They're going to kill her if we don't go back to Dover. She says that.'

'But does she mean it? And don't say Yes . . . Well, never mind. She wrote that letter under duress. I'm sure of it. More, if they could murder her with impunity, why haven't they done so already. Something else is different. In all her previous messages, La Comtesse has told me to burn the letter but here she doesn't. And there's our cue. She means us to go on. We're going to draw their fire. We'll leave as soon as it's dark and take the road we would have gone if we'd never read this letter.'

Glodstone got up and went down the corridor to the bathroom with a box of matches. He returned to the room with a fresh wave of euphoria seething up inside him to find Peregrine staring out of the window.

'I say, Patton,' he whispered, 'I'm sure we're being watched. There's a Frenchie on the corner and I swear I've seen him before somewhere.'

'Where?' asked Glodstone peering down into the street.

'I don't know. He just looks like someone I know.'

'I don't mean that,' said Glodstone, 'I mean where is he now?'

'He's gone,' said Peregrine, 'but he's been hanging about all day.'

'Good,' said Glodstone with a nasty smile. 'Two can play that game. Tonight we'll be followed and so we'll go armed. I'd like to hear what our watcher has to tell us. And let me know if you spot him again.'

But Slymne did not put in another appearance. He had had an appalling day and his feeling about thriller-writers was particularly violent. The sods ought to try their hands at skulking about French towns pretending to be peasants and attempting to keep a watch on a hotel before they wrote so glibly about such things. His feet were sore, the pavements hard, the weather was foully hot and he had drunk more cups of black coffee than were good for his nervous system. He had also been moved on by several shopkeepers who objected to being stared at for half an hour at a time by a shifty man wearing dark glasses and a beret. He'd also had the problem of avoiding the street outside the hotel and this meant that he had to walk down a back-alley, along another street and up a third to vary the corners from which he watched. All in all Slymne made a rough calculation that he must have trudged fifteen miles during the course of the day. And for all his pains he had learnt nothing except that Glodstone hadn't left the hotel, or if he had, he hadn't used the Bentley.

And it was the Bentley that most interested Slymne. As he wandered the streets or stared so menacingly into shop windows his mind, hyped by too much caffeine, tried to devise ways of following the car without keeping it in sight. In books it was quite simple. Reality was something else again. So were boys. On the other hand, if he could only bring the Bentley to a halt in some lonely spot, Glodstone would have to leave the car and go for help. Slymne remembered the time when an enterprising fourteen-year-old at Groxbourne had stuffed a potato up the exhaust pipe of the Art master's car to such good effect that the man had had to have it towed away and the engine stripped before anyone had found out what was wrong. And there had been talk of another master's car which had been wrecked before the War by adding sugar to its petrol tank. Inspired by these memories, Slymne went into a café and ordered a calvados. Under its influence, and that of a second, he reversed his order of priorities. If Glodstone started south again, Slymne could stay ahead of him by sticking to the main roads. But not in the Cortina. One glimpse of its number plate would give the game away.

Slymne left the café in search of a garage where he could hire a car. Having found one, he moved his luggage from the Cortina to a Citroën, bought two kilos of sugar, another kilo of nails, several large cans of oil at different garages, and parked near the hotel. If

Glodstone left that night, he was in for a nasty surprise. Wearily he looked at his watch. It was nine o'clock. He would give Glodstone until midnight. But at ten-thirty the Bentley's bonnet poked cautiously from the garage, paused for a moment and then swung south. Slymne let it go and when it had turned the corner started the car and moved after it. Five minutes later he watched it turn onto the Anet road. Slymne put his foot down, doing ninety on the N183, and before Glodstone could have entered the Forêt de Dreux, the Citroën was six kilometres ahead of him.

Chapter 11

In the event, he need not have hurried. Glodstone was taking his time. Twice he had turned down side roads and switched off his lights.

'Because,' he said, 'I want to give them a chance to go by. They've been waiting to see what we're going to do and they'll follow. But they won't know which road we've taken and they'll have to look.'

'Yes, but when they don't find us, won't they watch the roads ahead?' asked Peregrine who was enjoying himself unstrapping the revolvers from their hiding places beneath the seats.

Glodstone shook his head. 'They may later on, but for the moment they'll assume we're travelling fast. I mean they would if they were in our shoes. But we'll move slowly. And France is a big country. If we lose them here they'll have a thousand roads to search much further south. And here, I think, they come.'

'How do you know?' whispered Peregrine as a Jaguar shot past the side road. Glodstone started the Bentley.

'Because French headlights are yellow and those were white,' he said, 'and if I'm not mistaken, our Englishman at Calais is the link man. He's probably above suspicion too. Some wealthy member of the Bar whose Club is White's and who moves in the best circles. Now a Jag may be a shade too flashy in London but it'll do very well in France for speed.'

And with this pleasing invention Glodstone drove the Bentley out into the road and turned sedately after the disappearing tail lights.

In the Forêt de Dreux, Slymne completed his preparations. He had chosen the end of a long straight with a tight corner on it for his ambush, had parked his car on a track well out of sight round the bend, and was ready to swill a can of oil on the road as soon as he saw the Bentley's headlights. It was a desperate measure but Slymne was a desperate and partially drunk man and the memory of being called Slimey had inspired him with a grim determination. Glodstone had to be stopped, and quickly. As he waited, Slymne made some further calculations. The Bentley would slow before the bend, would then hit the oil slick and skid. Slymne considered its next move and decided that a log in the road would help. He found a fallen branch and had just put it down when the headlights appeared. Slymne emptied the can of oil and crossed the road to be on the safe side. There he lay in the forest waiting for his man.

In the event, he was proved wrong. It was less a man than an entire family, Mr and Mrs Blowther from Cleethorpes and their two children, who were enjoying the privilege afforded by straight French roads of travelling at a hundred miles an hour in their brand-new Jaguar when they hit the oil slick. For a moment they continued on their way. It was a brief respite. A second later the car slewed sideways. Mr Blowther, under the misapprehension that both his front tyres had blown, slammed his foot on the brake. The Jaguar spun like a whirling dervish before encountering the branch and then somersaulted through the air. As it landed on its roof and with a crescendo of breaking glass and tearing metal shot upside down round the corner, Slymne knew he had made a ghastly mistake and was running for the car. Or trying to. After the brilliance of the now shattered headlights, the forest was pitch-black and filled with an extraordinary number of hollows, barbed bushes and invisible trees. As he came abreast of the wrecked car the Blowthers, still miraculously alive, were crawling from the windscreen and giving vent to their outraged feelings. Mr Blowther, convinced that the fallen branch had caused the catastrophe, was particularly vehement about fornicating French foresters and flaming firtrees, and only stopped when Mrs Blowther more maternally began moaning about saving the children.

'Save? Save?' yelled her husband still too deafened to hear at all clearly, 'Of course we'll have to save. It'll take ten years to save enough to buy another effing Jag. You don't think that crumpled conglomeration of craftsmanship was comprehensively covered? All we had was third-party insurance and for your beastly benefit, the only third party is that fractured flipping fir-tree.'

In the bushes the authentic third party shuddered. Not only had he wrecked the wrong car but he had just remembered the oil cans. He had left them in the wood and his fingerprints would be all over the things. Under cover of Mr Blowther's demented alliteration, Slymne slipped back into the forest rather more successfully now that his eyes weren't blinded by the headlights and had reached the cans when the Bentley appeared. Slymne slid into the undergrowth and prayed it would emulate the Jaguar But his hopes were dashed by Mr Blowther who scampered round the corner and was endeavouring to flag down the Bentley when he encountered the oil slick. For a moment, he waved frantically before losing his foothold and slumping down on the road. By the time he had got to his feet four times, had fallen three and had rolled into the ditch, he was not a sight to inspire confidence. Even Slymne could see that. Glodstone could evidently see more. He brought the Bentley to a halt and stared at Mr Blowther suspiciously

'Don't make another move,' he called out. 'You see we've got you covered.'

Mr Blowther took umbrage. 'Move?' he shouted. 'You must be out of your bleeding mind. I can't even shuffle without falling arse over elbow. And as for being covered, I don't know what you think I am now but the way it feels to me I'm a human Christmas tree That flaming holly '

'That's enough of that,' shouted Glodstone, for whom Mr Blowther's North country accent was further proof that he was a gangster and the whole thing an elaborate trap. 'Now get your hands above your head and walk backwards. And remember, one false step and you're a dead man.'

Mr Blowther stared into the darkness behind the great headlamps incredulously 'Listen, mate,' he said, 'If you think I'm going to stick my hands in the air and try to walk anywhere on this grease pan and not be a dead man, you've got another think coming.'

'I shall count to ten.' said Glodstone grimly. 'One, two ' But Mr Blowther had had enough He had been through a terrible car crash and was now in the middle of a second inexplicable night mare. He moved. To be precise he slid sideways and landed on his shoulder before rolling back into the ditch. As he went the Bentley started forward into the oil and, skidding this way and that, disappeared round the corner Thanks to this veering and the erratic swing of the headlamps, Glodstone was spared the sight of the wrecked Jaguar among the trees and of the distraught Mrs Blowther searching in the debris for her handbag and a handkerchief with which to blow the nose of a little Blowther. All his energies were concentrated on keeping the Bentley on the road.

'By God,' he said, when the car finally steadied itself, 'that was a damned near thing. It only goes to show the sort of swine we're up against.'

'Do you think they'll come after us?' asked Peregrine hopefully, toying with a revolver.

'Certain to,' said Glodstone, 'But we'll give them a run for their money. There's a crossroads coming up and I'm going to go left. From now on we'll drive straight through the night.'

Behind them, Slymne was struggling with two empty oil cans and his conscience. From Mr Blowther's vehement opinions and Mrs Blowther's complaints about using foul language in front of the children, he had gathered that, although he had been responsible for wrecking a very fine motor car, the occupants had somehow managed to escape unhurt. It was small consolation. The police would undoubtedly be called to the scene and it would be extremely difficult to explain his presence there or his possession of the oil cans, two kilos of sugar and a large quantity of nails. Worse still, he had the crested notepaper and the notes he had made for Glodstone's premeditated adventure in his suitcase. In the circumstances it seemed wisest to make himself scarce as quickly as possible.

Under cover of the Blowthers' acrimony, he stumbled back to the Citroën, put the cans in the boot and, driving without lights, followed the road by the gap of night sky between the trees. Ten miles further on, he wiped the oil cans clean of fingerprints, dumped them over a bridge into the river and buried his handkerchief in a ditch. To make doubly sure, he poured the sugar into the river too and drove on another mile before disposing of the nails. Finally he burnt the rest of the notepaper and the envelopes, and drove back to Mantes considering extradition treaties. For the first time in his life, Slymne was definitely against them. He was also very much against remaining in France. Whatever Glodstone might find when he reached the Château and even if he still had the forged letters in his possessions, Slymne and no intention of spending time in a French prison for destroying a car and endangering life. It seemed best to leave the Citroën at the garage and drive like hell for Calais in his own Cortina. With any luck, he would be across the Channel and safely home in Ramsgate before the police had made any headway in their investigations. And so Slyme drove quietly into Mantes and spent the rest of the night trying to get some sleep in the forecourt of the rent-a-car garage. At eight that morning, he was on the road for Calais.

Far to the south, the Bentley was still covering ground. Glodstone finally pulled into the side of a very minor road and yawned.

'We seem to have lost them,' said Peregrine, who had spent the night peering over the back of the car in the hope of taking a shot at their pursuers.

'Not the only thing we've lost,' said Glodstone gloomily looking at the map. 'I suppose we can find where we are when we come to the next town. All the same, we're not out of the wood yet.'

'Aren't we?' said Peregrine, too literally for Glodstone's taste. 'I mean we can see for miles around and they don't know where we are.'

Glodstone took out a pipe and lit it. 'But they know where we're heading,' he said, 'And if I were in their shoes I'd concentrate my forces on the roads leading to the Château. I mean I wouldn't waste my time any further afield when it is obvious where we're going.'

He laid the map out on the grass and knelt beside it. 'Now here's the Château and as you see it's devilish conveniently placed. Five roads lead into Boosat but only one leads from the village and past the Château. The drive must come from that road and by the look of the ground I'd say it goes up here. But first it has to cross the river and that means a bridge. That shows they've only to watch the road from Boosat to the north and Frisson to the south and guard the bridge to have us neatly in a trap. In short, if we drive there we're entering a killing ground. And so we won't Instead, we'll go south on this road here to Florial. It's about twenty miles away with empty country in between and no connecting road to Boosat. If we can find a base somewhere there we can travel on foot to these heights overlooking the Château. They may be guarded but I doubt it. All the same, we'll have to move cautiously and take our time And now let's have some breakfast. After that we'll lie up for the day and get some rest.'

Peregrine climbed back into the Bentley and fetched the camping-gas stove and the picnic hamper and, when they had breakfasted, Glodstone unrolled a sleeping bag. 'We'll take it in turns to keep watch,' he said, 'and remember, if anyone stops, wake me. And stop toying with those damned revolvers. Put them away. The last thing we want is to draw attention to ourselves.'

While Glodstone lay on the far side of the Bentley and slept, Peregrine kept vigil. But the road was little more than a track and the country flat and quiet and nothing passed. Seated on the running-board, Peregrine basked in the morning sun and was intensely happy. In a less literal person, the thought might have crossed his mind that his dreams had come true; but Peregrine had accepted dreams as reality from his earliest childhood and had no such gap to bridge. All the same, he was excited, and endowed the countryside around him with dangers it didn't obviously possess. Unlike Glodstone, whose heroes were romantic and born of nostalgia, Peregrine was more modern. Seated on the running-board, he was not Bulldog Drummond and Richard Hannay, he was Bond and The Jackal; a man licensed to kill. Even a cow which peered at him over a gateway seemed to sense its danger and retreated to browse more safely further afield.

So the morning passed with Glodstone snoring in his sleeping bag and Peregrine eyeing the world for lethal opportunities. The afternoon was left to Glodstone. Leaning on the gate and sucking his pipe, he planned his campaign. Once the base was found, they would need enough supplies of food to keep them off the roads and away from towns for several weeks if necessary. He took out a notebook and made a list, and then, deciding that their purchases should be made as far from the Château as possible, he woke Peregrine and they drove on to the next town. By the time they left it the back of the Bentley was filled with tinned food, bottles of Evian water, a comprehensive first-aid kit and a quite extraordinarily long strand of nylon rope.

'And now that we are well prepared,' said Glodstone, stopping to study the map again, 'we'll make a detour so far to the south that no one will suspect our destination. If anyone should ask, we're on a mountaineering holiday in the Pyrenees.'

'With all these torches and candles I'd have thought potholing would be more likely,' said Peregrine.

'Yes, we'd better get them out of sight. What else? We'll need a good supply of petrol to see us there and out again without using local garages. And that requires two jerrycans as a reserve.'

That night, they took the road again but this time their route was further east and through wider and more barren country than any they had seen before. By four in the morning Glodstone was satisfied they had come sufficiently far to turn towards the Château again without risk.

'They'll be watching the north-south roads,' he said, 'but we are coming from the east and besides, the Floriac road is off the beaten track.'

It was. As the sun rose behind them, they breasted a hill and looked down into a shallow wooded valley beyond which a panoply of oaks and ancient beeches rose to a crested range before falling again. Glodstone brought the Bentley to a halt and took out the binoculars. But there were no signs of life on the road below them and no habitation of any sort to be detected among the trees.

'Well, now we have our route in and out secure and if I'm not mistaken, there's a track down there that might prove useful.' He let in the clutch and the Bentley slipped forward almost silently. When they came to the junction, Glodstone stopped. 'Go and take a look at that track,' he said, 'see if it's been used lately and how far it leads into the woods. By my reckoning it points towards the Château Carmagnac.'

Peregrine got down, crossed the road and moved through the trees with a silent expertise he had learnt from Major Fetherington on the Survival Course in Wales. He returned with the news that the track was almost overgrown with grass and ended in a clearing.

'There's an old sawmill there but it's all tumbled down and no one has been down there for ages.'

'How can you tell?' asked Glodstone.

'Well if they have, they didn't use a car,' said Peregrine. 'There are two trees down across the path and they'd have had to move them to get past. It's not difficult because they're not heavy but I'd swear they had been like that for a couple of years.'

'Splendid. And what about turning-room?'

'Plenty up by the sawmill. There's an old lorry rusting outside the place and you can put the Bentley in a shed behind it.'

'It sounds as though it will do for the moment,' said Glodstone and presently the Bentley was stealing up the track. As Peregrine had said, it was overgrown with tall grass and the two fallen trees were light enough to move aside and then replace. By the time they reached the disused sawmill, Glodstone was convinced. An atmosphere of long disuse hung over the crumbling buildings and rusty machinery.

'Now that we're here, we'll use the track as seldom as possible and for the rest we'll move on foot. That's where we'll score. The sort of swine we're up against aren't likely to be used to fieldcraft and they don't like to leave their cars. Anyway, we came here unobserved and for the moment they'll be occupied watching the roads for a Bentley. I'd say they'll do that for two days and then they'll start to think again. By that time we'll have proved the ground and be ready to take action. What that action will be I don't know, but by nightfall I want to be in a position to observe the Château.'

While Peregrine unloaded the stores from the Bentley and put them in neat piles in what had evidently been the manager's office, Glodstone searched the other buildings and satisfied himself that the place was as deserted as it seemed. But there was nothing to indicate that the sawmill had been visited since it had closed down. Even the windows of the office were unbroken and a calendar hanging on the wall and portraying a presumably long-dead kitten and a bowl of faded flowers was dated August 1949.

'Which suggests,' said Glodstone, 'that not even the locals come here.'

Best of all was the large shed behind the ancient lorry. Its corrugated iron doors were rusted on their hinges but by prising them apart it was possible to berth the Bentley under cover and when the doors had been shut there was nothing to show that the place was inhabited again.

'All the same, one of us had better sleep beside the car,' said Glodstone, 'and from now on, we'll carry arms. I doubt if we'll be disturbed but we're in the enemy's country and it's foolish to be unprepared.'

On that sober note he took his sleeping bag through to the office while Peregrine settled down beside the Bentley with his revolver gleaming comfortingly in a shaft of sunlight that came through a slit in the door.

Chapter 12

It was mid-afternoon before Glodstone was prepared to leave for the Château.

'We've got to be ready for every eventuality and that means leaving nothing to chance,' he said, 'and if for any reason we're forced to separate, we must each carry enough iron rations to last us a week.'

'I can see why they're called iron rations,' said Peregrine as Glodstone stuffed another five cans of corned beef into his rucksack. Glodstone ignored the remark. It was only when he had finished and was trying to lift his own rucksack that its relevance struck him at all forcefully. By then each sack contained ten cans of assorted food, a flashlight with two sets of spare batteries, extra socks and shirts, a Calor-gas stove, ammunition for the revolvers, a Swiss army knife with gadgets for getting stones out of horses' hooves and, more usefully, opening bottles. On the outside was a sleeping bag and groundsheet beneath which hung a billycan, a water bottle, a compass and a map of the area in a plastic cover. Even the pockets were jammed with emergency supplies: in Peregrine's case four bars of chocolate, while Glodstone had a bottle of brandy and several tins of pipe tobacco.

'I think that's everything,' he said before remembering the Bentley. He disappeared into the garage and came out ten minutes later with the sparking plugs.

'That should ensure nobody steals her. Not that she's likely to be found but we can't take risks.'

'I'm not sure we can take all this lot,' said Peregrine who had only just managed to get his rucksack onto his back and was further burdened by a long coil of nylon rope round his waist.

'Nonsense. We may be in the field for some time and there's no use shirking,' said Glodstone and immediately regretted it. His rucksack was incredibly heavy and it was only by heaving it onto a rusting oil drum that he was able to hoist the damned thing onto his back. Even then he could hardly walk, but tottered forward involuntarily propelled by its weight and by the knowledge that he mustn't be the first to shirk. Half an hour later he was thinking differently and had twice stopped, ostensibly to take a compass bearing and consult the map. 'I'd say we are about fifteen miles to the south-east,' he said miserably. 'At this rate we'll be lucky to be there before dark.'

But Peregrine took a more optimistic line. 'I can always scout ahead for an easier route. I mean fifteen miles isn't really far.'

Glodstone kept his thoughts to himself. In his opinion fifteen miles carrying over half a hundredweight of assorted necessities across this diabolically wooded and hilly country was the equivalent of fifty on the flat, and their failure to find any sort of path, while reassuring in one way, was damnably awkward in another. And Peregrine's evident fitness and the ease with which he climbed steep banks and threaded his way through the forest did nothing to help. Glodstone struggled on, puffing and panting, was scratched and buffeted by branches of trees and several times had to be helped to his feet. To make matters worse, as the leader of the expedition he felt unable to complain, and only by staying in front could he at least ensure that Peregrine didn't set the pace. Even that advantage had its drawbacks in the shape of Peregrine's revolver.

'Put that bloody thing away,' Glodstone snapped when he fell for the second time. 'All I need now is to be shot in the back.'

'But I'm only holding it in case we're ambushed. I mean, you said we've got to be prepared for anything.

'I daresay I did but since no one knows we're here and there isn't a semblance of a path, I think we can safely assume that we aren't going to be waylaid,' said Glodstone and struggled to his feet. Twenty minutes and four hundred yards of wooded hillside later, they had reached the top of a ridge and were confronted by a dry and rocky plateau.

'The Causse de Boosat,' said Glodstone again taking the opportunity to consult the map and sit on a boulder. 'Now if anyone does see us we've got to pretend we're hikers on a walking tour and we're heading for Frisson.'

'But Frisson is over there,' said Peregrine, pointing to the south.

'I know it is but we'll make out we've lost the way.'

'Bit odd, considering we've got maps and compasses,' said Peregrine. 'Still if you say so.'

'I do,' said Glodstone grimly and heaved himself to his feet. For the next hour they trudged across the stony plateau and Glodstone became increasingly irritable. It was extremely hot and his feet were beginning to hurt. All the same, he forced himself to keep going and it was only when they came to a dry gully with steep sides that he decided to revise his tactics.

'No good trying to reach the Château tonight,' he said, 'and in any case this looks like a suitable site for a cache of foodstuffs. We'll leave half the tins here. We can always comes back for them later on if we need them.' And unhitching his rucksack he slumped it to the ground and began to undo his bootlaces.

'I shouldn't do that,' said Peregrine.

'Why not?'

'Major Fetherington says you only make your feet swell if you take your boots off on a route march.'

'Does he?' said Glodstone, who was beginning to resent Major Fetherington's constant intrusion even by proxy. 'Well, it so happens all I'm doing is pulling my socks up. They've wrinkled inside the boots and the last thing I want is to get blisters.' For all that, he didn't take his boots off. Instead he unstrapped the sleeping-bag, undid his rucksack and took out six tins. 'Right, now we'll dig a hole and bury the emergency supplies here.'

While Peregrine quarried a cache in the side of the gully, Glodstone lit his pipe and checked the map again. By his reckoning they had covered only six miles and had another nine to go. And nine more miles across this confoundedly stony ground in one day would leave him a cripple.

'We'll go on for another hour or two,' he said when Peregrine had finished stowing the tins in the hole and covered them with soil. 'Tomorrow morning we'll make an early start and be in a good position to spy out the land round the Château before anyone's up and about.'

For two hours they tramped on across the causse, encountering nothing more threatening than a few scrawny sheep, one of which Peregrine offered to shoot.

'It would save using any of the tins and I don't suppose anyone would miss just one sheep,' he said. 'The Major's always telling us to live off the land.'

'He wouldn't tell you to go around blasting away at sheep if he were with us now,' said Glodstone. 'The shot would be heard miles away.'

'I could always slit its throat,' said Peregrine, 'nobody would hear anything then.'

'Except a screaming bloody sheep,' said Glodstone, 'and anyway it's out of the question. We'd still have to cook it and the smoke would be spotted.'

But Peregrine wasn't convinced. 'We could roast bits of it over the Calor-gas stoves and that way –'

'Listen,' said Glodstone, 'we've come here to rescue the Countess, not to butcher sheep. So let's not waste time arguing about it.'

Finally they found a hollow with several thorn trees and bushes in it and Glodstone called a halt. 'We can't be more than three miles from the river and from there we'll be able to view the Château,' he said as they unrolled their sleeping-bags and put a billycan of water on a stove. Above them, the evening sky was darkening and a few stars were visible. They ate some sardines and baked beans and made coffee, and Glodstone, having added some brandy to his, began to feel better.

'Nothing like the open-air life,' he said, as he climbed into his sleeping bag and put his dentures in the empty coffee-cup.

'Hadn't one of us better stay on guard?' asked Peregrine, 'I mean we don't want to be taken unawares.'

Glodstone groped for his false teeth. 'In the first place, no one knows we're here,' he said when he'd managed to find them and get them back in his mouth, 'and in the second, we've come the devil of a long way today and we're going to need all our strength when we reach the Château.'

'Oh, I don't know. We've only come about twelve miles and that's not all that far. I don't mind taking the first watch and I can wake you at midnight.'

'I shouldn't if I were you,' said Glodstone, and put his teeth back into the mug. He lay down and tried to make himself comfortable. It wasn't easy. The ground in the hollow was uneven and he had to sit up again to dislodge several stones that had wedged themselves under his sleeping-bag. Even then he was unable to get to sleep but lay there conscious that his hip seemed to be resting on a small mound. He shifted sideways and finally got it settled but only at the expense of his right shoulder. He turned over and found his left shoulder on a stone. Once more he sat up and pushed the thing away, upsetting the coffee mug in the process.

'Damn,' he mumbled and felt around for his teeth. As he did so, Peregrine, who had been peering suspiciously over the edge of the hollow, slid down towards him.

'Don't move another inch,' said Glodstone indistinctly.

'Why not?'

'Because I've mislaid my bloody dentures,' Glodstone mumbled, aware that his authority was being eroded by this latest admission of a physical defect and terrified that Peregrine would step on the damned things. In the end, he found the top plate resting against something that felt suspiciously like sheep droppings. Glodstone shoved it hurriedly back into the mug and made a mental note to wash it carefully in the morning before having breakfast. But the bottom plate was still missing. He reached across for his torch and was about to use it when Peregrine once more demonstrated his superior fieldcraft and his night vision by whispering to him not to turn it on.

'Why the devil not?' asked Glodstone.

'Because there's something moving around out there.'

'Probably a blasted sheep.'

'Shall I slip out and see? I mean if it's one of the swine and we captured him, we could make him tell us how to get into the Château and what's going on there.'

Glodstone sighed. It was a long, deep sigh, the sigh of a man whose bottom plate was still missing while the other was in all probability impregnated with sheep dung and who was faced with the need to explain that it was extremely unlikely that one of the 'swine' (a term he regretted having used so freely in the past) was wandering about on a barren plateau at dead of night.

'Listen,' he hissed through bare gums, 'even if it is one of them, what do you think they're going to think when the ... er ... blighter doesn't turn up in the morning?'

'I suppose they might think –'

'That we're in the neighbourhood and have got him and he's told us he knows. So they'll be doubly on the *qui-vive* and –'

'On the what?'

'On the lookout, for God's sake. And the whole point of the exercise is that we take them by surprise.'

'I don't see how we're going to do that,' said Peregrine. 'After all they know we're coming. That oil trap in the forest –'

'Told them we're coming by road, not across country. Now shut up and get some sleep.'

But Peregrine had slid quietly back up the bank and was peering intently into the night. Glodstone resumed the search for his teeth and finally found them covered in sand. He dropped them into the mug and transferred this to a safer spot inside his rucksack. Then he wormed down into his sleeping bag again and prayed that Peregrine would let him get some rest. But it still took him some time to fall asleep. A lurking feeling that he had made a mistake in bringing Peregrine with him nagged at his mind. He was no longer a young man and there was something about Peregrine's fitness and his blasted fieldcraft that irritated him. In the morning, he'd have to make it quite clear who was in charge.

In fact it was only an hour or so later when he was woken. The weather had changed and it had began to drizzle. Glodstone stared bleakly from his one eye into a grey mist and shivered. He was stiff and cold and doubly aggravated to see that Peregrine had covered his own sleeping-bag with his ground-sheet and pools of water had gathered in the folds. In Glodstone's case it had soaked through the bag itself and the bottom half felt decidedly damp.

'Stay in here any longer and I'll go down with pneumonia,' he muttered to himself and, crawling out, put on a jersey, wrapped the groundsheet round his shoulders and lit the stove. A cup of coffee with a bit of brandy in it would take off the chill. Blearily, he filled the billycan with water and had put his top dentures in his mouth before being reminded by their earthy taste and something else where they had been. Glodstone spat the things out and rinsed them as best he could. Presently, huddled under the groundsheet, he was sipping coffee and trying to take his mind off his discomfort by planning their stategy when they reached the Château. It was rather more difficult than he had foreseen. It had been all very well to drive across France, eluding pursuit, but now that they were so close to their goal he began to see snags. They couldn't very well march up to the front door and ask for the Countess. In some way or other they would have to let her know they were in the vicinity and were waiting for her instructions. And this would have to be done without giving the game away to anyone else. The phrase brought him up short. 'The *game* away'? In the past he had always thought of the great adventure as a game but now in the cold, wet dawn, squatting in a hollow in a remote part of France, it had a new and rather disturbing reality about it, one involving the genuine possibility of death or torture and something else almost as alarming. For one brief moment, Glodstone sensed intuitively the unlikelihood that he should have been asked to rescue a Countess he had never met from villains occupying her own Château. But a raindrop dribbling down his nose into his coffee-cup put an end to this insight. He was there in the hollow. He had received her letters and two attempts had been made, at Dover and again in the forest of Dreux, to stop his coming. Those were undeniable facts and put paid to any doubts about the improbability of the mission. 'Can't have this,' he muttered, and stood up. Over the edge of the hollow drifts of light rain shifted across the plateau obscuring the horizon and giving the broken terrain the look of No-Man's-Land as he had seen it in photographs taken in the Great War. He turned and prodded Peregrine. 'Time to be moving,' he said and was horrified to find the barrel of a revolver pointing at him.

'Oh, it's you,' said Peregrine, who was all too evidently a light sleeper and one who woke instantly, 'I thought –'

'Never mind what you bloody thought,' snapped Glodstone, 'Do you have to sleep with the damned gun? I could have been shot.'

Peregrine scrambled out. 'I didn't have it cocked,' he said without any attempt at apology, 'it was just in case anyone attacked us in the night.'

'Well, they didn't,' said Glodstone. 'It would have been a dashed sight more helpful if you'd let me know it was raining. As it was, I got soaked.'

'But you told me I wasn't to wake you. You said –'

'I know what I said but there's a difference between blathering on about sheep being people and letting me get pneumonia.'

'Actually it was a pig,' said Peregrine. 'When you started snoring it started moving this way and I thought I'd better go out and head it off.'

'All right, let's get some breakfast,' said Glodstone. 'The one good thing about this drizzle is that we'll be able to approach the Château without being seen, especially if we move off as soon as possible.'

But getting anywhere near the Château proved easier said than done. They had covered a couple of miles when the plateau ended on the edge of a deep ravine whose sides were thick with thorny undergrowth. Glodstone looked over and hesitated. There was no question of fighting their way down it. 'I think we'd better head round to the north,' he said but Peregrine was consulting his map.

'If I'm right,' he said, adopting an expression Glodstone considered his own and consequently resented, 'we're too far to the north already, the Château lies three miles south-south-west from here.'

'What makes you so sure?' said Glodstone, once more feeling that Peregrine was getting the upper hand.

'I counted the paces.'

'The paces?'

'We've come about three thousand yards and if we'd been going in the right direction we should have come to these woods by now.'

'What woods?' said Glodstone looking round wearily.

'The ones on the map,' said Peregrine, 'they're marked green and the river is just beyond them.'

Glodstone peered at the map and was forced to agree that they were woods opposite the Château 'Must be something wrong with my compass,' he said 'All right, you lead the way but for God's sake go carefully and don't hurry We can't afford to take any chance of being spotted now And having tried to ensure that Peregrine wouldn't march off at some godawful speed he plodded along behind him. This time there was no mistake and an hour later they had entered the woods marked on the map They sloped away from the plateau and then rose to a ridge

'The river must be on the other side,' said Peregrine, 'We have only to get to the top and the Château should be opposite us.'

'Only,' muttered Glodstone, disentangling his sodden trousers from a bramble bush. But Peregrine was already pushing ahead, weaving his way through the undergrowth with a cat-like stealth and litheness that Glodstone couldn't emulate. Before they had reached the ridge, he had twice had to retrieve his monocle from bushes and once, when Peregrine suddenly froze and signalled to him to do the same, had stood awkwardly with one foot poised over a pile of twigs.

'What the devil are we waiting for?' he asked in a hoarse whisper. 'I can't stand here like a damned heron on one leg.'

'I could have sworn I heard something,' said Peregrine.

'Another bloody sheep, I daresay,' muttered Glodstone but Peregrine was immune to sarcasm.

'You don't get sheep in woods. They're ruminants. They eat grass and –'

'Have two blasted stomachs. I know all that. I didn't come all this way to listen to a lecture on animal physiology. Get a move on.'

'But you said –'

Glodstone put his foot down to end the discussion and, shoving past Peregrine, blundered on up the hill. As he crested the rise, he stopped for a moment to get his breath back only to have it taken away again by the view ahead. Like some holy shrine to which he had at last come, the Château Carmagnac stood on a pinnacle of rock half a mile away across the Gorge du Boose. Even to Glodstone the Château exceeded a life-time's devotion to the unreal. Towers and turrets topped by spire-like roofs were clustered around an open courtyard which seemed to overhang the river. An ornate stone balustrade topped the cliff and to the south, beneath the largest tower, was an archway closed by a massive pair of gates.

Then, realizing that he might be seen from its windows, he dropped to the turf, and, reaching for his binoculars, scanned the place in an ecstasy mixed with anxiety, as if the Château was some mirage which might at any moment disappear. But the glasses only magnified his joy. Everything about the Château was perfect. Window-boxes of geraniums hung from the first floor as did a stone balcony; a tiny belvedere perched on a slim promontory above the cliff; orange trees in tubs stood on either side of the steps leading down from doors set in a round tower whose walls were pierced at intervals to indicate the passage of a staircase that circled up it. In short, all was as Glodstone would have had it. And as he looked, the sun broke through the clouds and the spires and the flagstones of the courtyard gleamed silver in its light.

Glodstone put down the binoculars and studied the surrounding landscape. It was rather unpleasantly at odds with the Château itself and while the latter had a festive air about it, the same couldn't be said for its environs. To put it bluntly, the country was as bleak and barren as the Château was ornamental. A few rather desiccated walnut trees had been planted, and presumably irrigated ever since, to provide an avenue for the portion of the drive closest to the main gates but for the rest the Château was surrounded by open ground which afforded no cover. And the drive itself was formidable. Cut into the rock to the south of the Château, it writhed its way up the cliff in a series of extraordinary bends which suggested a truly maniacal desire for the spectacular on the part of its designer. Finally, to make the approach by road still more secure, a wooden bridge without a guard rail spanned the river.

'Dashed cunning,' Glodstone muttered. 'There's no way of crossing that bridge without signalling your coming.' As if to prove the truth of this observation, a van turned off the road below them and rattled slowly across the planks before grinding its way in bottom gear up the quarried drive. Glodstone watched it reach the walnut trees and disappear round the rear of the Château. Then he turned hopefully to the north in search of an easier way up. True, the slope was less perpendicular than the cliff but the few stunted thorn trees managing to grow among the rocks afforded little cover. And the rocks themselves seemed untrustworthy, to judge by the number that had rolled down and now formed a barrier along the river bank. Last but by no means least in the list of natural hazards was the river itself. It swirled round the base of the cliff with a dark and malevolent turbulence that suggested it was both deep and subject to dangerous currents.

'Well, we've had a preliminary look at the place,' he told Peregrine. 'What we need now is to establish a base camp out of sight and get something warm inside us while we consider the next move.'

They crawled back off the ridge and found a suitable space among the bracken There. while Peregrine heated up some baked beans on the stove, Glodstone sat on his rucksack sucking his pipe and pondered what to do.

Chapter 13

For the rest of the day Glodstone lay in the sun drying himself out and keeping a close watch on the Château.

'They're bound to have some system for watching the roads,' he told Peregrine, 'and for signalling when someone suspicious puts in an appearance and once we find out what that is we can bypass it.'

'Yes, but we're not on the road,' said Peregrine. 'I should have thought the simplest thing would be to swim the river and shin up the cliff . . . What's the matter?'

'Nothing,' said Glodstone when he could bring himself to speak, 'And when do you propose we do this? In broad bloody daylight?'

'Well, no, we'd have to do it after dark.'

Glodstone gnawed on the stem of his pipe and tried to control himself. 'Listen,' he said finally, 'if you're seriously suggesting that we try to climb what amounts to the north face of the Eiger, on a miniature scale, in pitch darkness, you must have less between the ears than I thought you had. We've come here to save the Countess, not to commit bloody suicide. Why do you think the Château is walled on three sides but there's only a balustrade above the river?'

Peregrine considered the question thoughtfully, 'I don't suppose it's very safe to build a high wall on top of a cliff,' he said, 'I mean you never know with cliffs, do you? I've an auntie in Dorset and she's got a bungalow near some cliffs and she can't sell it because some of the other bungalows are slipping over and -'

'To hell with your blasted aunt,' said Glodstone, savaging a can of corned beef with a tin-opener. 'The reason there's no wall on this side is because they don't have to protect it. Only a blithering idiot would try to scale that precipice.'

'Clive did,' said Peregrine unabashed.

'Clive? What on earth are you talking about now?'

'When he captured Quebec. He sailed his –'

'Wolfe, for God's sake. Can't you get anything right?'

'All right, Wolfe then. I never was much good at history.'

'So I've noticed,' said Glodstone, skewering bits of corned beef into the billycan. But Peregrine hadn't finished.

'Anyway, it's not really a cliff And we wouldn't have to start at the bottom There's a ledge near the top and we could get onto it from the drive.'

'Which they've left unguarded just to make things easier for us, I suppose,' said Glodstone.

'We could always make our way round to the south and climb up there,' Peregrine continued. 'That way we'd be coming down the drive from the top instead of the other way round. They'd never expect us to do that.'

'I'll grant you that,' said Glodstone, absentmindedly putting the billycan on the Calor-gas stove and lighting it, 'and if I were in their shoes I wouldn't expect anyone to do such an asinine thing either.'

'Then once we're on that ledge ' He stopped and stared at the smoking billycan. 'I say, I've never seen corned beef cooked like that before. Shouldn't you stir it round a bit?'

Glodstone wrenched the pan off the stove and burnt his hand in the process 'Now look what you've made me do, he said lividly

'I didn't make you do it,' said Peregrine, 'all I said was '

'Once we were on that bloody ledge That's what you said. Well, let's get something straight. We're not going anywhere near that ledge. That cliff is unclimbable and there's an end to the matter '

'What I meant was I didn't tell you to fry that corned beef like that Major Fetherington always taught us to put cans in hot water and heat them that way You open them first, of course, otherwise they might explode.'

'And doubtless he also taught you to climb cliffs in the middle of the fucking night too ' said Glodstone. resorting to foul language as a safety value against exploding himself.

'Well, actually, yes.' said Peregrine 'Mind you, we used tampons.'

'You used what?' demanded Glodstone. momentarily diverted from his burnt hand by the extraordinary vision this conjured up

'Steel things you hammer into the rock,' said Peregrine.

'For your information they're called crampons. Otherwise known as climbing-irons.'

'That's not what the Major calls them. He said always to call them tampons because if you didn't ram them into some bleeding crack really tight you'd end up looking like a jam-rag yourself. I don't know what he meant by that.'

'I do,' said Glodstone miserably.

These revelations of the Major's revolting teaching methods were having an adverse effect on his morale. He had come on an adventure to rescue a noble lady and already the idyll was turning into an unnerving and sordid experience. To get some temporary relief he told Peregrine to shut up, crawled back to the lookout and went through the notes he'd made on the occupants of the Château as he had observed them during the day in an attempt to discern some sinister pattern to their movements.

The van he had seen drive up at 7 a.m. had left twenty minutes later; at 8 a young man in a track suit had come out onto the terrace, had run round it thirty-eight times and had then touched his toes fifty times, done twenty-two press-ups, had lain on his back and raised his feet in the air too erratically for Glodstone to keep count, and had finally wandered exhaustedly back to the door in the round tower on the right under the watchful eye of a portly woman in a floral dressing-gown who had appeared on the balcony above. Glodstone had switched his own observations to her but she had disappeared before he could deduce anything very sinister from her appearance except that she seemed to be wearing haircurlers. At 8.30 an old man with a watering-can had ambled from the gate tower and had made some pretence of watering several flower-beds, which considering the rain there had been through the night, Glodstone found distinctly suspicious.

But it was only at 10 that Glodstone's interest was genuinely aroused. A group of men came out onto the terrace engaged in heated argument. They were joined presently by the woman he had seen on the balcony. Training the binoculars on her, he hoped she wasn't the Countess. His image of her had been more petite and vulnerable. On the other hand, the men lived up to his expectations.

'That's as unpleasant a bunch as I've seen in a long while,' he told

Peregrine, handing him the binoculars. 'Take a good look at the bald-headed bastard with the moustache and the co-respondent shoes.'

'The what?'

'The . . the two-tone shoes. It's my guess he's the leader of the gang.'

'He seems to be having a row with a swine in a grey suit.'

'Probably because they lost us on the road. I wouldn't like to cross his path.'

Peregrine thought this over 'But we're bound to,' he said at last. 'That's what we've come for, isn't it?'

'Yes, said Glodstone, 'Yes, it is. I just meant   Never mind. I'm just pointing him out as a particularly nasty piece of goods.'

'It's a pity we didn't bring a rifle,' said Peregrine a few minutes later 'I could have picked a couple of them off from here with no trouble.'

'Doubtless. And given our position away into the bargain. For goodness' sake, try to understand we mustn't do anything to put the Countess's life in danger. When we strike we're only going to get the one chance. Miss it and she's done for.'

'I'd have done for some of them too. Anyway, I don't miss.'

'Thank God we didn't bring a rifle,' said Glodstone. 'And now let's go and have some lunch. They're going in and I'm feeling peckish myself.'

They crawled back to the dell and settled down to a meal of stale French bread and over-ripe Camembert washed down with vin très ordinaire. 'You'd think they'd have some sentries posted,' said Peregrine as Glodstone lit his pipe

'No doubt they have. But not here. They'll be on the roads or on the far side of the Château. It's nice and flat over there and it's the direction they'd expect an attack to come from.'

'I wouldn't. I'd -'

'I don't want to know. said Glodstone, 'I'm going to take a kip and I'd advise you to do the same. We've got a long night ahead of us.'

He climbed into the sunlight and lay looking up at the cloudless sky If it hadn't been for Peregrine's lust for action and preferably for killing people at the drop of a hat, he'd have been perfectly happy. He'd have to keep him under control. With this thought in mind he drifted off to sleep. But when he awoke it was to find Peregrine squinting up the barrel of a revolver.

'It's nice and clean and I've oiled them both.'

Glodstone asserted his authority. 'Look,' he said, 'tonight's expedition is simply a recce. It's highly unlikely we're going to find an easy way in. We're going to check every avenue . . . Yes, I know there's only one fucking avenue of walnut trees. Just keep your trap shut and listen. We're going to see how many ways there are of getting into the place. And only when we've worked out a definite and foolproof plan will we act. Get that clear in your head.'

'If you say so,' said Peregrine. 'All the same I'd have thought we –'

'I am not interested in what you think. I'm in charge and those are my orders.' And without waiting for an answer, Glodstone went back to the lookout. That ought to keep the stupid bastard quiet, he thought. It did.

Later that night they set out. Peregrine was grimly silent. 'We're going up-river,' Glodstone told him, 'I've an idea we'll find some shallows there.'

Peregrine said nothing but when half an hour later they scrambled down the hillside and crossed the road to the water's edge it was obvious that Glodstone had been mistaken. The Boose ran darkly past and curved away towards the cliff at the top of which the Château loomed weirdly against the starlit sky. Not even Glodstone's imagination could endow the place with anything more romantic than grim menace and when a car swept round the bend in the road above them, its headlights briefly illuminating the river, he was frankly shocked. Dark swirls of water indicated that the Boose was both deep and fast-flowing.

'Well, at least one thing is clear,' he said. 'We know now why they're not watching this side. It's too well protected. The river sees to that.'

Beside him, Peregrine merely grunted.

'And what's that supposed to mean?' asked Glodstone.

'You told me to keep my trap shut and just listen,' said Peregrine. 'Those were your orders and that's what I'm doing.'

'And I suppose you don't agree with me?' said Glodstone.

'About what?'

'That it's impossible to get across here,' said Glodstone and immediately regretted it.

'I could swim across easily enough if that's what you mean.'

'It's not a risk I'm prepared to allow you to take. We'll have to try further on.'

But though they stumbled along the bank for half a mile the river grew wider and less inviting. Glodstone had to admit defeat. 'We'll just have to look for another route downstream in daylight tomorrow,' he said.

'I don't see why you won't let me swim across with the rope,' said Peregrine. 'I could tie it to something on the other side and you could haul yourself over on it.'

'And what about the guns and the equipment in the rucksacks? They'd get soaked.'

'Not necessarily. Once you're over I can come back and get them. The Major –'

But Glodstone had had enough of Major Fetherington's methods. 'If you get across.'

'I shall,' said Peregrine and taking the coil of rope and winding it round his waist he waded into the river.

Left to himself, Glodstone sat disconsolately in the darkness. To conjure up some courage he concentrated his thoughts on the Countess. She had warned him that the affair would be hazardous and she had obviously been telling the truth. On the other hand she had taken a terrible risk herself in writing to him. Above all she had appealed to him as a gentleman, and gentlemen didn't flinch in the face of a mere river. After all, his father had fought at Jutland and a maternal great-uncle had assisted in the bombardment of Alexandria in 1881. There had even been a Midshipman Glodstone at Trafalgar. With such a nautical tradition in the family he couldn't fail in his duty now. And in any case it would never do to show the slightest fear in front of Peregrine. The brute was cocky enough as it was.

All the same, he was decidedly disappointed when Peregrine returned with the news that there was nothing to it. 'A bit of a current, that's all, but it's all right if you swim upstream and anyway you'll have the rope.'

Glodstone took off his boots and, tying the laces together, looped them across his shoulders The main thing was to act quickly and not to think. Even so, he hesitated as he took hold of the wet rope. 'You're absolutely certain you saw nothing suspicious over there? The last thing we want is to walk into a trap.'

'I didn't see anything except rocks and things. And anyway you said they're not watching this side because –'

'I know what I said. You don't have to keep repeating it all the time. Now as soon as I'm over I'll give a tug on the rope as a signal. Have you got that straight?'

'Yes,' said Peregrine, 'but shouldn't I get the rope taut and tied to something?'

Glodstone didn't hear him. He had already plunged into the river and was experiencing to the full what Peregrine had described as 'a bit of current'. To Glodstone's way of thinking – not that he had much opportunity for thought – the lout didn't know a current from a maelstrom. And as for swimming upstream . . . Desperately fighting to keep his head above water and failing (tying his boots round his neck had been a ghastly mistake, the bloody things had filled with water and acted as sinkers), holding his breath when he went under and spouting when he came up, Glodstone clung to the rope for dear life and was swept downstream at a rate of knots. Only the rope saved him and just as he knew he was drowning, he banged into a rock, found himself bobbing in some slightly less turbulent water, and his feet touched ground. For a moment he lay there before scrambling up onto a rock ledge. It was still below water but it served as a seat and when the water had drained from his eye he saw that he was at the base of the cliff. He hadn't much use for cliffs but in the circumstances they were infinitely preferable to the swirling river. Glodstone edged himself away from it and stood up. As he did so he gave a tug on the rope.

Upstream, Peregrine responded. He'd been having some difficulty getting his hands on the cord in the darkness but had finally found it. And now came the signal that Glodstone was safely across. Peregrine dragged on the rope. So, for a moment, did Glodstone,

109

but the imminent prospect of being hauled back into that infernal torrent combined with his inability to stand upright on the slimy rock proved too much for him. With a groan he slumped down and let go. He knew now with a terrible certainty that he should never have brought Peregrine. 'The bloody moron,' he muttered, before realizing that his only hope lay in the moron realizing what had happened. It was a faint hope but he clung to it as desperately as he did to the rock. As usual he was wrong. Peregrine was busy devising a method of carrying the guns and rucksacks across without getting them wet. On their way up the river he had noticed what looked like a rubbish tip. Worming his way along the bank he made a number of other interesting discoveries, among them an ancient bedstead, a rotted garden frame, several plastic sacks filled with garbage, something that felt and smelt like a dead dog and finally an old oil drum. This was just what he needed. He dragged it back and was about to put the rucksacks in when it dawned on him that it wouldn't float upright unless weighted down. After searching around for some rocks he climbed back to the road and brought down a painted concrete block which marked the verge. He dumped it in and tying the drum to the rope, let it out. The thing stayed upright. Only then did he put the guns and rucksacks in and, wedging the thing against the bank, undid the rope from the tree.

Five minutes later he was on the opposite bank. 'I've got everything ready to pull across,' he whispered. There was no reply. Crouching down he stared up the rocky hillside and was wondering where Glodstone had got to when something moved and a boulder rolled down to his left followed by a cascade of small stones. Evidently Glodstone had gone ahead to recce, and as usual was making a bad job of it. Presumably he'd be back in a minute or two and in the meantime the equipment had to be brought across.

Setting his back against the slope and bracing his feet against a large rock, Peregrine grasped the rope and began to haul. For a moment the oil drum seemed to resist his efforts and them with a surge it was out into the mainstream and swirling away almost as fast as Glodstone. Certainly it followed the same course, and Glodstone, who had just taken his sodden pipe out and was sucking it morosely, was suddenly aware that a new and possibly more dangerous element than the river itself had entered his limited domain. With a metallic thud the drum slammed into the rock he was crouching on and it was only by throwing himself to one side that he avoided having his legs crushed. Then as he glared at this latest threat, the thing moved away upstream leaving him to ponder on its purpose. Clearly whatever it was that had attempted to kill him couldn't be making headway against the current unless it was being pulled . . . Glodstone got the message but it was too late to grab the drum. In any case the notion that Peregrine's idea of trying to rescue him consisted of letting heavy metal objects batter the ledge he was on suggested that the lout was insane. Standing well back against the cliff he waited for the next attempt. It never came.

Having pulled the drum up the bank Peregrine hurriedly unloaded it, untied the rope and stowed it on the rocks. Only then did he begin to wonder what to do next. If Glodstone had gone ahead he would presumably come back or send a signal for Peregrine to join him. But as the minutes went by and nothing happened a new and more ominous thought came to mind. Perhaps Glodstone had walked into a trap. He'd said they wouldn't be watching this side of the Château because it was too well protected but that was just the opposite of what Major Fetherington had taught. 'Remember this,' he had said, 'the one place you don't expect the enemy to attack is the one they'll choose. The secret of strategy is to do what your opponent least expects.' But Glodstone hadn't seen it that way. On the other hand, why hadn't they waited to capture him too? Again Peregrine found an easy answer: the swine had thought Glodstone was on his own and didn't know there were two of them. Besides, his fieldcraft was hopeless and you could hear him coming a mile off. And he'd definitely got across because there had been that tug on the rope.

With all the stealth of a dangerous predator Peregrine put the coil over his shoulder, stuffed one revolver in his belt, cocked the other one and began the slow ascent of the hillside. Every few yards he stopped and listened but apart from a goat that scurried off across the rocks he heard and saw nothing suspicious. At the end of twenty minutes he had reached the top and was standing in the dry moat under the walls of the Château itself. To his left was the cliff while to his right was a corner tower. For a moment he hesitated. The notion of climbing in by way of the cliff still appealed to him but it was too easy now. He was about to move round the tower when he found what he wanted to make a genuinely dangerous entry. A metal strip ran down the wall of the tower. A lightning conductor. Shoving his hands behind it, he pulled but the copper strip held. Five minutes later he had reached the top of the tower and was on the roof. He crawled forward and peered down into the courtyard. It was empty but a few windows on the first floor were still alight and opposite him under the archway that led to the main gates a lamp shone down on the cobbles. That put paid to his idea of letting himself down on the rope. He'd be seen too easily.

He got up and moved across the roof towards the tower, and saw a square box-shaped trap protruding from the lead. Kneeling down beside it, he eased the top up and peered down into the darkness. It was obviously a means of access to the roof but what was below? Shoving it still further over, he lay down and put his head through the opening. Silence. Nothing stirred below and after listening carefully he took out his torch and flashed it briefly down. He was looking into a corridor but, best of all, some metal rungs were set into the wall. Peregrine switched off the flashlight, swung his legs over the edge and, hanging onto the top rung, eased the cover back over the trap. Then he climbed down and moving with the utmost caution, crept along the passage to a door at the end. Again he waited with every sense alert for danger but the place was silent. He opened the door and by the light shining through a slit window found himself at the head of a curved turret staircase.

Keeping close to the outer wall, he went down until he came to another door. Still silence. He opened it a fraction and saw a long corridor at the end of which a light was shining on a landing. Peregrine closed the door and went on down. If Glodstone was imprisoned anywhere it would be in an underground cell. Perhaps the Countess would be there too. Anyway it was the first place to look. Peregrine reached the ground floor and, ignoring the door into the courtyard, followed the steps down below ground. Here everything was pitch-dark and after taking the precaution of waiting and listening again, he switched on his torch. The base of the turret had brought him to the junction of two tunnels. One led off to his right under the east wing while the other disappeared into the distance below the main body of the Château. Peregrine chose the latter and was halfway along it when through an open doorway on one side he heard the murmur of voices. That they didn't come from the room itself was obvious. It was rather that people in the room above could be heard down there. He flashed his torch briefly and saw that the place had once been a kitchen.

An old black iron range stood in the chimney breast and in the middle of the room a large wooden table stood covered with dust. Beyond it was a large stone sink and a window and a door which led out into a sunken area. To one side of the sink, a chain hung down over the walled lip of what seemed to be a well. A wooden lid covered it now. Peregrine crossed the room, lifted the lid and shone the torch down and very faintly saw, far below, its reflected light. It might come in handy for a hiding place in an emergency but in the meantime he was more interested in the voices. The sound of them came, he realized, from what looked like a small lift-shaft set into the wall at the far end of the kitchen. Peregrine switched off his torch and stuck his head through the opening. Two men in the room above were engaged in heated argument.

'You're not reading me, Hans,' said an American, 'You're taking a non-power-oriented standpoint. Now what I'm saying is that from the proven experimental evidence of the past there is no alternative to Realpolitik or Machtpolitik if you like . . .'

'I don't like,' said a man with a foreign accent, 'and I should know. I was there at the Battle of the Kursk. You think I liked that?'

'Sure, sure. I guess not. But what happened there was the breakdown of Machtpolitik powerwise.'

'You can say that again,' said the German. 'You know how many Tigers we lost?'

'Jesus, I'm not talking logistically. You had a pre-War situation which was unbalanced.'

'We had a man who was unbalanced too. That's what you fail to take into account. The human psyche. All you can see is the material, the non-personalistic and dehumanized product of an economically dependent species. But never psychical impulses which transcend the material.'

'That is not true. I admit the interdependency of the individual and the socio-economic environment but the basis remains the same, the person is the process.'

The German laughed. 'You know, when I hear you talk that way I am reminded of our Soviet colleague. The individual is free by virtue of the very collectivity which makes him unfree. With you the collective imposes a freedom on the individual which he does not want. In the Soviet case there is the stasis of state capitalism and in the American the chaos of the free-market economy, and in both the individual is tied with the halter of militaristic power monopolies over which he has no control. And that you rationalize as Realpolitik?'

'And without it you wouldn't be sitting here, Heinie,' said the American savagely.

'Professor Botwyk,' said the German, 'I would remind you that we neither of us would be sitting here if twenty million Russians hadn't died. I would ask you to remember that also. And so, good night.'

He left the room and for a while Peregrine could hear the other man pacing the room above. He had understood nothing of what they had been talking about except that it had had something to do with the War. Presently, the American moved out of the room. Below him in the passage Peregrine followed the sound of his footsteps. Halfway along the passage they turned away. Peregrine stopped and flashed his torch briefly. Some steps led up to a door. Very cautiously he climbed them and softly opened the door. A figure was standing on the terrace and had lit a cigar. As Peregrine watched he walked away. Peregrine slipped after him. Here was the perfect opportunity to learn what had happened to Glodstone. As the man stood staring contemplatively over the valley puffing his cigar Peregrine struck. To be precise he sprang and locked one arm round his victim's throat while with the other he twisted his arm behind his back. For a second the cigar glowed and then grew dim.

'One word out of you and you'll die,' whispered Peregrine gratuitously. With rather more smoke in his lungs than he was in the habit of inhaling and with what felt like a hangman's noose in human form round his neck, the advocate of Machtpolitik was for once speechless. For a moment he writhed but Peregrine's grip tightened.

'What have you done with him?' he demanded when the struggling stopped. The American's only answer was a spasm of coughing. 'You can cut that out too,' continued Peregrine and promptly made the injunction entirely unnecessary. 'You're going to tell me where you've put him.'

'Put who, for Chrissake?' gasped the professor when he was allowed to breathe again.

'You know.'

'I swear –'

'I shouldn't if I were you.'

'But who are you talking about?'

'Glodstone,' whispered Peregrine. 'Mr Glodstone.'

'Mr Gladstone?' gurgled the professor whose ears were now buzzing from lack of oxygen. 'You want me to tell you where Mr Gladstone is?'

Peregrine nodded.

'But he's been dead since –'

He got no further. The confirmation that Glodstone had been murdered was all Peregrine needed. With his arm clamped across Professor Botwyk's windpipe he shoved him against the balustrade. For a moment the professor fought to break loose but it was no use. As he lost consciousness he was vaguely aware that he was falling. It was preferable to being strangled.

Peregrine watched him drop without interest. Glodstone was dead. One of the swine had paid for it but there was still the Countess to consider. With his mind filled with terrible clichés, Peregrine turned back towards the Château.

Chapter 14

For the next hour the occupants of the Château Carmagnac were
subjected to some of the horrors of Peregrine's literary education.
The fact that they were a strange mixture, of British holidaymakers
who had answered advertisements in the *Lady* offering a quiet
holiday *au château* and a small group of self-styled International
Thinkers sponsored by intensely nationalistic governments to
attend a symposium on 'Détente or Destruction', added to the
consequent misunderstanding. The Countess's absence didn't help
either.

'Haven't the foggiest, old chap,' said Mr Hodgson, a scrap-iron
merchant from Huddersfield whom Peregrine had caught in the
corridor trying to find the lightswitch. 'You wouldn't happen to
know where the loo is, would you?'

Peregrine jabbed him in the paunch with his revolver. 'I'm not
asking again. Where's the Countess?'

'Look, old chap. If I knew I'd tell you. As I don't, I can't. All I'm
interested in now is having a slash.'

Peregrine gave him one and stepping over his body went in search
of someone more informative. He found Dimitri Abnekov.

'No capitalist. No roubles. No nothing,' he said taking hurriedly
to broken English instead of his normally fluent American in the
hope that this would identify him more readily on the side of
whatever oppressed masses Peregrine's anti-social action might be
said to express. In his pyjamas he felt particularly vulnerable.

'I want the Countess,' said Peregrine.

'Countess? Countess? I know nothing. Countess aristocratic
scum. Should be abolished like in my country. Yes?'

'No,' said Peregrine. 'You're going to tell me where . . .'

Dr Abnekov wasn't. He broke into a spate of Russian and was
rewarded by one of Major Fetherington's Specials which left him

unable to say anything. Peregrine switched out the light and hurried from the room. Outside he encountered Signor Badiglioni, a Catholic Euro-Communist, who knew enough about terrorism to have the good sense to hurl himself through the nearest door and lock it behind him. That it happened to be the door to the room of Dr Hildegard Keister, a Danish expert on surgical therapy for sexual offenders, and that she was cutting her toenails with a pair of scissors and exposing a good deal of thigh in the process, rendered Signor Badiglioni totally incoherent.

'You want me? Yes?' asked the doctor in Danish, advancing on him with a Scandinavian broadmindedness Signor Badiglioni entirely misinterpreted. Babbling frantic apologies, he tried to unlock the door but the good doctor was already upon him.

'Terrorist outside,' he squealed.

'The reciprocated sensuality is natural,' said the doctor and dragged him back to the bed.

Further down the corridor, Peregrine was engaged in an attempted dialogue with Pastor Laudenbach, the German who had been through the Battle of the Kursk Salient and whose pacifism was consequently sufficiently earnest for him to refuse to give in to Peregrine's threat to blow his head off if he didn't stop saying his prayers and tell him where the Countess was. In the end, the Pastor's convictions prevailed and Peregrine left him unscathed.

He was even less successful with his next victim. Professor Zukacs, an economist of such austere Marxist-Leninist theoretical principles that he'd spent a great many years in Hungarian prisons to save the country's industrial progress and who had been sent to the conference in the vain hope that he would defect, was too used to young men with guns patrolling corridors to be in the least disconcerted.

'I help you find her,' he told Peregrine. 'My father was with Bela Kun in the First Revolution and he shot countesses. But not enough, you understand. The same now. The bourgeoisification of the masses is detrimental to the proletarian consciousness. It is only by –'

They were interrupted by the Mexican delegate who poked his head round the door of his bedroom and expressed the wish that they would shoot countesses somewhere else and said that he had enough trouble with insomnia without having proletarian consciousness added to it.

'Trotskyite,' snapped Professor Zukacs, 'imperialist lackey . . .' In the ensuing row Peregrine made his escape. Even to his limited intellect it was obvious the Countess wasn't in this wing of the Château. He hurried along the corridor and found a passage to the right. He was just wondering which room to enter when the matter was decided for him. Someone was moaning nearby. Peregrine moved towards the sound and stopped outside a door. The moaning was quite distinct now. So was the creak of bedsprings.

Peregrine had no difficulty interpreting them. Someone who had been gagged and tied to a bed was struggling to escape. He knew who that someone was. Very gently he tried the handle of the door and was surprised to find it opened. The room was as dark as the passage and the sounds were even more heartrending. The Countess was obviously in agony. She was panting and moaning and the depth of her despair was rendered more poignant by the occasional grunt. Peregrine edged silently towards the bed and reached out a hand. An instant later he had withdrawn it. Whatever other physical peculiarities the Countess might have, one thing was certain, she had a remarkably hairy and muscular behind. She was also stark naked.

Anyway she had got the message that help was on the way. She'd stopped bouncing on the bed and Peregrine was about to explain that he'd have her out of there in a jiffy when she moaned again and spoke.

'More, more. Why've you stopped? I was just coming.' It was on the tip of Peregrine's tongue to say that she didn't have to because he was there and would untie her when a man's voice answered.

'How many hands have you got?' he asked.

'Hands? Hands? How many hands? Is that what you said?'

'That's exactly it.'

'That's what I thought,' muttered the woman, 'at a time like this you've got to ask fool questions? How the hell many hands do you think I've got, three?'

'Yes,' said the man, 'And one of them is cold and horny.'

'Jeepers, horny! Only thing round here that's horny has got to

118

be you I should know So come on, honey. lay off the gags and give it to me.'

'All right,' said the man doubtfully, 'All the same I could have sworn . . .'

'Don't be crazy, lover. Get with it.'

The bouncing began again though this time it was accompanied by rather less enthusiastic grunts from the man and by frantic requests for more from the woman. Crouching in the darkness by the bed Peregrine dimly understood that for the first time in his life he was in the presence of a sexual act. He wondered what to do. The only thing he was sure of was that this couldn't be the Countess.. Countesses didn't writhe and moan on beds with hairy men bouncing on top of them. All the same, he was interested to see what they were doing but he couldn't stay there when the Countess's life was at stake. He was just getting up when the mat on the floor slid away from him. To stop himself from falling Peregrine reached out and this time grasped the woman's raised knee. A strangled yell came from the bed and the bouncing stopped. Peregrine let go hurriedly and tiptoed to the door.

'What's the matter?' asked the man.

'Hands,' gasped the woman. 'You did say hands?'

'I said one hand.'

'I believe you. It just grabbed my knee.'

'Well. it wasn't mine.'

'I know that. Where's the lightswitch? Get the lightswitch.'

As her voice rose hysterically. Peregrine groped for the door-handle and knocked over a vase. The sound of breaking china added to the din.

'Let me go,' shrieked the woman, 'I've got to get out of here There's something awful in the room. Oh. my God. Someone do something!'

Peregrine did. He wasn't waiting around while she screamed blue murder. He found the door and shot into the corridor. Behind him the woman's screams had been joined by those of her lover.

'How the hell can I do anything if you won't let me go?' he bawled.

'Help.' yelled the woman.

As doors along the passage opened and lights came on. Peregrine disappeared round the corner and was hurtling down a large marble staircase towards the faint light illuminating the open doorway when he collided with the British delegate, Sir Arnold Brymay, who had been trying to think of some rational argument to the assertions of all the other delegates that Britain's colonial role in Ulster was as detrimental to world peace as the Middle East question, U.S. involvement in South America and Russia's in Afghanistan and Poland, about which topics there was no such agreement. Since his expertise was in tropical medicine, he hadn't come up with an answer.

'What on earth . . .' he began as Peregrine ran into him but this time Peregrine was determined to get a straight answer.

'See this?' he said jamming the revolver under Sir Arnold's nose with a ferocity that left no doubt what it was. 'Well, one sound out of you and I'm going to pull the trigger. Now, where's the Countess?'

'You tell me not to utter a sound and then you ask me a question? How do you expect me to answer?' asked Sir Arnold, who hadn't been debating the Irish question for nothing.

'Shut up,' said Peregrine and forced him through the nearest doorway and shut the door. 'Any funny tricks and your brains will be all over the ceiling.'

'Now look here, if you'd kindly remove that firearm from my left nostril we might be able to get down to the agenda,' said Sir Arnold, jumping to the natural conclusion that he was either dealing with one of the other delegates who'd gone clean off his head or, more probably, with the I.R.A.

'I said where's the Countess,' growled Peregrine.

'What Countess?'

'You know. If you don't answer it's curtains.'

'It rather sounds like it,' said Sir Arnold, buying time.

Upstairs a fresh problem had obviously arisen. 'Let me out,' bawled the erstwhile lover.

'I can't,' screamed the woman, 'I'm all tensed up.'

'As if I didn't know. And stop pulling my legs, you bastards. You want me to be disembowelled or something? Can't you see I'm dog-knotted?'

'Dear God,' said Sir Arnold, 'This is terrible.'

'Answer the question'

'It rather depends on which countess you mean.'

'The Countess of Montcon.'

'Really? An unusually revealing name, and one that by the sound of things upstairs that young man would have found infinitely more inviting, don't you think?'

'Right,' said Peregrine. 'You've asked for it and you're going to get it.' And shoving Sir Arnold against the wall he aimed the revolver at him with both hands.

'All right, all right As a matter of fact she's not here,' said the expert on bilharzia, deciding that, while he hadn't asked for anything. the time had come to invent something in preference to being shot 'She's at Antibes.'

'And where's she live, this aunt?' asked Peregrine.

'Live?' said Sir Arnold. his sangfroid crumbling under this line of questioning and the discussion going on above. Some voluble woman who claimed to know all about dog-knotting from personal experience with her bull terriers had just tried throwing a bucket of cold water over the loving couple with predictably aggravating results.

'Shit,' yelled the young man. 'Get it into your stupid head I'm not a fucking bull terrier Do that again I'll be clamped in a corpse.'

Sir Arnold dragged his attention away from this academic question and faced up to his imminent death. Peregrine had begun the coundown.

'Antibes is a place, for God's sake. he said, beginning to gibber.

'I know that. but where?' demanded Peregrine.

'Near St Tropez.

'And what's the address?'

'What address?'

'Aunt Heeb's.'

But the strain of being held at gunpoint by a maniac who thought that Antibes was a person while a couple who claimed they weren't bull terriers were being drowned upstairs was proving too much for Sir Arnold.

'I can't stand it I can't stand it.' he gibbered, and proved his point by slumping down the wall For a moment Peregrine hesi tated He was tempted to kick some life into the swine but the sound of footsteps and someone talking excitedly in the hall deterred him. Besides he fairly sure now that the Countess wasn't in the Château, and there was no point in risking capture. Opening a window, he checked that the courtyard was clear and then jumped lightly across the flowerbed. Five minutes later he had reached the roof and was scrambling down the lightning conductor with a lack of vertigo that would have appalled Glodstone.

Not that Glodstone needed appalling. Ever since he had scrambled onto the ledge at the bottom of the cliff he had come to feel differently about adventures. They were not the splendid affairs he had read about. Quite the contrary, they were bloody nightmares in which one stumbled across miles of foul countryside carrying an overweight rucksack, spent sleepless nights shivering with cold in the rain, ate burnt corned beef out of tins, learned what it felt like to be drowned and ended up soaked to the skin on rock ledges from which the only escape had to be by drowning. Having experienced the Boose's horrid habit of sucking things down like some torrential lavatory pan, he knew he'd never be able to swim across.

On the other hand there was little enough to be said for staying where he was. The simile of the lavatory didn't apply there; it was literal. The Château's sewage system was extremely primitive and, in Glodstone's opinion, typically French. Everything it carried issued from some encrusted pipe in the cliff above and was discharged into the river. In practice, a good deal of it landed on Glodstone and he was just wondering if it wouldn't be preferable to risk drowning than be treated as a human cesspit when he became aware that something more substantial was bouncing down the cliff. For a moment it seemed to hang on the pipe and then slid forward out into the river. With the demented thought that this would teach Peregrine not to be such a stupid idiot as to climb cliffs in the middle of the night, Glodstone reached for the body and dragged it onto the ledge. Then he groped for its mouth and had already given it the kiss of life for half a minute before it occurred to him that there were one or two discrepancies between whatever he was trying to resuscitate and Peregrine. Certainly Peregrine didn't have a moustache and wasn't entirely bald, added to which it seemed unlikely that he had suddenly developed a taste for brandy and cigars.

For a moment or two Glodstone stopped before his sense of duty forced him to carry on. He couldn't let the bastard die without doing anything. Besides, he'd begun to have a horrid suspicion what had happened. Peregrine must have assumed he'd been drowned while trying to cross the river and instead of coming to his rescue had somehow got into the Château and was evidently bent on murdering everyone he could lay his hands on Glodstone wanted to dissociate himself from the process. Rescuing Countesses was one thing, but bunging bald-headed men off the top of cliffs was quite another In any case the blithering idiot would never make it. He'd get himself killed and then   For the first time in his life Glodstone had a glimmering sense of reality.

That was more than could be said for Professor Botwyk Thanks to Peregrine's gruesome handling he had been unconscious during his fall and his limpness had saved him Now he began to come round. It was a doubtful relief. For all his convictions that the future of the world depended on stock-piling weapons of mass, not to say universal, destruction, the Professor was an otherwise conventional family man and to find himself lying soaked to the skin being inflated by someone who hadn't shaved for three days and stank like a public urinal was almost as traumatic as being strangled with a lungful of cigar smoke still inside him. With a desperate effort he tore his mouth away from Glodstone's

'What the fucking hell do you think you're doing? he snarled feebly Glodstone recoiled He knew exactly what he'd been doing, reviving one of the most dangerous gangsters in the world It didn't seem the time to say so

'Now just take it easy,' he muttered and hoped to hell the swine wasn't carrying a gun He should have thought of that before. 'You've had a nasty fall and you may have broken something.'

'Like what?' said Botwyk, peering at his shape

'Well, I don't really know I'm not an expert in these things but you don't want to move in your condition

'That's what you fucking think said Botwyk whose memory of some of the horrors he had been through was slowly returning

123

'Just wait till I lay my hands on the bastard who strangled me.'

'That's not what I mean,' said Glodstone, who shared his feelings about Peregrine. 'I'm just advising you not to move. You could do yourself an injury.'

'When I get out of here I'm going to do more than an injury to that son of a bitch. You'd better believe me. I'm going to –'

'Quite,' said Glodstone to prevent hearing the gory details. He didn't want any part of that retribution. 'Anyway, it was a good thing I happened to be passing and saw you fall. You'd have been dead by now if I hadn't rescued you.'

'I guess that's so,' said Professor Botwyk grudgingly. 'And you say you saw me fall?'

'Yes. I dived in and swam across and managed to pull you out,' said Glodstone, and felt a little better. At least he'd established an alibi. Professor Botwyk's next remark questioned it.

'Let me tell you something, brother. I didn't fall. I was pushed.'

'Really?' said Glodstone, trying to mix belief with a reasonable scepticism. 'I mean, you're sure you're not suffering from shock and concussion?'

'Sure I'm not sure,' said Botwyk, whose latent hypochondria had been understandably aroused, 'the way I feel I could have anything. But one thing's certain. Some goon jumped me and the next thing I'm down here. In between being strangled, of course.'

'Good Lord,' said Glodstone, 'and did you . . . er . . . see who . . . er . . . jumped you?'

'No,' said Botwyk grimly, 'but I sure as shit mean to find out and when I do . . .'

He tried to raise himself onto an elbow but Glodstone intervened. It was awful enough to be stranded on a ledge with a murderous gangster without the swine learning there was nothing much the matter with him.

'Don't move,' he squawked, 'it's vital you don't move. Especially your head.'

'My head? What's so special about my head?' asked Botwyk, 'It's not bleeding or something?'

'Not as far as I can tell,' said Glodstone, edging round towards the Professor's feet. 'Of course, it's too dark to see exactly but I'd –'

'So why the spiel about not moving it?' said Botwyk eyeing him nervously.

'I'd rather not say,' said Glodstone, 'I'm just going to . . .'

'Hold it there,' said Botwyk, now in a state of panic, 'I don't give a dimestore damn what you'd rather not say. I want to hear it.'

'I'm not sure you do.'

'Well, I fucking am. And what the hell are you taking my shoes off for?'

'Just making a few tests,' said Glodstone.

'On my feet? So what's with my head? You start yapping about my fucking head and not moving it and all and now you're doing some tests down there. Where's the goddam connection?'

'Your spine,' said Glodstone sombrely. The next moment he was having to hold the Professor down. 'For Heaven's sake, don't move. I mean . . .'

'I know what you mean,' squealed Botwyk. 'Don't I just. Sweet Jesus, I've got to. You're telling me . . . oh my God!' He fell back on the rock and lay still.

'Right,' said Glodstone, delighted that as last he'd gained the upper hand. 'Now I'm going to ask you to tell me if you feel anything when . . .'

'Yes, I do,' screamed Botwyk, 'Definitely.'

'But I haven't done anything yet.'

'Guy tells me he hasn't done anything yet! Just tells me my spine's broken. And that's nothing? How would you feel if you'd been strangled and dropped over a cliff and some limey at the bottom gives you mouth-to-mouth and then says you've got a broken spine and not to move your fucking head? You think I don't feel nothing? And what about my fucking wife? She's going to love having me around the house all day and not being able to get it up at night. You don't know her. She's going to be hot-tailing it with every . . .' The prospect was evidently too much for him. He stopped and glared up at the sky.

'Now then,' said Glodstone, getting his own back for being called a limey, 'if you feel . . .'

'Don't say it,' said Botwyk, 'no way. I'm going to lie here and not move until it's light enough for you to swim back over there and get an ambulance and the best medical rescue team money can buy and . . .'

It was Glodstone's turn to panic. 'Now wait a minute,' he said, wishing to hell he hadn't boasted about swimming across so readily, 'I've sprained my ankle rescuing you. I can't go back into

'Ankle yankle, shouted Botwyk, 'you think I care about ankles in my fucking condition, you've got to be crazy Somebody is for sure.'

'Oh well, if you feel like that about it,' said Glodstone rather huffily only to be stopped by Botwyk.

'Feel?' he yelled. 'You use that fucking word again and someone's going to be sorry.'

'Sorry,' said Glodstone; 'All the same . .'

'Listen, bud,' said Botwyk, 'It's not all the same. Not to me it isn't. Your ankle and my spine are in two different categories, right?'

'I suppose they'd have to be,' said Glodstone.

'You don't need a fucking ankle to get it up and feel and all. Well, it's not that way with spines. Not the way I read it So lay off the feeling part.'

'Yes,' said Glodstone, not too sure now if he'd been wise to raise the issue in the first place. 'All the same . .'

'Don't,' said Botwyk menacingly.

'I was going to say . . .'

'I know what you were going to say And I've answered that one already. It's not the fucking same. Same is out, same as feel is.'

'Even so, said Glodstone after a pause in which he had searched for a phrase which wouldn't infuriate the blighter 'for all we know there may be nothing the matter with your spine The way to find out is to

'Take my fucking shoes off like you did just now, said Botwyk, 'I've got news for you

But whatever he was about to impart was drowned by the sound of sirens A car followed by an ambulance hurtled along the road opposite and turned over the bridge to the Château

'For hell's sake do something, yelled Botwyk 'We ve got to get their attention.

But Glodstone was too preoccupied to answer Whatever

126

Peregrine had done had included more than dumping this foul-mouthed swine over the cliff and if he was caught . . . The notion horrified him. In the meantime, he had better keep on good terms, or as near good as he could get, with the sod.

'Did you notice that?' he enquired, jabbing his finger into the sole of Botwyk's foot when the professor had stopped shouting.

Botwyk sat bolt upright. 'Of course I fucking did,' he snarled, 'What do you expect me to fucking notice if you do a thing like that? I've got sensitive feet for Chrissake.'

'That's a relief,' said Glodstone, 'for a while there I thought you'd really broken your back.'

'Jesus,' said Botwyk, and sank back speechless on the rock.

Chapter 15

He was not alone in this. Mr Hodgson, the scrap-iron merchant who had been dying for a slash and had been the recipient of one of Major Fetherington's Specials, was still incapable of doing more than scribble that he'd been the victim of an attack by one of those damned foreigners and the sooner he got home to Huddersfield the safer he'd feel. Dimitri Abnekov's opinion, also given in writing, was that a deliberate attempt had been made by a CIA hit-team to silence the Soviet delegate and was a violation of the UN Charter and the Helsinki Agreement as regards the freedom of speech. Signor Badiglioni, having been subjected to Dr Keister's clinical approach to what she called 'reciprocated sensuality' and he didn't, wasn't prepared to say anything. And Sir Arnold Brymay preferred not to. Professor Zukas had been too engaged in a polemic with the Mexican delegate on the question of Trotsky's murder and the failure of the Mexican government to collectivize farms it had already distributed to the peasants to remember anything so contemporary as his encounter with Peregrine. Finally, Mrs Rutherby and Mr Coombe once they have been extricated from one another by Dr Voisin. were blaming their agonizing ordeal on Mrs Branscombe, the bull terrier judge. who denied that she made a habit of entering other people's bedrooms to indulge her latent lesbianism by hurling buckets of water over heterosexual couples.

Only Pastor Laudenbach approached the problem at all rationally 'The question we must ask ourselves is why a young man should want so desperately to find a countess. It is a phenomenon not easily explicable. Particularly when he was obviously British.'

'Oh, I wouldn't say that.' said Sir Arnold, who could see an extremely awkward international incident heading his way

'I would. said Dr Grenoy the French delegate He had slept through the whole affair but the honour of France was at stake and in any case he was looking for an opportunity to divert the symposium away from his country's rôle in Central Africa. On the other hand, he was anxious to prevent the scandal reaching the media. 'I am sure there is a simple hooliganistic explanation for this regrettable occurrence,' he continued. 'The essential factor is that while we have all been put to some inconvenience, no one has actually been hurt. In the morning, you may rest assured that adequate protective measures will have been taken. I myself will guarantee it. For the moment, I suggest we return to our rooms and . . .'

The Soviet delegate was protesting. 'Where is the American Botwyk?' he whispered, 'In the name of the Union of –'

'Let's not get too excited,' pleaded Dr Grenoy, now as anxious as Sir Arnold to avoid an international incident. 'The Professor's absence is doubtless due to a comprehensible prudence on his part. If someone will go to his room . . .'

Pastor Laudenbach volunteered but returned in a few minutes to announce that Professor Botwyk's room was empty and that his bed had not been slept in.

'What did I say?' said Dr Abnekov, 'There has been a deliberate conspiracy to destabilize the conference by elements . . .'

'Oh Lord,' said Sir Arnold, appealing uncharacteristically to his French counterpart, 'can't someone bring an element of commonsense to this trivial affair? If that damned Yank had instigated anything he wouldn't have been idiotic enough to disappear. Anyway, there were no political implications. The lunatic simply wanted to know where some Countess was. I told him she was in Antibes. He's probably pushed off there by now.'

'Countess? Countess? Mere subterfuge,' said Dr Abnekov, finding his voice. 'Typical imperialistic tactics to obscure the real issue. There are no Countesses here.'

Dr Grenoy coughed uncomfortably. 'I am afraid to announce that there are,' he said, 'The proprietor of the Château . . .' He shrugged. The name Montcon was not one he wished to announce to the world.

'There you are,' said Sir Arnold more cheerfully, 'The woman has some lover . . .'

He was interrupted by the arrival of one of the ambulance drivers.

'There appears to be an explanation to the disappearance of Professor Botwyk,' Dr Grenoy announced after a whispered consultation with the man. 'He has been found on a rock in the river.'

'Dead?' asked Dr Abnekov hopefully.

'No. In the company of another man. The Emergency Services have been alerted and they should be rescued at any moment.'

The delegates trooped out onto the terraces to watch. Behind them Dr Grenoy and Sir Arnold consulted one another on the need to re-establish Franco-British collaboration, at least for the time being.

'You keep the British out of this and I won't spread the word about Madame de Montcon,' said Sir Arnold.

'It's the wretched American I'm worried about,' said Dr Grenoy. 'He may demand an enormous security operation. Thank God we don't have a representative from Libya.'

They went out onto the terrace in time to see Professor Botwyk and Glodstone being ferried across the river by several frogmen with an inflatable dinghy.

'I just hope he doesn't insist on holding a press conference,' said Sir Arnold, 'Americans make such a song and dance about these things.'

Beside him Dr Grenoy made a mental note to see that the State-controlled French television refused facilities.

But Botwyk was no longer interested in anything to do with publicity. He was more concerned with the state of his own health. In addition to being strangled, dropped into the river and made the victim of Glodstone's suggestion that he might have broken his back, he had also been subjected to the attentions of the Château's sewage disposal system. Being hit in the face by an unidentified sanitary napkin had particularly affected him. With a haunted look he was hauled up the bank and helped into an ambulance. Glodstone was brought up too and together they were driven up to the Château. Only then did Botwyk open his mouth briefly.

'Just get me into a disinfectant bath and a bed,' he told Dr Voisin as he stumbled out into the dawn light. 'If you want any further information, ask him.'

But Glodstone had his own reasons for being reticent. 'I just happened to be in the right place at the right time,' he said. 'I was passing and saw him fall. Swam across and got him out.'

And conscious that he was now in the enemy's camp, he followed Botwyk and the doctor miserably up the stairs to the bathroom.

From the far side of the valley Peregrine watched these proceedings with interest. It was good to know that Glodstone was still alive but rather disappointing that the swine who had said he was dead had somehow survived. Anyway, there was nothing he could do now until darkness came again. He wriggled back to the bivouac and hung his clothes out to dry and climbed into his sleeping bag. For a moment he wondered if he shouldn't take the precaution of moving somewhere else in case they tortured Glodstone into telling them where the base was, but Gloddie would never talk no matter what they did to him. On this reassuring note he fell asleep.

Deirdre, Comtesse de Montcon, never slept in the Château during the holiday season. She would never have slept there at any other time if she could have helped but during the summer she had her anonymity to think about, and besides, by staying the night in Boosat, she was sure of getting the best vegetables in the market and the finest cuts of meat at the butcher. Nobody at the Château Carmagnac could complain that the cuisine wasn't excellent or the service poor. Nor would they know that the expert cook was a countess. More importantly, no one would suspect that the woman who drove up in the Renault van each morning and spent the day scurrying about the kitchen and shouting orders to the other servants was English or that her greatest ambition was to retire to an even greater anonymity in her bungalow in Bognor Regis. Above all, they must not know that she had a past.

Born Constance Sugg, of 421 Selsdon Avenue, Croydon, she had risen by a series of changed identities and useful adulteries to her present title. In fact it could be truthfully said that she had a great many pasts. She had been Miss Croydon at seventeen, a starlet in Hollywood at nineteen, a masseuse in an extremely dubious parlour in San Francisco at the age of twenty-two, a hostess at a dude-ranch three years later and for ten years the wife of Siskin J. Wanderby. By then Wanderby, a man who believed in putting his money where his mouth was, had made and lost several fortunes and Constance, now Anita Blanche and mother of Anthony B. Wanderby, had divorced him on the grounds that never knowing from one week to another whether she was the wife of a millionaire or something destined for Skid Row constituted a particularly sadistic form of mental cruelty. At the time, Wanderby had been on the point of making a fortune out of capped oil wells in Texas and had looked good for a gigantic alimony. Instead, the oil glut had put paid to her hopes and she had been forced to provide for her own future. Since she was in Las Vegas she had changed her name to Betty Bonford and had stayed on as sucker-bait at Caesar's Palace. It was there she met her future husband, Alphonse Giraud Barbier, Comte de Montcon.

At fifty, the count had already gained a considerable reputation as a playboy, a gambler and a piss-artist, a consequence of his having followed his widowed mother's advice to the letter. 'Don't marry for money, Alphonse,' she had told him, 'go where money is.' And Alphonse had. By the time he landed in Las Vegas he had been to almost every expensive hotel, ski-resort, exclusive club and casino in Europe and was down to his last million francs and the Château Carmagnac. He was also under orders to marry the first rich woman who would have what was left of him. Again the Count had done what he was told and had proposed to Deirdre Gosforth (she had changed her name once more for this eventuality) in the mistaken belief that a woman who could win a hundred thousand dollars three nights running in crap games had to be loaded. The fact that it was the dice that were, and that she handed back her winnings to the management, never occurred to him, even when she had steered him in an alcoholic haze through a marriage ceremony and onto a jet to Paris taking with her, for once, all her winnings.

It was only when they reached the Château that the Count realized his mistake and the new Countess knew that in hooking her last sucker she had been hooked herself. Worse still, there was no way she was going back to the States with a hundred grand of the Syndicate's money. She had reconciled herself with the knowledge that any man who breakfasted on black coffee laced with Armagnac was heading for the hereafter at a rate of knots and as his widow she'd be able to flog the Château. The illusion hadn't persisted. The Count's constitution proved stonger than his intellect and while the Château might be in his possession it couldn't be in his will. Without an heir it would revert to the family and the Count's two sisters had no intention of losing it to a Yankee gold-digger. In fact they had done their damnedest to get the marriage annulled. Deirdre had fought back by keeping the Count's alcohol level too high for him to remember where he'd been married, or to care.

In the ensuing vendetta neither side could be said to have won. Deirdre's premature announcement that she was pregnant had driven the two sisters to consult the family lawyers while her efforts to achieve the only partially desired result had killed the Count. Since the traumatic moment when she had realized his brandy droop was terminal and that for the past ten minutes she had been having coition with nothing more responsive than a corpse with a strangulated hernia, the Countess had come to an accommodation with the family.

'You want me out, you buy me out,' she told the relatives after the funeral, 'and that means a million.'

'Francs?' asked ancient Uncle René hopefully.

'Dollars.'

'Impossible. Impossible. Where would we get such a fantastic sum?'

'By selling this dump.'

'Only a madman would pay . . .'

'Not as it stands,' said Deirdre, 'We turn it into a château de luxe. Best food in France, the finest wines, get top ratings in the *Guide Bleu*. We climb on the cuisine gravy train and charge through the nose.'

The relatives had looked at one another thoughtfully. Money talked, but they had their family pride to consider.

'Are you expecting us to become restauranteurs?'

'Leave it to me,' Deirdre told them, 'I run the joint and –'

'The name Montcon means something still in France. We are not petit bourgeois,' said one of the sisters.

'So we don't muddy the name. I'll take the flak. You can keep your hands clean and inside five years we put it on the market and scoop the pool.'

After a great deal of argument, the family had agreed and the Countess, now plain Deirdre, had set to work only to discover that she had been taken for a sucker yet again. The family had no intention of ever selling. She could have her cut of the profits but that was all. Even her threat to drag the name of Montcon through the mud of the courts had backfired. The family no longer existed and the sisters and nieces were content with their husband's names and the income they drew from Deirdre's efforts. Worse still, the youngest sister of the late Count had married Dr Grenoy, the Cultural Attaché to the Embassy in Washington, who had used his position to look a little more closely into Deirdre's background. From that moment, Deirdre had become a dependant. Dr Grenoy had made that clear enough. 'There are . . . how shall I say? . . . certain gentlemen in a town renowned for gambling and violence who have long memories. It would interest them to know where their money has been invested.' Deirdre's eyes had hardened and Dr Grenoy continued. 'However that need not concern us. In France we are more civilized. Naturally we will have to readjust your percentage to prepare for any unfortunate contingencies . . .'

'Hold it there,' said Deirdre, 'I work my butt off and you tell me . . .'

'Madame,' interrupted Dr Grenoy, 'there are additional advantages I have yet to mention. I need not stress your understandable desire for anonymity but I have something to offer. Conferences funded by international corporations, UNESCO, the World Wildlife Conservation. I am in a position to influence the venue and with the service you provide . . . Need I say more?'

'And the cut off my percentage goes to you?'

Dr Grenoy nodded. Deirdre had agreed, with the private reservation that she'd keep meticulous records of Dr Grenoy's new source of income. Two could play that game. And one of these days she would skip France and resume her original identity in her bungalow at Bognor Regis. Constance Sugg was not a name she'd have chosen for herself but it had the great advantage of being on her birth certificate.

Now as she drove the little van back from Boosat her mind was concerned with a new problem. Once it had been impossible to get money out of Britain and easy to shift it from France. The situation had changed and the little gold bars she had slowly accumulated over the years, while they had appreciated enormously in value, made the matter even more difficult. Perhaps if she bribed a fisherman to take her across to Falmouth . . . At least there would be no trouble with Immigration Officials. She was a British subject born and bred . . . But the problem was never to be resolved.

As she drove into the courtyard and saw the ambulance, her mind switched to the terrible possibility that one of the visitors had gone down with food poisoning. Those mushrooms she had used in the *coq au vin* . . . She got out and hurried into the hall and was stopped by Dr Grenoy.

'What has happened?' she asked.

'I can't explain here,' said Grenoy, hustling her into the dining room and shutting the door. 'They've found you. A man with a gun was here during the night looking for you.'

The Countess sat down. She felt sick. 'For me?'

'He demanded of the guests where you were. He asked specifically for the Countess.'

'But no one knows. Except you and Marie-Louise and some of the servants,' she said. 'This is all your fault. They must have traced me through you and your stupid enquiries in the States.'

'I didn't make enquiries myself. I hired a detective. He didn't know who I was.'

'He knew you were French. And doubtless you paid him by cheque.'

'I paid in cash. I am not indiscreet. You think I wanted my wife's family to be known to be involved with such people? I have my reputation to consider.'

'And I've got my life.'

'Exactly,' said Dr Grenoy, 'You must leave here at once. Go to Paris. Go anywhere. This affair could become a national scandal. Professor Botwyk has already had to be rescued from the river and the Russian delegate and the dreadful Englishman, Hodgson, were both assaulted. Not to mention other most unpleasant events concerning the wife of Mr Rutherby and Mr Coombe. The situation is extremely awkward.'

Deirdre smiled. It had occurred to her that there was another explanation. They wanted her out of the Château and she had no intention of leaving except in her own good time. 'Dr Grenoy,' she said, 'with your influence I am sure I shall be well protected. In the

135

meantime, no one knows who I am and, if what you say is correct, no one need know. I shall speak to the servants. You need have no worry. I can take care of myself.'

She went down to the kitchen and found Dr Voisin gleefully helping himself to coffee from the pot on the stove. 'Ah, madame la Comtesse,' he said, 'my illusions of a lifetime have been destroyed. I had always believed that French women, my dear wife in particular, were the most possessive in the world. But now I know better. Madame Voisin, and I thank the good God for it, is only interested in possessing material things. True, one may count the male organ as material, though for myself I prefer a more personalistic approach. Monsieur Coombe shares my prejudice. But Madame Rutherby . . . what a woman! Passion and possessiveness to that degree are fortunately beyond my experience. And one speaks of women's liberation . . .'

'What on earth are you talking about?' asked the Countess, when she could get a word in. 'I understood a gunman was here . . .' She stopped. The less said about the purpose of his visit the better.

'The English,' continued Dr Voisin. 'An amazing species. One cannot designate them as a race. And one would not describe Madame Rutherby as a particularly desirable woman. It is all a mystery. And finally to find that the American has been rescued by an English eccentric with one eye who claims to be on a walking tour in the middle of the night, no, that is not explicable either. And when I offered him a sedative it was as though I was trying to poison him.'

'An Englishman with one eye rescued Mr Botwyk? Did he give his name?'

'I think he said Pringle. It was difficult to tell, he was in such an agitated state. And how the American came to be at the foot of the cliff is another mystery. But I must be off. I have my other patients to think of if I can bring my thoughts to bear on anything except the English.'

And muttering to himself about barbarians he went out to his car and drove off. In the kitchen, the Countess busied herself with the preparations for breakfast but her thoughts were still on the bizarre events of the night. A one-eyed Englishman? Where had she heard of such a person before? It was only when Marie-Louise brought the two men's clothes down to be laundered and dry-cleaned that the puzzle was resolved. And made more mysterious. Inside Glodstone's shirt and underpants were sewn little labels on which were written his name. It was something the school laundry demanded and he had entirely forgotten.

Chapter 16

In the case of Mr and Mrs Clyde-Browne there would never be any forgetting their holiday in Italy. From the first it had been an unmitigated disaster. The weather had been lousy; their hotel accommodation had included cockroaches; the Adriatic had been awash with untreated sewage and the whole damned place, in Mr Clyde-Browne's opinion, polluted by ubiquitous Italians.

'You'd think they'd have the gumption to go to Greece or Turkey for their own blasted holidays instead of cluttering up the beaches here,' he complained, 'their economy's on the brink of collapse and without the money they get from tourism the lira would be worth even less than it is now.'

'Yes, dear,' said Mrs Clyde-Browne with her usual apathy when politics came up in their conversation.

'I mean, no sane Englishman would dream of going to Brighton or even Torquay in August. Mind you, you'd have less chance of bumping into a turd in the Channel than you do here.'

In the end a bout of Adriatic tummy had persuaded them to cut their losses and fly home a week early. Mr Clyde-Browne waddled off the plane at Gatwick wearing one of his wife's tampons and determined to institute legal action against the travel agent who had misled them. His wife, more philosophically, looked forward to being with Peregrine again. 'We've hardly had a chance to see him all year,' she said as they drove home, 'And now that he's left Groxbourne '

'He'll be lounging about the house all day unless I can get him into the Army.'

'All the same, it will be nice . . .'

'It won't,' said Mr Clyde-Browne. 'It'll be pure hell.'

But his attitude changed when he found among the mail cluttering the floor in the hall a letter from the Headmaster apologizing for the cancellation of the Overactive Under-achiever's Survival Course in Wales owing to unforeseen circumstances. 'Unforeseen circumstances, my foot, every circumstance ought to be foreseen. That's what we're given brains for, to foresee circumstances and make contingency plans. Now if that infernal idiot at the travel agent's had done his homework, he'd have foreseen that our bloody holiday would be a downright catastrophe.'

'Yes, but where's Peregrine?' asked Mrs Clyde-Browne before her husband could launch too thoroughly into an impassioned rehearsal of his claim against the firm.

'Peregrine? What do you mean, where is he? He's bound to be at the school. You don't imagine they'd be mad enough to let him try and find his own way home?'

But Mrs Clyde-Browne had already gone into the study and was dialling the school's number. 'I want to speak to my son, Peregrine Clyde-Browne,' she told the School Secretary, only to be told in turn that Peregrine wasn't there.

'He's not there? Then where is he?'

'I'm afraid I've no idea. If you'll just hold the line I'll try and find out.'

Mrs Clyde-Browne held the line and beckoned to her husband who was examining a gas bill suspiciously. 'They don't know where he is.'

'Probably lurking in the school bogs.'

'He isn't at Groxbourne. He's somewhere else.'

'If he isn't there, he's bound to be somewhere else. It stands to reason . . . What?'

'The secretary's gone to see if she can find out where he went to.'

But the strain of his holiday and his fury at the travel agency had been exacerbated by the gas bill. Mr Clyde-Browne seized the phone. 'Now listen to me,' he shouted, 'I demand to know . . .'

'It's no use bawling like that, dear,' said Mrs Clyde-Browne pacifically, 'There's no one there to hear you.'

'Then who the hell were you talking to?'

'The School Secretary I told you she's gone to see if anyone knows where Peregrine –'

'Damn,' said Mr Clyde-Browne, cursing both the school and the state of his bowels. 'Then call me back the moment ' He shot into the downstairs lavatory and it was left to his wife to learn that Peregrine had gone to stay with his uncle

'His uncle?' she asked, 'You wouldn't happen to know which one?'

The secretary didn't. Mrs Clyde-Brown put the phone down, picked it up again and called her sister-in-law in Aylesbury only to find that Peregrine wasn't there. It was the same with Uncle Martin and all the other uncles and aunts. Mrs Clyde-Browne broke down. 'They said he'd gone to stay with one of his uncles but he hasn't,' she moaned through the lavatory door. Inside, Mr Clyde-Brown was heard to mutter that he wasn't surprised and gave vent to his paternal feelings by flushing the pan.

'You don't seem to care,' she wept when he came out and headed for the medicine cupboard. 'Don't you have any normal feelings as a father?'

Mr Clyde-Brown took two tablespoonfuls of kaolin and mor-phine before replying. 'Considering I have just flown halfway across Europe wearing one of your sanitary napkins to contain myself, what feelings I have whether as a father or not can't by any stretch of the imagination be called normal. When I think what might have happened if the Customs officer you tried to bluff about that silk had given me a body search, my blood runs cold. As a matter of fact, it's running cold now '

'In that case, if you're not prepared to do anything, I'm going to call the police,' said Mrs Clyde-Browne realizing for the first time in her married life that she was in a strong position.

Mr Clyde-Browne, who had been heading for the stairs and bed, stopped in his tracks. 'Police? What on earth are you going to do that for?'

'Because Peregrine is a missing person.'

'He's certainly missing something, though I'd qualify the word "person", but if you think for one moment the police are going to be involved '

It was an acrimonious exchange and was only ended by Mr Clyde-Browne's inability to be in the lavatory and to stop his wife reaching the phone at the same time. 'All right,' he conceded frantically, 'I promise to do everything humanly possible to find him as soon as I'm physically able provided you don't call the police.'

'I can't see why not. It seems the sensible thing to do.'

'Because,' snarled her husband, 'if there's one thing a prospective employer – and God know they're few and far between in Peregrine's case – dislikes as a reference it is a police record.'

'But Peregrine wouldn't have a police record. He'd be . . .'

'Listed on the Missing Persons Computer at New Scotland Yard, and where the Army and banks are concerned that constitutes a police record. Oh, damnation.' He stumbled back into the lavatory and sat there thinking dark thoughts about dysentery and idiot sons. He emerged to find his wife standing by the front door.

'We're leaving now,' she said.

'Leaving? Leaving for where?'

'Groxbourne. You said you'd do everything possible to find poor Peregrine and I'm holding you to it.'

Mr Clyde-Browne hung onto the door sill. 'But I can't drive all that way in my condition.'

'Possibly not,' said Mrs Clyde-Browne, 'but I can. And since we haven't unpacked, we can leave straight away.'

Mr Clyde-Browne climbed submissively into the seat beside her. 'I just hope to hell you know what you're doing,' he moaned, 'and you'd better be prepared to stop fairly frequently.'

'I do and I am,' she said with a terseness he'd never heard before.

An hour later, his experience of the three motorway toilets his wife had allowed him to use had been so revolting that he was half disposed to think more highly of Italians. 'If further proof were needed that this country's gone to the dogs . . .'

'Never mind about the country,' snapped Mrs Clyde-Browne, hurtling past a petrol tanker at ninety miles an hour, 'What I want to know is where Peregrine has gone to. You don't seem to realize our son is lost.'

Mr Clyde-Browne checked his safety belt again. 'Not the only thing we'll lose if you continue to drive   Mind that flaming motorbike! Dear God!'

All in all it had been a hair-raising journey and by the time the car skidded to a halt outside the school office Mr Clyde-Browne was in a state of shock and his wife wasn't to be trifled with

'I'm not trifling with you,' said the School Secretary indignantly, 'I am simply telling you that the Headmaster is on holiday.'

'Where?'

'On the Isle of Skye. I can find the address of his cottage if you like. He's not on the phone.'

But Mr Clyde-Browne had heard enough. To ward off the terrifying possibility that his wife might insist on driving through the night to the West Coast of Scotland he interposed himself between them. 'Our son Peregrine is missing,' he said, 'He was supposed to go on the Survival Course in Wales He has not returned home. Now since Major Fetherington was in charge of the course he's *in loco parentis*, and . . '

'He's not,' said the secretary, 'he's in the Sanatorium. If you ask Matron nicely she may let you see him. It's across the quad and up the steps by the chapel.'

'Impudent hussy,' said Mrs Clyde-Browne when they left the office. Her husband said nothing. As they marched across the grim quad and past the looming chapel, he was praying that Peregrine hadn't been left in Wales. The notion of being driven there was almost as bad as Scotland.

'Is there anyone about?' Mrs Clyde-Browne shouted when they found the Sanatorium and had tried several empty rooms in vain. At the end of the passage a door opened and a woman peered out.

'We want to see Major Fetherington,' said Mr Clyde-Browne.

The woman looked doubtful. 'I'm just giving him a bed-bath.' she muttered, 'If you'll just wait a minute . .'

But Mrs Clyde-Brown wasn't waiting for a second. Pushing past her husband, she bore down on the Matron. For a moment there was a confused scuffle and then the Matron managed to shut the door and lock it.

'Bed-bath indeed!' said Mrs Clyde-Browne, when she had got her breath back. 'If you'd seen what I saw . .'

'Which, thankfully I didn't,' said her husband, 'now for goodness sake try and get a grip on yourself . . .'

'Grip on myself? I like that. If you ask me those two were . . .'

'I daresay,' snapped Mr Clyde-Browne, 'but if we're to get the Major's co-operation you're not going to help matters by intruding on his private affairs.'

'Private affairs indeed! That depraved creature was stark naked and wearing a French tickler and if you call that a bed-bath, I most certainly don't,' said Mrs Clyde-Browne, managing to combine a sexual knowledge her husband had never suspected with a grievance that he'd never bothered to use one. But before he could reply the bedroom door opened and the Matron appeared. Mr Clyde-Browne was grateful to note that this time she was wearing a skirt.

'Well I must say . . .' she began.

'Don't,' begged Mr Clyde-Browne, 'We're extremely sorry to have . . .'

'I'm not,' interrupted his wife, 'considering that that filthy man in there –'

Mr Clyde-Browne had had enough. 'Shut up,' he told her violently and, leaving her speechless, explained the situation as swiftly as he could to the Matron.

By the time he had finished she was slightly mollified. 'I'll go and see if the Major is prepared to see you,' she said, pointedly ignoring Mrs Clyde-Browne.

'Well I like that,' Mrs Clyde-Browne exploded when the door was shut. 'To think that I should be told to shut up in front of a –'

'Shut up!' roared Mr Clyde-Browne again. 'You've already done enough damage and from now on you'll leave the matter in my hands.'

'In your hands? If I'd had my way none of this would have happened. In the first place –'

'Peregrine would have been aborted. But since he wasn't you had to delude yourself that you'd given birth to a bloody genius. Well, let me tell you –'

By the time he had got his feelings about Peregrine off his chest, Mr Clyde-Browne felt better. In the next room Major Fetherington didn't. 'If he feels like that about the poor sod I'm not surprised Perry's gone missing. What I can't understand is why that maniac wants to find him. He'd be better off in the Foreign Legion.'

'Yes, but what are you going to tell them?' asked the Matron.

'Lord alone knows. As far as I can remember, he told me he was going to stay with his uncle and then pushed off. That's my story and I'm going to stick to it.'

Five minutes later, Mr Clyde-Browne's legal approach had changed his mind. 'Are you suggesting, Major, that my son was guilty of a deliberate falsehood?'

The Major shifted uncomfortably under the bedclothes. 'Well, no, not when you put it like that. All the same he did say he'd phoned his uncle and . . .'

'The inescapable fact remains that he hadn't and that no one has seen him since he was left in your care.'

Major Fetherington considered the inescapable fact and tried to elude it. 'Someone must have seen him. Stands to reason. He can't have vanished into thin air.'

'On the other hand, you were personally responsible for his welfare prior to his disappearance? Can you deny that?'

'Prior to, old boy, prior to. That's the operative word,' said the Major.

'As a matter of fact it's two words,' said Mr Clyde-Browne, getting his own back for being called an old boy.

'All right, two operative words. Doesn't make any difference. As soon as he said he was going to his uncle's and shoved off I couldn't be responsible for his welfare, could I?'

'Then you didn't accompany him to the station?'

'Accompany him to the station?' said the Major indignantly, 'I wasn't capable of accompanying anyone anywhere. I was flat on my back with a fractured coccyx. Damned painful I can –'

'And having it massaged by the Matron no doubt,' interrupted Mr Clyde-Browne, who had taken out a pocket book and was making notes.

Major Fetherington turned pale and decided to change his tactics. 'Look,' he said, 'I'll do a deal.'

'A deal?'

'No names, no packdrill. You don't mention anything to the Headmaster about you-know-what and . . .' He paused to see how Mr Clyde-Browne would respond.

The solicitor nodded. 'Do go on,' he said.

'As I was saying, no names, no packdrill. The chappie you really want to see is Glodstone . . .'

Outside, Mrs Clyde-Browne sipped a cup of tea reluctantly. It was a peace offering from the Matron but Mrs Clyde-Browne wasn't mollified. She was wondering how her husband could have condemned her Peregrine to such a terrible environment. 'I blame myself,' she whimpered internally.

In the school office her words would have found an echo in Slymne. Ever since he had wrecked the Blowthers' brand-new Jaguar he had been cursing himself for his stupidity. He had been mad to plan Glodstone's prepackaged adventure. In an attempt to give himself some sort of alibi he had returned to the school, ostensibly to collect some books, only to learn that events had taken another turn for the worse.

'I've never seen parents so livid,' the School Secretary told him. 'And rude. Not even Mr and Mrs Fairchild when their son was expelled for tying a ferret to the crotch of Mr Paignton's pyjamas.'

'Good Lord,' said Slymne, who remembered the consequences of that awful occasion and had examined his own pyjamas very carefully ever since.

'And all because that stupid Peregrine Clyde-Browne hasn't gone home and they don't know where he is.'

Slymne's heartbeat went up alarmingly. He knew now why the youth he had seen washing the Bentley in Mantes had seemed so familiar. 'What did you tell them?' he asked tremulously.

'I told them to see the Major. What I didn't tell them was that Mrs Brossy at the Post Office says she saw a boy get into Mr Glodstone's old banger down at the bus-stop the day he went away.'

'Who went away?' asked Slymne, his alarm growing by the minute.

'Mr Glodstone. He came back here all excited and –'

'Look,' said Slymne, 'does the Headmaster know about this?'

145

The secretary shook her head. 'I said he was on holiday on the Isle of Skye. Actually, he's in his caravan at Scarborough but he doesn't like that to be known. Doesn't sound so respectable, does it?'

'But he's on the phone?'

'The campsite is.'

'Right,' said Slymne, coming to a sudden decision, rather than have them bothering you, I'll deal with them. Now what's the number of the campsite?'

By the time the Clyde-Brownes left the Sanatorium Slymne was ready for them. 'Good afternoon,' he said briskly, 'my name is Slymne. I'm the geography master here. Miss Crabley tell me you're concerned about your son.'

Mr Clyde-Browne stopped in his tracks. Mr Slymne's reports on Peregrine's lack of any academic ability had always struck him as proving that at least one master at Groxbourne was neither a complete idiot nor a barefaced liar.

'More than concerned,' he said. 'The boy's missing and from what I've been able to gather from that man Fetherington there seems to be good reason to suppose he's been abducted by Mr Glodstone.'

Slymne's mouth dried up. Mr Clyde-Browne was evidently an expert investigator. 'Mr Glodstone's abducted your son? Are you quite sure? I mean it seems , . .'

'Of course I'm not sure. I'd have called the police if I were,' said Mr Clyde-Browne, bearing in mind the law on slander. 'I said I'd been given reason to believe it. What's your opinion of Glodstone?'

'I'd rather not comment,' said Slymne, glad to be able to tell the truth for the time being, 'my relations with him are not of the best and I might be prejudiced. I think you ought to consult the Headmaster.'

'Who happens to be in the Outer Hebrides.'

'In the circumstances I'm sure he'll return immediately. I'll wire him to say that you're here. Now would you like me to find some accommodation locally? There's an excellent hotel in Leominster.'

When they left, the Clyde-Brownes were slightly happier in their minds. 'Thank God someone round here seems to have his head screwed on the right way,' said Mr Clyde-Browne.

'And he did seem to think that Peregrine was in safe hands,' said his wife, 'I do hope he's right.'

Mr Clyde-Browne kept his thoughts on the subject to himself. His hopes were rather different. He was wondering how best to intimidate the Headmaster into paying considerable damages for the loss of a son.

In the school office Slymne picked up the phone and dialled the campsite in Scarborough. About the only bright spot he could see on the horizon was that the Clyde-Brownes were evidently reluctant to call in the police.

Chapter 17

It was mid-morning before the Headmaster arrived to be met by a haggard and desperate Slymne. His conversation with the Major the previous night, assisted by a bottle of whisky, had appalled him. Glodstone had told the Major where he was going. And since he had confided so much it seemed all too likely that he had kept those damning letters. Slymne had spent a sleepless night trying to think of some way to dissociate himself from the whole ghastly business. The best strategy seemed to be to show that he had already acted responsibly.

'I've checked the railway station and the bus people,' he told the Headmaster, 'and it's clear that Clyde-Browne didn't leave by bus or train on the 31st, which is the day he went missing.'

'That's a great help,' said the Headmaster. 'What I want to know is where he *did* go. I've got to have something to tell his bloody parents.'

'Well, Mrs Brossy at the Post Office thinks she saw Glodstone pick a young man up outside her shop around midday.'

The Headmaster slumped into a chair behind his desk. 'Oh, my God! And I don't suppose anyone has a clue where the lunatic took him?'

Slymne played his ace. 'Strictly in confidence, sir, I did manage to get Major Fetherington to tell me that Glodstone had said he was going to France by way of Ostend.'

'Going to France by way of Ostend? Ostend's in bloody Belgium. Are you seriously telling me that that one-eyed maniac has dragged the son of a prominent solicitor out of this country without asking his parents' permission?'

Slymne demurred. 'I'm not exactly saying that, sir. I'm merely repeating what the Major told me in strict confidence and I'd appreciate it if you kept my name out of the business. I mean –'

'Damn Major Fetherington. If Glodstone's gone to France with that ghastly boy we'll all have to go into business. We'll certainly be out of teaching.'

'Quite,' said Slymne. 'Anyway, acting on the Major's tip I phoned the Channel ferry services at Dover to ask if they could confirm it.'

'And did they?'

'Not in so many words. They wanted to know who I was and what my interest was and I didn't think I'd better say anything more until I'd spoken to you. Mr Clyde-Browne didn't strike me as a man who'd take kindly to the news that his son had gone abroad with Glodstone.'

The Headmaster closed his eyes and shuddered. From his previous dealings with Peregrine's father he'd gained the distinct impression that Mr Clyde-Browne didn't count kindliness as one of his strong points. 'So that's all the information we have? Is that what you're saying?'

Slymne hesitated. 'I can't speak for the Major but I have an idea he knows more than he was prepared to tell me.'

'By God, he'll tell me,' said the Headmaster savagely. 'Go and get the fellow.'

Slymne slipped out of the room and crossed the quad to the San. 'The old man wants to see you,' he told the Major, whose physical condition hadn't been improved by a dreadful hangover, 'and if I were in your shoes, I'd tell him everything you know.'

'Shoes?' said the Major. 'If I had shoes and wasn't in a wheelchair I'd have been out of here long ago. Oh well, into the firing line.'

It was an appropriate metaphor. The Headmaster was ready to do murder. 'Now then, I understand Glodstone told you he was going to France by way of Ostend,' he said, ignoring Slymne's plea for discretion. The Major nodded unhappily. 'Did he also tell you he was taking Clyde-Browne with him?'

'Of course not,' said the Major rallying, 'I wouldn't have let him.'

'Let him tell you or let him take the boy?' asked the Headmaster, glad to take his feelings out on a man he'd never much liked anyway.

'Take him, of course.'

'What else did he tell you?'

Major Fetherington looked reproachfully at Slymne. 'Well, if you must know, he said he'd been asked to undertake a secret mission, something desperately dangerous. And in case he bought it. . .'

'Bought it? Bought what, for Heaven's sake?'

'Well, if things went wrong and got himself killed or something, he wanted me to look after his interests.'

'Interests?' snapped the Headmaster, preferring not to dwell on 'killed'. 'What interests?'

'I really don't know. I suppose he meant let the police know or get him a decent funeral. He left it a bit vague.'

'He needn't have. I'll fix his funeral,' said the Headmaster. 'Go on.'

'Not much else to tell really,' said the Major hesitantly but the Headmaster wasn't deceived.

'The lot, Fetherington, the lot. You leave out one jot or tittle and you'll be hobbling down to join the ranks of the unemployed and I don't mean tomorrow.'

The Major tried to cross his legs and failed. 'All right, if you really want to know, he said he'd been asked by the Countess of Montcon— '

'The Countess of Montcon?'

'Wanderby's mother, he's a boy in Gloddie's, the one with allergies and whatnot, to go down to her château . . . You're not going to believe this.'

'Never mind that,' said the Headmaster, who appeared to be in the grip of some awful allergy himself.

'Well, she wanted him to rescue her from some gang or other.'

'Some gang or other? You mean to tell me . . . The man must be off his bloody rocker.'

'That's what I told him,' said the Major. 'I said, "Listen, old boy, someone's having you on. Get on the blower and call her up and see if I'm not right." But you know what Glodstone's like.'

'I'm beginning to get a shrewd idea,' said the Headmaster. 'Mad as a March fucking hare. Don't let me stop you.'

'That's about the lot really. I had no idea he was going to take Perry with him.'

'So you've said before, and it's not the lot.'

The Major tried to focus his thoughts. 'About the only other thing I can think of is that he asked me to let him have a couple of revolvers from the Armoury. Naturally I wasn't buying that one –'

'A couple of revolvers from the School Armoury? Jesus wept! And that didn't tell you anything?'

'Only that he was obviously dead serious about the whole business. I mean obviously

'A couple of revolvers, you moron,' shouted the Headmaster, 'not just one. Who the hell do you think the second one was for?'

'Now that you come to mention it –'

'Mention it? Mention it?' yelled the Headmaster 'What I want to know is why you didn't mention it at the bloody time?'

'Well, since he didn't get them there didn't seem much point,' said the Major. 'If Glodstone wanted to go off on some wild goose chase that was his affair and –'

'Slymne,' interrupted the Headmaster before the Major could say it was no skin off his nose what Glodstone did, 'take him to the Armoury and see that there aren't two revolvers and half a dozen rifles missing. I want every weapon accounted for.'

'But I've just told you –'

'I know what you've told me and I'm not taking any chances on your opinion. Now get out.'

As Slymne bundled the Major's wheelchair through the door, the Headmaster put his head in his hands. The situation was far worse than he had imagined. It had been bad enough to suppose that Glodstone had merely taken the wretched boy on some jaunt round the country, but that he'd almost certainly gone abroad with the lout on a so-called 'secret mission' to rescue another boy's mother verged on the insane.

The Headmaster corrected himself. It *was* insane. Finally, collecting what thoughts he could, he reached for the phone.

'Get on to International Enquiries and put a call through to Wanderby's mother in France. Her name's the Countess of Montcon. You'll find the address in the files. And put her straight through to me.'

As he slammed the phone down he saw the Clyde-Brownes car drive up. The moment he had dreaded had come. What on earth was he going tell them? Something soothing, some mild remark No, that wouldn't work. With an almost manic smile he got up to greet them. But Mr Clyde-Browne had come to be heard, not to listen. He was armed with a battery of arguments.

Peregrine had been in the school's care; he had last been seen on the school premises (the Headmaster decided not to mention Mrs Brossy's sighting in the village); the school, and on a more personal level, the Headmaster, had been and still were responsible for his well-being; Mr Clyde-Browne had paid the exorbitant sum of ten thousand pounds in advance fees; and if, as seemed likely, his son had been abducted by a possibly paedophilic master he was going to see that the name Groxbourne went down in legal history and was expunged from the *Public Schools Yearbook*, where, in his opinion, it should never have been in the first place. And what had the Headmaster to say to that?

The Headmaster fought for words. 'I'm sure there's a perfectly simple and straightforward . . .' he began without any conviction, but Mrs Clyde-Browne's sobs stopped him. She appeared to have gone into premature mourning. 'I can only promise . . .'

'I am not interested in promises,' said Mr Clyde-Browne, 'my son is missing and I want him found. Now, have you any idea where he is?'

The Headmaster shuddered to think, and had his agitation increased by the telephone.

'I can't get any number,' said the School Secretary when he picked it up, 'International Enquiries say there's no Countess de . . .'

'Thank you, Miss Crabley, but I'm engaged just at the moment,' he said to stifle any shrill disclosures. 'Please tell the Bishop I'll call him back as soon as I'm free.' And, hoping he had impressed the Clyde-Brownes, he replaced the receiver and leant across the desk. 'I really don't think you have anything to worry about . . .' he began and knew he was wrong. Through the window he could see Slymne crossing the quad carrying two revolvers. God alone knew what would happen if he marched in and . . . The Headmaster got to his feet. 'If you'll just excuse me for a moment,' he said hoarsely, 'I'm afraid my bowels . . . er . . . my stomach has been playing me up.'

'So have mine,' said Mr Clyde-Browne unsympathetically, but the Headmaster was already through the door and had intercepted Slymne. 'For God's sake put those beastly things away,' he whispered ferociously.

'The thing is . .' Slymne began but the Headmaster dragged him into the lavatory and locked the door. 'They're only replicas.'

'I don't care what . . . They're what?' said the Headmaster.

'I said they're replicas,' said Slymne, edging up against the washbasin nervously.

'Replicas? You mean –'

'Two real revolvers are missing. We found these in their place.'

'Shit!' said the Headmaster, and slumped onto the seat. His bowels were genuinely playing him up now.

'The Major is checking the ammunition boxes,' continued Slymne, 'I just thought you'd want to know about these.'

The Headmaster stared bleakly at a herb chart his wife had pinned up on the wall to add a botanical air to the place. Even the basil held no charms for him now. Somewhere in Europe Glodstone and that litigious bastard's idiot son were wandering about armed with property belonging to the Ministry of Defence. And if the Clyde-Brownes found out . . . They mustn't.

Rising swiftly he wrenched the top off the cistern. 'Put the damned things in there,' he said. Slymne raised his eyebrows and did as he was told. If the Headmaster wanted replica firearms in his water closet that was his business. 'And now go back to the Armoury and tell that Fetherington not to move until I've got rid of the parents. I'll come over myself.'

He opened the door and was confronted by Mr Clyde-Browne, for whom the mention of stomachs and lavatories had precipitated another bout of Adriatic tummy. 'Er . . .' said the Headmaster, but Mr Clyde-Browne shoved past him and promptly backed out again followed by Slymne. 'The toilet's not working. Mr Slymne here has been helping me fix it.'

'Really?' said Mr Clyde-Browne with an inflection he relied on in cases involving consenting adults charged with making improper use of public urinals, and before the Headmaster could invite him to use the toilet upstairs he was back inside and had locked the door.

'You don't think .' said Slymne injudiciously.

'Get lost,' said the Headmaster 'And see that , . . the Major doesn't stir.'

Slymne took the hint and hurried back to the armoury. The Major was looking disconsolately at several empty boxes in the ammunition locker. 'Bad news, Slimey old chap,' he said. 'Two hundred bloody rounds gone. The Army isn't going to like it one little bit. I've got to account for every fucking one.'

'Not your fault,' said Slymne. 'If Glodstone chooses to go mad and pinch the key . . .'

'He didn't. Peregrine had the thing. And to think I used to like that boy.'

'Well, the Head's got his hands full with the Clyde-Brownes and I don't think he's having an easy time.'

The Major almost sympathized. 'I don't see how he can avoid sacking me. I'd sack myself in the circumstances. More than flesh and blood can stand, that bloody couple.' He wheeled himself across to a rack of bayonets.

'Don't tell me they've taken some of those too,' said Slymne.

'I wish to God they had,' said the Major. 'The Army wouldn't worry so much. Mind you, I hate to think what Perry would get up to. Born bayoneteer. You should see what he can do with a rifle and bayonet to a bag of straw. And talking about guts I suppose if I were a Jap the Head would expect me to commit Mata Hari.'

Slymne ignored the mistake. He was beginning to feel distinctly sorry for the Major. After all, the man might be a fool but he'd never been as malicious as Glodstone and it had been no part of Slymne's plan to get him sacked.

'They probably won't use any of those bullets,' he said by way of consolation and wondered what he could do to save the Major's job.

It was not a consideration that had top priority with the Headmaster. Mr Clyde-Browne's eruption from the lavatory clutching the two replica revolvers he had dredged from the cistern in an attempt to make the thing flush had honed to a razor's edge the Headmaster's only gift, the capacity for extempore evasions.

'Well I never,' he said. 'Would you believe it?'

'No,' said Mr Clyde-Browne.

'Boys will be boys,' continued the Headmaster in the face of this blunt refusal to accept his rhetoric, 'always up to some practical jokes.'

Mr Clyde-Browne fingered the revolvers dangerously. He had yet to realize they were replicas. 'And maniacs will presumably be maniacs. Since when have you and that man Slymne made a habit of hiding offensive weapons in the cistern of your lavatory?'

'Are you suggesting –'

'No. I'm stating,' said Mr Clyde-Browne, 'I intend to present these firearms to the police as proof that you are wholly unfit either by virtue of insanity or criminal tendency to be in charge of anything more morally responsible than an abattoir or a brickyard.'

The Headmaster struggled with these alternatives but Mr Clyde-Browne was giving tongue again. 'Marguerite!' he yelled, 'Come here at once.'

Mrs Clyde-Browne crept from the study 'Yes, dear,' she said meekly.

'I want you to bear witness that I have discovered these two guns in the water closet of this –'

But the sight of her husband aiming two revolvers at the Headmaster was witness enough.

'You're mad, mad, mad!' she wailed and promptly had a fit of hysterics.

The Headmaster seized his opportunity. 'Now look what you've done,' he said appealing to Mr Clyde-Browne's better feelings in vain. 'Your poor wife .'

'Keep your hands off that woman,' snarled her husband, 'I give you fair warning .' He waved the revolvers as the Headmaster tried to calm her.

'There, there.' he said. 'now come and sit down and

Mr Clyde-Browne was more forthright. Putting the guns on a side table, he whisked a bowl of faded roses from it and did what he had been longing to do for years. It was not a wise move With water running down her face and a Wendy Cussons in her hair, Mrs Clyde-Browne's hysterics turned to fury

'You bastard,' she yelled and seizing one of the guns. aimed it at her husband and pulled the trigger There was a faint click and Mr Clyde-Browne cowered against the wall.

The Headmaster intervened and took the gun from her. 'Toys,' he explained, 'I told you it was simply a prank '

Mr Clyde-Browne said nothing. He knew now where Peregrine had got his demonic gifts from and he no longer cared where the sod was.

'Come into the study,' said the Headmaster, making the most of the domestic rift. 'The School Secretary will see to Mrs Clyde-Browne's needs and I'm sure we could all do with a drink.'

The respite was only temporary. By the time the Clyde-Brownes drove off half an hour later, Mrs Clyde-Browne had threatened to divorce her husband if Peregrine wasn't found and Mr Clyde-Browne had passed the threat on in terms that included legal damages, the end of the Headmaster's career and the publicity that would result when the *News of the World* learnt that Major Fetherington, instead of being *in loco parentis*, had been *in loco matronae* and wearing a french tickler to boot. The Headmaster watched them go and then crossed the quad at a run to the Armoury.

'Off your butts,' he shouted, evidently inspired by the place to use Army language and ignoring the Major's patent inability to do more than wobble in his wheelchair. 'You're going to France and you're going to bring that bloody boy back within the week even if you have to drug the little bugger.'

'France?' said Slymne with a quaver. That country still held terrors for him. 'But why me? I've got –'

'Because this stupid sex-maniac can't drive. By this time tomorrow you'll be at the damned Château.'

'More than I will,' said the Major. 'You can sack me on the spot but I'm fucked if I'm going to be hurtled across Europe in a fucking wheelchair. I can't put it plainer than that.'

'I can,' said the Headmaster, who had learnt something from Mr Clyde-Browne when it came to blunt speaking. 'Either you'll use your despicable influence on your loathsome protégé, Master Peregrine Clyde-Bloody-Browne, and hopefully murder Glodstone in the process, or that damned man will have the police in and you'll not only lose your job but you'll be explaining to the CID and the Army why you gave those guns to a couple of lunatics.'

'But I didn't. I told you –'

'Shut up! I'll tell them,' said the Headmaster, 'because you were screwing the Matron with a french tickler and Glodstone threatened to blow your cover.'

'That's a downright lie,' said the Major without much conviction.

'Perhaps,' yelled the headmaster, 'but Mrs Clyde-Browne

evidently didn't see it that way and since her husband claims to be a personal friend of every High-Court Judge in the country, not to mention the Lord Chancellor, I don't fancy your chances in the witness box.'

'But can't we phone the Countess and explain   ' Slymne began

'What? That the school employs maniacs like Glodstone to come and rescue her? Anyway the secretary's tried and the woman isn't in the directory.'

'But the cost ·'

'Will be funded from the school mission on the Isle of Dogs which is at least designated for the redemption of delinquents and no one can say it's not being put to its proper purpose.'

Later that afternoon, Slymne drove down the motorway towards Dover once again Beside him the Major sat on an inflated inner tube and cursed the rôle of women in human affairs. 'It was her idea to use that beastly thingamajig,' he complained, 'I couldn't stop her. Had me at her mercy and anyway I couldn't feel a thing. Can't imagine why they call them French letters.' Slymne kept his thoughts to himself He was wondering what the Countess had had to say about the letters she hadn't written.

Chapter 18

He needn't have worried. For the moment the Countess had other problems in mind. In fact the day had been fraught with problems. Mr Hodgson had refused to spend another night in a place where he was liable to be mugged every time he went to the loo and had left without paying his bill; Mr Rutherby had added to his wife's and Mr Coombe's little difficulties by threatening to commit a *crime passionnel* if he ever caught them together again, and Mr Coombe had told him in no uncertain terms that Mr Rutherby wouldn't know what a *crime* fucking *passionnel* was until he'd been clamped in Mrs Rutherby for three bloody hours with people pulling his legs to get him out.

But it had been the delegates who had given the most trouble. Dr Abnekov still maintained that he'd been the victim of a CIA conspiracy to silence him, while Professor Botwyk was equally adamant that a terrorist group had tried to assassinate him and demanded a bodyguard from the US Embassy in Paris. Dr Grenoy had temporized. If the American delegate wanted protection he would have him flown by helicopter to the nearest military hospital but he could rest assured there would be no recurrence of the previous night's dreadful events. The Château had been searched, the local gendarmerie alerted, all entrances were guarded and he had installed floodlights in the courtyard. If Professor Botwyk wished to leave the symposium he was perfectly welcome to, and Grenoy had hinted his absence wouldn't be noticed. Botwyk had risen to the taunt and had insisted on staying with the proviso that he be given the use of a firearm. Dr Abnekov had demanded reciprocal rights, and had so alarmed Botwyk that he'd given way on the issue. 'All the same I'm going to hold the French government fully responsible if I get bumped off,' he told Dr Grenoy with a lack of logic that confirmed the cultural attaché in his belief that

Anglo-Saxons were incapable of rational and civilized thought. Having settled the problem temporarily he had taken other measures in consultation with the Countess. 'If you refuse to leave,' he told her, 'at least see that you serve a dinner that will take their minds off this embarrassing incident. The finest wines and the very best food.'

The Countess had obliged. By the time the delegates had gorged their way through a seven-course dinner, and had adjourned to discuss the future of the world, indigestion had been added to their other concerns. On the agenda the question was down as 'Hunger in the Third World: A Multi-modular Approach', and as usual there was dissension. In this case it lay in defining the Third World.

Professor Manake of the University of Ghana objected to the term on the reasonable grounds that as far as he knew there was only one world. The Saudi delegate argued that his country's ownership of more oil and practically more capital in Europe and America than any other nation put Arabia in the First World and everyone not conversant with the Koran nowhere. Dr Zukacs countered, in spite of threats from Dr Abnekov that he was playing into the hands of Zionist–Western Imperialism, by making the Marxist–Leninist point that Saudi Arabia hadn't emerged from the feudal age, and Sir Arnold Brymay, while privately agreeing, silently thanked God that no one had brought up the question of Ulster.

But the main conflict came, as usual, in the differing interpretation by Dr Abnekov and Professor Botwyk. Dr Abnekov was particularly infuriated by Botwyk's accusation that the Soviet Union was by definition an underdeveloped country because it couldn't even feed itself and didn't begin to meet consumer demand.

'I demand a retraction of that insult to the achievements of the Socialist system,' shouted Abnekov. 'Who was the first into space? Who supports the liberationist movements against international capitalism? And what about the millions of proletarians who are suffering from malnutrition in the United States?'

'So who has to buy our grain?' yelled Botwyk. 'And what do you give the starving millions in Africa and Asia? Guns and rockets and tanks. You ever tried eating a goddam rocket?'

'When all peoples are freed –'

159

'Like Afghanistan and Poland? And what about Czechoslovakia and Hungary? You call killing people liberating them?'

'So Vietnam was freeing people? And how many murders are there in America every year? You don't even know, there are so many.'

'Yeah, well that's different. That's freedom of choice,' said Botwyk, who was against the uncontrolled sale of hand-guns but didn't feel like saying so.

Dr Grenoy tried to get the meeting back to the original topic. 'I think we ought to approach the problem rationally,' he pleaded, only to be asked by Professor Manake what rational rôle the French Foreign Legion were playing in Central Africa in solving anyone's problems except those of French Presidents with a taste for diamonds.

'I suppose the Foreign Legion absorbs some of the scum of Europe,' said Sir Arnold, trying to support Dr Grenoy, 'I remember once when I was in Tanganyika –'

'Tanzania,' said Professor Manake. 'You British don't own Africa any longer, in case it's escaped your attention.'

Dr Zukacs stuck his oar in. 'Untrue. Financial imperialism and neo-colonialism are the new –'

'Shut up, you damned Magyar,' shouted Dr Abnekov, who could see the insult to Ghana coming, 'not every country in Africa is a neo-colony. Some are highly progressive.'

'Like Uganda, I suppose,' said Botwyk. 'And who gave support to that cannibal Idi Amin? He kept heads in his deep-freeze for a quick snack.'

'Protein deficiency is rife in the Belgian Congo,' said Sir Arnold.

'Zaïre,' said Professor Manake.

Dr Grenoy tried again. 'Let us examine the structuralism of economic distribution,' he said firmly. 'It is a functional fact that the underdeveloped nations of the world have much to contribute on a socio-cultural and spiritual basis to modern thinking. Lévi-Strauss has shown that in some parts of . . .'

'Listen, bud,' said Botwyk, who imagined Dr Grenoy was about to bring up the question of Israel, 'I refuse to equate that bastard Khomeini with any spiritual basis. If you think holding innocent US citizens hostage is a Christian act . . .'

In the tumult that followed this insult to the Muslim world the Saudi delegate accused both Botwyk and Lévi-Strauss of being Zionist and Pastor Laudenbach advocated an ecumenical approach to the Holocaust. For once Dr Abnekov said nothing. He was mourning the loss of his son who had been captured and skinned alive in Afghanistan and anyway he loathed Germans. Even Dr Grenoy joined the fray. 'I wonder if the American delegate would tell us how many more Americans are going to prove their spiritual integrity by drinking orange juice spiked with cyanide in Guyana?' he enquired.

Only Sir Arnold looked happy. He had suddenly realized that Zaïre was not Eire and that the question of Ulster was still off the menu.

The Countess finished clearing up in the kitchen. She could still hear the raised voices, but she had long ago come to her own conclusions about the future of the world and knew that nice ideas about peace and plenty were not going to alter it. Her own future was more important to her and she had to decide what to do. The man who called himself Pringle was undoubtedly Glodstone. She had taken a good look at him when she had gone up to his room with his supper tray and had returned to her room to compare his drawn face with that in the school photograph Anthony had brought back. So why had he lied? And why had someone broken into the Château looking for her? She had already dismissed Grenoy's suggestion that the mob in Vegas had caught up with her. They didn't operate in that way. Not for a measly hundred grand. They were businessmen and would have used more subtle means of getting their money back, like blackmail. Perhaps they'd merely sent a 'frightener' first, but if that were the case they'd employed a remarkably inept one. It didn't make sense.

Now, sitting at the big deal table eating her own dinner, she felt tired. Tired of pandering to men's needs, tired of the fantasies of sex, success and greed, and of those other fantasies, the ideological ones those fools were arguing about now. All her life she had been an actress in other people's dream theatres or, worse still, an usherette. Never herself, whatever her 'self' was. It was time to find out. She finished her meal and washed up, all the while wondering why human beings needed the sustenance of unreality. No other species she knew of did. Anyway she was going to learn what Glodstone's real purpose was.

She climbed the stairs to his room and found him sitting on the bed draped in a sheet and looking bewildered and frightened. It was the fear that decided her tactics. 'So what's Glass-Eye Glodstone doing in these parts?' she asked in her broadest American accent.

Glodstone gaped at her. 'Pringle,' he said. 'The name is Pringle.'

'That's not the way I read your Y-fronts. They're labelled Glodstone. So's your shirt. How come?'

Glodstone fought for an excuse and failed. 'I borrowed them from a friend,' he muttered.

'Along with the glass eye?'

Glodstone clutched the sheet to him hurriedly. This woman knew far too much about him for safety. Her next remark confirmed it. 'Look,' she said, 'there's no use trying to fool me. Just tell me what you were doing sneaking around in the middle of the night and rescuing so-called people.'

'I just happened to be passing.'

'Passing what? Water? Don't give me that crap. Some hoodlum breaks in here last night, beats up the clientèle, dumps one of them in the river, and you just happen to be passing.'

Glodstone gritted his dentures. Whoever this beastly woman was he had no intention of telling her the truth 'You can believe what you like but the fact remains

'That you're my son's housemaster and at a guess I'd say he wasn't far out when he said you were a psycho.'

Glodstone tended to agree He was feeling decidedly unbalanced. She couldn't be the Countess. 'I don't believe it. Your son told you   It's impossible You're not the Countess.'

'OK, try me,' said the Countess.

'Try you?' said Glodstone, hoping she didn't mean what he thought Clad only in a sheet he felt particularly vulnerable.

'Like what you want me to tell you. Like he's circumcised, got a cabbage allergy, had a boil on his neck last term and managed to get four O-levels without your help. You tell me.'

A wave of uncertain relief crept over Glodstone. Her language might not fit his idea of how countesses talked, but she seemed to know a great deal about Wanderby.

'Isn't there something else you want to tell me?' he asked finally to put her to the test about the letters.

'Tell you? What the hell more do you want to know? That he hasn't got goitre or something? Or if he's been laid? The first you can see for yourself or Miss Universe 1914 can tell you. And the second is none of your fucking business. Or is it?' She studied him with the eye of an expert in perversions. 'You wouldn't happen to be an asshole freak, would you?'

'I beg your pardon?' said Glodstone, stung by the insult.

'No need to,' said the Countess nastily. 'It's not my sphincter you're spearing and that's for sure. But if I find you've been sodomizing my son you'll be leaving here without the wherewithal.'

'Dear God,' said Glodstone crossing his legs frantically, 'I can assure you the thought never entered my head. Absolutely not. There is nothing queer about me.'

'Could have fooled me,' said the Countess, relaxing slightly. 'So what else is on your mind?'

'Letters,' said Glodstone.

'Letters?'

Glodstone shifted his eye away from her. This was the crunch-point. If she didn't know about the letters she couldn't possibly be the Countess. On the other hand, with his wherewithal at stake he wasn't going to beat about the bush. 'The ones you wrote me,' he said.

'I write you letters about Anthony's allergies and you make it all the way down here to discuss them? Come up with something better. I'm not buying that one.'

But before Glodstone could think of something else to say, there was the sound of a shot, a scream, more shots, a babble of shouting voices, and the floodlights in the courtyard went out. Peregrine had struck again.

Unlike everyone else, Peregrine had spent an untroubled day. He had slept until noon, had lunched on baked beans and corned beef and had observed the comings and goings at the Château with

163

interest Now that he knew Glodstone was alive, he wasn't worried People were always getting captured in thrillers and it never made any real difference. In fact he couldn't think of a book in which the hero got bumped off, except *The Day of the Jackal* and he wasn't sure the Jackal had been a hero But he had been really cunning and careful and had nearly got away with it Peregrine made a mental note to be even more cunning and careful No one was going to bump him off. Quite the reverse.

And so through the long hot afternoon he watched the floodlights being installed and the police van being stationed on the road by the bridge and made his plans Obviously he wouldn't be able to go up the cliff as he'd wanted and he'd have to make sure the lightning conductor hadn't been spotted as his route in. But the main thing would be to create a diversion and get everyone looking the wrong way Then he'd have to find Glodstone and escape before they realized what had happened He'd have to move quickly too and, knowing how useless Glodstone was at running cross-country and climbing hills, that presented a problem The best thing would be to trap the swine in the Château so they couldn't follow But with the guards on the bridge He'd have to lure them off it somehow. Peregrine put his mind to work and decided his strategy

As dusk fell over the valley. he moved off down the hillside and crawled into the bushes by the police van Three gendarmes were standing about smoking and talking. gazing down at the river That suited his purpose He squirmed through the bushes until they were hidden by the van Then he was across the road and had crawled between the wheels and was looking for the petrol tank In the cab above him the radio crackled and one of the men came over and spoke Peregrine watched the man's feet and felt for his own revolver But presently the fellow climbed down and the three gendarmes strolled up the ramp onto the bridge out of sight Peregrine reached into the knapsack and took out a small Calor-gas stove and placed it beneath the tank Before lighting it he checked again. but the men were too far away to hear and the noise of the water running past would cover the hiss of gas Two seconds later the stove was burning and he was back across the road and hurrying through the bushes upstream He had to be over the river before the van went up

He had swum across and had already climbed halfway up the hill before the Calor stove made its presence felt. Having gently brought the petrol tank to the boil, it ignited the escaping vapour with a roar that exceeded Peregrine's wildest expectations. It did more. As the tank blew, the stove beneath it exploded too, oil poured onto the road and burst into flames and the three gendarmes, one of whom had been on the point of examining a rear tyre to find the cause of the hiss which he suspected to be a faulty valve, were enveloped in a sheet of flame and hurled backwards into the river. Peregrine watched a ball of flame and smoke loom up into the sunset and hurried on. If anyone in the Château was watching that would give them something to think about, and take their minds off the lightning conductor on the northern tower. It had certainly taken the gendarmes' minds off anything remotely connected with towers. Only vaguely thankful that they had not been incinerated, they were desperately trying to stay afloat in the rushing waters. But the Calor stove hadn't finished its work of destruction. As the flames spread, a tyre burst and scattered more fragments of blazing material onto the bridge. A seat burnt surrealistically in the middle of the road and the radio crackled more incomprehensibly than ever.

But these side-effects were of no interest to Peregrine. He had reached the tower and was swarming up the lightning conductor. At the top he paused, heaved himself onto the roof and headed for the skylight, revolver in hand. There was no one in sight and he dropped down into the empty corridor and crossed to the window. Below him the courtyard was empty and the smoke drifting over the river to the west seemed to have gone unnoticed. For a moment Peregrine was puzzled. It had never occurred to him that the gendarmes were really policemen. Anyone could dress up in a uniform and gangsters obviously wouldn't bring in the law to protect them, but all the same he'd expected them to have been on the lookout and he'd gone to a lot of trouble to draw their attention away from the Château. But no one seemed in the least interested. Odd. Anyway he was in the Château and if they were stupid enough not to be on their guard that was their business. His was to rescue Glodstone and this time he wasn't going to mingle with people in passages and bedrooms. He'd strike from a different direction.

He went down the turret to the cellar and searched the rooms again. Still there was no sign of Glodstone. But in the abandoned kitchen he could hear people arguing. He went to the dumb-waiter and listened but the voices were too many and too confused for him to hear what was being said and he was about to turn away when it occurred to him that he was in a perfect position to kill all the swine in one fell swoop. Swoop wasn't the word he wanted, because coming up in a diminutive lift wasn't swooping, but it would certainly take them by surprise if he appeared in the hatchway and opened fire. But that wouldn't help Glodstone escape. Peregrine suddenly realized his mistake. They were holding Glodstone hostage. That was why they'd only had three guards on the bridge and had put floodlights on the terrace. They knew he'd return but because they'd got Glodstone there would be nothing he could do except give himself up. It explained everything he found so puzzling.

In the darkness Peregrine's mind, as lethal as that of a ferret in a rabbit warren, gnawed at the problem: and found an answer.

Chapter 19

In the grand salon the members of the symposium had long since abandoned the topic of World Hunger. There were no experts on nutrition or agricultural techniques among them and even Dr Grenoy had failed to rally them around the topic by recourse to those generalities which, as a cultural attaché, and a French one, were his forte. In fact his attempt had made things worse. Only the multi-modular approach remained and, thanks to the enormous dinner and now the brandy, found increasing expression in national prejudices and personal feelings.

Curious bonds had been formed. Dr Abnekov's antipathy to American capitalism had been overcome by Professor Botwyk's observation to the Saudi delegate that any man who couldn't hold his liquor ought to stop spouting about the power of petroleum products, and Pastor Laudenbach had brought them even closer together by supporting the refusal of Muslims to touch alcohol. Even Professor Manake and Sir Arnold had found a common interest in big-game hunting. Only Dr Zukacs remained obstinately doctrinaire, explaining to no one in particular that the only way the under-developed countries could free themselves from imperialism was by developing heavy industry and collectivizing farms. Since he was sitting next to the Polish delegate, who was under orders to keep his mouth shut and who knew what collective farming had done to his own country, and who resented the imputation that Poland was under-developed anyway, only Dr Abnekov's threat to beat their collective heads together unless they shut up prevented a fight. Pastor Laudenbach's appeal for peace brought Botwyk to his feet.

'Listen, you dirty kraut,' he shouted, 'Don't you start yammering about peace. Two world wars your lousy country's started this century and don't think we've forgotten it. Six million died in the gas chambers and it wouldn't surprise me to learn you were the camp doctor at Auschwitz.'

'That's a lie,' snarled the Pastor inadvisedly, 'I spent four years on the Eastern Front in Panzers. I was at the Battle of the Kursk while you were bombing innocent civilians to death by the hundred thousand. I know about war. At Kursk I learnt and –'

It was too much for Dr Abnekov. 'You murdering Hitlerite,' he yelled, 'just let me get my hands on you and I'll show you what we did to butchers like you. At Kursk were you? By God –'

'Gentlemen,' appealed Dr Grenoy, 'let us try to forget the past and –'

'Shut up, you damned Frog,' shouted Botwyk. 'Without the boys who died on Omaha beach you'd be still doing what Heinie here told you even if you weren't a goddam collaborator which is open to question.'

'I was five at the time –' began Dr Grenoy, but neither Botwyk nor Abnekov were to be silenced. As Abnekov hurled himself drunkenly at the Pastor, Botwyk cursed Dr Grenoy for getting out of Vietnam and NATO, not to mention teaming up with a load of Huns in the Common Market. And what about Marshall Aid?'

'Amazing,' Professor Manake observed to Sir Arnold. 'You Europeans never seem to realize how extraordinarily barbaric you are.'

'I wouldn't call myself a European, you know,' said Sir Arnold. 'We're an island race with a seafaring tradition –'

But as he spoke, Peregrine, following another English tradition, acted. Firing with all the deadlines Major Fetherington had taught him he put his first bullet through Professor Botwyk's forehead, then shot the lights out and with two more bullets plunged the courtyard into darkness as well. As the screams and shouts of the delegates echoed through the Château he dashed for the cover of the gateway tower. There was a little office there and from it he could command a view of the entire terrace and the stableyard where the cars were parked at the back. In short, no one could move out of the buildings without being shot. Best of all, he had the swine trapped in the Château and until they released Glodstone he didn't intend to budge.

Three floors above, the Countess felt the same way about

budging. From the sound of the shots, the screams and the confusion below, she realized she had been wrong. Dr Grenoy had known what he was talking about. Some hit-man had come looking for her last night and she should have left while the going was good. Right now it was bad. Whipping to the door, she locked it and switched the light out. 'If anyone comes don't utter,' she told Glodstone. 'And wedge that bed against the door.'

For some time they sat on the floor in silence listening for more sounds of trouble and separately wondering how the hell they were going to get out of the mess. 'Must have shot one of the guests,' whispered the Countess finally.

'Guests?' said Glodstone.

'Either them or the think-tank merchants.'

'Think-tank merchants?'

'The futurologists. Though what they know about the future beats me. Still, they pay well. Or did. I can't see this being the world's favourite venue for conferences after tonight.'

Glodstone tended to agree, though he wasn't at all clear what futurologists were. Certainly international gangsters would be inclined to avoid the place.

'What beats me,' continued the Countess, 'is why that goon last night was looking for me and now he's shooting those poor egg-heads down there. Unless it's the gendarmes doing the shooting.'

'The gendarmes?' said Glodstone. 'You mean they've had the nerve to call the police in?'

'You don't seriously imagine an international gathering of some of the world's most eminent intellectuals are going to sit on their fannies when there's a contract killer on the loose? It's a miracle we haven't got the United States Marines on call, the way that Professor Botwyk was carrying on this morning. Wanted to phone the Embassy.'

'The Embassy?'

In the darkness the Countess looked at him suspiciously. 'Do you always repeat everything anyone says to you?' she asked.

'No, but . Well, you wouldn't think men like that would have the nerve to ask for government protection.'

'I can't think why not.'

Glodstone could, but in the present circumstances it didn't seem advisable to say so. On the other hand he had the increasing feeling that there had been some terrible mistake and for a moment he began to wonder if they'd come to the wrong château, before remembering that this woman had claimed to be Wanderby's mother. Perhaps all this talk about international scholars and the police was subtle means of getting him to talk. 'It all seems very odd,' he muttered.

'You can say that again,' said the Countess as another shot rang out below. Peregrine had just winged Dr Abnekov who had made the mistake of urinating out of one of the windows and had learnt what it felt like to be circumcised by a revolver bullet. As his yells receded the Countess got to her feet. 'Where's your car?' she asked.

Glodstone hesitated. He still couldn't make head or tail of the woman but there was nothing to be gained from lying. 'I left it hidden in an old sawmill. I didn't want anyone to steal it.'

'Yeah, well I'd say you showed good sense,' said the Countess. 'We'll just have to chance it. This place is beginning to feel like the condemned cell and I don't fancy sitting here waiting. Help me move the bed. But quietly.'

Glodstone got to his feet and clutched the sheet to him. It was beginning to feel like a premature shroud. 'Is that wise?' he asked as another shot rang out, 'I mean it sounds like a battle out there.'

'Which is why we're moving now So long as they're occupied we've got a chance.'

They moved the bed and the Countess unlocked the door and went out into the passage. Glodstone followed her unwillingly and stopped.

'So what's holding you?' demanded the Countess. 'Got cold feet or something?'

'It's just that I've got no clothes and   well   I wouldn't want to compromise you,' he murmured.

'Jesus, at a time like this he talks about compromising. If we don't hurry I'm going to get compromised by a bullet.'

Glodstone gave in and traipsed nervously down the steps after her. 'In here,' whispered the Countess when they reached a large open landing directly above the gateway. Opening a door she pushed him inside. 'You'll find some of my husband's clothes in

170

the bedroom. He was twice your size but you'll look better in something dark. That sheet goes with your complexion.'

Glodstone shuffled across the carpet into the next room and found some suits in a wardrobe. Whoever the woman's husband might be she hadn't been lying about his build. The brute must have stood six foot in his socks and his waistband was in the upper fifties. Still, anything was preferable to that sheet. Glodstone put on a shirt while the Countess busied herself in the other room. By the time he was dressed and could move about without tripping (he'd had to roll the bottom of the trousers up eight inches to achieve this feat) she had finished packing a suitcase.

'Right,' she said, fastening a rope ladder to a hook above the window that overlooked the drive and the avenue of walnut trees, 'exit one Countess followed by bear. You can hand the case to me when I'm out. And then we'll head for your car.'

'But I'll never make it dressed like this,' said Glodstone, 'where are my own clothes?'

'If they're back from the dry-cleaners they'll be in the the office down below but I wouldn't advise trying to get them. That way the only place you'll make is infinity. Let's hit the fire escape.'

She dropped the ladder out of the window and climbed over the sill. 'Now the case,' she said. Glodstone handed it to her. It was remarkably heavy. As she disappeared he stood irresolute. He had no doubt now that she was the Countess and to some extent he could be said to be rescuing her, but the thought of trying to walk fifteen kilometres in oversize men's wear and lugging that suitcase appalled him. And where was Peregrine? A shot from below should have told him. It certainly decided him. Glodstone climbed over the sill and slithered down the rope ladder.

In the little office Peregrine was in high spirits. This was the life, the world, the action he had read and dreamt about and had been prepared for. It was no longer imaginary. It was real and exciting, a matter of life and death and in the case of the latter he'd undoubtedly been successful. He'd certainly shot one swine stone-cold dead and had just potted another who'd appeared at a window. The only thing that puzzled him was that no one had fired back. He'd have welcomed an exchange of shots. But none had come and he was

171

trying to work out what this meant when a sound outside gave him the answer. Something had just bumped against the wall of the Château and he heard voices. So the bastards had managed to get round behind him and were preparing to attack him from the rear. Cunning. He'd soon put a stop to that.

Checking that the courtyard was still empty he crossed to the tiny window that gave onto the drive. As he watched, a figure appeared with a suitcase. They were going to blast him out with a bomb. Peregrine aimed the revolver through the window and then hesitated. It was a woman, and he hadn't been trained to shoot women. All the same, he was taking no chances. Slipping out to the gates he gently unlocked them. A man was out there too. He could hear him whisper. He'd strike now. Shoving the gate open with his foot he aimed the revolver with both hands. 'OK, freeze,' he shouted, now identifying with the heroes of every American thriller he'd read. 'Get your hands on your heads and don't move.'

But the woman had already done so. She was off down the drive running as fast as she could. For a second Peregrine was tempted but Bulldog Drummond prevailed. At least he'd got the man and he wasn't giving any trouble. He was wheezing and gasping but his hands were up.

'For God's sake don't shoot,' he whimpered. Peregrine recognized the voice.

'Gloddie,' he said, 'Is that you?'

'Of course it's me,' said Glodstone with a moan and sat down on the suitcase. 'Oh my God!'

'Are you all right?'

Glodstone felt his heart and thought not.

'So who's the frail?' asked Peregrine, reverting to Mickey Spillane.

'I am,' said Glodstone.

'I mean the woman.'

'That happened to be the Countess.'

'And we've rescued her. That's terrific.' Glodstone didn't reply. To his way of thinking the adjective was wholly inappropriate.

'Then we can go,' said Peregrine, 'or do you want me to finish the swine off?'

Glodstone tried to get up and promptly trod on the bottom of his

172

trousers and fell over. 'I don't want you to do another thing,' he said savagely as Peregrine helped him to his feet, 'except see if my clothes are in an office in there and bring them out. And hurry. There's murder going on.'

'Oh I don't know,' said Peregrine, 'They're –'

'Well, I fucking do,' said Glodstone.

'Oh, all right,' said Peregrine sulkily. 'Just when it was getting to be fun.'

All the same he went into the office and presently returned with a brown paper parcel. 'Just one more thing to do,' he said and before Glodstone could protest that even one more thing would be too much for his heart he was gone. Glodstone flapped off down the drive with his clothes. If what he expected occurred he wanted to be behind a walnut tree when it did. For a few minutes everything was quiet and then a volley of shots rang out and Peregrine ran from the Château.

'That should keep them quite while we make our getaway,' he said. 'I've dumped that rope ladder and locked the gates.'

'And shot someone too, I suppose.'

'Nobody to shoot.'

'Well, get that bloody suitcase,' said Glodstone, hobbling along. He couldn't wait to put as much distance between himself and the Château as was humanly possible. The place had nothing romantic about it now.

In the grand salon the delegates crouched in the darkness surrounded by broken glass. Their concern for the future of mankind had assumed a personal and more interested dimension, but they were still at odds with one another. Dr Abnekov particularly objected to Sir Arnold Brymay's insistence that the only way to treat a badly wounded penis was to apply a tourniquet. 'But not around my scrotum,' shouted Abnekov.

'It stops the venom getting into the bloodstream,' said Sir Arnold, with a peculiar logic that stemmed from his experience of treating snakebite victims in the Tropics.

'Not the only thing it stops,' yelled the Russian. 'You want to castrate me or something?'

'I suppose we could try cauterizing it as well,' said Sir Arnold, getting his own back for the Soviet delegate's accusations that he was personally responsible for the atrocities committed by the British Army in Ireland.

Dr Keister intervened. 'Perhaps I may be of assistance,' she said. 'In Denmark I have had experiences with the genitals of sexual offenders and –'

'I am not a sex offender, you filthy cow. You do what you like in your rotten little country with all your pornography but if you touch me you'll learn what a sex offence is.'

'In Africa,' said Professor Manake, 'Some of the less progressive peoples still practise female circumcision. In Ghana it is naturally unknown but elsewere I have studied initiation rites among males. They are a symbolic preparation for manhood.'

'And what's that got to do with me, you bloody witch-doctor?' yelled Abnekov. 'There's nothing symbolic about my manhood. And stop twisting that piece of string, you imperialist pig.'

'Actually, it's my last pipe-cleaner,' said Sir Arnold. 'Still if you want to bleed to death I suppose you're entitled to.'

Under the table Dr Grenoy and Professor Badiglioni was arguing about the threory and origins of international terrorism. The Italian placed the blame squarely on Robespierre, Babeuf, Blanqui, Sorel and any other Frenchman he could think of, while Dr Grenoy countered with the Carbonari, the Mafia, Mussolini and Gramasci, whom he'd never read. The shooting of Botwyk had put all thought of the Countess' connection with gangsters in Las Vegas out of his mind.

Only Pastor Laudenbach and Sheikh Fahd bin Riyal, united by their faith in a spiritual future and certain unspoken prejudices, remained unmoved. 'It is the will of Allah. The Western world is decadent and the infidel Botwyk was clearly a Zionist. He refused to acknowledge that the return of Jerusalem and all Arab lands can only be achieved by force of arms. It is the same with Berlin and the occupied East Bank of your country.'

'I hadn't thought of it like that before,' said the Pastor. 'We have much to feel guilty about.'

In the darkness the Saudi delegate smiled. He was thinking wistfully of Eichmann.

*

Far to the north, Slymne drove down the N1 at ninety miles an hour. He wasn't wasting time on side roads and the ·Major's suggestions, made at frequent intervals, that they stop the night in a hotel had been ignored. 'You heard what the Head said,' he told the Major. 'This could be the ruination of us all.'

'Won't be much of me left to ruin at this rate,' said the Major and shifted his weight on the inner tube.

Chapter 20

Halfway down the drive the Countess paused in her flight. Too
many days in the kitchen hadn't equipped her for long-distance
running and anyway she hadn't been shot at Nobody had chased
after her either She sat down on the wall to get her breath back and
considered the situation grimly. She might have saved her life but
she'd also lost her life savings. The seven little gold bars in the
suitcase had been her guarantee of independence. Without them
she was tied to the damned Château and the kitchen stove. Worse
still, she might have to go elsewhere and struggle on satisfying the
whims and lusts of men, either as someone's cook, housekeeper and
general bottle-washer or, more distastefully still, as a wife. She
would lose the bungalow in Bognor Regis and the chance of
resuming her interrupted identity as Constance Sugg safe in the
knowledge that her past was well and truly behind her It was an
appalling prospect and wasn't helped by the fact that she was fat,
fair and forty-five. Not that she cared what she looked like. The
three Fs had kept the fourth at bay but they wouldn't help her in a
world dominated by lecherous men.

It was all the more galling that she would have escaped if it hadn't
been for Glodstone's clumsiness. Another damned man had fouled
things up for her, and an idiot at that Baffled by the whole affair,
she was about to move on when another thought struck her.
Someone had certainly come looking for her and having found her
they'd let her get away Why? Unless they'd got what they'd wanted
in her suitcase. That made much more sense. It did indeed. With a
new and nasty determination the Countess climbed off the wall and
turned back up the drive She had gone twenty yards when she
heard footsteps and the sound of voices. They were coming after all.
She slipped into some bushes and squatted down.

'I don't care what you think,' said Glodstone, as they passed, 'if you hadn't come out with that bloody gun and yelled "Freeze" she wouldn't have run off like that.'

'But I didn't know it was the Countess,' said Peregrine, 'I thought it was one of the swine trying to get round behind me. Anyway we rescued her and that's what she wanted, isn't it?'

'Without her suitcase with all her clothes in it?'

'Feels jolly heavy for clothes. She's probably waiting for you at the bridge and we can give it back to her.'

Glodstone snorted. 'Frighten the wits out of the poor woman and you expect her to hang around waiting for me. For all she knows I'm dead.'

They passed out of earshot. In the bushes the Countess was having difficulty understanding what she had just heard. Rescue her? And that was what she wanted? What she wanted was her suitcase and the madman with the gun had said they could give it back to her? The statements resolved themselves into insane questions in her mind.

'I must be going crazy,' she muttered as she disentangled herself from the brambles and stood in the roadway trying to decide what to do. It wasn't a difficult decision. The young lout had her suitcase and whether he like it or not she wasn't letting him disappear with it. As the pair rounded the bend she took off her shoes and holding them in one hand ran down the drive after them. By the time they reached the bridge she was twenty yards behind and hidden by the stonework above the river.

'What's that over there?' asked Glodstone, peering at the wreckage of the police van and the remains of the driver's seat which had burnt itself to a wire skeleton in the middle of the bridge.

'They had some guards there,' said Peregrine, 'but I soon put paid to them.'

'Dear God,' said Glodstone, 'when you say 'put paid to' . . . No, I don't think I want to hear.' He paused and looked warily around. 'All the same, I'd like to be certain there's no one about.'

'I shouldn't think so. The last I saw of them they were all in the river.'

'Probably the last thing anyone will see of them before they reach the sea, if my experience of that bloody torrent's anything to go by.'

'I'll go over and check just in case,' said Peregrine. 'If it is all clear I'll whistle.'

'And if it isn't I'll hear a shot I suppose,' muttered Glodstone but Peregrine was already striding nonchalantly across the bridge carrying the suitcase. A minute later he whistled but Glodstone didn't move. He was dismally aware that someone was standing behind him.

'It's me again, honey,' said the Countess. 'You don't get rid of me quite so easily.'

'Nobody wants to get rid of you. I certainly . . .'

'Skip the explanations for later. Now you and me are going to walk across together and just in case that delinquent gunslinger starts shooting remember I'm in back of you and he's got to drill you before he gets to me.'

'But he won't shoot. I mean, why should he?'

'You tell me,' said the Countess, 'I'm no mind-reader even if you had a mind. So, let's go.'

Glodstone ambled forward. In the east the sky had begun to lighten but he had no eyes for the beauties of nature. He was in an interior landscape, one in which there was no meaning or order and everything was at variance with what he had once believed. Romance was dead and unless he was extremely careful he might join it very shortly.

'I'm going to tell him not to do anything stupid,' he said when they reached the ramp.

'It's a bit late in the day for that, baby, but you may as well try,' said the Countess.

Glodstone stopped. 'Peregrine,' he called, 'I've got the Countess with me so its all right. There's no need to be alarmed.'

Behind the wrecked police van Peregrine cocked the revolver. 'How do I know you're telling the truth?' he shouted, and promptly crawled away down the bank so that he could get a clear line of fire on the squat figure silhouetted against the sky.

'Because I say so, you gibbering idiot. What more do you want?'

'Why's she standing so close to you?' said Peregrine from a different quarter. Glodstone swung round and the Countess followed.

'Because she doesn't trust you with that gun.'

'Why did she ask us to rescue her?' asked Peregrine.

But Glodstone had reached the limits of his patience. 'Never mind that now. We can discuss that later. Just let's get off here and out of the way.'

'Oh all right, said Peregrine who had been looking forward to bagging another victim. 'If you say so.'

He climbed up the bank and Glodstone and the Countess scurried past the shell of the police van.

'OK, so what's with this business of my wanting to be rescued?' asked the Countess. pausing to put her shoes on 'And who's our friend with the itchy trigger finger?'

'That's Peregrine,' said Glodstone, 'Peregrine Clyde-Browne. He's a boy in my house. Actually, he's left now but '

'I don't need his curriculum vitae. I want to know what you're doing here, is all.'

Glodstone looked uneasily up and down the road. 'Hadn't we better go somewhere more private?' he said. 'I mean the sooner we're out of the district the less chance they'll have of following us.'

It was the Countess's turn to hesitate. She wasn't at all sure she wanted to go anywhere too private with these maniacs On the other hand there was a great deal to be said for getting the hell away from burnt-out police vehicles She didn't fancy being questioned too closely about the little gold bars in her suitcase or what she was doing with several different passports, not to mention her son's housemaster and a schoolboy who went round shooting people. Above all she wanted to put this latest piece of her past behind her Bognor Regis called.

'Nothing like burning your bridges, she said 'Lead on. Mac Duff.' And picking up her bag she followed Glodstone across the road and up the hillside Behind them Peregrine had taken her words to heart and by the time they reached the ridge and paused for breath, smoke had begun to gather in the valley and there came the crackle of burning woodwork.

'That should keep them quiet for a bit.' he said as he joined them. Glodstone stared back with a fresh sense of despair He knew what he was going to see. The Château looked deserted but the wooden bridge was ablaze.

'Quiet? Quiet? every bloody fire-engine and policeman from here to Boosat is going to be down there in twenty minutes and we've still to break camp. The idea was to get back to the car before the hunt was up.'

'Yes, but she said –'

'Shut up and get moving,' snapped Glodstone and stumbled into the wood to change into his own clothes.

'I'll say this for you, boy,' said the Countess, 'when you do something you do it thoroughly. Still, he's right, you know. As the man said, the excreta is about to hit the fan.' She looked round the little camp. 'And if the snout-hounds get a whiff of this lot they be baying at our heels in no time.'

'Snout-hounds?' said Peregrine.

'Tracker dogs. The ones with noses the cops use. If you'll take my advice, you'll ditch every item back in the river.'

'Roger,' said Peregrine, and when Glodstone finally emerged from the undergrowth looking his dejected self it was to find Peregrine gone and the Countess sitting on her bag.

'He's just destroying the evidence,' she said, 'in the river. So now you can tell me what this caper is all about.'

Glodstone looked round the empty dell. 'But you must know,' he said. 'You wrote to me asking me to come down and rescue you.'

'I did? Well, for your information, I . . .' She stopped. If this madman though she'd written asking to be rescued, and it was quite obvious from his manner that he did, she wasn't going to argue the toss with him in the present fraught circumstances. 'Oh well, I guess this isn't the time for discussion. And we ought to do something with Alphonse's suit. It reeks of mothballs.'

Glodstone looked down at the clothes he was holding. 'Can't we just leave them?'

'I've just explained to young Lochinvar that if the police bring dogs they're going to track us down in no time.'

But it was Peregrine who came up with the solution when he returned from the river. 'You go on ahead and I'll lay a trail with them that'll lead in the wrong direction,' he said, 'I'll catch you up before you get to the sawmill.' And taking the suit from Glodstone he scrambled down to the road. Glodstone and the Countess trudged off and two hours later were on the plateau. They were too preoccupied with their own confused thoughts to talk. The sun was up now and they were sweating but for once Glodstone had no intention of stopping for a rest. The nightmare he had been through still haunted him, was still with him in the shape of the woman who quite evidently didn't know she had written to him for help. Even more evidently she didn't need helping and if anyone could be said to have been rescued Glodstone had to admit she'd saved him. Finally, as they reached the woods on the far side of the Causse de Boosat, he glanced back. A smudge of smoke drifted in the cloudless sky and for a moment he thought he caught the faint sounds of sirens Then they were fighting their way through the scrub and trees and after another half an hour stumbled across the overgrown track to the sawmill.

The same atmosphere of loneliness and long disuse hung over the rusting machinery and the derelict buildings, but they no longer evoked a feeling of excitement and anticipation in Glodstone Instead the place looked sinister and grim, infected with death and undiscovered crimes Not that Glodstone had time to analyse his feelings They rose within him automatically as he made his way across to the shed and thanked God the Bentley was still there. While he opened the doors the Countess dropped her suitcase and sat down on it She had ignored the pain in her right arm and her sore feet. and she tried to ignore them now At least they had a car. but what a car Yeah. well, it fitted. A vintage Bentley You couldn't beat that for easy identification A one-eyed man in a Bentley Even if they didn't have road-blocks up the cops would still stop them just to have a look at it On the other hand. vintage car owners didn't usually go around knocking off Professors And there was no going back now She'd just have to say she'd been kidnapped and hope for the best

In the shed. Glodstone replaced the plugs and started the car He had just driven it out when Peregrine appeared, panting and dripping with sweat 'Sorry I'm late,' he said, 'but I had to make sure they wouldn't come this way Went down-river a couple of miles and found an old man who'd been fishing so I stuffed those clothes in the bag of his moped and waited until he rode off That'll keep them busy for a couple of hours Then I had to swim about a bit before doubling back Didn't want to leave my own trail.'

'Go and shift those trees.' said Glodstone, getting out and shutting the shed doors. The countess climbed into the back seat and five minutes later they were on the road. On the wrong side.

'Drive on the right for Chrissake,' squawked the Countess. 'We aren't in England and at this rate we won't be. And where do you think you're going?'

'Back to Calais,' said Glodstone.

'So why are we on the road to Spain?'

'I just thought . . .' said Glodstone, who was too exhausted to.

'From now on, don't,' said the Countess. 'Leave the brainwork to me. Spain might not be such a bad idea, but the frontier's the first one they'll watch.'

'Why's that?' asked Peregrine.

'Because, dumkopf, it's the closest. So Calais makes a weird sort of sense. Only trouble is, can Old Father Time here last out that far without writing us all off?'

'Of course I can,' said Glodstone, stung into wakefulness by the insult.

'Then turn left at the next fork. And give me that map.'

For a few miles she pored over it while Glodstone concentrated on keeping to the right. 'Now then,' said the Countess, when they had swung onto a road that led through thick oak woods, 'the next question is, did anyone round here see this car when you came down?'

'I shouldn't have thought so. We did the last two hundred miles at night and we were on roads to the South.'

'Good. That's a bonus. So the car's not what they're going to be looking for. It's clean and it's too conspicuous to be likely for a getaway. But if they do stop us those guns are going to put you inside for a long, long time. So you'll ditch them, and not in any river. The *flics* have a penchant for looking under bridges.'

'What's a penchant?' asked Peregrine.

'What those gendarmes didn't have when you blew that van up. Now shut up,' said Glodstone.

'Yes, but if we get rid of the guns we won't have anything to defend ourselves with and anyway they're supposed to go back in the School Armoury.'

Glodstone's knuckles whitened on the steering wheel. 'Listen, you damned moron,' he snarled, 'hasn't it got through your thick

rogated. They too were convinced they had been the victims of a terrorist attack.

'The crisis of capitalism expresses itself in these barbaric acts,' Dr Zukacs explained to a bemused gendarme. 'They are symptomatic of the degenerate bourgeois mentality and the alliance between monopoly fascism and sectors of the lumpen proletariat. Until a new consciousness is born . . .'

'And how many shots were fired?' asked the policeman, trying to get back to the facts.

Dr Zukacs didn't know.

'Fifteen,' said Pastor Laudenbach with the precision of a military expert. 'Medium-calibre pistol. Rate of fire, good. Extreme accuracy.'

The cop wrote this down. He'd been told to treat these members of the intelligentsia softly. They'd be in a state of shock. Pastor Laudenbach obviously wasn't.

'Your name, monsieur?'

The Pastor clicked his heels. 'Obergruppen . . . er . . . Pastor Laudenbach. I belong to the Lutheran Church.'

The policeman made a note of the fact. 'Did anyone see the assailant?'

Dr Hildegard Keister pushed Badiglioni forward. 'You met him in the passage,' she said.

The Professor cursed her under his breath. 'That was the night before. It may not have been the same man.'

'But you said he had a gun. You know you did. And when you –'

'Yes,' said Badiglioni, to cut short the disclosure that he had taken refuge in her room, 'he was a young Englishman.'

'An Englishman? Can you describe him?'

Professor Badiglioni couldn't. 'It was dark.'

'Then how did you know he was a young Englishman?'

'By his accent. It was unmistakably English. I have made a study of the inter-relationship between phonetics and the socio-economic infrastructure in post-Imperial Britain and I would say categorically that the man you are looking for is of lower-upper-middle-class extraction with extreme right-wing Protestant inclinations.'

'Sod that for a lark,' said Sir Arnold. Ulster was going to be on the agenda again at this rate. 'You were into Dr Keister's room before he had a chance to speak to you. You told me that yourself.'

'I heard what he said to Dr Abnekov. That was enough.'

'And where did you pick up your astounding capacity for analysing the English language? As an Eyetie POW, no doubt.'

'As a matter of fact I was an interpreter for British prisoners of war in Italy,' said Professor Badiglioni stiffly.

'I'll put him down as English,' said the policeman.

Sir Arnold objected. 'Certainly not. I had a fairly lengthy discussion with the fellow and in my opinion he had a distinctly foreign accent.'

'English is a foreign language in France, monsieur.'

'Yes, well I daresay it is,' said Sir Arnold, getting flustered. 'What I meant was his accent was European-foreign if you see what I mean.'

The cop didn't. 'But he did speak in English?'

Sir Arnold admitted grudgingly that this had been the case. 'Doesn't mean he's British though. Probably a deliberate ploy to disguise his real nationality.'

Another helicopter clattered down onto the terrace and prevented any further questioning for the time being.

In Bordeaux Dr Abnekov was undergoing micro-surgery without a general anaesthetic. He wanted to make sure he kept what was left of his penis.

Chapter 21

'Shit, that's torn it,' said Major Fetherington as they ground to a halt at a road block beyond Boosat. Three gendarmes carrying sub-machine-guns circled the car while a fourth aimed a pistol at Slymne and demanded their passports. As the man flicked through the pages, Slymne stared in front of him. He had been staring at the road ahead for hundreds of miles while the Major had dozed beside him and it had all been in vain. Obviously something catastrophic had happened. Even the French police didn't man road-blocks and keep the occupants of cars covered with machine-guns without good cause, but Slymne was almost too tired to care. They'd have to send a cable back to the Headmaster and then find a hotel and he could get some sleep. That would be some consolation. What happened after that didn't matter now. He wasn't even worried about the letters. If Glodstone had kept them, nobody could prove he'd sent them. And in a sense he was relieved. It was all over.

It wasn't. He was woken from this rhapsody of exhaustion by the car doors being opened and with the guns aimed at them they were ordered out.

'Can't,' said the Major adamantly, 'Ce n'est pas possible. Ma bloody derrière est blessé et je m'assis sur une tube de pneu.' But in spite of his protests he was dragged out and made to stand against a wall.

'Bloody disgraceful,' he muttered, as they were frisked, 'I'd like to see a British bobby try this sort of thing with me. Ouch!'

'Silence,' said the sergeant. They were prodded apart while the car was searched and their luggage was laid out on the road. It included the inner-tube and a bottle the Major had used to save himself the agony of getting out for a pee. After five minutes two police cars drew up on the far side of the barrier and several men in plain clothes moved towards them.

'Seem to be taking an interest in our passports,' said the Major and was promptly told to keep his trap shut. Slymne stared over the wall at a row of poplars by the river and tried to keep his eyes open. It was hot in the sun and butterflies soared and dropped about the meadow in the still air, alighting for no apparent reason on a small flower when there was a larger one only a foot away. Slymne took comfort in their random choice. Chance is all, he thought, and I am not responsible for what has happened. Say nothing and they can do nothing.

To the little group of policemen studying his passport, things looked rather different. The ferry ticket was in it. 'Entered France yesterday and they're here already?' said Commissaire Ficard, 'They must have driven all night without stopping.'

He looked significantly at the Major's bottle and its murky contents. 'Occupation, schoolmaster. Could be a cover. Anything suspicious in their luggage?'

Two plain-clothes cops emptied the suitcases onto the road and went through their contents.

'Nothing.'

'And what's the inner-tube doing there?'

'The other man was sitting on it, Monsieur le Commissaire. Claims to have a wounded backside.'

The mention of wounds decided Commissaire Ficard. 'Take them in for questioning,' he said, 'And I want that car stripped. Nobody drives here from Calais that fast without good reason. They must have exceeded the speed limit in any case. And check with the ferries. I'm interested in these two.'

As the Major was hustled into the van he made things worse. 'Keep your filthy paws off me, you oaf,' he snapped and found himself lying on the floor. Slymne went quietly. Being arrested had come as a relief to his conscience.

Outside Poitiers the Countess put the boot in. 'So we need gas. Now if you want to pull in at the next station with a description of a glass-eyed man circulating that's your problem. I don't want any part of it. You can drop me off here and I'll walk.'

'What do you suggest?' asked Glodstone. He had long since given up trying to think for himself.

'That you drive up the next quiet road and you and Al Capone Junior take a break and I drive on and have her filled up.'

'A car like this isn't easy to drive, you know. You have to have had experience of non-synchromesh gears and . . .'

'You double-declutch. I'll practise.'

'I suppose it might be a good idea,' Glodstone admitted, and turned onto a side road. For ten minutes the Countess drove while Peregrine sat in the back and Glodstone prayed she wouldn't strip the gears.

'OK?' she asked finally.

Glodstone nodded but Peregrine still had reservations. 'How do we know you'll come back? I mean you could just drive off and . . .'

'Leave a clever boy like you for the cops to pick up? I've got more sense. Besides, I wanted to be rescued and that's what you're doing. But if it'll make you any happier I'll leave my passport with you.'

She got out and, rifling in her suitcase, found the right one. 'I'll buy some food while I'm about it,' she said. 'Now you just take it easy in the field. Have a nap and if I'm not back inside two hours, call the cops.'

'What did she mean by that?' asked Peregrine as she drove away. Glodstone heaved himself over a gate into a field.

'She was joking,' he said hopefully and lay down in the grass.

'I still think –' said Peregrine.

'Shut up!'

Three miles further on the Countess pulled off the road again and spent some time stuffing the gold bars down behind the back seat. Then she changed into a summer frock and put on sunglasses. All the time her mind was busy considering possibilities. They could still be nabbed but, having come so far without being stopped, it seemed unlikely an alert was out for two men and a woman in a vintage Bentley. To be on the safe side, she took two of the little bars out and, making sure no one was in sight, hid them in the hedge behind a telephone pole.

An hour later she was back. The tank was full, she'd bought all the food they'd need, plus some very black coffee in a thermos, and a trowel. With this she dug a hole beside the hedge and buried the two gold bars. If the Customs found the others she wanted something to fall back on; if not she could always pick them up later. But best of all, as she drove on to where Glodstone was asleep and Peregrine still suspicious, two motor-cycle cops passed without more than a glance at her.

'Back on the trail, boys,' she said, 'We've nothing to worry about. The *flics* aren't looking for us. I've just seen two. No problems.' She poured Glodstone a mug of coffee laced with sugar. 'Keep a sloth awake for a week it's so strong, and you can eat as we go.'

'I'm not going to be able to make Calais all the same,' said Glodstone, 'not today.'

'We're heading for Cherbourg and you will.'

By midnight they were in the car-park outside the Ferry Terminal and Glodstone was asleep at the wheel. The Countess shook him awake. 'Galahad and I will cross as foot-passengers tonight,' she said, 'you come over the first boat in the morning. Right?' Glodstone nodded.

'We'll be waiting for you,' she went on, and got out with Peregrine and crossed to the booking-office. But it was another two hours before she passed through Customs and Immigration on an American passport in which she was named as Mrs Natalie Wallcott. Ahead of her, a youth called William Barnes settled himself in the cafeteria and ordered a Coke. He too was asleep when they sailed. The Countess bought a bottle of Scotch at the Duty-Free shop and went up on deck with the plastic bag and leant over the rail with it. When she came down again the bag and the bottle and any documents that might have suggested she had been the Countess de Montcon or Anita Blanche Wanderby were sinking with the Scotch towards the bottom of the Channel. By tomorrow she would be Constance Sugg once more. By today. She must be getting tired.

Slymne wasn't. He had passed through the exhaustion barrier into a new dimension of light-headedness in which he wasn't sure if he was asleep or awake. Certainly the questions being put to him by the two detectives who sat opposite him suggested the former. They were put quite nicely, but the questions themselves were horrible. The contrast made him feel even more unreal. 'I am not a member of any subversive organization, and anyway the British Secret Service isn't subversive,' he said.

'Then you admit you belong to a branch of it?'

'No,' said Slymne.

The two men gave him another cup of coffee, and consulted a file on the table. 'Monsieur Slymne, on 12 April you arrived in France and on the 22nd you left again. On the 27th you came once more and departed 3rd August. The night before last you returned and drove 900 kilometres without resting. It will help if you explain.'

Slymne tended to agree but a seemingly distant portion of his mind took over. 'I teach geography and I like France. Naturally I come frequently on visits.'

'Which is presumably why you speak our language so fluently,' said Inspector Roudhon with a smile.

'That's different. I'm not very good at languages.'

'But an incredible student of geography to investigate the country for 900 kilometres without stopping. And at night too. Unless . . .' He paused and lit a cigarette. The room stank of stale tobacco. 'Unless, Monsieur Slymne, and I merely hypothesize, you understand, you were already in France and someone provided you with an alibi by booking a crossing to Calais in your name.'

'An alibi? What would they do that for?' said Slymne, trying to keep his eyes in focus. The situation was getting madder every moment.

'That is for you to tell us. You know what you have been here for. What mission you and Major Fetherington are on.'

'Can't,' said Slymne, 'because we aren't on one. Ask the Major.'

'We have. And he has had the good sense to tell us.'

'Tell you? What's he told you?' Slymne was wide awake now.

'You really want to know?'

Slymne did, desperately. The detective left the room and returned with a signed statement a few minutes later.

'Major Fetherington admits to being a member of the Special Air Services. He was parachuted into the forest near Brive from a light aircraft . . .'

'From a light aircraft?' said Slymne in the grip of galloping insanity.

'Yes, monsieur, as you well know. He has even named the type and the airfield from which he flew. It was a Gloster Gladiator and left from Bagshot at 0400 hours Tuesday morning –'

'But . . . but they haven't made Gladiators since God knows

191

when,' said Slymne. What on earth was the Major up to? And there couldn't be an airfield near Bagshot. The man must have gone off his rocker.

'On landing he hurt his back but buried his parachute and made his way to the road above Colonges where you picked him up,' continued the detective. 'You were to give him his orders . . .'

'His orders?' squawked Slymne. 'What orders, for Lord's sake?'

The detective smiled. 'That is for you to tell us, monsieur.'

Slymne looked desperately round the room. Major Fetherington had landed him up to his eyeballs in it now. Talk about passing the buck. 'I don't know what you're on about,' he muttered. 'I haven't been anywhere near Brive and . . .' He gave up.

'If you will take my advice, Monsieur Slymne,' said the Inspector, 'you will tell us now what you know. It will save you from meeting certain gentlemen from Paris. They are not of the police, you understand, and they use different methods. I haven't met such men myself and I hope I never have dealings with them. I believe they are not very nice.'

Slymne cracked. But when, an hour later, he signed the statement and the Inspector left the room, he was still denied the sleep he so desperately wanted. Commissaire Ficard wasn't having it.

'Does the clown think we're mentally deficient?' he shouted. 'We have the assassination of one of America's top political theorists and the mutilation of a Soviet delegate and he asks us to believe that some English schoolmaster is responsible? And the other one has already admitted being SAS. Oh, no, I am not satisfied. The Minister is not satisfied. The American Ambassador is demanding immediate action and the Russian too and we have this buffoon telling us . . .' The phone rang. 'No, I will say nothing more to the Press. And I'd like to know who leaked the story yesterday. The media is crawling all over the ground in helicopters. What do you mean they can't crawl in 'copters? They land in them and then . . .' He slammed the phone down and lumbered to his feet. 'Just let me lay my hands on this English turd. I'll squeeze the truth out of him if it has to come out of his arsehole.'

'Monsieur le Commissaire, we have already told him some special agents are coming from Paris,' said the Inspector.

'They needn't bother. By the time I'm through with him there'll be nothing left for them to play with.'

Major Fetherington lay on his stomach with his head turned sideways and contemplated the wall uncertainly. Like everyone else in the Boosat gendarmerie, he hadn't the foggiest notion what had really happened at the Château Carmagnac but for the moment he'd spared himself the ordeal Slymne was quite clearly going through. To the Major it sounded like an advanced form of hell and he thanked God he'd given the sods what they'd wanted – a load of codswallop. And in another way it was satisfying. Old Gloddie must have done something pretty gruesome to have warranted road-blocks, helicopters and accusations that he and Slymne were agents of the Secret Service, and good luck to him. The Major had never had much time for the French and Gloddie had given it to them where it hurt and got away with it. And he wasn't sneaking on the old ass to a lot of Frog cops who were doing whatever they were doing (the Major preferred not to think about it) to Slymne. Reaching over the side of the bed he found his socks and tried to block his ears with them and had partially succeeded when Slymne stopped yelling and the cell door opened.

'What about my clothes?' asked the Major with a quaver as they dragged him to his feet. Commissaire Roudhon studied his stained Y-fronts with disgust.

'You're not going to need any where you're going,' he said softly. 'You may require shoes though. Give him a blanket.'

'What's happening?' said the Major, now thoroughly frightened.

'You're taking us to the spot where you buried that parachute.'

'Oh, my God,' whimpered the Major. He could see now he'd made a terrible mistake.

Chapter 22

The Countess sat in the coffee-lounge in Weymouth waiting for the Bentley to come through Customs. She had sent Peregrine along to the statue of George III and would have made herself scarce too if it hadn't been for the gold bars. She had bought the *Daily Telegraph* and had learnt that the assassination of Professor Botwyk was already causing an international furore. Like Slymne, she knew the efficiency of the French police and she was lumbered with two halfwits. Without her to think for them they'd end up in the hands of Scotland Yard and with the American government now involved the FBI would backtrack her to California and through her various aliases to her arrival in the States and Miss Surrey and finally to Selsdon Road and Constance Sugg. She could see how easily it would be done. Anthony at Groxbourne, the missing revolvers – she'd made a terrible mistake there – Glodstone's account of her 'letters' and Peregrine's pride in being such a good shot . . . Worst of all, whoever had set her up had done a spectacular job.

Once again she cursed men. All her life she had had to fight to maintain her independence and now just when she had it all made to be her quiet surburban self she was being forced to think ruthlessly. And think she did. By the time the Bentley nosed off the ferry, she had made up her mind. She got up and walked down the road where Glodstone could see her and waited for him. 'No problems with Customs?' she enquired as she climbed in behind him.

'No,' said Glodstone glumly. 'Where's Peregrine?'

'By the statue. He can wait. You and me is going to have a quiet talk.'

'What about?'

'This,' said the Countess and put the newspaper on his lap.

'What's it say?' said Glodstone, almost killing a pedestrian on a zebra crossing in his anxiety to get away.

'Nothing much. Just that the French government have assured the State Department that the killers of Professor Botwyk will be caught and brought to justice. The Russians appear to be taking a dim view too. Apparently your boyfriend shot their delegate as well, which must confuse the issue more than somewhat.'

'Oh my God,' said Glodstone and turned down a side street and stopped. 'What on earth possessed you to write those bloody letters?'

'Keep moving. I'll tell you when to stop.'

'Yes, but . . .'

'No buts. You do what I say or I'm cutting loose and calling the first cop I spot and you and Master C-B will be facing an extradition order inside a week. Turn right here. There's a parking lot round the corner.'

Glodstone pulled in and switched off and looked at her haggardly.

'Firstly I didn't write those letters,' said the Countess, 'and I want to see them. Where did you stash them?'

'Stash them? I didn't. You told me to burn them and that's what I did.'

The Countess breathed a sigh of relief. But she wasn't showing it. 'So you've no proof they ever existed?'

Glodstone shook his head. He was almost too tired and frightened to speak.

'Well, get this straight. You can think what you like but if you seriously imagine I needed rescuing you've got to be insane. Right now, you're the one in need of a rescue operation and with what you've got between the ears that's not going to be easy. Every cop in Europe is going to be hot on your trail before the day is out.'

Glodstone dragged his mind out of its stupor. 'But no one knows we were at the Château and . . .'

'Whoever wrote those letters does, doesn't he just. You've been set up, and a little anonymous call to the police is all it's going to take to have you in the net. You haven't a plastic bag's hope in hell of getting away. One glass eye, this old banger and a youth with an IQ of fifty. You were made for identification and if you ask me that's why you were chosen.'

Glodstone gazed at a bowling green and saw only policemen,

court rooms, lawyers and judges and the rest of his life in a French prison. 'What do you suggest we do?' he asked.

'*You* do. Count me out. I don't mind thinking for you but that's as far as it goes. First off, I'd say your best bet is to do a Lord Lucan but I don't suppose you've got the money or the friends. And anyway that still leaves that juvenile mobster on the loose. What's his background?' Glodstone told her.

'Then one eminent solicitor is in for a very nasty shock,' said the Countess when he'd finished, 'though from what I've seen of his offspring I'd say he'd been cuckolded or his wife had a craving for lumps of lead when she was pregnant. Doesn't make your situation any cosier. Mr Clyde-Browne's going to have his son plead insanity and hurl the book at you.'

'What on earth can I do then?' whimpered Glodstone.

The Countess hesitated. If she suggested going to the police he might just do it and she wasn't having that. 'Isn't there any place you can hang out for a few days and nobody ever comes?'

Glodstone tried to concentrate. 'I've got a cousin near Malvern,' he said, 'She may be away and anyway she'd put us up.'

'Until the police came. Think, for Chrissake. Think where you wouldn't go.'

'Margate,' said Glodstone suddenly, 'I wouldn't be seen dead there.'

'Then that's where you'll go,' said the Countess, with the private thought that he probably would be seen dead there. 'And buy a pair of dark glasses and shave your moustache. And if I were you I'd sell treasure here to the first dealer you can find.'

'Sell the Bentley?' said Glodstone. It was the final straw. 'I couldn't do that.'

'In that case, stew in a French hoosegow for the rest of your natural. You don't seem to know what your prospects are. Well, I'm telling you. They're zero minus forty. Permafrost all the way to the Judgement Day. Amen.'

'Oh God. Oh God! How did this ever happen? It's too horrible to be real.'

For a moment the Countess felt a twinge of pity for him. The world was full of people like Glodstone who played at life and only discovered reality when it kicked them in the face. 'Roast lamb and abattoirs,' she said inconsequentially and was surprised when he picked up the message.

'Or to the slaughter.' He paused and looked at her. 'What are you going to do?'

'Think about it. You go and fetch Butch Cassidy. On foot. If I'm not here when you get back stay at the Marine Hotel in Margate and register as Mr Cassidy. I'll call you there.'

'Is there a Marine Hotel in Margate?'

'If there isn't, choose one with two AA stars and I'll call them all.'

Glodstone trudged disconsolately from the car park and found Peregrine eating an ice-cream and studying some girls in bikinis with an almost healthy interest. When they returned to the car the Countess had vanished. She was sitting in the bus station waiting for one that would take her to Bournemouth and from there she'd catch a train to London.

'I don't trust that woman,' said Peregrine grimly.

'You'd better,' said Glodstone. 'She's all that stands between us and the reintroduction of the guillotine.'

'I tell you the whole thing was a joke,' said the Major, 'I did not drop by parachute so I don't know where it's buried.' He was standing by the roadside surrounded by armed gendarmes. Nobody else thought it was a joke.

'Monsieur chooses to play games with us,' said the Commissaire. 'Ah well, we too can play games. Back to the station.'

'Now hang on,' said the Major, 'I don't know what Glodstone's done but . . .'

'Glodstone? Who is this Glodstone?'

'Hasn't Slymne told you? I thought . . .'

'What did you think? No, I want to hear from you what this man Glodstone is.'

Major Fetherington told him. He wasn't going through Slymne's experience before he cracked and obviously Glodstone had asked for it.

'It fits the description of the one who called himself Pringle,' said the Inspector when he had finished, 'but he rescued Botwyk. Why should he then shoot him?'

'Who knows why the English do things? Only the good God

knows that. In the meantime, put out a full alert for him. All airports, frontier posts, everywhere.'

'Do we ask Scotland Yard?'

Commissaire Roudhon hesitated. 'I'll have to check with Paris first. And I want these two grilled for every bit of information they've got. They must have known more about the operation than they've admitted so far or they wouldn't be down here.'

He drove off in a hurry and the Major was shoved into the back of a van and taken back to Boosat. For the rest of the day he sat answering questions and at the end of it no one was any the wiser. Inspector Ficard made his report to an incredulous Commissaire.

'An adventure? The Countess wrote to him asking to be rescued? He came down in an ancient Bentley? And they come looking for a boy called Peregrine Clyde-Browne because his father wanted him back? What sort of madness is this?'

'It's what the other one, Slymne, told us.'

'So they had a ready-made story. We have a major political assassination to deal with and you expect me to believe it was carried out by an English schoolteacher who . . .' He was interrupted by the telephone. When he put it down Commissaire Roudhon no longer knew what to think.

'A man answering that description and driving a Bentley crossed from Cherbourg this morning. Ticket made out in the name of Glodstone. I'll inform Paris. They can decide how to play it from now on. I am a policeman, not a bloody politician.'

'What shall we do with these two?'

'Put them in a cell together and tape every single word they say. Better still, install a video camera. If they pass messages I want to know. In any case, it's the sort of thing that'll impress the Americans. They're flying ten anti-terrorist specialists in from Frankfurt, and they're going to need some convincing.'

Slymne was still gibbering when they came for him. He was too feeble to resist and what he said made even less sense than before but they carried him down the passage and put him in a larger cell.

'God Almighty,' said the Major when he was led in too. 'You poor sod. What did the buggers do to you, use electrodes on your bollocks or something?'

'Don't touch me,' squealed Slymne squinting at him.

'I don't intend to, old boy. Count me out. All I do know is that Glodstone's got something coming to him.'

In his hotel room in Margate, Glodstone looked at himself in the mirror. Without his moustache and wearing dark glasses he did look different. He also looked a great deal older. Not that that would help matters in the slightest if they caught him. He'd be over eighty by the time he was released – if they ever bothered to let people out who had been partly responsible for assassinating American political advisers. He rather doubted it. He was also extremely dubious about having followed the Countess's advice but he'd been too exhausted and numb with terror the day before to be able to think for himself. And Peregrine had been no help. He'd made matters worse by wanting to lie low in a hole in a hedge like the man in *Rogue Male*.

'Nobody would think of looking there,' he'd said, 'and when it's all blown over . . .'

'It isn't going to blow over, damn you,' said Glodstone, 'and anyway we'd come out stinking like a couple of ferrets with BO.'

'Not if we found somewhere near a stream and bought some soap. We could stock up with tins of food and dig a really deep burrow and no one would ever know.'

'Except every farmer in the district. Anyway, cub-hunting's coming up shortly and I'm not going to be chased across country by a pack of hounds or earthed up. Use your loaf.'

'I still don't think we should do what that woman said. She could have been lying.'

'And I suppose you think the *Daily Telegraph*'s lying too,' said Glodstone. 'She told us it was an international gathering and she was bloody well right.'

'Then why did she write you those letters? She asked us to –'

'She didn't. Can't you see that? They were forgeries and we've been framed. And so's she.'

'I can't see why. I mean . . .'

'Because if we're caught and we say she wrote those letters she can't prove she didn't.'

'But you burnt them.'

Glodstone sighed, and wished to hell he hadn't. 'She didn't know

199

that. That's how I knew she was telling the truth. She hadn't a clue about the damned things. And if she'd been going to do us down she'd have gone to the police when she went off to get petrol. Surely that told you something?'

'I suppose so,' said Peregrine, only to bring up the question of the revolvers. 'The Major's going to be jolly angry when he finds they're missing from the armoury,' he said.

Glodstone stifled the retort that what Major Fetherington felt was the least of their problems. If the damned man hadn't trained Peregrine to be such an efficient killer they might not have been in this terrible mess. And mess was putting it mildly. Their finger-prints were all over the Château, the French police must be looking for an Englishman with a glass eye, and even if they'd had the revolvers to put back the forensic experts could easily match them with the bullet that had killed Professor Botwyk. Finally, what made it insane to imagine they could resume their old lives or pretend they'd never been to France was what the Countess had said; whoever had set them up would undoubtedly drop the word to the police. After all, it would pay the bastard to. He hadn't killed anyone and they had, and it would get him off the hook. And only the Countess could save their necks – if she chose.

So Glodstone had driven to London, had changed his travellers' cheques and, leaving the Bentley with a reputable dealer in vintage cars with orders to sell as soon as he received the registration and licence papers, had caught the train to Margate. Peregrine had travelled in a separate carriage and he'd found himself a room in a guest-house. Glodstone spent half an hour changing and shaving in a public lavatory and had booked into the first Two-Star hotel to have a spare room. He hadn't been out since. Instead, he had hung about the bar, had watched the news on TV and had read the latest report in the papers of the terrorist attack in France. But for the most part he had stayed in his room in an abyss of self-pity and terror. Life couldn't be like this. He wasn't a criminal; he'd always detested murderers and terrorists; the police were always right and they should never have stopped hanging. All that was changed and he was particularly grateful that capital punishment had been abolished in France. He'd lost faith in the police too. It had been all very well to talk about going outside the law but now that he was there he knew no self-respecting policeman who would believe his story and if he did it would make not the slightest difference. And being inside meant just that. Whatever some damn fool poet had said about stone walls and iron bars, Glodstone knew better. They made prisons, and French ones at that. He'd never have a chance to urge his House on at rugger or knock a ball about in the nets again and the train-set in the basement . . . He'd be known as Glodstone the Murderer and go down in the school infamy as Groxbourne's equivalent of Dr Crippen. And how Slymne would gloat . . . He was just plumbing this new hell when the phone rang beside his bed.

Glodstone picked it up and listened to a now familiar voice.

'My, my, brother John, it's just taken me for ages to reach you.'

'Yes, well, the thing was . . .' Glodstone began before the Countess cut him short. She was thinking about girls on switchboards.

'I'm down by the pier so meet me there in five minutes and we'll have ourselves some lunch. Alone.'

'Yes,' said Glodstone. The phone went dead. With as much nonchalance as he could muster, he walked downstairs and out into the sunshine. The promenade was crowded with the sort of people he would normally have avoided at all costs, but today he was grateful for their presence. The Countess had known what she was doing when she had picked on Margate. All the same, he approached the pier cautiously, horribly conscious that he might be walking into a trap.

But the Countess was sitting on a bench and rose as he came up. 'Darling,' she said to his surprise, and put her arm through his. 'Gee, it's just marvellous to see you again.'

She dragged him across the road and down a side street to a car. 'Where's Peregrine?' she asked as they got in.

'In the amusement park probably, shooting things,' said Glodstone. 'It's called Dreamland.'

'Appropriately,' said the Countess. 'Right, so that's where he stays temporarily while I debrief you.'

'Debrief me?' said Glodstone, uncertain after that 'Darling' how to interpret the word.

'Like with astronauts, and guys that have been taken prisoner.

Somewhere along the line there's got to be a connection.'

'Between what?' said Glodstone more confused than ever.

'Between you and me. Mister Letter-Writer. Someone who wanted to screw us both and succeeded. Go back over those letters again. Was there anything peculiar about them?'

'Yes,' said Glodstone vehemently, 'there bloody well was. They . . .'

'No, sweetheart, you're not reading me. Did you see where they were posted?'

'In France. Definitely in France and in your envelopes. The ones with the crest on the back.'

'And in my handwriting. You said all that but how could you be so sure?'

'Because I've got your other letters to me about Anthony's allergies and whatnot. The handwriting was identical.'

'So that puts it back in my court. Now what did they say, and I mean exactly.'

As she drove slowly out of town Glodstone went through the details of the letters and their instructions with a total recall born of fear.

'Hotels you were booked into? Crossing via Ostend? Your whole route mapped out for you? And you did just what they said?'

'Until we got to Ivry. There was another letter there saying we had to turn back or you were going to die.'

'So you had to come on,' said the Countess, shaking her head sadly. 'And that was the only one that made sense.'

'That night they tried to stop us by putting oil on the road in the forest. We could have been killed. As it was, a man tried to hold us up –'

'Stop right there. Can you describe him?'

Glodstone visualized the figure of Mr Blowther covered in oil and leaves, and found it difficult.

'But he was English? You're sure of that?'

'I suppose he was. He certainly sounded English. And there was another one at Calais who told the ferry people my wife had died. I don't have a wife.'

'I can believe it,' said the Countess. 'Which doesn't help any.

202

Whoever used my notepaper and knew my hand and posted the letters in France, booked you rooms in hotels, tried to stop you . . . No way they can't be crazy. And how did they know you'd come? Come to that, why *did* you?'

Glodstone blushed. 'I couldn't leave you in the lurch,' he muttered. 'I mean I'd always thought of you as a lady and, well . . . it's difficult to explain really.'

'And what do you think now? Am I still a "lady"?'

'You're certainly very nice,' said Glodstone judiciously. 'You'd have gone to the police if you weren't.'

The Countess sighed. It still hadn't dawned on the poor dumb cluck that she'd have done just that if she hadn't had something to hide. Like seven gold bars and a past that would make his romantic hair stand on end. Talk about knight errant, operative word 'errant'. It was only in Britain they made them so innocent. 'And you're nice too,' she said and patted his knee. 'It wasn't your fault you were framed. So we can't let them take you to prison, can we?'

'Hopefully,' said Glodstone quivering with new devotion under the influence of the pat on the knee and the baby-talk. Her next remark blew his mind.

'So we go back and get the Sundance Kid and put the bite on the Clyde-Brownes.'

'We do what?'

'Put the squeeze on them. You're going to need money, and if they're what you say they are, and I think, they'll pay through the nose to keep themselves out of the media. I can't see Papa C-B wanting to be thrown out of the Reform.'

'I won't do it,' said Glodstone. 'It wasn't Peregrine's fault that . . .'

'He's wanted by the police in every country this side of the Iron Curtain? And he did the killing, not you. So Mr Clyde-Browne is going to have to work hard to pull both your irons out of the fire. And he has got influence. I've looked him up and he reeks of it. His brother's Deputy Under-Secretary at the Department of Trade and adviser to the EEC Commissioner for the Regularization, Standardization and Uniformity of Processed Food Products. Meaning fish fingers.'

203

'Good Lord, how did you find that out?'

'Holborn Public Library's latest copy of *Who's Who*. So we've got some muscle. And we're going to use it tonight.'

'Tonight? But we'll never drive all the way to Virginia Water . . . I mean it'll be after midnight by the time we get there.'

'I can't think of a better time to break the news,' said the Countess, and drove back to the Amusement Park.

Chapter 23

In fact it was almost 2 a.m. when they parked the car at the end of Pine Tree Lane and rang the doorbell of The Cones. A light came on upstairs and presently the door opened on the chain and Mr Clyde-Brown peered out. He'd had a hard evening listening to his wife argue that it was time they called in the police, and had only managed to get to sleep with a cup of Horlicks laced with yet more whisky and two Mogadons.

'Who is it?' he mumbled.

'Me, Dad,' said Peregrine stepping under the porchlight. For a moment Mr Clyde-Browne was prey to the ghastly thought that two Mogadons and a quarter of a bottle of Scotch didn't mix too well. Certainly he had to be hallucinating. The voice sounded horribly right but the face, and in particular the hair, didn't gel with his memory of Peregrine. The last time he'd seen the lout he'd been fair-haired and with a fresh complexion. Now he looked like something the Race Relations . . . He stopped himself in time. There was a law about saying things like that.

'Where the hell have you been?' he asked instead, and undid the chain. 'Your mother's been at her wit's end worrying about you. And who –'

The Countess and Glodstone stepped through the doorway after Peregrine. 'Let's hit the lounge,' said the Countess, 'Somewhere nice and private. We don't want the neighbours in on this.'

Mr Clyde-Browne wasn't sure. The arrival of his son with black hair in the company of a woman in dark glasses and a tall haggard man who looked vaguely familiar and definitely sinister, and this at two in the morning, seemed to suggest he might need every neighbour within shouting distance. The Countess's language didn't help. With the feeling that he had stepped into a Cagney movie he went into the sitting-room and turned on the light.

205

'Now what's the meaning of this?' he demanded, trying to muster some authority.

'Tell him, baby,' said the Countess, checking the curtains were closed to unnerve Mr Clyde-Browne still more.

'Well, it's like this, dad,' said Peregrine, 'I've been and gone and shot a professor.'

Mr Clyde-Browne's eyes bulged in his head. 'I'm not hearing right,' he muttered, 'It's those fucking Mogadons. You've been and gone . . . Where the hell did you pick up that vulgar expression?'

'His name was Botwyk and he was an American and we thought he was a gangster and I shot him through the head,' said Peregrine. 'With a .38 from the School Armoury.'

Mr Clyde-Browne's knees buckled and he slumped into a chair. 'I don't believe it,' he moaned. 'This isn't happening.'

'No, not now,' said Peregrine. 'But it did. It's in all the papers. I shot a Russian too, but he didn't die. At least, he hasn't yet.'

Mr Clyde-Browne shut his eyes in an attempt to convince himself that he was having a nightmare. It failed. When he opened them again Peregrine and these two awful people were still there. The Countess handed him a copy of *The Times*.

'I've ringed the latest piece,' she said. 'Right now they're looking for a terrorist. Well, he's standing there in front of you.'

Mr Clyde-Brown hurled the paper aside. He'd read all about the murder on the train the day before and had expressed his sense of outrage. With another sense of outrage he got to his feet. 'If this is some sort of fucking joke,' he yelled, 'I'll –'

'Cool it, baby,' said the Countess. 'You want the cops in on this just keep bawling your head off. That's your prerogative. Or you can phone them. I guess the number's still 999.'

'I know what the fucking number is,' shouted Mr Clyde-Browne rather more quietly.

'So he's your son. You want him up on a murder rap, call them up. It's no skin off my nose. I don't go round bumping people off.'

Mr Clyde-Browne looked from her to Peregrine and back again. 'You're bluffing. He didn't shoot anyone. It's all a lie. You're trying to blackmail me. Well, let me tell you –'

'Oh sure. So go ahead and phone. Tell them you've got two

blackmailers and a son who just happens to be a murderer on your hands and you don't know what to do. We'll wait here for you. No sweat.'

Beads of it broke out on Mr Clyde-Browne's forehead. 'Tell me you didn't do it,' he said to Peregrine, 'I want you to say it and I want to hear it.'

'I shot a Professor, dad. I've told you that already.'

'I know you have . . .'

He was interrupted by the entrance of his wife. For a long moment she stood in the doorway gazing at Peregrine.

'Oh, my poor boy,' she cried, rushing forward and gathering him to her. 'What have they done to you?'

'Nothing, mum. Nothing at all.'

'But where've you been and why's your hair that colour?'

'That's part of the disguise. I've been to France . . .'

'And shot an American Professor. Through the head, didn't you say?' said Mr Clyde-Browne, helping himself to more whisky. He didn't give a damn what the stuff did with Mogadons any longer. A quiet death was preferable.

'Oh my poor darling,' said Mrs Clyde-Browne, who still hadn't got the message, 'I've been so worried about you.'

In the corner Mr Clyde-Browne was heard to mutter something about her not knowing what worry was. Yet.

The Countess got up and moved towards the door. Mr Clyde-Browne hit it first. 'Where do you think you're fucking going?' he shouted.

Mrs Clyde-Browne turned on him. 'How dare you use that filthy word in my house!' she screamed. 'And in front of Peregrine and these . . . er . . .'

The Countess smiled sweetly. 'Let me introduce myself,' she said. 'My name's Deirdre, Countess de Montcon. And please don't apologize for your husband's language. He's just a little over-wrought. And now if you'll excuse us . . .'

Mr Clyde-Browne didn't budge. 'You're not leaving this house until I've got to the bottom of this . . . this . . .'

'Murder?' asked the Countess. 'And of course there's the little matter of kidnapping too but I don't suppose that's so important.'

'I didn't kidnap you,' said Peregrine and blew his father's mind still further. If the sod was prepared to deny kidnapping while openly admitting he'd murdered, he had to be telling the truth.

'All right,' he said. 'How much do you want?'

The Countess hesitated and made up her mind not to go back to American slang. Kensington English would hit Mrs Clyde-Browne's gentility harder. 'Really,' she said, 'if it weren't for the obvious fact that you're not yourself I would find your attitude extremely sordid.'

'You would, would you? Well let me tell you I know sordidity when I see it and I know blackmailers and add that lot to your calling yourself a countess and –'

'But she is a countess,' said Peregrine as his father ran out of words, 'I saw her passport and she lives in this jolly great Château. It's called Carmagnac and it's ever so nice. And it's there I shot the professor.'

'Oh, you never did,' said Mrs Clyde-Browne reproachfully, 'you're making it up.'

'Christ!' said Mr Clyde-Browne, and downed his Scotch. 'Will you keep out of this. We've enough . . .'

'I most certainly won't,' retorted Mrs Clyde-Browne, 'I'm his mother . . '

'And he's a fucking murderer. M – U – R – D –'

'I know how to spell, thank you very much. And he's not, are you, darling?'

'No,' said Peregrine. 'All I did was shoot him. I didn't know he was –'

'Know? Know? You wouldn't know mass murder from petty larceny,' shouted his father, and grabbed the paper, 'well, the rest of the bloody world knows . . .'

'If I might just get a word in,' said the Countess. 'The rest of the world doesn't know . . yet. Of course, in time the French police will be in touch with Scotland Yard but if we could come to some arrangement . . .'

'I've already asked you how much you're demanding, you blackmailing bitch. Now spit it out.'

The countess looked at him nastily but kept her cool. 'For a man supposedly at the top of your profession you are really remarkably obtuse,' she said. 'The truism about the law applies. You are an ass.

And what's more, if you don't moderate your language I shall call the police myself.'

'Oh, you mustn't,' wailed Mrs Clyde-Browne on whose dim intelligence it had slowly dawned that Peregrine really was in danger. Mr Clyde-Browne edged onto a chair.

'All right,' he said, 'what are you suggesting?'

'Immunity,' she said simply. 'But first I would like a nice cup of tea. It's been a hard two days getting your son out of France and –'

'Get it,' Mr Clyde-Browne told his wife.

'But, Oscar –'

'I said get it and I meant get it. And stop blubbing, for God's sake. I want to hear what this blo . . . this lady has to say.'

Still sobbing, Mrs Clyde-Browne left the room. By the time she returned with the tea-tray Mr Clyde-Brown was staring at the Countess with something approaching respect. He was also drained of all emotion except terror. In a life devoted to the belief that all women were an intellectual sub-species whose sole purpose was to cook meals and have babies, he had never before come across such a powerful intelligence. 'And what about that?' he asked, glaring with horror at Glodstone.

'I have arranged his future,' said the Countess, 'I won't say where, though it may be in Brazil . . .'

'But I don't want to go to Brazil,' squawked Glodstone, and was promptly told to hold his tongue.

'Or it may be somewhere else. The point is that Mr Glodstone is going to die.'

On the couch Glodstone whimpered. Mr Clyde-Browne perked up. This woman knew her onions. 'And about time too,' he said.

'And isn't it time you phoned your brother?' asked the Countess. 'The sooner he can get the ball rolling the sooner we can wrap this up. And now if you'll excuse us . . .'

This time Mr Clyde-Browne didn't try to stop her. He knew when he was beaten. 'How will I get in touch with you if –'

'You won't, honey,' said the Countess patting his ashen cheek, 'from now on in the ball's in your court.'

'Well, really!' said Mrs Clyde-Browne, 'She didn't even touch her tea.'

'Bugger tea. Take that murderous bastard upstairs and bleach his hair back to normal.'

'But we haven't any peroxide and –'

'Use whatever you pour down the lavatory. Even if his hair falls out it'll be better than nothing.' And he hurried down the passage to the study and phoned his brother.

The Countess drove steadily towards London. She didn't want to be stopped by a patrol car and she had to get back into the sprawl of the metropolis and anonymity in case Mr Clyde-Browne's brother refused to cooperate.

'I've booked you a room at Heathrow,' she said.

'But I don't want to go to Brazil,' said Glodstone.

'So you're not going. You flew in on a Dan-Air Flight from Zimbabwe, arrival time 6 a.m., name of Harrison. And you're not to be disturbed. It's all arranged. I'll pick you up around noon for the funeral.'

'Funeral? What funeral?'

'Yours, sweetheart. Mr Glodstone's going to die. Officially. And don't take on so. You'll get used to the after-life.'

Glodstone doubted it.

Slymne didn't. Given the choice he'd have willingly died. Once again he was being interrogated. This time by three American agents from Frankfurt who were under the impression that he had spent time in Libya. In another room Major Fetherington was getting the same treatment. Unfortunately, he had.

'In the war,' he moaned, 'in the bloody war.'

'Yom Kippur or the Seven Days?'

'In the Eighth Army. A Desert Rat, for God's sake.'

'You can say that again, bud. You and Gaddafi both.'

'I'm talking about the war, the real war. The one against the Afrika Korps.'

'The who?' said one of the men who'd obviously never heard of any war before Vietnam.

'The Germans. You must know about Rommel.'

'You tell us. He train you or something?'

'Damned near killed me,' said the Major, rather wishing he had.

'So you were threatened into this, is that what you're saying?'

'No, I'm not. I'm not in this, whatever it is. I was sent down here by the Headmaster to try to find Clyde-Browne . . .'

'Tell us something new. We've been through that routine before.'

'But there's nothing else to tell. And what are you doing with that fucking hypodermic?'

In the passage outside Commissaire Roudhon and the man from the Quai d'Orsay listened with interest.

'The space shuttle and truth drugs and not an inkling of history,' said Monsieur Laponce. 'So much for the special relationship. The President will be pleased.'

'Monsieur?' said the Commissaire, who hadn't a clue what the Foreign Office man was talking about.

'Between London and Washington. We are standing at the end of an era.'

Commissaire Roudhon looked up and down the passage. 'If you say so, monsieur,' he said. Eras meant nothing to him.

'From now on Britain will be what she should always have been, a dependency of France,' continued Monsieur Laponce, indulging his taste for rhetoric. 'The idiots in Whitehall have played into our hands.'

'You really think the British government sent these men?'

'It is not what I think that matters, Commissaire. It is what those charming Americans in there report to Washington.'

'But Gaddafi –'

'– has nothing to do with this. Nor have the Red Brigade or any other terrorist group. It was a stratagem to worsen our relationship with the United States and it has failed.'

'I hadn't thought of it like that,' said the Commissaire.

'You will, Monsieur Roudhon. From now on you will. Bear that in mind. And no press releases. You will simply tell the press that the affair is of too delicate a nature diplomatically to speak about since British Intelligence Officers . . . You will stop yourself there in some confusion and demand that what you have just said is not to be reported. Is that clear?'

'Absolutely.'

'If you fail in the duty, you will have failed France,' said

Monsieur Laponce. 'Remember that. And now, to avoid listening to that terrible noise, I will report to the Minister.'

Inside the interrogation room Major Fetherington under the influence of the drugs he had been given was living up to Henry Ford's dictum that history was bunk.

'I'll tell you something,' said the chief American investigator after the Major had babbled on for the tenth time about dog-turds in Shrewsbury, 'you can say what you like about the limeys but when they make 'em they make 'em tough.'

'Not the other one,' said the medical expert, 'he's plain loco. Give him a shot of this stuff and he'll be psychotic for life.'

'What's all this shit about letters mean?'

'Zero. He's scrambled eggs cerebralwise.'

'So what've we got? Two names, Glodstone and Clyde-Browne. They're not going to like this in Washington.'

In Whitehall, Deputy Under-Secretary Cecil Clyde-Browne, CBE, sat staring dismally at a pigeon on the roof opposite and wondered what was being decided. Somewhere nearby, the Home Secretary, the Secretary of State for Foreign Affairs, the Police Commissioner and the Head of MI5 held his future in their hands. More accurately, they held a telex from the British Ambassador in Paris.

'Well?' asked the Foreign Secretary, when they'd all had their fill of the ghastly news. 'Do we hand the little bugger over or do we not?'

The Chief Commissioner of Police and the Head of MI5 shook their heads.

'Out of the question,' said MI5, 'I've had a look at the imbecile and if the French get their hands on him I've no doubt they can programme him to say anything. Not that they'd need much for him to say. Nobody'd believe his story anyway.'

'I'm not sure I do,' muttered the Foreign Secretary. 'This couldn't be some frightful CIA plot, could it? I've never been entirely happy about your American counterparts since they tried those damned explosive clams on Castro.'

'I can't see what they could possibly gain from it. It's more likely to be KGB-inspired.'

The Foreign Secretary looked nostalgically at a globe of the World which still showed India as part of the Empire. 'Where have you got the brute?' he asked presently.

'In a safe house in Aldershot.'

The name inspired the Foreign Secretary. 'I don't suppose you could arrange for him to have an accident, or Lassa fever, or something?'

'It's feasible, but with the man Glodstone on the loose . . .'

The Home Secretary intervened. 'I'm not prepared to be party to an unofficial execution,' he said hurriedly, 'I mean if this got out . . .'

'It is out, damn it. Whatever it is. And we've got to decide something now. The American Ambassador is due at two and with the confounded French putting it about that there's an SAS hit-squad conducting an assassination campaign to worsen Franco-US relations, I've got to tell the fellow something credible. I know he's from Arkansas but . . .'

'The truth perhaps?' murmured the Home Secretary. 'They say it always comes out in the end.'

'They can say what they bloody well please, but I haven't spent forty years in the foreign service to believe that one, and from what I can tell no one knows what the truth is.'

'I suppose we could always put the blame on the IRA,' said MI5. 'It's as good a ruse as any and it won't do the Irish lobby in Washington any harm to get a kick in the teeth!'

'And what the hell do we do with Clyde-Browne? Call the little bastard O'Brien? I know this fellow from Arkansas thinks Bombay is part of a B52, but he's not going to fall for anything as dumb as an Irish dimension.'

It was the Police Commissioner who came up with the answer. 'I should have thought the obvious thing to do was put the lad in the SAS. He's obviously a born killer and it's the last place they're going to look.'

'The first, you mean,' said the Foreign Secretary, but the Police Commissioner held his ground.

'The last. If we had organized a hit-squad along these lunatic lines with vintage Bentleys and men with glass eyes nobody would think the SAS were involved. They're experts and professionals.'

213

'But this raving Major Fetherington's already admitted . . .'

'Which makes it certain no one seriously believes he is. The man's in his mid-fifties. In any case he has nothing to do with it. He was in the UK at the time of the murder.'

The Home Secretary backed him up. 'It's the same with Slymne. The Headmaster sent them both off.'

'Splendid,' said the Foreign Secretary, 'so how do I explain to this Arkansas beef baron that the bloody boy isn't in the SAS when he is?'

MI5 smiled. 'I think you can safely leave that to me,' he said.

The Foreign Secretary had his doubts. He was thinking about Blake, Philby and Blunt. 'Safely?' he asked.

MI5 nodded.

By the time the American Ambassador arrived a hooded figure was standing in the ante-room.

'Of course, we wouldn't disclose the identity of any of our men in the Special Air Services,' said the Foreign Secretary after asking politely about the health of the Ambassador's cattle and learning that he was actually into natural gas and came from Texas, 'in ordinary circumstances, that is. But we're prepared to make an exception in this case.'

He pressed a bell on his desk and the hooded figure entered. 'Sergeant Clyde-Browne, remove your balaclava,' he said.

'We're going to want more identification than than,' said the Ambassador, staring at the large individual with the walrus moustache.

'Fingerprints? I mean the French have got those of the assassin, haven't they?'

'I guess so.' He was still guessing when the man, having given his fingerprints, weight, size of shoes and height in centimetres (to confuse the issue still further) donned his balaclava helmet and left the room. 'Haven't I seen him some place else?' enquired the Ambassador.

'Possibly,' said the Foreign Secretary loftily. 'Between ourselves I understand him to be in charge of certain . . . er . . . unmentionable security operations at Buckingham Palace.'

'I guess that explains it then. Those goddam Frenchies seem to have screwed things up again. I'll have our security chief check the

214

details but they don't fit the description I'd been given. The killer was shorter and twenty years younger.'

'And doubtless French,' said the Foreign Secretary, and saw him to the door.

'Who on earth was that grisly-looking blighter?' he asked MI5 when the Ambassador's armour-plated limousine was safely out of the way. 'And what are those unmentionable duties at Buck House?'

'Actually he's Captain of the Queen's Heads,' said MI5. 'I thought that was rather a nice touch.'

'Captain of . . . you mean he's a lavatory attendant? Good God, man, no wonder that blasted Yank guessed he'd seen him before ' He stopped and looked at MI5 suspiciously. 'He's not another swine like Blunt, is he? Has he had positive vetting?'

'Oh absolutely. Comes from an eminently respectable Catholic family in the Falls Road area of Belfast. Anyway he's only in charge of the visitor's loos. Don't suppose he's set eyes on Her Majesty.'

'I should bloody well hope not. And if I were in your shoes I'd see to it she doesn't set eyes on the wallah. Wouldn't blame her for setting those damned Corgis on the brute. Anyway, thank the Lord that's settled. Even the present American administration wouldn't have the gall to start checking the Palace.'

Chapter 24

As the Cortège drove slowly out of the Crematorium, Glodstone
stared miserably at the back of the chauffeur's head. It was one of
the ironies of having attended his own funeral that he should now
recall that 'chauffeur' came from the French for stoker; presumably
even modern furnaces had to be attended by somebody to take out
the ashes. Whoever had just been incinerated (probably an unidentified tramp or something they'd finished with in the dissecting-
rooms at one of the teaching hospitals) had gone to his Maker
bearing Glodstone's name. It was there on the death certificate and a
little obituary would shortly appear in the *Old Groxbournian*. The
Great Adventure had gone up in smoke.

'I know just how you feel,' said the Countess, patting his hand.
'*Mourir c'est partir un peu.*'

'What?' said Glodstone.

'To die is to part a little. But it won't be for long. By the time the
surgeon's finished with you you'll be a new man.'

'Surgeon?' said Glodstone. 'What bloody surgeon?'

'The plastic one. He's said to be terribly good with burns.'

'Burns? Considering where I'm supposed to be he'd have to be
fucking miraculous.'

'There's no need to use that sort of language,' said the Countess
sharply, 'I haven't gone to all this trouble and expense to have you
swearing like a trooper.'

Glodstone considered the change in her own language and said
nothing. There was something about this extraordinary woman that
frightened him and it was only when she stopped the car at the top of
Hampstead Heath and they were walking down to the tube station
that he brought up the matter of burns and plastic surgery.

'What the hell do I need plastic surgery for? Apart from whoever
went up in that coffin. . .'

'Well, we won't go into that now,' said the Countess, 'that's all past and done with. You've got to look to the future and since you refuse to go to Brazil you'll just have to do what I tell you. The main thing will be to alter the shape of your ears. They're the give-away and the police always look at them first. Then –'

'But with this wig on no one can see my blasted ears,' said Glodstone.

'I'm not going to be married to a man with a toupee. It's unbecoming and anyway it won't fit your image. As far as the rest of you . . .'

But Glodstone wasn't listening. 'Did you say "married"?' he asked.

'Of course I did. You don't imagine for one moment that I'm going to live in sin with you, do you?'

Half an hour later Glodstone entered a clinic near Portland Place. On the door a brass plaque seemed to suggest its main business lay in abortions, but Glodstone no longer cared. It was enough to know he was going to be married. It was infinitely preferable to spending the rest of his life in Brazil.

'My hero,' said the Countess, kissing him lightly on the cheek, 'Now don't forget to sign your name as Mr Smith.'

'Slymne's *where*?' said the Headmaster when Major Fetherington returned a week later, in the company of two Special Branch officers.

'Rampton,' said the Major.

'Rampton? But that's that ghastly hospital for the criminally insane, isn't it? And what on earth have you been doing to your face?'

'Dog-turd in Shrewsbury,' said the Major, who hadn't fully recovered from the effects of the truth drug and his hours of interrogation.

'But that was your backside. Now you come back here with a face looking like a . . .'

'Dog-turd in Shrewsbury,' said the Major.

'Christ,' said the Headmaster. If Slymne was sufficiently off his rocker to be in Rampton, the Major could do with some treatment himself. 'And what about Glodstone?'

'That's what we've come to see you about,' said one of the men and produced his identification. The Headmaster examined it cautiously.

'Special Branch?' he asked weakly.

The man nodded. 'Now about Mr Glodstone, sir,' he said, 'we're going to require access to his rooms and we'd be glad if you answered a few questions. For instance, were you aware that he had any Communist inclinations?'

'Communist inc . . . I thought the sod belonged to the Monday Club. He certainly read the *Daily Telegraph*.'

'That could have been cover. Homosexual tendencies? Excessive drinking? Chip on his social shoulder? Anything of that sort?'

'All of it,' said the Headmaster fervently and glanced out of the window. A number of soldiers had driven up in a lorry and were debussing on the drive. 'What the hell are they doing here?'

'If you'll just sign this,' said the Special Branch man and placed a document on his desk.

The Headmaster read it through with increasing alarm. 'The Official Secrets Act? You want me to sign –'

'Just a simple precaution, sir. Nothing more. Of course if you'd prefer to face criminal proceedings in connection with certain offences again the person committed in Belfast . . .'

'Belfast? I've never been anywhere near Belfast,' said the Headmaster, beginning to think he'd shortly be joining Slymne in a padded cell. 'You come here and tell me to sign the Official Secrets Act or be charged . . . Dear God, where's that pen?' He scrawled his signature at the bottom of the form.

'And now the key to the School Armoury, if you don't mind.'

The Headmaster handed it over and while one of the men took it out to the officer in charge of the squad the other settled himself in a chair. 'I think I must warn you that should anyone make enquiries about Mr Glodstone or a certain ex-pupil it will be in your interest not to say anything,' he said. 'The Belfast charges are still outstanding and having signed the Official Secrets Act the consequences could be slightly unfortunate. Need I say more?'

'No,' said the Headmaster indistinctly, 'but what am I going to tell Mr Clyde-Browne?'

'Who, sir?'

218

'Christ,' said the Headmaster. Outside the soldiers had begun to load the lorry with all the weapons from the Armoury. That was a relief anyway. He'd never liked the bloody things.

'And now if you'll just take me up to Glodstone's rooms.' They crossed the quad and climbed the staircase. 'Not that I suppose we'll find anything of interest,' said the Special Branch man. 'When the Russians employ a sleeper they do things thoroughly. Probably recruited the traitor when he was at Cambridge.'

'Cambridge? I never dreamt that Glodstone had been anywhere near a University. He certainly never mentioned it.'

'Obviously not. The man's clearly an expert. One only has to look at the sort of books he surrounded himself with to see that.'

The Headmaster gazed at the collected works of Sapper and felt peculiar. 'I really can't believe it even now,' he said. 'Glodstone was a ghastly man but he didn't have the brains to be a . . . what did you call it?'

'A sleeper,' said the Special Branch man, putting the cigar box containing the Countess's letters in a plastic bag. 'Probably in code.'

The Headmaster tried to look on the bright side. 'Well, at least I won't have the damned man around me any more,' he said. 'That's some relief. Have you any idea where he is?'

The Special Branch man hesitated. 'No harm in telling you now. We found his Bentley parked near Tilbury yesterday. An East German tramp steamer sailed on Wednesday night.'

They went back to the Headmaster's study.

'I think that'll be all we'll require for the moment, sir. If anything should occur to you that might be of use to us, we'd be grateful if you'd call this number. It's a phone drop, so just leave your name.'

'And what about him?' asked the Headmaster glancing anxiously at Major Fetherington.

'What about him?'

'I can't have a master going about muttering "Dog-turd in Shrewsbury" in front of the boys all the time. He's as mad as a hatter.'

'You should see Mr Slymne,' said the Special Branch man

grimly. 'The Major's all right. He's a hero by comparison. And you can always use him as a groundsman.'

But it was in Pine Tree Lane that feelings were most mixed.

'I'll never forgive you. Never,' wailed Mrs Clyde-Browne, ignoring the presence of ten undercover agents dressed in overalls who had already installed double glazing and were now redecorating the entire house. 'To think that I'll never see poor Peregrine again!'

'Oh, I don't know,' said Mr Clyde-Browne cheerfully, 'he'll probably get leave once in a while. They can't keep a garrison in Antarctica for ever.'

'But he isn't used to the cold and he's got such a delicate chest.'

'There is that,' said Mr Clyde-Browne almost gaily. 'You can always go out and put flowers on his grave. And he certainly won't need embalming. Things keep for ever on ice.'

'You murdering . . . No, I don't want flock fleur-de-lys in the kitchen,' she yelled, as one of the agents tactfully interposed a wallpaper pattern book between them, 'and you can stop painting the hall pink. That's a William Morris design.'

Mr Clyde-Browne made himself scarce. He had an interesting divorce case to consider involving custody of a domestic cat and now that Peregrine was out of the way it might be advantageous to goad his own wife a little further.

In Bognor Regis Glodstone looked at his face in the bathroom mirror, and failed to recognize himself. It wasn't the first time, but it still shook him to see someone he didn't know staring with such horrid amazement back at him. And horrid was the word. The Countess had been right in claiming the plastic surgeon was good with burns, though, in Glodstone's livid opinion, she ought have said 'at' them.

'Just let me get my hands on the sod,' he had shouted when the bandages had been removed and he had finally been allowed the use of a mirror. 'He must have used a bloody flamethrower. Where are my blasted eyebrows?'

'In the disposal bin,' said the Sister in charge. 'Anyway, you specifically asked for total non-recognitive surgery.'

'Non-recog . . . bugger it, I did nothing of the sort. I came in here expecting to have my ears adjusted, not to be turned into something that'd frighten a fucking punk dalek into a fit. And why am I as bald as a coot?'

'We did a scalp transplant with another patient. He had alopecia totalis. It's taken very well.'

'And what have I got then, galloping fucking ringworm?'

'It'll save you having to brush your hair again.'

'And shave,' said Glodstone, 'Who did you swop my face with, some terminal leper?'

'That's called the Spitfire effect,' said the Sister. 'Lots of pilots who crashed in the Battle of Britain looked like that.'

'In that case I'd have thought the Messerschmidt effect would have been more appropriate,' said Glodstone. 'Am I going to have to spend the rest of my life with these pustules? There's one actually swelling on what's left of my nose.'

'They're just leeches. We use them for scavenging –'

'Shit,' said Glodstone and had to be held down to prevent him from trying to dislodge the things.

'We'll have to give you a sedative if you don't behave like a good boy.'

'Madam,' said Glodstone, managing to rally some dignity under threat of the needle, 'I have had some considerable experience of boys and no sane one would allow his face to be used as a watering hole for scavenging leeches. I could get tetanus, or die from loss of blood.'

'Nonsense. We ensure they're all perfectly healthy and they're only cleaning up the scar tissue.'

'In that case they'll get bloody awful indigestion,' said Glodstone, 'they've got enough grub there for the Lord Mayor's banquet. And get that sod out of my left nostril. I can't with my hands in bandages. And what's that for?'

'Fingerprint removal,' said the Sister, and left Glodstone to contemplate a life without any physical means of identification. Even his closest friends wouldn't know him now. Or want to.

But at least the Countess had been delighted. 'Darling,' she said when she came to collect him, 'you look wonderful.'

'You've got fucking peculiar tastes is all I can say,' said Glodstone bitterly and was promptly rebuked for using filthy language.

'You were something hush-hush in the War and you'd rather not talk about it. That's the line you'll have to take,' she said, 'and from now on you're to call me Bobby.'

'But that's a boy's name,' said Glodstone, wondering if he was about to marry some sort of lesbian with a truly horrific lust for disfigured men. It was a wonder he hadn't had a sex-change operation.

'It's nice and thirtyish. Lots of girls were called Bobby then and it'll blend with the Peke.'

Glodstone shuddered. He loathed Pekes and it was clear he was no longer going to be allowed to call his life his own, let alone his face.

It had proved only too true. After a swift registry marriage at which he had had to declare himself to be Clarence Sopwith Hillary, a combination of names Glodstone found personally humiliating, unnecessarily provocative and, in the case of the last, in exceedingly bad taste, they had driven on in Bobby's dinky Mini ('We mustn't be thought to consider ourselves a cut above the neighbours, Clarence,' she told Glodstone, who knew damned well he was a hell of a lot of cuts just about everywhere else) to the bungalow in Bognor Regis. It had fulfilled his direst expectations. From its green-tiled roof to the petunias bordering the weedless lawn and the cubistic carpet in the drawing room, it represented everything he had most despised.

'But it's pure art-deco, Clarence. I mean it's us.'

'It may be you,' said Glodstone, 'but I'm damned if it's me. And can't you call me something other than Clarence? It's almost as foul as Cecil.'

'I shall call you Soppy, darling. And this is Beatrice.'

'Hell,' said Glodstone, who had just been bitten on the ankle by the Peke.

Now as he stood gazing at his own nonentity in the bathroom he knew he was beaten. They would play bridge all evening with the Shearers and he'd get told off for bidding badly and have to make the coffee and have to take that bloody Beatrice for a pee before

222

going to bed. And he knew what they'd drink. Crême de menthe. Constance Sugg had returned to her roots.

In a hedge in South Armagh, Peregrine, now Number 960401, stared through the night-sight of his rifle at the figure moving in the field below. It could be a Garda but he didn't care. He'd already notched up five IRA men, two poachers and an off-duty RUC constable, not to mention an Army Landrover, to such awful effect that even the local Protestants had joined with the IRA in declaring his sixteen square miles a No-Go Area, and the Army avoided the place. Peregrine didn't care. He was in his element, doing what he had been trained to do. And every few weeks an unmanned balloon (there'd been an unfortunate incident with a helicopter) would drift over for him to shoot down and collect his ammunition and supplies.

Not that he needed the latter. He'd already bagged a sheep for his supper in the burrow he'd dug halfway down an old well and was rather looking forward to it. The Major had said one should live off the land, and he did. He squeezed the trigger and watched the man drop. Then he obeyed another of the Major's dicta, that an army marched on its stomach, and crawled the two miles back to his hide-out. Presently, in the happy knowledge he was doing exactly what he'd been told, he pulled his rifle through and oiled it, and settled down to leg of lamb.

Alexander Kent
Special limited edition
The Collected Adventures of Richard Bolitho 1792–1806
Three Richard Bolitho adventures for the price of one!

ALEXANDER KENT
'One of our foremost writers of naval fiction'
Sunday Times

Spring, 1792. In the brief lull before war breaks out with Revolutionary France, Richard Bolitho accepts the thankless task of recruiting for the fleet. And in the West Indies and at Cape Town, new battles await . . .

Sail with Richard Bolitho, and the men of King George's Navy, in these action-packed seaborne adventures from Alexander Kent. The three stories here, collected in one volume for the first time, follow Bolitho's rise from Captain to Vice-Admiral.

WITH ALL DESPATCH (1792)
'Impeccable naval detail and plenty of action'
Sunday Telegraph

THE ONLY VICTOR (1804)
'As a former naval officer, Alexander Kent knows what it is like to be at sea. Well crafted, well written, an exciting story'
The Times

HONOUR THIS DAY (1806)
'Spellbinding force and authority . . . moving, almost elegiac'

Dick Francis
Special limited edition
Enquiry   Risk   The Danger £4.99
Three champion thrillers for the price of one!

From the undisputed champion of the racing crime thriller, three classic
bestselling tales of murder, mystery and intrigue – set against the colourful
background of the Sport of Kings . . .

ENQUIRY
'Suspense, high drama and the bristling hatred of revenge'
New York Times

RISK
'An amateur jockey who won the Cheltenham Gold Cup is kidnapped . . . a
tangled tale of crookery and corruption'
Daily Mirror

THE DANGER
'Francis is on a winner all the way'
Observer

'Dick Francis at his brilliant best'
Sporting Life

Carl Hiaasen
Special limited edition
Skin Tight/Native Tongue £4.99
Two bestsellers for the price of one!

A double dose of satire from Florida's finest – and funniest – crime writer

The Sunshine State's very own Carl Hiaasen is the modern master of the comic crime thriller. Straight from the murky waters of the Florida badlands, here's a manic double bill of Hiaasen at his zany and original best. First, *Skin Tight* – a wonderful indictment of the American obsession with beauty and success. (Not to mention barracudas.) To follow, *Native Tongue* – a brilliant rollercoaster farce at the expense of the Island theme park industry. (Abandon your sanity at the gateway to the Amazing Kingdom of Thrills.)

But be careful! As humorist P.J. O'Rourke puts it: 'Reading Carl Hiaasen will do as much damage to the Florida tourist industry as an actual visit to Florida itself . . .'

'Reading him is violently pleasurable – a bit like being on a terrifyingly good rollercoaster'
Daily Mail

'Hiaasen is seriously funny, and highly recommended'
Irish Times

All Pan Books are available at your local bookshop or newsagent, or can be ordered direct from the publisher. Indicate the number of copies required and fill in the form below.

Send to: Pan C. S. Dept
                Macmillan Distribution Ltd
                Houndmills Basingstoke RG21 2XS

or phone: 0256 29242, quoting title, author and Credit Card number.

Please enclose a remittance* to the value of the cover price plus £1.00 for the first book plus 50p per copy for each additional book ordered.

*Payment may be made in sterling by UK personal cheque, postal order, sterling draft or international money order, made payable to Pan Books Ltd.

Alternatively by Barclaycard/Access/Amex/Diners

CardNo.

Expiry Date

Signature

Applicable only in the UK and BFPO addresses.

While every effort is made to keep prices low, it is sometimes necessary to increase prices at short notice. Pan Books reserve the right to show on covers and charge new retail prices which may differ from those advertised in the text or elsewhere.

NAME AND ADDRESS IN BLOCK LETTERS PLEASE

. . . .

Name _____

Address _____

_____

_____

_____

6/92